Books By Rick Bentsen

The Blademaster Chronicles
The Blademaster
Willowdale
The Age of Darkness
Dragonsbane

The Chronicles of Xarin
The Crucible

Gamma Strike
+* Dawn of a New Age
The Dawning of a New Age

The Chocolate Sheriff

** The CIRCLE

+ Out of print
* Released through iUniverse
** Forthcoming

Dragonsbane

By Rick Bentsen

Steel Drake Press
Taunton

Dragonsbane
Book 4: The Blademaster Chronicles

First Print Edition

Cover image: © Dusan Kostic | Dreamstime.com

For information, contact the author at
rickbentsen@gmail.com

www.facebook.com/RickBentsenAuthor

ISBN: 099845981X
ISBN-13: 978-0994859813

Praise for The Blademaster

"Up until I'd read "The Blademaster" by Rick Bentsen, the closest thing I'd come to reading or seeing a story in this genre was "The Lord Of The Rings" that I saw at the theater several years ago because my husband wanted to see it.

I wanted to read "The Blademaster" because Rick and I have been cyber friends since around 2000 and I wanted to support him and his new book.

So, kind of to my own surprise, when I started reading the saga of Alana Steeldrake (First Blademaster to be named in over 300 years) and Colwyn Starseeker (Protector to Alana Steeldrake and heir to the title of First Lord of the Valendale Territory) I found myself really enjoying it!

The story flows with just enough descriptions that keep the story moving and on course.

All the characters, even the secondary ones, are really well developed. I felt like I knew all the characters in the book, even the bad guys, by the time I'd finished it.

I'm impressed with Rick's writing ability. I'm amazed at his imagination. I'm intrigued with the names of places, characters, and phrases he came up with and how they perfectly fit the tone of the story. And I appreciated the underlying moral code of love and honor that he threaded throughout the story.

And I can totally see this story becoming a movie!"

--Pat Ballard, author (Abigail's Revenge, Wanted One Groom, and others... The Queen of Rubenesque Romances...)

Foreward

March 15, 2017

So this book was a lot less of a struggle to write than Age of Darkness. It was a lot of fun to write though. And it was a lot of fun to explore some things that I wasn't sure I would ever get to explore in this series. Especially the goings on at the Tower of the White.

The first section of the book wherein William becomes the Dream Weaver originally wasn't going to actually appear in this kind of detail, but once I started plotting out the book, I realized that I had to show his journey.

I am happy with the result.

The second section of the book was also not going to be in this book. Originally Tunera was to be introduced in The Age of Darkness. As some of you might remember from my notes in the last book, she decided she did not want to appear in that book. I was afraid that she would continue to cause issues and not want to be a part of the story, but here she is. In the end, I think this introduction to the character is stronger than what I originally planned.

There are several pop culture references in this book. This is something I haven't really done in my Blademaster books before, but these ended up making the story better in one way or another.

Sharp-eyed readers will notice the name of the very first Dream Weaver when he appears in the book. Some of my older readers may even recognize the name. Who is he? Well, when I was trying to come up with the name for the very first Dream Weaver, I was having a hard time coming up with a suitable one. In fact, I just left a ____ in the manuscript for a long time. I just could not come up with something... appropriately wizardly.

I was watching "Dr. Scuss's How the Grinch Stole Christmas" around Christmastime (the cartoon, not the Jim Carrey weirdness) when the perfect name for the first Dream Weaver came to me. It was right there in print on the back of the case... Thurl Ravenscroft. For those of you who don't know who he is, Thurl Ravenscroft is the man that sang the Grinch song in the cartoon. He's also notable for being Tony the Tiger in Frosted Flakes commercials for years. And he has a sufficiently wizardly sounding name. So I stole it. Other than the name, there is not, I don't think, any similarities between the character and the man he's named after.

The other pop culture reference is a bit of a running joke with a friend of mine. There was a show a few years back called Babylon 5. (IF you like shows like Star Trek, you should give it a watch if you haven't. The writing is excellent.) In it, there's a minor recurring character called Zathras. Actually, it's more than one character, all played by the same character. My friend Mike Romero, over the years, has channeled Zathras in our chats. So when it came time to come up with the guardian of the vortex in the Tower of the White... Well, he's not much like the Zathrases in Babylon 5, but he was very clearly modeled after those Zathrases.

And with this book, we have just one more adventure before the Great War of Souls begins. I hope you stay with me on this ride. It's going to be a fun one.

Dia duit,
Rick Bentsen

Acknowledgements

I can hear it now. "Oh, goodness me, the author is about to blather on and on about who did what to help him... Do we really have to read this?" First of all, I love the word blather and I now firmly promise to use the word far more often.

Second, no, you don't have to read this. But I would be remiss if I did not include my thanks. So, yes. Feel free to skip this section, but I shall now blather (told you I would use the word more often) on about Team Rick Bentsen and all they've done.

First of all, thanks to God for the gifts that make the writing possible. A little bit of imagination goes a long way, it would seem.

To my parents, who have been arranging many in person appearances for me to sign and sell my books. It has been a very interesting journey over the past several months, but I have enjoyed every bit of it.

To my brother without whom I would likely never have been introduced to Dungeons and Dragons. Without which.... No Blademaster.

To my continuity expert and editor, Joanna, for everything she does. As I said in *The Blademaster*, Joanna knows the characters as well, if not better, than I do. It makes it easier to hand these books off to her when I know she will take good care of them.

To my readers, because without you, there would be no point to doing this. I love each and every one of you.

Finally to Alana and Colwyn. You came into my life like a whirlwind and have made the past several years very interesting. You two are very special to me. Thank you for letting me tell your story to the world.

*For the woman who keeps me
always on the hunt...*

Dragonsbane

The fourth book in
The Blademaster Chronicles

Chapters

The Prophecy of the Coming of the Age of Darkness
As prophecied by Bahalla Maranal, the Dream Weaver
31 Years after the Great Purge

In the waning days of the Age of Light, one who wears the white shall fall to the rites of the Dark One. Only the true power of the Child of Light can save her soul.

When the One born of the Light goes to the twice dead city, she shall fall to the darkness, as one of her own shall betray her. Only the slim blade of the Second Law of the Blades can save her.

When the twice dead city falls empty a third time, the storm clouds will gather, and sabres will rattle in their scabbards. The blight of war shall be upon the land, and only the One born of the Light can lead the charge against the darkness.

On the wings of war comes the Age of Darkness.

What came before...

In *The Blademaster...*

 n the town of Ravendale in the Southern Dales of Calthea, a warrior woman, Alana Steeldrake, who knows nothing of her parentage awoke one morning. The man she loved, Colwyn Starseeker came to find her that morning to bring her to see the High Priest of Taelin.

When they got to the Temple of Taelin, they were sent on a quest to discover what happened to a priestess in Tornith, a city in the northern part of the continent of Calthea. Tornith is a dark city dedicated to the Dark God, Thraal.

On their way to Tornith, Alana, Colwyn, and their companions, William Stonehands (a mage), Meryn Swiftfoot (a halfling), and Balaam Otakis (the High Priest of Taelin) journeyed to the city of Valendale to consult the sage, Isaiah Talon.

They found the city completely deserted, save for some warriors of Thraal who were there to try to catch them. After defeating the warriors, Alana consulted the sage who directed her to the Elven Woods, where she would finally learn her destiny.

In the Elven Woods, the companions were given directions to a hidden temple at the heart of the forest. In the Temple of the Blades, Alana learned that she is the first Blademaster in 300 years. After hearing all that is entailed with her new position and that she must marry someone she truly loves, Alana and Colwyn agreed to get married. Colwyn underwent the Test of the Blades and succeeded, thereby earning the right to marry Alana.

After the wedding, the companions started north towards Tornith. Along the way, they found a new companion, a dragon named Cobalthaxillius.

Once they crossed the border from the Southern Dales into Dracomyr, the companions came to the Stonegate Mountains where they were taken prisoner by goblins. The goblins began to take the companions to Tornith in cages. Partway there, the companions escaped and made their way the rest of the way to Tornith.

In Tornith, Alana tried to infiltrate the ziggurat of Thraal, but was captured. She was told she would be sacrificed to Thraal.

When the time came for the sacrifice, she was bound to the altar on the top of the ziggurat. Before she could be sacrificed, Balaam threw himself over her body, forcing the ceremonial dagger to kill him instead of her.

Alana got free and killed the High Priest of Thraal.

Balaam was sent to Limbo, where he freed the people that had been sent there by the High Priest of Thraal when he sacrificed them. Also freed was the Dark God himself.

The companions buried Balaam's body at sea and then returned to Ravendale, knowing that their next adventure would come soon...

In *Willowdale*...

Not long after the companions defeated the High Priest of Thraal and leave the ziggurat of Thraal, the Dark God appeared to his new High Priest, Adouon Darkholme. Thraal gave his High Priest instructions on how to create a fighter to counter the Blademaster called the Nightstalker. Kera Rayden was turned into the first Nightstalker and sent to Willowdale to wait for the Blademaster and her companions.

In Ravendale, Alana and her companions spent a month recovering from their trip to Tornith before their next adventure comes along. One day, the proprietor of the White Horse Inn in Valendale, Marcus Whelan, appeared at the Lucky Minotaur in bad shape. Alana made sure he was taken care of.

Marcus told Alana and Colwyn about how the people of Valendale were captured and taken to Willowdale. The Blademaster agreed to go help the people of Valendale.

After hearing prophecies from the sage Isaiah Talon, the companions left for Willowdale.

Just outside the city limits, the companions were stopped by a woman named Silvestra Knightwing. Silvestra, as it turned out, was an old friend of William. She gave them a tour of Willowdale, but the companions were captured on their way back out of the city.

The companions escaped from the dungeons in the palace, but only Colwyn was able to get away.

Colwyn flew to the Elven Woods so that he could go to the Temple of the Blades and consult with the Legacy of the Blademasters about the situation in Willowdale. While in the Elven Woods, Colwyn was tempted to stray from his marriage by the Queen of the Forestwalker Elves. After turning aside the Queen's advances, Colwyn went to the Temple of the Blades and got what information he could about the situation in Willowdale and the Nightstalker.

When he returned to Willowdale, Colwyn freed the rest of his companions. They went to a cavern overlooking the city so they could plan their attack.

The companions scouted the city so that the Blademaster would have all the information she could when she planned the attack. After listening to all of the reports, Alana planned out the attack on the Zeraphim forces that were holding the city.

During his watch during the night before the attack, William talked to Silvestra about their past. They realized that they still loved each other and were supposed to be together. Meryn overheard their conversation and went to the Nightstalker in Tornith in a fit of jealous anger and gave away the plan for the attack.

The next morning when Meryn was discovered missing, William and Silvestra went to rescue her while Alana and Colwyn roused the leaders of the Resistance in Willowdale to fight for themselves. Lord Taelin himself spoke to the leaders of the Resistance to get them to help themselves.

Alana issued the challenge to the Nightstalker and Colwyn led the citizens of Valendale into battle against the Zeraphim.

During the course of battle, the Nightsalker's undead dragon attacked. Cobalt fought the dragon, but ended up losing the battle and dying. Silvestra Knightwing assumed her dragon form and fought the undead dragon, ultimately destroying it.

Alana and the Nightstalker fought one on one in the ramparts of the palace. When her undead dragon was defeated, the Nightstalker escaped through a portal to Tornith.

With the Zeraphim and the Nightstalker defeated, Alana and her companions brought the people of Valendale back to their homes before returning to Ravendale themselves.

In *The Age of Darkness...*

In the city of Talondale, the man known as the Dream Weaver woke after having a dream about the Great War of Souls and the army of darkness. He wrote down the information about the weaving and prepared for his journey to tell the Blademaster what he knew.

In Tornith, Kera Rayden returned to the ziggurat of Thraal after her defeat in Willowdale. Once there she was sent to the Wilds to take command of the army of undead.

On the Isle of Dragons, Silvestra Knightwing and Taelin spoke to the Council of Dragons about the need to send new dragons to protect the new Blademasters that would be named soon. Eliazar, the leader of the Council, attacked the god, forcing Taelin to kill the ancient dragon. Once his replacement to the council was named, the dragons agreed to send dragons to the Temple of the Blades.

In Ravendale, the Dream Weaver arrived and told the Blademaster about the army of undead that he had seen in his weaving. He also told her that she would need to go to Barandale to seek out a Blademaster among the halflings.

While he was there, the Dream Weaver spoke with William Stonehands about becoming his replacement as the Dream Weaver. William told the Dream Weaver that he would need to consult with Silvestra before he could give a decision.

Before they could leave for Barandale, a guard from Arvendale arrived to give Colwyn a message from his father demanding that the younger Starseeker return to Arvendale to speak with his sister.

The Blademaster and her companions set out to Arvendale. When they arrived, Colwyn's father was less than responsive to Alana being Colwyn's wife. After much discussion, however, the First Lord of Arvendale accepted their marrage.

Colwyn spoke with his sister Bella and discovered that she was a Blademaster. She and the palace guard she had fallen in love with agreed to travel to the Temple of the Blades with Alana and Colwyn.

Silvestra returned to the companions just as they were getting ready to leave Arvendale. She flew the companions to Barandale, saving them weeks of travel time.

In Barandale, they met with the halfling Council of Elders. After speaking with the Council, they were taken to the Swiftfoot compound where they met Talby Swiftfoot. Alana recognized Talby as the Blademaster they had been sent to Barandale to find.

Before leaving Barandale, Alana and her companions, as well as the Lady Laeyra, bore witness to the marriage of Meryn Swiftfoot to one of her oldest friends, Odway Thistlethumb.

Silvestra flew the companions back to the Temple of the Blades where Tests of the Blades were performed for the two Protectors. After they successfully completed the Tests, the two Blademasters were bonded to their Protectors.

After the bondings were completed, they went out to the clearing to find dragons arriving from the Isle of Dragons. After the dragons paired off with the Blademasters they would protect, they were all immediately tested by an attack on the clearing by undead led by Kera Rayden.

Once the undead were driven off, the Blademasters returned to Ravendale, where they reported what they had seen to the King.

William told Alana and Colwyn that he was leaving for the Tower of the White to become the next Dream Weaver.

Dragonsbane

Just as he was leaving on Silvestra, winter arrived with the first snow.

And so begins the next part of The Blademaster Chronicles....

Dragonsbane

pRoLogue
CDaLachai ORazonsdane

he man sat in the corner of the tap room. From where he sat, he could clearly see everything going on in the room. It was his preferred location when he was in a tap room or tavern. It was the only way he could make sure that no one snuck up on him.

He was a man that needed to control everything that he possibly could.

The man sat sipping an ale. He did not, as a general rule, get drunk. That would be a giving up of control. In his line of work, giving up control like that would be fatal.

He leaned back in his chair, and he looked at where the bard was just getting ready to begin playing. He loved listening to a good bard play. Although he had no idea if the bard that was about to perform would be any good. He would happily listen, though, and make a determination from there.

The serving wench that had brought him his ale earlier came by with a bowl of stew. The stew was thick, with large chunks of meat, potatoes and vegetables. He had eaten in this tap room before, as it was where he tended to stay when he was home in Darcandale. He was not home near often enough though. He had been home for a long while this time, and he was itching to go out on a new adventure. Sitting at home did not appeal to him. The man was one that needed constant adventure in his life.

He was a hunter.

He did not currently have a prey, though, so there was nothing for him to hunt. He knew that the lack of prey would change, and that it would likely change soon.

It always happened that way.

The bard began to sing. It was a new song that the man had never heard before. He took a bite of his stew as he listened to the song, which was about the rescue of the citizens of Valendale. He listened carefully to the words of the song. He had heard about this new Blademaster. Like many people in the Southern Dales, the man had a deep respect for the Blademasters of old and all that they were said to have done for the Southern Dales throughout history.

As he listened to the song, though, he realized just how little he knew about the Blademasters.

As the bard sang, he weaved together the story of the great battle in Willowdale. The song brought the images of the battle to the man's mind as all good songs of heroic deeds should. He could see the great skeletal dragon wreaking havoc in the skies over the battle. He could see the great gold dragon give his life to protect the Blademaster and the people of Valendale. He could see the silver dragon attack out of nowhere and defeat the skeletal dragon.

He had not known that the Blademasters consorted with dragons.

The man opened his eyes and set his spoon down. He waved over the serving wench. It was time to settle up his bill.

For Malachai Dragonsbane was about to go on the hunt once more.

Dragonsbane

Part 1
The Tower of
the White

Chapter 1
The Tower of the White

inter set in quickly in the Southern Dales.

The snows had come fast and furious once they started falling. The people of the Southern Dales barely had time to recover and clean up from one storm before the next one set in. It made travelling especially difficult.

Even when one was travelling by dragon.

They had gotten halfway to the Tower of the White before Silvestra Knightwing and William Stonehands could travel no further due to the weather. They found refuge in a cave so that they could wait the snows out. With how hard the snow was whirling during this particular storm, it was just too dangerous for her to continue flying.

It took three days for the snow to clear enough for her to fly again. While it was nice to have time together where they were alone without having to worry about anyone else, William was nervous and wanted to get on with their journey. His journey was a treacherous one, and he would just as soon be done with it.

If he even survived the journey, that is.

William knew that his journey to the Tower of the White could be his last one. It was a thought he tried hard not to dwell on. It all depended upon what the magic sensed within him when he surrendered himself to the vortex in order to take his place as the new Dream Weaver.

While he knew that this was where his destiny lay, he still found himself nervous about the prospect of entering the vortex. Few mages actually surrendered themselves to such a ritual. Only the Mages of the Inner Circle, sages, and the Dream Weaver had to endure the vortex. All he had to go on were vague rumors about what the vortex was like.

All he knew was that the vortex was nothing more than the purest essence of magic.

The wrong person entering the vortex would find himself claimed by the magic itself and never leave. Even the right person was monumentally changed by the experience. As he had no idea what to expect from the experience, he looked to it with dread.

If he had not been travelling with Silvestra, he may have chosen to turn around and head back to Ravendale to forget the whole ordeal.

Silvestra, though, was his rock. She believed in him. And that belief buoyed his spirits. It allowed him to move forward when he did not think he would be able to.

He understood, now, how his friends Alana and Colwyn were able to go forward as they prepared to lead the Southern Dales in the Great War of Souls.

He had often wondered why Taelin and Laeyra had built the powers of the Blademasters on the foundation of the love they shared with their husbands. But now that he had a wife of his own, he had come to realize the power to be found in the love shared with a partner.

It would seem that Lord Taelin is, indeed, wise, he thought to himself, a rue smile sneaking across his face.

"You have a look, my love," Silvestra broke the silence of the cave. "What deep thoughts are you having?"

"I was just thinking about how wise it was to base the power of the Blademasters on a foundation of love," he said, stroking her hair. "I never realized how powerful it was."

"Did you not?" she looked over at him. "You have loved deeply, but you've never understood the power of it?"

"Well, to be fair, I did have that love taken from me once before," he said.

"True," she nodded. "But it has returned to you."

"And for that, I am profoundly grateful," he laughed.

They sat in silence, watching the snow whirl outside the cavern entrance. William took a great deal of comfort from having Silvestra by his side. He knew that she would always be by his side now.

Despite the best efforts of the Council of Dragons to keep them apart, they had found each other earlier in the year when the Blademaster and her companions had gone to the city of Willowdale to rescue the citizens of Valendale that had been taken there. Silvestra had been amongst the people in Willowdale.

Their love had instantly rekindled as soon as they had seen one another.

Their love had caused problems amongst the companions, including a betrayal of the companions by Meryn Swiftfoot. But it had been the right thing to pursue. The time alone together had helped to solidify that in William's mind.

There was little Silvestra could do on this journey other than to provide support for her husband. That did not stop William from being happy she was here. This was, though, his journey. He had agreed to undergo the test to become the Dream Weaver. Had he not, he and Silvestra would still be warm in Ravendale helping Alana and Colwyn plan the defense of the Southern Dales.

Still, being with a dragon definitely had its advantages. She was able to get a roaring fire going far quicker than he would have been able to, even with his magic. It made it easier to hole up in a cavern for a few days if they had a nice warm fire to sleep by.

On the fourth morning that they were in the cavern, they looked out the entrance to see that the snow had stopped sometime during the night. William put his arm around Silvestra's shoulders as they looked out at the glistening snow covering the ground outside. He knew that they would be able to continue their journey that day. As much as he wanted to stay in the cavern with Silvestra for the rest of the winter, he knew he could not.

He sighed deeply, and Silvestra squeezed him gently in comfort.

"I suppose we should get on with it," he said.

"Yes," she nodded. "The sooner we get to the Tower of White, the sooner you can complete your Test of Magic and return to the Blademaster's side."

"Silvestra, I hate to admit it, but the Test of Magic scares me," he admitted.

"As it should," she nodded. "Entering the vortex is not easy. That is why it is only for some mages to do. But it is your destiny, and I know you will pull through to the other side."

"How can you be so sure?" he asked.

"Because I know you, William," she smiled over at him. "I know that, now that we are together once more, you will not leave me again."

"That is true enough," he smiled back. "Let's go before I decide to never leave this cavern."

Silvestra nodded. Within minutes, she had transformed back into her dragon form and they were once more flying towards the Tower of the White.

The Tower of the White was one of three towers for the training of Mages in Calthea. Located deep in the heart of the Southern Dales, only mages who have felt the call can find where it is. Anyone else who got close to the towers found themselves turning away from the tower's location without realizing it.

It had always amazed William that no one noticed the giant tower of white marble rising up from the countryside. And yet no one that was not meant to find the Tower of the White could see it.

But after seeing similar protections on the Temple of the Blades, William realized that this was a protection that the gods of magic themselves had put on the Towers of Magic.

When William had been to the Tower of the White for his training, he had been amazed by a great many things to do with the Tower and his training. Now that he was returning after being out in the world, he was far less amazed. He had seen many wonderful things out in the world. Terrible things too. The thought of the undead army that his Blademaster was about to lead the Southern Dales against still gave him shivers.

And yet, he knew that all he had seen would not prepare him for what was to come. Nothing out in the world could prepare someone to enter into the vortex. The vortex was a unique bit of magic all to its own. He had heard it said that no one could prepare you for what you would see in the vortex, because it was not the same for any two people. It took from your experiences to build itself out into what you saw.

He hoped it was going to be something friendly to him and not, say, the interior of the Ziggurat of Thraal in Tornith.

It did not matter. Friendly confines or no, he had to enter the vortex if he was to take the Test of Magic. And while he still could turn around and decline to take the test without penalty, he knew that it was his destiny to become the next Dream Weaver. In order to do that, he had to enter the vortex and take the Test of Magic.

After several hours of flying, the Tower of the White came into view. Silvestra glided down for a landing about an hour's walk away from the tower, knowing full well that she would not be able to fly right up to the tower. Safeguard would bring her down long before she reached the tower, which would lead to both she and William being injured or killed. An hour of walking was a small price to pay for living.

When she landed, William slipped off her back and she began the transformation back to her human form. She slipped back into her robes, and William handed her her pack. Without a word, they began the walk towards the Tower of the White.

William had a momentary vision of déjà vu as he walked up to the iron wrought gate leading to the grounds of the Tower of the White. He did not have the nerves that he had had the first time he had walked up to those gates hoping to be accepted as an adept. He had not known as he entered the grounds that the fact that he had been able to enter the gates was proof that he had been accepted.

He stopped with his hand on the gate. The iron was ice cold beneath his hand. It took all of his willpower not to pull his hand away. William knew that this would be his last chance to walk away from the Test of Magic. He would not be able to do so once he walked through this gate.

He looked at Silvestra, and she nodded once to him, smiling sadly. She would accept whatever decision he made at this point, he knew, but she had known from the time that they were studying at the Tower of the White that this was where his destiny lay. Having her by his side made it at least a little easier. But it was still not going to be easy.

Determined to see this through, William pushed the gate open and stepped through. Boldly, he strode up the walk to the main door of the tower, Silvestra by his side. When he got to the door, he thumped on the door with the butt of his staff.

It was not long before the door opened and a mage that William recognized as one of the teachers at the tower opened the door.

"William Stonehands?" the mage said, surprised. "You have returned to the Tower of the White?"

"Yes, Master Arwyn," he nodded. "I have come as I have been bid to by Roald Vilas. I have come to enter the vortex and take the Test of Magic to become the next Dream Weaver."

"Then come inside," Arwyn Bronnen said. "Suitable quarters shall be found for both of you."

William and Silvestra followed the mage inside the Tower of the White. He knew now that there was no turning back from his destiny.

Chapter II
The Master Adept

he Room that William had been shown to turned out to be the room that had been his during his training at the Tower of the White. William was not a firm believer in coincidence, so he suspected that the choice to house him in the same room as when he was an adept was a conscious choice.

As was the choice to separate him from Silvestra.

He chose not to fight the decree that he and Silvestra would be in separate quarters. There would be a time and a place for such battles. He knew that, and he knew that Silvestra knew as well. Besides, he knew that he would need time alone in order to practice the skills he would be taught during his training.

Still, he knew he would miss having Silvestra by his side every day. They had missed so much time that he did not want to miss any more time with her. They had had years stolen from them. And while they were able to be together finally, there was a part of William that was afraid that something would happen to cause them to be parted once more.

He could not bear to be parted from her again.

William looked around the little room that would be his home for the next little while. It had not changed since he had been there as an adept. A small room with wooden walls, the domicile had only the basics, a bed, a washstand with an ewer of water, and a small wardrobe. He knew that the Master Adept frowned on mages having any ostentatious trappings. He felt that mages should live simple lives and the living quarters in the Tower of the White reflected that attitude.

The one thing that he was happy about was that the small room was peaceful. He had always found his quarters at the Tower of the White to be that way. The bed was not as comfortable as his bed at home in Ravendale was, but that could also have been because he was sleeping by himself in it. He mused as he sat on the bed that a bed was far more comfortable when there was a beautiful silver haired woman sharing it with you.

He had just leaned his staff against the wall by his bed when the door opened. A young adept stood at the door waiting to be acknowledged.

"Yes?" William asked.

"The Master Adept summons you, William Stonehands," the adept squeaked, clearly nervous to be summoning a mage that had already passed his tests to graduate from the Tower of the White.

"As expected," he nodded. He stood and grabbed his staff once more. "Will my wife be in attendance for this meeting?"

"I cannot answer that, sir," the adept blanched. "I was only told to bring you. It is possible that someone else was sent to bring her."

"I suppose it does not matter," William shrugged. "We will find out soon enough. Where does the Master Adept wish to see me?"

"He is in the Star Chamber awaiting your presence," the adept said.

This was not pleasing news for William. The Star Chamber was oft times used as a disciplinary chamber for troublesome adepts. It appeared that the Master Adept was going to cause problems with William's training to become the new Dream Weaver.

It was not unexpected. William had never been one of the Master Adept's favorite pupils. He had once told William that he did not believe that the young man would ever amount to anything in the world of mages. William had surprised the Master Adept when he had successfully completed his tests and graduated from the Tower of the White.

And now, he had come back to become the new Dream Weaver, further proving the Master Adept wrong about William's future. He knew that it was something that the Master Adept would not be pleased by.

There was little he could do about it, though, but to confront the Master Adept once more and go forward with the training required to become the Dream Weaver.

"The Star Chamber it is then," William spoke softly. "Lead on. I shall follow."

William followed the adept out of his quarters, the butt of his staff thumping on the floor with every step.

The Star Chamber was at the very top of the Tower of the White. A transparent dome allowed for starlight to filter into the large round room. It was the room that mages learned to take star sightings and learn their constellations in.

It was also the room that the Master Adept meted out punishment in.

The punishments varied depending on the offense, but, without fail, the Master Adept carried out the punishments in the Star Chamber. William had been whipped more than once in the Star Chamber.

There were few mages that had fond memories of the Star Chamber. So being summoned to the Star Chamber so soon after arriving back at the Tower of the White did not sit well with William.

He could only imagine that the Master Adept was going to cause trouble.

It had been over eight years since William was an adept at the Tower of the White, but the Master Adept still struck fear into his heart. He knew that the Master Adept had to be strict and, at times, cruel in order to keep the adepts in line and make sure they stayed on the right path. A mage of the white robes could easily slide to the gray, or worse, the black robes if they were not careful. It was easy to be seduced by the magic. And it was easy to be corrupted by it.

William had worked hard since he had first been lured by the call of the magic to not be seduced by the darker forms of the magic. It was a daily struggle, as it was for all mages that wore the white. Having Silvestra by his side helped a great deal. He knew that without her, the seductive nature of the dark magical arts would have an easier time calling to him.

His love for her protected him. Much like the love the Blademasters shared with their Protectors was their protection. He wondered once again at the wisdom of Taelin to build the Blademasters' powers on true love.

The young mage kept his head held high as he walked into the Star Chamber. He knew that he had done nothing that he could be punished for. He had only just arrived at the Tower of the White, after all. He also knew that he was no longer an adept, so the Master Adept had no direct authority over him anyway.

As he entered the Star Chamber, William noticed that the Master Adept was standing in the exact center of the chamber, standing in a pool of light. It was a gesture that was meant to be intimidating. William had fought many intense battles alongside the Blademaster. He was no longer intimidated by the Master Adept.

"Summoned, I have come," William said in a soft voice.

"You were not summoned to the Tower of the White," the Master Adept's voice cracked. "What are you doing here, Mage."

"Summoned, I have come," William repeated, his voice remaining calm and soft.

"What are you doing at the Tower of the White, Mage?" the Master Adept demanded. "And why are you in possession of the Staff of Cirricus?"

William took a step closer, frowning slightly. There were protocols to be observed and the Master Adept was outright ignoring the protocols of the Tower of the White.

It was not a good sign.

"Summoned, I have come," William said a third time.

"Then come," the Master Adept nodded.

William stepped forward and entered the pool of light in the center of the Star Chamber. He stood at the edge of the pool of light, far enough that the Master Adept would have to move to physically touch William. He stood with his arms folded before him, his hands clasping the opposing wrist. His staff lay in the crook of his right elbow where it was ready to be used at a moment's notice.

"I have come as I was bid to by Roald Vilas," William said. "I have come to submit myself to the vortex."

"You?" the Master Adept snorted. "You are hardly fit to take on the mantle of the Dream Weaver."

"I do not disagree," William shrugged. "And yet, here I stand. Ready to enter the vortex to submit myself to the Test of Magic."

"Bah," the older mage waved his hand. "You are not ready. You would perish in the attempt."

"That is for the magic to decide," William said. "Not for you."

"You are willing to throw your life away for this?"

"If need be, yes," William nodded. "I was called. You know as well as I do that a mage called to the vortex must enter."

"Indeed," the Master Adept frowned. He turned around and walked to the other side of the circle before turning back to face William. "Where did you get the Staff of Cirricus, Mage?"

William looked at the staff in the crook of his elbow and studied it long and hard before answering.

"It was entrusted to me by the High Priestess of the Blades," William answered in the same calm voice he had used the entire time he had been in the Star Chamber. "Cirricus had left it in her care."

"Why did she give it to you?"

"My guess would be that she knows what Blademaster Alana is about to face and wanted to make sure that the mage that had sworn himself to her service was able to protect her as best he could," William said. "I have seen the army the Blademaster is about to lead the fight against. Have you?"

"Have care, mage," the Master Adept narrowed his eyes at William. "I am still the Master Adept of the Tower of the White. You will accord me the respect of that position."

"I am no longer an adept, Master," William said. A flash of anger in his eyes was the only indication that William might be losing his calm demeanor. His voice was kept under control, though. "I have been out in the world these past few years. I have seen horrors that would give any sane man nightmares. I have seen a skeletal dragon cutting down brave warriors. I have watched, unable to do anything, as a lich held my charge prisoner and prepared to sacrifice her to the Dark God. I have seen the Zeraphim leave their mighty keep to enslave the citizenry of an entire town. And I have seen the army of the undead that prepares to invade the Southern Dales. No, I am no longer an adept. I am a mage that has been called by the vortex. And whether I feel I am ready or not, I will enter the vortex and accept my fate. Because to do less would be to deny all that my Blademaster fights for. And that, Master, is something I do not believe you fully understand."

"You shame me to no purpose, mage," the Master Adept growled. "Very well. You will see the Inner Circle. And they will decide your fate as to whether or not you will enter the vortex. May Lord Ferrin have mercy on you if you are deemed unworthy by the magic."

"If I am deemed unworthy by the magic, it will consume me," William shrugged. "And Roald Vilas will have to simply find another to take his mantle. It will be as it will be."

"So be it," the Master Adept nodded. "Go. You will be summoned by the Inner Circle soon."

William bowed slightly to the Master Adept and made his way out of the Star Chamber, happy to leave the presence of the Master Adept.

Tannen Silverheart watched as William left the Star Chamber. While he would never admit it to the young mage, he was very proud of how William had grown since leaving the Tower of the White.

As the Master Adept of the Tower of the White, Tannen had seen many mages come and go over the years. Some had had great talent. Others had only been able to master the most basic of magics. But William had always been special.

Although the young mage had never sought to have an advanced position among the ranks of mages, William had an unquenchable thirst for knowledge. Knowledge itself was the only power that William actively sought.

In the end, Tannen suspected that that thirst for knowledge was what attracted the Dream Weaver to the young mage.

Tannen had hoped that William would one day replace him as the Master Adept. He saw, now, that Ferrin had other plans for the young mage.

He could only hope that William could handle the Test of Magic he would have to undergo to become the Dream Weaver.

The old man drew a ragged breath and let it out in a deep sigh. William was right that dark times were coming. It was for that reason that he did object to William undergoing the Test of Magic now. William was needed by his Blademaster's side more than ever. It was a great risk to undergo the Test of Magic. If William were to fail, it would be fatal for the young mage.

William seemed to know the risks, though. And if William had, indeed, been called to the vortex then there was little that Tannen could do. It was unheard of for a mage to be denied the Test of Magic after being called to the vortex.

The thought of losing the young man to the magic made Tannen's stomach a little queasy.

"I am not through with young William just yet, Tannen Silverheart," a voice called from behind the Master Adept.

Tannen whirled around, far quicker than someone his age should have been able to. When he finished turning about, he found himself face to face with the god of white magic, Ferrin.

"Lord Ferrin," Tannen bowed slightly at the waist. "To what do I owe the honor of your presence in the Tower of the White?"

"William Stonehands," Ferrin said, shrugging his shoulders slightly in a "what else" gesture. "I find him to be a very interesting young mage. He was trained well, a true credit to his Master Adept and his teachers in the Tower of the White."

"Thank you," Tannen bowed again. "He was an excellent student, if not a sometimes troublesome one."

"You will find, that many of the best mages throughout the ages have all been sometimes troublesome ones," Ferrin smiled. "I suspect that young William, when all is said and done is going to be amongst the greatest of our order."

"I hope you are right," Tannen nodded. "He is a special mage. I can only hope that he will succeed in the Test of Magic. It would be a very bad thing to lose him. He is needed."

"Indeed he is," Ferrin said. "I have seen what the Blademaster is up against. There will be great need of William's magic before this war is over. Of that I am sure. Passing the Test of Magic will only make him stronger. And that, in turn will make him better able to protect his Blademaster."

"The Inner Circle will not so easily let William take the Test of Magic, Lord Ferrin," Tannen sighed. "Never has one so young been called. And he has flouted edicts set down by the Inner Circle. That will not go over well."

"You speak of his wife," Ferrin said, a frown crossing his face. "Yes, separating those two was a mistake. But it was not just the Inner Circle's mistake. The Council of Dragons also tried to separate them."

"And now they are together again," Tannen said. "The Inner Circle will not like that."

"Did you know Lord Taelin himself joined them?" Ferrin raised an eyebrow.

"I did not," Tannen said, a note of awe in his voice. "I do not know that that will sway the Inner Circle, but it is good to know that their union is blessed by the Lord of Light."

"That is why I am at the Tower of the White, Tannen Silverheart," Ferrin smiled at the Master Adept. "I am here to ensure that the Inner Circle does not block William's Test of Magic. Roald Vilas selected William. And he had good reasons for his choice. I will not let the Inner Circle deny the Dream Weaver a proper successor for foolish reasons."

"I think that the Inner Circle will be difficult to persuade, my Lord," Tannen said softly. "But I am glad William will not have to face them alone."

"So long as William wears the white, he will never face anything alone," Ferrin smiled warmly. "As with any of my mages, I will always be by his side."

Before Tannen could respond, Ferrin had faded back into nothingness. He always found it amazing that the gods could appear and disappear so easily. Tannen chuckled to himself as he worked to ready himself for his own part of the battle ahead of him.

For he had decided that, although he did not want to risk William to the Test of Magic, he would argue for the young mage.

Dragonsbane

Chapter III
The Inner Circle

here were reasons to be nervous, William knew. Although he had once stood before the three Mages of the Inner Circle who represented the Mages of the White, he had never before been in the presence of the entire Inner Circle. He did not know any mages that had been. Well, he supposed, the Dream Weaver must have appeared before the Inner Circle when he prepared to take his own Test of Magic. But no one that he had trained with had ever appeared before the Inner Circle.

And now he would be doing so.

He thought about the edict that he had received just before leaving the Tower of the White. He had been forbidden from ever seeing Silvestra Knightwing again. He was told that such a relationship could only end poorly for him.

And yet, here he was. Back at the Tower of the White to take his Test of Magic to become the new Dream Weaver and Silvestra Knightwing was by his side as his wife.

He knew that the Inner Circle would not be pleased to know that he had openly defied their edict to him. And he suspected that they would not be moved that their union had been blessed by no less than Lord Taelin himself. He knew that Lord Ferrin also approved of their union, but he doubted seriously that the Inner Circle would ever accept his marriage, no matter how many deities approved of it.

In the end, William supposed, it did not matter if they accepted his marriage or not. All that mattered was that they did not bar him from undergoing the Test of Magic. He had sought in the magic the truth of things as he had been taught to. But he knew that no one that had been called to take the Test of Magic was ever denied access to the vortex in the end.

He had seen the vortex once. All mages were shown the vortex before they graduated from the Tower of the White. But he had not been permitted to enter it. To enter the vortex without being called was tantamount to committing suicide. The mage would be lost to the magic immediately. Even when called, entering the vortex was highly risky. There was every chance that the slightest thing would cause the mage to fail the Test of Magic and be consumed by the magic.

It was a daunting prospect, but he was committed to the course set before him. He knew that this was what he was supposed to do, no matter how nervous the thought of entering the vortex and taking the Test of Magic made him.

While he waited for the Inner Circle to summon him, he sat in his small room and studied the Staff of Cirricus. He had not tried to do anything with the staff since he got it from the Temple of the Blades. There had been very little time for him to do much in the way of experimentation with the staff. There had been some down time between their adventure in Tornith and their journey to Willowdale, but he had been concerned with studying the new spell books he had purchased prior to their trip to Tornith.

And after returning from Willowdale, he was deep in worry over his wife.

He had heard stories about how powerful a staff it was. It had, after all, been made by one of the most powerful mages to ever serve on the Inner Circle, Cirricus Silverflame. The stories he had heard said that only the most powerful mages could master even the smallest tasks with the Staff of Cirricus.

He doubted that he would be able to do much of anything with the staff as he was, but he suspected that once he completed the Test of Magic and became the new Dream Weaver that he would have sufficient power to at least light the crystal of the staff.

Even though he knew that he would not be able to succeed, he had to at least make the attempt to light up the crystal. He was not sure if the incantation would be the same as it had been for his staff, but it was the only thing that he knew to try.

"Sentalusin Cirricus," he whispered.

Although it did not light fully, the crystal at the top of the Staff of Cirricus began to glow with a very pale glow. It was not enough that it would light a dark room, but it was more than William had expected. He looked at the crystal in surprise. It continued to glow faintly to William's surprise and delight.

"Davalas," he whispered.

The glow from the crystal winked out. William stared at the crystal for a few seconds after the glow disappeared. He was surprised that it had lit at all, but now that it had, he knew that it would light whenever he commanded it to. He suspected that it would be a more powerful light the next time.

It was an interesting thing that he was able to light the crystal on his first attempt. But it was also a worrisome thing. He knew that Colwyn and Alana were worried about the amount of power he seemed to be acquiring at so young an age. He appreciated their worry because it was one he shared. He knew that he was getting to be a powerful mage. He also knew that once he had the mantle of the

Dream Weaver, he would be far more powerful than he was now.

The thought of having so much raw magical power scared him quite a bit.

He was counting on Silvestra to keep him grounded. He knew that it was one of the benefits of his marriage to Silvestra. She would keep him from succumbing to any temptation to go bad due to the power he'd gained. It would be very easy for him to cross the line into grey magic. Or worse, the black. But he also knew that Silvestra would do everything she could to keep that from happening.

Perhaps that was why Taelin had made a point of putting them back together.

The mage said a quick prayer of thanks to Taelin for his wisdom in putting Silvestra and he back together. He knew that Taelin's decision to marry him to the silver dragon would one day lead to his safety. Perhaps, it would even help in the upcoming Test of Magic. At the very least, that love would keep him grounded while he underwent the Test of Magic.

The support of her love would see him through the trials that were to come. Starting, he hoped, with his appearance before the Inner Circle.

He knew that the Inner Circle would be summoning him soon. He could only hope that this appearance would go well for him. Although he knew that no mage who had been submitted for a Test of Magic had ever been denied access to the vortex, he decided it would be the height of foolishness to assume that he would be able to take the Test of Magic uncontested. He figured that it would be safe to assume that objections would be raised by at least two members of the Inner Circle. The head of the Evocation Order would object to a member of his order being appointed to such a high profile posting in a different order. And the head of the Divination Order would object to the Dream Weaver coming from an order other than his.

These were not new concerns for him, though. He had known that these would be the issues he had to deal with from the moment he had accepted the Dream Weaver's invitation to become his replacement.

He knew that he would have to find a way to work through these objections. There was no choice. He was determined to see his decision through to the end, no matter what it actually meant for him.

There was a soft knock on his door. William nodded to himself, knowing that it would be the summons to the Inner Circle.

Finally, I can get this part over with, he thought to himself.

He crossed over to the door and opened it. The same adept that had summoned him to the Star Chamber to meet with the Master Adept was standing in the doorway, looking no more comfortable to be bringing William to the Inner Circle than he had before.

William stifled a smile. He remembered when he was an adept. He had been just as nervous when he had been tasked with bringing a full mage somewhere. It was, he knew, the way of things.

"I am here to bring you to the Inner Circle," the adept managed to get out.

"As expected," William nodded.

Without another word, the adept turned and started down the hallway. William followed behind, the butt of his staff thumping softly against the floor with every step.

He did not try to engage the adept in conversation as they walked. William knew that the adept was probably thankful for that, but there was more to his silence than consideration for the poor adept. He was channeling his energies, for he knew that before the meeting with the Inner Circle was out, he would have need of all of the energy at his disposal. He did not think that magic would be required in front of the Inner Circle, but he chose to be prepared for anything.

And so it was that when he walked through the entrance to the chambers of the Inner Circle that he was fairly crackling with collected power. If the adept that was leading him noticed the power building in the mage, he did not give any notice. William knew that mages building up power in the Tower of the White was a fairly commonplace occurrence, so the young adept was likely used to such displays.

William strode into the chamber and stopped in the center. The Inner Circle sat at a long semicircular table that curved around the center of the room. Where William stood was the exact center of the room, putting him right in the center of the semicircular table as well. He stared straight ahead at the Mage of the Inner Circle sitting at the center of the table. He knew that this would be the leader of the Inner Circle, traditionally the Mage of the Inner Circle representing the History Order.

"Summoned, I have come," William said softly into the pure quiet of the chamber of the Inner Circle.

"So you have," Alric Dalphain, the Mage of the Inner Circle for the History Order, nodded. "We were told you would be coming to submit yourself to the vortex."

"As much as the thought of entering the vortex worries me, I have been called to the vortex," William said in the same soft voice. "I dare not deny its call."

"You are wise to fear the vortex, William Stonehands," a voice called to his left. William turned to face the head of his order, the Evocation Order, Balor Windham. "The vortex is not for everyone."

"This is true, Master Balor," William nodded. "And if I did not feel the call so strongly, I would not have come."

"I see that you have brought the Staff of Cirricus back to the Tower of the White," Balor said in a gruff voice. "We thank you for returning this priceless staff back to the Inner Circle where it belongs."

"No," William said. He could tell that the one word caught the leader of his order by surprise.

"No?" Balor raised one bushy white eyebrow. "What mean you by saying no?"

"The staff was entrusted to me," William said. "And it has bonded to me. You know that a staff bonded to a mage will work for no other so long as that mage is living."

"Preposterous," Balor scoffed. "You are not advanced enough in magic to bond with the Staff of Cirricus."

"Sentalusin Cirricus," William said boldly.

Unlike before when the crystal lit with a feeble glow, this time the crystal blazed with an intense white light as William knew it would.

"I do not believe it!" Balor thundered.

"And yet, the evidence is in front of your eyes, Balor Wyndham," a voice called from behind William.

William recognized the voice immediately, so he was not surprised when he turned to see Ferrin standing behind him. He nodded in respect to his god before turning back to Balor.

"Lord Ferrin, this is unusual," Balor growled. "You never appear before the Inner Circle."

"Well, I am here now," Ferrin shrugged. "It is not the first time I have stood before the Inner Circle. Nor, I think, will it be the last."

"I assume you are here because of the young mage in front of us?" Balor asked.

"Indeed," Ferrin nodded. "Young William here intrigues me. I want to see what happens here."

"Very well," Balor nodded.

"If I may, Balor," another one of the mages at the table said. William recognized him as the head of the Conjuration Order and the most senior of the Mages of the White, Darim Valan. He groaned a little on the inside, for he knew what was coming. "This mage has chosen to disregard edicts of the Inner Circle. He is not fit to enter the vortex."

"You are speaking of my wife, I assume?" William said, keeping his voice under control as much as he could.

"You were forbidden to see her ever again by the Inner Circle," Darim thundered. "And here you are, returned to the Tower of the White to beg to be allowed to enter the vortex with her by your side. No, I see no reason why we should allow this when you cannot abide by a simple edict."

"Things in the world are not so black and white, Master Darim," William said. "It was pure chance that Silvestra and I were reunited. I would remind you that it was you who assigned me to serve and protect Blademaster Alana Steeldrake."

"What of it?" Darim demanded.

"Were I not in the service of my Blademaster, I doubt I would have gone to Willowdale to encounter Silvestra once more," William shrugged. "Once I was there, I had little choice. I could either be in Silvestra's presence, or I could abandon the Blademaster. I know which of the two would be looked upon worse by the Inner Circle. And so I chose to stay and serve my Blademaster. Nor do I regret that choice."

"That is as may be," Balor interrupted. "But once that situation was resolved, you should have left Silvestra Knightwing's presence."

"Ah, see, that would have proved quite difficult," William shrugged. "During the battle at Willowdale, the dragon that was serving as Blademaster Alana's nathair an aeir a chosnaíonn was killed. Lord Taelin himself appointed Silvestra as her new nathair an aeir a chosnaíonn. And so again, I could stay in her presence or leave the Blademaster. I was forced to the same decision as when I first encountered Silvestra in Willowdale. I could not leave then any more than I could when I first saw her again."

"But you married her!" Balor thundered. "Against the express wishes of the Inner Circle."

"Do you know, I think I did, yes," William nodded. He scratched his chin. "What a wonder. I suppose you will wish the name of the person who bonded Silvestra and I against your will. I am sure you will want to deal with them as well."

"Indeed," Balor nodded. "You will tell us who performed this bonding against the express decree of the Inner Circle."

"Actually, I will tell you," Ferrin said from behind William. "The bonding was conducted by Lord Taelin himself. But if he had not done so, I likely would have myself."

That caught William's attention. He turned and gave his god a slight smile of appreciation. He made sure to wipe the smile off his face before turning back to the Inner Circle.

"It does not matter who performed the bonding," Balor waved his hand dismissively. "The fact remains that

William has violated a direct edict of the Inner Circle. We cannot allow him to enter the vortex when he cannot abide by edicts of the Inner Circle."

"So if I had bonded the two of them myself, it would not have made a difference to you?" Ferrin raised an eyebrow. "Do you forget who I am, Balor Wyndham?"

"I do not forget who you are, Lord Ferrin," Balor snapped. "But we cannot allow someone who cannot follow edicts from the Inner Circle to become the Dream Weaver. It is too important a position. Who knows what he would do? He could reveal things to his Blademaster that she should not know."

"In all of the years that there has been magic on Calthea, no mage has been denied access to the vortex when the mage has accepted the calling," William said softly. "I have been called. I am here."

"You will be the first to be denied," Balor thundered. "It is the decision of the Inner Circle that Roald Vilas must find another."

"No," Ferrin said softly from behind William. "William is the correct successor to the Dream Weaver. And he will enter the vortex to take the Test of Magic."

"This is a matter for the Inner Circle, Lord Ferrin," Balor snapped. "And we have decided that he will not."

"It is rare when Ferrin, Chemish and I agree on something, but in this we are in agreement," a deep booming voice called from behind William. "This mage is the right one to take the Test of Magic to become the next Dream Weaver."

"Lord Torval, you honor us with your presence," Alric said from the center of the table.

"If you are so honored, then you will allow this mage to take the Test of Magic," Torval thundered.

"We will discuss this new development," Alric said. "Please wait outside. All of you."

William bowed and turned to walk out of the chambers. He got to where Ferrin was standing but was stopped when his god put his hand on William's shoulder.

"No," Ferrin said. "There is to be no discussion. This has been decided. William Stonehands is to be the next

Dream Weaver should he pass the Test of Magic. I have every confidence that he will."

"Lord Ferrin," Balor called. "Why are the gods of magic so insistent upon this mage becoming the next Dream Weaver when it is clear that the Inner Circle is so opposed to it?"

"We have reasons of our own, Balor," Ferrin said with a shrug. "And they shall remain reasons of our own. In this, we are overriding the Inner Circle."

"This has not been done before," Alric said. "It is very disturbing."

"Disturbing or no, it is what is to be," Torval rumbled.

"Very well," Alric sighed. "If this is what the gods of magic wish, William Stonehands will be trained. In one month's time, if he is deemed ready, he will enter the vortex. What happens from there is not our concern. Remember, William, if you fail, you will not return from the vortex."

"I understand," William nodded.

"Go, then," Alric said. "Your trainer will see you tomorrow."

William bowed slightly to the Inner Circle before turning to face the two gods of magic. He bowed to them respectfully and mouthed "Thank you" to Ferrin.

He could feel the eyes of the entire Inner Circle on his back as he left the room.

Chapter IV
Training

William awoke the next morning to a banging on his door.

After throwing his robes over his head, William went over to open the door. The adept was once more at his door looking as if he wanted to be anywhere else. William squinted at the adept, the muted light in the hallway bright compared to the darkness of his chambers.

"Master William, I have been sent to summon you for your training," the adept said. "Please come."

"All right," William grimaced. "I will be out in a moment."

He closed the door against the adept's protests. Staring longingly at his bed, he sighed. He knew that too long a delay would result in the poor adept being disciplined. He would not be the cause of the adept visiting the Star Chamber. He took as little time as he could to make himself presentable.

Five minutes later, staff in hand, William followed the adept down the hallway.

The adept took him to a part of the Tower of the White to which he had never been. He knew that all nine orders, even Necromancy, had parts of the Tower where mages of that order trained. William had been of the Evocation Order when he had been at the Tower of the White before, so he had only spent time in the Evocation area.

Today, the adept was leading him to the Divination area.

It felt weird entering a new part of the Tower of the White, but he knew that, although he would retain his abilities as an evoker, the abilities he was about to learn belonged solely to the realm of Divination. It was only appropriate that any training for those abilities take place in the Divination section of the Tower of the White.

The adept led him to a small round room. There were no windows in the room. The room was well lit by light globes embedded into the wall of the room. There was no furniture in the room, only two thick pads on the floor, which William assumed would be where they practiced.

"I have been instructed to tell you to sit on one of the pads and wait for your instructor," the adept said. "I am to leave you now."

"There will come a day when you will terrify a young adept yourself, young one," William smiled kindly at the adept. "When that day comes, I pray you look back on this experience and it makes you smile."

The adept nodded and backed out of the room.

William sat on one of the pads with his legs crossed. He lay his staff across his knees and closed his eyes. Since it seemed like he would have some time before his instructor appeared, he figured it would be best to take some time to clear his mind and ready himself for the training that was to come.

With his mind clear, his senses were sharpened. He could hear the buzzing of a fly near one of the light globes. The faint odor of sweat wafted up from the mat he was sitting on. And the sound of shuffling feet outside the room came closer. Focusing on the shuffling steps, he tried to identify the gait of the mage that was coming to train him. He thought he recognized the pattern of the foot falls, but he could not be sure.

The shuffling steps came into the room and stopped at the mat across from William. The young mage could hear the other man grunt softly as he sat down on the mat. The grunt was enough to tell William who was in the room with him.

He opened his eyes to look at the Dream Weaver sitting across from him.

"Of course, you would be the one to train me," William bowed his head slightly. "Who else would know what it is I need to know?"

"Of course," Roald Vilas nodded to William. "Who but a Dream Weaver can teach a Dream Weaver? It has always been this way. It will always be this way. When it comes time for you to pass the mantle on to another, you will train that person just as I train you now."

"It only makes sense," William nodded. "What happens if a Dream Weaver dies before he can name his successor?"

"It has happened, but it is rare," Roald said. "In such a case the spirit of the Dream Weaver does the training of whoever it is that comes to take the mantle."

"I see," William frowned. "So he would not merge with the magic until his replacement is trained. I suppose that is part of the magic of the Dream Weaver."

"It is."

William thought on this for a while. He thought that it was a wise precaution to ensure that the line of Dream Weavers went unbroken. It was just one more way that magic continued to amaze him.

"Let us begin," Roald said. "Close your eyes and clear your mind of all thoughts..."

The Dream Weaver trained William for a month. Unlike when he was training to be an evoker, William cast no spells during his training. What Roald Vilas was training him to do was to open his mind to the predictions that would come when he wove dreams.

Although there were no actual spells that he was learning, William's training was still difficult. It was one thing to master a new spell. It was something altogether different to focus one's mind so that it could do something that it had never done before.

There were moments where he wanted nothing more than to give up. But he had committed to his path, and he was determined to see it through. And so he put in the work.

He saw very little of Silvestra during his training. It was hard for him to be so close to her and not spend time with her, but he spent all day every day in training. And when he was done training for the day, he only had energy to get something to eat on his way to collapse into his bed. William knew that she understood what he was going through and was supportive. He also knew that the lack of time together upset her as much as it did him. Moreso, probably, since she did not have training to take up her days and all of her energy. It made him feel bad to know she was so sad all the time.

There came a day about halfway through the training that the Dream Weaver surprised him.

As usual, William had arrived before the Dream Weaver had. He sat on his mat and placed his staff across his crossed knees as he had done every morning. Closing his eyes, he began to run through the exercises to open his mind. He had just expanded all of his sense when the Dream Weaver shuffled into the room.

"Open your eyes, William," the Dream Weaver said softly. "We will not be training your mind today."

William frowned and opened his eyes to look at the Dream Weaver. "Then what will we be doing today?"

"Today we will be discussing the most important thing you need to know as the Dream Weaver," Roald said softly. "It is also the most tricky. You must learn what you can and cannot tell others about the weavings that you dream."

"This sounds like something that is not going to be easy to understand," William frowned.

"Actually, it is very easy," Roald sighed. "Very easy to understand. Not quite as easy to do."

"Teach me, Master," William nodded.

"When you have a weaving, you will see the meaning of the weaving," Roald said. "And you will see the words that you can give and, often, who the words are intended for. You can only tell the words. You cannot tell any more about the weaving than that."

"I don't quite understand," William frowned.

"Do you remember the weaving I gave the Blademaster on the day that we met?" the Dream Weaver asked.

"OF course I do," William nodded. "It sounded ominous."

"It was far more ominous than it sounded," Roald said, his voice shaking. "Recite the words to me."

"As you wish," William said. He closed his eyes and sought out the memory of the words that were on the parchment the Dream Weaver gave Alana that day. "When the twice dead city falls empty a third time, the age of darkness will spread across the land.

"A wave of shadows shall block out the sun. The undead shall spread across the land in waves. Their number will be as close to endless. And they shall be led by the red eyed demon.

"Only the one truly born of the light can lead the army of light against the army of darkness."

William opened his eyes and looked at the Dream Weaver, who looked pleased that William remembered the words so exactly.

"Your memory is excellent, as it should be for a mage," Roald said. "But knowing the words does not begin to convey the pure horror of the weaving."

"How so?" William asked.

"Close your eyes, and open your mind," the Dream Weaver instructed. "I will show you the weaving and the words. But you can tell your Blademaster no more than what she has already been told about this weaving."

"I understand," William nodded once.

William closed his eyes and went through the exercises to open his mind to the visions that were going to come. He knew that the visions were not going to be easy to see, and he wanted to prepare himself as best he could.

After a few moments, he could feel the Dream Weaver press two fingers against each of his temples. Immediately, darkness in his mind's eye lifted.

William stood looking at a large field filled with soldiers. But they were not normal soldiers. William could tell by how they were moving that these soldiers were not alive. At least not in the conventional sense.

From where he was standing, he could not get a sense of just how large the army was, but he could not move. He was in a memory of a vision and could only experience what the Dream Weaver experienced in the original vision.

As the Dream Weaver moved, so did he. They shuffled their way to a hill overlooking the field. From the top of the hill, William could see that the army stretched out in an almost endless sea of writhing bodies. He felt sick at seeing the army. There was no way he could count the endless soldiers.

The Dream Weaver had been right that the mere words of the prophecy he had given Alana could never adequately prepare her for this sight.

He was moving again. The Dream Weaver was jostling through the army once more, heading towards the command tents that William had seen in the distance. William followed along, jostling past skeletons and zombies as he went.

It took what felt like hours to shove their way through to the command tents. William was amazed that they passed through unnoticed, but he imagined that was part of the magic of the Dream Weaver. He could only hope that the magic held.

When they arrived at the command tent, William could hear two voices, one of which he recognized immediately. He was disheartened but not surprised to hear the Nightstalker's voice. She had led the attack at the Temple of the Blades, after all. Still, even though he knew she was involved in the War of Souls, it was nonetheless disconcerting to hear her talking about the fate of people he cared about.

"As you can see, my army will sweep through the Southern Dales quickly once the snows allow for passage,"

the other voice said. It was a deep masculine voice, full of strength with just a touch of menace in it.

"I don't care what you do to the rest of the Southern Dales, General Atreus," the Nightstalker said. "Just make sure that the Blademaster and her companions are dealt with by no one but me."

"That is your part in this, then?" Atreus said.

"The Blademaster has bested me once," Kera Rayden spat. "It will not happen again. She and her companions are mine to kill. I will kill anyone who gets in my way."

"But, my dear Kera, we are already all dead in this army," Atreus said. William could swear he heard the man smile a wicked smile. But how could he hear a smile? "What have we to fear from such threats?"

"I give you free reign to do whatever you want to the Southern Dales, General," Kera growled. "Raze the entire kingdom to the ground for all I care. But the Blademaster and her companions are mine."

"Very well," Atreus said. "I—"

"What is it?" Kera said.

"We are not alone," Atreus said.

Could this Atreus have sensed them? William did not know how it could be possible, but it certainly sounded like he had sensed their presence through the magic of the weaving. William willed Roald to leave, but he could do nothing while the Dream Weaver stayed where he was. It was a memory, after all.

The flap to the tent opened, and the leader of the undead army emerged from the tent, Kera Rayden behind him.

As soon as William saw the general, he understood why this weaving had shaken the Dream Weaver so much.

Dressed head to toe in all black, General Atreus was a menacing sight. A black tunic tied all the way up to his chin, black breeches, black boots, black gloves, and a long black velvet cape clung to the man like they were painted on, leaving little to the imagination. He had an impressive physique. His face was pale, and exceedingly so. Long black hair was tied back with a velvet band that matched the cape he wore. But it was the eyes that arrested William's attention. They were blood red.

And they were staring directly at him.

It was as if the man, if he really was a man, was looking not at William, but at his soul. And everything was laid bare to this creature. All of William's wants and desires were there for the general's taking.

And then the general smiled.

Atreus had elongated canines filed to the sharpest of points. William tried not to think about those canines ripping into his neck to feed on his lifeblood. For he knew at that moment what the creature was.

When the general smiled, William snapped out of the memory...

William opened his eyes in the small room in the Tower of the White. He was panting heavily and his hands were wrapped around the Staff of Cirricus so tightly that his knuckles had gone white.

"I understand why this weaving scared you," William said through parched lips.

Roald said nothing. He passed over a skin of wine, and William lifted the skin to his lips, drawing off a mouthful.

"And are all weavings as vivid as that?" William asked.

"Not all, no," Roald said. "Many are simple with little in the way of detail. But some are like this. Incredibly vivid and detailed visions, much of which we cannot share with anyone. It is our burden."

"General Atreus is a vampyre," William said. He had regained control of his breathing and was starting to think about what this would mean for his Blademaster.

"A particularly old one too," the Dream Weaver nodded. "He will not be easy to defeat."

"And I cannot tell Alana what she will be facing," William said. He frowned. "She will be walking into this encounter blind."

"You must not tell her what he is before she meets him," Roald admonished. "To do so would be to introduce hesitation. She must meet the red eyed demon in her own time."

"And once she meets this General Atreus the first time?" William asked.

"Then you are free to tell her what you can about how to destroy this vampyre," Roald nodded. "But until then, you will be bound by the magic to not interfere."

"I understand," William nodded.

"There is something else you need to know about this vampyre," Roald said. "He is old enough that your magic will not harm him. Even SIlvestra's considerable magic, both human and dragon, will have little effect against a vampyre of this advanced age."

"What can we do then?" William frowned.

"Protect Alana from the other undead while she fights the vampyre on her own," Roald said, a sad note in his voice. "It will not be an easy battle for her, and she will need to use all of her skill."

"That we can do," William nodded.

"Good," Roald smiled. "And now you understand the difference between a weaving and the words that can be passed on in a weaving."

"I do."

"You are one step closer to being ready to enter the vortex," Roald said. "Come. We have more work to do."

Dragonsbane

Chapter V
Into the Vortex

n the morning that William was to enter the vortex to take the Test of Magic, he awoke when the light of the morning sun crept into the window of his small domicile.

He knew that he should be nervous about entering the vortex, but he was, much to his surprise, instead quite calm. He had trained hard for this moment. And he was glad that the time for the Test of Magic had finally come. He had been training hard, and he did not want to put off his return to the Blademaster any longer than he had to.

He knew that she was going to need him soon.

He was not sure what had him so convinced that the Blademaster would need him soon, but he knew without a doubt that the time was fast approaching when he would be needed by the Blademaster's side. He would have to be back to her when that time came.

Assuming of course, he passed the Test of Magic.

He shoved all thoughts of doubt away from the forefront of his mind. It would not do to dwell on even the slightest of doubts as he went into the Test of Magic. Such doubts would prove fatal once inside the vortex.

Besides which, he actually had little doubt that he would succeed in the Test of Magic.

He was certain that he would succeed. His work for the Blademaster was far too important for him to not be able to return to her. And while he knew that another mage would be assigned to Alana should he not make it through the Test of Magic, he knew it had to be he that was by her side during the War of Souls.

The best thing he could do would be to get started on his day, he decided. There were meditations he needed to do before entering the vortex, but those could wait.

First, he wanted to have breakfast with his wife.

He found Silvestra sitting by herself in the dining chambers. She looked miserable, and he knew that it was because they had seen so little of each other while he was training. He walked over to her table and sat down.

"I assume that I can sit here, my lady," he said softly as he sat.

"Of course!" she said. Her face transformed into a smile as soon as she saw him. "I am glad to see you."

"As I am to see you, my love," he said with a smile of his own. "We have things to discuss, but I do not have a great deal of time."

"You're entering the vortex tonight," Silvestra said. "I know. I have been keeping tabs on your progress."

"I need you to be there when I enter the vortex," he said.

"That will not make the Inner Circle happy," Silvestra reminded him. "Of course I will be there."

He reached across the table and took her hand. She smiled again and gave his hand a squeeze. William wanted nothing more than to just sit like that with her until it was time for the Test of Magic. He knew that he could not, though.

"Will you be ready to fly when I am done?" he asked.

"I am ready to fly now, William," Silvestra said. "Why?"

"We have been away from Alana too long, Silvestra," the mage sighed. "I fear what is happening with the preparations for the War of Souls in our absence."

"I understand," Silvestra nodded. "I am worried too. I scryed this morning. They are still in Ravendale. The snows have not stopped. At the moment, our friends are safe. But you and I both know that they will not be for long. I agree. We must return soon."

"Silvestra, listen to me," William said after a moment. "I am going to tell you something. You must return to Alana immediately if I do not return from the vortex. You must stay by her side."

"You will return, William," she said. "But if you do not, I will return to Alana's side. And may the gods have mercy on any enemy that gets in my path if you do not return, for I will have none."

"There is one more thing you will need to do if I fail to return, my love," William said. "And it will not make the Inner Circle happy, but I believe that it must be."

"What?"

"You must take the Staff of Cirricus back to the Temple of the Blades for safekeeping," William said. "There is something about this staff that is important to the War of Souls. I do not know what or how, but there will be a time when this staff is needed. It must be at the Temple of the Blades if I am no longer able to bear it."

"I understand," Silvestra nodded again. "It will be as you ask. But you will return. I believe it."

"I believe I will return too," he gave her a reassuring smile. "But I must make these plans in case I do not."

"I know."

William leaned forward and gave her a gentle kiss.

"I must go, love. There is much to do before I enter the vortex tonight."

He gave her hand another loving squeeze and stood. As he turned and left the dining hall, he could feel the happiness drain from Silvestra's face. And after leaving the dining hall, he realized he had not eaten.

He did not think he could eat at that point anyway.

William stood before Roald Vilas. The two mages were alone in a small room. It was almost time for William to enter the vortex to take the Test of Magic. But in order for him to do so, he needed to speak to the Dream Weaver one last time.

It was, after all, Roald he was to replace once he completed the Test of Magic.

"You have done well, William," the Dream Weaver said in his soft voice. "I am confident that I will be able to join with the magic this evening when you are done."

"I am honored that you had enough faith in me to choose me to be your replacement, Dream Weaver," William smiled. It was a sad smile, because he knew that he would never see the old mage again after he left the room. "I hope that I will prove to reward your faith in me."

"Oh, you will," Roald smiled. "Of that I am sure. You will do well as the Dream Weaver. Perhaps you will do better than I."

"We will see what we will see, I suppose," William shrugged. "I am as ready as I will ever be to take the Test of Magic."

"Yes, you are," the older man nodded. "You are anxious to get back to your Blademaster. I can assure you that the army of undead will not launch their attack until after you return to the Blademaster's side."

"You have had a weaving," William said. It was not a question. He knew the signs by now.

"I have," the Dream Weaver sighed. "It troubles me. I will tell you, but you cannot reveal what I say to the Blademaster. It might cause her to refuse to act, and she must see events through as they may be."

"What have you seen?" William asked.

"Before the War of Souls begins, a Blademaster will die," the Dream Weaver pronounced. "I do not know who, but I know that it is not Alana Steeldrake. I believe that you will be there when it happens, William. Or at least near enough. But there will be nothing you or anyone else can do to prevent this death. It will be a senseless death, but it will serve to save the lives of all the rest of your companions."

"Except for that Blademaster," William frowned.

"And her Protector," the Dream Weaver added. "Both will die. It will be a quick death, but both will die."

"And do you know where this will happen?" William asked.

"I do not know exactly where," the Dream Weaver shook his head. "All I can tell you is that they appeared to be in some form of castle. It appeared to be a stronghold dedicated to the One God."

"The One God," William's frown deepened. "We've fought servants of the One God before. In Willowdale."

"Yes," the Dream Weaver nodded. "I do not know if it is the same servants of the One God or others. I am sorry, William. I have given you all of the information I can give you. When you take on the mantle of the Dream Weaver, you will understand the frustration I feel at this moment. You, too, will be unable to give as much information as you would like to at times."

"It is all right, Dream Weaver," William smiled. "I understand the restrictions you live by. You have trained me well in that regard. Be comforted in the knowledge that I will take the information you have given me and use it as I can."

"You have learned your lessons well, William," the old man's eyes crinkled in a smile. "You are, indeed, ready for the vortex."

"Will you accompany me to the vortex, Roald?" William asked.

"I cannot," the old man said. "You will see me again only when you merge with the magic many years from now. Now go with my blessing."

The old man crossed the room and embraced William. William patted the old man's back and then broke the embrace, knowing that he needed to go prepare to enter the vortex. There was little time.

William smiled at the Dream Weaver one last time before stepping backwards through the door to the room.

Only when the door was closed did William allow the tears he had been holding back to fall.

The Inner Circle was at the table in the center of their chamber when William and Silvestra walked in. William's staff thumped with every step, and he walked with great purpose. He knew that Silvestra appearing in the Inner Circle chambers with him would cause anger and resentment amongst the members of the Inner Circle towards him, but he had valid reasons for wanting her there.

"I am ready," William announced. "Roald Vilas has deemed me ready to take the Test of Magic in order to become the new Dream Weaver."

"So we have been told," Alric said from the center of the table.

"What is *she* doing here?" Balor snapped.

"My wife is here at my request," William said. "She is here for several reasons. First, upon my successful completion of the Test of Magic, we will need to leave immediately to return to the Blademaster. There are matters that I must attend to there."

"And the other reasons?" Balor rumbled.

"She is to care for the Staff of Cirricus while I am in the vortex," William shrugged. "Silvestra has instructions to return the staff to the Temple of the Blades where it will be safe if I do not return from the vortex."

"Intolerable!" Balor thundered. "The staff will remain here if you do not succeed in your Test of Magic."

"Do not test me, Master Balor," William said softly. "While I am sure that you could best me one on one, there is more at stake here than the simple location of the staff. There is a reason that Cirricus left the staff at the Temple of the Blades. I believe that the staff will be integral in saving the Southern Dales from the army that is coming. Therefore, I will ensure that it will be where it is needed."

"How can you be so sure that you are right about the staff being needed?" Balor demanded.

"I am not completely sure," William shrugged. "But my instincts tell me that the staff would not have been given to me were it not going to be important."

"It is the instinct of a Dream Weaver," Wyric Janus, the head of the Divination Order, said softly. "I see now why Roald chose you, young William. If I may be so bold as to give you some advice?"

"Advice is always welcome from the head of an order, Master Wyric," William bowed his head in respect.

"Your instincts are sharp, William," Wyric said. "They will serve you well if you trust them. I do not doubt that your instincts will prove to be correct about the staff being needed in the War of Souls. I do not know how it will be, but I will consult the books of prophecy that I have access to in order to see if I can find out more for you. If I find anything, I shall send word to you in Ravendale."

"Thank you, Master Wyric," William bowed. "Your advice is welcome as is your aid."

"This is assuming he passes his Test of Magic," Balor scoffed. "Which I do still doubt he will."

"I do not," Wyric said, his eyes glazing over as he gazed inside himself. "I can see that we will be placing the mantle of Dream Weaver on this young mage this very evening."

"You have been wrong before, Wyric," Balor said.

"I have," Wyric nodded. "I am not wrong now, though."

"We shall see," Balor snapped. "Let us get this foolishness over with. If William Stonehands wishes to kill himself in the Test of Magic, I say let us have done with it."

Alric stood from the center of the table and motioned for the rest of the Inner Circle to join him.

"William Stonehands, you have been named as the successor to the Dream Weaver," Alric intoned. "Are you ready to submit yourself to the vortex to see if you are worthy to succeed Roald Vilas as the next man to wear the mantle of the Dream Weaver?"

"I am, Master Alric," William nodded once.

"Then follow," Alric said. "The Inner Circle and the dragon woman known as Silvestra Knightwing shall bear witness to your entrance into the vortex. Should you not return by this time tomorrow, we shall know you are not returning."

"I understand," William nodded.

"Very well," Alric nodded. "Then follow us to the vortex."

Alric led the members of the Inner Circle out of the chambers. William and Silvestra followed behind. The couple walked in silence, each knowing that the other had some nervous feelings about the upcoming Test of Magic for William. Neither wanted to say anything to worry the other though.

It was not a long walk from the chamber of the Inner Circle to the room with the vortex. William took the time offered to clear his mind, knowing that he would have to have his full faculties about him when he entered the vortex if he were to succeed.

His hand found Silvestra's, and he gave her hand a squeeze. She squeezed his hand back.

When they got to the room with the vortex, William let go of her hand and took a step forward.

"From here, you must go alone, William," Alric turned to the young mage and said. "We will stand and watch for you to return."

"Thank you," William nodded. He turned to Silvestra and held out the Staff of Cirricus to her. "Should I fail to return, you know what to do."

"You will return," Silvestra smiled. She took the staff from him. "I know you will."

William took a step forward and took Silvestra's face in his hands. He leaned down and kissed her, a deep and passionate kiss that made his heart race. He could feel the eyes of the Inner Circle on him, and he knew that at least one of them was looking at him disapprovingly.

He did not care.

He knew that entering the vortex would be difficult, as would whatever faced him on the other side of the singularity. He wanted the last thing he did before walking into that room to be something so loving and meaningful that it would help carry him through the Test of Magic. His love for Silvestra would be the light to lead him home, he knew.

The kiss lasted longer than he had intended it to, but he did not care about that either. When his lips parted from Silvestra's, they were both out of breath. It was a moment he would remember for the rest of his days.

"I love you, Silvestra Knightwing," he said, almost too soft to be heard.

"I know," she smiled up at him. "I love you too, William Stonehands. But you knew that too."

"I did," he returned the smile. He gazed at her smiling face, memorizing every wrinkle and every freckle. "There. Now I have a memory of perfect beauty to carry me through."

"Go," she said. "And come back to me soon."

He nodded once and turned back to the Inner Circle. The Mages of the Inner Circle parted to form a sort of human tunnel for him to pass through to get to the vortex.

William started walking, his eyes staring straight ahead. He kept his eyes focused on the vortex, not on the wizards he was passing by. It was the vortex that was calling him, and it was the vortex that was the most dangerous thing in the area. He would be foolish to take his eyes off it.

When he reached the vortex, he stopped. He could see ripples in the fabric of the singularity. He reached out and put his hand in the vortex. Ripples radiated out from his hand. He pulled his hand back out, and the singularity smoothed out.

William closed his eyes and stepped through...

Silvestra watched William step through the singularity and disappear. She fought down a moment of panic. She knew he would return. In the limited visions of their future that she had had, she had seen events that had not happened yet, so she knew he must return.

Unless those visions were ripples of what could be, not necessarily what would be.

She put that thought from her mind immediately. It would not do to dwell on that kind of thought. He would return.

She looked at the Mages of the Inner Circle. Only Balor Wyndham was looking away from the singularity. She frowned at that. The leader of the Evocation Order had been the most vocal about keeping William and her apart, and he had been the most vocal about keeping William from the vortex. Now, he was not watching the vortex as he was supposed to be.

This did not bode well, but she did not know what it could mean.

About five minutes after William entered the vortex, she felt the Staff of Cirricus start to tug against her grip. She looked at the staff with a quizzical expression. She could see the staff trying to pull itself from her grasp. This was not something she had expected.

Suddenly, the staff pulled free of her grasp and whipped forward towards the vortex. Silvestra took two steps towards the vortex trying to recover the staff, but it was gone in a blink.

"What happened?" Balor demanded. His voice was nothing short of accusing. "Did you throw the Staff of Cirricus into the vortex?"

"It pulled free from my hand," Silvestra said. "I was not expecting that to happen."

"The staff has gone to aid its master," Alric said. "It is not completely unexpected."

"If he fails, that means the Staff of Cirricus is lost to Calthea, Alric," Balor thundered. "Surely you cannot allow this!"

"What would you have me do, Balor?" Alric raised a bushy eyebrow. "Enter the vortex and retrieve the staff myself?"

"No," Balor backed down. "No, I suppose not. We shall just have to hope that Stonehands succeeds."

Chapter VI
The Test of Magic

illiam was not sure what he had expected when he entered the vortex. He wasn't sure what he would see on the other side of the singularity. From the side through which he entered, it looked to be a formless void full of chaotic lights and sounds.

He was not expecting to end up in what appeared to be a room in the Tower of the White.

And yet, that was where he landed upon stepping through the vortex. He looked around the room he found himself in. It looked like the room he lived in when he was training at the Tower of the White. The same small bed, washstand and wardrobe stood in the places he expected them to. The same wooden walls he had known for years while training stood around him.

Somehow, he knew he should not have been surprised. Roald had told him that the vortex would draw upon his experiences during the Test of Magic. The vortex must have pulled the room from his mind and decided that it would work as a place to put him when he arrived.

The thought was slightly disconcerting.

William looked around, with a frown. There was something that was bothering him about his surroundings. It wasn't the room itself. It was a perfect reproduction of his room in the Tower of the White. No, there was something else that was bothering him. It took him a moment, but finally, it came to him.

There were no background sounds.

The Tower of the White was always filled with the hum of power and the sounds of various spells being cast. There was always a background cacophony of sound.

But now, there was nothing.

It was as if he was the only person in the Tower of the White. He supposed that, since he was in the vortex, he was not actually in the Tower of the White, so it was possible that he actually was the only one in the Tower of the White.

It felt weird to not have his staff. He'd carried it with him every day since it had been entrusted to him in the Temple of the Blades. He understood why the Inner Circle had asked him to leave it behind. But it did not feel right attempting to make it through the Test of Magic without it. Frowning, he thought hard about the Staff of Cirricus, thinking that it might be something that he needed to get through the Test of Magic after all.

He heard a clunk behind him.

When he turned around, his jaw dropped when he saw the Staff of Cirricus lying on the ground behind him. He bent down and picked the staff up, looking it over from end to end. It was indeed the Staff of Cirricus. It had come to its master because it had felt his call.

He was amazed that he had been able to become enough of a master to the staff that it obeyed his summons like that.

He wondered what the Inner Circle must have thought when the staff disappeared into the vortex. The young mage allowed himself a quick smile at the consternation it probably caused the Inner Circle. He allowed himself the one moment of amusement. But not more than that. He knew that he would have to get on with the Test of Magic.

If he did not, he would never pass and he would end up becoming a part of the magic.

William made his way over to the door of the little room, his staff thumping the floor with every step. When he threw open the door, he found himself looking into darkness. All of the light globes in the corridor were out.

"*Sentalusin,*" he called out.

William was not exactly surprised when the light globes did not light at his command. He would have been far more surprised had they done so. It was no matter. The fact that the Staff of Cirricus had made its way to him in the vortex meant that he had his own light source.

"*Sentalusin Cirricus,*" he whispered.

The crystal at the top of the Staff of Cirricus lit up immediately, shining a bright glow around William. The glow did not fully drive out the darkness, but it gave him enough light to see at least a few feet in every direction around him. It was a small comfort to know that he would not have to navigate the Tower of the White in the darkness.

William was not sure where he was supposed to go in the Tower of the White for his test. He had an inkling as to where it would be, but it was only an inkling. It was more to go on than he would otherwise have. But he had to be sure. He thought that the best thing to do would be to go to the chambers of the Inner Circle. If this simulacrum of the Tower of the White were anything like the original, then that would be the place where he was most likely to get information as to where to go.

Decided on a plan of action, the young mage began to make his way down the corridor. He had taken no more than a few steps when he stopped short. There was a short stooped man standing in the corridor directly ahead of him.

"Hello?" William called to the man.

"Hello yourself," the man replied, turning to face William. "You're here for the Test of Magic, yes?'

"Yes," William nodded.

"Figures."

The old man turned and started to hobble away from William. The young mage hurried to catch the old man before he disappeared.

"Wait." William called. "What do you mean by saying figures??"

"No one ever comes in here just to visit me," the old man grumbled. "It's always for the test."

"Who are you?" William asked as he caught up to the old man. "What are you doing here anyway? I did not think anyone could stay in the vortex for too long or they would merge with the magic."

"Thought wrong then," the old man grumbled. "I've always been here. I will always be here."

"Who are you?"

"My name is too difficult for you to say," the man looked over at William. "Call me... Zathras. Yes. Zathras. That will work."

"OK, er, Zathras," William said, clearly flustered with the old man. "Maybe someday I can come visit you."

"You say that, but you'll never visit," Zathras sighed. "No one ever does. It is a sad existence for me."

"What is it that you do here?" William asked.

The old man shuffled forward a few steps before stopping. William kept walking for a few steps before he realized that the old man was no longer right next to him. William turned to look back at the old man with a raised eyebrow.

"I am a guide, of sorts," Zathras explained. "I am to take you to your Test of Magic. And I am to witness it. But I can give you no help other than taking you to where it is that your test will take place. Once I do that, you are on your own."

"I understand," William nodded. "It is, honestly, more assistance than I expected to get while I was inside the vortex. So, Zathras. Where am I going?"

"You already know, young mage," the old man smiled. "There is only one place that a Test of Magic could take place for you."

"The Star Chamber," William groaned. "It would be the Star Chamber."

"Of course it is," the old man wheezed. "There is no other place that would be appropriate for you to take your test of magic. You should go there now. He is waiting for you."

"Who is he?"

"You will see."

William looked at the old man, but it was clear that there was nothing more that Zathras was going to say to him. Shrugging, William turned and started walking towards the Star Chamber.

As he walked, William thought about everything that Roald had told him about the Test of Magic. Roald had said that there was no way to know what he would be required to do ahead of time. The Test of Magic was different for each person. But it would, the Dream Weaver said, test his character and intellect. As the Dream Weaver was an important position amongst the mages, it was imperative that they get the right person installed with the mantle of the Dream Weaver. William supposed that it was much the same way as it was with finding the Protectors for Blademasters. Only the right person for the job would do.

As he walked through the corridors of the Tower of the White, he thought about how he had come to be where he was. He had come a long way from when he first arrived at the Tower of the White as a teen. His training had been difficult, and he had caused no end of trouble, but his teachers had all told him that he was destined to be a great mage. Even the Master Adept had admitted, grudgingly, that William might one day become an above average mage.

From the Master Adept, that was high praise indeed.

His training at the Tower of the White had not sufficiently prepared him for his adventures, though. When he was training, no one had known that he would become a companion to the first Blademaster in three hundred years. Nor could anyone have prepared him for what he would see at the Blademaster's side.

And no one could have prepared him for his part in the Great War of Souls.

While the prophecy of the Great War of Souls was well known to many in the divination order, it was not common knowledge to the rest of the mages. Had it been, William would have known of it before they found the prophecy in the caves above WIllowdale. But he had not known. And so, he was surprised to find out that he was about to be embroiled in such a conflict.

And then there was the army of undead.

He knew that it was going to be a difficult war because of the enemy they would be fighting. It was hard to kill something that was already dead. The Blademaster and her companions would have a difficult time cutting through this enemy like they had done so many others. And the fate of the entirety of the Southern Dales was at stake.

William knew the real reason he had agreed to take the Test of Magic to become the Dream Weaver. It had nothing to do with the power he would be accorded in his new position. For William, this was about knowledge. Everything he had done towards acquiring his mage skills had been about knowledge.

That was the true power he sought.

In this case, though, he knew that the knowledge he sought would not be just to help himself. He knew that he sought the ability to help his Blademaster. And, in turn, the Southern Dales.

William had been to the Star Chamber so many times, he could walk there with his eyes closed. And he figured that, even though this was not the Tower of the White he had trained in, the Star Chamber would be located in the same place.

The only question in William's mind, though, was who would be waiting for him in the Star Chamber?

Were he still in the Tower of the White, he knew, it would be the Master Adept waiting for him in the Star Chamber. But he did not see how the Master Adept could be here inside the vortex. And yet, he would put nothing past the Master Adept. If there was a way that he could be here to conduct William's Test of Magic he would be.

William's impression of the Master Adept had changed somewhat since he had arrived at the Tower of the White. He had been surprised by how the Master Adept had argued for him in front of the Inner Circle to take the Test of Magic. He had honestly thought that the Master Adept had not liked him all those years ago when he had been at the Tower of the White for training.

Now he was starting to believe that the Master Adept had only been trying to push him.

It would appear that experience brought not only knowledge but wisdom as well.

As William pondered these things, he had kept right on walking towards the Star Chamber, his feet carrying him automatically onwards towards his test. He was surprised to suddenly find himself staring at the door to the Star Chamber.

William took a deep breath, steeling his nerves, and then threw open the door to the Star Chamber.

In the center of the circle of light cast by the stars' light filtering through the domed ceiling of the chamber, there stood a single robed figure. Whoever it was wore the crushed velvet robes of a Mage of the White. William found nothing odd about this. They were in the Tower of the White after all. William wasn't sure, but he thought there might be others in the Star Chamber. He could not see them for sure, but he did not believe that he and the white robed mage in the center of the chamber were the only two there for this Test of Magic.

"Summoned, I have come," William called out boldly.

"Then come into the light and be seen," the figure in the center of the Star Chamber said. It was a deep masculine voice, full of strength and power.

William stepped forward into the light, his staff thumping against the floor as he walked forward. He kept his eyes locked on the figure in the center of the room. While he did not know who it was, William knew that this was the person who would decide whether or not he was acceptable to replace Roald Vilas as the Dream Weaver.

"I am William Stonehands," William said after he stopped inside the circle of light. "Companion to the Blademaster, Alana Steeldrake and husband to the dragon, Silvestra Knightwing. I have come as I was bid to submit myself to the Test of Magic. Roald Vilas bid me come, for he intends me to replace him as the Dream Weaver."

"Companion to a Blademaster and husband to a dragon," the figure said, his voice soft and silky. "You do seem to be a figure that events of import would gravitate towards."

"So it would appear," William shrugged. "I asked for none of it. All I can do is make the most of the situation I find myself in."

"Yes," the figure nodded. "That is all any of us can do."

"And who are you, sir?" William asked. "If I am to be judged, I think it only fair to know who is judging my ability to become the Dream Weaver."

"I am Thurl Ravenscroft," the man said. He pulled his hood back to reveal long silver hair and intense blue eyes. He had a long silver beard that tapered to a point above his breastbone. "I am the first."

"The first?"

"The first Dream Weaver," the other wizard said. "Before me, no one wove the dreams to teach the others of what was to come. I was the first, and I am the only one who can judge who is to become the next one."

"If I may be so bold, how did you become the Dream Weaver if no one before you had woven the dreams?" William asked, his curious nature taking over.

"It was I that created the magic responsible for the weavings," Thurl Ravenscroft said. "I am the weaver of the magic. That is why only I can properly judge the fitness of a new potential Dream Weaver."

"But how did you create such a magic?" William asked. "It seems quite a massive undertaking."

"It was a challenge," Thurl smiled. "I have never been one to back away from a challenge. That was my weakness. And my strength. You have what seems an undying thirst for knowledge. That is your weakness. Turn that weakness into a strength and you could become one of the best of us."

"It is true that the only power I seek is knowledge," William said quietly. "That quest has brought me both pain and joy. I would not change anything about the way my search for knowledge has shaped my life."

"Very good," Thurl nodded. "You have already passed the first test."

"And how many tests are there?"

"As many as it takes for me to be satisfied," Thurl replied. "It will take what it takes."

"As is always the way," William nodded.

"You will wait here until I return," the first Dream Weaver said. "I will not be long. And when I return, we shall talk some more. I will know all your secrets before this night is out."

William did not like the sound of that, but he had no choice. If he was to survive the Test of Magic and become the new Dream Weaver, there was only one thing that he could do, and that was to keep going on the path that was before him.

He had no idea how long he would have to wait before Thurl returned. It did not matter. He would wait as long as he had to. Unlike a lot of his companions, William had a great deal of patience. It came with a thirst for knowledge. One could not rush through a book, after all, if one wished to retain the knowledge within. A true grasp of knowledge required long study.

While he waited for Thurl to return, William went through all he knew about the Dream Weavers and thought about what might be expected of him in the coming tests. He knew that there would be a test of magical ability as well as a test of his character. He was confident enough in both to believe that he would pass both. But he was not sure that Thurl would see him as a fit candidate to become the Dream Weaver. He was not sure what he could do to convince the first Dream Weaver of his fitness.

It would be if it was meant to be.

"I have heard told that you are a talented evoker, young William Stonehands," Thurl said, surprising William. He had not seen the first Dream Weaver return, and yet Thurl was standing right in front of him once more.

"I have studied well," William shrugged. "Whether or not I am talented is for others to judge."

"And so I shall," Thurl nodded. "Defend yourself!"

William did not wait for Thurl to complete his attack. He stepped back one step and brought he Staff of Cirricus in front of him, planting the butt of the staff firmly on the floor.

"*Sentreus malleus*," William whispered.

Instantly, the strongest shield William knew, a shield of thick air that would change with the attack against him, sprang up around him in a sphere. It started as air interwoven with threads of ice. The jet of flame that Thurl cast at him sputtered against the shield but did not breach it.

William grunted against the onslaught of fire, but the shield held.

Thurl said a word of command, and the jet of fire turned to lightning. William's shield adjusted itself accordingly, and the threads of ice turned into splinters of wood swirling through the shield of air.

"Most impressive," Thurl said. "A malleable shield like that is a very advanced bit of magic."

"That's the first time I've been able to adjust the shield on the fly like that, to be honest," William shrugged maintaining his concentration on the shield. "It's the first time I've cast that with this staff. Perhaps that is the reason why."

"Perhaps," Thurl nodded. "It is a powerful staff. I can feel that from here."

"It was owned by a Mage of the Inner Circle once," William said.

"That would explain the powerful feel," Thurl nodded. "Now. Attack me."

"No."

"No?" Thurl stopped and looked at William oddly. "You would risk failing the Test of Magic by ignoring a command given during the test?"

"If it means holding to my vows, yes," William nodded. "When I took the white, I vowed to protect life. If I were to just attack you without provocation, and it really would be without provocation, which would be a violation of my vows."

"But you have killed, surely?" Thurl said.

"I have when it has been to preserve life," William nodded sadly. "But it is never without cost. And it is never something I do unless I have absolutely no other choice. I always try to subdue rather than kill whenever possible. There are times when it is unavoidable. Part of why I serve the Blademaster that I serve is that she believes in the sanctity of life as much as I do. She and her Protector do not take lives if they can avoid it. I have seen them attack with the flats of their blades to knock out their opponents rather than striking to kill."

"Very interesting," Thurl stroked his chin. "You have given me a great deal to think about. You will wait here."

William was not surprised when Thurl vanished once more. He wondered how long he would have to wait this time. It did not matter. He would wait however long it took. The way was the way, as it had always been said.

As it turned out, he did not have to wait long. It was just a few minutes later when the first Dream Weaver reappeared in the Star Chamber facing William once more.

"I am satisfied that you are the correct person for the mantle to be passed to, William Stonehands," Thurl said in a soft voice. "The Test of Magic has ended."

With those words, Thurl disappeared for one final time. And William knew he would not return again.

William stared at where Thurl Ravenscroft had been standing. The first Dream Weaver's sudden disappearance had caught William by surprise. He supposed it shouldn't have, because Thurl kept disappearing suddenly throughout the entire test. But it did not matter. Because William knew by Thurl's last words that he had passed his Test of Magic.

He was now the Dream Weaver.

The magic came upon him all at once, buffeting him with magical energies. The magic came from all around him, pummeling him with force. It was almost too much to bear, but he knew that he must bear it, for this was the way he was to receive the mantle of the Dream Weaver. If he faltered in accepting this magic, it would be as if he had failed the Test of Magic outright.

He would not do that.

And so he stood there and let the magic surround him and flow through him. He could feel the power crackle through his body, infusing him with the power and the mantle of the Dream Weaver. He reveled in the feeling of added power. He could see the ebb and flow of eddies in the currents of magic, and he ran his hands through those eddies, caressing them like he would Silvestra's skin.

As quickly as it had started, it was over. The buffeting magic subsided, and he stood there alone in the center of the Star Chamber. And he knew that he had successfully received the mantle of the Dream Weaver. He had survived the ordeal.

He looked once more to where the first Dream Weaver had stood before, and he caught sight of a glint of silver on the floor. Slowly and cautiously, William stepped forward and squatted down.

There on the floor was the ring of the Dream Weaver.

William picked it up and looked at it. Intricately woven of fine silver threads, the setting of the ring was made of four interwoven curved leaves woven into a spiral pattern. He had, of course, seen the ring before, but the last time he had seen it, the ring had been on Roald Vilas's finger.

"That is yours now," Roald's voice came to him on the breeze. "You have done well, William Stonehands. And now, it is time for me to join with the magic and begin the long sleep. Farewell. You will see me again when it is your time to become one with the magic."

"Farewell, Roald," William said softly. "Go unto your sleep, for you have earned it. And go with peace."

William slipped the ring on his finger and stood. When he turned to leave the Star Chamber, he saw Zathras standing in the doorway waiting for him.

"I have come to guide you out of the vortex, Dream Weaver," Zathras said. "You have passed your Test of Magic, I see."

"I have," William nodded.

"And now you will leave me alone once more," Zathras said, his voice bitter.

"Zathras, I believe that I will see you at least one more time before I bring my successor to the Tower of the White for his Test of Magic," William said, looking at the old man oddly. "I do not know why I believe this, nor do I know when, but I know that I will enter the vortex at least one more time in my life. And it will be specifically to speak to you. I had this flash of insight when I put the ring on."

"You would be the first Dream Weaver to do so," Zathras grumbled. "I think you would be the first mage of any kind to enter the vortex just to speak to me. Why would you say this to me?"

"Because I believe it to be the truth," William shrugged as he started to walk out of the Star Chamber. "I do not know when or how, but there will come a time when you will have answers for me. When that time comes, I will have to come to where you are to get those answers."

"You would seek me out for answers, Dream Weaver?" Zathras stared at William. "No one listens to Zathras."

"I would, yes," William nodded. He gently placed his hand on the old man's shoulder. "I know you have a hard time believing me since no one has ever come into the vortex just to speak with you, but the time will come when I will need your knowledge."

The old man nodded. The two men walked for a few minutes in silence before Zathras put his hand out to stop William. He turned to face the younger man.

"Then take some of my knowledge now, for what I would tell you is critical to your Blademaster," Zathras said softly.

"I am listening," William nodded.

"Do not trust the necromancers," Zathras said. "Caliban has forsaken his vows of non-involvement. He is working directly for the Dark God to bring down the Southern Dales. Caliban is working on a magic that will allow his necromancers to instantly raise any soldier that one of their army slays. Your Blademaster must find a way to stop him before this happens, or else it will be next to impossible for the Southern Dales to win this war."

"Why would you tell me this?" William asked, surprised at the old man's betrayal of the Inner Circle.

"Because I believe in the Blademasters," Zathras said. The old man smiled, showing crooked teeth. "And I believe in what your Blademaster is trying to do in saving the

Southern Dales. I can give this help to her. Heed my words, young one."

"I will bring this warning directly to the Blademaster," William nodded once. "You have my word. And my thanks."

"That you would heed my warning without question is thanks enough," Zathras rumbled. He turned to lead William the rest of the way out of the vortex. "Finally, someone listens to poor Zathras."

Part II
Tunera Ironmoon

Chapter VII
Iron and Feathers

S far south in the Southern Dales as Talondale was, the winter was not as harsh. There was still snow, but not nearly as much as there had been in other parts of the Southern Dales. It was a decided benefit to living in the southern port city.

Despite the lack of snow, though, trade still lagged in the winter. Deliveries of goods from other parts of the Southern Dales were delayed due to impassable roads. But the residents of Talondale did the best they could with what they had. They always did.

On High Street, a variety of stores flourished even with the delays in goods arriving in Talondale. There were stores of all kinds. The general store was owned by a big bear of a man named Talor Ironmoon. He was considered to be one of the fairest shop owners in Talondale. He never overcharged his customers, even when he easily could. He had always considered such to be bad business.

Talor had owned the store for a number of years, ever since his father had handed over the keys to him. It had been in his family for generations. He had hopes that his daughter, Tunera, would inherit the store from him someday. She showed an aptitude for business, even if her head was sometimes in the clouds.

Even with her periods of daydreaming, he was hopeful that she would take over the business when the time came. Tunera was his only child. His wife had died years before, and he had never remarried. He had never had any interest in doing so. He lived life for himself and for his daughter. It was enough for him.

The store was his second love. His daughter, though, would always take precedence over the store. She was his heart. He did not know what he would do without her. He supposed that was the way all fathers felt about their daughters, but it did not change that it was how he felt.

All he did, he did for her. He wanted to provide her the best life that he could. And the store allowed him to do so. She worked with him in the store, often out running errands or making deliveries. It helped to have her close by like that, even though she no longer lived with him. She had purchased a small house not far from his where she lived by herself.

Talor hoped that she would not be by herself in that little house for long.

There was a man in his daughter's life, he knew. And he liked the young man. Tomas Fletcher was an apprentice for the blacksmith, Gareth Wayland. He was a good man, and he treated Tunera well. There was little more that Talor could ask of a suitor for his daughter. He had a good trade, and he was a kind man.

And Tomas loved Tunera.

There was talk that Tomas and Tunera might get married one day. Talor had no objection to such a marriage. In fact, he welcomed it. He could not think of a better match for her. And he believed that she would be happy married to Tomas.

Things nagged in the back of Talor's mind, though. Whispers of a memory told him that marrying Tomas would bring Tunera great sadness as well as great joy. But he did not dwell on such thoughts. He chose to dwell only on Tunera being happy. Even though he knew that that happiness would be tinged with tragedy, he still wanted her to have happiness.

It was a lovely day for winter and Talor was in his shop, preparing some sandwiches that he would sell from his shop throughout the day. As he was cutting some meat into thin slices, he whistled softly to himself. Talor enjoyed making sandwiches for his customers. It was a service that most shop owners did not think to provide to their customers. It did not cost much to make the sandwiches, and it would allow his customers to shop on a full stomach. And his customers appreciated the gesture.

The daily cutting of the meat had been getting more difficult recently. So when he was done slicing the meat for that day's sandwiches, he looked at his knives carefully. Frowning, he tested the edges. They had all grown dull on him.

Well, he knew someone who could fix the knives.

And he was sure that Tunera would not mind taking them over to the blacksmith to hone the edges for him. After all, that would allow her to see Tomas. Tunera would never go to visit Tomas at work unless it were related to business for the store. But Talor also knew that she would not turn up the chance to go see him.

"Tunera!" Talor bellowed.

The young woman came out of the back room where she had been doing inventory. Dust covered her face and hands. She wiped her hands on her smock and then used it to wipe her face clear of dust.

"Yes, Father?" she said.

"I need you take these knives over to Gareth to have them honed," Talor said pointing to the knives on the counter.

"As you wish, Father," Tunera nodded.

She packed the knives carefully in a crate to carry them over to the blacksmith. After the knives were packed, she went back into the back room and grabbed her cloak.

"And I don't want you back until they're ready," he winked at her on her way out the door.

"Yes, Father," she said with a twinkle in her eye.

Talor watched her go. He recognized the light step of someone in love. He had once walked like that back when his wife, Taryn, was still alive. It did his heart good to see his daughter so thoroughly in love.

Love was a good thing, no matter how you looked at it.

As soon as he could no longer see his daughter through the doorway, Talor went back to making the sandwiches for his customers. Overall, the man was happy with the way his life currently stood. He supposed that he would be happier had his Taryn still been alive, but other than that, his life was good.

As he put the sandwiches together, he paid little attention to the door. So he was surprised when he heard someone clearing their throat on the other side of the counter.

The shopkeeper looked up, startled. There was a man wearing long white crushed velvet robes standing on the other side of the counter. He was an older man with greying hair and piercing blue eyes.

Talor immediately decided that this man was trouble.

"We're not really open yet, but can I help you?" Talor asked the strange visitor.

"Are you Talor Ironmoon?" the man asked in a soft voice.

"I am," Talor nodded. "This is my shop. What can I do for you?"

"I am looking for your daughter, Tunera," the old man said.

"I'm afraid she's not here," Talor frowned. The fact that the old man was looking for Tunera confirmed to Talor that he was trouble. "What do you want with my daughter?"

"You already know," the old man said. "Surely, you remember the Dream Weaver telling you that Tunera would leave Talondale at some point in the future."

"I remember," Talor nodded, his suspicions now completely confirmed. This man was trouble. "What of it?"

"It is time for her to go on her journey," the old man sighed. "I am here to send her on her way."

"No!" Talor yelled. "It is too soon! She just found true love! You can't take her now."

"I take no joy in this, Talor, but this is the time for her to go," the old man said. "The fate of the entirety of the Southern Dales depends on her going and fulfilling her destiny. The fact that she has found true love will only help her."

"This is not fair!" Talor growled.

"Nowhere is it written that life will ever be fair, Talor," the old man sighed again. "Were the consequences for Tunera not going to face her destiny not so dire, I would be happy to leave and never return."

"Then go," Talor snapped. "Go and be gone."

"I cannot."

"Why? Why is my daughter so important?" Talor demanded.

"I cannot tell you that," the old man said. "I have said too much already. I can only tell you that this is necessary."

"It always is with you mages," Talor sighed deeply. He leaned forward against the counter, happy for its support. "Do what you must and be gone from Talondale. I do not want to see your face again."

"You will not," the old man assured him. "Nor will you remember this conversation. I will cast a spell to help you forget you even saw me."

"Wait!" the shopkeeper said. "If you're going to make me forget, at least tell me where my daughter is going before you do."

"She is going to the Temple of the Blades," the old man said softly. He thrust forward his staff and placed the butt of it firmly against the floor.

"But that means she's going to be—"

"Oblivus!" the old man roared cutting Talor off.

A blinding pulse of light flashed from the crystal on the staff, causing the shopkeeper to freeze. The old man slumped from the loss of energy used on the spell and sighed. He took two of the sandwiches that Talor had made and dropped two gold coins on the counter in return. It was far more than the two sandwiches would have cost, the old man knew, but the gold meant nothing to the old man.

He walked out of the shop. Talor remained frozen in place until after the old man had vanished from sight.

When Talor was able to move again, he looked around the shop for whoever had cleared their throat. When he didn't see anyone, he turned back to the sandwiches he'd been working on. He saw the two gold coins and saw that there were two sandwiches missing.

"Well, at least whoever it was, was honest about taking my sandwiches," he grumbled.

Tunera Ironmoon was in a good mood. It was a beautiful day and she was getting to go see her love in the middle of the work day. It was not a luxury she got to take advantage of often. Only when her father had work for the blacksmith could she get away with such a visit while they were working.

But with her father's knives needing to be sharpened, there was no choice but for her to go visit Gareth's shop and to spend time with Tomas Fletcher.

It had been two years since their courtship had started. Tomas had asked her to dance at the harvest festival. With her dark skin and exotic looks, she got many an offer for a twirl, but she almost never accepted an invitation to dance.

For some reason she had accepted Tomas's.

She had seen the blacksmith's apprentice many times when she had gone to Gareth's shop on business. But she had given the young man little thought prior to that dance at the festival. She had assumed that Tomas was all brawn. As she got to know the young man, she realized how wrong she was. Gareth had insisted that his apprentices learn to read and write, but Tomas had already learned both skills.

Tunera found that Tomas was a learned and intelligent young man who just happened to have a strong aptitude for the smith trade. And the more she got to know him, the more she fell for him.

It had taken Tomas a full month after the harvest festival to work up the courage, but when he did, Tomas went to Tunera's father to ask for permission to court his daughter. Her father had been impressed that the young man chose to show respect towards him by asking for permission rather than just going to Tunera. It was a respect that was slowly fading from the world, but Talor was happy to see that some of the younger generation still chose to show respect to their elders.

He had, of course, reacted to this respect positively. He had given the young man permission to court Tunera.

Now, a year and a half later, Tomas had recently asked Tunera to marry him. And she had said yes. She could not imagine being with anyone else. And she believed that he felt the same way.

As she made her way down the road towards Gareth's blacksmith's shop, Tunera smiled to various people as she passed them. She had always been a friendly person, and that had gone a long way to keeping the customers coming into her father's store. And when she took the store over in the future, she knew that it would help her keep customers that might have otherwise left.

It was not far from her father's store to the blacksmith shop. So it did not take long for her to get there. Gareth, himself, was in the entry when she arrived. He was an older man, older than her father was, but still strong. His hair was starting to go grey at the temples, and there were a fair few wrinkles around his eyes.

"Good morning, Master Gareth," she said in a merry tone when she walked in.

"Ah, young Tunera," the middle aged blacksmith said with a warm smile. "Here with some work for me from your father, I take it?"

"Yes, Master Gareth," she nodded. "His knives have dulled and he asked me to bring them to you to give them fresh edges."

"Ah yes," Gareth nodded. "Well, I would, of course, be happy to put nice sharp edges on them for your father. But I believe Tomas is free to do the work, and I would imagine that you would much rather sit with him while he did the work than sit with me."

"You know I don't like to disturb Tomas at work, Master Gareth," Tunera said.

"That is why I have no problem with you going back now to have him do the work, Tunera," the blacksmith smiled broadly at her. "You have respected my place of business this entire time. It will take him some time to sharpen all of your father's knives. I cannot begrudge you sitting with him while he does so."

"Thank you, Master Gareth," Tunera smiled and nodded.

She hefted the crate with the knives in it and made her way back to the work area of the smithy shop.

She had been to the smithy any number of times on errands for her father, and it never changed. Always covered in soot and ash, and it always smelled of smoke and ash.

She took the crate over to where she saw Tomas working. The young man was studying a piece of metal, and she knew that he was looking it over to see if he could identify any flaws in the piece before he started to work on it. She set the crate down and watched him, not wanting to interrupt his inspection.

When he was satisfied with what he was seeing, he set the piece of metal down and turned around. He smiled when he saw her. He always smiled when he saw her.

"Hello, Tunera," he said, his voice soft. "I take it that since you are here while I am working, this is not a social visit."

"Father's knives have gone dull," Tunera shrugged. "He sent me here to have them sharpened. Master Gareth told me to have you look at them."

"He did, did he?" Tomas's smile grew broader. "Well, let me have a look then."

Tomas took the crate from her and opened it. As he pulled out each knife, he inspected the edge, nodding to himself as he looked over each one. He made small grunts as he worked.

There were five knives in all. Each of them had grown dull. But Tomas was a deft hand and Tunera knew that it would not take him long to put a sharp edge on all five.

The blacksmith's apprentice worked quickly, honing each knife to a keen edge. Although he worked quickly, he was also careful to sharpen the blades evenly. It would not do to have an uneven edge.

Soon enough, though, he was done. He carefully repacked the knives into the carrying crate and closed it up.

"Your father's knives should be fine for quite some time," Tomas said. "We will add it to his bill and he can pay at the end of the month."

"Of course," Tunera nodded. She picked up the crate and started out of the smithy shop. She turned, though and smiled at Tomas. "Come have dinner tomorrow. I shall make you a fine beef stew."

"I will never turn down a chance for your beef stew," he said. "I will be there."

"Good," she said, her smile widening. "I will see you then."

She walked back over to Tomas and planted a kiss on his cheek. Even as quickly as she turned away, she could see his face reddening. She knew he would have some explaining to do to Gareth later.

Tunera could feel his eyes on her the entire way out of the smithy shop.

Dragonsbane

Chapter VIII
Visit from the Sage

T was a sunny morning in mid winter, and Tunera was tending the garden outside her house. It was a small garden with various vegetables and herbs that helped to feed herself and her father. The garden was a passion of hers, and it had served to save her family a good amount of money over the years.

She was careful in tending the vegetation, making sure to remove all of the weeds, but making sure that the good plants remained untouched. It was a slow process, but it gave her great joy to kneel in the dirt and care for her plants.

As she worked, she hummed to herself. It was an old tune that her mother had sang as a lullaby years before. She remembered the lullaby even if she did not remember her mother so well. Tunera's mother had died when she was very young. Her father told her that she had been ill for a long time before dying. Knowing that did not make it hurt any less to lose her.

Now all that Tunera had of her mother was a necklace and the memories of her lullabies.

She often hummed one of her mother's lullabies while she worked in her garden. It helped to keep her focused. She needed to stay focused in order to keep up with the work in the garden.

The weeding was slow, but she was meticulous, making sure every weed was pulled while making sure that she was careful to leave the good plants. The garden had not been weeded in a while, even though she had been careful to tend it otherwise. She had just not had the time to pull weeds.

It still amazed her that she could grow things year round in Talondale. She knew that her garden would never have survived in other parts of the world, and she felt fortunate to be able to have fresh vegetables even in the middle of winter.

It was a lovely day for working in the garden, and she was happy. She would be seeing Tomas later, which always made her happier. The two of them worked well as a couple, everyone said. Tunera agreed. Which is why she had agreed to marry Tomas. Her father was pleased with the arrangement. Tomas was good for her, he thought.

She was going to make a lovely dinner for Tomas this evening, and it helped that there would be fresh vegetables for the dinner.

When she was done with the weeding, Tunera gathered some carrots and potatoes for dinner. The carrots were the bright orange that you could only get from freshly pulled carrots. And the potatoes were nice and big.

As she was gathering up the carrots and potatoes into a basket, she noticed someone coming up the street towards her house. Normally, someone coming up to her house wouldn't make her stop and take notice, but there was something about this person that had her attention from the moment she noticed him.

He was wearing long white robes of soft crushed velvet. The robes had somehow managed to stay pristine white despite his clearly having travelled a long way. He appeared to be tiring and was leaning heavily on a thick oaken staff. As he walked, she could see flashes of well work black leather boots under his robes. He had short greying hair and deep blue eyes, the kind of eyes someone could get lost in. He radiated power, but did not radiate a physical threat. It was more an internal power, the power of a deep and aged wisdom.

There was no question that this man was a mage of some kind or another. Tunera had no idea what such a man would have to do with her, but she had a feeling that he was coming to see her.

And she sensed that he was about to radically change her life somehow.

She finished putting the vegetables in the basket and stood. By that time, the man was at the gate leading to the walk up to her house. She frowned at the man, who had stopped at the gate and was looking at her.

"I am looking for Tunera Ironmoon," the man said.

"You have found her," Tunera said in a soft voice. "What do you want with me?"

"A cup of tea would be nice," the man said. "It has been a long journey and it was not as temperate where I came from."

"Well, come in then," Tunera sighed. She started towards the door. "But don't say I did not warn you. I do not make a very good cup of tea."

Tunera walked into the house and put her basket of vegetables on the table. She paid no attention to the man as he walked in. She'd already assessed that he wasn't a physical threat to her. Whatever it was that he wanted from her, it was not physical harm, she knew that.

She set to making some tea, boiling water over her cook fire. She worked quickly, and soon two cups of tea were steeping on the table. That done, she started peeling potatoes, deftly stripping the skin from the spuds with her knife. She could feel the man watching her work, but she said nothing. Whatever it was that he came to say, she would wait until he was ready to tell her.

The peeling went quickly. First the potatoes and then the carrots were peeled and then chopped into small chunks. When that was done, she put them aside and started cutting up some beef that she had gotten at the market. It was going to be a lovely beef stew, which was one of Tomas's favorite meals. It made Tunera happy to know that the man she loved would eat well this evening.

The man sat there and watched her, sipping his tea. He seemed in no hurry to get on with what he was there for. And Tunera was in no hurry to rush him. If she was right that he was about to change her life in a profound way, she was in no hurry to hear how.

When the beef was cut up into small cubes, she dusted the meat with flour and put everything into a pot with some water, onions and fresh herbs. She covered the pot and set it next to the cook fire where it would slowly stew all day long.

She sat back down at the table and sipped her tea looking at the man who had decided to pay her a visit. The man looked back at her and nodded once.

"You are, in fact, the one," he said softly.

"You're probably going to notice this quickly about me, sir, but I do not take kindly to riddles," Tunera said. "Either say what you came to say and have done, or leave and have done. I don't much care which."

"Oh, yes," he nodded. "You are certainly the one."

He smiled in satisfaction and pulled a piece of parchment from his robes. Tunera eyed the parchment warily, knowing that whatever was written on that parchment would change her life forever.

"The one for what?" she asked, despite her promise to herself that she would not push the man for more information.

"You are quite adept with that knife of yours," he said, avoiding her question. "I have never seen potatoes and carrots dispatched in quite so quick a fashion."

"I see," she said. She stood up and walked to the door. "You are only here to give me backhanded compliments. I've heard enough. You can leave now, sir."

"Sit down," he said, his voice cracking in the air like a whip. "I am not done with you yet, Tunera Ironmoon."

"Then say what you have to say and be done with it, old man," she snarled. Tunera had always had a distinct lack of patience, and it was showing now. She found the old man before her increasingly infuriating.

"How impudent of you," the man sighed. "But I expected nothing less. I've already seen this conversation, after all. But we all have a part to play in this great dance of life, and these steps are mine to take."

"Who are you?" she asked.

"I am no one of consequence," the old man said.

"But you must have a name!"

"I do," he nodded. "Names, however, have power. And in this case, it would do me great harm to give you my name. Although I suspect the harm will come anyway."

"You talk in riddles," Tunera frowned. "I do not like riddles, as I said."

"I am sorry, my dear," the old man sighed. "It is my way, ingrained after many years of being who I am. And you, you are at a crossroads, I think."

"What do you mean?"

"I see when I look at you someone who is both content and not," he said. "You are content in your life here in Talondale. Who wouldn't be? You have a lovely garden and house, a secure job and future working for your father, and a mate who dotes on you."

"I am content, yes," she nodded.

"And yet, you are also not," he said. "I see someone who wants to travel and see the rest of the Southern Dales. I see someone who wants adventure. Someone who wonders what it would be like to be someone other than who you are."

Tunera said nothing. She started mixing ingredients to make a loaf of bread to go along with the stew. She thought about what he said while mixing the ingredients. It was hard to hear the old man lay out so clearly the things she'd thought late at night when no one was around.

To buy some time, she kneaded the dough some getting it ready for the first resting. She carefully avoided looking at the old man while she worked, carefully thinking about how best to respond. When she was done kneading the dough and it was ready to rest she looked up at him again.

"I may have had such thoughts," she said, finally. "But what of it? My life is here. It is a good life, and I am content with it."

"You can lie to me, and you can lie to Tomas and your father," the old man said. "But you cannot lie to yourself. You say you are content, but you and I both know that it is a lie. You are no more content in this life than I would be. You crave adventure."

"And so what if I do?" she asked again. "My life is here."

"It does not have to be," he said, almost too softly to hear.

"I'm sorry?" she said. "What was that?"

"I said, that your life does not have to be here in Talondale. You and Tomas can go off and have an adventure."

Tunera stared for a moment. Then she turned away to check to see how the bread dough was rising, even though she'd only left it alone for a few moments. It would need at least an hour before she could continue making the bread, but it was a good thing to turn to in order to take her attention from the old man.

She did not dare to dwell on what he had said. There was no way she could go off on an adventure. She and Tomas were both needed here in Talondale, after all. Besides, what would her father do without her? He was getting older and needed caring after.

No, there was no way they could go running off on an adventure, no matter what the crazy old man said.

"I have a life here," she repeated. "I cannot go running off to see the world."

"I have seen it in the flames," he said in a soft voice. "You will, indeed, leave Talondale behind. And soon."

Tunera busied herself with cleaning up from her meal prep. She washed her knife carefully, then checked it for nicks and the honing of its edge. When she was done, she cleaned the table itself.

She did not know how to respond to such an enigmatic man. He seemed to have an answer for anything she might come up with. It was infuriating, but she knew that that was the way of the mages.

Finally she sat and took a sip of her tea, grimacing at the taste. It was worse than her normal attempts at tea. The old man had not seemed to mind. He had simply drank his tea as if it were the best tea he had ever had. That did not help Tunera feel all that much better about the old man.

"Why?" she said finally. "Why do you say I will leave Talondale?"

"As I said, I have seen it in the flames," the old man shrugged. "What know you of the Blademasters?"

"Warrior women that serve the gods Taelin and Laeyra," she shrugged. "That's about all I know. I've heard rumors that they have returned to Calthea after a long time."

"Indeed they have," the old man nodded. He smiled, but it was not a kind smile. "I have seen them. Well, I've seen two of them at least."

"Why now?" she asked. "Why have they returned now?"

"Because they are needed," the old man said. "There is a great war coming to the Southern Dales. Indeed, it is almost upon us. When the spring thaw comes, a great army will sweep out from the Wilds and lay siege on the Southern Dales. The Blademasters will lead the armies of the Southern Dales against the army of darkness that is coming."

"War is bad for business," Tunera sighed. "Fewer people will be coming through Talondale for trade while war is going on."

"It is far worse than that," the old man said. "If the Southern Dales does not repel the army of darkness, there will be no one left."

"It's that bad?"

"I'm afraid it is," the old man nodded.

"Then I guess it is good that the Blademasters are back to lead the forces of the Southern Dales," Tunera said. She stood and went to check on the bread again. It still wasn't ready, but checking on it gave her the excuse to take the time to form the next question. "That does not explain why you are here."

"No, it does not," the old man agreed.

Tunera saw that the old man was not going to continue, so she went over to stir the stew. Even though it had not been cooking long, the pleasant smell of stewing meat was already starting to waft throughout the house. She pulled a jar of minced garlic down from her pantry and added a small spoonful to the bubbling stew. After stirring the stew again, she decided she was satisfied and put the cover back on the pot. She went back to the table and sat.

Finally, she said what she needed to ask.

"Why are you here?" she asked softly. "The real reason. No games. No more redirections. What is it you want from me?"

"I said that I saw you leaving Talondale, and I meant it," the old man said. He drained the last of his tea and set his cup aside. "I have seen that you must leave Talondale, you and Tomas. You must journey to the Temple of the Blades hidden deep within the Elven Woods. There, you will take on the mantle of a Blademaster."

"And why will I do this?" Tunera asked.

"Because if you do not, all is lost," the old man sighed deeply. "You, Tunera Ironmoon, are to be the Blademaster that leads the Southern Dales against the army of darkness. For if you do not, we are lost."

"I see," Tunera looked down at the table. This was not what she had expected to hear. "I do not know if I can do this."

"You must," the old man said. He stood, leaning heavily on his staff. "You are our only chance, Tunera."

"I must think on this," she said.

"Of course, you must," the old man nodded. "But do not take too long. Winter is advancing slowly and soon the snows will thaw. With the end of winter, the army of darkness will be on the move once more." The old man started out of the little house. He stopped and tossed the parchment he'd been holding onto the table. Tunera saw that it was sealed with wax. "When you go to the Temple of the Blades, give that to the High Priestess. But know that if anyone other than the High Priestess opens the letter, it will explode in a fireball of vast proportions."

With that, the old man shuffled his way out of the house. Tunera watched him go. There was so much more that the old man could tell her, she knew. But she also could tell that he had told her all that he was going to.

It was up to her to make any sense of what she had been told.

Isaiah Talon drew the hood of his cloak up over his head as he shuffled away from Tunera Ironmoon's house. While he knew he had done what he had to, he did not like himself very much. He knew that there would be consequences for his actions.

There were always consequences.

His leg was bothering him from all the walking he had done trying to find Tunera's house to begin with. He was happy to have his staff to lean on as it helped. All he could do was to hobble his way out of town the best he could.

He was thankful that no one stopped him on the way out of Talondale. It was normal for people to stop the sage to ask him for help or for him to give them a glimpse into their future. He supposed that the fact that he spent so very little time in Talondale helped to keep people away from him. Still, it was a relief not to be pestered with insignificant requests.

When he left the city limits, he found a rock to sit down on to rest for a while. He was getting older, and he knew that his time would be coming soon to join with the magic. All he wanted was to help get the Southern Dales through the Great War of Souls before that time came.

He drew back the hood of his cloak and let the sun hit his face as he sat there and rested. The sun felt good. He was not looking forward to going back to his home in Valendale where it was considerably less pleasant in temperature in the middle of winter. But it was where he needed to be should he be called upon to assist during the War of Souls.

He knew it would not be the Blademaster that called on him.

He reflected on what he had done with Tunera. No matter how things played out amongst the Blademasters, he knew that Alana would not look upon his actions in a positive light. He knew that he had interfered in Alana's life one too many times, but there was little he could do. Events were moving fast, and he had to make sure that he helped shape events to ensure the best outcome for the Southern Dales.

As much as he hated himself for putting the young woman in harm's way, he knew that Tunera played a key to ensuring the success of the Southern Dales in the Great War of Souls.

"Hello, old friend," a soft voice called from behind him.

Isaiah knew who it was, so he did not hurry to turn around. His joints would not have liked him to whip around at any rate. As he expected, Ferrin was sitting on a rock behind him when he finally turned around.

"Hello, Lord Ferrin," Isaiah nodded his head.

"Is it done?" Ferrin asked.

"It is," Isaiah nodded. "I do not know for sure that she will decide to heed my words, but I have done all I can."

"She will, I think," Ferrin said. "A great deal depends on her doing so."

"I know, Lord Ferrin," Isaiah sighed. "I fear the reaction that Alana Steeldrake will have to my actions, however."

"All actions have consequences, my dear Isaiah," Ferrin said. "Something that Lord Taelin so wisely put in the Law of the Blades. The Twenty Fourth, I think."

"He is wise to remind the Blademasters of that," Isaish nodded. "What will the consequences of my interfering with Alana be, Lord Ferrin?"

"I do not know," Ferrin shrugged. "But I doubt that she will be happy to seek your guidance in the future."

"I doubt she was inclined to before this," Isaiah scoffed. "She blames me for what happened to the people of Valendale."

"She would," Ferrin frowned. "She cares about those people a great deal. It is part of what makes her such a good Blademaster. She loves unconditionally."

"With what I have done, will the Southern Dales prevail in the War of Souls?" Isaiah asked.

"You have seen what will be in the flames," Ferrin said. "Why ask me?"

"I have not seen how it will end."

"As war always does," Ferrin sighed. "With a great deal of pain and loss. Many will lose their lives in this war. It remains to be seen if we have done enough to swing the tide to the side of light."

"I wish there was more I could do to ensure victory for the Southern Dales," Isaiah said. "But I am getting old, and I fear I have little left to offer Calthea."

"Yes," Ferrin nodded. "You will be merging with the magic soon, my old friend. You have, I think, one last task. If the Southern Dales does prevail, I believe you will be called upon to provide one last service to the Blademasters. And I believe Alana herself, should she survive the war, will be the one to ask you for help."

"I will provide whatever aid I can give the Blademasters," Isaiah bowed his head.

"Good," Ferrin smiled at Isaiah. "Now go home, my old friend. Go home and rest. You have earned it."

"Somehow, it does not feel like betraying the one born of the light should earn me anything," Isaiah grumbled.

But there was no one there to hear him.

The old man sighed and stood back up, his joints creaking and popping with the movement. He held his staff in front of him with the butt of the staff pushed firmly into the ground.

"*Ashintias Valendale*," he whispered.

There was a roar of power and then the old man disappeared with a pop.

Where the old man had been standing was nothing more than rocky beach. The sound of the surf was the only sound left in the afternoon sun.

Dragonsbane

Chapter IX
Decisions

here was a bench in the front of her father's store that Tunera loved to sit on whenever she was troubled about something. After the sage left, it was where she went immediately to think about what the sage had said. The sage had given her a great deal to think about.

Tunera did not like prophecy, and she hated that prophecy was about to take a firm control of her life. But if the sage was right about what it would mean if she failed to heed his words, she knew that she had no choice but to go where he was sending her.

It was all so overwhelming, though. She knew that she had to speak to Tomas about it. Especially since the sage had made it clear that Tomas had to go with her. Tunera did not understand what that was about, but she was glad that she would not be parted from Tomas.

She sat on the bench watching people go by as she thought about what the sage had said to her. There was

Dragonsbane

not a lot that she knew about the Blademasters. She had heard the old stories and songs, of course. Everyone had. But the stories and songs did not actually tell all that much about being a Blademaster. She had no idea what it meant to be one. Nor did she have any idea what it entailed to become one. The fact that Tomas had to go with her to the Temple of the Blades was interesting.

Why was he needed too?

It made no sense. She knew that Blademasters were women. Obviously, Tomas could not become a Blademaster, so why did he need to journey with her.

Tunera decided that it did not matter why Tomas had to go with her to the Temple of the Blades. She was just happy that she would not be parted from him. She wasn't sure how Tomas would feel about the journey. And then there was the matter of telling her father.

That was the conversation she was looking forward to least.

She shook her head. The very fact that she was thinking about what conversation was going to be the one she looked forward to least brought her up short. If she was thinking in that line of thought, it was clear that she had already decided what to do about the sage's words.

But if what he had said about her being the key to the Southern Dales' survival was right, she had had no choice but to comply with his demands that she leave Talondale. And she had known it from the moment he had said it.

She sighed deeply. She wasn't ready to leave, but it was clear that she did not have a choice. She would go and find this Temple of the Blades, even though she had no idea where in the Elven Woods it might be.

All she needed to do now was to convince Tomas to go with her.

Tunera pulled her legs up onto the bench and wrapped her arms around her knees. Laying her head on her knees, she sighed softly to herself. Her life was about to get very complicated. What she did not know was why it had to be her. Why another couldn't be found to take on this burden was what she had been wondering ever since the sage had told her about what she was supposed to do. It did not seem fair that she had to uproot her life just because someone thought she was the one that the fate of the entire Southern Dales revolved around.

She remembered something that her father had always told her. Life is not always fair. You must make the most of what you are given and hope for the best.

Moaning about how unfair the situation was would not change anything. She had made her decision, and she needed to act on that decision. She needed to be a woman of action if, indeed, she was to become a Blademaster.

Her mind made up, Tunera stood from the bench and made her way into the shop to talk to her father.

As she had expected, he was behind the counter unpacking items from crates to the shelves of the store. She watched him work for several long minutes. It seemed odd to think that she would miss working in a store like this. She had expected that she would inherit the store when her father was ready to retire, but now that seemed impossible. Now it appeared that her destiny lay elsewhere.

Tunera made no sound, simply waiting for her father to notice her. She'd decided that it would be better if she did not interrupt him in his work to tell him that she was leaving. It was not going to be an easy conversation as it was.

It took several minutes, but he finished what he was doing and turned around. When he saw her, he smiled broadly at her. Her father doted on her. But when he saw the expression on her face, his smile faded quickly.

"What is it, Tunera?" he asked in a soft voice. "What has happened?"

"I just had a visitor, Father," Tunera said. She walked over to the counter and rested her hands on it. "I do not really understand why he came to see me."

"What did he say?" her father said, his eyes narrowing.

"He told me that I am to leave Talondale immediately," she said, a tear leaking from her eyes. Now that she had started, it all came out in a rush. "Tomas and I are to travel to the Elven Woods where we will find the Temple of the Blades. He said that the fate of the Southern Dales rests on my going. So even though I want to stay in Talondale, I am going."

Her father studied her with a blank expression on his face. That scared her more than anything. She had not known what to expect when she told him, but an expression completely devoid of emotion wasn't it.

Finally, he turned away from her and went back into the back room. She could hear him going through the back room looking for something. She wasn't sure what he was doing. For that matter, she wasn't sure if he would come back out and talk to her again. She was scared. Her father had always ben open with her and this was not something she was used to. Nor was it anything she knew how to react to.

After several minutes, her father came back out of the back room carrying two brand new travel packs, one in each hand. He laid the packs on the counter and sighed.

"I knew this day was coming," he said in a voice barely above a whisper. "I have dreaded that this day would come so soon."

"What do you mean you knew this day was coming?" Tunera frowned. This was news to her. She had never planned on leaving Talondale, so how could her father know that such a journey was coming.

"Go," he whispered, fighting tears. "Go and tell Tomas that you two are leaving. Tell Gareth that I will compensate him for the loss of his apprentice."

"Father,   I—"
"Go," her father said, his voice cracking. "I will get your supplies ready for you. Your packs will be ready for you when you are ready to leave."

Tunera tried to engage her father again, but he had turned away from her. She did not know how to react to how her father had reacted to what she said. So she did the only thing she could do. She left to go find Tomas.

Unlike the day before, the trip to Gareth's smithy took a fair amount of time. Tunera could not bring herself to go very quickly, even though she knew that putting off another conversation would not help her.

She slowly made her way through the streets of Talondale, taking a longer route than she normally would to get to the smithy. She kept her eyes turned down to the ground, not wanting to meet anyone's gaze. It was unusual for her to walk that way, and she knew that she was drawing stares. But she did not care.

She worked through in her head what she would say to Tomas. There was little doubt that she had to succeed in convincing him to go with her. There was also little doubt in her mind that she would fail. Tunera knew that he would go wherever she chose to go.

It took her a while, but she finally found her way to the smithy shop. When she entered, Gareth Wyland was polishing a helm on display. He nodded once when he saw her, but he did not flash her his usual smile for her.

He knows why I am here, she thought. *I wonder how he knows.*

"Good morning, Master Gareth," Tunera said in a soft voice.

"Good morning, Tunera," the smith said. "I had a visitor yesterday after you left. He had a fascinating story for me. Why do I get the feeling you are about to confirm what he said to me?"

"I would suppose it would depend on what he told you, Master Gareth," Tunera averted her gaze.

Gareth put the helmet back on the display and placed the cloth on the counter. He walked over to her and put his hands on her shoulders. She looked up at him, tears leaking from the corners of her eyes.

"I am not mad, Tunera," Gareth said in a kind voice. "I could never be mad at you. You have treated me with a great deal of respect, and I know that you are worried that what you are about to tell me will cause me to feel like you no longer respect me. The fact that you feel that way tells me everything."

"But—" she started.

"I know what the old man told you, for he told me much the same thing," the smith cut her off. "I understand what is at stake."

"Thank you for that," Tunera said. And she meant it. It made it easier to go forward knowing that he understood the why. "I still feel horrible taking Tomas away from you."

"He has served me well," the smith said. Then he smiled. "And he has learned all that I can teach him. I would be losing him to his own shop soon anyway. At least this way I don't' have to compete with my protégé."

"Father told me to tell you that he would compensate you for the loss of your apprentice," Tunera remembered to tell him.

"Bah," Gareth waved away her words. "Your father is a good man, but neither he nor you owe me anything."

"I am going to miss Talondale," Tunera admitted. "And the people."

"You're going to save us all, Tunera," Gareth reminded her. "Never forget that. The people of Talondale will not."

Tunera nodded, completely at a loss for words. The big smith wrapped her up in a big hug, which she gratefully returned.

"I should go talk to Tomas," she said.

"You will find he already knows. He was here when the old man visited, and heard everything," Gareth said. "It should ease your mind to know that he has already told me that if you decide to agree to go on the journey the old man has told you to go on, that he would join you."

"That does make it easier, yes," she nodded. "I am a little scared."

"Good," Gareth nodded. "A warrior that does not fear is not a warrior."

"That is an odd saying," Tunera frowned.

Gareth laughed, a deep and booming laugh. "Odd or no, it is no less true. Now go, Tunera. Go talk to your Tomas."

"Thank you, Master Gareth," she said softly. "For everything."

The smith patted her on the back one more time before letting her go

Tunera went back to the workroom where Tomas was working. The young blacksmith's apprentice was wiping down a freshly forged blade when she walked in. He did not look up from his work, but nodded once to acknowledge that she had walked in. She did not say anything to him until he finished what he was doing. She did not want to risk his cutting himself accidentally. When he was done, he lay the blade aside and looked at her.

"So, I hear we're going on a bit of a journey," he said.

"Assuming you choose to go with me," she nodded. "I am going regardless, but I would like it if you came with me."

"When do we leave?" he shrugged.

"Tomorrow," she said. "The sooner we leave, the sooner we get where we're going."

"Tomorrow, then," he nodded. "Do I still get my beef stew tonight?"

Dragonsbane

Chapter X
Journey Towards Destiny

The next morning, Tunera and Tomas rose early. Tunera had decided that, since they had decided to act on the sage's words, there was no need to delay their departure any longer than necessary.

She knew that it would be a long journey to get to the Temple of the Blades. The sage had told her that it was in the Elven Woods located between Arvendale and Ravendale. It would take several weeks to get there, and that was assuming that the roads were passable.

The longer they took to start their journey, the longer it would take to get there.

When she woke, she worked quickly to pack the things she would need in a pack she had purchased the day before. It helped that her father owned a general store. She was able to get everything that she and Tomas would need for the journey.

Her father's reaction to their decision was puzzling. She had tried to engage him further about what he meant by saying that he had always known that she would leave, but he refused to say anything more. He merely helped her gather what she would need for their journey.

Tunera thought he should be mad for her leaving him. Or happy that she was finally discovering what she was meant to be. She thought he should feel something other than sadness. And she wished she understood why he was so sad.

Tomas told her that Talor was just having trouble seeing her go off into the world. Tunera hoped that was all there was to it, but she doubted it. Her instincts were telling her that there was a lot more to the story.

But she knew that her father would not tell her what was bothering him until he was good and ready. So it really did not make any sense to dwell on problems that had no resolutions.

Instead, she focused her efforts on getting ready for the journey. She worked quickly, and soon, the two packs were ready to go. She looked once more around her bedroom to make sure she had everything she would need. When she was satisfied that she had everything, Tunera picked up the two packs and made her way out of her house. She made sure the door was locked and then made her way to her father's store.

Tomas was already there waiting for her when she arrived. He had gotten them both a horse and tack. He'd also brought them both swords. Both were sensible things for him to have acquired, Tunera thought.

"You have our packs?" Tomas asked her.

Tunera held up the packs. Tomas took them and hooked them on the saddle horns on the horses. She was glad he had thought through what they needed as far as horses and tack. While she had made the decision that they were going to go on this journey, she had not given nearly as much thought as to how they would get there.

"Talor was looking for you," Tomas said. "I believe he is inside. I will wait out here for you."

Tunera nodded and walked into her father's store.

This was the part she had been dreading. She knew that her father had accepted her decision to go on this journey, but it did not make it any easier for her to say goodbye to him. Nor did she think it would be easy for her father to watch her go. There was definitely something that her father was hiding from her. She hoped that he would tell her what it was before she left, but Tunera doubted that he would.

She found her father sitting in the chair he always sat in when there were no customers in the store, just as she had expected she would. Although she tried to hide it with a brave face, she knew that her leaving was hurting him somehow.

"Father," she said in a soft voice. "Tomas said you were looking for me."

"Yes, Tunera," the burly shop owner said. "I wanted to see you one last time before you left. I know that this journey is important. And I know you must go. But I could not bear to have you leave without saying goodbye."

"I would not have even dreamed of not saying goodbye to you, Father," she smiled a weak smile.

"I know," her father nodded.

Talor Ironmoon did not often show his emotions. And Tunera could tell that he was fighting hard to keep a brave face for his daughter. But she could see the tears leaking from the corners of his eyes. She stepped forward, her arms wide.

Her father embraced her. It was a warm bear hug of an embrace, and Tunera wanted to just stay there in her father's arms where she would stay safe.

But she knew that she couldn't. She could still hear the sage's words in her ears. There was no way that she could keep from following through on the decision to go to the Temple of the Blades. Far too much rode on her becoming a Blademaster. Far too many people would die if she did not go.

It wasn't a fair burden to lay on her shoulders, but it had been, and there was little she could do but to see it through.

"I wish I could stay, Father," she said into his shoulder.

"I know you do," he said, squeezing her a little tighter. "I don't want to let you go. But neither of us are going to get what we want. There is nothing more I would wish than to see you live a long life with your Tomas. He is a good man, that one."

"I know he is," Tunera smiled. "I am glad he has your blessing."

"From the moment you two first met as children, I knew he would be the one to win your heart," Talor said. "We fathers know these things, you know."

"Yes, I know," Tunera's smile widened.

She pulled away from his embrace, no matter how much she wanted to stay in it. Talor sighed and let her. He turned back to his chair and pulled a box from under it.

It was a long box, and she found a well-crafted long sword inside. She pulled it out and tested out how it felt in her hand. It was balanced perfectly for her, but she was not surprised to see that. Her father would know how she would have wanted a blade to be balanced. She did not understand, though, how he had gotten it made so quickly. She had only decided to leave yesterday. There was no way that he could have had the blade made overnight. A blade such as this would have taken days to make.

"I told you that I knew this day was coming," Talor said, subdued. "I had this made some time ago so that it would be ready when you were ready to leave. I wanted to make sure you had a reminder of home with you, as well as having the best available sword with you as you ride into battle."

"I do not know what to say, Father," she said. She was unable to keep the tears from leaking from her eyes any longer. "Thank you."

"That is enough," Talor nodded. "Promise me that you will train well with that blade so that it becomes a part of you. It will, I think, save your life, a fine blade like that."

"Of course, I will train," she smiled through the tears.

"Good," Talor said. "You should get going if you are going to go. The Temple of the Blades awaits you, my daughter."

Tunera rushed forward and hugged her father a second time. Somewhere deep inside, she felt like there was a finality in the hug as if she would never see him again. She pushed that feeling aside. Of course she would see her father again when this war was over with! She'd come home and make him a big pot of her finest beef stew to thank him for the sword that kept her alive.

When she parted from the embrace, she saw the lines that tears had traced along his face, but there were no more tears running from his eyes.

"Goodbye, Father," she said. "Until I see you again."

"Goodbye, Tunera," he replied. "Go save the world."

Tunera smiled at that and turned away before she was unable to. She made her way back out to the horses. Tomas was already in his saddle, so she mounted her horse next to his.

Talor followed behind her to the porch of the store. He held his hand up in a wave.

Tunera waved back at him before turning her horse to canter off out of Talondale.

She did not turn back to see her father fall into the chair on the porch, tears freely flowing down his handsome face.

Tunera and Tomas traveled for a week before they were forced to seek shelter for a winter storm. Fortunately, they had packed plenty of rations for just this sort of occurrence.

They found a cavern out of the way of the storm where they thought they would be able to stay warm and dry. As soon as they made their way into the cave, Tomas built a small fire that they could cook with and keep warm by.

"Perhaps we should start a stew," Tunera said after they'd sat in the cave for a bit. "It would give us something to do while we sit here. And we will get hungry at some point. Something warm would be good when that happens."

"As you wish," Tomas said.

Tunera began rummaging through her pack for the things she needed to make a stew. She pulled out some dried meat and some vegetables. She diced them all together and put them in a pot with a little bit of snow for liquid.

They sat and watched the pot bubble in silence. Neither had had much to say during the journey, and Tunera suspected that neither would have a whole lot to say as the journey continued.

When the stew was ready, Tunera rummaged in her pack for her bowl and spoon. As she rummaged, she felt something in the side of her pack that caused her to frown. She handed the bowl over to Tomas to fill while she tried to figure out what it was she was feeling.

Eventually, she found that there was a pocket on the inside of the pack. Curious, she reached into the pocket to pull out a folded bit of parchment. She turned it over in her hands and saw her father's seal in wax sealing the parchment together.

"What is that?" Tomas asked.

"Apparently a letter from my father," Tunera said.

"Well?" Tomas prodded. He handed her a full bowl of the stew. "What does it say?"

Tunera took a spoonful of the stew. It was a tasty stew for what had gone into it. Sitting back down, she broke the seal of the letter and began to read it aloud.

"My dear Tunera,

I have hidden this letter in your pack in the hopes that it will take you some time to find it. I want you to be well on your way to the Temple of the Blades before you read it. I do not want you to be tempted to turn around and come home.

I told you that I knew the day when you would leave Talondale was coming. And it is true. I did. I have expected as much for some months, in fact.

Many years ago, back before Taryn died, the Dream Weaver came to see us. You were still just a child, but the Dream Weaver could see the importance that you would hold in the future of the Southern Dales even then.

He told us that there was a great war coming to the Southern Dales, although he did not know when it would start. The Dream Weaver had been guided to our house, for he had seen that you, Tunera, would have a key hand in the Southern Dales surviving the war. He did not know how, though.

When word came that the Blademasters had once again come to the Southern Dales, I knew that it was likely that this Great War was coming. After all, why would the Blademasters return if not for that?

And then word came from the First Lord that preparations should be made for war. It was then that I knew that this day was fast approaching.

I don't know what your part in this war will be, Tunera. But I do know that I will not see you again. That was the other thing that the Dream Weaver told us all those years ago. He told us that once you left Talondale, you would not see us again. I do not know if that means that you will die before you return or if I will. Either way, when I said goodbye to you, I knew it would be the last time I said it.

I know that you are tempted to return to Talondale because of this. You cannot. Remember the words of the sage. He told you that if you do not accept your destiny, the Southern Dales will not make it through the War of Souls. I believe him.

The Southern Dales is more important than you and I seeing each other again. Know, though, that I am proud of you. IF, somehow, the Dream Weaver is wrong and I will see you again in this life, I will rejoice in that. If not, I will see you when we have both joined the walk with the gods. If that is the way I see you again, then I will rejoice when I see you then.

Until that day comes, do your best to do what needs to be done. And know that I am proud that you have embraced your destiny.

With all my love,
Your father,
Talor Ironmoon."

There were tears running down Tunera's cheeks when she finished reading the letter. Tomas looked over at her, but said nothing, knowing her well enough to know that there was nothing he could say at that point.

Tunera turned her back to him and leaned against him. She fell asleep crying in his arms.

Two weeks later, Tunera and Tomas found themselves on the edge of the Elven Woods. It had been a long and difficult journey, and they were both relieved to be so close to the end of the journey. They only had to go through the Elven Woods to the Temple of the Blades.

The only problem was that they did not know where in the Elven Woods the temple was. Tunera supposed that they would just wander through the woods until they got to the temple.

It was far from the best solution, but Tunera did not have another idea of how to figure out where the temple was.

The two of them stood just outside the forest. The trees looked very uninviting because they were so large. They both knew that there was a large clan of elves that lived in the forest, although neither of them had ever been there before. Tunera wasn't sure how that would affect their ability to get to the temple. She wasn't sure if she would have to honor the elves in some way.

"Looks pretty imposing," Tunera said softly.

"Yup," Tomas nodded.

"Guess we better go in," Tunera said.

"Yup."

Tunera checked that her pack was secure and then took a step forward on the path into the forest. Tomas kept in step beside her. The two of them slowly made their way into the forest.

It was not long before they heard the rustling of leaves. Before they had gotten more than a few hundred feet into the forest, they found themselves surrounded.

"Scoirfidh ag gluaiseacht ina bhfuil tú. Ná teacht ar bith eile," one of the elves ordered in a deep commanding voice. Even though Tunera and Tomas did not understand his words, the swords brandished in their direction made the meaning clear.

They stopped walking and held their hands up showing they were not holding weapons.

"I don't understand you," Tunera said in her soft voice.

"What are you doing in our forest?" the lead elf demanded.

"We were sent by a mage to speak with the High Priestess of the Blades," Tunera said.

The elves whispered amongst themselves for a few moments before the leader held up his hand for silence.

"This is bad business," the elf said softly. "But we will guide you to the path to the Temple of the Blades."

The leader turned to one of the elves and fired out an order in Elven. The other elf nodded and started running through the forest. Tunera was amazed at how fast the elf could move. And how silently. She supposed, though, that if you lived in the forest all your life, you would learn how to travel through it quickly and quietly.

The leader of the elves motioned for them to follow. Not knowing what else they could do, Tunera and Tomas followed.

They walked through the forest for several long hours. Tunera suspected that they were going around in circles. She knew that they would never find the way to the temple again on their own. It was likely that this was by design, she supposed.

After what felt like a full day of walking, the leader of the elves stopped. Tunera had caught sight of a flash of white marble in the distance just before they stopped.

"Here," the leader of the elves said.

"Where?" Tunera said. "There's no path."

"Of course there isn't," the elf laughed. "Do you think the Temple of the Blades would be so easy to find?"

"No," Tunera sighed. "I don't suppose it would."

"You saw the flash of marble?" the elf asked.

"I did," she nodded.

"Good," the elf said. "You will have to cut your way through the forest to get to the clearing. Keep going in the direction of where you saw the marble. You will keep seeing flashes of the temple as you go. It will take you some time to get there, but you will get there eventually."

"Thank you, sir," Tunera bowed her head slightly in respect. "I am not sure how we would have found the temple without your help."

"You would not have," the elf shrugged. He studied Tunera intently. "I do not know why you are here. But you are here, now. Honor the words of the Master Blademaster and you will do well."

With that the elves vanished into the woods. There was nothing for Tunera and Tomas to do but to start cutting their way through the forest to the Temple of the Blades.

Chapter XI
The High Priestess of the Blades

The white marble temple rose out of the clearing. Tunera had gotten flashes of the temple as she and Tomas fought through the dense foliage, but the flashes she had gotten had not prepared her for the immense size of the temple.

They stopped to look at the temple. For the first time, Tunera truly had misgivings about their choice to follow this path.

The temple was large, made out of shining white marble. As they got closer, though, they noticed that there were veins of darker marble winding throughout the pristine white. High marble parapets gave the temple a palatial feel. Banners from the parapets flapped in the breeze. Tunera noticed that the banners were all the same: a dark blue background with a stylized gold shield in the foreground. The shield was crossed over at the center by two silver long swords.

As they slowly walked around the temple, they saw the same stylized shield and swords inlaid into the walls. These inlays were made of silver and gold. The mottling in the marble seemed to be in constant motion, dancing in a pattern, although neither Tunera nor Tomas could draw any meaning from the dancing.

Tunera moved closer to the temple, and she put her hand on the marble. The marble was warm to the touch, almost as if life blood was flowing through the marble walls. The thought of the temple being alive was disturbing to Tunera.

As they made their way back around to the front of the temple, they stopped and stared.

Standing at the foot of the steps of the temple were a man and a woman. Tunera was sure that they were not there before.

The woman had long blonde hair that was combed back into a loose pony tail. She had deep blue eyes and thin red lips. She wore blood red leather armor, low cut down to her navel. And she had a long sword out in each hand. The man standing next to her looked no less intimidating in his chain mail. He had black hair and hair and hazel eyes. He wore a full beard. And in his hands was a great sword.

Tunera was feeling much less comfortable about this situation seeing two heavily armed warriors standing in her way. But she had been sent, and there was little she could do about it now.

"Hold," the woman in front of her said. "You are strangers to the temple. Why are you here?"

"We were sent," Tunera said softly.

"Sent by?" the woman asked.

"A mage," Tunera replied. "He sent us to speak with the High Priestess of the Blades."

"Alyssa," the man bellowed.

A redheaded woman wearing similar armor to the woman with the swords in front of Tunera glided down the stairs of the temple, stopping just to the right of the burly man.

"Yes, Richard?" the redhead asked.

"Go get the High Priestess," Richard said. "Tell her we have two strangers who wish to see her."

"Right away," the redhead nodded. She took one look at the two strangers and frowned. Then she ran back up the stairs into the temple.

"And now we wait," the woman with the swords said.

Solara Moonfire was deep in meditation in her sanctuary. The coming war was stressful, and it had been made more so with the constant training of the Legacy of the Blademasters that she had to oversee. Many of the women that made up the Legacy of the Blademasters had not held a sword since their spirit had been locked in the Temple of the Blades. It was to be expected, though, that they had gotten lax.

Without a foe to fight, why was there a need to train?

She was as guilty of it as the rest of them. Solara had gotten complacent in her time as the High Priestess of the Blades. It had been over a century since she had even bothered to do daily exercises with her blades.

She was rusty.

The prophecy of the Great War of Souls was clear, though, that the Legacy of the Blademasters would once again take the field of battle. Even though she was not mentioned in the prophecy, she knew that, if the Legacy of the Blademasters took the field, so, too, would the High Priestess of the Blades.

And so she had joined in with the training, knowing she needed it as much as the Legacy of the Blademasters did. The fact that her body was so sore after each training session told her just how much she actually needed the training.

After training came the meditation.

Solara believed that the mind needed to be as sharp as the body's skills were. It was something that she often made sure that the Blademasters kept in mind. It was, after all, the Sixteenth Law of the Blades. The sharpest weapon a Blademaster has are her mind and her wits. Without either, even the sharpest blade would fall as dull as a club.

As Solara had gotten to know Alana Steeldrake, the High Priestess of the Blades began to respect that Alana understood and honored the Sixteenth Law of the Blades in ways that even Solara had not understood. Her understanding that the Laws of the Blades were intended as a series of guiding principles for the Blademaster Corps rather than an inviolate set of laws, for instance, was a wisdom beyond that shown by any Blademaster that came before.

Alana was, perhaps, the first Blademaster to actually understand Lord Taelin's intent of the Law of the Blades.

Solara knew that understanding of the Law of the Blades was what caused her to dislike and mistrust Alana at first. It had taken time to understand that Alana was always the right choice to lead the forces of the Southern Dales in this war. There was, after all, great wisdom in Lord Taelin's decisions. But once she had come to see that wisdom, she had fully supported Alana's actions.

What had originally been anger at the Blademaster for dragging the Southern Dales into war slowly turned into wonder as to how the young woman was able to make the moral choices whenever possible, even though she knew that the right choices often had the worst consequences.

If it was the right choice to make, the consequences, no matter how bad, made the choice no less correct.

Solara had never had the wherewithal to make decisions such as the ones that the Blademaster had had to make since taking on the mantle of the Blademaster the spring before. So much had happened for that young woman in such a little amount of time. And yet, Alana had managed to always make the choice that needed to be made.

The High Priestess of the Blades found herself envious of Alana.

At the same time, though, she was proud of the young Blademaster. Alana's journey so far had not been an easy one, and yet she had handled herself with grace and dignity. She had never once railed at the unfairness of her lot in life, even though she certainly could have. Instead, Alana had considered herself fortunate that she had been able to marry the man that she loved. And she had already saved countless lives in just her short time as the Blademaster.

Solara no longer had any misgivings about naming Alana to the post of Master Blademaster. She had seen how the Blademaster had cared for others. Solara herself would never have gone to Willowdale to rescue the people of Valendale. And yet, Alana had gone without giving it a second though. She had seen the people in need, and she had given her aid without hesitation. It was a quality that Solara admired in the young woman. Solara had no doubt that, with Alana Steeldrake in command of the armies, the Southern Dales would make it through to the other side of the War of Souls. They may not make it through unscathed, for no one ever makes it through a war unscathed, but they would see the other side. And a great many people would owe their lives to Alana and her companions.

It calmed Solara to think about how Alana and her companions would do well when it came to leading the forces of the Southern Dales. It helped her to believe that the Southern Dales was in good hands. And she did believe that. It was a common saying that Lord Taelin picks his Blademasters well. In this case, she knew that Lord Taelin had, indeed, chosen wisely when he had chosen Alana Steeldrake.

The meditation had done wonders to clear Solara's mind. It had been a particularly rigorous training session, and she was tired. But it was a good tired. She could feel all her muscles loosening, and she knew that she had trained well. She was beginning to regain the form she had before she died and became the High Priestess of the Blades. Solara had been a formidable swordswoman once, and she felt it all coming back to her the more she trained.

The army of darkness would see just how much she remembered about her craft when she took the field.

There was a soft knock at the door to her sanctuary. It was the only time that the Legacy of the Blademasters did not just barge through a door or, worse, just float through a wall. When Solara was in her sanctuary, they respected that she needed her privacy and gave it to her.

It was the little things that mattered.

Solara opened her eyes and stood. Walking over to the door, she worked out the kinks in her legs. She had been kneeling too long.

When she opened the door, she saw Alyssa Nesbitt standing there, looking nervous.

"What is it, Alyssa?" Solara frowned. She could not remember seeing Alyssa anything but cheerful. "What's going on?"

"High Priestess, there are strangers in the clearing," Alyssa said. "Raven and Richard met them while out patrolling the clearing. They are demanding to see you."

"A man and a woman?" Solara asked.

"Yes, High Priestess," Alyssa nodded. "Armed, the both of them."

"I have, after a fashion, been expecting them," Solara sighed. "I had a visitor in the night from the Forestwalker Elves. They warned me about these two. They claim to have been sent by a mage in white."

"William?" Alyssa asked hopefully. Solara could understand the hopeful tone. If it were William, that would mean these two had Alana's blessing.

Solara did not think it was William that sent them through.

"I don't think so, but perhaps," Solara said. She tapped her thumb on her sword hilt. "Bring them into the Great Hall. I will see them there."

"Yes, High Priestess."

Alyssa nodded and ran off to pass on the High Priestess's words. Solara grimaced to herself as she watched the Blademaster go off. She had a feeling that these two visitors were going to cause trouble. The Southern Dales had enough trouble without adding more.

Solara heaved a deep sigh. She knew that this was going to be trouble. She wasn't sure how the Master Blademaster would navigate through this particular trouble. Solara knew, though, that Alana would have to. And there was no advice that Solara could give her.

Especially since Solara did not really know the true nature of the trouble that was coming.

Solara readied herself and made her way out to the Great Hall. She wanted to be there when Raven and Richard brought the two strangers in. She wanted to see them for herself as soon as possible. It would be good to take the measure of the two strangers. Such would give her a better idea of what to expect as she went forward with the two of them.

When she got to the Great Hall, Solara noticed that there were many members of the Legacy of the Blademasters lining the walls of the Great Hall. It was less than surprising. She knew that word about the two strangers had spread through the Temple of the Blades like wildfire. She couldn't blame the Blademasters for being curious. It was exceedingly rare that someone who was not already expected by the High Priestess of the Blades showed up out of the blue like this.

Solara could think of only one other time, and that had nearly been the end of the Temple of the Blades.

It was not something that was often discussed in the Temple of the Blades. Serina Thames was the only Blademaster that had ever been denied entry into the Legacy of the Blademasters. Even four hundred years later, Solara wasn't sure if it was wise to keep her from the Legacy of the Blademasters. How could the Blademasters learn from her mistakes if she was not there to answer questions about them after all?

But because of Serina Thames, Solara was concerned about these strangers. She feared a repeat of those mistakes.

The High Priestess of the Blades stood tall in front of the altar, her black leather armor cleaned and buffed so that it would shine in the torchlight of the Great Hall. She wanted to be the first thing that the two strangers saw when they entered the Great Hall.

This was, after all, her temple.

The door to the Great Hall opened, and Raven Windrider walked in first, followed by the two strangers with Richard Kale, Raven's Protector, following behind. The fact that Raven and Richard were guarding the two strangers like that told Solara how on edge the first Blademaster and Protector were.

The fact that Raven's swords were drawn and in a ready position drove the point home.

Solara stepped forward, causing Raven and Richard to break off and step to the side. They were both still on their guard, Solara saw, which pleased the High Priestess of the Blades.

As Solara looked over the two strangers, she frowned. They did not look like much in the way of fighters, although the man was burly. Solara did not know how well they would do as Blademaster and Protector, but she knew that they were heare to become such.

"I am Solara Moonfire, the High Priestess of the Blades," Solara said softly. "Explain yourselves. Who are you? Why are you here at the Temple of the Blades?"

"I am Tunera Ironmoon of Talondale," the dark skinned woman said in a soft voice. "We were sent here."

"Sent?" Solara raised an eyebrow. "Sent by whom?"

"There was a mage who visited me at my home in Talondale," Tunera continued. "He told me about the coming war and told me that I must be a part of it were the Southern Dales to survive. And he sent me here."

"Give her the letter, Tunera," the man beside her said.

"Letter?" Solara stepped forward. "What letter?"

"The mage gave me a letter to give to you. He said that it would explain everything, but that only you were to open it," Tunera said. She took the sealed letter from inside her cloak and held it out to Solara.

Solara waved Raven off as she took the letter. She'd recognized the handwriting on the paper, and was sure she would recognize the seal once she looked at it. The recognition of the handwriting put her at ease. Although they had often been at odds with each other over the years, Solara knew that the sage Isaiah would never intentionally cause trouble. He felt that protecting the Southern Dales was partially his job, and Solara knew that he would do whatever he had to in order to make sure the Southern Dales made it through the War of Souls.

When her hand touched the letter, she felt a crackle of static electricity snap through her hand. She knew that Isaiah had spelled the letter so that if anyone other than she had opened it, it would ignite before whoever it was could read it. Solara frowned. Such a protection was not normal, but if Isaiah had felt that it was that important to protect the letter, he must have had a good reason for it.

She looked at the blue wax seal. It was definitely the seal of the sage. A single eagle talon was pressed into the blue wax. Satisfied that the letter was from Isaiah Talon, she broke the seal and unfolded the letter. As she read, her frown grew deeper.

"Lady Solara,

You and I have not always seen eye to eye as to what needs to be done in order to make sure the Southern Dales survives the War of Souls. One thing that there is no argument about is that the Blademaster Alana Steeldrake is the keystone to the Southern Dales successfully winning this war.

The bearer of this letter, one Tunera Ironmoon, has a part to play in what is to come. I am afraid that she thinks her part to play is different than the one she is to play. There was little I could do. I had to convince her that she needed to make the journey to the Temple of the Blades.

Alana was to have found Tunera before now and brought her to the Temple of the Blades. Why she has not done so, I do not know. But if Tunera does not join the ranks of the Blademaster Corps, then Alana Steeldrake will die before the War of Souls begins.

Therefore, I have sent her to the Temple of the Blades along with her man, Tomas Fletcher. They are good people, and I am afraid I have used them for my own ends. But the fact remains that they are the right people for this purpose.

I implore you to tell Tunera none of what is in this letter. Tell her that this letter contains whatever you need it to in order to convince you that Tomas is to undergo the Test of the Blades.

This is, I think, the last time you and I will speak, even by letter, Lady Solara. I near the end of my time on Calthea. Lord Ferrin says I have one task left before me. And I know now what that task is.

Although Alana thinks I have hindered her at every path, you know that all I have done, I have done for the protection of the Southern Dales.

Goodbye, Lady Solara. May we all successfully fill our roles in the battles to come.

Signed by my hand,

Isaiah Talon."

Solara read the letter two more times. She fought the urge to shed a tear, for she knew that Isaiah was right. They would never speak again after this. It was sad to think that another old friend would leave her behind.

She folded the letter and slipped it into her armor. Turning, she looked at the new Blademaster once more and sighed softly.

"Raven, take Tunera and Tomas to a room where they can wait," she ordered softly. "I will be in to speak to them after I ready the Test of the Blades for Tomas."

Part III
Hunter, Prey

Dragonsbane

ChapⲦeR XII
The Councⁱⱡ of ⱲaR

Ɩⱡana SⲦeelⸯⸯdRake was ᵬoRed.
And she was growing angry

For the previous seven weeks, she had been stuck in daily meetings of the Council of War. Had they been productive meetings, she would not have minded. But the Council of War had done nothing as far as preparing the Southern Dales for war.

All that they had done was argue with each other.

It was pointless. Alana knew that the army was coming. She knew that the Southern Dales had to be prepared to meet the army. But unless the Council of War started actually making plans, there was no point to such a meeting taking place anymore.

The spring was coming fast, and the snows had already started to melt. Alana knew that it was only a matter of time before the army of undead was on the move.

The Southern Dales would need to be ready when that happened.

The problem was that many of the members of the Council of War did not yet believe that such a war was even coming. Some of them even outright scoffed at Alana's authority over the armies of the Southern Dales.

The Southern Dales would be lost if the Council of War could not be made to see what was coming.

There were three members of the Council of War that she knew were supportive of her assertions about what was coming. King Roland Stonehammer, Dargan Starseeker of the Arvendale Territory, and Marcus Whelan of the Valendale Territory all accepted her word without argument. The King had pledged the loyalty of the Southern Dales to her. Lord Dargan was her father in law and had come to see the wisdom of Taelin in her words. And Marcus would not even be at the council had she and her companions not saved the lives of the citizens of Valendale the previous summer.

But the rest of the Council did not believe her.

The councilor from Solvendale and the councilor from Talondale were arguing about trade disputes between their two territories. The councilor from Darcandale had gone to sleep. And the councilor from Parciandale was doing his best to shout over everyone he could.

Alana had had enough. Her eyes met those of the king, and he nodded once, as if he knew in that glance what she wanted to do. She nodded back.

Quietly, so as to not draw attention, she drew one of her swords from its scabbard. She had been the only one allowed to wear her blades openly during the Council sessions. It was by the King's order that she be allowed to wear her weapons at all times.

She had not wanted to draw attention to the fact that she had drawn her weapon, but she need not have worried. No one at the table but the King had noticed that she was now holding naked steel.

And so it was that everyone other than the King was shocked when she brought the flat of her blade against the table with a resounding clang. The councilor from Darcandale snorted awake at the noise. The rest of the councilors stared at her.

"You dare!" one of the councilors yelled.

"Have I got your attention now?" she asked, her voice intentionally kept soft. She sheathed her sword now that it was no longer needed to get the attention of the councilors.

There was some murmuring, but she ignored it. She jumped on the table and stood in the center so all the members of the Council of War had no choice but to look at her.

"I have listened to your insipid banter for weeks," she began. "You have argued amongst yourselves about trade routes and borders and all manner of things that do not matter."

"They do matter!" the councilor from Parciandale shouted.

"No, they do not," Alana said. "Trade routes and borders will matter little when everyone is dead."

"What do you mean by this?" another of the councilors barked at her.

"Have you not been paying attention to what the King and I have been trying to tell you these past seven weeks?" she raised an eyebrow. "War is coming to the Southern Dales. And soon. If we do not prepare for the defense of the Southern Dales, everyone will die."

"You can't know that," someone said.

"I can, and I do," Alana sighed. "Do you know the prophecy of the Great War of Souls? Because that war is almost upon us."

"I have never heard of this prophecy," the councilor from Parciandale scoffed.

"The Dream Weaver gave it three hundred years ago," the King said.

"And now, you're saying that this prophecy is coming true?" someone called.

"I am," Alana said. "Listen and learn, for this is coming true. The prophecy of the Great War of Souls

"After three hundred years of peace in the world comes the Age of Darkness. The Dark God will return to begin his conquest of the world once more.

"In the early days of the Age of Darkness, after the Blademasters have returned to the world of Calthea, the army of the dead shall arise in service to the Dark God.

The dead shall rise and wage war across the face of Calthea.

"When the twice dead city falls empty for a third time, the storm clouds will gather and the sabres will rattle in their scabbards. The blight of war shall be upon the land and only the one born of the light can lead the charge against the darkness.

"The army of the light must uncork the magic of the bean sidhe to turn back the darkness. The one born of the light must lead the legacy of the Blademasters onto the field of battle.

"When the soul of the captured bean sidhe wails, the stones of the stronghold of the light will shatter and crumble upon one another. The spirits of the chosen of Taelin will once more take the field of battle in the war against the darkness.

"The fire of the sun and the moon will dim and fade to darkness. The one born of the light must walk out from the shadow of the fire of the sun and the moon and lead the chosen of Taelin.

"The Twenty Third Law of the Blades will be violated for some of the chosen of Taelin.

"If the one born of the light does not lead the charge against the army of the dead, the world will fall into a darkness that will be without end. Only the power of the First Law of the Blades can guide the hand of the one born of the light.

"In this battle as in all others the one born of the light will fight, there will be no guarantees. Only by following the wisdom of Taelin and by the luck of Laeyra will the one born of the light prevail.

"Should the one born of the light be successful in leading the forces of the light, the world will live in relative peace for a time, but only for a time for the Dark God shall never give up his quest.

"If the one born of the light wishes to undo the damage caused by the wailing soul of the captured bean sidhe, she must find the Light of Taelin and use its magic to once more build the stronghold of the light.

"In the years after the end of the great war of souls, should the one born of the light in turning back the darkness for a time, she will extend the light three times. But with the third, she will take her place among the spirits of the chosen of Taelin.

"So ends the words of the final prophecy of Bahala, the Dream Weaver. With the gifting of this prophecy, I turn the mantle of power of the Dream Weaver over to a new and much younger Dream Weaver. Heed these words, for all that is written here shall come to pass.

"May these words one day find their way to the one born of the light. The one who protects her will be able to translate these words for her, although neither will know the meaning behind the words when they find them."

"And you believe that this prophecy has been invoked?" the councilor from Parciandale scoffed. "What proof do you have?"

"The proof is sitting right there," Alana said, pointing to Marcus Whelan. "The people of Valendale were held captive in the city of Willowdale As you know, the city of Willowdale is often referred to as the twice dead city. When the people of Valendale were returned to their city, that meant the twice dead city had fallen empty for a third time."

The councilors began to mumble amongst themselves, and Alana was afraid that they would start turning on Marcus. She looked over at King Roland, and saw that he was thinking much the same thing. She was relieved when he held up his hands to quiet the crowd.

"Councilors, please," the King said. "The matter of whether or not the people of Valendale should have been left there is not up for debate. When I heard about their plight, I personally implored the Blademaster and her companions to go rescue Marcus and his people. And yes, I knew of this prophecy at the time. But there was no way I could leave those people there."

The King's words had the intended effect, and the whispering died down. Alana nodded to the king in thanks before turning back to the councilors to continue.

"What the King does not know is that had I not gone to Willowdale to rescue the people of Valendale, they would have all been killed and the Zeraphim would have started over with the citizenry from another city," Alana said softly. "And another. And another. Until I showed up. Who knows how many people's lives I saved by saving the people of Valendale?"

"But you've condemned us all to war!" the councilor from Parciandale, who Alana now realized was going to be the toughest one to convince, bellowed.

"The war was coming," Alana shrugged. "If it had not been now, it would have been another time. But it was coming. Nothing I did or did not choose to do changes that."

There was more muttering. Alana let them mutter. She knew that they would have to talk this through and work through to the correct conclusions on their own. She had given them the information she could. It was up to the individual councilors to believe or disbelieve her as the case may be.

Finally, the muttering ceased.

"Alana, tell them what we are up against in this war," Dargan said, his strong voice unusually quiet. "They need to know everything."

Alana nodded to Dargan in appreciation. She turned back to the councilors and began to slowly walk around the perimeter of the table, looking down at each councilor as she passed.

"This is a war like no other the Southern Dales has faced," Alana began. "Yes, there will be the shadow warriors that the Dark God has used before. But this army is made almost entirely of the undead. Let me repeat that. Their entire army is already dead. So how are we to fight that?"

"How do you know what the army is like?" It was the councilor from Paricandale again. She had known he would be the one to ask.

"Because, my dear councilor, I have already fought a part of this army," Alana said crossing over to stand in front of him. She dropped to a knee so she could stare him in the eye. "I assure you. They are as tough to destroy as you might be fearing. Were it not for the fact that they chose to attack the Temple of the Blades when there were three Blademasters and four dragons present, things may have gone differently. Dragon fire is a very effective deterrent to the undead. But they fight fiercely. They do not tire. And they keep coming."

"How large an army are we talking?" Marcus asked.

Alana stood and pulled a folded piece of paper from her armor. She walked over to the King and handed the paper to her.

"The Dream Weaver gave me this weaving prior to our leaving for Arvendale this past fall," she said. "Please read it to the council, Your Highness."

The King took the paper and unfolded it. He read over the words once to himself, his face paling slightly.

"It is indeed from the Dream Weaver. I recognize his hand," the King said. He cleared his throat and read the words of the weaving aloud. "When the twice dead city falls empty a third time, the age of darkness will spread across the land.

"A wave of shadows shall block out the sun. The undead shall spread across the land in waves. Their number will be as close to endless. And they shall be led by the red eyed demon.

"Only the one truly born of the light can lead the army of light against the army of darkness."

He looked up from the paper and stared at Alana. She nodded once before taking the paper back from him.

"Their number will be near to endless," she said softly. "And they will fight without tiring."

"Then what are we to do?" Marcus asked. "It sounds as if all is lost for us."

"I am the one truly born of the light," Alana said. "I do not want to lead. It has never been my intention to lead. I just wanted to live a simple life with the man I love. But I know that cannot be."

"We would have wished for that too, Lady Blademaster," Dargan said, a smile threatening to spread across his face. "But we know that you will lead our armies to victory. The armies of the Arvendale Territory are yours to command."

"I am surprised at you, Lord Dargan," the councilor from Parciandale said. "I figured you would be the last of us to believe this tale."

"We have believed since we first heard the prophecy about this war," Dargan said. "We were told the prophecy by our son, Colwyn. We have the utmost trust in our son. And in our son's wife, who stands before you now. We ask that you trust her as well."

That got the councilors murmuring. They had not heard that Colwyn had married, it seemed. And to an outsider. That Lord Dargan would allow such a marriage must be shocking to the rest of the Council.

Alana let them murmur. She hopped down from the table and stood at her seat. She had said all that she could. There was nothing more that could be said that could convince the Council of War about the seriousness of what was to come.

Ironically, it seemed that the news of the fact that she was Colwyn's wife did more to help convince the council than any of her words did. Had she known that would be the case, she would have led with that.

But she was someone who wanted people to see the truth of a situation. And now, it appears that the council had and was ready to begin the actual preparations for the defense of the Southern Dales.

"What must we do?" the councilor from Parciandale slumped back in his chair. "What can we do to stop this horde that you are telling us is coming."

"Now that you are all understanding of what's coming, let us begin," Alana said.

Alana stood as the Council began to slowly file out of the room. While she was happy that she had been able to convince the Council of the seriousness of the coming threat, she was tired from the effort. It should not have been such a chore to convince the Council.

It had helped to have Lord Dargan argue so eloquently on her behalf though.

Alana wondered, not for the first time, if part of the reason that Taelin had put her and Colwyn together was so that she would have the support of his family through the difficult times that were ahead. She would not be surprised if that turned out to be the case. The whole purpose of the bond between the Blademaster and her husband was for her protection, after all. By connecting her to one of the noble houses of the Southern Dales, Taelin would ensure that Alana had extra protection.

As Dargan Starseeker came around the table to leave, he stopped next to her.

"We would ask you to join us for dinner at Arvendale Manor two nights hence," he smiled at her. "You and our son. We would love to see you in a setting other than council chambers."

"I'd like that, Lord Dargan," Alana smiled broadly. She turned to walk out the door by his side. "I want to thank you for your support in the Council meeting. It has been difficult."

"You are trying to protect the Southern Dales, Alana," Dargan said. For the first time, Alana realized how tired he sounded. "We must support you. If the reports that our son has brought us are to be believed, and we do not doubt them to be anything other than accurate, we must support you in all that you do."

"You have no idea how much your support means to me right now," Alana said. They walked for a short time before she continued. "There are times when I do not know if I am the right person to lead the forces of the Southern Dales, Lord Dargan."

Dargan put his hand on her arm to stop her. She turned to face him, looking deep into his eyes. She saw lines around his eyes that had not been there when she first met him in Arvendale. It was clear that the war was taking its toll on more than just her.

"We understand your doubts, Alana," he began. "But know that we believe in you."

"There are times when I wish someone else was chosen for this, Lord Dargan," she said. She did not know why she felt comfortable telling him this when she had not even told Colwyn. But then, she knew that Colwyn already knew how she felt. It was a token of how much he loved her that he had not mentioned it. "Leading the forces of the Southern Dales is something I would never have sought out to do."

"There is something we heard once that we think you should hear now," Dargan said quietly as he laid his hand comfortingly on her shoulder. "We believe that it is part of your Law of the Blades, in fact. Power is not given to those who seek it. We speak not of political power, such as what we hold. That is not true power. What you have is the power to save lives, Alana. You have the power to save everyone. Such power as that is not given to those would seek it. Because those who would seek such power would be corrupted by it. Only someone like you who does not wish to hold the power you hold but has it thrust upon them as you have can do what must be done."

Alana stared at Dargan. She had never thought about such concepts that way before. But she knew that he was right. She had had a great deal of power thrust upon her. And she knew that not anyone could hold that power and do what she needed to do.

"I think I understand," she nodded finally. "Thank you, Lord Dargan. I needed to hear that."

"You are welcome, my child," Dargan smiled at her. He leaned over and kissed her on the forehead. "We will expect you and our son at Arvendale Manor two nights hence for dinner then."

"We will be there."

Chapter XIII
Reunion

Alana and Colwgn made their way back to their house. Alana was tired from yet another session of the Council of War. It seemed like they were not getting anywhere as far as preparing for the war. She knew that the time was coming when she would have to step away from the Council and let them sink or swim on their own.

She knew that the time was quickly approaching where she would have to take the field of battle.

When that time came, she could only hope that the rest of the Southern Dales were ready for the war. There was only so much that she could do to prepare them. At some point, they would need to take a step on their own. She had to hope that they were able to do so. It helped that King Roland and Lord Dargan were two of the leading voices in the Council of War. Both of them were dedicated to the defense of the Southern Dales, and Alana felt that they would make sure that the Southern Dales were prepared for the war.

Alana had other concerns, though. She knew that the Nightstalker was still out there. And she had a feeling that there would be more than one of them at some point. She knew that she would have to make sure that the other Blademasters were ready for such opponents.

She also knew that, according to the prophecy that the Dream Weaver had brought them before their journey to Arvendale, there was still the red eyed demon to deal with. She was not sure what the red eyed demon was. The Dream Weaver had only brought her the text of the prophecy. He had not shown her what he had seen.

She was rather thankful for that.

When the time came for her to face this demon, she did not want to be paralyzed with fear. And Alana was afraid that if she knew what it was before she faced it, she would be.

And she was worried about William. The snows had melted and he had not returned from the Temple of the White. She could only hope that he was successful in his quest to replace the Dream Weaver. But Alana knew that she would need Silvestra back very soon, and so she hoped that her friends would return. Every night, she had spent time outside the front door of her house looking towards the direction that Silvestra had flown off in prior to the snows arriving in the Southern Dales.

She had yet to see them coming.

Colwyn shared her worry for the young mage. But he had told her that William would either return or he wouldn't. There was nothing they could do to help him by worrying.

Alana wished that she could so easily stop worrying about her friends, but it was not in her nature. She was always going to be a worrier. It was the way she was, and she did not want to change for it would mean that she was no longer the same person that she had always prided herself on being.

And so, night after night, she kept up her lonely vigil waiting for her two friends to come flying back to Ravendale from the Tower of the White. Some nights, Colwyn joined her in her vigil, but most nights, she stood alone. She couldn't explain to anyone why it was so important for her to watch for them every night. No one would understand if she tried.

Alana felt that if she gave up on William's returning, he would not do so.

It was silly superstition, but she did not want to be the cause of his failure if she stopped watching for him. It was a silly thought, and she knew better, but it made her feel like she was doing something to help her friend.

After dinner, she made her way out to stand in front of her house. Something told Alana that this night would be different. This night would be the night that would see William return. The Blademaster did not know why she had that feeling, but she had learned long ago to trust her instincts. They had kept her alive at times when she should not have been able to survive, after all. So if something inside was telling her that Silvestra and William would be coming home this night, she would not doubt that feeling

She would wait and she would watch.

She could feel her heart beating faster with anticipation as she waited. If William was, indeed, returning tonight, it meant that he had been successful in his Test of Magic. Alana knew that it would have been difficult on the young mage, and she wanted to know all about what had happened at the Tower of the White.

She promised herself, though, that she would let the poor man get settled back in Ravendale before she pestered him with questions about what he had been doing while he was at the Tower of the White. She knew that William would tell them everything that he could when he was able to. And she figured that there would be things that he would not be able to tell them about his experiences at the Tower of the White.

It would be good to see her friends again. Aside from being worried about William and his Test of Magic, Alana and Colwyn both missed William's companionship. And, as

Alana's nathair an aeir a chosnaíonn, Silvestra would be needed before too long.

If Alana were going to start to launch her own part of the defense of the Southern Dales, she would need her nathair an aeir a chosnaíonn with her to insure her safety. At least as much as Alana's safety could be assured considering they were headed into a war.

As she thought about her friends and how much she wished they would arrive safely, Alana thought she caught a flash of silver far off in the distance, but she could not be sure. Straining to see, Alana could not be sure she actually had seen what she thought she had seen.

"Col," she called, not taking her eyes from where she thought she'd seen the flash of silver. "Come here please. I need your eyes."

The chair that Colwyn liked to sit in creaked as he stood up. He walked out to where she was standing and put his arms around her from behind.

"What is it?" he asked.

"Look over in that direction," she said, pointing. She saw the flash of silver again, just for a second. "There. Did you see that?"

"Looked like it might be the flash of the moon off silver scales to me," Colwyn said after a moment. "But as far away as that looks to be, it could be another hour or more before they land if it is, in fact, Silvestra."

"We've waited this long for them, another hour shouldn't be a problem," Alana smiled back at him. "But if it is Silvestra, it will be nice to have them back."

"It will indeed," Colwyn returned the smile. "I only hope that William is with her. There is, after all, a real chance he failed in the Test. I know you don't want to hear that, Alana, but you need to prepare yourself just in case he's not coming back."

"He's coming back, Col," Alana said softly. She turned back to watch the flash of silver coming closer. "He has to come back. I'm not ready to say goodbye to anyone else. It's bad enough I'll be saying goodbye to Meryn soon when we send Talby back to Barandale."

"That's not goodbye though," Colwyn said, giving her a squeeze. "We will see the halfling again at some point during this war, I am sure."

"You know what I mean, Col."

"Yes, I do," he nodded.

They watched as the flash of silver slowly came closer to Ravendale. It seemed to take an agonizingly long time, but after an hour, they could start to see movement in the flash of silver. Alana supposed that it was the movement of Silvestra's wings as she flew through the air towards Ravendale. She still could not tell if William was on the silver dragon's back or not.

Alana leaned her head back against Colwyn's chest and closed her eyes. She knew that Colwyn would let her know when he could see whether or not William was with Silvestra. But it was a moment of peace that she might not otherwise have been able to grab during the preparations for the war.

She did not like to fail to take advantage of such small moments of peace.

It was a half an hour that they stood there like that. Alana kept her head leaned against his chest and he kept his arms around her.

"I can see Silvestra clearly now, Alana," he said softly after a while. "And there is definitely someone on her back. I can't tell yet if it is William, but I think it is. Whoever it is, they are wearing white robes."

"Has to be William then," she said without opening her eyes. "I suppose we will know for sure soon."

"Yes," he rumbled. "It looks like they are coming directly here, so we will know when they land."

"Good," Alana nodded. "At least we won't have to wait too much longer to find out how William did at the Tower of the White."

Alana opened her eyes. She could see the silver dragon more clearly herself, although she could not make out a rider on the dragon's back. The fact that Colwyn could see the rider was good enough, though. Her Protector had always had sharper vision than she had. She suspected that it had to do with training with the elves as much as he had.

As the minutes wore on, Silvestra drew closer and closer. Eventually, Alana could make out the rider. And soon enough, she was able to make out that it was, in fact, William She smiled when she saw the young mage sitting on Silvestra's back. It was good to see that her friend had survived his Test of Magic, even if she did not know exactly what it had entailed. She knew, though, that it likely had not been easy.

As the silver dragon flew closer, Alana could see that William looked to have aged some from his time at the Tower of the White. While he did not exactly look old, there was definitely a lightening in the hairs of his mustache. There were also more lines around his eyes than she remembered there being. Whatever had happened at the Tower of the White had certainly taken its toll on the young mage.

She doubted that he would give her a straight answer as to what had transpired during the Test of Magic though.

It did not matter. Alana did not need the details. All that mattered was that William had kept his promise and returned. It wasn't just that she knew she would need his magic during the war. He was a dear friend to her and one of the few that had believed in her from the start. There were so few people that Alana counted as true friends, she could not afford to lose any of them.

Soon enough, Silvestra was close enough that they could feel the wind from her powerful wings. The two of them stepped back into the doorway to their house so that Silvestra had an unobstructed landing spot.

The silver dragon coasted in for a gentle landing, kicking up some dust as her wings slowly beat to keep her aloft long enough to gently alight on the ground.

When she landed, William slid off her back. As soon as his boots hit the ground, Silvestra began her transformation back into her human form. Soon enough, Alana's two friends were standing there on her porch.

Alana could not help herself, and she launched herself at William, engulfing the young mage in a bear hug.

"I guess this means you missed us," William laughed after extricating himself from the Blademaster's embrace.

"You could say that," Alana nodded, a smile twitching across her face. "When the spring thaw came and you still hadn't come back from the Tower of the White, we worried you weren't coming back."

"It took some time to recover from the Test of Magic," the mage said. His voice had a haunted quality to it, and Alana could only wonder at what he had gone through in the Test of Magic. "I came back as soon as I was able to travel."

"I take it you were successful in your Test of Magic, William?" Colwyn asked from behind Alana.

"I would not have returned had I not been," the mage nodded. "I am now the Dream Weaver."

"And Roald Vilas?" Alana asked.

"Has merged with the magic," Williams sighed. "As I one day will. But not, I think, for many years."

"Come inside, my friends," Alana said softly. "I am sure that it has been a long journey. The least I can do is make you some tea."

"Tea would be lovely," Silvestra yawned. "It was a long flight."

"We cannot stay long," William said. "It was, as Silvestra said, a long flight. And I would very much like to sleep in my own bed. But I think a cup of tea with friends would be nice."

Alana led the way into the house. Colwyn led Silvestra and William over to the table while Alana went into the kitchen to fix some tea.

When Alana came back in with the tea, she set a cup in front of William, Silvestra and Colwyn before sitting down with her own cup.

"So, William," she said after a moment. "You are now the Dream Weaver."

"Yes, Alana," William nodded. He took a sip of his tea and put his cup down. "Excellent tea, as always."

"You don't have to tell us about the Test of Magic," Colwyn said. "But you know we are always here to listen should you decide you need to talk about it. Believe me, I understand better than most what going through such a test is like."

"I can no more talk about it than you can discuss the Test of the Blades with a new Protector, Colwyn," William said, his voice soft yet haunting. His hand found Silvestra's without his looking for it. "I do not know that I would have made it through the Test of Magic were it not for Silvestra waiting for me."

"That I understand all too well," Colwyn smiled a sad smile. He reached over and gave Alana's hand a squeeze. "True love is a very powerful thing. As Alana and I know well."

"And as I am learning," William smiled. "Still, that is not why we came here first before going to our own bed, as inviting as our bed is."

"Have you had a weaving already, William?" Alana raised an eyebrow. "Somehow, I did not think it would be so quick."

"No, I have had no weaving," the mage sighed. "I was told that it may yet be several years before I have a weaving. But I received information while I was in the vortex that you must know about."

"As far as we know, it has never happened that information has passed on through the vortex like this during a Test of Magic," Silvestra said. "It would cause great concern if the members of the Inner Circle knew that something like this happened. So we did not tell them."

"The only people that know about information being given to me during the Test of Magic are Silvestra, myself, and the guardian of the vortex," William continued. "And now the two of you."

"We would ask that you keep our counsel on this," Silvestra said. "As I said, if word of it got out, it would cause a great deal of trouble. For us, and, more than likely, for you. The Inner Circle would seek to eliminate all who know about such an event. The Southern Dales can ill afford to lose you now."

"I understand," Alana nodded. "You have our word."

"There's something we need to explain about the mages of Calthea," William said after a moment. It was clear to

Alana that he was trying hard to decide whether or not he could divulge the information he was about to give. "Without this explanation, the information I am about to pass on will not necessarily have the import that it should."

"What we're about to explain, though, is not something often discussed outside of our orders," Silvestra continued. She took a sip of her tea and looked Alana directly in the eyes. "Some would say that it is a betrayal of our vows that we explain these things to you."

"I understand," Alana nodded. "Please go on."

"There are nine orders within the mage community," William explained. He took a gulp of tea and swallowed before continuing. "Each of them specializes in a different kind of magic, although members of one order can use some magic from a different order too."

"The nine orders are alchemy, conjuration, divination, enchantment, evocation, history, illusion, necromancy, and wild magic," Silvestra said. "This applies only to human magic. Dragon magic does not obey the rules of the orders imposed on human magic."

"Each of the orders specializes in a different kind of magic," William explained. "Alchemists change things from one thing to another. Conjurors create things from nothing. Divination deals with prophecy, and is the order that sages and the Dream Weaver belong to. Enchanters can take an object and give the object some kind of magical property."

"Evokers can make things happen with different forms of energy, such as fire and electricity. William was of the evocation order before becoming the Dream Weaver," Silvestra continued for William. "The historical order is charged with maintaining books of magic and prophecy. Unlike any of the other orders, they do not have any magic specific to their order. Illusionists can create elaborate illusions to trick others. And practitioners of wild magic can manipulate nature to suit their needs."

"And necromancy?" Colwyn said. "I noticed you did not explain that order."

"The eight orders we told you about are the orders that most mages go into," William said after a few minutes.

"They can be good, neutral or evil mages. But none of the mages of those eight orders like to associate themselves with members of the necromancy order. They are vile. Even the Mage of the Black most dedicated to bringing about the Dark God's wishes keeps their distance from necromancers."

"But why?" Alana asked. "What are necromancers?"

"Necromancy is the magic of death," Silvestra spat with distaste. "You remember that skeletal dragon I fought in Willowdale?"

"How can I forget?" Alana shuddered. "I worried about you fighting that thing after what it did to Cobalt."

"That was a creature of necromancy," Silvestra explained. "It was created by a necromancer from the skeleton of a long dead dragon. It is a terrible form of magic. And while there are some that claim that some good might come from necromancy..."

Silvestra trailed off, unable to continue. It did not matter, though. Alana and Colwyn both understood that it was not something that she enjoyed talking about. And Alana could understand why. The skeletal dragon had been an abomination. And it had killed Cobalt, the first dragon to serve as Alana's protection. Had Silvestra not been there, Alana shuddered to think what havoc that creature could have wrought upon the citizens of Valendale that were fighting for their lives and for their freedom.

"I think I get the picture," Alana shuddered. "I think I understand about the orders of magic, now. But why do I need to?"

"While I was in the vortex undergoing the Test of Magic, some information about one of the orders was revealed to me," William said. "I do not know if it was supposed to be, but it was. The head of the necromancy order, a particularly nasty mage named Caliban, has ordered all of the mages in his order to assist Thraal in the Great War of Souls."

"Well, with an army of undead, that's hardly unexpected news," Alana said sourly. "So I expect there is more to it."

"There is," William nodded. "The fact that a Mage of the Inner Circle has taken direct involvement in such a conflict is troublesome. The Inner Circle is supposed to cut themselves off from actively having a hand in events on Calthea. Caliban has broken that rule."

"That doesn't sound good," Alana frowned.

"It is not," Silvestra said. "The Inner Circle is made up of the most powerful mage of each of the nine orders. That is why they keep themselves from interfering in the goings on here on Calthea. Were they to take a side in conflicts, it would tip the balance."

"Won't the others step in to stop him?" Colwyn asked, although he suspected he knew the answer.

"That would be taking a side," William shook his head sadly. "No, they will leave it up to the rest of us to stop Caliban. It is likely that Silvestra and I will have to fight him before the end of the War of Souls. Whether we will persevere or not, I do not know."

Alana frowned at that. She did not fear for her friends so much in this battle, for she knew that they would do their best to make it through to the other side of the battle. And there were still tricks that both William and Silvestra had hidden away that Alana knew they would pull out for this fight. But she feared what it would mean for Calthea if they failed.

It was the same fear she felt about Calthea if she were to fail herself.

Alana busied herself in refilling everyone's teacups, knowing that there was more coming from the mage, but not wanting to push. What he had already told them was bad enough. But she did need to know the rest. She gave him some time to collect his thoughts.

"There's more, isn't there?" she finally prodded.

"Yes," William sighed. "There is. The worst part of it. Caliban has ordered his necromancers to develop a new magic. One that would allow them to immediately resurrect our soldiers that fall during battle and bring them into the battle on their side."

"That is horrible," Alana gasped, covering her mouth with her hand.

"It's worse than that, Alana," Colwyn said. "Think about it. If they perfect that magic, then their army will grow exponentially while our army shrinks."

"You have the right of that, Colwyn," William nodded. "That is their plan. At this point, they do not have such a magic, but the necromancers are working hard to perfect it."

"We need to keep them from doing that," Alana said. "I don't know what we can do to stop it, but we must find a way to."

"William and I will work on that, Alana," Silvestra smiled. "In the meantime, I am working on a magic of my own that I hope will help you. I will say nothing more on it than that, but when I am ready, I will give you the aid I can with it."

"Any help is appreciated," Alana returned the smile. "This is not going to be a good war."

"There are rarely other kinds," William raised an eyebrow. "But we will do what we can to help. For now, though, it has been a long journey and I would like to sleep in my own bed tonight."

"Of course, my friend," Alana laughed. "Go get some sleep. I am sure we will talk more on this soon."

Chapter XIV
Consulting Dargan

lana had never really given any thought to the manors on High Street that were set aside for the First Lords when they visited Ravendale for council meetings. She had never had the need to go to any of the manors before. And, although Colwyn, as the son of the First Lord of Arvendale, could have stayed in Arvendale Manor at any point, they had never set foot inside the manor before now.

There had been no need to with the comfortable little house that Colwyn had built for the two of them.

But they had been invited to dinner at Arvendale Manor by Colwyn's father, and it meant that they would have to go there. That Dargan Starseeker had invited the both of them, not just Colwyn, said volumes about how far he had come in accepting their marriage. It would be a true family reunion, as Colwyn's sister, Bella, would also be there.

Alana was not sure why Dargan wanted to see them. She knew that he had a reason other than just having dinner with his son and daughter. Her instincts told her that there was a problem. She did not know what the source of the problem was, but she doubted that Dargan was there to cause them trouble.

It had taken divine intervention, but Dargan had accepted his children's marraiges that had both gone against his wishes. Alana held no illusions that Dargan was happy about both of his children flaunting the noble traditions. But she had the feeling that Dargan actually liked her.

And so, she and Colwyn were on their way to Arvendale Manor for dinner.

She had dressed in her hunter green dress that Colwyn loved so much. Since she was going to the manor of a First Lord, she had left her swords in their house. But she had secreted several daggers inside her dress. Colwyn had approved of that decision. He had not wanted her to go unarmed, but as she had no noble standing, it would not have been acceptable for her to openly carry her blades into the manor.

She was happy to see that Colwyn had also chosen to dress up for the occasion. He wore a white shirt that had puffy sleeves with gold buttons on the cuff and black pants tucked into hard soled black boots that came halfway up his calves. Unlike Alana, he did wear a sword, but he was allowed to as the son of the First Lord.

They left the house a bit earlier than they needed to in order to get to Arvendale Manor, as they chose to walk rather than to ride over. While it still got chilly at night, spring had arrived and brought warmer weather with it. They wanted to enjoy the walk over to the manor and relax some before they met with Dargan. Even though they expected that this meeting would go far more cordially than it had when they had visited Arvendale before the winter, they nonetheless wanted to make sure they were ready for whatever the meeting was to bring.

The streets of Ravendale were busier than they had been in a while as the citizenry was happy that the thaw had finally arrived and were starting to spend more time out of their houses. It was good to see the people getting out of their houses again. The city had felt very empty during the winter time.

Alana had not remembered seeing the city so empty before. But she also did not remember a winter as bad as the one they had just experienced either. It had been an incredibly rough winter in Ravendale. She had heard that several older people and children had succumbed to the elements during the winter.

There was a part of her that wondered if the especially harsh winter had been a part of Thraal's plan. She wasn't sure how he could control the weather to make such a rough winter though.

As she and Colwyn made their way through the city towards Arvendale Manor, they waved to people who smiled at them when they passed. Even before Alana had been named a Blademaster, the two of them had been popular amongst the citizens of Ravendale, and people were always happy to see them out and about. Alana had never been completely comfortable with the attention. That Colwyn was by her side and she did not have to deal with the attention by herself did help some, but only so much.

Colwyn had let her set the pace and she led them quickly through the streets, not wanting to dawdle where the citizens would fawn all over them All she wanted to do was to get to this dinner and get back to her house. While she did not mind spending time with Colwyn's family, she had a bad feeling that there would be some kind of bad news delivered at Arvendale Manor.

She wasn't sure what made her think that, but she could not shake the feeling. She had shared her thoughts with Colwyn before they left their house. To her great relief, Colwyn did not dismiss her feelings. She knew that they had gone through too much together for him to dismiss her instincts.

She knew that Colwyn was expecting trouble as well. She could always tell when he was expecting some kind of trouble. There were little hints like checking the sharpness of his blades. The fact that he had put his chain mail on under his clothes cinched it for her though. He would not have worn the chain mail to a family dinner had he not been expecting trouble.

Alana doubted that Lord Dargan or anyone in his service would want either of them harmed, but it never hurt to be cautious. She appreciated Colwyn's caution, especially when it so perfectly matched her own feelings of worry.

When they got to Arvendale Manor, Colwyn led the way up the steps to the manor. Alana smiled slightly as she watched him go up the stairs ahead of her.

Her smile faded as soon as she saw the armed guards step in front of the door barring their way.

"The First Lord of Arvendale is not seeing anyone this evening," one of the guards growled.

"The First Lord of Arvendale sent for us," Colwyn said to the guard.

"That may be, but we were given orders not to let anyone in," the guard said. The guard's hand strayed towards his weapon. "You will turn around and leave."

"Oh, really?" Colwyn raised an eyebrow. He turned to Alana. "We really must get home more often, Alana. None of the guards appear to know who I am." He sighed and turned back to the guard. "I highly doubt that Lord Dargan said to you that if his children were to arrive at the gate that you should turn them away."

"Ah, no. We were given no such orders," the guard blanched. "You... Oh."

"Right. Oh." Colwyn crossed his arms. "Well?"

Alana suppressed a giggle as she watched the guards part to let Colwyn lead the way into the manor. She could not help herself completely though, and she tossed a little wave to the guard that had challenged Colwyn as she walked by.

Colwyn led the way through the manor. Alana was content to follow him. After all, as the heir to the title of First Lord of Arvendale, he would know where everything in the manor was better than she. But she frowned when she realized they were not heading anywhere near where she expected that Lord Dargan would be.

"Where are we going, Col?" she asked after a few minutes.

"I want to talk to Victor for a moment before we go meet my father," Colwyn said.

"All right then," Alana nodded.

They walked down to where the guards were housed in the manor. Alana did not know what Colwyn wanted to talk to Victor about, but she knew that it had to be important if they were delaying going to have dinner with his father to see him. When they got to the guard barracks, Alana peeked in to see that there were only two men inside. One was Victor.

Colwyn leaned on the frame of the open door and crossed his arms. When the guards in the room failed to notice him, he looked back at Alana and winked.

"You know, time was a Starseeker showed up to speak to the guards and they actually made an effort to find out what he wanted," Colwyn said in a soft voice.

Victor's head whipped towards the door violently fast. Alana was concerned that he might have hurt himself, but she could tell right away that he had not.

"Colwyn!" he exclaimed as he made his way over to where the young noble was leaning against the wall. "You've come for dinner with your father, I suppose."

"I have," Colwyn nodded as he clasped forearms with his old instructor. "I wanted to see you before I went up to dinner with him, however."

"Of course," Victor nodded. He motioned for Colwyn to enter the barracks. Colwyn walked in at his invitation, Alana close behind. Victor chuckled when he saw her. "Ah, where one is, so is the other. Welcome, Blademaster."

"Thank you, Victor," she bestowed a wide smile on him.

"Now, Colwyn, my boy," the captain of the guard asked after the two were seated. "What can I do for you?"

"I wanted to know how preparations are going amongst the soldiers," Colwyn said softly. "I know that Lord Dargan ordered the standing armies to ready for war, but I also know he left the actual preparations to you."

"Yes, he has," Victor nodded. "And, for the most part, the preparations go well."

"For the most part?" Colwyn said, quirking an eyebrow up.

"Colwyn, the men are scared," Victor sighed. "The army of Arvendale has not fought a battle in many years. That is to your father's credit. Lord Dargan prefers to resolve his conflicts with words rather than swords. The fact that he is not even attempting a diplomatic solution is so out of character for him that the men are scared. They will fight to the last man if need be, for they will honor your father's commands without question. But they know it is going to be a very serious conflict."

"Do they know what they will be fighting?" Alana asked.

"No, they don't," Victor sighed. "None of us really do."

"We do," Alana said in a quiet voice. A haunted look flashed across her face for a moment. It was long enough for Victor to see it, though.

"I see," Victor frowned. "That bad?"

"Yes," Colwyn nodded. "Look, Victor. I'm not going to try to say it isn't serious. It is. The conflict the Southern Dales is about to enter is, frankly, the most serious conflict since the days of the very first Blademaster."

"It is that serious, then," Victor frowned.

"I am afraid that it is, yes," Colwyn nodded. "Can you get all of the guard that are here together in two days? Alana and I will speak to them."

"Of course, Colwyn," Victor nodded. "It will be done."

"Good," Colwyn nodded. He and Alana stood. "Well, we have to go up and have dinner with my father now, Victor."

"I believe your sister and young Cayden Antioch are here as well," Victor smiled.

"Good," Colwyn nodded. "Good that the whole family is getting together for dinner. It has been far too long."

"Indeed," Victor smiled broadly. "Go. Enjoy time with your family."

Colwyn clasped Victor's forearm again and turned to leave. As they were leaving, Alana leaned in close, a mischievous look on her face.

"Maybe after we meet with all the soldiers in two days, they'll remember who you are next time you visit Arvendale or the manor here in Ravendale," she teased.

He glared down at her, suppressing the urge to laugh.

They found Lord Dargan in the Great Hall. He and Lady Serina had been waiting for them. Bella and Cayden were also in the Great Hall. It appeared that Alana and Colwyn were, in fact, the last to arrive.

"We are pleased that you could come," Dargan said as he approached his son. "Although you are a bit later than we expected."

"I am sorry to be late, Father," Colwyn bowed his head slightly. "But I have not had a chance to check in with Victor Tram about the war preparations and I wished to avail myself of the opportunity to be able to do so."

"Your attention to duty is commendable, our son," Dargan nodded. "Come. Dinner should be ready for us soon."

Colwyn and Alana fell into step behind Dargan, Serina, Bella and Cayden. The six of them left the Great Hall and meandered their way through the halls of the manor until they reached a small private dining hall. There was a long table in the center of the room that was set with six service settings. Dargan sat at the head of the table, and Serina sat at the other end. Bella and Cayden took one side while Colwyn and Alana took the other side.

"Did you have any trouble getting into the manor, Colwyn?" Bella asked.

"Well, the guard wanted to refuse me entrance at first," Colwyn shrugged. "I guess he did not recognize me at first. I will have to try to spend more time in Arvendale so that I am not forgotten."

"The guard tried to arrest Cayden," Bella said, her voice angry. "For desertion."

"We did not authorize such orders," Dargan frowned. Clearly this was the first time that he had heard of the attempted arrest. "Cayden has left the service of the palace guard with our permission."

"I know, Father," Bella said softly. "I think the guard just wanted to cause trouble for some reason."

"We will speak to the captain of the guard about this," Dargan growled. "This will not happen again."

They lapsed into silence as several servants entered the dining hall bearing platters of food. The servants set the platters down and started to serve out the food to the six of them. When the servants were done and had left, the family began to eat.

"Thank you for having us for dinner, Father," Colwyn said after a few bites. "It is nice to have the family together again, even if only for one night."

"We are afraid that it is not just for the pleasure of your company that we have asked you here tonight," Dargan sighed. He wiped his mouth with his napkin and leaned back in his chair. "We have heard disturbing things that we feel you need to be aware of."

"More disturbing than an army of undead bearing down on the Southern Dales?" Alana asked. "Because I'm not sure I can handle anything more disturbing than that right now."

"It is not something more disturbing than that, no," Dargan said. Alana could swear the corners of his mouth twitched up in a smile for just the slightest of moments. "But it could complicate matters for you."

"What have you heard, Lord Dargan?" Alana nodded.

"Malachai Dragonsbane has left Darcandale," Dargain said. "It is said that he is on the hunt."

Alana looked at Colwyn, frowning. She could tell that he knew the name, but it meant nothing to her.

"I don't understand," she said, her frown deepening. "Who is Malachai Dragonsbane and why should it matter to me that he is on the hunt?"

"Dragonsbane is a dragon hunter," Colwyn said softly. "The best of all of them. If he is on the hunt, then he has found a prey that truly excites him."

"He has found three preys that truly excite him," Dargan said. "Their names are Greytonix, Timeanalia, and Silvestra Knightwing."

"Well," Alana said after a moment. "That certainly does pose a problem."

"That is why we are telling you what we have heard," Dargan said. "Dragonsbane will stop at nothing to see your dragons killed. We know that the dragons are a large part of the protection for the Blademasters. We would not see you stripped of their protection."

Alana looked over at Bella. She could tell the other Blademaster was a little shaken at the thought of someone hunting their dragons. She nodded once to the other woman, telling her that she too was concerned by this.

"Thank you for telling us this, Lord Dargan," Alana said softly. "I suppose that we will have to deal with this before the war starts. It would not be good for this Malachai Dragonsbane to show up right in the middle of a battle to kill our dragons."

"That is what we thought," Dargan nodded. "We will send someone over to your house with all the information we have on Dragonsbane's whereabouts. And I have ordered my guards to report to me instantly if he is sighted anywhere near Ravendale."

"Thank you," Alana nodded.

They finished their dinner in silence. As they were getting up to leave, Dargan came around the table and took Alana by the arm.

"We are sorry about how we treated you when we first met you, Alana," Dargan said softly. "We know that we have apologized for this already, and we know that our relationship with you has already improved. But we are really beginning to see just how you are truly a fit match for our son. And that you are the right person to lead the forces of the Southern Dales in this battle. That is why you have had our unceasing support as you rally the forces of the Southern Dales. There is little that we can do to make up for how we treated you however."

She reached up and placed a hand against his cheek. He looked taken aback at her touch, but he did not pull away.

"Lord Dargan, you are the father of the man I love," she began, a smile playing across her lips. "I cannot fault you for reacting as you did. You were surprised when I appeared in Arvendale at Colwyn's side. You did what you felt you needed to do to protect your family. I could not love Colwyn as much as I do and not understand why you reacted the way you did."

"You are a very rare person, Lady Alana," Dargan smiled at her. "We are honored to have you as a daughter in law."

"And I am honored to be a part of the Starseeker family, Lord Dargan. The aid that you have given Colwyn and I as we go forth to lead the Southern Dales has far outweighed any mistreatment that I might have received at your hand," she said. She took her hand from his cheek and took his hand. "There is no need to be sorry for how you treated me, Lord Dargan. Your actions have already spoken the words."

Dargan bowed his head at this, a single tear rolling down his cheek.

"Lord Taelin chooses his Blademasters well."

Alana leaned up and kissed him gently on the cheek.

"And he chooses the Protectors for his Blademasters well too," she whispered in his ear. "I could do no better than your son."

Chapter XV
War Preparations

wo days later, Alana and Colwyn found themselves walking towards Arvendale Manor once more. Colwyn had asked the captain of the guard to gather all of the generals and officers of the Arvendale army that were in Ravendale together.

Alana was about to tell them what they needed to know about the army of darkness that was coming for the Southern Dales.

She did not relish the duty of telling these men what they were up against, but someone had to. And as she was the one who was supposed to be leading them, it fell on her shoulders. She was thankful, once more, for the confidence that Dargan Starseeker had shown in her. That confidence allowed her to go forward.

They walked with a purpose down the streets of Ravendale. Alana knew that a difficult road was in front of all of them. But as the leader of the forces of the light, she knew that she had it the most difficult.

She thought once more about the prophecy of the Great War of Souls. The prophecy had made it perfectly clear that if Alana did not lead the forces of the Southern Dales, then the side of light would lose the War of Souls. It was a heavy responsibility that was laid on her shoulders. She sometimes wished that it was otherwise, but what was to be was to be, and there was little she could do about it now.

She was determined to see it through to the end.

Colwyn's love was a comfort, as it was meant to be. It made it at least a little bit easier to go forward and do what she needed to do. She shuddered to think about how it would be if she had to lead the side of light without Colwyn by her side.

Fortunately, she did not have to know what that would be like.

As they walked, they thought about what she was going to say to the generals. She knew that they needed to know what it was they were about to face when it came to the army of darkness. But she knew that without seeing the army, it would be hard for the generals to fully grasp what they were dealing with. And there was no way that they could see the army without actually fighting it. She had to make them understand what they were dealing with, without their actually having seen the army of darkness.

She had to be their eyes.

She was their leader, after all, and she had seen what the army was like, even if she had not seen the entirety of the army. She knew enough to know what they were facing. And she knew how hard it was to destroy the army.

It was bad enough that the Council of War was not able to grasp what they were up against. She knew that she needed to get the message across to the generals. If the Southern Dales was going to make it through the War of Souls, the generals would have to do their part in leading the troops. In order to do that, they had to accept the truth about what it was they were fighting.

It was a beautiful early spring day, and Alana was enjoying the touch of warmth in the air. After the brutal winter that the Southern Dales had just endured, she was happy that the weather had turned back towards the warmth, even if it meant that the war was coming fast.

There were birds singing in the sky, and that always made Alana smile. She was happy to see nature starting to awaken from its long winter slumber. The world just felt more alive.

It was what Alana was fighting to protect.

When they arrived at Arvendale Manor, Victor Tram met them. He bowed slightly to them and then smiled at Colwyn.

"Welcome, Colwyn, my boy," Victor greeted his former student. "I have gathered the generals together as you requested. They await your presence in the Great Hall. Your father is also there."

"Why is Lord Dargan there?" Alana asked.

She wasn't exactly upset to hear that Dargan was in attendance to the meeting. She had a feeling that his support would be helpful in getting the generals to understand what she was telling them. Still, it was a bit of a surprise that he was taking time out of his day to be a part of the meeting.

"Lord Dargan wishes to hear what you will tell the generals," Victor shrugged. "I suspect he also wishes to vocalize his support for you during this meeting."

"As he has during the meetings of the Council of War," Alana nodded. "Support for which I am extremely grateful."

"Lord Dargan has impressed upon me as the Captain of the Guard how important it is to follow the commands of the Blademaster Alana Steeldrake," Victor said. He smiled at Alana. "Not that I needed any encouragement. I was already determined to follow your commands in the war that is coming. I've read the prophecy. I know that you are the one that will keep us from falling into darkness."

"I am glad my father has understood this," Colwyn nodded once. He looked at Alana before turning back to Victor. "I was afraid, at first, that he would fight us on the topic of the War of Souls."

"As you know, Colwyn, your father sees his first duty as being to the people of Arvendale," Victor said.

"As it should be," Colwyn nodded.

"You have brought to him a credible threat to the people of Arvendale," Victor continued. "And you have brought him the means to see the people of Arvendale through the threat. Is it so hard to believe that he would, as a result, accept the very means of survival that you have presented him?"

"You saw how he reacted to Alana when I first introduced her," Colwyn sighed. "I feared he would not see the truth of it. I am glad to be wrong."

"You do your father a great disservice, Colwyn," Victor said, shaking his head. "You know as well as I do that Lord Dargan will do whatever it takes to keep his people safe. The moment you presented him with this threat to the Southern Dales, you should have known that he would do whatever was needed to make sure that the people of Arvendale were kept safe."

"You're right, Victor," Colwyn nodded. He clasped the captain of the guard on his shoulder. "I should have. I let his initial reaction to my wife color my perceptions. I should not have done so."

"No, you should not have," Victor smiled. "But you are your father's son and are just as stubborn as he is."

"So, Victor, there's something I need to talk to you about other than this war that's coming," Colwyn said, deciding that it was the right time to bring up the topic.

"And what might that be, young man?" Victor raised an eyebrow.

"When Bella and Cayden came to the manor the other night, the guards tried to arrest Cayden for desertion," Colwyn said.

"I have never termed Cayden a deserter and would never have issued orders for his arrest," Victor frowned.

"I know you wouldn't, my old friend," Colwyn smiled. "And yet, the attempt to arrest him was made. It failed of course."

"Of course," Victor nodded. "I daresay your sister gave them what for."

"You would think that people who have been around my family as long as some of these guards have been would know better than to upset Bella."

"You would think, but clearly they do not," Victor laughed. He clasped Colwyn on the shoulder. "Come, my friend. We will talk to them about that as well."

Colwyn nodded. He and Alana followed Victor to the Great Hall. Alana had no idea what to expect as far as how many people would be there. Colwyn had told her that there were a number of generals in the Arvendale armies. And he told her to expect that some of their subordinate officers would also likely be there. While he couldn't tell her how many people would be there, he told her to be prepared for a fairly large number.

Thankfully, their experience in Willowdale had given her practice in speaking before a large number of people that were not necessarily likely to take her at her word.

As had the meetings of the Council of War.

She hoped that, with Lord Dargan there to support her, it would be easier to convince these men of war. At least they were more disposed to the thought of war than the councilors had been.

Alana was not prepared for the sheer number of people in the Great Hall when they arrived. One look over at Colwyn told her that he was surprised as well. It appeared that far more than just the generals had shown up for the briefing. The Great Hall was packed to overflowing. There was one thin corridor empty amongst the throng of people. That one corridor led straight down to the dais where Lord Dargan was standing, waiting for them.

"When word got out that you would be addressing the generals about the war that was coming, others wanted to come and hear your words for themselves," Victor said softly. "Almost every soldier with us here in Ravendale is here. Everyone not currently on guard duty appears to be here."

"Just as well," Alana nodded. "The message will not be lost in translation this way."

Victor led Alana and Colwyn down the clear corridor to the dais. There were mutterings as the three walked past the throng. Whisperings about the Blademaster and about Colwyn made their way through the crowd of soldiers.

Alana paid them no mind. She was gathering up her energies for the task ahead of her.

Getting people to see the truth, it turned out, was much harder than fighting out in the field.

When they got to the dais, Alana bowed just slightly at the waist in respect to her father in law. He returned the gesture before turning to his son and offering his hand. Colwyn clasped arms with the elder Starseeker.

Then Alana and Colwyn turned to face the soldiers that were assembled.

A hush spread over the room as Colwyn raised his hands towards the crowd in an effort to silence them.

"Before we get to why we are here, there is something I would like to say to all of you," Colwyn said, his voice soft. "Cayden Antioch is not a deserter and should not be treated as if he is. He has left the service of the palace guard with my father's blessing. The war that is coming will be hard enough for the Blademasters to fight without their Protectors being thrown into the dungeons for no reason."

"We echo what our son has said," Dargan spoke. "We will not stand for Cayden being harassed over his leaving the palace guard. As he is now our daughter's husband and, as such, a member of the Starseeker family, we would be greatly displeased to hear of another attempted arrest, and we would be forced to severely punish those who attempted the arrest. Have we made ourselves clear enough on this matter?"

When no one challenged him on it, Dargan turned to Alana and nodded once. He turned back to the assembled soldiers once more and raised his hands.

"The Blademaster has come to address you about what it is we will be facing in the coming war," the First Lord continued. "We would have you hear her words and truly listen to them. Then go back to your commands and spread the word of what is coming so that we can all be ready once the fighting starts."

Alana stepped forward at that point and looked out over the soldiers. She hoped they would heed her words and not just dismiss them because she was a woman. She knew that some soldiers were like that. And she knew that was a problem she would likely continue to face as she went to lead the Southern Dales in this war.

"I am the Blademaster, Alana Steeldrake," she began. "My husband is your lord, Colwyn Starseeker. We have both seen what the army that is coming is like, and we are here to make sure you are ready for that army. I will tell you about the army and then I will open up the floor for questions. Let us begin."

Dragonsbane

Chapter XVI
The Parting of the Ways

Lana stood looking at herself in the mirror. It was not something that she often did for she did not really like the way she looked. Something about today, though, made her want to look.

She knew that today would be the day that the war actually started.

Oh, there would be no battle today, she knew. But today was the day that she would first issue orders to the other Blademasters. There were things that had to happen if the Southern Dales were going to be ready for the war that was coming. And in order for that to happen, her Blademasters would have to go on missions to gather information for her. There was no way she could help plan the defense of the Southern Dales without knowing fully what she was up against.

While she knew what the army of undead was like, she did not know the full extent of that army. And so she would have to send one of her Blademasters into the Wilds to determine the strength of the undead army.

She was starting to understand what it was like for King Roland to order men into battle. The Blademasters were her responsibility and no one else's. As a result, she was the one that had to order them into situations that could result in their deaths.

It was a heavy responsibility.

What bothered her more than knowing she was sending others into danger was the fact that she would be parting with an old friend.

She would be sending Talby Swiftfoot on a mission, and she knew that Meryn would be going with her. It would be the first time in quite a while that Alana would be going on a journey without the halfling. It would be odd not having the gregarious little one with her. She knew that Colwyn, for the most part, would be happy not to have Meryn along. But she also knew that even Colwyn would miss the halfling.

When someone saved your life, you tended to miss them when they were gone, after all.

Alana knew that it was for the best that Meryn went with Talby. Things just hadn't been the same since the incident in Willowdale. While Alana had forgiven Meryn for her betrayal, the others had not. It had been uncomfortable for Meryn, and it had been made even more so whenever William and Silvestra were both around.

So while she would miss Meryn, she knew that the mission she was sending Talby on was a better place for her little friend.

As she looked in the mirror, she sighed and straightened her armor. She was happy that she at least looked the part of the Master Blademaster even if she did not feel it. As she had told her father in law, there were times when she just did not feel like she was capable of being the person to lead the Southern Dales when it came to this battle. She knew, though, that she was the one spoken of in prophecy, so she knew that she had to do whatever she could to put those doubts behind her.

Satisfied with the way her armor looked on her, Alana pulled her hair back and tied it back with a hunter green feithidí silk ribbon. She nodded once and turned back to the bed where her boots were sitting on the floor waiting for her. She sat on the edge of the bed and slipped her bare feet into her boots.

When she stood back up, she had steeled her face into a blank expression, resolved to not be bothered by the upcoming parting of the ways. She buckled on her sword belt and made her way out of the house she shared with Colwyn.

When Alana opened the door to the tap room of the Lucky Minotaur, she could smell the aroma of Albert's famous spiced potatoes. She knew that Colwyn had told Albert that they would be leaving on a journey today. She also knew that it would not be practical to have one of Albert's farewell breakfasts before each journey that they took over the course of this war, but she could not begrudge the old innkeeper this one. She would feel better about sending Talby and Meryn on their way if they all had stomachs full of good food.

Colwyn had moved the tables together for the companions, and he was sitting there talking to Gwen when Alana walked into the tap room. He smiled over at her and she returned the smile brightly.

Alana knew that some women would feel threatened by the young bar maid if they found her talking to their husband. But Alana knew that Colwyn looked at Gwen like a little sister.

She also knew that Colwyn had eyes for only one woman.

Suddenly, though, Alana frowned as she looked at the table. Colwyn had set fourteen chairs around the tables. Alana ran though her companions and the other Blademasters and counted thirteen.

"Col, you counted wrong," she said as she got to the table. "There's one too many chairs here."

"No there isn't," Colwyn shrugged. "Martin asked me to set an extra chair out."

"Did he tell you why?" Alana asked.

"Nope," he shook his head. "Just said that we needed one more chair for breakfast. I figured it was easier to just set out another chair rather than ask for explanations I would never receive."

"Good point," Alana nodded.

She gave Gwen a quick hug and then sat next to Colwyn. Gwen jumped up and made her way over to the kitchen to bring Alana back a kava juice.

Alana smiled at Gwen as the young woman set the kava juice down in front of her. Gwen had always been a very thoughtful young woman and always remembered Alana's favorite things. Alana had no doubt that one of Albert's famous chocolate pies would likely make its way to Alana before too much longer.

The thought made her grin broadly.

Alana knew that if it were not for the fact that she was always on the go and always training, Albert's amazing food would have her unable to fit into her armor in no time. Especially with the chocolate pies. She loved those pies. But if she did not train heavily on a daily basis, the way she would always eat them would make her gain a great deal of weight.

Apparently, being a Blademaster was good for her figure.

The smell of the potatoes was making Alana realize just how hungry she actually was. She had a feeling that she would definitely eat more than her fair share of the feast that Albert was preparing. Then again, she always did. It was a running joke amongst the companions, one that Alana joined in on, that Alana sometimes seemed like she had a bottomless pit for a stomach.

She knew that they would not start eating until all of the others arrived, so she hoped they would start arriving soon. She wanted to get on with the business at hand.

She had a feeling that trouble was coming fast.

While she knew that trouble was indeed incoming with the revelation that Malachai Dragonsbane was hunting their dragon companions, Alana knew that that was not the sense of trouble she was feeling. Perhaps it was the impending war, but Alana did not think that was it either. She trusted her instincts, and her instincts told her that there was at least one more source of trouble on the way to confront her.

And that whatever it was would arrive prior to the war starting in earnest.

She looked sideways at Colwyn. Although he appeared to be smiling on the outside, she could see the worry in his eyes. Apparently, he was also feeling that there was more trouble on the way.

The door opened and William entered with Silvestra by his side. She had her arm through his. It made Alana smile to see them so openly showing affection for each other. She was, once again, happy to see that they had been able to make true love work out.

She reached over and squeezed Colwyn's hand, for she was happy that they had been able to make true love work out for each other too. He looked over and smiled at her. Unlike the forced smile he had on earlier, this smile was genuine, and she knew that it was a smile just for her. She returned it with the special tight lipped smile she only gave him.

"Oh, good," William said as they arrived at the table. "We're going on a journey."

"It's a bit of a parting of the ways, actually," Colwyn said.

"Oh?" Silvestra quirked an eyebrow up. She sat down next to William. "I know you're not sending us away."

"No, we're not," Alana chuckled softly. "I expect you and William to stay by our side during the War of Souls."

"Good," William nodded. "Because we were about to ignore any order you gave that would have us anywhere else."

"You were, were you?" Alana suppressed a smile.

"I was assigned by the Inner Circle to protect the Blademaster," William shrugged. He leaned the Staff of Cirricus against the wall behind him where it would be within easy reach should he need it. "I cannot exactly fulfill that duty if I am not with her. And she will need me during the War of Souls. Of that, I have no doubt."

"Of that I have no doubt either, old friend," Alana nodded once, all pretext at levity gone. "I would not have you or Silvestra anywhere else but by my side."

"Good," William nodded, happy that that was settled.

"As if there was any question," Silvestra snorted.

Alana chuckled at Silvestra. She turned back to William to explain what she meant by a parting of the ways.

She had just opened her mouth to speak when the door to the tap room thudded open once more. Alana turned to see Greytonix and Timeanalia enter the tap room. The two dragons were in their human forms but could be no different from one another even were they in their dragon forms. Greytonix was a big bear of a man whereas Timeanalia was a slight sapphire haired woman. From the moment that Alana had first met the two dragons, her opinion of the two of them was as different from each other as they were. She had immediately liked Greytonix, but there was something in Timeanalia's haughty attitude that had rankled at Alana from the start.

While she had warmed to the sapphire dragon somewhat since then, their relationship could not be considered anything other than cold. Fortunately, Timeanalia got along quite well with Bella, the Blademaster she had been paired with.

"Ah, a feast!" Greytonix boomed as he looked to where Alana and her friends were sitting. "Good. I'm hungry!"

"You're always hungry, Grey," the sapphire haired dragon woman hid a smile.

"Not always!" the big man protested. "Sometimes I am just thirsty."

Timeanalia rolled her eyes as the two dragons joined Alana and her companions at the table.

Alana turned back to William to tell him what she meant by a parting of the ways. She was interrupted by the door once more. Eventually, she would get to tell him what she meant. She was starting to think, though, that perhaps she should just wait until the rest of the companions were there.

Bella Starseeker and Cayden Antioch were the next to enter the tap room. Bella went straight over to her brother and gave him a hug from behind.

"You're looking good this morning, brother," she said in a cheerful tone.

That was one thing that Alana liked about Colwyn's sister. It did not matter what was going on, she was always cheerful. While Alana knew that some would find her constant cheerfulness to be quite annoying, Alana herself found it refreshing. There were times when she knew that she would rely on that cheerfulness during the war to come, although she did not know how Bella would be able to stay so cheerful in the midst of the war with the army of undead.

"Thank you, Bella," Colwyn smiled. He stood and gave his sister a proper bear hug. "You are looking quite fetching as always."

"Aw, shucks," Bella blushed.

Colwyn turned to Bella's Protector and clasped forearms with the younger man. "Sword kept sharp, Cayden?"

"Always, Colwyn," the former palace guard nodded.

"Good," Colwyn said. "I have a feeling our blades will be of use to us very soon."

"Excellent," Cayden smiled. "Being cooped up this winter has been hard. It will be good to get out and stretch my legs."

"I think we are all in agreement there," Colwyn chuckled.

Colwyn straddled his chair once more and had just turned back to Alana when the door opened once more. This time, the four halflings entered and made their way over to the table.

Alana looked around at the people around the table and counted to herself. When she was done, she nodded once.

"Looks like we're all here except for Martin and whoever he wanted a fourteenth chair set out for," she said. "I think it's safe for Albert to start bringing out the food now."

"Yes!" Greytonix bellowed. "More food! Less talk!"

"I can't take you anywhere," Timeanalia growled at him.

For the first time, Alana looked at the two dragons in a new light. Could it be that Greytonix and Timeanalia were a dragon couple? It was not something she had thought about at all, but the banter between the two would make so much sense if it were the case. As would the fact that they were the two that came to the Temple of the Blades in the first place. To Alana'a knowledge, for the most part, only good aligned dragons served the Blademasters. She supposed that it wasn't so unusual a concept for a neutral dragon to serve. After all, the Lady Laeyra was a neutral aligned deity. But it was not something she had expected.

She turned to Colwyn to comment on her observation when the door opened one last time. Alana whipped her head around to see who had entered. She saw Martin Faolin, as she had expected to. The High Priest of Taelin had agreed to stay on as one of her companions through the end of the Great War of Souls, which she had appreciated. She would have been just as happy had he sent on a replacement priest for her had he chosen to remain in Ravendale to oversee the Temple of the White's day to day activities. But she got along well with the young priest, so she was fine with his continuing to travel with them.

Martin was leading a young priestess of Taelin that Alana did not know. She suspected that she knew why he had brought her. If she was not mistaken, he had decided to assign a priestess of Taelin to travel with Bella. Alana approved of this. Talby had a priest of Laeyra with her, and Alana had Martin. She was relieved to know that Bella would have a priestess along with her as well.

Alana nodded and wave the priests over. When they settled down at the table, Alana smiled over at Martin.

"Good morning, Martin," Alana said. "I take it this is our mysterious fourteenth person that you asked Colwyn to set a chair for?"

"Indeed," Martin said. "This is Alura Dayne, one of the brightest young priestess at the Temple of the White. She's not very experienced, but I think she would do well as a companion to a Blademaster. Lady Bella, if you are willing, I would like her to travel with you, as I travel with Alana.

Lady Talby, as I recall, your Protector is a priest of Laeyra, so I won't send a priest with you."

"I can handle the priestly needs for Talby," Tovar nodded from the halfling Blademaster's side.

"Well, now that that is all settled," Alana said, standing. "This morning we are gathered together to feast. It is likely the last time we will all be together before the end of the War of Souls should we all make it to the end of the war. Today marks a parting of the ways, as it were."

There were glances amongst the companions. No one had expected that they would be parting from each other so soon.

"We go where we need to," Talby Swiftfoot said. "What do you need from us, Lady Alana?"

"Talby, I have a mission for you and your companions," Alana said. "And I need you to leave right away for it. Grey, are you up for a lengthy flight?"

"So long as I get my fill of this wonderful food," the big man nodded. "Where am I flying them to?"

"They need to go back to Barandale," Alana said. She turned to Talby. "I need you to rally whatever troops you can. Before you leave, I will give you a letter to present to the Council of Elders giving you the authority over the army of Barandale. Get them ready to fight. You've seen what they're going to be fighting. Make sure they're ready."

"I will," Talby nodded. "We will leave as soon as we have provisions, probably later today."

"Good," Alana nodded. She turned to Bella. "Bella, you heard what your father told me about Malachi Dragonsbane. You and I, with our Protectors, dragons and priests, we are going hunting."

"What is this about Malachai Dragonsbane?" Silvestra said, her nostrils flaring.

"Apparently, Dragonsbane is on the hunt," Alana said, turning to her friend. "For you three. I am going on the hunt to make sure he ends his quest to kill you."

"A worthy goal," William said. "But a dangerous one."

"Less dangerous than doing nothing and having him come upon us in the middle of the war," Alana said.

Dragonsbane

"There is some truth to that," William nodded. "What is your plan?"

"I am waiting for word of a sighting. Once he has been sighted, we go on the hunt and stop him," Alana said. "However we have to."

"Very well," William said.

"We will also be leaving soon," the Master Blademaster said. "Possibly as early as today. I will make sure we are well provisioned. I am sure Albert can have our packs filled today."

Chapter XVII
Dragonsbane Sighted

Iana sat on a chair on the porch of her house. She was waiting for Talby and her companions to say goodbye before they headed out to Barandale. They had promised to stop by before Greytonix took them out of the city.

Alana knew that it was going to be weird to travel around without Meryn by her side. And she had been thinking about that ever since she had realized that Meryn would be accompanying her cousin on her travels. Meryn had been one of her companions for so long. She knew that it was better for the halfling to travel with the other halflings, but she was going to miss Meryn.

She knew Colwyn wouldn't, though.

She did not begrudge Colwyn his dislike of Meryn and others of her race. Halflings did have the reputation for being thieves, a reputation that was well earned, and most nobles felt about them the way that Colwyn did.

But Alana had never felt that way about halflings in general or Meryn in specific. She had come to depend on Meryn's childlike innocence to bring a little light to Alana's life. Of course, Meryn caused no end of trouble. The incident in Willowdale where Meryn had betrayed the party's plans came to mind. Even so, Alana would miss Meryn's incessant chatter and cheerfulness.

But was for the best that she go with Talby. The halfling Blademaster would need Meryn. Alana was still not sure why Lord Taelin felt it was necessary to have a halfling Blademaster active during the War of Souls, but she figured there must be a good reason for it. And when that reason was discovered, Alana was determined that the halfling Blademaster still be alive. That meant sending Meryn with Talby as an extra level of protection.

Alana had seen Talby fight, though. She wasn't sure just how much protection the halfling needed. She was fierce for someone so tiny with a completely unorthodox fighting style that worked for her. She was, Alana mused, fun to watch in a fight. It was interesting how Talby moved from weapon to weapon in the course of a battle. Alana had never seen anyone flight like that before. She knew that she wouldn't be able to do that. Alana needed to have weapons that she was comfortable with in her hands whenever possible. If one of her swords were to break during a battle, she would pick up another, but that was the only way she would switch weapons in the midst of a battle.

In a way, Alana mused, Talby was more of a Blademaster than any other with the way she fought. Talby was truly comfortable with any weapon in her hand.

Alana was glad that Talby was on her side!

Alana saw Colwyn leading a small group of people towards the house. She stood and turned to face the group. She saw William, Silvestra, Bella and Nalia following behind Colwyn. Not for the first time, she noticed that Nalia was giving Silvestra a wide birth, and, every now and then, an unkind look. She wondered what that was about.

She hoped there would not be trouble between the two dragons.

Alana needed the dragons to get along. The dragons were supposed to be one of the best defenses for a Blademaster, after all. It was why she was trying to get the situation with Malachai Dragonsbane resolved quickly. She needed the dragons to be able to focus on protecting their Blademasters.

She would have to monitor any situations between Silvestra and Timeanalia to make sure that they did not turn into a problem.

But for now, it was not a problem she would have to worry about. She needed to worry about the dragon hunter now. And then she had to worry about leading the Southern Dales into war. She did not need this to turn into a problem that she actually needed to worry about.

Alana embraced Colwyn when the group got to the porch. She loved feeling his arms around her. His touch had always made her feel safe from the very first. It was part of why their relationship felt so easy. Considering what they had had to go through to end up together, she supposed that she couldn't really call their relationship easy, but it did feel that way.

She supposed that when you were with the right person it always felt easy.

"The halflings are on their way," Colwyn said. "My father asked to see us when we've seen them off."

"You told him we would, of course," Alana said.

"Of course," Colwyn nodded. "But I told him we wanted to see Talby off. It's the first time we've split a Blademaster off from the others, so best to see her off. He understood. Or at least he said he did."

"He's a good man, your father," Alana said. "A bit set in his ways, but a good man."

"I won't tell him you said that," Colwyn laughed. "He might get a swelled head."

She squeezed him in answer. Then she pulled away from him. She stretched and looked around. A ways behind Colwyn and the others, she could see the halflings coming. The big bronze haired man walked behind them, looking even larger than he was walking amongst the halflings.

Alana caught the light flash in Nalia's eyes. She'd been looking for it, as she wanted confirmation of what she suspected. Now she knew. Nalia loved Greytonix. She suspected it was mutual. It did seem an odd pairing, but, the more she thought about it, no odder than Bella and Cayden were. Or even Colwyn and herself.

Love did not matter who you were so long as you loved each other.

When Talby and her companions arrived at Alana's house, the Master Blademaster walked out to meet them.

"Are you ready to go, Talby?" Alana asked.

"I am," the halfling Blademaster nodded. "Don't you worry, Alana. The soldiers of Barandale will be ready to do their part in the war. We will be there when you need us."

"Good," Alana nodded. She pulled a folded and sealed piece of parchment from inside her armor. "Take this and give this to Lady Maren. It is a set of instructions and authorizations for you to do what you need to do in order to ready the soldiers of Barandale for war. Tell her that, on the authority of King Roland Stonehammer, I have assumed overall command of the forces of the Southern Dales. As my representative, you are my general in command of the forces of Barandale."

"It will be as you say," Talby nodded once. She took the parchment and whisked it away into one of her pouches. "I think Grandmother will be proud of me for this."

"I am sure she will," Alana smiled warmly.

She held out her hand to Talby and the halfling Blademaster shook it once. When she'd gotten her hand back, Alana turned to face Meryn.

"Ah, Meryn, my old friend," she smiled. "I'm going to miss you."

"I know, Lady Alana," Meryn squeaked. "But this is really for the best."

"I know," Alana nodded. "I was just thinking about how I am going to miss your unceasing good humor. I don't think I realized just how much I depended upon you always being around to cheer me up just by being you."

"Don't be sad, Alana," Meryn said, coming forward to give Alana a hug. "You'll see me again."

Alana gave her friend a hug. When she stood up, she smiled.

"My coin purse, please, Meryn," Alana smiled. "You know better."

"Just keeping in practice!" Meryn laughed, tossing Alana back her pouch of coins.

Finally, Alana turned to Greytonix. She strode over to stand before the large bronze haired man. Greytonix bowed his head in respect towards her.

"Keep them safe, Grey," Alana said in a soft voice. "I don't know why, but I believe that Talby has a very special part to play in this war. I need her to be alive to play that part. I need you to stay vigilant and keep her safe."

"You have my word, Lady Alana," Gretonix nodded once. "No harm will come to Talby Swiftfoot or any of her companions so long as I am able to prevent it."

"Thank you for that," Alana smiled. She lowered her voice so, she hoped, only Greytonix would hear her. "I think there's someone else you need to say goodbye to. Better not keep her waiting."

The look on Grey's face was worth it. Clearly, the dragon thought that they had kept their relationship low key enough that no one had known. He hadn't counted on Alana being as observant as she was.

He walked over to where Nalia was standing, waiting for him.

"They know," he said to her softly. "Or at least Alana does."

"I thought as much," the sapphire haired woman said. "Alana is a very good study of character. I did not think we'd been able to keep it from them."

"You'll be safe?" he asked.

"I'll probably be in more trouble than you will," she said. "You're just going to be surrounded by halflings. I'm going to be helping the Blademaster deal with Dragonsbane." She stopped and smiled. "On second thought, I think I have the easier task ahead of me."

Grey turned to face Silvestra. "I charge you to keep my lady Nalia safe, Silvestra Knightwing. I expect to see her safe and sound when I return."

"You have my word," Silvestra inclined her head in respect. "I will look after her for you."

"Her word means nothing," Nalia hissed. "She has already broken one vow. What is to keep her from breaking this one?"

And just like that, Alana understood why Nalia had been giving Silvestra dirty looks. She understood all too well. And she realized that she should have expected that this would come up.

"I never gave the Council my word that I would not see William again," Silvestra said in a voice almost too soft to hear. There was definite danger in her words. "Eliazar forced their decree on us. I never once agreed to it."

"Be that as it may, you are here now with him when you were told by the Council to never see him again," Nalia said. "How can I trust you when you go against the Council?"

"Let me ask you this, Timeanalia," Silvestra said. "Who should the dragons honor more? The Council or Lord Taelin?"

"Lord Taelin of course," Nalia said without hesitation.

"Then I have done no wrong," Silvestra shrugged. "The Lightbringer himself put William and I together. Alana and Colwyn bore witness if you do not believe me."

"Bah," Nalia said. "I still do not trust you."

"But I do, Grey said. "And I trust that you will keep Nalia safe."

"I will," Silvestra nodded.

Grey turned back to Timeanalia. There was little else to be said, so he gathered her up in a giant hug and kissed her. It was a tender kiss for someone so large to give someone.

Colwyn choked when he saw the two dragons kissing.

"You mean, him... and her... are... Really?" he stammered.

"You didn't know?" Alana looked over at him with an amused look on her face.

"You did?"

"I suspected," she nodded.

"And you didn't tell me?"

Alana laughed as he watched the tender moment between the two dragons. She hoped that they could keep Nalia safe for Grey. But it was dangerous where they were going. There were no guarantees that they would be able to keep either dragon from dying during the encounter with Dragonsbane. True, the odds were better with their making the encounter at a time and place of their own choosing. But it was still going to be a dangerous encounter for the two dragons.

"You better go, Grey," Nalia said tenderly. It was the first time that Alana had truly seen a tender side to the sapphire dragon. It was a nice change.

"Yes, I know," Grey said. He finally pulled away from Nalia and turned to the halflings. "Are you all ready to go?"

"We are, noble dragon," Talby answered for the group.

"Then let us be off!"

Grey roared as he began the transformation to his dragon form. In minutes, where the big man had been standing was one of the largest dragons Alana had ever seen. The dragons scales were the same bronze color that Grey's hair had been as a human.

When the transformation was finished, Grey lowered himself to the ground. The halflings settled on the great wyrm's back. When he was sure they were secure on his back, Greytonix launched himself into the sky.

Alana and the rest of the remaining companions watched him go, getting smaller and smaller in the sky with every beat of his great wings. After what seemed like only a few minutes, they could no longer see the great dragon in the distance.

"Let's go, then," Colwyn said to Alana. "Lord Dargan awaits."

Dargan was waiting for them in a smaller room in the manor that had been converted to his war room. It was certainly that. The long table running down the center of the room was covered in maps. The maps showed the region of the Southern Dales governed by Arvendale.

Dargan was hard at work with his generals planning the best defense for the territory.

Alana was glad to see that the First Lord of Arvendale was taking the defense of his territory seriously. She knew that other members of the Council of War were not taking the threat as a serious one. There was little more that she could do about that. She had tried her best to make sure that they knew exactly what it was that they would be facing. The fact that they were not listening to her was not on her. She could only hope that they would make plans before it was too late.

This war was going to start soon, Alana knew. Whether the Southern Dales was ready for it or not, it was coming.

Alana truly appreciated the faith that Lord Dargan was showing in her words by his in depth preparations for the defense of Arvendale. She knew that she would never be able to fully express her gratitude to her father in law for believing in her. Nor would she ever be able to tell him how much it helped her self-confidence for him to act on her words without hesitation like he had.

"No, this squad needs to be here, otherwise Bellfrost will be lost," Dargan was saying. He moved the token for the squadron he was talking about to the place he wanted them.

"Yes," one of the general said. "Yes, that would be better. You are right, Lord Dargan. From there they can protect both Bellfrost and Misthaven."

"Exactly our point," Dargan nodded. He looked up and noticed Alana and Colwyn standing there. "Ah, good. You're here."

"Colwyn said you wanted to speak with us," Alana said.

"We did, yes," Dargan nodded. He turned back to the general. "Go get the scout that had information about Dragonsbane, please."

"Right away, Lord Dargan," the general nodded and bowed.

"Looks like you've got the defense of Arvendale pretty well planned, Father," Colwyn said as he looked over the maps. "If I may make one small suggestion?"

"Of course, Colwyn," Dargan nodded. "If there is something we have missed, we would be glad to hear of it."

"This squadron here," Colwyn pointed to a squadron in the southern part of the territory. He shifted the token slightly to the west. "If you put them here instead, they will completely cut off access to the southern border of the territory. Where they were before, there was a gap that troops could have gotten through without being challenged."

Dargan studied the change that Colwyn had made to the defensive alignment thoroughly, stroking his chin. He frowned as he studied it.

"We have been studying this defense for hours," Dargan said. "We do not understand how we could have missed that."

"You were focusing on the defense of the northern part of the territory," Colwyn said. "And that's important considering the north is where the army is coming from. But it is also important to make sure the southern border is secure too."

"That way if the army skirts around and tries to enter Arvendale's territory from the south, they are equally as stymied, yes," Dargan nodded. "That change will be made. Thank you for seeing that, our son."

"I'm sure you would have seen it soon enough, Father," Colwyn smiled.

Alana loved seeing her husband smile, especially in the presence of his father. She knew that the praise he had just given Colwyn was something that he had needed to hear. And she knew that a compliment from his father about tactics would help Colwyn's confidence as well.

The general returned with a scout in tow. The scout blanched at seeing both the First Lord and his son in the room. Alana was amused. Surely it wasn't the first time the scout had to report to Lord Dargan for something?

"You wanted to see me, Lord Dargan?" the scout managed to get out.

"Yes, we did," Dargan nodded. "I was told you have information on the whereabouts of Malachai Dragonsbane."

"Yes, sir," the scout nodded, more comfortable now that he knew that he was there to provide information. "I passed a large group of riders with a man with an iron helm shaped like a dragon at the head. I can only assume that is Malachai Dragonsbane and his men."

"That would be him," Colwyn nodded. "I remember well that helm from the one hunt I did with Dragonsbane."

"Where is Dragonsbane now?" Alana asked.

"My lady, he is several hours ride to the west of Ravendale," the scout said. "He sent a scout into the city. I'm not sure what the scout is looking for, but I would imagine that Dragonsbane is waiting for that scout's report before entering the city."

"The scout is looking for me," Alana said softly. "Lord Dargan, might I trouble you for a piece of parchment, some ink and a pen, and some sealing wax?"

"Of course," Dargan nodded. "What are you going to do?"

"I am going to issue a challenge," Alana said as she began to scrawl a note on the parchment. She read over what she wrote, nodded in satisfaction and then passed the note to Colwyn to read.

"Well, that will certainly rile Dragonsbane up," Colwyn nodded. "He's sure to accept your challenge. Odds are good he will try to beat us there and set up an ambush."

"Of course," Alana nodded. "But it is what it is."

She handed the letter over to Dargan, who looked it over as well.

"A dangerous game you play, Lady Alana," the First Lord said. "But we do not see you have a better option."

"Less dangerous than waiting for him to come upon us in the middle of a battle," Alana said.

She took the letter back and folded it. She dribbled some wax on it and pressed her seal into it.

"May we see your seal?" Dargan said. "That way we will know for sure a sealed letter is from you if we should see one in the future."

"Of course," Alana nodded. She passed the sealed letter over to Dargan so he could study the seal.

When he handed the letter back to her, she slid it into her armor.

"Lord Dargan, would you be so good as to accompany me to the meeting of the Council of War that is about to begin?" Alana said. "I must inform the Council that I will be leaving Ravendale."

"When do you think you'll be leaving?" Dargan said.

"Within an hour of running into the scout, which I am sure will be soon," Alana said.

"Best get on with telling the Council, then," Dargan nodded.

The Council of War was seated at the table when Dargan and Alana arrived. Colwyn had accompanied them but was waiting outside. Alana had sent Bella to round up the companions so that they could be ready to go within a moment's notice.

The Council, as usual, made no notice of Alana's arrival. They were arguing loudly with each other. Only King Roland noticed that she had entered.

The King looked at her with sad eyes. He knew that most of the Council was a lost cause at that point. While they seemed to understand that a war was coming and, to a degree, what that might entail for the Southern Dales, very few of them seemed to be at all interested in preparing for that war. The delegates of the Council were too interested in their petty squabbles between the Dales to worry about the defense of the entire kingdom. Ravendale, Barandale, Arvendale, and Valendale were the only territories that were taking the threat of the war seriously. That meant that less than half of the Dales were actually making preparations for war.

If the rest did not start preparations, the war would go badly.

There was little more that Alana could do to convince them of the seriousness of the situation. And it was getting to the point where she was no longer going to try. She could only work with what she was given. If she was only going to get support from the four Dales, then that would be what she would use to defend the Southern Dales.

She cleared her throat, but none of the Council looked her way. Fine. They could have it that way. She would make sure they listened to her.

Alana pulled one of the knives from her belt. Flipping it in the air so that she caught it point first, she whipped it towards the center of the table. It dug into the exact center of the table, the hilt quivering in the air. The display had the desired effect. Conversation trailed off and everyone in the room turned to look at her.

"Have I got your attention now, gentlemen?" she asked.in a soft voice.

"That was hardly necessary, Blademaster!" the councilor from Parciandale bellowed. "You have damaged an ancient table!"

"I'll have my mage fix it," Alana shrugged. She hopped on the table and walked over to her knife. Pulling it free, she inspected the point. When she was satisfied, she slid the knife back in its sheath. "And if I hear one more word from you, Councilor, the next one goes in your right eye. If you doubt I can do that, I would have you consider how exactly in the center of the table I threw that knife."

The Councilor from Parciandale opened his mouth to say something but thought better of it. Instead, he slumped back in his chair and folded his arms across his chest.

"I am leaving Ravendale for a time," Alana said. "I do not know how long I will be gone, but it is a necessary errand I must run before the war begins."

"You're abandoning us?" one of the councilors asked. "Now?"

"I am hardly abandoning you," she said. "The First Lord of Arvendale has brought to my attention a situation that is critical to my Blademasters. It is a situation that I must attend to in my own way rather than letting it develop into a problem later on."

"And what is this situation?" King Roland asked.

"Malachai Dragonsbane is on the hunt," Alana said. "His prey are the dragons that accompany the Blademasters. Those dragons are a part of our protection. I will not have them killed. And if I do not attend to this, he will come upon us in the middle of a battle when we cannot do anything to prevent it. So I go now. I am hoping that I can turn Dragonsbane away from his quest to kill our dragons. There is a chance that a dragon hunter of his caliber might be needed in defense of the War of Souls."

"Do you think you can convince him?" King Roland asked.

"I do not know," Alana shrugged. "I hope I can. If not, I will have to kill him. I do not want to do that."

"I'd generally prefer if you didn't kill any of my subjects unless you have no other choice, Lady Alana," the king said. "But I will understand if that ends up being the case."

"Thank you, King Roland," Alana sighed. "I take no joy in the choices I must make."

"A sign of a good leader," the king smiled. "When do you and your companions leave?"

"Dragonsbane has a scout in the city. As soon as I make contact with that scout and give him a message to pass on to Dragonsbane, we will head out towards the Wilds. I expect that will be within the hour."

"Good journey to you, Blademaster," the king nodded. "Report to the Council when you return as to what happened."

"Of course, Your Highness," Alana said. She hopped off the table. "But for now, I take my leave. Please keep working on planning the defense of the Southern Dales while I'm gone. If you can get the councilors to actually work on it, that is."

She did not wait to see what the councilors reactions were to that last jab. She turned on her heel and walked out of the council chambers.

She had a scout to find.

Dragonsbane

Chapter XVIII
hunter, prey

addles creaked in the early afternoon air as the riders sat waiting for orders. They had ridden a long way from Darcandale. Now, they were just a few hours ride from Ravendale, but their leader had stopped them.

Malachai Dragonsbane sat on a large black stallion at the head of the group of riders. He leaned against the saddle horn, waiting for the scout that he had sent into the city to return with news of the Blademasters and their dragons.

Not long after the scout had ridden off towards the city, a large bronze dragon had lifted off from the city and soared away. Dragonsbane had watched it go until it was no longer visible. He knew that one of his preys had gotten away. At least for the moment. He hoped that the scout would be able to tell him where the dragon had gone. They would go after that one when they finished with the two in Ravendale.

Dragonsbane settled in to wait for the news that the scout would bring him about the Blademasters and their dragons. He had time.

This hunt had only just begun.

The streets of Ravendale were usually safe for Alana to walk around in. And while she felt safe on that day, there was still something in the air that made her feel like trouble was about. She had woken that morning feeling like there was trouble in the air.

The feeling of trouble had not left her the entire day.

She and Colwyn were headed back to their house from the Council meeting. It was a walk that they knew well, having walked home from a number of Council meetings in the previous few months.

As they walked, Alana could feel someone watching them. She looked around as they walked, hoping to find out who was watching them.

As it turned out, it was very easy to figure out.

There was a man following them at some distance. He made no effort to hide himself when she saw him.

"Colwyn," she said.

"I see him."

"Think he's part of Dragonsbane's party?" she asked.

"Don't know for sure," he shrugged. "But probably."

"Good," she nodded. "Let's give him a surprise."

They kept an eye out for a turning that would work for what they wanted. When they saw one, they took it and slipped between two buildings right after making the turning so they would be out of view.

The man that was following them made the turning and shuffled past where they were hiding. When he stopped and looked around, Colwyn slipped out from his hiding place and grabbed him from behind. Colwyn pinned the man's arms to his side and placed his forearm across the man's throat so he couldn't get away and he couldn't scream.

When he was secured, Alana slipped out from the hiding space as well and came up to stand in front of the man.

"Nod your head for yes. Shake your head for no, but say not a word or I will let Colwyn crush your windpipe," she snarled. "Do you understand me?"

The man nodded once, his eyes wide.

"Good," she said. "Do you know Malachai Dragonsbane?"

A nod.

"Did you travel to Ravendale with him?"

Another nod.

"Do you know where he is right now?"

A third nod.

"Good," she nodded. She pulled a folded parchment from inside her armor. The parchment was sealed with her symbol, a dragon clutching a sword in each of his front paws. "This is a message for Malachai Dragonsbane. You are to deliver it to him. You are to ride out of Ravendale right now and deliver it. If I find that you did not deliver the message, I will kill you. If I find out that you read the message before delivery, I will kill you. If you delay leaving Ravendale for any reason other than getting to your horse, I will kill you. Are we crystal clear?"

The man nodded once more.

"Good," she said. She looked at Colwyn. "Let him go, Col."

Colwyn dropped the man who fell to the ground like a sack of potatoes. He slowly stood up to face Alana. She handed him the parchment.

The man did not wait for her to say anything more. He took off in the direction of his horse. Alana knew that the man would head right to Dragonsbane.

"That was a little harsh, Alana," Colwyn said. "Not your usual style."

"I don't have time to deal with Dragonsbame trying to kill the dragons, Col," she said. "This needs to be dealt with soon. This is the way to do that."

"I guess," he said.

"Come," she smiled at him. "We need to get the others and get ready to set out ourselves. We need to get to the Wilds before Dragonsbane does."

Colwyn nodded and followed her back to their house where the others were waiting.

The riders were fidgeting with impatience, but Dragonsbane sat still, waiting for the scout to return. He knew that it could take time for the scout to find the information he sought. There would be time for action later. Dragonsbane was cautious. He would not act until he had all the information he needed to act properly.

He knew, though, that his companions did not like sitting and waiting. It was fine. They would have plenty of action soon. All they needed was to know where their targets were. And then they would act.

Dragonsbane was intently looking upon the western edge of Ravendale, knowing that would be where the scout would return from. He was rewarded for his patiently watching the city by seeing the rider immediately as he left the city.

The rider was riding hard, Dragonsbane noticed, frowning. He had not wanted the scout to tire his horse, but something was up, apparently. This was interesting. He loved when prey did something unexpected. He felt like his pray was about to do something completely unexpected, and he was looking forward to seeing what.

The rider took little time in riding from Ravendale to where Dragonsbane was waiting with the other riders. Dragonsbane watched him the entire ride.

As the scout drew closer, Dragonsbane could see that his face was white as a sheet. Something had happened in Ravendale that had scared his scout senseless. What could have possibly scared his scout, he wondered.

The scout stopped in front of him, breathing hard. Dragonsbane gave him a minute to catch his breath, knowing that it would be easier to get a report if the man could breathe to give it.

"Speak," Dragonsbane said, finally.

"One of the Blademasters flew out this morning," the scout said. "I was able to find out that they went to Barandale."

"Barandale," Dragonsbane spat. "Halflings. They'll give us no trouble. We'll go there after taking care of the other two. What of them?"

"I... ran into one of the Blademasters," the scout grew even paler. Dragonsbane hadn't thought that would be possible.

But now he knew what had scared his scout. Clearly the Blademaster knew that he was after her dragon. Good. As far as Dragonsbane was concerned, that would make the hunt that much more interesting. He enjoyed a challenging hunt, and this was certainly turning into an interesting one.

"And what did this Blademaster have to say?" Dragonsbane asked.

"She bade me bring you a message," the scout gulped. "She was rather... insistent. I have it here for you, still sealed. I have no idea what it says."

The scout pulled the parchment Alana had given him out of his saddlebag. The wax seal was unbroken.

Dragonsbane studied the seal with distaste. The woman used a dragon for her sigil. Maybe he should rid the world of her too. It might make the world a safer place.

He slid his finger through the wax seal breaking it open. Dragonsbane carefully unfolded the letter and began to read it.

"Malachai Dragonsbane,

I know that you have come to hunt the dragons who travel with my fellow Blademasters and I. My husband, Colwyn Starseeker, tells me you are a relentless hunter who will not stop until you have killed your prey.

The Southern Dales is about to be embroiled in a war that, if we have any hope to survive, I must lead. I cannot lead the war if I am worrying about you coming at any time to kill our dragons.

Therefore, I am telling you where we are going now so that you can come to me. I hope that there is a way we can work out a compromise that will allow us to work together to keep the Southern Dales safe. But do not think I will just let you kill our dragons. You will have to go through my sisters of the blade and I if you want to kill them.

I assure you. That will not be easy. We are called Blademasters for a very good reason.

We ride to the Wilds within the hour to investigate the news of a necromancer in the Wilds adding to the army of darkness that is soon to be unleashed on the Southern Dales. Come to the ruins of El Coran if you wish to find us. We will be there.

No tricks. We will not run. But we will not let you kill the dragons.

This is your only chance to end this peacefully without facing our wrath.

If you do not come, may Taelin have mercy on you. For I will not.

Signed by my hand,
Alana Steeldrake
Master Blademaster"

Dragonsbane blinked as he read the words a second time. The Blademaster certainly had a great deal of nerve to dictate terms to him. But he had always liked a challenge. And this would certainly add to the thrill of the hunt.

He was surprised to see that this Blademaster had married Colwyn Starseeker. He knew the young Starseeker heir. They had hunted a dragon together once. Colwyn was good with a blade and had a good amount of mettle.

Dragonsbane had no quarrel with him.

For that matter, he had no quarry with the Blademasters either. He did not want to fight them. He had heard of their prowess with the blade which lent credence to their name. Alana was right about that in her letter. They were called Blademasters for a very good reason. While he had not actually seen a Blademaster fight, he had heard the stories. The Blademasters were fighters without peer. And there would be more than one Blademaster there. He did not fancy that he had much of a chance against one Blademaster let alone multiple.

So he would go to the ruins of El Coran. But he would not be dissuaded from his mission of killing the dragons. The Southern Dales would be better off without them.

"Dragonsbane, look," one of the riders said.

Dragonsbane looked where the rider was pointing. Riding out from the northern end of the city was a column of riders. While he could not make out who was on the horses, he knew that it would be the Blademasters and their companions. It was interesting that they were riding out on horses. Surely they could have flown on the backs of their dragons!

"That is our quarry," Dragonsbane spoke. "They are headed to the ruins of El Coran. If we ride hard, we can beat them there."

"And what then, Dragonsbane?" the rider who had pointed out the column of riders asked.

"And then we kill the dragons."

Dragonsbane

Part IV
Showdown

Chapter XIX
Into the Wilds

vast expanse of land between the kingdoms of the Southern Dales and Dracomyr, the Wilds stretched from the eastern coast of the continent to the western. The expanse of land varied in distance between the two sides depending on where in the Wilds you were. At its thinnest, the Wilds stretched only twenty or so miles, while at its thickest, a good two to three hundred miles of vast emptiness.

There were many towns in the Wilds. The people who lived in these towns claimed fealty to neither of the bordering regions, making the Wilds the third region of Calthea. Each of the towns in the Wilds was, in essence, its own little kingdom, for each town in the Wilds was self-governing. Unlike the Southern Dales and Dracomyr, there was no central council or government for the region and, for the most part, the region was the better for it. That was not to say that there were no squabbles between the towns. But, for the most part, the setup of the Wilds worked for everyone that lived there. The only times that the Wilds were not an ideal place for the people who lived there was during the times of active war between the Southern Dales and Dracomyr. Many of the battles in those wars were fought in the Wilds. But such periods of war were exceedingly rare. It had been several centuries since the last war between the Southern Dales and Dracomyr, and the Wilds had been a good and peaceful place to live that entire time.

But now, war was coming once more. The people of the Wilds could feel it coming. They knew that when the Southern Dales and Dracomyr went off to war once more, it would come right through their lands. Many of their people would, inadvertently, be killed in the conflict, even though neither side particularly wanted to kill anyone in the Wilds.

It was the way of things.

There were small towns scattered throughout the Wilds. Some of those towns had been abandoned and left to ruin for whatever reason. There were few in the Southern Dales or Dracomyr who knew or cared why towns in the Wilds had been abandoned. The information on the how and the why was lost in time, although Ana, the Goddess of History, was like to have written down in her collected journals of Calthea the details of such lost towns. But one would first need to learn where the goddess kept her journals and then have the patience to flip through all of them in order to find the details. Such a task would take several hundred lifetimes, however, as Ana recorded several tomes for each year that Calthea existed. Only the goddess herself could know where any given event was located amongst her journals.

And she was not inclined to help mortals find what they wanted in her books.

Near the center of the Wilds was the largest of the ruined cities in the Wilds, a place called El Coran. Much like the other ruined cities in the Wilds, no one alive knew what had happened in El Coran, but it was clear that something terrible had happened in that once proud city. Even so, the ruined city was easy for most everyone to find in the Wilds, and it was often used to give directions in the Wilds.

It made sense for Alana to set El Coran as the location for the confrontation with Malachai Dragonsbane.

Alana had been in the Wilds before. She did not like going into that part of Calthea, but she did when she was required to. She was far more comfortable staying in the Southern Dales. Sometimes, though, her duties took her into the Wilds or even into Dracomyr. She had not been back into the Wilds, though, since returning from Dracomyr when she had destroyed the lich, Drakkhous.

She tried hard not to think about the lich, but she still had nightmares about her captivity, brief as it had been. The lich had been terrifying. And had it not been for her friends, she may well have been sacrificed to the Dark God.

It was part of the reason she was so sad to see the halfling go off with her cousin. Meryn, more than any of the others, had saved her on the roof of the ziggurat of Thraal. She owed Meryn a debt that she might never be able to repay.

But now Meryn was with Talby on their way to Barandale, far away from Alana and her companions. Alana could only hope that Meryn would keep Talby safe the same as she had helped to keep Alana safe.

But now, Alana needed to focus her thoughts not on the little sneak thief but on the task at hand. She was leading her companions into the Wilds to have a final confrontation with Malachai Dragonsbane so that she did not have to deal with him in the middle of the War of Souls. It would be hard enough leading the forces of the Southern Dales into war as it was. It would be harder still if she had to keep looking over her shoulder to make sure that her dragons were not about to get killed.

She knew that the scout had left Ravendale with her message. And she was sure that she had put enough fear of her in the scout to ensure that he road straight to Dragonsbane to deliver her message. Not for the first time, she wondered how the dragon hunter would react to her challenge. Colwyn had told her he would accept the challenge and then go about attempting to set an ambush in El Coran before they got there.

Dragonsbane would have ample time to do so.

Alana knew that she needed to take the opportunity while in the Wilds to scout the enemy forces. She intended to take that opportunity to start tracking the movements of the army as well as starting to find out where the necromancers were working. It was her hope that she could gather some information about the necromancers' whereabouts while dealing with Dragonsbane. She also hoped that she might be able to determine how far along they were on creating the magic to instantly raise her fallen soldiers in the midst of battles.

That magic needed to be stopped before it could begin to cause trouble for the Southern Dales.

The night before they entered the Wilds, Alana decided to tell the rest of the companions her plans.

As Colwyn prepared the fire to make dinner, she worked on preparing the ingredients for a stew. They had a fair amount of dried meat left for the stew, but they'd likely have to resort to hunting soon to make sure they could stretch what they had. It was fine. Colwyn and Cayden were both accomplished hunters. Alana had no doubt that they would be able to find sufficient meat to keep their supplies full.

Alana worked quickly, and by the time that Colwyn had the fire crackling, she'd filled a pot full of meat, vegetables, potatoes, herbs and water. It would be a delicious stew when it was done. When she put the pot on the fire, the smell of cooking stew almost immediately wafted through the clearing. The rest of the companions, upon smelling the cooking stew, started to gather about the fire.

"Stew will be ready in about an hour," Alana grunted as she sat back from the fire.

"It smells good," William said.

Alana pulled out her knives and started to work on them, making sure each of them was as sharp as possible. She checked for nicks in the edges that could cause the blade to break if it struck something the wrong way. She was careful to maintain her blades. The last thing she needed was to have one of her blades break in the middle of a fight.

"So I thought I should tell you why I am having Dragonsbane confront us in the Wilds," Alana said.

"I was wondering when you'd tell us that," William smiled. "There's more to it than just Dragonsbane, isn't there?"

"Yes, William," Alana nodded. "Dealing with Dragonsbane is important, but we need information. As you know, the War of Souls is coming fast. While we have had some trouble convincing the Council of War about the fact that the war is coming, there are those who are making preparations."

"I love how you say that we've had some trouble with that," Colwyn roared with laughter. "You've all but torn their heads off trying to get them to see the truth of it."

"They just don't want to believe that the Southern Dales is in danger," Alana sighed. She'd finished checking over her knives and had moved to her swords. "They would rather be content in their palaces and pretend nothing is wrong."

"Except for my father," Colwyn said. "And Marcus Whelan."

"And the King," Alana added. "But those are the only three who are actively working on preparing their armies for battle. I'm hopeful that when Talby and Meryn get back to Barandale, they will be able to get the halflings to rally to the cause."

"So what are we doing in the Wilds?" William asked. "What are we doing here besides confronting the man who wants to kill my wife, that is?"

"We need information, William," Alana said. She was satisfied with how her swords looked, so she set them aside. "We need to know how the army is coming along, and we need to know how the necromancers are coming along with that magic you told me about. We need to know what they're planning. We can't find that out sitting in Ravendale."

"Of course not," William nodded. He looked over at the stew and sniffed at it. "I've been waiting to see when you would decide to go on the offensive like this."

"I had to wait until we could get into the Wilds," Alana shrugged. "It's still cold, but at least it's not snowing."

"So what is the plan, Alana?" Colwyn asked. He stirred the pot of stew. "Obviously you have a plan in mind."

"I picked El Coran to have the confrontation with Dragonsbane for a reason," Alana smiled. "It's in almost the exact center of the Wilds. While we're travelling to the ruins, we can scour the Wilds for signs of necromancers and undead."

"That will undoubtedly allow Dragonsbane and his hunting party to arrive in El Coran before we do," William pointed out.

"Unfortunately," Alana nodded. "There is little to be done about that, though. We need to gather this information."

"It is a dangerous game you play, Blademaster," Nalia said from her spot near the fire. "The dragon hunter needs to be stopped before he kills us."

"He will be stopped," Alana turned to face the sapphire haired woman. "Would you counsel me to pass up an opportunity to gather information about the foe we will be fighting in this war, Nalia?"

"No, you are right that we must do this," Nalia said. "I just do not like the idea of the dragon hunter having an opportunity to prepare an ambush for us before we can get to El Coran."

"Dragonsbane and his companions would have arrived at El Coran before us anyway, Nalia," William said. He looked into the fire. "Of all the non-dragons in the party, I have the most to lose if Dragonsbane is not stopped. I do not like the idea of Dragonsbane's having time to set up an ambush, either, but he would have had that time regardless. I trust Alana to lead us through to the other side of the ambush."

Alana looked over at William with gratitude. She knew how much the young man worried about Silvestra being hurt or killed by the dragon hunter. The fact that he was still expressing his complete trust in her even though she was delaying their confrontation with Dragonsbane meant the world to her.

She turned her attention back to the stew and gave it a stir. It was still a ways away from being ready but it was getting closer. But tending the stew gave her something to focus on other than Nalia's accusing gaze.

"We're going to do this whether everyone in the party agrees with it or not," Colwyn said in a soft voice. "We are desperately in need of any information we can find about the enemy and soon."

"Of course we need information," Nalia grunted. "But it is just as important to make sure your dragons are safe too, Blademaster."

"And we will do so," Alana nodded. "I do not doubt that you will be needed before the end of the war if we are to succeed in protecting the Southern Dales. Do not ever think I am discounting the importance of you and Silvestra, Nalia. You weren't in Willowdale. Silvestra was and she knows what she had to face there. I am sure she still has occasional nightmares about that fight. I would not be surprised if the necromancers did not try to create such a monstrosity again. Or worse."

"I do, indeed, still have nightmares about the fight in Willowdale," Silvestra nodded. "I will probably never forget fighting that skeletal dragon for as long as I live."

"And you're probably right that they will try to recreate it," William said. "The Nightstalker will remember how effective that dragon was and will ensure there is at least one such beast to take the field of battle for their side. Unless they come up with something worse."

"Unless they come up with something worse?" Colwyn stared at the mage. "What could be worse?"

"I do not know," William shrugged. "But there is no end to the lengths that the Dark God will go to conquer the Southern Dales."

"Then we must be equally as diligent in our protection of the Southern Dales," Alana nodded. "Eat up and get to bed early. I want to get an early start in the morning."

Alana lay in her bedroll nestled up against Colwyn. She was staring up at the stars unable to sleep. She had been having a lot of trouble sleeping for the past few weeks as the War of Souls neared. There was so much to do and so much to worry about. It did not help knowing that the defense of the Southern Dales rested solely on her shoulders. She felt the weight of that responsibility all the time.

It helped to have Colwyn to lean on, but the burden was hers to bear. Alana knew that Colwyn wished he could take the burden from her, but he could not.

Colwyn had been kind enough to not comment on her lack of sleep, but Alana knew that he'd noticed the nights she'd left their bed to pace while she thought about things.

It was why she was so determined to seek out any information she could while they were in the Wilds. While she did not think it would help her sleep any, it would at least help her form a plan of defense for the Southern Dales. Dargan, Marcus and the King were dedicated to helping her, but there was only so much those three could do. It was up to her to really lead the defense. And so it fell on her to make the majority of the defense plans.

"Colwyn, are you still awake?" she whispered.

"Yes," he grunted. "I can't sleep either."

"Do you think William is right that they'll come up with something worse than the skeletal dragon?" she asked.

"I don't want him to be, but we should be ready for it if he is," Colwyn said after a few moments' thought.

"Just one more thing to worry about," Alana sighed.

"Just one more reason to make sure the dragons are safe," Colwyn agreed.

"What do you think we'll find in the Wilds?"

"Trouble," Colwyn said. "With you, we always find trouble."

Alana smiled and snuggled closer to him. After a few minutes, she fell into a fitful and restless sleep.

Chapter XX
Gathering Information

The path that the companions followed deeper into the Wilds appeared to be well worn. Hundreds of thousands of pairs of feet had kept the path cleared over the centuries. And, while Alana could not be perfectly sure, the path appeared to have been very recently used.

Although the path would, she thought, eventually lead to El Coran, it was not the most direct route to the ruined city, and she doubted that Dragonsbane and his companions would have taken this path to get to the city. Which begged the question. Who was using this path? And why?

Her instincts told her that the path needed to be investigated. While it could have just been inhabitants of the Wilds going from one place to another, the way that the path led straight out to the Southern Dales made her think that was not the case.

So she pressed the companions forward to investigate.

They had been riding for several hours when William stopped. Alana called a halt to the rest of the companions and turned to face the wizard.

"Find something, William?" she asked.

"Maybe," he said.

The wizard dropped from his horse and went over to something that he'd seen on the side of the road. He knelt down next to a bush with wilting leaves.

"Vakaris dolamadin," he whispered as he held his hands over the bush. When they glowed a sickly yellow color, his frown deepened.

"What is it?" Alana asked.

"Come and look at this, Alana," the wizard said without turning towards her. "If I am not mistaken, this is evidence of necromantic activity in the area."

"How can you be sure it's not just a dying bush?" Alana asked as she knelt beside him.

"When we study at the Tower of the White, mages focus in one school of magic, but we are taught how to recognize magic from other schools," he explained in a soft voice. "The spell I just cast over this plant was designed to detect the touch of necromancy. It's not necessarily close by, but this plant has been touched by necromancy."

Alana reached towards the bush but stopped when she felt a dreaded chill run up her arms as she got close to the bush.

"Do you feel that?" she asked the wizard.

"Yes," William nodded. "That is the touch of death. This bush will likely be completely dead within just a few more hours. This is very recent activity."

"So there is a necromancer somewhere nearby actively working?" Alana asked.

"Could be around the corner or he could be a hundred miles away," William shrugged. "There's no way to know how close he is, to be honest. Magic is funny like that."

Alana nodded and turned to get back onto her horse. But she stopped and turned back to the wizard.

"It's still the first clue we've seen that necromancers are actively working, though," she said to him. "It's more than we had, and it is important information."

"Of course it is," William nodded. "But there's little to be learned from this one bush. We will have to do more searching to figure out where the necromancer or necromancers might be."

"Well, let's see if we can't find some more hints about the necromancers in the Wilds while we're riding to El Coran," Alana nodded.

Later that evening when they camped for the night, the companions talked about all they had seen during their journey through the Wilds. They had not learned as much as Alana might have liked, but every bit of knowledge was helpful.

They had found more evidence of the necromancers working in the Wilds, but nothing that they found led them in any specific direction. It was frustrating for Alana, because she needed more information about what the necromancers were doing in order to form a plan for dealing with them.

At one point, they had come across boot and horse tracks. It was an odd thing to come across in the middle of the Wilds, especially considering how many tracks there were. Alana had wanted to investigate, but Colwyn had, wisely, suggested that it was something they could investigate after dealing with the dragon hunter.

Alana did not think the prints were related to the coming war. They were too precise and deep to have been made by undead troops. Colwyn was right, though. The tracks would keep until after they dealt with Dragonsbane. It was far more important to make sure their dragon companions would be safe than it was to chase after tracks that might or might not be related to the coming war.

Still, the tracks nagged at Alana. There was something about them that made her think they were important. Her instincts had never let her down before, so she knew that it was something they would eventually have to look into. Whether it was something to deal with before or after the War of Souls, she did not know. Her instincts said before, though.

Dinner was subdued that evening. All of the companions had a great deal on their minds. It made for a quiet evening.

After dinner, they all turned in, save for Colwyn who took the first watch.

Colwyn stood where he could watch both the camp and all of the approaches to the camp. He was taking no chances that the hunters could sneak up on them in the middle of the night and kill the dragons.

He was on the lookout for things that might be even worse than that, as well. He feared that with the army of undead somewhere in the Wilds, some of those undead would attack the party. He wanted to make sure that the party was safe from the undead on his watch.

He was not surprised when someone came to talk to him during his watch. There were few watches that he took that he spent completely by himself. What did surprise him was who came to talk to him.

The sapphire dragon was the last person that he expected to come talk to him.

And yet, near the end of his watch, the sapphire haired woman came stealing up to where he was keeping watch over the camp.

It was surprising to Colwyn that Nalia sought him out. They had talked very little since the sapphire dragon had joined the party, even though she was the nathair an aeir a chosnaíonn for his sister, Bella. But despite that, he did not think the sapphire dragon much cared for him. Or for his Blademaster, Alana.

He watched the sapphire haired woman make her way over to where he was standing, frowning slightly at her. He did not know what she wanted, but he knew that he likely was not going to like whatever it was that she was about to say to him.

"Nalia," he nodded once when she stopped beside him.

"Protector," she nodded back.

They stood in silence for several long minutes, neither looking at each other. Finally, Colwyn broke the silence.

"What is bothering you?" he asked.

"I am concerned," the sapphire dragon said. "I know that the Blademaster is doing what she needs to in order to be able to lead the forces of the Southern Dales in the War of Souls, but I fear that she has forgotten that Silvestra and I are in danger. Worse, I fear that her plan for dealing with Dragonsbane will lead to either Silvestra or I being killed."

"I understand your concerns," Colwyn said after a few moments. "I have not known Alana to do anything without thinking it through. I do not know what is going to happen when we get to El Coran, but I know that she and I will do all that we can to make sure you and Silvestra make it through. We both realize the importance of the dragons to the Blademasters."

"Do you?" she challenged him.

"You weren't there in Willowdale, Nalia," Colwyn turned ot her. "You didn't see the abomination that Kera Rayden put into play. It killed one nathair an aeir a chosnaíonn. If Silvestra had not been there, I do not think any of us would have survived Willowdale. So yes, I do know how important the nathair an aeir a chosnaíonn is for a Blademaster."

"I am sorry, Protector," she turned away. "I did not realize just how much your Blademaster has been through."

"It's all right, Nalia," he smiled sadly. He reached over and put his hand on her shoulder. "We're all still learning. I dare say we will all still be learning our duties until the day we die."

"You are wise, Protector," Nalia said. The trace of a smile crossed her lips. "For a human."

"Well, thank you," Colwyn smirked. "Look, I can't guarantee your safety. But you knew that this would not be a safe duty when you chose to be the nathair an aeir a chosnaíonn to a Blademaster."

"True," Nalia nodded.

"We must be able to trust each other," Colwyn reasoned. "You must be able to trust Alana and I. And we need to be able to trust you."

"I understand, Protector," Nalia nodded. "You have given me a great deal to think about."

"I am in no way dismissing your concerns, Nalia," he smiled gently at her. "I understand your concerns, in fact. But we can only do what we can do. We will do our best to keep you and Silvestra safe."

"Thank you for that," the sapphire dragon smiled weakly. "I'll go back to bed now."

Colwyn watched Nalia go, sighing softly. He did understand her concerns, but he hoped that they were nothing to really worry about in the end.

And yet... He began to worry about them anyway.

Chapter XXI
Ambush

lana stopped the companions just outside of the ruins of El Coran. Something had not felt quite right to her. She suspected that there was an ambush waiting for them in El Coran. The Blademaster had no doubt that the dragon hunter was lying in wait for them in an effort to catch them off guard.

Even though she suspected as much, Alana was not sure how she could keep such an ambush from succeeding. Unless they were to actually see the dragon hunter and his hunting party before they actually leapt out upon the companions, there was little they could do but to just be as aware as possible so that they would not be as surprised when the ambush happened.

So she had stopped them far enough away from El Coran that they could look around without having Dragonsbane's ambush happen.

They were on a wooded hill overlooking the ruins of El Coran. Alana and Colwyn had gotten down off their horses and crept forward to stand between two trees. The ruins looked to be empty at first glance, but Alana knew that they were in there somewhere.

"I can't see them," Alana said quietly to Colwyn.

"They're there," Colwyn assured her.

They continued to watch, hoping to catch even the slightest bit of movement.

They had left the horses in the forest back a ways. Alana had thought that going through the ruins of El Coran would be easier without the horses. At the very least, she thought they would have a better chance of being able to slip into the ruins without the hunters seeing them if they were not riding in a column of horses.

"Looks empty," Alana muttered.

"They're there," Colwyn muttered back.

"How do you know?" she turned to him, "I can't see any of them out there."

"They're there," Colwyn repeated. "I can't see them either but I know they're there. Dragonsbane makes sure his hunters are excellent at hiding. They're there somewhere. Waiting for us."

"You're sure?" Alana frowned.

"I'm sure."

Alana studied the ruins some more. She thought she might have caught the faintest sight of movement, but she couldn't be sure. When she pointed it out, the movement, if there had been any, had stopped.

"We have no choice," she said. "We'll have to go in there anyway."

"If we want to end this, yes," Colwyn nodded. "But it's not going to end without a fight."

"Is there anything you can think of about Dragonsbane that might help?" she asked.

"Malachai Dragonsbane follows a strict code of honor, even though it may look nothing like yours or mine," Colwyn said softly. "But he will always do exactly as he says. He believes that he is protecting the Southern Dales. If you can somehow appeal to that protective nature, you might be able to delay his hunt. But I do not think you can stop it."

"I never thought this was going to be easy," Alana sighed. "But you make it sound impossible."

"Getting Malachai Dragonsbane to call off a hunt once he's started it is as close to impossible as it gets," Colwyn shrugged. "Getting him to delay the hunt might be a little less so."

Alana stared off towards the ruins for a while. Finally, she sighed and backed away from the hill they were looking over.

"Guess we can't put this off any more," she said. "Let's go get the others and get in there to end this."

Timeanalia was not happy. While she trusted the Blademasters, she did not feel that the situation with Dragonsbane was being handled in the best way. She would have preferred to just kill the man and be done with it. He was a clear threat to the dragons and, by extension, the Blademasters they were sworn to protect.

And now they were going to go parlay with him.

Nalia knew that this was not going to end well. She just hoped that it would end with two living dragons and one dead dragon hunter. That would be the best way for it to end.

Silvestra had suggested that she and Nalia stay behind while the Blademasters went in to deal with Dragonsbane and his hunters, but Alana had shot that idea down. Alana said that she thought it would be best if everyone stayed together. That way, if something happened, there would be a better chance of getting help to whoever needed it.

Nalia was glad that the Blademaster had the sense to keep the party together. While she could see the wisdom of keeping the dragons out of the ruins where the hunters would definitely be, she knew that the hunters would expect such a strategy and prepare for it. Rovers would be sent for some distance to catch the two dragons if they chose to stay out of the city.

If they weren't with the rest of the party, they could die without anyone knowing until it was far too late.

But this did not make the sapphire dragon any happier about the situation.

It was what it was, though. They needed to deal with Dragonsbane and soon. Alana was right about that. But Nalia could not help but feel like Alana was leading them into a trap. She did not believe the Blademaster was leading them into a trap on purpose, but Nalia felt that they were headed into a trap anyway. She had let her opinion known, but everyone else had just shrugged as if to say "what else can we do?"

So she trudged along with the rest, doing her best to keep her eyes open for any trace of the trap she was expecting.

Even so, though, she did not see the attack coming until it was too late.

They were just entering the ruins of the city of El Coran when the hunters struck from nowhere. It was a terribly effective ambush, Nalia thought to herself as she tried to defend herself from the attack.

The dragon hunters had waited until most of the party had gone past before launching their assault on the party. It had the intended effect of separating the dragons from most of the fighters. It was an effective tactic, especially when the dragons were in their human forms. They were far more vulnerable in that form without their natural defenses or their dragon magic.

Worse, Nalia had no human magic having never felt the need to learn it.

She was, however, decent with a sword, and she pulled the sword she wore at her hip as soon as she saw the attackers coming. The leader of the hunters, Malachai Dragonsbane, had fixed on her sapphire colored hair and was coming straight for her.

The hunter swung his sword at Nalia's head, trying to lop it off. The sapphire haired woman dropped to a knee so that the sword would whistle uselessly over her head. She brought her own sword up and attacked his belly, but the big man just brushed her attack aside, knocking her off balance.

She didn't see the knife in his other hand until he pushed it into her side. The knife burned as it entered her side, and she knew that there was poison on the blade.

Nalia pitched forward towards the ground, screaming as she fell.

Alana turned quickly when she heard the scream. She knew at once that one of the dragons had been hurt. The sapphire haired dragon woman lay on the ground bleeding.

Springing into action, Alana launched herself between the hunter and Nalia, but she knew that she was too late. In the back of her mind, she identified that it was Dragonsbane himself that had attacked Nalia.

"William, a little separation would be nice," Alana called.

William nodded and looked around at where the hunters were in relation to his companions.

"Altasin!'" William shouted.

A wall or air stretched out curving around the companions and separating them from the hunters. The air was thick and impassable, but would not hurt anyone attempting to break through it. Alana gave the wall little thought after it went up other than to approve of William's choice to put up a wall that would not hurt the hunters. The wall of air was sufficient that she felt she did not have to keep an eye on the hunters. She knew that Colwyn would be, though.

Alana's full attention was on Timeanalia.

While Alana had not been able to get close to the sapphire dragon, she nonetheless did not want her to be hurt. The Blademaster moved over to where the dragon woman was lying. A stream of blood was flowing from a deep stab wound on lower right side of the woman's front. It was a deep wound and would need to be treated immediately or the woman would most certainly die.

Alana was not sure how to treat such a wound, though.

"Martin!" she bellowed. "I need you."

The priest made his way over to her and knelt down beside the Blademaster. He looked over the wound with a frown on his face.

"This is beyond my ability to heal, Lady Alana," the priest said softly. "Perhaps the mages can do something for her. Or perhaps there is a dragon magic that can save her. Were I a priest of Terra, I could do more."

"Silvestra?" she looked up at the silver dragon who had just knelt down beside her.

The silver haired dragon woman carefully examined the wound without touching it. She leaned in close and sniffed at the wound, growling at what she smelled.

"I can heal her," Silvestra said quietly. "But it will be difficult. We need to get to her to a sheltered location."

Alana looked around and her gaze settled on a large ruined building a ways away from where they were.

"What about there?" she asked, pointing to the ruins.

Sivlestra nodded when she saw where Alana was pointing.

"That will work," Silvestra said. "William can place wards around that while I work."

"Colwyn and Cayden can carry her," Alana said. "The rest of us will make sure that Dragonsbane and his hunters don't attack until you are safe inside the ruins."

Colwyn and Cayden carefully picked up the sapphire haired dragon woman and started off towards the ruined building Alana had pointed out. The others followed behind them protecting them from the hunters.

Dragonsbane felt the wall of air go up between him and his quarry. He knew that he had hurt one of the dragons. He'd seen her go down with the wound in her side. But he was not able to go in for the kill while the wall of air was up.

Worse, from the way his quarry was talking, they might be able to heal the wound he had dealt the dragon before he could finish the job.

That would not do.

He tracked the dragons and their companions towards the ruined building. He was sure that his hunters could catch up to them at any time, but he was in no hurry. He could see where they were going. They would stay holed up in the ruins while they healed the dragon. He could bide his time and attack when it was to his advantage.

"Soon, Blademaster," he rumbled as he watched them go. "Soon, I will kill your dragons. Whether you try and stop me or not."

He set in to wait. He would wait all night if he had to.

And then he would attack.

Dragonsbane

Chapter XXII
Dragon Magic

The building that they carried Nalia to appeared to have once been a temple of some sort. It was a very large open aired room. The room was empty, which gave Silvestra plenty of room to work.

The two Protectors lay Nalia down on what might have been an altar once, but was now nothing more than a slab of stone. She groaned when they put her down, despite the fact that they were as gentle as they could be.

Silvestra walked up to the altar and looked at Nalia. She studied the wound that Dragonsbane had inflicted on the sapphire dragon and frowned. She closed her eyes and hovered her hand over the wound.

She stood like that for several long minutes, using her magic to probe the wound to find the extent of the damage. When she was done, she opened her eyes and looked at Nalia.

"I can heal it," she said in a soft voice. "But it will be painful. For both of us."

"What... what was on the sword?" Nalia asked.

"It was poison," Silvestra confirmed. "The juice of the death blossom berry. Very rare and very deadly, especially to dragons."

"Hurts," Nalia moaned.

"Yes," Silvestra nodded. "It will."

Alana made her way to Silvestra's side. She looked down at Nalia with sad eyes.

"Will she be all right?" Alana asked Silvestra.

"I can heal her," Silvestra said. "But it will not be easy. I need you all to leave. I will need to be in my dragon form to perform the necessary magic. There is not enough room in here for me to take that form if you are all underfoot."

"I understand," Alana nodded. "The rest of us will make sure you remain undisturbed while you work."

"I appreciate that, Alana," Silvestra smiled over at her friend. "William will need to stay here. He can set wards around the building that will help keep Dragonsbane out if he were to get by. He may be protected from dragon magic, but human magic should still work on him."

"Of course I'll stay, Silvestra," the mage said. "Whatever you need me to do."

Alana placed her hand on Nalia's shoulder and looked down at the sapphire dragon.

"You hang in there, Nalia," Alana said. "Silvestra will heal you up, good as new. You just hold on and let her do what she needs to to set you right."

"Seems like her promise to Grey is going to be tested," Nalia winced.

"So it would appear," Silvestra nodded. "I have no intention on failing to keep my word, though. This will be a complex healing, though. It will be very difficult. And as I said. It will hurt. Both of us. But it is the only way I know how to heal you."

"Do as you must, Silvestra," Nalia wheezed. "The pain will tell me I am still alive."

"Go now, Alana," Silvestra said. "Go and keep anyone from coming in."

Alana nodded and motioned for the others to follow her out. Soon, it was just Silvestra, William and Nalia in the temple.

"William, go put up your wards," Silvestra said to him without turning. "I think we will need them before this night is over."

"Of course," William said.

She did not watch to see if he was setting the wards as she had asked. She was too busy preparing herself for the dangerous bit of dragon magic she was about to use.

William set himself to the task of setting wards around all the entrances and windows. Any gap that someone could conceivably enter the building from, he warded. They were strong wards that would physically bar entry from anyone not allowed to enter the building. He had keyed the wards to allow the companions in, however. But Dragonsbane could not use that to follow one of them in. Even if he had his arm around a companion when they entered, he would be flung away from the building. It was a complex ward, but he felt that it was necessary to make as complete a protection as possible while his wife worked.

When he was done, he turned to watch his wife slowly transform into her dragon shape. It was a transformation that he always found amazing. He knew, always, that there was a dragon inside the silver haired woman that he had fallen for. And he knew that the human figure she wore most of the time was a façade. But it did not change how he felt about her. He was thrilled every time he saw her, whether it be in her human form or her dragon form.

When the transformation was complete, William walked over to Silvestra's head and put his hand on her snout. Her eye swiveled to look at him, and she nodded once.

"It is time," she said.

"What do you need me to do?" he asked.

"This healing will be difficult," Silvestra said. "I will need to borrow some of your energy during the process. And there is a part that I will be unable to do. You will need to complete that part of the healing. I will walk you through it."

"Of course, Silvestra," William nodded.

"No," Nalia said weakly. "You must not do dragon magic in front of him."

"If I do not do this, you will die," Silvestra looked down at the sapphire dragon woman. If I do not act as I must then you are lost. The Blademasters are too important to sacrifice one of our number over foolish notions."

"It is not a foolish notion," Nalia said. "It is the law."

"It is a law that I have already broken and suffered the consequences for breaking," Silvestra said. "And I will break it again now because I must. I cannot heal you with dragon magic alone. This healing requires both human and dragon magic. I can only perform the dragon component. If William does not perform his part of the healing, my magic will have been spent for nothing."

William shifted uneasily from one foot to the other. He knew that it was dangerous for Silvestra to do her dragon magic in front of him. The laws of dragonkind forbade them from displaying their dragon magic in front of human mages. He knew that the penalty was severe. It was one of the reasons that Eliazar had attempted to keep Silvestra away from him. The gold dragon had been afraid that Silvestra would try to teach William some of her dragon magic.

Eliazar needed not have worried. William respected and loved Silvestra too much to be tempted to learn her magical secrets. Besides, he had more power now than he had ever imagined that he would. Having been imbued with the power of the Dream Weaver had amplified his already immense abilities.

William knew that he was now one of the most powerful mages on Calthea. Balor Wyndham was concerned that the power of the Dream Weaver would corrupt William. It was why the head of the evocation order had been so vehemently opposed to William's ascension to the title of Dream Weaver. William had had a moment of concern about the possibility of being corrupted by the power. But he was a Mage of the White, and he would always be a Mage of the White.

And he had Silvestra to keep him from becoming corrupted.

Sometimes he wondered how he got so lucky to have a woman like Silvestra by his side. He put it to divine intervention. In this case, it literally was divine intervention. The Inner Circle of mages and the Council of Dragons had done their best to keep the two of them apart. If Lord Taelin had not decided that they should be together, then they would still be parted. He believed that there was a reason that the Lightbringer had seen fit to put them back together. Perhaps a part of that was to keep William on the path of the White.

It would not surprise him if that were the case. Lord Taelin had, after all, taken a great interest in all of Alana's companions.

And so William found himself standing by Silvestra's snout while she prepared to begin a complicated healing spell that William could not even hope to be able to do on his own. And she needed his help. He would gladly do whatever she needed him to do if it meant not being sent away while she worked. He would feel better about her devoting all her energy to healing the wounded dragon woman if there were someone else in the ruins able to protect her while she worked.

William did not trust that Dragonsbane would not find a way through his wards.

All he could do was to hope that his friends would be able to keep Dragonsbane away from the ruins while they worked.

"I am ready," Silvestra said softly. "Let us begin."

As soon as they walked outside, Alana realized that there was going to be trouble. With just the six of them she was not sure that they would be enough to protect the entirety of the building. Especially since she was not sure what kind of a fighter the young priestess, Alura Dayne, would turn out to be.

There was little to be done. She could only work with the fighters she had.

Alana spread the companions out around the exterior of the ruins. She put the two clerics on one side. The two Protectors and Bella each took a side, and Alana herself took it upon herself to slowly circle the ruins so that she could pitch in wherever she was needed.

It was nowhere near enough, she thought, but it was what she could do with the fighters she had. She had to hope that the wards that William set around the inside of the ruins would be enough to keep Dragonsbane and his men at bay while Silvestra worked.

But it was their job to make sure the wards would not be tested if at all possible.

Alana stalked the outside of the ruins. The Blademaster intended to be up all night protecting her friends if she had to. It did not matter that she had not been sleeping well. The dragons were important for the Blademasters' protection, so she had to make sure they were safe.

As she patrolled the outside of the ruins, she kept a close eye out for members of Dragonsbane's hunting party. She did not doubt that the hunters would take advantage of the fact that both dragons were incapacitated while one healed the other. They all had expected that the hunters would be after the dragons in force. Alana was surprised they were able to get into the ruin and get protection set up before they arrived. But they had, and now all that remained was to be the shield against the hunters.

Alana was happy to see that her companions were all staying diligently awake and searching out the possibility of hunters attacking the ruins. It made her slightly more comfortable to know that she was not the only one that was taking the threat seriously.

As she started to turn around one corner of the ruins, she heard the sound of steel on steel coming from up ahead. She broke into a run, wanting to be there to assist her friend. As she got closer, she saw Colwyn taking on one hunter. She picked up speed and barreled into the hunter, hitting him shoulder first right in the middle of his side. The hunter went flying backwards, his sword flying from his hand.

Alana strode forward and grabbed the hunter by the front of his tunic. Bringing his face close to hers, she snarled at him.

"Tell Dragonsbane that in order to get to the dragons, he will have to get through me," she growled into his face. "Tell him that it will not be easy. I am totally willing to go to war to protect them. Is he willing to go to war with me? You tell him my words."

She threw the hunter back and he sprawled back down on his back. He scurried back away from her and picked up his sword again. Alana scowled at him again and sent the hunter running.

"You can be kind of scary when you want to be, Alana," Colwyn chuckled.

"I intend to be more than a little scary if I have to be," she scowled. "Keep an eye out. I expect they'll be back before morning."

Silvestra worked quietly throughout the night. The healing took all of her energy plus a good amount of William's stored reserves. There was no other way. If Silvestra did not expend all of the energy she had available into the healing then the sapphire dragon would die.

As it was, with the healing, there was still a chance that she could die.

Silvestra's part of the healing process was the more difficult part. It fell to her to knit together the flesh rent by the sword tearing through Nalia's body. Before the two mages could go any further on the healing, though, Silvestra needed to staunch the bleeding. It was a difficult magic to cast. She needed to mend the broken blood vessels one by one. The process took over an hour, and Silvestra's silver scales shone with the exertion.

William kept a hand pressed against her snout, feeding her energy as he could.

"William, the next part you need to do," Silvestra said. "It is difficult, but you must use your magic to pull the poison from her. I cannot do this, or it could kill me. The poison would, very likely, start to kill me even as I was drawing it off from her."

"I understand," William nodded. "Tell me what I must do."

Silvestra moved aside slightly so that William had better access to the wound. William looked into the wound with distaste. The mage had never liked the sight of blood. But there was little that could be done. He had to do his part in this healing or both dragons would die. The mage pushed aside his revulsion at the sight of so much blood and concentrated.

As Silvestra talked him through the intricate process of drawing the poison off from the wound, William listened to every word. It was a healing he had never attempted. It would draw on much of his reserve energy to accomplish. There was a part of him that worried that he would not have enough energy available to be able to complete the process.

It was a worry he had no time for.

He concentrated on the wound and placed his hands over the entrance. Concentrating carefully, he sent his magic probing into the wound. He felt pain as the magic came into contact with the poison, but he knew that the pain was far less than Silvestra would have experienced had she tried to do this healing. Gritting his teeth, he worked, ignoring the pain. He let the magic flow, gathering up the poison. Pouring more magic into the wound, he made sure he found every drop of the death blossom berry juice. He knew that if he left any, it could still kill Nalia.

And Silvestra when she went to complete the healing.

When he was sure he had found every drop, he let the magic bring all of the poison together into one compact ball. Carefully, he wrapped the ball of poison around with layers of his magic. Once the poison had been wrapped about with magic, he slowly drew the ball of liquid out of the wound.

When the ball was safely out of Nalia, William flung the ball of magic and poison to the far wall on the other side of the altar. It hit the stone with an acidic splat, but it did not splatter like liquid normally would. He gave the magic a pulse and the poison turned into a solid disk that melded into the wall.

He sent a thread of magic back into the wound, probing to make sure he had gotten every last drop of the poison. When he was satisfied that he had, he withdrew his magic and nodded to Silvestra.

William slumped with the exertion, happy that his part in the healing was done.

"Now I can finish the healing," Silvestra nodded. "This will likely hurt, Nalia."

"Just do it," the sapphire dragon grimaced.

Silvestra nodded once and began the process of knitting the torn flesh back together.

The companions were still well alert deep in the middle of the night. Alana was pleased that none of them had slacked from being alert. It was tough, though, all of them staying up all night. If Alana had felt that they could have gotten away with watches, she would have happily let her companions get some sleep.

The Blademaster knew that the hunters would take advantage of a single watcher, though.

The fact that they had gotten through as much of the night as they had with only one attempt to get to the dragons was surprising. The Blademaster had expected that they would have to fight the whole night through. But after the one hunter she'd tackled, they had not seen any of the others come near the ruins.

She knew that would not last.

She remained alert, knowing that they could be coming at any time. The rest of the companions kept walking back and forth along the side of the ruined building they were on so that they would stay awake.

Deep in the middle of the night, one of the hunters came stalking up to the ruins, heading straight for Alana. The Blademaster tensed, checking her grip on her swords. The hunter stopped just outside of the reach of her blades. Alana looked at him, waiting for him to make a move.

"I am looking for the Blademaster," the hunter said.

"Well, you've certainly come to the right place," Alana said, fighting the urge to cross her arms over her chest. "What do you want?"

"I have a message for you from Malachai Dragonsbane," the hunter said. "He bade me tell you that he is coming for the dragons at first light. If you are still here when he comes, then your life is forfeit."

"Is that what he told you to tell me?" Alana raised one eyebrow.

"Indeed," the hunter nodded.

"Then I have a message for you to bring to Malachai Dragonsbane."

"And your message is?"

"Bring it."

The Blademaster watched as the hunter ran off to relay her message to Dragonsbane. She sheathed her swords, hoping they would not be needed before morning. Turning, she started back around the ruins to where Colwyn was patrolling.

Colwyn smiled when he saw her coming, although the smile was short lived. Her expression was one of pure anger.

"He's coming for the dragons with first light," she said without preamble when she got to him. "Go tell everyone to be ready for him to make his move an hour before that."

"You think he'll come before he said he's going to?" Colwyn asked.

"Why else would he tell me when he was coming?" Alana shrugged.

"You have a very suspicious mind," Colwyn sighed. "But it makes sense."

"My suspicious mind has kept us alive, Col," she smiled at him. "Now go and tell the others. I will let William and the dragons know."

Colwyn nodded and turned to go relay the message to the others. Alana watched him go, taking a moment to, once again, appreciate how lucky she was to have him. She turned and headed towards the entrance to the ruined temple.

She felt a static buzzing against her skin as she stepped through the entry to the temple. She knew that it was the wards that William had set reacting to her intrusion. For a moment, she wondered what would have happened had she not been one of the companions. After a moment's thought, she decided she didn't want to know.

Slowly, so as not to startle them, Alana walked over to where William was sitting by Silvestra. The great silver dragon had her head down on the floor, and she appeared to be dozing. William looked up at Alana's approached and smiled weakly.

"Alana," he said. "How goes it out there?"

"Well, the hunters are staying away for now," she said. "But one of them just informed me that they will be coming in force at first light. I figure that means they're probably coming about an hour before that."

"That would stand to reason," William nodded. "The wards should hold, but you'll probably still need to fight them."

"I know," Alana nodded. "We'll keep them out. How goes the healing?"

"Timeanalia will be fine. It was a very difficult healing, and both Silvestra and myself are tired," William said. "But we were able to heal her. We expended far more energy than is wise. I do not know how much help either of us will be when it comes to the confrontation with Dragonsbane."

"I understand, William," Alana nodded. "You rest. We'll take care of Dragonsbane and his hunters."

"Thank you," William nodded. "I will rest now."

William leaned back against his wife's body and closed his eyes. Alana nodded once and then headed back out to patrol the ruined temple once more.

Dragonsbane

Chapter XXIII
The Showdown

IST WAS RISING FROM the
ground when the sun started to peek over
the hills to the east of the ruins of El Coran.
Alana stretched against the wall of the
ruined temple as she looked around for the
dragon hunter and his men.

The Blademaster was surprised that the hunters had
not attacked before now. She had fully expected that they
would attack long before the time that Dragonsbane had
told her he would be attacking. It was not that she didn't
trust his word. It was that she knew that most people in
Dragonsbane's situation would try to give themselves an
advantage by attacking earlier than they had indicated that
they would in order to get an advantage over their
opponent.

That he had not spoke to his character.

Colwyn had called Dragonsbane an honorable man.
He'd said that the dragon hunter lived by a code of honor,
but that he had a singlemindedness of purpose. It was

hard for Alana to reconcile that he had honor when his singlemindedness of purpose was to kill her dragons. And yet, he had acted with honor in keeping his word about when he would attack.

A man like that would be helpful in defending the Southern Dales in the War of Souls. If only she could figure out how to turn the man away from his purpose of hunting her dragons to help her defend the people of the Southern Dales against the very real threat of the army of undead.

She had given the problem a great deal of thought, but she had not yet come up with a solution to how to convince the dragon hunter.

She wasn't sure there was a way.

She had spent much of the night patrolling around the ruined temple. She'd taken only brief stops to rest and refresh herself. The hunters were coming, whether it was before the dawn came or at sunrise, and Alana would have to be ready to fight Dragonsbane when they did. It would not do for her to be so tired she could not swing her swords.

The key was to find a way to subdue Dragonsbane without having to kill him. As misguided as his hunt for the dragons was, he was not an evil man and did not deserve to die.

Alana expected that Dragonsbane would be a difficult opponent for her. Perhaps he would even be more difficult than Kera Rayden had been, and she had been a difficult fighter to overcome. Dragonsbane would likely be stronger, although she doubted he would be as skilled with the blades as the Nightstalker had been. Skill didn't matter if he cracked her head open with his strength.

In the end, it would come down to her skill. It always did. She was confident in her skill being better than her opponent, but she just had to make sure she did not become overconfident. Overconfidence could kill a warrior as fast as a lack of skill.

Still, the confidence she had in her own skills told her she would prevail somehow in the coming fight.

Off in the distance, she saw the hunters beginning to move towards the temple. She knew that they would attack as soon as they got in sight of the temple. She looked over at where Colwyn was standing and saw that he had noticed them coming too. He nodded once to her and ran off to get the others.

By the time the others had arrived at the side of the ruined temple that she was on, the hunters had gotten close enough that she could make out which one was Dragonsbane.

It was he who she would have to focus on.

"We've come for the dragons," Dragonsbane hollered. "Stand aside, Blademaster. I have no wish to harm you. Last time warned."

"You want the dragons, you will have to go through us," Alana said, drawing her swords. "I suggest you turn around and go home, Dragonsbane. Last time warned."

"Not leaving without killing those two dragons," Dragonsbane growled. "I don't want to fight you, but I will."

"Then bring it," Alana shrugged.

"Tobias, go into the temple and grab the dragons and bring them out here," Dragonsbane ordered one of the other hunters.

The hunter named Tobias started running towards the temple. Alana held up one sword to the rest of her companions. She knew the hunter would not get into the temple, but she knew that when he ran into the ward, it would alert William that the hunters were out here.

She wanted the mage to know so that he could prepare whatever defenses he needed to.

The others caught her intent and did not stop the hunter from reaching the temple. The hunter continued his headlong rush towards the temple unmolested.

Until he got to the temple itself, that is.

The ward activated as soon as he came in contact with it, sending him flying backwards to slam into the wall of another ruined building.

"Guess we will have to do this the hard way," Dragonsbane growled. "Attack!"

Alana gritted her teeth as she made her way forward. The other hunters in the party did not matter. Only Dragonsbane did. He was the one that wanted to kill her dragon companions and he was the one that needed to be stopped. If he were stopped, the rest of the hunters would likely flee. The Blademaster knew that Malachai Dragonsbane was the key, and so he was the one she was completely focused on. She knew that she could trust the rest of her companions to keep the other hunters away from her while she took on the leader.

She stopped just short of Dragonsbane. Alana was just far enough out of his reach that, in order to attack her, he would have to take a step forward. It would be enough of a delay for her to be able to easily defend against his attack. It was a conscious choice. She would not be the one to launch the attack. She would fight if necessary, but Dragonsbane would have to take the first swing.

She knew that the man would.

Arrogent men could not often help themselves when they thought they were the stronger and better fighter. Dragonsbane might be stronger than Alana was, but she was confident that she was a more skilled fighter. It did not take a lot of finesse to attack a dragon. But to fight a moving human sized target took a great deal of skill. While she did not doubt that the hunter was skilled with his blade, she was willing to safely bet that she was more skilled when it came to actual hand to hand swordplay with another human.

By the same token, she did not want to kill Dragonsbane. He was not an evil man. He was just misguided when it came to wanting to kill her dragons. She would much prefer to subdue him if possible, so that she could find a way to convince him to leave her dragons alone.

She was not sure she could convince him, though.

Colwyn had told her that, once Dragonsbane got his sights set on a prey, he did not let go of that prey until he had succeeded of killing whatever dragon he had set his sights on. That would be fine if the dragons he had decided on as prey were not the dragons that the three Blademasters were depending on for their protection during the War of Souls.

As she stood watching him, waiting for the hunter to make his move, she studied him. Malachai Dragonsbane was a big man. He was probably double her weight, and his heavy armor did make him look intimidating. She knew, though, that the heavier armor would slow him down during the fight. That would be to her advantage. His arms were longer, so he had a reach advantage on her as well. But she had speed and agility on her side. She would use those skills to the best of her ability.

"I have no quarrel with you, Blademaster," Dragonsbane said, keeping his voice low. "Move now before I have to hurt you."

"If you want to get to my dragons, you will have to go through me to get to them," Alana shrugged. She drew her swords and stood with the points touching the ground in a ready position. From that position, she could quickly react and block any attack Dragonsbane threw her way. "But you should know that, as a Blademaster, I was born to fight with my blades and my wits, and I will use both to stop you."

"Bah," Dragonsbane scoffed. "You're just a slip of a girl. I take no pleasure in killing you, but if I must to rid Calthea of two more dragons, I will."

"You won't be the first to underestimate me," she shrugged. "I'm willing to bet that you won't be the last either."

"I don't want to have to kill you, Blademaster," Dragonsbane rumbled. "Last warning. Stand aside."

"I'm thinking," Alana said. She looked him over once more. Finally she smiled and gripped her swords tighter. "No. I'm not going anywhere. As I said. To get to them, you have to go through me."

"So be it," Dragonsbane rumbled.

The dragon hunter's attack was as strong as it was basic, a heavy overhand slash coming straight down towards Alana's head. It was, she thought, the single most expected opening strike he could have gone for. She dropped to a knee and brought her swords up, crossed, to block his strike. She grunted when his sword hit hers. She was right, he was much stronger than she was. Grimacing, she stood, his sword still caught between her crossed blades.

She was not going to be able to trade blows with him. With his strength, he'd be able to wear her down, even though she had the more advanced skill. His choice of opening strike had cemented in her mind his level of skill.

Of course, she knew that he could have just used that to see what she would do. It was likely he had more skill than just simple strikes, and it would not do to underestimate him like she accused him of underestimating her.

She flung his sword away and cut low towards his right knee. No matter how big a person was, if you took out their legs, they would go down. His plate armor protected the joint, but if she aimed just right, she knew that she could hack right at the joint of two plates. Plate armor was designed to not let that happen, but she'd noticed that there were the slightest gaps between some of the plates. It was possible that Dragonsbane had gotten the armor when he was a smaller man.

Dragonsbane was faster than she expected and he deflected her attack away from his leg.

Alana hopped backwards out of the range of his swing again. The two of them began to slowly circle around each other, looking for the weakness in the other's defense. Alana prided herself in being able to quickly size up an opponent. She had been wrong about Dragonsbane's speed, but after that first parry, she'd modified her appraisal of him. While she still believed that she had the advantage over him when it came to speed and skill, the advantage was not nearly as great as she had first thought. She would have to use all of her skill and cunning if she wanted to best Dragonsbane.

"You're faster than I expected," Alana remarked.

"Slow dragon hunters end up dead dragon hunters," Dragonsbane shrugged.

"I suppose that's true," Alana nodded.

As she watched him move, she tried to pick up on any hint as to where his next attack was come from. She had just noticed him start forward in a slashing attack when the world went white.

Not far from where the two of them were circling each other, a large bolt of lightning struck the ground, blinding all of the fighters   The lighting had the effect of stopping all combat.

"Enough!" William Stonehands bellowed from the entrance to the ruined temple.

Dragonsbane

Chapter XXIV
Bargain Struck

illiam stood at the doorway to the temple that Silvestra had healed the sapphire dragon. His arms were opened wide, his staff clutched tight in his right hand. His robes were whirling in a breeze that no one else could feel.

It was an intense display of power, meant to intimidate the dragon hunter and his companions.

He looked around at the various people around the structure. Most everyone had weapons out, which only made sense since there was fighting right up until he'd shouted and called down lightning. It had been an effective trick to get the fighting to stop, and William was pleased that it had worked.

"Enough," he shouted again.

"Who are you to dictate to us when to stop fighting, wizard?" Dragonsbane yelled back.

"I am the Dream Weaver," William declared. "I am he who weaves the dreams. And I am the one who can make you stop."

"You're but one wizard," Dragonsbane scoffed. "You can't stop all of us. Besides. I'm protected from magic."

"Protected from dragon magic, yes," William nodded. "But Malachai Dragonsbane, I am no dragon. My magic will work on you. Do you care to test my word?"

"You're a human," Dragonsbane said. "You can die just as any other human. Antus and Wellin, kill him."

Two of Dragonsbane's companions started towards William with their swords drawn. William marked their progress. When they were far enough away from anyone else, he murmured a word and fire flowed from his hands. He directed the fire to form a circle around the two men. It was a large enough circle that the men could move without being burned, but they could progress no further towards the mage.

"Do you even understand why the Blademasters need the dragons?" William demanded as he slowly advanced towards where Dragonsbane was standing.

"They are abominations!" Dragonsbane roared. "They need to be destroyed!"

"Abominations, you say?" William arced an eyebrow. "Truly?"

"Yes," Dragonsbane spat. "Every last dragon is an abomination and should be removed from the world."

William took another step towards the dragon hunter. The wizard had completely forgotten about his own companions, so intent was he on the dragon hunter and his hunting party. Alana called out to him, but he ignored her.

"Would you like to see an abomination?" William asked as he took another step towards the dragon hunter. "I can show you one that is far worse than any of the dragons currently protecting Blademasters."

"There is nothing worse than a dragon!" Dragonsbane thundered.

"So you claim, but I have seen it," William said. He stopped an arm's length away from the dragon hunter. "And now, so shall you. See and remember always." The wizard reached up and touched two fingers to the dragon hunter's temple. "Membius!"

Dragonsbane cried out, unable to move, as his mind was assailed by images.

In his mind's eye, he was transported to Willowdale during the final battle for the people of Valendale. He was fighting against a Zeraphim soldier when a dark shadow passed overhead. He looked up, completely shocked at what he saw.

The great skeletal dragon caused mass panic when he appeared. Some of the men of Valendale dropped their weapons and ran from the field of battle, the Zeraphim soldiers chasing them, trying to stab them in the back. Even Colwyn and Alana were momentarily shaken when they saw the great beast. Alana grabbed the summoning statue from around her neck, hoping that Cobalt would be able to handle the massive skeletal dragon. She did not know how or even if Cobalt could handle such a monstrosity, but she hoped he could.

It did not take long for Cobalt to soar onto the scene. The skeletal dragon was easily half again the size of the gold dragon. It was not going to be an easy battle, nor would it be a pleasant one to watch. But knowing that Cobalt was attacking the great skeletal dragon, Alana and Colwyn were both able to turn back to their respective battles, wading into the fray. Alana's way was suddenly clear in front of her, and she dashed towards the palace, running as fast as she could so that she would not be stopped by the Zeraphim.

The scene shifted, and Dragonsbane realized he was seeing the attack from the eyes of the gold dragon. It was an odd feeling to be flying, but he found it exhilarating. And a bit scary. But he could understand why dragons loved to take to the air.

Cobalt had seen the giant skeletal dragon take the field. He kept his fear in check and forced himself to launch into the air to take on the giant bone dragon. It was a fearsome prospect. For the first time, he actually doubted the bravado that he had shown Alana in the skeletal dragon's lair.

Cobalt actually did not know if he could best such a beast.

There was nothing he could do but to try though. With a cry, Cobalt loosed a humongous blast of flame at the skeletal dragon as he soared towards it. The great gold dragon tried to show no fear. He knew that his Blademaster was counting on him to take on this abomination.

Cobalt quickly ran through what he knew about skeletal dragons as he flew towards the monstrosity. Unfortunately, that knowledge did not amount to much. He figured that the only way to really kill the creature, if that was even the appropriate word, would be to remove its head.

It sounded a lot easier than Cobalt knew it would be. He kept the torrent of flame going as he flew towards the skeletal dragon, hoping that the dragon would be afraid of the fire.

The skeletal dragon roared a challenge back at Cobalt and the two dragons flew towards each other.

As he approached the skeletal dragon, Cobalt noted that, although the dragon had no flesh, he still had very sharp teeth and talons. He would have to be careful as he knew that those talons could tear his wings as easily as a living dragon's talons could. He was afraid of what extra surprises might be in store for him with the dragon being undead.

The skeletal dragon was easily twice as long as Cobalt was. The bones were bleached white, not showing a single speck of dirt. The head was massive with a snout twice as long as Cobalt's. The talons were razor sharp and the skeletal dragon kept flexing his paws and Cobalt could imagine the talons ripping through his flesh.

It was not a feeling the great gold dragon had any desire to actually experience.

The skeletal dragon was coming from a higher level, so Cobalt swooped low under the great undead beast. He hoped that he could make his way under the larger dragon and swoop up over his back. The skeletal dragon seemed to know what Cobalt was planning though and twisted in midair so that his talons were facing up when Cobalt finished his maneuver.

Cobalt kept circling around the larger dragon, but the skeletal dragon kept barreling around so that his talons were always directed at Cobalt.

The gold dragon was getting frustrated. He did not want to get too close to those claws. He kept faking moves to try to get the skeletal dragon to drop his guard, but the undead beast seemed to know everything that Cobalt wanted to try even before the gold dragon did.

Cobalt blew a short burst of flame at the skeletal dragon. It hit the skeletal dragon's ribs, causing the larger dragon to roar, although Cobalt did not think that he felt pain.

Cobalt reversed direction and took to the air, putting distance between the two dragons. He was frustrated, but he refused to be forced into a hasty attack. Such an attack would not go well for the gold dragon, he knew. He had to find a weakness. By the same token, he was not sure that the skeletal dragon had a weakness. There was something very disturbing about the skeletal dragon.

Cobalt watched the skeletal dragon as it lazily flew a circle under him. The gold dragon wondered what kind of dragon it had been in life. From its size and shape, Cobalt supposed that the dragon had probably been a red dragon in life. It certainly had the arrogance of an ancient red.

What accursed magic could bring it back across the veil like this though?

What had the Dark God done to imbalance the scales to create something like this?

It was an abomination like nothing that Cobalt had ever seen in his life. All he could do is pray to Taelin that there were no other undead dragons like this one on Calthea. One was enough. More than enough, really. Despite his bravado to Alana in the creature's cave, he was not sure he could actually defeat this creature on his own. It was not in his nature to ask for help, however. It had always been one of his biggest flaws. That and his stomach.

He had to keep the skeletal dragon interested in him rather than the troops that were attacking the Zeraphim. He was afraid that if he did not kill this beast, then many of the people that his Blademaster were trying to save would die.

He could not allow that to happen.

He circled twice more then dove straight at the skeletal dragon.

It was a sudden dive and it had actually caught the skeletal dragon off guard, which was what Cobalt had hoped. Cobalt got to the skeletal dragon before he could shift, and the great gold dragon latched his jaws onto a rib.

The skeletal dragon howled, and this time, Cobalt knew that the larger dragon actually felt pain. The gold dragon stayed with it, keeping his jaws locked onto the rib. He twisted his head, trying to jerk the rib free. He had decided that it might be easier to pick off individual bones this way rather than try to go for a killing blow. It would be harder, he felt, to latch onto the neck of the dragon. The larger dragon was proving to be far more maneuverable than he had at first expected.

With a last wrench, the rib came free. Cobalt dropped it from his jaws as the skeletal dragon howled in pain. The larger dragon craned his neck trying to reach Cobalt, but the smaller dragon did his best to keep out of reach of the massive jaws of the skeletal dragon. It was not an easy task, and the larger dragon kept trying.

Cobalt lashed out with a blast of fire aimed directly at the head of the skeletal dragon. The fire seemed to be doing nothing to the skeletal dragon, however. Despite that, Cobalt felt the need to keep at it in the hopes that it might distract the larger dragon at any rate.

The skeletal dragon proved to be too observant to be distracted by such ploys. Cobalt had all he could handle to keep himself out of the jaws of the larger dragon. It was not an easy trick, as the skeletal dragon was showing itself to be incredibly flexible. The skeletal dragon's massive jaws kept snapping at Cobalt, trying to latch onto anything that was vulnerable.

Cobalt knew that if the skeletal dragon got his jaws on him he was dead.

He could not die without being sure that his Blademaster would be safe. In this, though, he knew he was not alone. If for some reason he did fail in defeating the skeletal dragon, he knew that Silvestra would take his place in the battle. He did not want the young silver dragon to have to risk herself in that battle, however.

Cobalt broke off and flew high into the air trying to regroup. The skeletal dragon lazily swooped around in a circle below him, watching him. Cobalt hovered several hundred feet higher than the skeletal dragon. It was a height from which he could launch a devastating diving attack on the other dragon. He surveyed the skeletal dragon trying to figure out where the best place to attack the other dragon would be. He thought that maybe if he tried to sever the dragon's tail, the skeletal dragon would have a tougher time flying.

Quick as a flash, the great gold dragon dove at the skeletal dragon. The larger dragon knew what Cobalt was planning, however and was ready for the gold dragon. The skeletal dragon rolled on his back and let his talons rip along the gold dragon's sides. Cobalt screamed in pain and fury as drops of dragon blood fell on the battleground below.

Cobalt tried to latch his jaws on the skeletal dragon's tail, but the larger dragon kept it out of his reach.

Cobalt flew off to regroup. He surveyed the damage that the skeletal dragon had caused. Cobalt had lost a few scales and had some ragged gashes on his sides, but he was not heavily injured from the skeletal dragon's assault. He needed to be more careful in the future attacks he launched on the larger dragon. He had almost gotten caught by the great bone dragon's jaws.

He knew that the skeletal dragon was the better dragon on the battlefield, and that gave Cobalt pause. He knew that this would be his final battle. And that realization saddened him. He had simply gotten too old to be able to hold his own in battle.

Cobalt was desperate to end the battle quickly. He launched himself at the other dragon once more. The skeletal dragon caught Cobalt with a slash of talons across his right wing. Cobalt screamed in fury as his wing tore. He knew a torn wing was the one thing he could not recover from in the middle of battle. It was as good as a death sentence. He knew that he would not be able to carry his own weight for too much longer. He had to end it quickly.

He launched himself at the skeletal dragon and landed on the larger dragon's back. He tried to latch his jaws on the larger dragon's neck, but the skeletal dragon kept snaking his neck out of reach

It was then that the skeletal dragon got his jaws around Cobalt's neck.

Cobalt screamed in fury, but he knew that it was too late. The skeletal dragon closed his jaws around Cobalt's neck and slowly began to apply the pressure. It did not take long for the bones in Cobalt's neck to crack and splinter. The great gold dragon screamed one last howl of fury before he was incapable of such an expression.

I hope I have served my Blademaster well enough to find my redemption, was the gold dragon's final thought.

When Cobalt had breathed his last breath, the skeletal dragon opened his jaws, and the great gold dragon fell to the ground below them, knocking over several small buildings as he landed. The gold dragon twitched once and then was still.

The skeletal dragon roared in triumph and started circling the battlefield in search of easy prey.

Dragonsbane could still feel the teeth of the skeletal dragon around his neck when the viewpoint of the battle changed once more. He realized that he was in a second dragon. And he realized by looking at the wings of the dragon he was in that it was the silver dragon that was currently with the Blademasters even now in the Wilds.

Silvestra examined the skeletal dragon as she flew towards it. The dragon was massive, far larger than she had first thought. She had no idea how she would be able to best it. Her only thought was that she had to keep out of the way of the massive jaws of the beast. If she could do that, she had a chance to survive.

She let off a blast of lightning to get the skeletal dragon's attention. The lightning did not connect with the dragon's bones, but it was not meant to. It was meant to get the dragon's attention, and it succeeded in doing so. The skeletal dragon roared in fury and started to chase the much smaller silver dragon. She prayed to Taelin that she knew what she was doing by taunting this evil monstrosity.

She did not want to face the skeletal dragon right over the city. She was afraid that people she cared about might get hurt if she or the skeletal dragon fell to earth at the end of the battle. She did not want that to happen. She had not seen if there had been anyone under where the great gold dragon landed. She hoped there wasn't.

Her plan was simple. Get the skeletal dragon to follow her into the mountains. From there, she was not sure what the best course of action would be.

When she saw the skeletal dragon coming her way, she twisted her body and started to fly as fast as she could towards the mountains. She looked behind her several times to make sure that the skeletal dragon was, in fact, following her. She smiled grimly to herself when she realized that he was. The problem was that he was slightly faster than she was. She did not understand how that could be. He was far larger than she was, so she should be the faster of the two. She figured it had to do with how the skeletal dragon had been reanimated. There was clearly some evil magic at work here. She did not want to contemplate the kind of magic that went into creating such a creature.

She made it to the mountains before he did, though and so she whirled around a mountain so she could come at him from behind. She had timed it perfectly as she came around the mountain just as the skeletal dragon started to fly past the other side.

She let out another blast of lightning at the skeletal dragon, this time scoring a hit on the skeletal dragon's tail. The skeletal dragon roared and came at her. She used her smaller size to stay out of his way as much as she could, firing blast after blast of lightning at the larger dragon to keep him at bay and hurt him as much as she could before they closed in for the inevitable grapple.

Dragonsbane could see all of the fighting going on in Willowdale still. He could see the citizens of Valendale fighting against the Zeraphim soldiers. He knew that the citizens of Valendale would have had no chance against this skeletal dragon that the silver dragon was fighting.

He could just barely make out the Blademaster fighting against another woman. From what he'd heard about the events in Willowdale, the woman in black was called the Nightstalker. The stories about the battle said that the Nightstalker was the Blademaster's opposite number. It was a pitched battle, and the two women were evenly matched.

Far above and far to the west of where the two women were fighting for their very survival, Silvestra and Calindilarin were locked in heated battle, their jaws flashing at each other. Calindilarin was a little slower, having already fought one tough battle against Cobalthaxillius, but he was far larger, and he tried to use his size to every advantage. Silvestra writhed and twirled to keep out of the large skeletal dragon's jaws. She had seen what he had done to Cobalt and she was trying everything she could to keep the same thing from happening to her.

She had taken several bad cuts on her body during the battle though. The battle was wearing on both of them. They both knew it would have to end quickly or else neither of them would survive it.

Silvestra arced her neck and back away from Calindilarin and swirled away from him, flying slowly, turning lazily around. She sucked in a great breath of air and breathed a hefty bolt of lightning at the skeletal dragon. It struck home right in the skeletal dragon's ribcage, shattering two of the great ribs. Chunks of bone fell to the ground far below. Silvestra was thankful that they had moved away from the city. Someone would have been killed if they'd been hit by those chunks of bone.

The skeletal dragon screamed with agony and rushed Silvestra. She'd been waiting for the rush and flew to the side, raking her talons against the skeletal dragon's left wing, tearing large holes in the thin membrane and bone alike. Silvestra knew she had the advantage and that she had to press it while she had it. It would not do to gain the advantage and then lose the battle immediately following.

She waited until the great skeletal dragon had stopped spinning around and dropped onto his back, her talons *digging into his ribs. She reached down and latched her jaws onto the vertebrae of the great skeletal dragon's neck. She held on tight as the great skeletal dragon bucked. She tried to close her jaws and sever the vertebrae she had in her mouth. The bone was rock hard though and she was afraid she would break her fangs if she did so.*

So she did the next best thing she could think of. She twisted her neck with the vertebrae in her jaws trying to separate it from the next one in line. The skeletal dragon screamed with each twist of Silvestra's head.

Finally with a great wrench, she broke the connection between the two vertebrae. The neck of the skeletal dragon hung from her jaws and she spat it out. With a scream, she pulled her talons from the skeletal dragon's ribs, taking chunks of bone out when she pulled. She freed herself just before the great bone dragon fell to the earth with a jarring crash. The skeleton came apart as it hit the ground, and waves of released dark magic rushed out from the crash site. The waves of magic rushed all the way back to Willowdale, cracking foundations in the city's great walls.

As the dark magic released, the vision faded to black.

William watched the dragon hunter closely. He had never cast such an intense spell without having studied it before. It was pure instinct that he had been able to cast the spell in the first place. He hoped that there would be no side effects.

One of the members of Dragonsbane's huntimg party started towards where he was standing with Dragonsbane. It had only been a few moments since he had touched the dragon hunter. He knew that for Dragonsbane, a great deal of time would pass in the visions he was forcing the man to see. There was sure to be disorientation when Dragonsbane came out of the vision state, but there was nothing that William could do about that.

"Take your hand off Dragonsbane, wizard," the man said as he approached.

"Of course," William nodded. He removed his fingers from Dragonsbane's temple. "The spell has already been cast. Malachai Dragonsbane will see what I wish him to see whether I keep my fingers there or not."

"And what did you make him see, William?" Alana asked, a lot closer than he'd expected her to be.

He turned to face Alana and bowed his head slightly.

"A memory," he said. "Nothing more."

"How did you do that?" Colwyn asked.

"I do not know," William shrugged. "I suspect it is a part of the Dream Weaver's magic. Roald used the spell on me before the Test of Magic."

"What did he make you see?" Alana asked, intrigued.

"A memory," William smiled. "Nothing more."

Dragonsbane gasped as his eyes snapped open.

"What...." He gasped for air. "What was that, wizard?"

"You told me the dragons were abominations," William said. "I have now shown you an abomination. One that took two dragons to destroy. Did you feel the terror in the people in Willowdale when they saw that thing?"

"What was it?" Dragonsbane asked.

"A foul creation of magic," Willam spat. "A skeletal dragon. An animated skeleton as it were."

"It was powerful," Dragonsbane said. "I don't know how the dragons were able to defeat it."

"Silvestra is a very smart dragon," William's smile grew broader. "She's crafty. Even so, it could have easily killed her. Had it done so, it would have killed everyone in Willowdale. All those people we saved would have died if the dragons we had with us that day were not there."

"They are still abominations," Dragonsbane said, although he did not say it with anywhere near as much vehemence as he had previously.

"And they are still the protection the Blademasters need in the war to come," William countered. "I will make you a deal, dragon hunter."

"A deal?" Dragonsbane frowned. "What deal?"

"The War of Souls is coming, whether anyone wants to believe that or not," William said. "I do not know what it will bring as far as enemies, but I know that the dragons will be sorely needed to keep the Blademasters alive. Help us through the War of Souls. Help us defeat whatever evil dragons the army of darkness throws at us. If, at the end of the War of Souls, you are still alive, you are free to continue your hunt for Silvestra, Timeanalia, and Greytonix. But know, now, that they know you are coming now and will be ready for you."

"Bargain struck," the dragon hunter nodded.

William shook Dragonsbane's hand and turned back to Alana.

"Help me back to Silvestra, Alana," the mage whispered. "That spell took more out of me than I expected."

Alana helped her friend back to where his wife was waiting, still trying to figure out what she had just witnessed.

Dragonsbane

Chapter XXV
Home Again

The great bronze dragon flew quickly across the continent. It still took several days for him to fly all the way to Barandale with his charges, but it was still a lot quicker than had they gone by horse.

On the night before they would arrive at the gates of Barandale, they camped about two hours walk from the city gates. Talby had decided that it would be better to arrive at the gates when it was still light out. No one had disagreed with her thought.

They made a fire and had a late supper. Grey ate his fill and then started to doze. He was happy that he was done flying for this journey and wanted a good night's rest. For the rest of the halflings, they were happy to be almost home.

Meryn thought about the fact that she was going home. It was strange. She had spent so much of her adult life away from Barandale. She'd never really felt like she needed to return. Then, the previous fall, she had brought the Blademaster and the rest of her companions to her home. She realized then that she was a little homesick for Barandale. Meryn was happy that they'd be going to spend some time in Barandale now.

It would not be restful time, though. Alana was counting on them to raise Barandale's army up. It was true that Barandale did have an army, but they had not fought a battle in years and were in sore need of training.

It was going to take a great deal of work in order to get the army ready for a war.

Talby was determined to see her instructions through. And Meryn would be there to help. She wasn't that good with tactics, but she could help make sure they knew how to fight. That was something that she was good at.

There were other things she could help train the army in. She was passingly good at field dressings after helping patch Alana up many times over their travels together. She smiled as she thought about her tiny fingers sewing closed a particularly nasty gash on Alana's forearm. How that gash had healed without a scar, Meryn would never know. And Alana had just sat there without even so much as a whimper while Meryn had sewed the gash closed.

Meryn doubted that she would ever have been able to remain as calm as that while having a gash like that sewn shut. She wasn't even sure she'd be able to stay awake. That much pain and blood would surely make her pass out from the shock!

Meryn stared into the fire, for once not sleepy. Or talkative. She was... pensive would be a good word. It was true that Meryn was definitely a woman of action. But this night, she was a woman of thought.

She thought about how her life had changed since the moment she had met Alana. She'd gone from being a half bit thief to being a hero. And while she had not quite processed what that meant to her and to her future, she was proud of herself just the same. And her grandmother, Maren, was proud of her too. That made it even better.

The halfling looked over at where Talby was dozing. Her cousin had been named the first ever halfling Blademaster. Meryn was jealous, but did not begrudge her cousin the title. After all, she'd seen Talby fight. If ever there was a halfling that deserved to be called a Bladmaster, it was Talby. The way she fought was spectacular! Meryn could never be comfortable with all the different blades she'd seen Talby use even in just the few battles they'd fought together. Meryn was happy just using knives and a short sword.

But Talby had used everything she could get her hands on. She'd even used a great sword like the one Colwyn carried once. The sword had been taller than she was! Meryn had laughed at her cousin taking off a skeleton's head with the great sword. It was a sight to behold!

Meryn was jealous of Talby's easy with weapons. But only so much. It was clear that Meryn had her own part to play in this upcoming war. If it weren't so, she would never have gotten involved with Alana and her companions to begin with.

What that role might be, Meryn had no idea. In time, it would reveal itself. It was the way of these things.

She had thought that her part would have to do with William. But she had been wrong about that too. Looking over at her husband, Odway, she decided that it was OK to be wrong sometimes. Odway was a good enough man. Had she not left Barandale years before, it was likely that they would have married long before they did. Her grandmother had wanted them to be married. It was only Meryn's own stubbornness that had kept it from happening.

But now she was married to the man that she figured she'd always been meant to marry. What that meant for her part in the War of Souls, she could only guess. But she would find out with Odway. It was the way of things when you were married.

Content for the first time in a long time, Meryn lay down and went to sleep.

The next morning, Talby led her companions into the city of Barandale. As a member of the Swiftfoot clan, she faced no questions from the guards at the entrance to the city. Nor did they question anyone who was with her.

She grabbed one of the guards by his arm and spun him around to face her.

"Go tell my grandmother that I've returned and I need to meet with the Council of Elders straightaway," Talby ordered the guard.

"Who are you to give me orders, Talby Swiftfoot?" the guard growled.

"I'm the one who will put my foot through your behind if you don't do what I tell you," Talby growled right back. "Hurry on, now. Lady Maren will want to know we've returned."

The guard grumbled again, but ran off. Talby and her companions followed along, much slower in pace. It really did not matter how long it took for Talby to get to the Council of Elders. She knew that they would wait to hear what she had to say.

They weren't going to like it.

Talby fully suspected that she was about to experience some of the annoyance that the Master Blademaster had been dealing with wile trying to get the Council of War to understand the need for rallying the troops. She doubted that most of the Council of Elders would understand the need for the halflings to get involved in this battle.

It would be up to Talby to convince them.

She did not know who would be the main elders to object. Maren, of course, would unconditionally support her. Talby was grateful for that. What she was going to have to do was difficult enough. Having the support of one of the elders before she even said a word would make it easier. She could lean on that support as she needed to.

She thought about what she would say to the council. She'd seen what the army was going to be like. How much should she tell them? Would telling them the whole truth about what they were about to face help her cause or hinder it?

She had the letter from Alana. What help that would be, she did not know. But it was a tool she had. Talby would take all the tools she could in order to succeed with the Council of Elders.

The standing army of Barandale was small. It was doubtful if it would be enough to really make a difference in the War of Souls, but it was Talby's job to raise the army and lead it. She would do her job.

When they arrived at the Hall of Elders, they were met by a guard. The guard looked the group over and nodded once. He motioned for them to follow him.

The door they entered to go in to see the Council of Elders was small enough that Greytonix had to almost double over to fit through it. As he started through, Talby was afraid he would get stuck. The council chamber itself was large enough for him to stand, though, which came as a great relief to everyone.

Talby strode forward with purpose and faced the Council of Elders, a determined expression on her face. Her eyes met those of her grandmother The sad smile that Maren gave her spoke volumes. She would, indeed, be in for a fight, but she was up for it.

"I am Talby Swiftfoot, granddaughter of Maren Swiftfoot," she began boldly. "I am the first halfling to ever be called to the Temple of the Blades. The blood of Lord Taelin and Lady Laeyra runs through my veins. Lady Maren, I come before the Council of Elders to inform you that I have come to take control of the standing army of Barandale on the orders of Lady Alana Steeldrake, Master Blademaster, and King Roland Stonehammer, King of the Southern Dales."

"You? Take command of the army?" an elder named Dramor Whistlethenn scoffed. "You are just a girl. You know nothing of battles."

"I am just a girl, yes," Talby looked coldly on the elder. "But I am a girl that could slice the skin off your ears where you sit without drawing a single drop of blood. Do I need to prove my worth with the blade to you, my lord?"

"Why is the standing army being called to action, Talby?" Maren asked. "Is it the War of Souls?"

"The War of Souls is just a myth," Dramor growled. "A tale to scare children."

"The War of Souls is real," Talby said softly. "And it is upon us. The army of undead marches on the Southern

Dales. I've seen it. I have fought it. And if our people are to survive, we must make ready to fight."

"You wouldn't know an undead if it came up and swatted you on your pretty little behind, Talby," Dramor sneered.

"If she were the only one to have seen the undead, perhaps that might be the case," Odway spoke from his place beside Meryn. "Or do you doubt the word of a priest of our Lady Laeyra, Lord Dramor? I doubt you would wish to experience my lady's displeasure for doubting her servant's word."

"Bah," was all Dramore said in response.

Talby took a step forward towards the Council of Elders. She pulled the letter that Alana had given her from her armor and looked at Maren.

"Grandmother, this letter is from Lady Alana to the Council of Elders," she said. "If you will permit me, I should like to read it to the Council."

"Of course, Talby," Maren nodded, a slight smile playing across her face. Clearly her grandmother was enjoying Talby putting the Council of Elders in their place.

Talby broke the seal on the letter and held it up to read.

"To the Council of Elders in Barandale," Talby began. "The bearer of this letter, Blademaster Talby Swiftfoot, is my messenger. You will heed her words as you would heed mine, or I will know the reason why.

"War is coming to the Southern Dales. There can be no discussion about this. It is coming. It does not matter if you believe or not. The army of undead and shadows will not stop coming just because you believe them to be a fairy tale to scare children.

"On my authority as the Master Blademaster of the Southern Dales and with the support of King Roland Stonehammer, I call all standing armies of the Southern Dales to the defense of the people of the Southern Dales. This will be a long and bloody battle, but it needs be fought or we all die.

"Blademaster Talby is hereby ordered to bring the army of Barandale to action. As one of my Blademasters, I hereby charge her to take command of the army of

Barandale with a field promotion to the rank of General. All armies and commands of Barandale are to immediately place themselves under her command.

"With spring approaching fast, the army of darkness also approaches. Therefore, training of the army must begin immediately. Any able bodied men and women who choose to join the fight are welcome.

"I am aware that there are few people that will stand side by side with the halflings. For that you have my deepest apologies. But there is little that can be done about that before the war comes. You must stand ready to defend your people.

"These are my orders. And the orders of King Roland Stonehammer. They are not to be questioned. Follow these orders and place your armies under the command of Blademaster Talby Swiftfoot. Train and be ready for war.

"For it is coming.

"Signed by my hand,

"Alana Steeldrake

"Master Blademaster of the Southern Dales"

When Talby finished reading, she met Maren's gaze. The elder Swiftfoot looked at her granddaughter with pride. There were few that would have trusted Talby with the command of an entire army. That Alana had trusted Talby to ensure that the army of Barandale was ready to fight spoke to the respect that the Master Blademaster already had for Talby.

"What do we do?" Maren asked.

"We be ready to fight," Talby shrugged. "Here's what I need..."

Sunrise hung low in the sky when Alana and her companions mounted their horses for the last ride to Ravendale. They'd camped not too far outside the city so as to arrive sometime in the late morning or early afternoon.

They had taken their time riding from the Wilds back to Ravendale. William had needed a lot of time to recover his energy. Even now, he was still looking a bit pale. The Blademaster knew that her friend had expended far more energy than he should have, both in helping to heal Nalia and with the memory spell he had cast afterwards. Had he had time to rest between the two, he'd have been fine, but there had been no time for him to rest. He had simply acted as he had needed to.

Alana, not for the first time, worried about the young mage. He had increased in power very quickly, and Alana feared for him. She knew, though, that love was a powerful bond. There was hope there. Hope that Silvestra would keep him from being seduced by the magic and turning away from the white. It would be a hard thing to watch if he were to succumb to the seduction of power.

Silvestra, for her part, had assured Alana that she knew that William would stay on the path of the white. Alana took what comfort she could from Silvestra's assurance, but it did little to ease her worry.

Worried or not, Alana had been impressed with how William had been able to put an end to the confrontation so completely. It had been an impressive display of magic from the start. From calling down lightning to the fire to the memory spell, it had been one long bit of impressive magic.

But it was also far more than she'd ever seen him do before. And that fed her worry. He had been able to control fire in new ways, turning it into a barrier to impede the hunter's companions. She'd never seen anything like that before. Especially not from William. She wondered what else the mage would be able to do now. The thought scared her. And yet, he had chosen to use the fire to stop the men, not kill them. He had made the conscious choice to prevent them from being able to attack without killing them. Alana respected that choice. It was the same choice she would have made herself.

Alana took comfort that William continued to respect the sanctity of life even with the new levels of power that he had developed. That was something that she would have to keep a watch on. The moment he stopped respecting the sanctity of life was the moment she would know he was starting to go bad.

She would have to do something to keep that from happening if it started.

For now, though, it was not a problem that she would have to worry about. That was good, as they had more than enough problems to complicate things as it was.

As they rode though the city gates, the guards waved them through. The guards, Alana knew, had express orders to let the Blademasters and their companions through the gates of Ravendale no matter what hour they arrived. Alana, for her part, preferred not to test whether or not they'd be challenged if they arrived in the middle of the night. It made it easier for the guards to recognize her for who she was if they rode in during daylight hours. It was hard to mistake her with her dark red hair and her dark brown armor, so traditional for a Blademaster. But she knew that, at night, it might not be as easy to make out those details.

She waved to the guards as they went through the gates. All she wanted was a warm bath and her bed. But those would have to wait. She needed to make sure that William was settled before anything else.

Bella and Cayden peeled off from the rest of the group to head to their house, where they, too, would rest up. Alana had told them that she intended to leave for the Wilds again very soon. She wasn't sure when, but she had told them that they'd best rest up for the journey.

Timeanalia followed Bella and Cayden. She still looked a little drained from her experience in the ruins of El Coran. Alana held some concern for the sapphire dragon, but Silvestra told her that Nalia would be fine. It would just take some more time for her to fully recover.

Alana hoped she could give the dragon that time.

William and Silvestra lived in a house not far from the small house that Colwyn had built for Alana and himself. It was convenient. That meant that they would be able to make sure that William was put to bed before they went home to make their own plans.

When they got to William's house, the young mage slid off his horse. Silvestra dropped to the ground next to him to make sure he was able to stand. The mage had recovered a bit on the journey home, though, and was able to stand without assistance from his wife.

"Thank you for your concern, Alana," William said as he faced his friend. "I am going to be fine. It is just taking some time to recover from so much magic. A couple days of normal sleep in my own bed, and I should be fine."

"We are leaving again soon, William," Alana said. "I don't know exactly when. I suspect that we will not be able to leave as soon as I would like, but it will be soon."

"And I will be ready," William nodded.

"Keep an eye on him, Silvestra," Alana smiled at the silver haired dragon woman. "I suspect we will need our mage before too long."

"I suspect you are right," Silvestra nodded. She smiled at Alana, but it was a weak smile. "Do not worry, Alana. I will look after William."

Alana looked intently at Silvestra. She knew that the silver haired dragon woman knew that Alana was concerned about William being corrupted by the magic. Looking at Silvestra now, Alana knew that she meant more than just keeping an eye on him to make sure that he was OK while he recovered his energies.

Apparently, Alana was not the only one who was concerned about how much power William had gained.

Alana nodded once and then wheeled her horse around towards home.

When they got to their house, they found Victor Tram leaning against the wall by the door. Alana was not surprised. Since they chose not to go talk to Lord Dargan straight away when they returned to Ravendale, he sent one of his most trusted guards to seek them out. Alana was not angry, but she did not want to go see Dargan. She wanted to sit in her house and plan out their next move. Or take her nice long hot bath. Probably the bath first. Then the planning.

"I can only assume you are here to take us to see Lord Dargan," Alana grunted as she dropped from her horse.

"The First Lord of Arvendale would like to see his son and daughter in law, yes," Victor nodded.

"Could you tell Lord Dargan that, if he wants to meet us at the palace tomorrow, we will tell both him and King Roland what happened in the Wilds?" Alana said. "I'm too tired to do much of anything more right now."

"Of course," Victor nodded. "Can I at least tell him if everyone made it back to Ravendale alive?"

"We're all here," Alana nodded. "A bit battered, some of us, but we're all alive. Anything more than that, he'll learn tomorrow. There is much to tell."

"Then I shall relay your words," Victor nodded. "Would you like me to take your horses to the Arvendale Manor stables?"

"If you would be so kind, that would be lovely of you," Alana smiled a weak smile.

"Then I shall let you be," Victor said. He took the reigns of the two horses. "Welcome home, Blademaster."

Alana and Colwyn watched the captain of the guard head off to Arvendale Manor, their horses following behind him before turning to head into the house.

Later that evening, Alana was laying cuddled up against Colwyn's chest. As tired as they were, neither could sleep. The events in the Wilds lay heavily on Alana's mind. She was happy that everyone had made it through all right, but it had been a close call.

If it had not been for William's magic, Alana doubted that the dragons would still be alive.

Even so, that wasn't what was bothering Alana. Spring had come into full bloom, and Alana knew that with the bloom, the attackers would come soon. She could no longer wait for the Council of War to finish debating whether or not the war was actually coming. Whether or not they wanted to believe it, the army of undead was coming, and coming soon. If the Southern Dales was going to have any chance of survival, then Alana needed to act. Sitting in Ravendale waiting for the army to arrive would cause the war to be lost before she had even begun to fight. She needed to find a way to bring the war to Thraal's army. They had seen evidence of necromancy in the Wilds. At the very least, it was a place to start. They would go and search for more signs of the necromancers.

There was still the matter of preventing the necromancers from figuring out how to instantly raise the troops that fell in the middle of battle. Should the necromancers figure out how to do that, then the war would be lost before it began. Alana could not allow that.

"You're right, Alana," Colwyn said in the darkness.

She looked up at him. Once she might have been surprised that he seemed to know exactly what she was thinking. But while she knew that he could not read her mind through the bond that they shared, the fact was that they had always been in tune with each other's thinking.

"We have to leave, Col," she sighed, settling her head back down on his chest.

"We will need to leave someone in charge who can rally the troops," Colwyn said. "I don't know when we'll get back to Ravendale once we leave to lead the fight against the Dark God's army."

"I think we should leave Victor in charge of the army in Ravendale," Alana said after some careful thought.

"He'll piss and moan about it," Colwyn chuckled softly. "But I agree that he is the best choice. He is someone we can trust."

"Then I think that after we meet with the King and Lord Dargan tomorrow, we should be off," Alana said. "I think we need to go back to the Wilds and find the necromancer that we saw signs of."

"It is as good a place to start as any," Colwyn said.

Having come to a decision, Alana closed her eyes and, within just a few minutes, fell into a fitful sleep.

Chapter XXVI
Tunera

When Alana woke the next morning, she felt rested for the first time in a long time. The fact that she had made her decision to go do what she needed to do to ensure the safety of the Southern Dales rather than continue wasting time in planning sessions with the Council of War had been very freeing. She knew that the King would understand even if the rest of the Council did not. Alana had to do what she felt was best if the Southern Dales were to make it through the war. In this case, that meant she would have to start actively working to ensure that she knew all she needed to do if she were going to lead the army of light.

Colwyn had, of course, agreed to her plan to go and find out what she needed to know. He had long felt that the Council of War was a waste of time. While some of the members, like his father and the King, were dedicated to the fight, other councilors did not believe the war was coming, and so they were not helpful in the Council meetings.

Alana had agreed that the Council meetings were a waste of time. She had spent time outside of the Council meetings strategizing with the King and Lord Dargan. The three of them had accomplished more in those strategy sessions than the entire Council of War had managed in three months.

But now the time had come for action. The army of Thraal was not going to sit and wait for the forces of the Southern Dales to come to them. They would attack, and the attack was coming soon. The Blademaster felt that it was best to be as prepared as possible for when that day came.

It did not matter to Alana whether the King and Lord Dargan understood her plan to leave Ravendale to seek out the army of undead. Understanding was not required. They had sworn that they would do what needed to be done to protect the Southern Dales.

This was what was required.

Alana was aware that not everyone on the Council of War would understand that she needed to excuse herself from the Council. She knew that some would think it cowardice. Others still would see it as a sign that she should not be leading the forces of the Southern Dales. And so she had sent a messenger to the King and to Lord Dargan that she wanted to meet with them. That meeting was to happen a little later in the day.

Alana thought that the King might already know why she wanted to meet. King Roland seemed to have an almost clairvoyant way about him. She never failed to be amazed that he knew something she was about to tell him before she said it. She suspected that, being King, he had a better spy network than she did and heard almost everything that happened in Ravendale and the surrounding territory.

It was a comfort to Alana that she knew that the King and Lord Dargan would understand why she had to leave. They would understand that it was because she saw this as necessary to protect the Southern Dales. The fact that they would understand that she was doing her duty was why she felt she needed their support when she explained to the Council that she was leaving and why.

She knew that they would support her no matter how much they might not feel that it was the wisest course for her to take.

It amazed her that her father in law had become one of her most trusted advisors and confidants. With the way their relationship had started so heatedly, it constantly amazed Alana that Lord Dargan was so much on her side.

With the support of the King and the First Lord of Arvendale behind her, Alana had felt like maybe she was the right person to lead the forces of the Southern Dales in this war after all.

Alana dressed carefully. She did not go to the Council of War meetings in her armor. There was something about the atmosphere of the meetings that had made her feel like her armor would not be welcome. But this day, for some reason, she felt that she needed to appear before the King as the Blademaster in all her glory.

Even though it was not proper to appear before a King armed, this meant wearing her long swords too.

"Expecting a battle today, love?" Colwyn asked when he saw her laying out her armor.

"I am always expecting a battle, Col," she said softly. "But something about today makes me nervous."

"My father and the King will both support your decision," he said as he came up behind her. "They know what is at stake."

"Still, there is trouble coming," she said, leaning back against him. "I can feel it."

"Alana, we're headed into a war," he gave her a squeeze. "There's bound to be a great deal of trouble coming."

"Not the war, Col," she said. She pulled away and turned to face him. "There is trouble coming today. At the palace. I don't know why or how I know this, but I do."

"Then in that case, perhaps I should follow your lead," Colwyn nodded.

Alana looked at him, relieved that he was taking her feelings seriously. But then, he always had. Her instincts had never led them wrong. In fact, her instincts had saved both of their lives many times over.

She watched as Colwyn went over to his wardrobe and pulled out his chain mail. He did not often wear it while in Ravendale, but with the spectre of trouble looming, it made sense to exercise caution.

They dressed in silence, each putting the mantle of their position on with their armor. There would be no question when they arrived at the palace as to who they were.

By the time that Alana had finished braiding her hair and donning her armor, Colwyn had drawn his forest garb over his armor. Alana nodded once at his choice of outfit. She knew that, when Lord Dargan saw how his son was dressed, he would understand that Colwyn was appearing in the palace solely as Alana's Protector.

It was a subtle but important distinction.

Alana buckled her sword belt on. Colwyn raised an eyebrow at that, knowing they were going to the palace, but he did not say anything. He followed suit and slung the scabbard for his big sword onto his back.

When they were ready, they slowly made their way over to the palace. Despite the fact that Alana and Colwyn were well known in Ravendale, it was not often that they were dressed in their full armor and fully armed. They drew a lot of whispered conversations behind them as they made their way to the palace. Neither of them thought anything of it, though. Alana knew that there would be a lot of whispers about the Blademaster walking around in full armor and what it might mean.

For the most part, the citizens of Ravendale had been shielded from the truth about the war that was coming. Alana knew that the time was coming where the citizens would have to be told that war was spreading through the Southern Dales. And there would likely be some panic in the streets when that happened. But that was not something she would have to worry about.

She knew that she wouldn't be there when the citizens were told.

The Blademaster intended to leave Ravendale the following day. She still wasn't quite sure where she was going to go, but she thought she might start by consulting the Legacy of the Blademasters. Maybe they would have some ideas as to what needed to be done to prepare the Southern Dales for war. It was as good a place as any to start, and a much better idea than just wandering around the Southern Dales would have been.

Alana and Colwyn swept up the steps of the palace. There were two guards standing at the entrance to the palace. When they saw that Alana and Colwyn were armed, they moved to bar their entrance.

"No blades," one of the guards grunted.

"Let me pass," Alana said quietly. "I am the Blademaster and the King is expecting me."

"Of course you may enter, Blademaster," the guard nodded. "As soon as you leave your blades with us."

"Not going to happen," Alana said. "Now get out of my way."

"No blades inside, ma'am," the guard said, not moving. "I am sorry, but I cannot let you pass."

"It's all right, guard," Dargan Starseeker said as he opened the door to the palace behind the guards. "The King has been expecting the Blademaster. He has expressly ordered that she is never to be denied entry to the palace, armed or no. We will bring her to the King now."

"But she is armed, Lord Dargan," the guard countered. "The laws of Ravendale prohibit all who are not palace guards from entering with weapons."

"A law that the Blademasters are exempt from by the King's order," Dargan reminded them. "Now let the Blademaster and her Protector through. We are to bring them to the King immediately."

"Very well," the guard nodded, stepping aside to let Alana and Colwyn pass. "Be it on your head if something happens to the King, Lord Dargan."

Alana and Colwyn followed Dargan down a corridor towards the council chambers. They walked in silence for a few moments before Dargan stopped and turned to face Alana.

"Why are you armed today, Blademaster Alana?" he asked softly.

"I woke up feeling as if trouble were coming, Lord Dargan," she said. "I felt it prudent to be armed because of that feeling."

"You were wise to be armed," Dargan heaved a deep sigh. Suddenly, he looked much older than he had. "We do not quite know what is going on, but there is a woman claiming to be a Blademaster in with the King as we speak. We knew only of three Blademasters; you, our daughter, and the halfling, Talby."

"Those are the only Blademasters that Colwyn and I know of, as well," Alana frowned. Could this be why Alana had been feeling like there was going to be trouble at the palace when she arrived. "We have not found any others."

"And yet there appears to be one in with the King now," Dargan said. "Be cautious, Blademaster Alana. We fear that she means to cause you trouble. The Southern Dales can ill afford to lose you as we head into this war."

"Thank you for the warning, Lord Dargan," she smiled at him. She checked around her neck where she had put the Bladestone earlier to make sure it was still there. Satisfied that the Bladestone was hanging about her neck, she drew herself up to her full height. "This would likely explain why I woke up with a feeling that trouble was coming. Well, let's go meet this other Blademaster."

Dargan nodded and turned back towards the council chambers, leading them once more down the hallway. Alana's right hand rested on the hilt of the sword on her right hip as she followed Dargan down the hallway. Colwyn did not comment on her readiness for a fight, but he did check that his own sword was clear in its scabbard so that if he needed to draw it, he could.

Alana steeled herself to be ready for the confrontation that was about to happen. She did not know who this new Blademaster would be, nor why she was in Ravendale, but Alana could not help but think that it meant trouble for her. It was trouble that Alana did not need at the moment, but she would deal with it.

When they got to the council chambers, Alana stopped them and motioned for them to get behind her. Dargan looked at Colwyn as if asking what he should do. Colwyn just shrugged. Dargan shrugged back and took a step backwards.

Alana took a deep breath and pushed through the doors and entered the council chambers. Colwyn and Dargan followed not too far behind her, neither wanting to miss what was about to happen.

"King Roland," Alana bowed her head in respect. "I am here for our meeting."

"I greet you, Blademaster Alana," King Roland bowed to her. "We appear to have one extra person at the meeting."

The king nodded at the woman sitting at the council table. Alana looked at the woman and raised an eyebrow in surprise.

"I know you," Alana said in a soft voice. "You are the daughter of the owner of the general store on High Street in Talondale. Tunera Ironmoon, isn't it?"

"I am Tunera Ironmoon, yes," the woman said, her voice chilly. "I am here to take command of the forces of the Southern Dales."

"I see," Alana said. She sat down on the table and pulled her legs up under her. "Yes, indeed, I see. This is interesting indeed."

"You will relinquish command of the Southern Dales forces to me," Tunera continued. "Immediately."

"Well, yes, I suppose I could do that," Alana said. She stroked her chin thoughtfully for a moment. "I suppose I could at that. But then again, I don't think I will."

"You have no choice."

"I don't?" She turned to Colwyn. "Col, go get Martin, please."

Colwyn stood rooted in place, looking between Alana and Tunera, frowning.

"What is happening, Alana?" Colwyn asked.

"Just go get Martin, please, Col," Alana said again. She turned back to face Tunera once more, her eyes locking with the other woman's. "I promise you nothing will happen until you return with him."

"All right," Colwyn nodded. "I'm going."

Colwyn could run when he needed to. And in this case, he felt that his haste was definitely warranted. He did not know who this other Blademaster was, but he had seen the Bladestone flash when they had entered the council chambers, so he had no doubt that she was who she said she was.

He did not understand why this woman thought she could wrest command of the forces of the Southern Dales from Alana, though. It was clear that the woman thought she had the right to command, but who had put it in her head that she had that right?

The Temple of the White was not far from the palace, which was good. It did not take long for Colwyn to run from the palace to the temple. He knew that Martin would be at the temple, for the young High Priest of Taelin would be nowhere else when they were not travelling. It made it easier to collect Martin when Alana asked for him.

Colwyn wasn't sure why Martin would be needed to mediate this dispute, but he did not argue. He had a feeling that there was more to the confrontation than first appeared. Somehow, he knew, Alana was going to have to either get the other Blademaster to back down or the two women would fight.

Colwyn suspected that a fight between two Blademasters would not be a pleasant thing to behold.

He hoped that Alana would keep her promise and keep her cool until he returned with the High Priest. It did not make Colwyn happy that he had been sent away to get the priest when there was a clear danger to Alana. He knew, though, that if a fight were to break out between the two Bladmasters, he would not be allowed to get between them anyway.

Much as the fight with the Nightstalker when they were in Willowdale had been for Alana alone, so too would this fight.

When he got to the Temple of the White, Colwyn stopped to catch his breath. Although it was not a long run from the palace to the Temple of the White, he chose to run full speed so that he could take as little time as possible in returning with Martin. But he did not want to enter the temple winded.

After catching his breath, Colwyn pushed through the doors of the temple, vowing to get the first person he saw in the temple to go find Martin.

As it turned out, Martin himself was the first person he ran into once inside the temple.

"Alana sent for me, Colwyn?" Martin asked, bringing Colwyn up short.

"Now, how could you have known that?" Colwyn gasped in surprise.

"I was in my meditations and Lord Taelin came to me," Martin shrugged. "He told me that you would be on your way to retrieve me momentarily because the Blademaster called for me. Something about trouble, I would wager."

"You have the right of it," Colwyn nodded, waving Martin on to follow him back out of the temple. "A Bladmaster that we don't know showed up at the palace demanding to have command of the armies of the Southern Dale ceded to her."

"Ah, yes," Martin nodded. "This would fit my definition of trouble. Let us go. Alana was right to call me. I will be needed before this day is over one way or the other."

Colwyn did not like the sound of that, but he led the High Priest to the palace anyway.

Alana and Tunera were still staring at each other when Colwyn returned with Martin. Neither had moved from where they had been when Colwyn left the council chambers. The tension was thick in the room, and it was clear that Alana was on the razor's edge of drawing her blades.

"I am here, Blademaster Alana," Martin spoke softly. "I can see that there is a problem here."

"There is no problem," Alana said softly. "Unless Tunera wishes one."

"I have no quarrel with you, Blademaster," Tunera said. "But you will cede command to me."

"No, I will not," Alana said flatly. "If the Southern Dales are to survive the war that is coming, I must be the one to lead them. I do not wish this power. It was, however, put on my shoulders and I will not walk away from my duty, nor will I pass it off to anyone else."

"And yet, you must," Tunera countered. "I was sent to take command from you."

"I highly doubt that," Martin interjected.

"This does not concern you, priest," Tunera growled. "I don't even know what you are doing here."

"That would be High Priest, young lady," Martin scolded her. He held up his hand so that she could see the ring of office that he wore. "Whether you are willing to recognize what is in front of you or not, I am the High Priest of Taelin. I speak for Lord Taelin. I have every business being here, and as you are challenging Lord Taelin's chosen, it very much concerns me."

Tunera's face flushed with embarrassment as she turned to look at Martin. Alana hoped that that embarrassment would lead to understanding in time. She did not want to have to fight Tunera. She knew, though that if the other Blademaster kept pushing the issue, a fight would be inevitable.

"I am sorry, my lord High Priest," Tunera bowed her head in respect. "I did not recognize you."

"Clearly not," Martin said. "Now. What is this about you being sent to take command of the forces of the Southern Dales? Lord Taelin has not indicated to me that he wishes Alana to be removed from her command as the Master Blademaster."

"The man that came to me to tell me I was to go to the Temple of the Blades to become a Blademaster explained to me that I needed to take command of the army if the Southern Dales were to survive," Tunera explained.

"Man?" Alana asked, her eyes narrowing at Tunera. "What man? What did he look like?"

"Well, he was tall," Tunera frowned, trying to remember. "Definitely a mage of some sort. He was wearing white robes. Short greying hair. Piercing blue eyes. I'm sorry, but I don't' remember much more than that."

Alana looked at Colwyn. She knew who it was. She knew who it was all too well.

"I'll kill him," she said softly. "This time I will kill him for sure. He's interfered one time too many. Never a help and always interfering. I'll kill him."

"Who is it?" Dargan furrowed his brow. "Who has you this worked up and angry?"

The Blademaster looked over at Dargan, surprised to see him standing there, for Alana had forgotten that the King and Lord Dargan were still there. She sighed and relaxed some, knowing, now, that there would be no battle. She had seen the way clear to keeping Tunera from challenging her, she believed.

"The sage, Isaiah Talon," Alana sighed again. "He has caused Colwyn and I a great deal of trouble. And I hold him partially responsible for the people of Valendale being taken, as he did not lift a finger to help them."

"But he sent me," Tunera protested.

"Tunera, this is not a burden you want, believe me," Alana smiled at her. "And if you read the prophecy of the Great War of Souls, you will understand that only I can lead the forces of the Southern Dales if we are to keep the Southern Dales from falling into darkness."

"Ugh, prophecy," Tunera spat with distaste. "Nothing but trouble comes from prophecy."

"Such wisdom for someone so young," King Roland laughed. "You are correct, Blademaster. Prophecy causes no end of trouble. Unfortunately, this prophecy is also set in its meaning. Blademaster Alana will lead the Southern Dales. I am sure she would welcome your help, though. I believe that there will be a great deal for all of the Bladmasters to do in this war."

"In that, you are very correct, King Roland," Alana grunted.

"Blademaster, forgive me for challenging your authority," Tunera bowed her head. "I will follow your leadership."

"Good," Alana nodded after a moment. "Wait for me outside, Tunera. I would speak with the King and Lord Dargan. And then you, Colwyn, Martin and I will have a long discussion about the war that is coming and what your part in it will be."

"Of course," Tunera nodded.

Alana watched as the other Blademaster left the council chambers. When Tunera had left, Alana hopped off the table and turned to face Martin.

"Go with her, Martin, please," Alana said softly. "Talk to her about what's coming. I think she is in over her head, but I cannot afford to turn anyone who wishes to help away."

"As you say, Blademaster Alana," Martin bowed slightly.

As Martin turned to leave the council chambers, Alana turned back to face the King and Lord Dargan.

"I intend to leave Ravendale tomorrow," she said without any further preamble. "While the Council of War is important to the defense of the Southern Dales, we are losing precious time with the bickering. Most of the council does not even believe that the war is coming. I don't think they will believe it until the army of undead is at their door."

"What do you intend to do?" the king asked.

"I intend to go gather as much information about the army of undead as I can. Maybe I can even learn how to stop any more undead from joining the army. I don't know. But I need information, and sitting here wasting time in council meetings is not going to help me prepare the Southern Dales for war."

"I understand," the King nodded. "But I would ask you to wait until after the next council meeting. Report to the council about what happened with Malachai Dragonsbane and tell them you are leaving."

"Very well," Alana nodded. "I will attend one more council meeting. But Colwyn and I will be leaving Ravendale the day after. The other Blademasters will be coming with me."

"So must it be," Lord Dargan said. "We would ask that you be careful, but you and the other Bladmasters must do as you need to in order to protect the Southern Dales."

"I will do my best to bring both your children back safely, Lord Dargan," Alana smiled at her father in law.

"That is all we ask," Dargan smiled back.

Dragonsbane

Epilogue
Warning on the Wind

"And so," Alana said, addressing the Council of War. "Malachai Dragonsbane has agreed not to hunt the Blademasters' dragons and will be willing to help defend the Southern Dales from the advance of Thraal's forces."

"Excellent," Roland Stonehammer nodded. "This is very good news, indeed."

"It is the First Lord of Arvendale you should be thanking, my liege," Alana smiled slightly. "Had he not warned me that Dragonsbane was rumored to be hunting my nathair an aeir a chosnaíonn, I would not have gone looking for him to turn to our side."

Alana looked over at Dargan Starseeker, and her father in law nodded once at her, stifling a smile. She smiled at him in thanks for all he had done. When she turned back to the King, she could see that King Roland was smiling. It was clear from that smile that he knew that the relationship between the Blademaster and her Protector's father had not started off easily. But the First Lord of Arvendale had come around to see how important the Blademaster would be to the Southern Dales and had turned into a valuable ally. Alana felt relief to have her father in law as an ally. His advice to her had already proven invaluable as she went forward in the defense of the Southern Dales. She could only hope that it would continue to prove so.

"Very good," the King nodded. "If there is nothing else?" He looked around the table. When no one spoke up, he continued. "Then I will call an end to this session of the Council of War. We will meet again this time next week to discuss the defense line at the border of the Wilds."

Alana put up her hand to stop the Council from leaving. She stood and looked at the Council, knowing that what she was about to say would not go over well with some members of the Council.

"I will not be here when the Council resumes," she said. When several members of the Council started to yell in response to her announcement, she held up her hands and continued over them. "I am not finished."

"Let her speak," King Roland said from his seat on the table. He turned back to the Blademaster. "Please continue, Blademaster Alana. I, for one, would hear what you would say."

Alana looked gratefully over at the King. Even though King Roland already knew what she was about to say, she was nonetheless grateful to have his support as she told the Council what they needed to hear.

"Thank you, King Roland," she bowed her head slightly to the King. Then she looked back up, her eyes blazing. "The time has come for my Blademasters and I to take the field. The Great War of Souls is coming fast. Many in this room choose not to believe that. I have tried my best to make this Council see the truth of what is coming. Don't try to deny it. I have eyes and I have seen the way that some of you look at each other when I speak of the army that is coming.

"But that army is, indeed, coming. And I can no longer waste time trying to convince you of that fact.

"The prophecy says that I am to be the one to lead the forces of light against this army. Some of you believe that I am not the right person for that job. I do not know if it is because I am a woman, that many of you do not really know me, or if it is just because you refuse to see that war is coming to the Southern Dales. In the end, it does not matter. I remind you that your King has committed the forces of the Southern Dales to my command. That should be enough for you.

"Some of you have believed me from the start." At this, she looked directly at Dargan Starseeker and then Marcus Whelan. "For that, I am grateful. It is to you that I give this charge. You must keep preparing the Southern Dales for war while I do what I must. I cannot tell you where I am going. But you must trust that I know what I am doing. This is what the Blademasters were created for.

"There are four of us now. We cannot be everywhere during the war. We must have the support of the rest of the Southern Dales or this war is lost before it begins.

"I leave you with this one last thing. It is not for those who are not members of the Blademaster Corps to know the Laws of the Blades, but in this, I must teach you the First Law of the Blades, for it is only by the light given by that law that we can drive away the darkness.

"You are commanded to love. Love your friends. Love your enemies. Love without reservation. Love without hesitation. Love without condition. Love without expectation of return. If you must fight, then fight with love in your heart. If you must kill, then kill with love in your heart. Never kill or fight with hate or anger in your heart. Hate leads to impotence, but love brings power. This is the law a Blademaster must live by more than any other or else she will be powerless to serve as she should. It is the First Law of the Blades because it is the most important. Live by it, or you will die.

"I want you all to think on what I have said. The Southern Dales is counting on all of you to do what is necessary in order for us all to survive."

Alana sat back down. Some of the Councilors looked at her defiantly, while others looked down at the table, having the good sense to look properly chastised. She wasn't sure if her message had really gotten through, but she did not have the luxury to keep trying to convince them.

King Roland stood up and nodded to Alana, smiling slightly. His smile told her that he understood why she could no longer wait for the Council to see the truth of her words. She hoped that he would continue trying.

"As there is nothing else, we will reconvene in one week's time," the King said quietly. "Go in peace, my friends and think on what our Blademaster has said to you."

Alana and the other members of the Council of War stood as one. They waited for the King to leave and then began filing out of the chamber. Only Dargan and Marcus looked Alana's way as they left the Council chambers. Dargan came over and clapped Alana on the shoulder. Without saying a word, the First Lord of Arvendale walked out of the Council chambers, leaving Alana alone in the room.

When she made her own way out of the Council chambers, she saw Colwyn sitting waiting for her. As he was not allowed in most of the Council of War meetings, he simply waited for Alana just outside the Council chambers to bring her home. She had assured him more than once that she was capable of walking home on her own, but she hadn't argued the point very strenuously. To be fair, she enjoyed walking home from the palace with him.

"I told the Council we were leaving," Alana said as they walked down the steps of Ravendale Palace. "They were not happy with me."

"They can deal with it," Colwyn grunted. "You have to do what you have to do if we are going to survive this war."

"I know," Alana smiled over at him. "Thank you for believing in me."

"Of course I do."

They walked along the streets of Ravendale in silence. It was a peaceful day with just a hint of a breeze, perfect for a walk.

They were halfway home when she heard it.

The dead are rising.

Alana wasn't sure where the voice had come from. She stopped, frowning. Slowly turning in place, Alana looked for the source of the voice she'd just heard, but she saw nothing.

"What is it, Alana?" Colwyn asked.

"Didn't you hear that voice?"

"No," he frowned. "I didn't hear anything."

"I must have imagined it," Alana shrugged.

They started walking again, but they had not taken more than a few steps before she heard it again.

The dead are rising.

Alana's hand automatically went to the hilt of her sword as she looked around.

"The dead are rising?" Colwyn frowned. "What does that mean?"

"You heard it this time?" Alana looked over at him.

"Yeah," he nodded. "Plain as day. Someone whispered that the dead are rising."

"But I don't see who said that," she said.

"There's no one out here," Colwyn said, looking around.

Beware the Zeraphim. The dead are rising in the Wilds.

"OK," Alana frowned. "This is getting a little creepy. Who is saying this?"

"I don't know, but I was hoping we were done dealing with the Zeraphim," Colwyn spat with distaste.

"I know," Alana looked at Colwyn. "Me too."

"I think we need to investigate this, Alana," Colwyn sighed. "If the Zeraphim are going to be trouble, we need to know."

"The tracks in the Wilds," Alana said quietly.

"The tracks?" Colwyn frowned.

"The ones that I felt like they were important?" Alana looked at him. "That's why I thought they were important. They're from the Zeraphim. We have to deal with this."

"You're right," Colwyn sighed. "We do."

"Send for Bella and Tunera, then," Alana nodded. "Have them come to the house and we will start planning how best to investigate this."

Dragonsbane

As they started walking back to their house, Alana could not help but feel uneasy about what was coming.

Appendix

Every effort has been made to keep things straight for the reader in the story, however, there are a lot of names and concepts. And so, I have provided this handy set of references for you. As the series grows, so too will this Appendix. I hope you all find this information handy.

The Appendix is divided into the following sections:

Deities
(Alignment of the Deity is in Parentheses)
(G = Good Aligned, N = Neutral Algined,
E=Evil Aligned)

Ana (*AH-nah*) (N) Goddess of History

Aram (*AH-rum*) (N) God of Balance

Ceres (*SER-ees*) (N) Goddess of Love

Chemish (*KEM-ish*) (E) God of Magic (for evil aligned magic users)

Ferrin (*FER-un*) (G) God of Magic (for good aligned magic users)

Isis (*EYE-sis*) (N) Goddess of Life

Laeyra (*lay-EHR-uh*) (N) Goddess of Luck

Raeven (*RAY-vun*) (G) God of Nature

Ranthos (*RAHN-thos*) (E) God of the Moon

Serrin (*SER-un*) (G) God of the Sun

Taelin (*TAY-lin*) (G) God of Wisdom and Justice, also known as the Lightbringer, the Lord of the Light, and the Bringer of Light

Terra (*TER-uh*) (G) Goddess of Healing

Thraal (*THRAHL*) (E) God of Chaos, often referred to as the Dark God or the Bringer of Chaos

Torval (*TOR-vul*) (N) God of Magic (for neutral aligned magic users)

Dragonsbane

Vash (*VAHSH*) (E) Goddess of the Seas

Veral (*ver-AHL*) (E) God of War

Xaria (*ZAHR-yuh*) (G) Goddess of Fertility

Zish (*ZISH*) (E) Goddess of Death

Places

The Southern Dales

The Southern Dales are the southernmost region located on the Continent of Calthea, in the world of Calthea. Home to many races championed by the gods of good and neutrality, the Southern Dales are a region governed by a king who resides in a palace in Ravendale. Nobles known as the First Lords govern each of the ten territories reporting to the king. They rule fairly, the wisdom of Taelin guiding the leader's hands.

Arvendale – A medium sized city that is deep in the heart of the Southern Dales, on the other side of the Elven Woods from Ravendale and noble seat of the Arvendale territory. Dargan Starseeker, Colwyn's father, is the First Lord of Arvendale, and, although he does not necessarily recognize the fact, Colwyn is the heir to that title.

Attendale – A city on the eastern coast of the Southern Dales and the noble seat of the Attendale territory.

Barandale – A city on the western coast of the Southern Dales and the noble seat of the Barandale territory. Home to the halflings.

Darcandale – A small city in the northwest of the Southern Dales and the noble seat of the Darcandale territory

Lovendale – A small port town on the southeast coast of the Southern Dales and the noble seat of the Lovendale territory.

Parciandale – A city in the north of the Southern Dales and the noble seat of the Parciandale territory.

Ravendale – The capitol city of the Southern Dales near the center of the Southern Dales and not too far from the Elven

Woods. The noble seat of the Ravendale territory and home of the High Priest of Taelin.

Solvendale – A small town on the southwest of the Southern Dales and noble seat of the Solvendale territory

Talondale – A small merchant city in the southern part of the Southern Dales and noble seat of the Talondale region. Alana's hometown.

Valendale – A town a week's ride south of Ravendale and the noble seat of the Valendale territory. Home to the sage Isaiah.

Willowdale – A city in the far northeast of the Southern Dales. Also known as the Twice Dead City, Willowdale was once the noble seat of the former Willowdale territory, but that area of the Southern Dales has become somewhat vacant. Willowdale is known from time to time to be home to various outlaws and cutthroats.

The Elven Woods – A dense forest to the southwest of Ravendale. Home to the Forestwalker clan of elves and the location of the Temple of the Blades.

The Temple of the Blades – The ancestral home of the Blademaster. Here, Blademasters learn what they are to become. The Test of the Blades and all Blademaster weddings happen here. In addition, the Temple of the Blades is the location of the Legacy of the Blademasters.

The Wilds

The Wilds are the lands between the Southern Dales and Dracomyr. Each town in the Wilds is its own little kingdom, governing over itself. Unlike the Southern Dales or Dracomyr, there is no central council or government for the region.

El Coran – A ruined village near the center of the Wilds.

Vikerin – A small village in the Wilds that is home to the largest temples for Taelin and Laeyra in the Wilds.

Dracomyr

Dracomyr is the northernmost part of the continent of Calthea. Dracomyr is home to the shadow creatures and the undead that Thraal loves. The capitol city is Tornith.

The Stonegate Mountains – A mountain range not too far from the Wilds that is home to several large clans of goblins.

Tornith – The capitol city of Dracomyr. The High Priest of Thraal serves in Tornith.

Outworld

Outworld refers to places that do not exist as part of the world of Calthea per se.

Limbo – Limbo is a prison where Taelin trapped the essence of the Dark God for several hundred years. It is protected by a multi-headed dragon known as Mahumet.

The Isle of Dragons – The Isle of Dragons is home to the dragons of Calthea. The Dragonic Council meets here to oversee law and order for the dragon nation. Although the Isle of Dragons does actually exist as an island on Calthea, it is considered to be part of Outworld as it is inaccessible to any but the gods and the dragons.

Dragonsbane

People

Aluthra, Idris – Mage of the Inner Circle – Illusion

Antioch, Cayden – Former Palace Guard in Arvendale, Protector to Bella Starseeker

Bothain, Albert – Proprietor of the Lucky Minotaur

Bronnen, Arwyn – A teacher at the Tower of the White

Bunten, Hubert – A brute that occasionally can be found at the Lucky Minotaur

Dalphain, Alric -- Mage of the Inner Circle – History

Dalphain, Caiaphas – High Priest of Taelin when the new Blademaster, Alana Steeldrake, is born. Dies of old age

Darkblade, Tokar -- Mage of the Inner Circle – Enchantment

Darkholme, Adouon – High Priest of Thraal after the death of Drakkhous

Dayne, Alura – Priestess of Taelin assigned to Bella

Delwyn, Merinda – Priestess of Taelin sacrificed to Thraal and beloved of Balaam Otakis

Doilin, Altas – Legate of the Goblins in the Stonegate Mountains

Dragonsbane, Malachai – A dragon hunter

Drakkhous – High Priest of Thraal. Killed by Alana Steeldrake

Eammon, Valur – Mage of the Inner Circle – Alchemy

Dragonsbane

Faollin, Martin – Priest of Taelin assigned to Alana Steeldrake's party

Fletcher, Tomas – Tunera's Protector

Greythistle, Tovar – Protector to Talby Swiftfoot

Ironmoon, Talor – Tunera's father

Ironmoon, Taryn – Tunera's mother (deceased)

Ironmoon, Tunera – A Blademaster

Jana, Deera – An acolyte of Taelin that Alana Seeldrake finds to show some promise

Janus, Wyric -- Mage of the Inner Circle – Divination

Kale, Richard – Protector of Raven Windrider

Kovalani, Mirian – Queen of the Forestwalker Elves and former lover of Colwyn Starseeker

Kovalani, Otan – Trainer of rangers for the Forestwalker Elves and brother of Mirian Kovalani

Marant, Lilliana – Priestess of Taelin that dies of the wasting sickness in the wilds and beloved of Darius Redwind

Mastairs, Naomi – High Priestess of Taelin after Balaam Otakis dies.

Otakis, Balaam – High Priest of Taelin after Caiaphas Dalphain dies. Killed by Drakkhous in Tornith while protecting Alana Steeldrake

Ravenscroft, Thurl – The first Dream Weaver

Rayden, Kera – The Nightstalker

Redwind, Darius – Priest of Taelin that becomes Drakkhous after he loses the woman he loves

Sapphire, Crystal – Last Blademaster named before the Great Purge

Starseeker, Bella – A Blademaster. Brother to Colwyn Starseeker

Starseeker, Colwyn – Protector to Alana Steeldrake and heir to the title of First Lord of the Valendale Territory

Starseeker, Dargan – First Lord of the Valendale Territory and Colwyn Starseeker's father.

Starseeker, Serina – Colwyn Starseeker's mother.

Steeldrake, Alana – First Blademaster to be named in over 300 years.

Stonehammer, Roland – King of the Southern Dales

Stonehands, William – Mage of the White that travels with Alana Steeldrake

Stoneheart, Tannen – Master Adept at the Tower of the White

Swiftfoot, Maren – Leader of the Council of Elders in Barandale. Meryn Swiftfoot's grandmother

Swiftfoot, Meryn – Halfling thief that travels with Alana Steeldrake

Swiftfoot, Talby – Halfling Blademaster. Cousin to Meryn Swiftfoot.

Talon, Isaiah – A sage

Dragonsbane

Tencis, Olianna – Priestess of Taelin in Tornith

Thames, Caliban – Mage of the Inner Circle – Necromancy

Thames, Mariska – Priestess of Thraal and beloved of Adouon Darkholme

Thistlethumb, Odway – Childhood friend of Meryn Swiftfoot, now her husband

Tram, Victor – Captain of the Palace Guard in Arvendale

Valan, Darim -- Mage of the Inner Circle – Conjuration

Vilas, Arthais – Senior Priest of Taelin in Tornith

Wade, Kassin -- Mage of the Inner Circle – Wild

Wayland, Gareth – Blacksmith in Talondale

Whelan, Marcus – Innkeeper of the White Horse Inn in Valendale.

Whistlethenn, Dramor – Elder in Barandale

White, Ash – Stable boy at the Lucky Minotaur. Brother of Gwendolyn White

White, Gwendolyn – Waitress at the Lucky Minotaur. Sister of Ash White

Windrider, Raven – The First Blademaster

Wyndham, Balor -- Mage of the Inner Circle – Evocation

Zathras – Guardian of the Vortex

Dragons

(Type is in parenthesis)
Good dragons are Gold, Silver, Bronze, Brass, and Copper
Neutral Dragons are Diamond, Ruby, Emerald, Sapphire,
and Amethyst
Evil Dragons are, Red, Green, Blue, Black, and White

Alpharin (amethyst) Member of the Dragonic Council

Alpharis (bronze) Member of the Dragonic Council

Calindilarin (undead) Undead dragon in service to Kera Rayden, destroyed during the battle in Willowdale

Centrus (brass) Member of the Dragonic Council

Cobalthaxillius (gold) Nathair an aeir a chosnaíonn to Alana Steeldrake, killed during the battle in Willowdale

Cyrus (green) Member of the Dragonic Council

Eliazar (gold) Leader of the Dragonic Council

Esmertas (emerald) Member of the Dragonic Council

Firegem (ruby) Member of the Dragonic Council

Greytonix (bronze) Nathair an aeir a chosnaíonn to Talby Swiftfoot

Mahumet (multi headed good dragon) Guardian of Limbo

Mintakis (diamond) Member of the Dragonic Council

Onyx (black) Member of the Dragonic Council

Pyrus (copper) Member of the Dragonic Council

Sephiras (sapphire) Member of the Dragonic Council

Shakaaris (red) Member of the Dragonic Council

Silvestra Knightwing (silver) Beloved of William Stonehands and nathair an aeir a chosnaíonn to Alana Steeldrake

Snowfang (white) Member of the Dragonic Council

Talonwing (silver) Member of the Dragonic Council

Timeanalia (sapphire) Nathair an aeir a chosnaíonn to Bella Starseeker

Trakkis (blue) Member of the Dragonic Council

Rick Bentsen

The Prophecy of the Great War of Souls

Tá an tuar an cogadh mór anamacha

Tar éis trí chéad bliain ar fud an domhain a thagann an Aois dorchadais. Beidh an Dia olc ar ais chun tús a conquest an domhain arís.

Sna laethanta tosaigh an Aois dorchadais, tar éis na máistrí na lanna ar ais go dtí saol na Calthea, déanfaidh an arm na marbh chun cinn i seirbhís an Dia olc. Déanfaidh an marbh ardú agus cogadh pá ar fud an aghaidh Calthea.

Nuair a thiteann an chathair faoi dhó marbh folamh ar feadh uair an tríú, beidh an scamaill stoirme a bhailiú agus beidh an claimhte fuaime i gcuid truaillí. Déanfaidh an dúchan cogaidh a bheith ar an talamh agus ní féidir ach an ceann a rugadh ar an bhfianaise an cúiseamh i gcoinne an dorchadas mar thoradh.

Ní mór don arm an solas scaoilte an draíocht na bean sidhe dul ar ais ar an dorchadas. An ceann a rugadh ar an cheo solais mar thoradh ar an oidhreacht na máistrí na lanna isteach ar an réimse an cath.

Nuair a ghlaonn an anam an bean sidhe a gabhadh amach, beidh na clocha ar an daingean ar an bhfianaise a bhriseadh agus titim ar a chéile. Beidh an bhiotáille an roghnaithe de Taelin uair níos mó a chur ar an réimse an cath i Cruinniú w i gcoinne an dorchadas.

Déanfaidh an tine an ghrian agus an ghealach dim agus céimnithe chun dorchadais. Ní mór don duine a rugadh ar an solas ag siúl amach as an scáth an tine an ghrian agus an ghealach agus an roghnaithe de Taelin mar thoradh.

Beidh an Dlí is Fiche ar an Tríú na lanna a shárú, i gcás roinnt de na roghnaithe de Taelin.

Mura ndéanfaidh an ceann a rugadh ar an bhfianaise thoradh an cúiseamh i gcoinne an arm na marbh, beidh an domhain titim isteach i dorchadas a bheidh gan deireadh. Ní féidir ach an cumhacht ag an Dlí Chéad na lanna threorú láimh an ceann a rugadh ar an solas.

Sa chath mar atá i ngach daoine eile a mbeidh an ceann a rugadh ar an solas troid, ní bheidh aon ráthaíochtaí. Ní ghlacfar ach le méid seo a leanas an eagna Taelin agus ag an ádh de Laeyra an ceann a rugadh ar an solas i réim.

Dragonsbane

Ba chóir an ceann a rugadh ar an bhfianaise a bheith rathúil i gceannas ar an fórsaí an tsolais, beidh an domhan beo go buan coibhneasta ar feadh tamaill, ach ní bheidh ach ar feadh tréimhse chun a Dhia olc a thabhairt ar a thóir suas.

Más mian leis an duine a rugadh ar an bhfianaise a Cealaigh an damáiste de bharr an anam glaoch ar an bean sidhe a gabhadh, ní mór di teacht ar an Solas de Taelin agus a chuid draíochta a úsáid chun aon uair amháin níos mó a thógáil an daingean ar an solas.

Sna blianta tar éis dheireadh an chogaidh mór anamacha ba chóir, an ceann a rugadh ar an solas i casadh ar ais ar an dorchadas ar feadh tamaill, beidh sí a leathnú trí solas huaire. Ach leis an tríú, beidh sí a hionad i measc na spioraid na roghnaithe de Taelin.

Mar sin deireadh leis an bhfocal an tuar deiridh Bahala, an fíodóir de greams. Leis an gifting an tuar, cas mé an maintlín de chumhacht an fíodóir an aisling thar a fíodóir nua agus i bhfad níos óige an aisling. Creid na focail seo, beidh ar gach a bhfuil scríofa anseo teacht chun pas a fháil.

Is féidir na focail seo lá amháin a mbealach chun an ceann a rugadh ar an solas. Beidh an té a chosnaíonn a bheith in ann aistriú na focail seo a son, cé go mbeidh a fhios ag an bhrí nach taobh thiar de na focail nuair a fhaigheann siad iad.

Scríofa ag mo lámh,
Bahala Maranal, an fíodóir an aisling
Tríocha seacht mbliana anuas an bás mór de na máistrí na lanna.

The prophecy of the Great War of Souls
After three hundred years of peace in the world comes the Age of Darkness. The Dark God will return to begin his conquest of the world once more.

In the early days of the Age of Darkness, after the Blademasters have returned to the world of Calthea, the army of the dead shall arise in service to the Dark God. The dead shall rise and wage war across the face of Calthea.

When the twice dead city falls empty for a third time, the storm clouds will gather and the sabres will rattle in their scabbards. The blight of war shall be upon the land and only the one born of the light can lead the charge against the darkness.

The army of the light must uncork the magic of the bean sidhe to turn back the darkness. The one born of the light must lead the legacy of the Blademasters onto the field of battle.

When the soul of the captured bean sidhe wails, the stones of the stronghold of the light will shatter and crumble upon one another. The spirits of the chosen of Taelin will once more take the field of battle in the war against the darkness.

The fire of the sun and the moon will dim and fade to darkness. The one born of the light must walk out from the shadow of the fire of the sun and the moon and lead the chosen of Taelin.

The Twenty Third Law of the Blades will be violated for some of the chosen of Taelin.

If the one born of the light does not lead the charge against the army of the dead, the world will fall into a darkness that will be without end. Only the power of the First Law of the Blades can guide the hand of the one born of the light.

In this battle as in all others the one born of the light will fight, there will be no guarantees. Only by following the wisdom of Taelin and by the luck of Laeyra will the one born of the light prevail.

Should the one born of the light be successful in leading the forces of the light, the world will live in relative peace for a time, but only for a time for the Dark God shall never give up his quest.

If the one born of the light wishes to undo the damage caused by the wailing soul of the captured bean sidhe, she must find the Light of Taelin and use its magic to once more build the stronghold of the light.

In the years after the end of the great war of souls, should the one born of the light in turning back the darkness for a time, she will extend the light three times. But with the third, she will take her place among the spirits of the chosen of Taelin.

So ends the words of the final prophecy of Bahala, the Dream Weaver. With the gifting of this prophecy, I turn the mantle of power of the Dream Weaver over to a new and much younger Dream Weaver. Heed these words, for all that is written here shall come to pass.

May these words one day find their way to the one born of the light. The one who protects her will be able to translate these words for her, although neither will know the meaning behind the words when they find them.

Written by my hand,
Bahala Maranal, the Dream Weaver
Thirty seven years past the Great Purge.

The Elvish Language

(Author's Note: When I first decided that the Forestwalker Elves were going to have their own language and that it would be represented in the book, I thought I was going to make a language up. Then, I realized just how difficult that really is. I wasn't going to create a language for the Forestwalker Elves, but I still wanted to have a distinct language for them. Last year I hit on the perfect solution to my problem, and I put it into action.

The language for the Forestwalker Elves is the Irish language. I am currently learning the language. Those of you folks who speak Irish fluently (And I know there are, sadly, not that many of you) will most likely see that the translations are not very accurate. That's OK. They don't have to be. They just have to be good enough. And that's what I have.

Less than two million people worldwide speak the Irish language. I do not want the language to die as it is a truly beautiful language, which is why I'm learning it. My hope is that maybe some of my readers will see that this language is a beautiful language that needs to be saved. When I have children, I hope to pass the language down to them. But, for now, all I can do to save the Irish language is to use it. As the series goes on, I am sure this Elvish Language dictionary will grow. –Rick Bentsen)

An máistir na lanna – Blademaster

An té a chosnaíonn a – Protector

Bhuel le chéile – Well met

Cíbé rud a tharlaíonn, deartháir, tá a fhios go bhfuil mé go raibh aon pháirt ann. – Whatever happens, brother, know that I have had no part in it.

Féadfaidh an ádh ar Laeyra agus an eagna Taelin leanann tú – May the luck of Laeyra and the wisdom of Taelin go with you.

feithidí – A type of insect that releases silk that is woven into clothing by the Forestwalker Elves.

Go dtí tú filleadh ar an gcathair sna crainn, mo dheartháir – Until you return to the city in the trees, my brother.

I ngach den saol, ní mór go mbeadh cothromaíocht. A chailleadh go bhfuil cothromaíocht a cuireadh chaos agus bás isteach Ní mór máistir na lanna a bheith i gcónaí ar comhardú i di féin agus ina cuid déileálacha le daoine eile. Sin é an fáth go bhfuil an dlí chéad cheann de na lanna chomh tábhachtach sin. Ní mór an grá roinneann sí lena fear céile bás caithfidh sí a chothromú déileáil ina seasamh – In all of life, there must be balance. To lose that balance is to invite chaos and death in. A Blademaster must always be in balance in herself and in her dealings with others. That is why the First Law of the Blades is so important. The love she shares with her husband must balance the death she must deal in her position.

Impigh mé de tú maithiúnas a thabhairt dom, mo dheartháir. Tá a fhios agat an grá agus meas agam duit féin agus do na mná grá agat. Ba mhaith liom rudaí a bhí difriúil ná ní mór cad a tharlóidh. Tá tú i gceannas ar feadh trialach nach raibh ach is féidir leat duine. Ní mór duit i réim. Gach ár saol ag brath air. Is é an meáchan ar an domhan ar do ghualainn. Tá eagla orm go bhféadfadh sé a bheith i bhfad ró-a iompróidh. Cuimhneamh nach bhfuil rudaí i gcónaí mar atá siad. – I beg you to forgive me, my brother. You know I love and respect you and the woman you love. I wish things were different than what must happen. You are headed for a trial that only you can face. You must prevail. All our lives depend on it. The weight of the world on your shoulders. I'm afraid it might be too much to bear. Remember that things are not always as they appear.

Is breá liom tú go mór – I love you very much

Is cuma cad a tharlaíonn sa lá atá inniu, tá a fhios go mbeidh tú féin agus an Alana Lady a bheith i gcónaí fáilte roimh chách sa chathair sna crainn, le haghaidh an banríon gheall an dílseacht na clan go siúlóidí i measc na foraoisí ar an máistir na lanna agus an ceann a chosnaíonn di. – No matter what happens today, know that you and the Lady Alana always be welcome in the city in the trees, for the queen has pledged the loyalty of the Forestwalker Clan to the Blademaster and her companions.

Is é sin é! Is é sin an réiteach! – I've got it! I figured it out!

Is maith a fheiceann tú arís, mo dheartháir. – It is good to see you again, my brother.

mo dheartháir – my brother

Mo dheartháir, le do thoil logh dom. Bhí mé ina páirtí do pian. Rinne mé rabhadh duit, ach tú a bheith gortaithe ar aon nós. Impigh mé de tú maithiúnas a thabhairt do mo mhuintir an pian go bhfuil muid ba chúis agat. Más rud é go mbeadh sé éasca do pian, a chur ar mo shaol mar íocaíocht as an méid atá déanta againn a thabhirt duit. – My brother, please forgive me for my part in the pain you have suffered. Although I did warn you, you have been hurt anyway. I beg you to forgive my family for the pain we have caused you. If it would ease your suffering, I offer my life as payment for what we have done to you.

Mo ghrá, Tá brón orm má ba chúis agam ort pian – My love, I'm sorry for the pain that I have caused you.

Múinteoir – A term of respect for a teacher of rangers in the Forestwalker Elves.

nathair an aeir a chosnaíonn – The dragon assigned to protect a Blademaster

Ní mór di a rachaidh isteach anseo chun aghaidh a thabhairt ar ndán di dul isteach le croí glan. Ní mór sí ag troid i gcomhréir leis an idéalacha Taelin agus Laeyra. Ní mór di cloí le Dlí na lanna má ghlacann sí ndán di. Teip ciallaíonn bás. – She who enters here to face her destiny must enter with a pure heart. She must fight according to the precepts of Taelin and Laeyra. She must abide by the Law of the Blades if she accepts her destiny. Failure brings death.

Scoirfidh ag gluaiseacht ina bhfuil tú. Ná teacht ar bith eile. – Stop where you are. Do not come any further.

Sí nach bhfuil grá nach bhfuil a fhios Taelin chun é Taelin ghrá. – She who does not love does not know Taelin for Taelin is love.

stát ndoimhneacht na tsíocháin inmheánach -- A technique used by elven rangers that allows them to be in a deep state of inner peace

Turas go maith duit, an ceann a chosnaíonn sí an máistir na lanna. Go dtí go mbeidh níos mó ná uair ár cosáin trasna. – Good journey to you, Protector to the Blademaster. Until next our paths shall cross.

The Laws of the Blades

The First Law of the Blades:

You are commanded to love. Love your friends. Love your enemies. Love without reservation. Love without hesitation. Love without condition. Love without expectation of return. If you must fight, then fight with love in your heart. If you must kill, then kill with love in your heart. Never kill or fight with hate or anger in your heart. Hate leads to impotence, but love brings power. This is the law a Blademaster must live by more than any other or else she will be powerless to serve as she should. It is the First Law of the Blades because it is the most important. Live by it, or you will die.

The Second Law of the Blades:

True love breeds true forgiveness. Nothing is more powerful than the ability to forgive the one you love. And nothing brings you closer than the forgiveness of your own misdeeds.

The Third Law of the Blades:

Dark and light. Good and evil. Black and white. These are two sides of the same coin. Both sides must exist or neither will.

The Fourth Law of the Blades:

Power is not given to those who seek it.

The Fourteenth Law of the Blades:

There are many things in life that arc but mere illusions. Things are not always as they appear. A Blademaster must depend on the wisdom of Taelin to understand what is real and what is an illusion. Confusion brought on by false realities can lead to a gruesome death.

Always remember to let Lord Taelin be your guide in everything you do. Remembering this will cause you to see through any illusion that is in your path.

The Fifteenth Law of the Blades:

In life as in battle, there are no guarantees. Victory and defeat teeter on the edge of a thin blade. It is belief in one's self that can make the difference between victory and defeat. A Blademaster must always believe in herself and be willing to seek the help of others in order to claim victory. This is the truth of life and battle. Live or die as you choose.

The Sixteenth Law of the Blades:

A Blademaster's mind needs to be as sharp as her body's skills and her blades.

The Eighteenth Law of the Blades:

In all of life, there must be balance. To lose that balance is to invite chaos and death in. A Blademaster must always be in balance in herself and in her dealings with others. That is why the First Law of the Blades is so important. The love she shares with her husband must balance the death she must deal in her position.

The Nineteenth Law of the Blades:

We all make mistakes. The true test of a person is their reaction to making a mistake. Only by accepting the mistake and doing one's best to make amends can a person keep on the correct path.

The Twenty First Law of the Blades:

The Blademasters only owe fealty to the balance. They serve only the Southern Dales. Their only quest is for the truth. Only in this way can they fulfill their purpose.

The Twenty Third Law of the Blades:

The war never ends. Only the battles change.

The Twenty Fourth Law of the Blades:

All actions have consequences.

The Twenty Fifth Law of the Blades:

All things must end. Nothing remains forever.

Dragonsbane

Blademasters and Protectors

Over the years of recorded history in Calthea, many women have held the title of Blademaster. Obviously, not all Blademasters have been mentioned in this series, but as Blademasters and their Protectors are mentioned, they will be listed here.

Blademasters of Old:

Raven Windrider and Richard Kale (The first Blademaster and her Protector)
Alyssa Nesbitt and Michael Westlund
Maria Davalos and Tarvan Draderis
Serina Thames and Arturin Barda
Crystal Sapphire and Markus Sharde

Blademasters of Now

Alana Steeldrake and Colwyn Starseeker
Bella Starseeker and Cayden Antioch
Talby Swiftfoot and Tovar Greythistle
Tunera Ironmoon and Tomas Fletcher

Dragonsbane

The adventures of Alana Steeldrake and her companions
will continue in

The Revenge of the Zeraphim

Coming April, 2018

The War of Souls is coming.

The dead are rising in the Wilds. But the army of undead is
not the only enemy that the Blademaster must face.

The Zeraphim were soundly defeated in Willowdale, and
they have not forgotten. Now, having retreated to their
stronghold on the boundary between the Southern Dales
and the Wilds, the Zeraphim plot their revenge on the child
of the light for her part in disrupting their plans in
Willowdale.

Now, the Blademaster and her companions must enter
Zhentaril Keep to confront the Zeraphim and defeat them
once and for all before the war begins.

But all is not as it seems with the followers of the One God.
Can the Blademaster and her companions make it through
the confrontation alive, or will the Southern Dales be left
defenseless when the army of undead arrives?

TURN THE PAGE
For a preview of **The Revenge of the Zeraphim,**
the fifth exciting book in
The Blademaster Chronicles

Prologue
Ambush

It was a beautiful spring day. It was midmorning, and the sun was shining brightly through the wispy clouds. Bella Starseeker and her Protector, Cayden Antioch, walked down a path that was not very well used. They moved swiftly considering the path was somewhat overgrown.

There had been rumors of undead incursions into the Southern Dales, and the Blademaster was following those rumors to try to find out where the undead were coming from. Alana Steeldrake had sent them into the Wilds to try to find the source of the undead.

While the undead had been trickling into the Southern Dales through the Wilds, Alana had known that they were actually coming through the Wilds all the way from Dracomyr. It was the way it had always been when Dracomyr had threatened the Southern Dales. So far, though, Bella and Cayden had not been able to find any clues to help explain the undead incursions into the

Southern Dales. Bella had never been one to give up easily, though. She knew that the undead were coming through the Wilds, and she knew that if they kept looking, they would find the information that Alana wanted.

She had struck on the idea to search a series of unused paths. The paths had been used during the ancient wars between the Southern Dales and Dracomyr. Bella had thought that these paths might be used by the forces of Dracomyr once more, so she had decided that they needed to search each and every one of them until they found what they were looking for.

Cayden had not liked the idea.

As a palace guard before becoming Bella's Protector, Cayden was not as comfortable with being out in the Wilds. He loved his Bella, though, and because she wanted to explore the paths, he went along with it.

"How long are we going to keep search these unused paths, Bella?" he asked. It was not the first time that he had asked the question.

"Until we find what it is we are looking for, Cayden," she smiled at him. She had given him the same answer every time he'd asked the question.

"Ugh," he groaned. But he kept walking.

"Don't be like that, Cayden," Bella laughed. It was a sound that he loved to hear. "I am sure that it won't be too much longer. We are bound to find something soon."

"Or something is bound to find us," he grumbled.

"Cheer up, Cayden!" Bella laughed harder. "We'll be back with the others soon enough."

They kept walking down the trail. They were in front of Nalia and the priestess Alura Dayne by a good distance. Neither had planned on getting so far ahead of their companions, but it had happened. And once they realized that they had a little bit of privacy, although not much for the others were still watching them, they decided to just go with it. There was little enough chance for privacy now that they were a part of the battle for the Southern Dales.

As they walked, Bella had a sense that they were being watched, but she could not tell where the feeling was coming from. She brushed off the feeling as simply being jittery from being away from the other Blademasters for so long.

Had she been paying more attention, she would have seen the soldiers before they surrounded her and Cayden.

And yet, she did not. Out of nowhere a ring of soldiers surrounded them.

"Keep your hands away from your blades or we will kill you where you stand," the leader of the soldiers stated.

Bella carefully moved her hands up in the air, far away from the hilts of her swords. She turned and caught Nalia's eyes and mouthed one word.

Run.

Without a word, she let herself be tied up by the soldiers and dragged off.

Nalia had no interest in talking to the priestess. They just walked in silence behind their charges. They were close enough that she could keep watch over her Blademaster, but far enough away to give the Blademaster and her Protector some privacy to talk.

But they were too far away to do anything when the soldiers surrounded Bella and Cayden. Nalia caught Bella's eye and saw the Blademaster mouth "run" to her.

"Shouldn't we help them?" the priestess asked as she started forward towards where the Blademaster was being dragged away.

"No," Nalia said softly. "Go and get the others. I will track them."

The sapphire dragon did not wait to see if the priestess followed her directions before changing into her dragon form and taking to the air.

Preview of Dragonsbane

About the Author

Rick Bentsen released his first novel in 2001. It was a simple science fiction story that was somewhat well received. Although it never sold very well, the people that read his first novel enjoyed it immensely. From that first moment, Rick was hooked.

Rick has long loved science fiction and fantasy books and movies and that love has turned into a writing passion. He has recently added a mystery/thriller series to his normal science fiction and fantasy series as projects to complete.

Rick lives in southeastern Massachusetts which he believes is the most beautiful place in the world. Fall in New England, he finds to be the most inspirational time of the year with all the colors.

Rick can be reached through his facebook page (www.facebook.com/RickBentsenAuthor).

Blauw Druk
"Mannen"

een verzameling verhalen waarin mannen hun hoofdrol spelen
in het spel dat ze het meest bezighoudt

Ets op de omslag gemaakt door: B.Kienjet
(*voorstellende het portret van de schrijver*)

ISBN 978-90-818898-2-7

Inhoudsopgave

Plaatsvervangend

Het komt de laatste tijd nogal eens voor dat, als de man en zijn vrouw samen boodschappen doen, ze na een korte tijd toch al een flink eind achter elkaar aan blijken te lopen. Hij loopt niet echt snel of heeft haast, maar zijn vrouw blijft steeds vaker een stukje achter onder het voortgaan. Dan moet hij dus even blijven wachten voordat ze weer naast hem loopt. 'Treuzelen' durft hij het weleens te noemen en soms vindt hij het ronduit vervelend. Bijvoorbeeld als hij zijn echtgenote kwijt is geraakt in de massa of ergens een opmerking over maakt in de veronderstelling dat ze binnen gehoorsafstand verkeert. Maar dan is ze daar in werkelijkheid te ver voor achterop geraakt.

Zijn grapje of vraag is erdoor opgelost in het niets. Herhalen wat hij zei als ze weer naast hem is aangekomen heeft meestal geen zin omdat het moment dan natuurlijk voorbij is. Hij heeft zijn opmerking gemaakt en die is in de tussentijd niet meer voor herhaling vatbaar. Het antwoord op een vraag doet er meestal niet meer toe omdat die òf reeds door de omstandigheden is beantwoord òf de grondslag ervoor is intussen te sterk veranderd. Er vervolgens een hele uitleg aan wagen is hem dan teveel moeite en het irriteert hem als het vaak achter elkaar voorkomt.

Op de Singel slaat hij de hoek om en gaat de straat naar hun huis in. Twee jonge meisjes gaan hem voor. Ze hebben allebei een strakke spijkerbroek met een wijd vallend shirt erboven aan en lopen op op elkaar lijkende platte schoentjes. Ze vormen zo een evenbeeld van elkaar en hij bedenkt dat ze dus wel vriendinnetjes zullen zijn. Volgens hem heten de schoentjes trouwens ballerina's, maar de man zou het zijn dochter moeten vragen of hij daar gelijk in heeft.

De dames voor hem zijn druk met elkaar in gesprek en zijn kennelijk uit een van de huizen pal om de hoek naar buiten gekomen. Hij weet niet welke precies, maar het valt 'm vooral op dat ze allebei uitbundig lopen te sloffen. Nu hij er op let ziet hij dat hun manier van voortbewegen voornamelijk lijkt op schaatsen. Ze zetten hun voeten een beetje dwars neer, alsof ze anders niet vooruit zullen komen. Daar is het momenteel echter geen weer voor. Het is godbeterehet al eind mei, of is het eigenlijk zelfs al juni?

Het kind dat links loopt heeft een blauwe fles in haar ene en twee glazen in de andere hand. In een ervan zit nog wat lichtgele vloeistof, het andere glas

7

draagt het meisje nonchalant op zijn kop tussen haar vingers. Volgens hem zijn de glazen overigens echte flûtes, maar het kunnen ook goedkope kopieën van die mooie champagneglazen zijn. Het andere meisje neemt net een slok uit degene die ze bij zich heeft. Omdat ze erbij stil is blijven staan heeft de man haar tot op een paar meter bijgehaald. Hij meent in haar een vriendinnetje van het buurmeisje dat vroeger tegenover hem en zijn vrouw in de straat gewoond heeft, te herkennen. Die is nu natuurlijk met haar ouders mee verhuisd naar het buitenland, maar hij herinnert zich dat ze weleens samen stoepbal speelden. Hij kon vanuit het raam van zijn kantoor boven, horen hoe ze al kwebbelend de bal van de ene stoep naar de rand van de stoep aan de overkant wierpen en dat ze er een soort puntentelling van bij hielden. Ze konden het heel lang volhouden en hij heeft er de indruk aan overgehouden dat ze er veel plezier bij hadden.

Hij moest uitgaan van de klanken die hij vanuit zijn raam kon waarnemen, maar die waren altijd opgewekt. Het meisje is onmiskenbaar wat ouder dan het spichtige kind van indertijd, maar ze zal nu toch hooguit zestien of zeventien jaar oud kunnen zijn. Hij probeert het snel uit te rekenen, maar kan zich niet herinneren of ze toen al in de brugklas zaten. Misschien verbleven ze nog op de lagere school, maar dan zeker in een van de hoogste klassen. Zijn buurmeisje zou naar het Gym zijn gegaan, daarvan is hij zeker. Hij kan 't zich allemaal niet meer exact herinneren.

Het andere meisje is eerst doorgelopen, maar staat nu op de stoeprand stil om haar glas opnieuw te vullen. Afgaande op de vlaggen met lege schooltassen eraan vast, ze hangen her en der aan de gevels, is de uitslag van de eindexamens binnengekomen. De man concludeert dat de twee hier voor hem waarschijnlijk hun diploma hebben gehaald en dit op deze manier aan het vieren zijn.

Ze steken over en blijven vlak voor hem uit lopen. De meisjes verkeren in hun eigen wereld en merken hem niet op. Jammer natuurlijk want hij had hen graag even naar hun resultaat gevraagd. Dan had hij ze vervolgens een compliment kunnen maken over het behalen van hun diploma. Het lijkt hem dat zoiets toch aardig op ze moet overkomen van een buurtgenoot. Al zal hij in hun ogen waarschijnlijk slechts een oude man zijn. Misschien vatten ze het op als bemoeien en kan hij het maar beter achterwege laten als de gelegenheid zich alsnog voordoet.

"Je moet me straks even met Jan Jaap alleen laten."

Het glas is weer helemaal volgeschonken en er moet heel vlug een slokje worden genomen om het schuim niet over de rand te laten lopen. Het glas dat ze bij het uiteinde van de voet vast heeft maakt er vreemde, zwaaiende bewegingen door de lucht bij. Hij vraagt zich af of dat allemaal heel blijft. Het komt natuurlijk door haar beweeglijkheid dat de drank zo sterk schuimt. Als

8

het meisje haar wijn heeft gered en het meeste schuim heeft weggezogen, is haar glas nog voor minder dan de helft gevuld. Hij schat dat het geen erg dure champagne zal zijn die ze bij zich hebben. Al meent hij op afstand in het etiket een gerespecteerd merk herkend te hebben.

"Ik verzin wel een smoesje en probeer hem dan even mee te tronen naar zijn kamer."

Het meisje dat vlak voor hem loopt antwoordt iets, maar hij kan het niet verstaan. Het doet er helemaal niet toe. Alleen al uit beleefdheid heeft hij niet echt geluisterd. De man blijft op een meter of twee achter het tweetal aan lopen. Ze moeten dezelfde kant op want hij meent te weten waar het onderwerp van hun conversatie woont. De woning van de Jan Jaap die hij kent staat ongeveer halverwege de straat. De meisjes moeten het over de zoon van die aardige vrouw hebben en volgens hem werkt ze bij het grote warenhuis in het centrum. Op welke afdeling is hem onbekend al heeft ze het hem zeker eens verteld toen ze samen een buurpraatje maakten. Een paar maanden geleden nog heeft hij haar even gesproken. Hij stond zijn auto te wassen van alle zout en aanslag van de winter. Zij liep met een kleine hond aan de lijn langs hem. Dat beestje was een logé, vertelde ze toen.

De jongen heeft hij trouwens onlangs nog gezien als vakkenvuller in de supermarkt. Hij vindt het een vrolijke knul en wilde hem jolig een compliment maken over hoe netjes de winkel er onder zijn zorgen uitzag. Maar voordat hij er de gelegenheid voor had werd er door een vrouw iets aan het joch gevraagd waardoor hij met haar mee moest lopen.

Waarschijnlijk werkt hij daar dus na schooltijd, misschien als vakantie baantje. De man is niet meer zo goed op de hoogte van het ritme nu zijn kinderen niet meer leerplichtig zijn. De naam Jan Jaap heeft hij trouwens vroeger al eens horen noemen, verder is de jongen hem nooit opgevallen. De meeste kinderen uit de buurt zijn een stuk jonger dan zijn eigen dochter dus daardoor is hij niet volledig meer op de hoogte.

Het voorste meisje is wat langzamer gaan lopen zodat het tweetal weer naast elkaar is uitgekomen. Ze draait zich wat naar haar vriendinnetje toe. "Ik wil me een keer hard door hem laten nemen."

De man aarzelt, hebben de meisjes hem echt niet opgemerkt of proberen ze hem met hun grove taal te provoceren?

Zouden ze zich schamen als ze wisten dat hij hun gesprek heeft opgevangen? De dames bellen intussen aan bij het verwachte huis. Jan Jaap doet zelf de deur open en het meisje met de fles houdt deze triomfantelijk omhoog.

"Ta da"!

De jongen maakt een stap naar buiten en laat zich het derde, nog lege glas in de hand drukken. Vlug schenkt ze het vol zodat ze een toast op elkaar kunnen uitbrengen. Alsof het limonade betreft klokken ze alle drie de drank naar bin-

9

nen, Het duurt tot de glazen helemaal leeg zijn. Ad fundum. Daarna laat de jongen hen binnen. Uitbundig zoenen ze eerst nog in de deuropening hun felicitaties. Het is inderdaad echte champagne ziet de man in het voorbijgaan.

Hij steekt in het voorbijlopen kameraadschappelijk zijn hand op naar de buurjongen. Hij hoopt dat die er een gebaar in ziet waarmee hij hem eveneens feliciteert met zijn slagen. De jongen aarzelt, herkent hem dan blijkbaar, glimlacht verlegen en sluit de voordeur. Zou hij weten wat hem te wachten staat?

De man doet een paar stappen en blijft dan staan. Zijn vrouw is weer een flink stuk achterop geraakt en komt net de hoek omgelopen. Ze zal van zijn waarnemingen dus niet zoveel hebben opgepikt. Moet hij haar er verslag van uitbrengen?

Zal hij haar vertellen over wat hij zojuist gehoord meent te hebben?

Hij kan zich eigenlijk niet voorstellen dat meisjes zo spreken. Opeens voelt hij zich ontzettend oud. Hij snapt het niet, hoe zijn de mensen toch zo ver gekomen dat er vrijwel niets meer heilig is?

Hoe komt het dat allerlei privézaken op straat lijken te liggen?

Van zijn eigen middelbare schooltijd kan hij zich niet herinneren dat meisjes zich ooit aanboden of aangeboden hadden. In ieder geval niet aan hem. Maar ook van andere jongens of klasgenoten heeft hij nooit gehoord dat hen zoiets overkomen zou zijn. Hij stelt zich voor dat ze daar onderling toch met een zekere trots over hadden gesproken. Ze zouden er minimaal stoer over hebben gedaan.

Hij kan zich nog goed herinneren hoe ze onderling klasgenoten en vooral de meisjes uit hun parallelklassen met elkaar bespraken. Maar altijd op een beleefde manier. Ze hadden het wel over hun uiterlijk en speciale kenmerken, maar het ging er nooit zo grof aan toe als hij tegenwoordig opmerkt. Zelfs niet in het geval van Karin. Al had die zulke enorme borsten dat iedereen er een uitgesproken mening over had. Daar was geen ontkomen aan tenslotte.

Weet zijn vrouw of het in deze tijd normaal is dat meisjes onderling zo over jongens spreken?

Heeft zij dat indertijd zelf ook gedaan of zoiets meegemaakt bij haar klasgenootjes?

Gedraagt hun dochter zich ook weleens zo?

Zijn vrouw is intussen bij hem aangekomen. De man kijkt naast zich en besluit het erbij te laten. Misschien kan hij dit soort vragen beter een andere keer eens ter sprake brengen. Als ze bijvoorbeeld zelf iets dergelijks, desnoods naast hem aan zijn arm, heeft kunnen waarnemen.

Op zijn woord zal ze hem vast en zeker niet geloven. Ze zal er eerder een reden in zien om hem terecht te wijzen, vertellen dat hij een oude man aan het worden is en dat hij zich dingen inbeeldt. Waarschijnlijk zal ze hem ook voor-

houden dat hij niet begrijpt dat mensen tegenwoordig anders met elkaar omgaan en dat jongelui een andere woordkeus hebben dan zijzelf vroeger onder
elkaar gebruikten.

Hij loopt voor haar uit naar het einde van de straat. Achter een van de deuren
iets verderop om de hoek wonen ze. Als hij in dit rustige tempo doorwandelt
zullen ze vrijwel gelijktijdig bij hun voordeur aankomen. Hij heeft dan voldoende tijd om die voor haar van het slot halen en zal even wachten tot zij
voor hem uit naar binnen is gegaan.

Herman

Er is een ding dat je niet over Herman kunt zeggen, namelijk dat hij dom te noemen is. Laten we eerlijk zijn, een mens maakt niet zomaar een Universitaire studie af, of behaalt zijn bul met het sparen van zegeltjes. Bijvoorbeeld van die exemplaren die je bij een pakje boter krijgt. Nou goed dan, toen Herman er studeerde heette het in Delft nog de Technische Hogeschool, kortweg de TéHa. Maar niemand zet na zo'n uitgebreide studie als hij volgde in een paar jaar tijd een goed lopend bureau op met veel opdrachten en flink wat klanten. Daar moet je tenminste toch een beetje slim voor zijn en dat is hem dus echt wel toevertrouwd. Laten we Herman alleen daarom dus al geen 'domme jongen' noemen! Toch heeft de verbintenis met Sonja ruim veertien jaar geduurd voordat hij erachter kwam dat hij zich niet helemaal gelukkig kon noemen. Helaas moeten we stellen dat hij er dus lang over heeft gedaan om te ontdekken dat zijn huwelijk hem niet paste. Dat hij er zich niet prettig bij voelde, zich erdoor geremd wist.

Even wat feiten op een rij: vlak na het eindexamen van hun middelbare school is hij met haar in het huwelijk getreden. Onmiskenbaar was Sonja het meisje dat voldeed aan de jongens dromen die hij tijdens zijn schooltijd had opgebouwd en die hij innig wilde koesteren. Hoewel het stel kinderloos gebleven is heeft hij haar altijd meer dan liefgehad. Ronduit gezegd heeft hij zijn echtgenote gedurende vele jaren op handen gedragen. Tot ruim een jaar geleden, toen hij tot de conclusie kwam dat er iets mis was met betrekking tot hun huwelijk, met de relatie zogezegd.

Feitelijk was het een gewone werkdag en hij zat te werken op z'n kantoor toen het hem opeens duidelijk werd dat hij niet anders was omdat hij afweek van zijn omgeving, maar de afwijking die hij al een tijdje bij zichzelf dacht waar te nemen werd veroorzaakt door wat zich op z'n minst als een soort handicap liet omschrijven. Opeens drong het tot hem door hoe hij binnen zijn relatie, zoals dat zo mooi heet, al een hele tijd van alles tekort was gekomen. Niet het vaderschap, een mooie auto en andere spulletjes, een fijn huis of zo nu en dan een leuke vakantie of fijne sex, hij heeft dat allemaal gedaan, meegemaakt, gehad. Als hij trouwens eens iets leek te missen, dan heeft ie in de loop der tijd geleerd er niet teveel om te geven.

Herman nam extra's die aan anderen toevielen met gemak voor lief. Als iemand in zijn omgeving iets tot zijn of haar beschikking kreeg, iets waar hij zelf niet aan toekwam of dat kennelijk niet voor hem was weggelegd, dan leerde hij het geluk van die collega of vriend, te aanvaarden. Hooguit was hij plaatsvervangend blij voor hen. Zo kon hij in het eventuele geluk dat eruit voortkwam, delen. Maar opeens werd het hem die ochtend duidelijk dat er iets onbestemds aan zijn bestaan miste. Iets dat zich niet een, twee, drie liet omschrijven of benoemen maar onmiskenbaar niet bij hem en Sonja te vinden was. Hij miste 't zogenaamde HET. Zonder 't overigens ooit bewust bezeten te hebben.

Vanaf dat ene moment wist hij plotseling wat HET betekent en om er zonder te moeten leven en hoe moeilijk 't hem viel om er niet over te kunnen beschikken. Het was hem nogal duidelijk dat je HET namelijk nergens kunt kopen, maar volgens hem zou HET wèl gewoon aanwezig moeten zijn. Helaas mis je HET namelijk pas als je weet dat HET er niet is. En het drong plotseling tot Herman door dat HET er bij hem en Sonja niet was.

Na korte tijd begon 't zich steeds duidelijker bij hem af te tekenen dat hij HET daadwerkelijk miste. Toen hij er eenmaal op begon te letten werd het hem helder dat er vooral in alle alledaagsheid vele gaten in zijn bestaan leken voor te komen. Het besef was van het ene op het ander moment ontstaan, maar naarmate de wetenschap zich in zijn gedachten nestelde stemde hem dat steeds ongeruster. Vooral omdat ie 't gemis voornamelijk aan zijn echtgenote en de relatie die hij met haar onderhield, verbond.

Na korte tijd begreep hij niet meer of en in hoeverre hij er zelf nog invloed op uit kon uitoefenen. Hij wist gewoonweg niet wat hij moest doen om HET er alsnog aan toe te voegen. Het gevoel begon meer en meer zijn ergernis te voeden en de sfeer in huis raakte daar vervolgens door verprutst. Hij richtte zich geleidelijk aan volledig op zijn werk, maar het late thuiskomen of overwerken maakte Sonja vervolgens boos omdat ze "alweer" met het eten op hem had moeten wachten. Vaak kwam hij namelijk pas thuis als haar favoriete serie op de tv al dreigde te beginnen. Zo konden ze niet gezamenlijk van de maaltijd genieten. Maar het was natuurlijk belangrijker dat zijn ongerief ternauwernood met haar te bespreken viel.

Hoewel hij altijd met grote liefde naar zijn echtgenote had opgekeken vielen hem tot zijn grote verontrusting een groeiend aantal tekortkomingen aan haar op. Ze namen zelfs buitengewone proporties aan naarmate hij er beter op begon te letten. Een paar weken later al waren het er intussen zoveel geworden dat 'uit elkaar gaan', een scheiding aan te vragen, de enig overgebleven optie leek te zijn. Vooral ook omdat Sonja slechts tegen zijn bevindingen in bleek te willen gaan.

Vanzelfsprekend had Herman er "niets van begrepen" en erover praten om tot een andere, wellicht betere of meer aanvaardbare oplossing te komen was

14

meestal onmogelijk omdat ze binnen de kortste keren als twee verhitte kemp-
hanen tegenover elkaar stonden. Misschien een teken dat ze nog iets om elkaar gaven, maar ze waren er niet aan gewend om op zo'n manier met iemand, dus ook elkaar, om te gaan. Iemand zo tegemoet te treden deed zeer.

Als Herman alleen was, in zijn auto bijvoorbeeld of op een leeg kantoor, dan
wist hij exact wat hij tegen zijn echtgenote op zou willen merken. Hij nam
zich dan voor om het zo en op een rustige manier met haar te bespreken.
Maar als hij eenmaal voldoende moed verzameld had om inderdaad de dis-
cussie aan te gaan, vervielen ze al snel in gekijf en het elkaar verwijten maken. Hoe goed hij een gesprek ook had voorbereid en zich voorgenomen had
om rustig te blijven. Hij wist dat hij zich niet moest laten verleiden tot haar
toon van spreken, maar de uitvoering van deze wijsheid bleek weerbarstig.

Herman haalde op de middelbare school redelijke cijfers. Hij kon zoals dat
dan heet 'heel aardig meekomen'. Hij was weliswaar nooit de beste van zijn
jaar, maar zijn resultaten waren altijd goed genoeg om zonder veel extra inspanning elke keer naar een volgende klas 'over te gaan'. Zijn eindexamen
heeft hij eveneens in een keer gehaald. Weliswaar was het spannend of hij
voor zijn talen een voldoende zou scoren, maar met een aantal bijlessen in de
laatste maanden van dat jaar is 't hem zonder noemenswaardige problemen
gelukt. Geen herexamen en helemaal zonder een enkele onvoldoende is hij
geslaagd voor zijn diploma. Hij werd er om geroemd in de afscheidsrede van
de rector en bleek de enige leerling te zijn die aldus dit Cum Laude resultaat
had weten te behalen.

"Het kost een paar centen, maar dan heb je ook wat" zou hij er nu ongetwijfeld over opmerken. De vraag is echter tegen wie Herman indertijd zo'n opmerking zou hebben moeten of kunnen maken. Zijn schooltijd onderscheidt
zich immers door een totaal gebrek aan maten, vrienden of kennissen. Na
schooltijd kwam er nooit eens iemand bij hem om bijvoorbeeld samen huiswerk te maken, of nog in de lagere klassen om gewoon eens een spelletje te
doen. Zelf werd hij daar trouwens ook nimmer voor uitgenodigd. Men liep
hem telkens voorbij, leek hem in al zijn kennelijke onopvallendheid niet op te
merken.

Meteen uit school ging hij dus op huis aan, er was niets dat hem bond. Nooit
eens met de klasgenoten mee voetballen of nog op de lagere school, toen er
na twee nachten vorst een laagje ijs op de sloot tegenover het schoolgebouw
lag, hier gearmd over heen en weer lopen zodat er barsten in ontstonden.
Hooguit bleef hij een keer kijken naar wat de kornuiten uitspookten, maar
daar hield zijn betrokkenheid mee op.

Herman fietste altijd alleen naar huis en kwam in zijn eentje naar school. Hij
hing niet samen met de anderen bij de poort totdat de lessen begonnen maar
bleef in de fietsenstalling rondlummelen tot de bel ging. In de pauze liep hij

een rondje door de buurt of zat nogmaals achter op een van de fietsen in de stalling te schuilen voor de regen. Hij at dan in alle rust zijn meegenomen boterhammen en dronk iets uit het flesje dat hij van thuis had meegekregen. Water geen frisdrank want dat vond hij eigenlijk helemaal niet lekker.

In de kantine hoefde hij dus evenmin te komen want op de toiletten in de gang kon hij het drinken evengoed aanvullen. Dat het hem gewoonweg te druk was in de grote zaal waar iedereen zich in de pauzes verzamelde vormde slechts een bijkomstigheid. Volgens zeggen zouden al die schreeuwende jongens en meisjes hem koppijn bezorgen en gebaseerd op deze medische reden had hij toestemming verkregen om zich er afzijdig van te houden. Zo iemand er al last van zou kunnen ondervinden, voor Herman vormde het gegeven een buitenkans en niemand bleek aanstoot te nemen aan deze afwijking.

Er waren over hem wel opmerkingen gemaakt in de lerarenvergadering. Iets in de trant van "die jongen loopt altijd alleen" of "hij heeft niet zoveel vriendjes", maar daar bleef het bij omdat hij er zoals gezegd geen last van bleek te ondervinden. In ieder geval heeft Herman er nooit zijn beklag over gedaan of de behoefte gehad er met iemand over te spreken. Hoewel er buiten het jaarlijkse gesprekje met zijn mentor, sowieso ternauwernood gesproken kan worden van enige aanspraak. Zijn ouders kwamen overigens slechts sporadisch op een ouderavond. De leraren hadden niets om over te klagen en omdat hij altijd braaf aan de lessen meedeed, viel er dus weinig te bespreken. Kortom Herman viel op in zijn onopvallendheid.

Hij had geen vertrouwelingen met wie hij zijn hartsgeheimen kon delen en de hele gang van zaken paste bij zijn rol van Einzelgänger. Dat viel op tussen de andere leerlingen, maar men liet het zo. De leiding van de school, het lerarenkorps, de rector en decaan, accepteerde het als zijn eigen, vrijwillige keuze. Tenslotte werden er op de school "mogelijkheden genoeg" geboden en daar werd "toch volop" gebruik van gemaakt. Het werd als zijn keuze gezien dat hij de afzondering zocht boven allerlei uitbundigheid en "meedoen."

Op andere sociale vlakken ging Herman trouwens evenmin op in de rest van de populatie. Hij toonde zich bijvoorbeeld nauwelijks geïnteresseerd in sport. Zodoende viel er in die richting dus evenmin uit te blinken en ontsloeg 't hem van de verplichting om op dat vlak 'ook eens ergens aan mee' te doen.

Op een gemengde middelbare school is meestal wel sprake van de een of andere vorm van actie, maar Herman wist zich telkens op de achtergrond te houden. Bij wijze van uitzondering, op aandringen van zijn moeder en voornamelijk om zijn solidariteit met haar te tonen is hij in de vierde samen met een meisje uit de klas, die overigens eveneens de eenzaamheid leek te verkiezen boven een ingewikkeld sociaal verkeer, op dansles gegaan. Daar heeft hij in levende lijve met Sonja kennis gemaakt. Op dat moment nog een meisje uit de parallelklas maar ze vormde wel een extra reden waarom hij die dansles-

16

sen wilde gaan volgen. Pas halverwege zijn eindexamenjaar liep de omgang met haar uit op wat we misschien 'verkering' mogen noemen.

Achteraf laat 't zich vaststellen dat Sonja, evenals Herman, van huis uit een nogal verlegen en terughoudend type is. Het maakte dat de manier waarop ze met elkaar omgingen niet hartstochtelijk genoemd kon worden. Pas toen ze het echt aandurfden om 'verkering' aan te gaan, liepen ze samen in de pauze hun rondje door de buurt van de school. Netjes naast elkaar, maar soms ook wat 'gewaagder' hand in hand. Na een paar weken kon er zo nu en dan een kusje af, maar openlijke en innige verliefdheid durfden ze niet aan de buitenwereld te tonen. Heel af en toe legde hij zijn arm om haar schouder, maar het leek erop dat ze dat niet eens prettig vond. Wellicht leek het haar niet gepast, vond ze dat het 'raar' stond en schaamde ze zich ervoor.

Intussen was vrijwel iedereen ervan overtuigd dat het tweetal beter genegeerd kon worden. Het was tenslotte het eindexamenjaar en men had wel iets anders aan het hoofd. Jongens en meisjes die met elkaar omgingen concentreerden zich op het maken van huiswerk en de voorbereidingen op het naderende examen. Al dan niet paarsgewijs. Het tweetal werd daarom vrijwel niet gehinderd door mensen die met hen mee wilden wandelen of er belangstelling voor toonden om eens met ze op te trekken na schooltijd of in de pauze. Een verjaardag of fuifje ging zodoende ook vaak aan ze voorbij. Uitsluitend als de klasgenoot zich een vriend of vriendin wilde tonen dan werden ze erbij gevraagd, maar van harte ging dat niet. Geheel in stijl met de tijd moeten we het een vorm van 'wederzijdse tolerantie' noemen.

Sinds de derde klas was Herman verliefd op Sonja maar zijn verlegenheid had hem nooit toegestaan dit aan zijn toekomstige bruid te bekennen. Het is er dus voornamelijk bij gebleven dat hij zuchtend haar naam in zijn agenda krabbelde.

Thuis op zijn kamertje, onder het huiswerk maken, schreef hij haar gepassioneerde zeer hartstochtelijke brieven en gedichten. Het had zijn bedoelingen zo duidelijker kunnen maken, maar helaas kon hij ze door hun expliciete inhoud niet aan haar versturen. Om dezelfde reden durfde hij ze ook niet in haar handen te duwen tijdens het langslopen tussen de lessen. Alle boeken die hij las en gelezen had, en het waren er nogal wat omdat hij er ruimschoots de tijd voor kon nemen om ze aan zijn literatuurlijst toe te voegen, boden een ruime inspiratie. Passages die hem bruikbaar leken, lieten zich herontdekken en toepassen bij zijn eigen liefdevolle ontboezemingen. Het zorgde ervoor dat hij, toen ze eenmaal in dezelfde klas zaten, met elkaar om durfden te gaan en regelmatig samen een wandelingetje gingen maken, beschikte over een voorraad materiaal waaruit hij vrijelijk kon citeren. Een gesproken woord heeft een beduidend andere impact dan een uitlating die zwart op wit neergeschre-

17

ven staat. Maar live aan haar ter berde gebracht, kon hij zijn liefde in gepaste glorie en met de juiste intonatie aan haar uiten.

Gedurende een groot deel van de vierde en ook nog tot na de grote vakantie had Sonja overigens nog verkering met een jongen uit een andere klas. Voor Herman heeft het echter nooit iets uitgemaakt. Dat die knul gezakt was en in een parallelklas terechtkwam pleitte slechts in zijn voordeel. Hij was net zoals Sonja immers zonder kleerscheuren in het examenjaar terecht gekomen en zoiets schept vanzelfsprekend een band. Allebei behoorden ze hierdoor trouwens tot de jongsten van de klas. Toen vlak voor de vakantie bleek dat haar verkering uit was geraakt, heeft hij al zijn moed verzameld en een vriendelijke kaart met kerst wensen naar haar huisadres gestuurd. Op die eenvoudige manier kon hij haar voor zich winnen zodat ze daarna 'een stel' genoemd mochten noemen.

Na schooltijd begonnen ze zich 's middags allengs vaker gezamenlijk voor te bereiden op het naderende examen. Eindelijk kwam er dus eens iemand bij hem op bezoek om huiswerk mee te maken of een belangrijke repetitie voor te bereiden. Het gebeurde niet omdat ze wilden handelen in de geest van hun klasgenoten, maar zo vonden ze elkaar natuurlijk wel. Het maakte overigens dat ze er allebei profijt van ondervonden. Hun resultaten gingen er zienderogen op vooruit. Ze merkten allebei dat hun cijfers allengs hoger werden. Inderdaad vond dat trouwen zo kort na het examen een beetje snel plaats, maar het paste feitelijk wel bij de no-nonsense houding die Herman altijd heeft gekenmerkt. Om het verhaal compleet te maken, moeten we concluderen dat Sonja evenmin een opvallende persoon wilde zijn. Als combinatie wekten ze in hun omgeving totaal geen opzien en dat wilden ze ook helemaal niet.

De omstandigheden, zoals het bij elkaar in de klas zitten, het samen huiswerk maken en de verdere manier van met elkaar omgaan, hebben gemaakt dat de twee al meteen vanaf het begin van hun relatie de indruk wekten, goed met elkaar op te kunnen schieten. Op het eerste gezicht leken ze dus een heel gelukkig stel te vormen. Leek, want zoals gezegd is Herman intussen tot de conclusie gekomen dat hij zijn leven een andere koers wil geven. Een koers waarbij Sonja wat hem betreft niet meer noodzakelijk aanwezig hoeft te zijn.

Juridisch gezien zou het wellicht verstandiger geweest zijn als ze een paar jaar eerder aan hun scheiding waren begonnen. Na de bijna veertien jaar die hun verbintenis heeft geduurd, kon Sonja bij de rechter betrekkelijk eenvoudig bedingen dat zij een alimentatie toegewezen kreeg. Ze waren weliswaar kinderloos en op Herman rustte daardoor geen directe 'zorgplicht', maar omdat zijn vrouw vrijwel de hele huwelijkse periode 'thuis' was gebleven, had ze daar volgens de rechter recht op. Hij kende haar een tijdelijke ondersteuning toe die ervoor moest gaan dienen dat zij aan een studie en 'n eventuele carrière voor zichzelf kon beginnen. De voorgestelde periode mocht tussen de twee en vier jaar duren. In principe was het geen vreemde gedachte voor zo'n jurist maar Herman had zijn vrouw nooit opgedragen om thuis de afwas te doen of een keer per week hun woning helemaal te poetsen. Het kostte hem trouwens geen moeite om te bevroeden dat de toegezegde periode geen dag korter zou duren dan wat de rechter als maximum voorgesteld had.

Gedurende hun huwelijk heeft hij Sonja regelmatig op een cursus of een interessante workshop gewezen. Daaraan kon zij naar zijn idee dan deelnemen om haar leven wat te verrijken. Hij heeft zijn echtgenote ook weleens zomaar aangespoord om 'iets buitenshuis' te ondernemen. Vrijwilligerswerk of desnoods een cursus bloemschikken of macramé. Weliswaar vond hij het gezellig als er een huiselijke sfeer in hun woning hing of dat het eten bij zijn thuiskomst op tafel kon, maar het stoorde hem dat ze het na hun eindexamen heeft gelaten bij een paar weken vormingsklas als vervolg studie. Daar heeft ze eigenlijk uitsluitend leren stofzuigen, afwassen, strijken en de was doen.

De studie aan te TéHa leverde hem veel bevrediging op en hij zou het op prijs hebben gesteld als zijn vrouw wat meer ambitie aan de dag had gelegd. Het ging hem er niet om dat ze een maaltijd niet smakelijk kon klaarmaken of dat zijn overhemden ongestreken in de kast hingen, maar ze had er haar horizon mee kunnen verbreden. Wat hem betreft had hij zich voor allerlei zaken heel goed zelf kunnen redden en het meeste deden ze in de praktijk sowieso het liefst samen. Noem het desgewenst burgerlijk, maar de omstandigheid dat ze meteen na school een gezamenlijk huishouden vormden betekende vanzelfsprekend wel dat er niet 'gepionierd' hoefde te worden. Zijn tijd als 'student' kreeg er een speciale kleur door, maar naarmate zijn studie vorderde viel hem het verschil in achtergrond soms op. Bijvoorbeeld als hij met een collega van gedachten wisselde en Sonja alleen als 'n soort stoorzender aan het gesprek leek deel te kunnen nemen. Zijn partner domweg naar bed of huis sturen ging hem te ver, maar hij wilde haar ook niet uitsluitend als serveerster of decoratie zien. Het leek hem dat ze zijn gelijke was, maar dat zag zijn omgeving helaas anders door de ronduit 'vrouwelijke opstelling' waar zij dan voor bleek te kunnen kiezen. Zijn studie was feitelijk een echte mannen aangelegenheid en dat maakte het onderscheid dan opeens opvallend.

Afgaande op de opvoeding die hij thuis genoten had, was het hem voorgekomen dat huishoudelijke taken min of meer automatisch van moeder op kind overgingen. Zowel zijn zusje als hij hadden zich thuis aan menig taakje overgegeven en ze zagen dat nooit als bezwaarlijk. Daarentegen leek Sonja voornamelijk van haar moeder opgestoken te hebben hoe ze damesbladen en romannetjes moest doornemen. Al sprak het in haar voordeel dat ze zo nu en dan een stukje daadwerkelijk gelezen leek te hebben. Daar had Herman zijn schoonmoeder namelijk nog nooit op weten te betrappen. Die hield het op bladeren en plaatjes kijken. Maar in die vaardigheid leek hem geen training noodzakelijk. Eens een - desnoods eenvoudige - bijscholing doen of bijvoorbeeld deelnemen aan 'n workshop - zoals ze toen genoemd werden - volgen, het zou de verveling die weleens van Sonja afstraalde, bestreden hebben.

Het was hem bijvoorbeeld opgevallen hoe het haar verbaasd had toen hij een keer bij het koken geen vast recept volgde. Of dat ingrediënten niet perse uit een blik of pakje hoefden te komen om eens iets speciaals klaar te maken. Dat je lekker kunt koken omdat je ergens trek in hebt en het speciale van een gerecht veroorzaakt wordt door de smaak die de afzonderlijke delen in combinatie met elkaar opleveren. Dat je zelf een smakelijke combinatie kunt maken door gewoon te proeven. Het leek een regelrechte openbaring en vervulde haar met een ontzag dat hij niet kon plaatsen. Nam ze hem in de maling of was het echt totaal nieuw voor haar?

Inderdaad experimenteerde Herman zo nu en dan eens in de keuken, maar voor Sonja bleek dat vrijwel onmogelijk. Dat had ze van huis uit niet in zich. Netjes woog ze de voorgeschreven ingrediënten af en die mochten pas aan een gerecht worden toegevoegd als het wekkertje voor het juiste moment had gerinkeld. Het smaakte dan wel goed en hij had niets op haar kookkunst aan te merken, maar het ontbreken van spontaniteit, de wil om eens iets te 'proberen' het ontbrak eraan en dat viel hem erbij op. Chili-con carne, macaroni of een andere pasta schotel ze smaakten altijd hetzelfde als de vorige keer en hij kon erop rekenen dat degene die ze voor deze keer aan het brouwen was, net zo zou smaken.

Zijn echtgenote bleek weinig begrip op te kunnen brengen voor wat haar overkwam tijdens het vieren van een verjaardag, bijvoorbeeld van een studiegenoot of collega. Ze begreep niet wat het betekende om eens deel te nemen aan een etentje in het studentenhuis van zijn vrienden. Dat er namelijk zomaar van vier verschillende soorten borden gegeten moest worden, er soms slechts één scherp mes te vinden was of maar twee soorten glazen aanwezig waren. Men was dan verplicht om in wat ze 'waterglazen' noemde, de meegebrachte wijn te serveerde. Het stuitte haar telkens zichtbaar tegen de borst, zelfs al beperkte het zich tot tussendoor even snel wat bordjes afwassen voor het toetje. Helaas kon ze haar onbegrip niet altijd voor zich houden en Herman prijsde zich dus telkens gelukkig als ze haar misprijzende opmerkingen pas op de terugweg en exclusief tegen hem maakte.

Zulke 'tekortkomingen' merkte hij vanzelfsprekend ook wel op, maar niet iedereen was voorzien van een nieuw servies en allerlei prachtig spullen toen ze het ouderlijk huis uitgingen om aan hun studie te beginnen. Dat geluk was hen, alleen al vanwege hun huwelijk natuurlijk, wèl ten deel gevallen. Maar in plaats van zich gelukkig te prijzen, koos Sonja ervoor om zich te ergeren. Het kostte Herman al veel moeite om enigszins in het studentenleven opgenomen te raken, maar de houding van zijn echtgenote belemmerde hem aanzienlijk om kontakt op te bouwen met een groep geestverwanten. Door haar houding koos hij er regelmatig voor om maar helemaal niet in te gaan op een uitnodiging. En 'ns iemand vragen voor een tegenbezoek aan hun huis stuitte meestal op zoveel verzet dat ook zoiets er nauwelijks van kwam. Het maakte dat ze op elkaar aangewezen bleven, waardoor er eigenlijk weinig verschil met hun eigenlijk nogal eenzame schooltijd bestond. Het maakte allemaal dat hun oude leventje gewoon door leek te lopen en er deden zich nauwelijks opwindende veranderingen voor. Ook niet naarmate ze ouder werden.

Het stel 'beoefende' regelmatig de liefde maar hoewel ze er hard aan werkten om Sonja zwanger te krijgen, leverde dat geen resultaat op. Het lag niet aan haar eicellen of de levendigheid van zijn zaad, maar ondanks alle inspanning met thermometers en het nauwkeurig bijhouden van statistieken op de kalender, bleek het niet mogelijk om haar langer dan 'voor een paar dagen' over tijd te krijgen. Iedere keer als de hoop toenam en ze naar alle waarschijnlijkheid een gezinnetje konden gaan vormen nam de teleurstelling toe als ze toch ongesteld werd.

De kinderwens groeide overigens aanzienlijk naarmate zijn studie vorderde. Het werd niet ingegeven door hun leeftijd, ze waren tenslotte nog jong. Maar het leek weleens of Sonja ermee wilde laten zien dat ze tegenover zijn prestatie er ook een van haarzelf kon plaatsen. Het bleef helaas voor zowel hen, de uroloog en gynaecoloog, een raadsel waarom ze maar niet zwanger raakte.

Zoals het hem past berustte Herman in de ontstane situatie. De financiële consequentie van zijn scheiding vatte hij op als een speling van het lot en hij droeg de last die het hem opleverde met geheven hoofd. Dat hij, verbitterd door de gerechtelijke uitspraak, zijn ex-vrouw niet meer wilde zien is echter begrijpelijk.

Min of meer geruisloos zijn de twee uit elkaar gegaan, gescheiden op de letterlijke manier. Herman is terug verhuisd naar zijn geboortestad en hij heeft Sonja de woning die ze al vlak na zijn afstuderen in Delft betrokken hadden, gelaten. Het was een gehuurde bovenwoning, maar met vier ruime kamers wel tamelijk groot voor een vrouw alleen. Het zou meer geschikt zijn voor hem en de praktijk die hij aan het opbouwen was, doch de keuze was gemaakt en zoals gezegd past berusting het beste bij hem. Al was het dus nieuw dat hij plotseling voor zichzelf op diende te komen en daarbij overduidelijk zijn mannetje moest gaan staan.

Pal nadat hij zijn studie had afgerond, kon Herman aan de slag bij een firma die computers en verschillende toepassingen hiervoor bouwde. Nu nauwelijks meer voorstelbaar maar nog uitermate nieuw voor die tijd. Hij vond het ontdekken van de vele mogelijkheden, heel erg aantrekkelijk en omdat de markt

21

voor die dingen nog volop in ontwikkeling was kon hij er in betrekkelijk korte tijd een carrière in opbouwen. Voornamelijk door zich steeds verder te specialiseren, het volgen van nadere studies en het opbouwen van ervaring bij het implementeren of aanpassen van de voor de tuinbouw, de branche waarop de firma zich speciaal richtte, noodzakelijke randapparatuur. De ontwikkelingen boden perspectief, maar de vraag nam in korte tijd zo sterkt toe dat het leek of er plotseling voor van alles en nog wat naar ontwikkelingen gezocht diende te worden. In betrekkelijk korte tijd overtrof de vraag in feite het aanbod.

Het werk stelde Herman in staat om zoals bij hem gewoonlijk, op de achtergrond te functioneren, maar hij kon zich met de vernieuwingen of soms slimme vondsten die hij deed, toch wel eens in de schijnwerpers plaatsen. Zij het dat zijn bescheidenheid hem remde. Op kantoor werkte hij gestaag en tamelijk stil door, maar in de buitendienst straalde hij een almaar groeiende zekerheid uit. Bij klanten bleek hij doortastend op te kunnen treden en was hij de diverse apparaten de baas. Hierdoor kon hij telkens nieuwe orders binnenhalen. Vaak omdat hij de oplossing van een vraagstuk al bedacht had voordat de klant deze had weten te formuleren. Zijn manier van omgaan met de apparatuur sprong zo in het oog dat hij er in korte tijd een reputatie mee opbouwde. Het duurde dus niet lang voor hij tot de conclusie kwam dat hij zoiets ook voor zichzelf, als zelfstandige dus, kon doen.

Vandaar zijn beslissing om er een aanvang mee te maken. Al dient hierbij te worden opgemerkt dat zijn werkgever de enorme groei van het bedrijf ook niet meer aan leek te kunnen. Het inhuren van mensen met een overeenkomstige specialisatie, bleek namelijk erg lastig. Herman ontving dus veel steun bij zijn beslissing. Het leek hen dat ze, als ze naast elkaar te werk gingen, beter konden presteren voor de klanten. Herman voor de implementatie en ontwikkeling van de apparaten en zijn op deze manier gecreëerde collega, voor de bouw ervan. Het scheiden van deze taken leek ze volop perspectief te bieden en beiden zagen ze dus uit naar de samenwerking. Het zou ze geen windeieren gaan leggen!

Op basis van deze steun, zijn achtergrond en behaalde titel, alles zo mooi anciënniteit genaamd, kostte het hem niet veel moeite om korte tijd later in Leiden een huis aan te schaffen. Niet zo groot als hij eerder samen met Sonja had bewoond, maar ruim genoeg om zich te vestigen en er zijn kantoor te verwezenlijken. Het krediet ervoor verwierf hij op zijn eerder gevestigde faam, al mogen we stellen dat banken in die tijd aan vrijwel iedereen een zowat onbeperkte hypotheek leken te willen verstrekken. Maar Herman droeg ook dit lot met overgave en bescheidenheid. Hij nam zich voor om op het nieuwe adres helemaal opnieuw te beginnen.

Zoals reeds gezegd, van huis uit schikt Herman zich eenvoudig, al is hij terughoudend voor grote veranderingen. Zeker als die ingrijpend dreigen te worden en een inbreuk vormen op de dagelijkse gang van zaken. Deze keer durfde hij echter de koe bij de horens te vatten en begon al zijn energie te steken in het nieuwe dat hij tegenkwam op de ingeslagen weg. Zijn besef dat hij niet langer zonder HET en zijn vrouw wilde leven, maakte dat hij vernieuwingen eerder als een uitdaging accepteerde dan ze als een bedreiging zag. Deze opvatting vormde natuurlijk een enorme breuk met vroeger, maar de verhuizing naar zijn nieuwe omgeving stond het een en ander toe. Hij ondervond er inspiratie, nieuwe kracht door. Herman durfde daarom vol overtuiging de confrontatie aan te gaan.

Hij ontwierp drukwerk voor zijn nieuwe zaak, kocht – toen natuurlijk nog heel modern – 'n computer voor de administratie, kleedde zijn huis mooi aan en zette alle zaken op een nieuwe leest op. Vormgeven bijvoorbeeld bleek een gave waarvan hij nooit eerder gebruikt had gemaakt en hij richtte met gevoel voor stijl en elegantie zijn kantoor in. Zo kreeg de kamer waarin hij zijn nieuwe klanten te woord wilde gaan staan een heel moderne, open uitstraling. De benodigde 'vijftiger jaren' meubels tikte hij op de kop door er in speciaalzaken naar op zoek te gaan en zo nu en dan kocht hij ze op veilingen, die hij tijdens tripjes in de buitendienst bezocht.

Aldus kostte het hem de nodige tijd voordat hij het een en ander volledig naar zijn zin voor elkaar had, maar wat gereed was zag er daarna tiptop uit. Herman kon met de resultaten voor de dag komen en hoewel hij nog niet alles meteen perfect van de grond kreeg, liepen de nieuwe klanten bij hem binnen. Bij oude leek het of ze er trots op waren om voortaan bij hem hun diensten af te nemen. Hij merkte dat zijn grondige manier van de dingen aanpakken, betrouwbaarheid uitstraalde. Al doende durfde hij niet uitsluitend zakelijk, maar ook op het persoonlijke vlak meer en meer van zichzelf te laten zien. Voorzichtig durfde hij incidenteel zijn kwetsbaarheid te tonen. Daar was zijn voormalige werkgever danig van onder de indruk en het lukte Herman zodoende om in korte tijd en van de grond af aan, iets degelijks op te bouwen!

Op het persoonlijke vlak leek Herman zich gaandeweg minder geremd te voelen. Zo op het oog had hij een zekere vervulling gevonden in de werkzaamheden rond zijn huis en de zaak. De manier waarop hij er zich volledig aan kon weiden om aan de uitvoering van de veranderingen en aanpassingen die hij wilde uitvoeren, een eigen vorm te geven het was opvallend. Ze leken terug te voeren op het idee dat hij niet meer voor van alles en nog wat eerst overleg moest plegen met Sonja. Of dat hij zoiets dus juist wilde. Hij kreeg vanzelfsprekend niet meer de kritiek en opmerkingen die zij vroeger automatisch tegen hem maakte. Haar intentie was altijd opbouwend en misschien bedoeld als ondersteuning, maar hij hoefde zich niet meer bij haar te verantwoorden. Dat was wennen, want zij stond altijd met haar mening klaar. Zo waren ze immers met elkaar getrouwd.

23

Herman leek op te leven uit de van hem bekende berusting. Natuurlijk leverde het vele werk dat hij bij de uitvoer van zijn plannen moest leveren een hoop inspanningen op, maar hij kon zich er daarnaast ook ontspannen bij voelen als het een en ander leek te lukken. Het kwam er op neer dat hij minder door de omstandigheden belemmerd werd, zich meer durfde te uiten, dat de beklemming van hem af begon te vallen. In zijn nieuwe omgeving liet hij zich bijvoorbeeld vaker zien dan hij eerder in Delft en onder de hoede van zijn echtgenote, ooit had aangedurfd.

Zo werd hij na het verbouwingswerk regelmatig op het terrasje bij hem om de hoek en later op de avond wel eens in het eetcafé verderop in de straat aangetroffen. Dit was dan weliswaar te wijten aan de keuken die in de woning nog grotendeels uit elkaar lag, bijvoorbeeld door de uitgestelde levering van zijn bestelde eethoek of de nog niet helemaal droge verf van de stoelen, maar het leek erop of Herman langzamerhand naar buiten durfde te komen. Vanzelfsprekend kon er hierdoor niet gekookt worden, er was geen plaats om een bordje neer te kunnen zetten of het ontbrak aan een plek om even rustig te gaan zitten, maar met je kont op een kratje plaats nemen en dan van je schoot je bord leeg lepelen is alleen voor een enkele keer wel aardig. Een mens wil zo nu en dan voor zijn maaltijd toch liever plaats nemen op een echte stoel die aan een echte tafel staat met een echt bord er op. Kamperen moet om het leuk te houden zoveel mogelijk tot de vakantie beperkt blijven en daar komt bij dat de benaming natuurlijk niet voor niets zo verdacht veel lijkt op 'creperen'.

Toen hij pas zijn intrek in het huisje had genomen en er dus nog volop in het woongedeelte aan het werk was, lag daar vaak zoveel rommel van de verbouwingen dat zelfs een biertje drinken er niet plaats kon vinden. Vanzelfsprekend had hij het op de rand van zijn bed kunnen doen. Of staand tussen de stapels materiaal en het gereedschap in de rommelige kamer. Eventueel moest hij er dan eerst een opruim beurt aan wagen om de mogelijkheid alsnog te creëren, maar vaak had hij daar geen zin in. Een paar dagen later zou hij toch weer verder gaan met de werkzaamheden. Een klusje is toch het gemakkelijkst uit te voeren als je al het materiaal om je heen hebt liggen, dan hoef je er niet naar te zoeken of het eerst klaar te zetten. Het maakt de moeite van het opruimen overbodig en er kan beter mee gewacht worden tot de uitvoering van het werk helemaal gereed is. Pas na de finale van een uitgebreide klus is schoonmaken aantrekkelijk. Dan spreekt het resultaat immers pas helemaal voor zich en is het gedane werk in alle glorie te bewonderen.

Zijn slaapkamer boven op de eerste verdieping en, hoewel nog niet zo grondig aangepakt als de rest ook de badkamer ernaast, waren gelijk vanaf de verhuizing naar Leiden bruikbaar. Niet meer dan dat want hij had in de korte tijd die hem ervoor ter beschikking stond, het huis uitsluitend 'bewoonbaar' kunnen maken. In dit geval dus een kamer om te slapen, plek waar hij iets te eten kon maken, tevens opeten en tenslotte een ruimte om te douchen. Maar hoe elementair danook, het maakte dat hij zijn werk gewoon kon blijven uitvoeren. Hij kon zich netjes maken, zag er niet continu uit als een bouwvakker of had alleen maar vieze kleren aan.

Eerst bleef Herman nog een poosje part-time in Delft bij zijn oorspronkelijke baas aan de slag, maar dat was omdat hij zich ernaast nog volop bezig moest houden met de opbouw van zijn eigen zaak. De beslommeringen die dit opleverde hadden gemaakt dat hij juist daarvoor zijn oude baan nog een poosje moest aanhouden. En het sprak vanzelfsprekend een aanzienlijk woordje mee dat de inkomsten die hij met zijn ZZP functie genereerde, niet meteen voldoende waren om aan alle verplichtingen te kunnen voldoen. Herman wilde zich zoveel mogelijk tijd gunnen om de 'eigen zaak' zo rustig en gedegen mogelijk op te bouwen. Dit werd overigens door de ondersteuning aan zijn ex noodzakelijk gemaakt. De overgang van de oude naar nieuwe omstandigheden werd er minder abrupt door. De in de loop der tijd gegroeide band met Delft raakte zo niet van het ene op het ander moment verbroken.

Beland in het café een stukje verderop bij hem in de straat, bleef Herman daar zoals te verwachten niet stilletjes in een hoekje zitten. In tegenstelling tot bijvoorbeeld zijn schooltijd maar vooral ook de periode waarin hij aan de TH studeerde, vormde hij er regelmatig het middelpunt van de belangstelling. In korte tijd werd duidelijk dat hij er erg goed en grappig anekdotes over zijn studententijd of werk kon vertellen. Hoezeer het wereldje voor zijn toehoorders weleens een wat vreemde voorstelling opleverde. Ze bleken niet bekend met het leven in een studentenhuis, rondlopen op een technische faculteit of het afleggen van bezoeken aan tuinders. In het Westland moest Herman regelmatig improviseren, maar het ging hem zoals gezegd heel goed af. Vaak werd hij door zijn nieuwe vrienden gevraagd om bij hen aan te schuiven. Een enkele keer leek het er zelfs op dat de gezelligheid pas goed begon nadat hij de gelagzaal binnen was komen lopen.

Een opvallende kwestie in deze nieuwe omstandigheid was dat Herman, ondanks dat hij altijd vol had gehouden een uitgesproken afkeer van kaarten te hebben, blijkbaar gegrepen door het samenspel aangetroffen kon worden aan het speciaal voor het pokeren gereserveerde tafeltje bij het raam.

Alles bij elkaar opgeteld kan gesteld worden dat Herman langzamerhand in de groep mannen opgenomen werd. Het kwam niet omdat hij daarmee gespannen een gemis uit zijn jeugd wilde compenseren, maar het bleek hem zomaar aan te komen waaien. Hij functioneerde steeds beter in de nieuwe situatie en bleek zich er ook steeds beter bij aan te kunnen passen.

Gedurende de eerste weken na de overdracht van het huis, de afwikkeling bij de notaris en een periode waarin hij zich nog voornamelijk bezig moest houden met het voorbereiden van het opknap werk aan het woongedeelte of zijn werkruimte, had hij zich beleefdheidshalve aan een aantal buren voorgesteld. Eerlijkheidshalve moeten we hierbij begrijpen dat hij zich toen nog voornamelijk toelegde op het weghalen van wat hem in het huisje in de weg leek te staan, wat hem er teveel was.

Het vele stof dat hij bij zijn sloopwerkzaamheden veroorzaakte maakte dat ie er regelmatig voor naar buiten, de straat op vluchtte. Op de stoep bleef hij dan een tijdje wachten tot de stofwolken enigszins waren opgetrokken of dat het ergste ervan was neergedwarreld. Overigens voornamelijk op de auto's die er vlak voor zijn huis, tot hooguit twee deuren links of recht verderop, geparkeerd stonden. Omdat veel buren door het warme weer ook op straat te vinden waren, vond hij er gemakkelijk aanspraak. Regelmatig werd hem al bij de eerste kennismaking aangeboden dat men hem 'best een keer' wilde komen helpen. Men leek graag bij te willen springen bij het vele werk en er werd hem regelmatig een aanbod gedaan, bijvoorbeeld om eens te komen schilderen. Maar ook voor loodgieten en zo nu en dan een timmer- of metselklusje wilde men zijn hand niet omdraaien. Voor zowat iedere kleinigheid bleken zijn buren, zowel de mannen als hun vrouwen, klaar te staan. In de praktijk leken ze zelfs bereid om hem, als de werkzaamheden dat noodzakelijk mochten maken, avonden lang, een heel weekend behulpzaam te zijn.

Iedereen stond voor hem klaar bij het verrichten van de vele werkjes die zich in de loop van de verbouwing en het aanpassen van zijn woning annex kantoor voordeden. "Zorg maar dat er voldoende bier in huis is, dan help ik je wel even", was de opmerking die hij telkens te horen kreeg bij weer zo'n nieuw aanbod. Dat was niet tegen dovemansoren gericht en eigenlijk lustte Herman er zelf ook wel een op zijn tijd. Dat zat dus wel snor, want ook als er een avondje niet zoveel te doen bleek was men welkom. De mannen voorzagen elkaar van advies, maakten met elkaar grapjes over de vorderingen en het werk dat er al verricht was of nog in het verschiet lag.

Omdat hij dit allemaal in zijn oude, oorspronkelijke leven niet gewoon was, voelde Herman zich weleens bezwaard. Vooral als bleek dat de aanpassingen die hij aan zijn huis wilde maken, meer tijd en inspanning kostten dan het zich oorspronkelijk had laten aanzien. Diverse keren kwam het voor dat een klein ideetje dat hij had willen uitvoeren, uitdraaide op aanzienlijk meer werk dan waarin hij eerste instantie had voorzien. Hij had zich dan bijvoorbeeld voorgesteld dat het doorslaan van een niet dragende muur een beter zicht op de keuken toeliet. Maar op aanwijzing van zijn vrienden liep het werk uit op veel meer dan beraamd. Er behoefde dan, niet alleen een nette afwerking gemaakt te worden, zo een waarbij hij alle hulp al nodig had. Maar er bleek dan vooral veel tijd in de voorbereidende werkzaamheden en de definitieve afwerking te gaan zitten. Dat kon hij meestal niet alleen af en tot zijn grote verbazing deed het er niet toe. Zijn nieuwe vrienden hadden elkaar allemaal naar beste kunnen en kennen geholpen tijdens het opknappen van hun eigen woning. Daarom waren ze het onderling niet anders gewend dan voor elkaar klaar te staan. Door dik en dun zoals Herman intussen zelf mocht opmerken!

In Delft waren Herman en Sonja in het laatste jaar voor zijn afstuderen eveneens naar een wijk met zogenaamde arbeiderswoningen verhuisd. Ze hadden er dus net zoals Herman nu in Leiden, te maken gekregen met mensen die hun huis in orde aan het maken waren om er zo riant mogelijk in te kunnen gaan wonen. Aanpassingen waren daardoor ook daar noodzakelijk maar bij de uitvoering ervan was hun hulp nooit echt nodig geweest. Veelal betrof het oud medestudenten en hierdoor hadden ze toch op een bepaalde vorm van aanspraak, van solidariteit moeten kunnen rekenen. Die is echter grotendeels aan ze voorbij gegaan.

De saamhorigheid rond de TéHa was beduidend anders geregeld dan in zijn nieuwe situatie een meer Alpha georiënteerde omgeving tenslotte. In Delft was hij indertijd hooguit gevraagd voor wat incidentele hulp bij het sjouwen tijdens een verhuizing, een deur verven omdat die veel teveel was afgebladderd of zo nu en dan een uurtje assistentie bij behangen en ophangen van een plank of kastje. Het was bijvoorbeeld handig als een medestudent kon beschikken over een boormachine of de noodzakelijke handigheid had om iets tot een goed eind te brengen, maar zo niet dan was er altijd wel een ander te vinden die daarbij beter bruikbaar was. Even goede vrienden.

Alle muren en plafonds afwerken, vrijwel al het kleine timmerwerk en schilderen het was in de woningen waarin Herman en Sonja terecht kwamen, telkens door haar vader uitgevoerd. Voornamelijk omdat hij dat "nou eenmaal een leuk werkje" vond. Als ambtenaar was hij vanwege zijn 'dienstjaren' op dat moment al enige tijd gepensioneerd. Al moet ook hierbij de alom om zich heen grijpende invoer van de automatisering een woordje mee hebben gesproken. De man zat in ieder geval verlegen om bezigheden en indertijd was ook hun nieuwe huis weer volledig door hem opgeknapt.

Ervoor heen en weer reizen tussen Oegstgeest en Delft scheen hij eveneens graag te doen, want hoewel Sonja en Herman hem indertijd voor al het werk hadden willen en kunnen betalen, moesten ze accepteren dat hij uitsluitend de afgelegde kilometers vergoed kreeg als hij incidenteel een keer met de auto kwam. Tegen een van tevoren afgesproken prijs, dus niet een volle tank benzine! Het stel had overigens al waargenomen hoe haar ouders elkaar steeds meer leken te irriteren. Ze begrepen dat zijn aanbod dus beter aanvaard kon worden en hoewel uitermate opportunistisch, hielden ze zodoende de weg naar de lieve vrede binnen de familie open.

In Leiden zagen alle huisjes rondom dat van Herman er keurig opgeknapt uit. Daardoor zou op korte termijn het leveren van een wederdienst waarschijnlijk

27

niet op handen zijn, maar hij kon erop rekenen dat die ooit aan hem gevraagd zou gaan worden. Het leek hem dus te voorzien dat hij met zijn beperkte ervaring dan flink tekort ging schieten in verhouding tot de hulp die hem op dat moment belangeloos werd geboden. Al zou hij met de kennis op zijn eigen vakgebied natuurlijk ook in een zekere vraag kunnen voorzien. Iedereen heeft tenslotte zijn eigen specialisatie en daar kwam bij dat Herman al doende het nodige opstak van zijn handige buren. Het was hem weliswaar niet duidelijk hoe het een het andere aanvulde of kon compenseren, maar hij durfde het onbezwaard zo te laten omdat niemand er aanstoot aan leek te nemen.

Hoe blasé dit in feite was, kwam hem wel als bezwaarlijk voor, maar er bleef hem geen andere keuze. Men keek gewoonweg niet te ver vooruit en hijzelf kon zich vinden in 'kwam tijd, kwam raad'. Telkens als hij het vraagstuk aan de orde stelde werd hem op het hart gedrukt zich "nergens zorgen over te maken." Met een eenvoudig "doe toch gewoon, we willen het graag voor je doen" liet hij zich vervolgens afschepen.

Hij kon al de aangeboden hulp overigens niet afslaan omdat hij de vakkennis om het werk alleen tot een goed einde te brengen, eenvoudigweg niet in huis had. Daarnaast miste hij de financiën om voor iedere speciale wens die bij hem opkwam, de vereiste vakkennis in te kopen bij een professional. Hij vond de samenwerking trouwens veel gezelliger dan alleen verder te moeten tobben. De mannen vormden op die manier gezamenlijk een team. Weliswaar trokken ze in steeds wisselende samenstellingen met elkaar op, maar Herman liet zich daar telkens met het grootste plezier bij betrekken.

Vanaf halverwege het vierde, voorlaatste jaar van de middelbare school stond het voor Herman vast dat hij naar Delft wilde om er te studeren. Hij wist nog niet welke richting hij exact op wilde, maar de plaats waar hij ging 'studeren' stond vast en dat was een aardig begin. In eerste instantie ging zijn voorkeur ernaar uit om er architect te worden. De opleiding zou aansluiten bij zijn belangstelling voor wiskunde en hij voorzag dat hij er zijn creativiteit erin zou kunnen uitleven. Dat een kennis van zijn ouders hem verteld had dat er goed belegde boterham mee te verdienen was, sprak ook een woordje mee.

Een poosje later zou hij iets met ruimtevaart en vliegtuigen gaan doen. Niet zelf aan de knoppen of daadwerkelijk mee gaan de ruimte in, maar vanuit zijn belangstelling voor de techniek wilde hij zich laten betrekken bij de bouw of zelfs het ontwerpen van satellieten en zulke vaartuigen. Een ruimtestation zoals er intussen boven onze hoofden zweeft dus. Al was daar in die tijd alleen in zogenaamde Science Fiction verhalen weleens sprake van.

Allengs tekende zich af dat een praktisch vak als natuurkunde en dan in het bijzonder de richting waarbij elektronica en elektronische apparatuur een rol spelen, hem waarschijnlijk het beste zou liggen. Nog op school werd er door sommige leraren weleens gesproken over "computers" en aan het speculeren over wat daar allemaal mee mogelijk gemaakt zou worden. Herman kon hier aan meedoen omdat hij er altijd zoveel mogelijk over las. Heel regelmatig kocht hij Engelse, Amerikaanse of Duitse tijdschriften die hem op de hoogte hielden. En als er eens eentje was kocht hij een Nederlandse uitgave.

Van hun woonplaats Leiden was Delft maar een kleine stap. Op en neer met de trein zou dus niet de allergrootste opgave opleveren, maar tot ieders verbazing kwam er, nota bene pal voordat de examenperiode aanbrak, via een tante van Sonja een verdieping beschikbaar. De ruimte lag niet eens erg ver van de binnenstad van Delft. Het vormde een uiterst gelukkige bijkomstigheid en dat bood vanzelfsprekend aanlokkelijke perspectieven!

Kamernood is een vervelend gegeven in alle steden met studenten. Dat gaat evenzo op voor de plaats waar de TH gevestigd en hun eigen woonplaats, die je net zomin een wereldstad kan noemen. Zowat alle klasgenoten van Herman en Sonja besteedden al ver voor hun eindexamen, al vanaf het moment waarop ze wisten waar ze hun studie zouden gaan volgen, veel tijd aan het doorspitten van advertenties. De opperste belangstelling ging uit naar berichtjes waarin kamers, een appartement of verdieping werden aangeboden. Een enkeling toog regelmatig naar de universiteitsstad van zijn of haar voorkeur om er in de supermarkten of een kantine van de grootste bedrijven een annonce op te hangen waarin ze om een plek voor een bed en tafeltje om aan te studeren bedelden. Voor Herman was zoiets gelukkig niet meer nodig!

De noodzaak om desnoods een heel andere studie te kiezen of uit te moeten wijken naar een andere Universiteit of Hogeschool kwam bij hem niet aan de orde. Allemaal door het eenvoudige aanbod van de tante van zijn vriendin!

Sonja had zich nooit uitgesproken over wat ze na haar examen wilde gaan doen. Ze had nooit verteld waarnaar haar plannen uitgingen of in welke richting haar verwachtingen zich leken te ontwikkelen. Ze greep dus met beide handen de mogelijkheid aan om zich minimaal een jaar te onderwerpen aan huiselijke zaken in Delft. Zij nam het zich voor om haarzelf toe te leggen op de inrichting van de woning en voeren van de huishouding. Er drukte namelijk een uitdrukkelijke voorwaarde op de verdieping. De woonruimte zou uitsluitend bewoond mogen worden door een getrouwd stel. Of de leeftijden van het samenwonende paar bij elkaar opgeteld moest hoger zijn dan 55 jaar. Daarvan moesten ze dan ook nog meer dan drie jaar onafgebroken en zelfs officieel 'samen gewoond' hebben.

Hun ouders wilden allebei wel voor het laatste een valse getuigenis afleggen voor bij hen op zolder. Maar alleen al qua leeftijd schoot het tweetal een flink aantal jaren tekort om aan de gestelde criteria te voldoen. Uiteindelijk was Herman slechts een halfjaar ouder dan Sonja en beiden moesten ze op het moment van slagen hun 19e verjaardag nog vieren. Noem het ongunstig geboren zijn of de druk van de babyboomers, maar helaas lagen de zaken niet anders dan dat ze dus 'moesten' trouwen wilden ze daadwerkelijk in aanmerking komen voor de onontbeerlijke woonvergunning. Alleen dus om er zich te mogen vestigen als ze dat wilden.

In verband hiermee besloten ze om tegelijk met het fuifje ter ere van het behalen van het eindexamen, een verlovingsfeest te geven. Het zou extra belangstelling opleveren bij hun kennissen. Het bespaarde trouwens aanzienlijk op de kosten van twee afzonderlijke festiviteiten en later nog een voor Herman z'n verjaardag. De eventuele cadeaus zouden daarbij een goede start opleveren voor als ze zich in Delft gingen vestigen. Zowel Sonja als Herman hadden namelijk nog nooit aan het sparen voor een uitzet gedacht en eraan toegekomen waren ze ook niet omdat ze er als scholier nog helemaal nooit aan hadden gedacht. Om heel eerlijk te zijn hadden ze 't altijd als erg 'burgerlijk' afgedaan als een oom, tante, of bijvoorbeeld oma erover begon.

Overigens was het mogelijk om een heel jaar lang in zogenaamde ondertrouw te blijven. Ook in die toestand mocht men zich alvast in de woonruimte vestigen. Het minimale vereiste was weliswaar dat er binnen dat jaar een huwelijksdatum moest worden vastgelegd, maar die mocht ook pas na die 12 maanden vallen, als de dag maar werd besproken. Het bood ze de tijd om zich op hun gemak in het huis van tante te vestigen, verschafte ze de mogelijkheid om de daadwerkelijke feestelijkheden rond hun huwelijk grondig voor te bereiden en in stijl te organiseren. Rond kerstmis leek ze trouwens een aardig uitgangspunt, vooral omdat Sonja een 'winter bruidje' wilde zijn. Het liefst wilde ze in het wit trouwen en vanzelfsprekend moest er dan in overvloed sneeuw neerdwarrelen.

Bij haar ouders thuis ontvingen ze een aantal klasgenoten en drie leraren voor het feest rond de verloving en net zoals bij de andere klasgenoten, het slagen voor hun eindexamen. Met dit gezelschap als getuige beloofden de twee elkaar plechtig hun toekomstige trouw en wisselden vervolgens een speciaal ervoor gemaakte set ringen uit. Zilveren, want Herman heeft een vreselijke hekel aan goud, "het is veel harder en dus duurzamer." Onder het genot van de aangeboden drankjes en voorzien van een bijpassend hapje, werden ook de gasten het erover eens dat de ringen prachtig waren. Unaniem werd besloten dat de edelsmid, die ze toch maar speciaal voor hen had gemaakt, er erg zijn best op had gedaan. De man had weliswaar in opdracht gehandeld van Sonja's ouders, het was uiteindelijk een voormalige collega van haar vader, maar hij had de speciale wensen van het tweetal uitstekend in zijn ontwerp weten te verwerken. De inscriptie vermeldde in ieder geval alvast de datum van hun verloving en die van dat huwelijk kon er nog gemakkelijk bij.

Na deze receptie zijn ze met haar ouders, zijn moeder, Sonja's oudere broer en de zusjes van Herman uit eten gegaan in een restaurant in de stad. Het feest kreeg zo een mooi slot en bij het toetje, toen de vader van Sonja een gepast toespraakje hield, een plechtige en serieuze bekroning.

Twee dagen later, op zaterdagochtend rond een uur op tien, zijn ze voor een gezamenlijke vakantie naar Brabant vertrokken. Allebei op hun fiets en met de bagage stevig achterop de bagagedragers vastgebonden. De afspraak was 'slapen in een jeugdherberg' en 'ongeveer zestig tot hooguit zeventig kilometer per dag'. Op dinsdag, ze namen in verband met het warme weer een dagje rust op het strand bij de IJzeren Man van Vught, heeft hij Sonja voor het eerst bloot gezien. Sowieso voor het eerst in zijn leven kreeg Herman een bloot meisje onder ogen. Eerder had hij er nooit belangstelling voor gehad en was er, behoudens eens een zusje dat over de overloop naar de douche snelde, geen aanbod geweest. Dat wil zeggen buiten de foto's die hij in de klas wel-eens langs had zien komen als oververhitte klasgenoten een porno blaadje uit-wisselden. Maar die afbeeldingen tellen niet omdat die bijgetekend schenen te worden en daardoor niet natuurlijk, niet eerlijk waren. Wat er op te zien was werd niet natuurlijk gevonden en scheen daarnaast zo buitenproportioneel te zijn dat men zoiets thuis niet aan zou kunnen treffen. Het was vanzelfspre-kend niet voor niets dat er een taboe op zulke tijdschriften rustte, dat ze onder de tafel doorgegeven en ronduit stiekem bekeken dienden te worden.

Het paar had zich vlak voor de lunch met meegebrachte broodjes op een afge-legen stukje van het strand geïnstalleerd. Voordat ze naar de jeugdherberg te-rug moesten, wilde Sonja zich nog "even snel verkleden." Vrijwel de hele middag hadden ze er van de zon en het water genoten, maar voor 's avonds wilde ze niet de hele tijd het badpak onder haar kleding aan hebben. Ze had "dat ding nou lang genoeg" aan gehad. Op de een of andere manier zag ze er tegenop om zich op de slaapzaal, waarschijnlijk door de aanwezigheid van de andere meisjes, te moeten verkleden en daarom wilde ze dat dus "nog even snel hier" op het strand doen. Er "voor die paar momenten" een kleedhokje voor huren vonden ze echter allebei te duur. In alle redelijkheid verstandig omdat ze nog steeds aan het begin van hun vakantie stonden en het budget niet ruim te noemen was. Wilden ze in de drie weken die ze ervoor beschik-baar hadden Zuid Limburg of zelfs Luxemburg bereiken, dan was enige zui-nigheid op z'n plaats. De vakantie hoefde allemaal niet op een koopje, maar ze hadden gezien dat het huren van z'n hokje wel zeven gulden vijftig moest kosten. "Dat geld konden ze ook op een andere manier besteden."

Terwijl ze vlak voor hem onder een groot badlaken met het omkleden in de weer was, heeft hij het speels een stukje opgetild. Ze had net het kledingstuk dat haar zo hinderde laten vallen en hij deed het ver genoeg omhoog om haar billen te kunnen zien. Koket probeerde ze een stapje achteruit te doen en sloeg, netjes met haar rug naar de bewoonde wereld gekeerd, de grote hand-doek een stukje terug om zich zo verleidelijk mogelijk aan hem te tonen. He-

31

laas vergiste ze zich in het struikgewas zodat de handdoek daaraan bleef vast-zitten toen ze verder achteruit liep. Het maakte dat ze plotseling in haar volle glorie voor hem en toch nog de wereld achter zich, terecht kwam. Op het moment dat hij hierdoor aangemoedigd naar haar wilde reiken, stapte ze achter-uit en buiten zijn bereik. Zo kon hij er dus niet meer bij om haar daadwerke-lijk aan te raken, vast te pakken of voorzichtig op zoek te gaan naar een daar-toe geëigend plekje. Bijvoorbeeld om haar daar even liefdevol te strelen.

Herman mocht dan nauwelijks tot geen ervaring met meisjes hebben, hij had telkens wel zijn oren de kost gegeven als klasgenoten die van henzelf met hun omgeving aan het delen waren. Al dan niet overdreven, hij wist dus dat er zul-ke 'heel speciale' plekjes te vinden moesten zijn. Zonder problemen had hij er graag bij zijn verloofde even naar gezocht. Het was hem namelijk eveneens bekend dat meisjes zoiets niet onaangenaam zouden vinden.

Zijn moeder had hem een aantal jaren geleden niet voor niets zo'n boekje ge-geven waarin de omgang tussen jongens en meisjes uit de doeken werd ge-daan. Zelf vond ze het een te lastig onderwerp om te bespreken en er volledig op vertrouwen dat de paters hem voldoende voorgelicht hadden durfde ze niet. In het drukwerkje zou beschreven staan hoe het een en ander in zijn werk diende te gaan. Ze had hem het boekje was er speciaal voor in z'n han-den gedrukt. Het ging niet alleen over hoffelijkheid en hoe een vrome Room-sche jongen, zich tegenover 'de leden van het andere geslacht' diende te ge-dragen. Ook 'eventueel een kusje' uitwisselen en zelfs 'de daad' stonden er verderop in beschreven. Zij het uiterst summier, maar bleu of helemaal on-kundig mocht hij dus zeker niet genoemd worden!

Alleen de praktische ervaring ontbrak hem nog, maar daar werd intussen aan gewerkt. Verderop langs het strandje trok Sonja, weer zorgvuldig verstopt on-der de inderhaast terug gegriste handdoek, zo snel mogelijk de kleren aan die ze eveneens mee had weten te pakken. Ze ging zo omzichtig te werk dat hij niet in de verleiding durfde te komen om alsnog tot actie over te gaan. Wat hem er vooral van afhield was dat zij een aantal keren ronduit bang naar hem om leek te kijken. Ze keek angstig en scheen op haar hoede of hij er niet aan-kwam om zich bruut aan haar te vergrijpen. Ze zat overigens zo ver buiten zijn reikwijdte dat hij, zonder dat het té gretig over zou komen, onmogelijk kon proberen haar aan te raken. Ervoor opstaan of door het zand naar haar toe kruipen leek hem eveneens nogal ver gaan.

Twee dagen later, in het bosgebied van de Campina vlakbij Oisterwijk, kwa-men ze terecht bij een vennetje. Voor onderweg hadden ze, het was intussen hun gewoonte geworden bij het ontbijt in de jeugdherberg, lunch pakketjes gemaakt. Die konden in de luwte van de bomen, grotendeels verborgen voor stekend ongedierte bij het water maar in de stilte die rondom het ven heerste, worden opgegeten. Ze vonden er een duinpan voor waarin ze zo ongestoord van de boterhammen, en enigszins beschut voor de nog steeds meedogenloos brandende zon, konden genieten.

Van de etappes van zestig à hooguit zeventig kilometer waren ze trouwens afgestapt. In verband met de warmte hadden ze besloten om hun reis verder op zijn beloop te laten. "Ze zouden wel zien waar ze terecht kwamen", of "hoeveel tijd het kostte om er ooit een keer te komen." Hun vakantie was uiteindelijk pas een paar dagen geleden begonnen en intussen waren ze al een flink eind gevorderd. Als je het uitrekende op de kaart hadden ze die eerste dagen ruimschoots voldaan aan de limiet! Nu kon het dus wel wat rustiger aan en mochten ze op de terugweg toch een keer een wat langere etappe af moeten leggen, dan waren ze daarvoor intussen beter getraind.

Een van de oorspronkelijke doelen van hun trip was Eindhoven, daar woonde een oud klasgenote, een voormalig "goede vriendin uit de tweede klas" van Sonja. Maar ze hadden van tevoren geen afspraak met elkaar gemaakt. Het meisje was overigens niet op hun verloving geweest en ze zouden haar dus met het heugelijke feit gaan verrassen. Maar het maakte niet uit of ze er dezelfde dag nog of misschien pas over een week aan zouden komen. Omdat het evenmin bekend was of ze überhaupt in Eindhoven aanwezig zou zijn, mochten ze er dus ooit aankomen. Intussen vonden ze het 'samen onderweg zijn' een stuk belangrijker dan misschien eens 'een doel bereiken'. Eindelijk werden Herman of Sonja niet meer gestoord. Niet meer door leraren, noch door klasgenoten of familieleden.

Hoewel allebei zeer terughoudend van aard was 't hen langzamerhand duidelijk aan het worden dat zowel hijzelf als zij erg veel aandacht aan hun omgeving besteedden. Dat ze altijd ronduit op hun hoede waren en dus uitermate oplettend door het leven leken te gaan. Bij mensen die verlegen zijn lijkt het immers vooral of de wereld een bedreiging vormt. Het is de basis onder het idee waardoor je altijd op je qui vive moet zijn, op moet letten voor de rest van de mensheid. Deze reis leek die druk geleidelijk van ze af te vallen. Het stel raakte hierdoor meer en meer op elkaar aangewezen en ze leerden op elkaar te vertrouwen. Dat was voor beiden een nieuwe ervaring waaraan ze erg moesten wennen.

Na de lunch wilden samen ze nog even een poosje van de zon blijven genieten. Alleen al vanwege de drukkende warmte die hen omringde lag zoiets voor de hand. Het verder fietsen lokte aanzienlijk minder dan nog een tijdje rustig blijven luieren in de zon. Nu ze zo samen en beschut van de buitenwereld waren, mocht hij nogmaals haar schoonheid bewonderen. Voorzichtig heeft hij haar eerst geholpen om het blijkbaar knellende shirt uit te doen. Het bovenstukje van haar bikini mocht hij daarna eveneens losmaken. De warmte maakte dat het dingetje haar vreselijk hinderde en omdat hij het in alle tederheid deed, verweerde ze zich niet tegen zijn behulpzaamheid. Voorzichtig

33

heeft hij daarna haar tepeltjes gekust, het zweet tussen haar borsten op gelikt en tegen de haartjes op haar buik geblazen. Het verbaasde hem dat ze zich onder zijn aanrakingen op leken te richten en hoe Sonja duidelijk hoorbaar van de attenties genoot. Dat maakte hem nieuwsgierig naar verdere reacties op zijn aanrakingen, strelen en kusjes. Toen hij even later zijn eigen broek ook uit durfde te doen liet ze zich zonder protest door hem 'nemen'.

Het was voor Herman de eerste keer dat hij intiem was met een meisje en het viel hem allemaal niet tegen. Of Sonja nu eveneens ontmaagd was wilde hij haar niet vragen. Het leek hem ongepast en al was ze misschien met die andere jongen ooit eerder 'naar bed geweest', nu was het fijn genoeg. Ze was met hem verloofd en ze zouden zeker en vast met elkaar gaan trouwen. Hij kon overigens niet beslissen of hij 't feit eigenlijk aan haar wilde bekennen.

Het leek hem niet 'stoer'. Dromerig is hij meer dan anderhalf uur naast haar blijven liggen. Dan weer met zijn hoofd tegen haar schouder of bovenarm en er even later mee op haar buik. Toen pas voelden ze hoe heet de zon was en dat het waarschijnlijk beter zou zijn om iets aan te trekken, om zich ter bescherming te bedekken tegen de hete stralen. Voorzichtig hebben ze elkaars verbrande plekken ingesmeerd met de olie die ze al die dagen al, in hun bagage hadden mee getorst. Het viel Herman op hoe teder Sonja kon zijn als ze dat klaarblijkelijk wilde. Pas om een uur of vijf stapten ze weer op de fiets om een slaapplaats voor de nacht te gaan zoeken.

Die avond in de jeugdherberg bij Mierlo waren ze de enige gasten. Omdat ze er aan een van de tafeltjes in de huiskamer aan een spelletje Monopoly begonnen waren, lieten de moeder en vader hen om een uur of negen alleen in de recreatiezaal. Herman won vervolgens met meer dan een miljoen aan reserve kapitaal, maar het was al kwart over elf voordat het zover was. Mijmerend dat het helaas namaak geld betrof en wat ze ermee zouden hebben gedaan als het echt zou zijn geweest, dronken ze hun cola op. Nog opgewonden van het eerdere succes leek het hem daarna wel zo charmant om zijn vriendin door het intussen donker geworden gebouw helemaal tot in de slaapzaal te begeleiden. Daar kwam van het een het ander en toen hij zich schielijk uit haar terugtrok om 'voor het zingen de kerk uit te gaan' was het de eerste keer dat dit daadwerkelijk lukte.

Kennelijk ging zoiets in een bed gemakkelijker dan in het zand, half onder de struiken die ochtend op de heide, of 's middags verscholen achter een dikke boom in het bos. Wellicht baarde de oefening het uiteindelijke kunstje of had hij langzamerhand geleerd om het ejaculeren tijdig aan te voelen komen. Onder indruk van de huisregels waaraan ze zich onderworpen hadden, durfde hij trouwens niet bij haar te blijven slapen op de meisjes slaapzaal. Al bleek achteraf dat zoiets door de leiding van de herberg niet eens vreemd geacht zou zijn. Eerder zeiden ze het 'opvallend' gevonden te hebben dat ze als 'aanstaand paar' de nacht apart op zaal door hadden willen brengen en niet een kamer hadden gewenst. De 'vader en moeder' waren over de hoed en rand blijkbaar ruimschoots ingelicht door Sonja's mama.

Onderweg terug naar huis, weer naar Leiden, vlak voordat ze de richting van Lage Zwaluwe en de brug over de Moerdijk in wilden slaan, bekende Sonja dat ze zich "vreselijke zorgen maakte." Na enig aandringen durfde ze hem in de beschutting van een bushokje te vertellen dat ze niet ongesteld was geworden. Daar had ze die ochtend op gerekend, want normaal was ze heel regelmatig. Samen rekenden ze uit hoe het zat en werden het erover eens dat ze zich niet vergist kon hebben. Op de vlucht voor een aanstaande regenbui bleven ze daarna een poosje in stilte achter elkaar aan fietsten. De route liep langs een drukke weg en er was geen vrijliggend fietspad. Ook vanwege het gevaar was dit dus de verstandigste keuze, maar Herman had toch liever naast zijn verloofde gereden om te overleggen wat hen te doen stond als ze inderdaad zwanger zou blijken.
Ondanks dat ze net de school voltooid hadden en hij er toch een hoog cijfer voor op zijn eindlijst had weten te behalen, kon hij zich van de biologielessen niet meer herinneren hoe het precies ging met de eisprong, vruchtbare periodes en de tijd dat zaad nodig had om bij eitjes aan te komen. Het stond hem vaag bij hoe het zat, maar uiteindelijk hadden ze daar natuurlijk van tevoren bij moeten nadenken. Indertijd was het theorie geweest en leek de eventuele praktijk heel ver verborgen. Maar op dat moment speet het hem dat hij over zulke zaken slechts af kon gaan op de stoere verhalen die erover waren rondgegaan in de klas. Sonja had daar ook bij stil kunnen staan natuurlijk, maar misschien was dat nu te laat.
Zo zwoegde hij een tijdje achter haar aan en streden de verwijten, schaamte en angstige visioenen over hoe hij het aan hun ouders zou moeten vertellen, om voorrang. Gezien de omstandigheden leek het hem voor de hand liggend dat die taak voornamelijk op zijn schouders terecht gekomen was. Hij kon zich weliswaar een voorstelling maken hoe zijn moeder zou reageren op een toekomst als oma, maar zijn schoonouders kende hij daarvoor nog niet goed genoeg. Helaas waaide het op de lange brug over het Holland's Diep veel te hard om er naast elkaar te kunnen fietsen en het onderwerp met Sonja te bespreken. Door schuin voor haar uit te blijven trappen probeerde hij zoveel mogelijk om zijn partner uit de wind te houden en 't was dus een geluk dat de regen nog niet naar beneden kwam kletteren. Al was dat de avond ervoor dus wel op het tv journaal voorspeld en hadden ze zich er uiteindelijk op gekleed. Nu hij erover nadacht zou een ander soort regenjasje waarschijnlijk ook verstandiger geweest zijn. Maar hoe je aan zulke zogenaamde kapotjes moest komen was hem, door de taboesfeer die er omheen hing, nooit helemaal duide-

lijk geworden. Aan de gevel van de drogist op de Haarlemmerstraat had hij ooit een condoomautomaat zien hangen. De klasgenoten hadden er in alle stoerheid ook regelmatig gewag van gemaakt dat de dingen bestonden, maar het hoe en wat is nooit tot hem doorgedrongen. Er was feitelijk nog nooit aanleiding geweest om zich in het gebruik te verdiepen.

Het lawaai van de auto's op de rijbaan naast hen maakte het eventueel met elkaar overleggen evenmin mogelijk. Eenmaal aan de overkant, aangekomen bij een snackbar, zijn ze op het terras gaan zitten. Niet om er op adem te komen of te lunchen, desnoods tegen de losgebarsten regen een extra jas aan te trekken, maar vooral om de bijsluiter van dat medicijn eens grondig door te nemen. Iedere dag nam Sonja een tabletje in voor het slapen. Het was de bedoeling dat die haar menstruatie zouden regelen en 't middeltje had haar tot nog toe inderdaad regelmatig weten te houden!

Herman kon door de intussen vallende regen met moeite de kleine lettertjes ontcijferen en omdat de snackbar nog niet open was konden ze er niet schuilen of gebruik maken van extra verlichting. Maar hij maakte zich tijdens het lezen opeens erg vrolijk. Hardop las hij voor dat de tabletten die ze slikte zogenaamde 'anticonceptie pillen' waren. Zonder dat Sonja het zich had gerealiseerd en blijkbaar ook al gedurende een hele tijd, slikte zijn vriendin de wereldberoemde 'pil'. Hoewel aanvankelijk beledigd door zijn hilariteit, zag ze na verloop van tijd de humor van de situatie in. De opluchting zal er waarschijnlijk een rol bij gespeeld hebben dat ze na een paar minuten toch met hem mee begon te lachen. Op hun verwarring terugkijkend waren ze Sonja's moeder dankbaar voor haar vooruitziende blik. Maar het kwam ze voor dat zij haar dochter toch minstens op de hoogte had kunnen stellen van haar bedoelingen. Sonja had trouwens al te kennen gegeven dat een deel van de verantwoording "natuurlijk bij haar lag."

Nadere bestudering van de bijsluiter, een halfuurtje later in een snackbar die wel geopend was, leerde hen dat waarschijnlijk door het fietsen, de extra beweging die ze door hun vakantie kreeg of de keren dat ze sex hadden gehad, haar periode uitgesteld was geraakt. Het stond uitgebreid beschreven in de bijsluiter en het behoorde tot de mogelijkheden die haar zogenaamde cyclus ontregeld zouden kunnen hebben. Inderdaad kwam het later die middag, ze waren vlakbij Ridderkerk, alsnog en blijkbaar nogal heftig in orde.

Herman had een nieuwe afvoer voor de wastafel in elkaar geplakt en buurman Kees voorzag een erachter liggend stukje muur van wat vlakker, in zijn termen 'lekker strak', stucwerk. Het leverde zoals intussen gebruikelijk leek te geworden een hoop extra werk op, maar het resultaat mocht er na alle inspanning weer zijn. Het leidde ertoe dat Herman na een avond flink doorpakken nog even met hem meeliep om samen 'een afzakkertje' te halen. Het was nog ruim voor half elf dus kon er niet gesproken worden van een een vreselijk nachtelijk moment op een doordeweekse vrijdagavond. Voor hun gevoel was de zon eigenlijk net onder gegaan, want de verlichting hadden ze pas tijdens het opruimen in hoeven te schakelen.

Patty de buurvrouw bleek bij binnenkomst al op bed te liggen. Toch kwam ze voor de gezelligheid even naar beneden. Ze maakte voor "haar mannen" een glaasje whiskey klaar. In verband met de warme avond, met veel ijs dat ze ervoor maalde in het machientje dat ervoor op het aanrecht stond. Ze zouden daar volgens haar aan toe zijn en vond dat ze er "veel te vermoeid voor" waren om zelf de glazen te pakken of de drank in te schenken. Er kwam bij dat "ze het graag deed."

Patty had vanuit haar bed naar een tv-programma liggen kijken waarin mensen elkaar iets moesten vertellen of juist geheim houden. Helaas kon ze niet reproduceren wat er precies gezegd was of waar het exact om draaide. Daarom leek het de mannen dat ze er weinig aan gemist hadden. Geen van drieën vonden ze het daarna de moeite waard om in de huiskamer gezamenlijk verder te kijken naar hoe het afliep. Dat het stel op hun slaapkamer een tweede tv had was Herman onbekend, maar het leek hem onmiddellijk een goed idee om zoiets bij zichzelf ook eens te installeren. Niet dat hij er nu met vrijwel iedere avond nog veel te doen aan het huisje meteen enig nut van inzag, maar wellicht zou de toekomst uitwijzen dat er met zo'n tweede toestel een hoop voordeel te behalen zou zijn. In bed genieten van een late uitzending bood eigenlijk wel wat perspectieven.

Patty, achter in de twintig en dus iets jonger dan haar echtgenoot of Herman, ging naast Kees op de bank zitten. Maar eerst schonk ze voor zichzelf een glaasje rosé in. Ze had een badjas aan die zo ruim viel dat Herman er klakkeloos vanuit ging dat die van haar echtgenoot moest zijn. Haar lange blote benen kwamen er zo nu en dan onder vandaan en voor zover hij er een glimp van opving, droeg ze er alleen een soort niemendalletje onder. Volgens hem heette zoiets een babydoll, maar hij was er niet zeker van omdat de ervaring met zulke kleding hem ontbrak. Onwillekeurig keek hij, terwijl ze redderend heen en weer liep, bewonderd toe. Hij genoot van de manier waarop ze bewoog en met haar heupen draaide. Daarbij leek ze hem een kort moment te betrappen zodat hij snel zijn glas oppakte en de aandacht daarop concentreerde. Met een glimlach en klein wiebeltje met haar achterwerk gaf ze te kennen zijn blikken te waarderen. Het was een kort privé momentje tussen hen beiden, want Herman zag dat Kees er geen notie van had.

Het ging hem natuurlijk niet aan hoe mensen zich kleedden of gedroegen, maar toen het leek dat ze steeds aanhankelijker tegen haar man begon te doen, dronk hij zijn glas snel leeg. Hij wilde niet dat ze hem als een indringer zouden gaan beschouwen en was met zulk gedrag eigenlijk niet bekend. Sonja

37

had weleens van die dagen gehad dat ze 'liever tegen hem deed dan gewoonlijk', maar in hoeverre dat normaal te noemen was of wat er eventueel de oorzaak van zou kunnen zijn, is hem nooit duidelijk geworden. Het leek hem vooral iets dat voorkwam in boeken die hij nooit gelezen had. 'Keukenmeiden romans' werden die tijdens de Nederlandse les genoemd en het was hem in de loop der tijd duidelijk geworden dat zijn vrouw ze samen met haar moeder in grote getale doornam. Zelf las hij voornamelijk literatuur boeken en daarin kwamen zulke expliciete scènes ternauwernood voor.

Omdat hij tamelijk moe was, sloeg de drank in als een bom. Wankelend stond hij dus op van zijn stoel en daarmee wekte hij de indruk dat hij slechts met moeite de juiste weg naar huis zou kunnen vinden. Zowel Patty als zijn collega van die avond, boden aan om even met hem mee te lopen, maar hij wilde ze niet langer tot last zijn. Hij vond dat hij zijn afgang er groter mee zou maken als hij inderdaad thuisgebracht zou moeten worden. Hij had maar twee glaasjes whiskey gehad!

Het was zeker niet de manier waarop hij zichzelf wilde laten zien, maar voor zover hij nog in staat was om erop te letten, lachten ze hem niet uit. Hij merkte dus ook niet op of ze opgelucht waren dat hij eindelijk vertrok. Het ontging hem of ze zoals even ervoor nog aangeboden, een extra glaasje met hem hadden willen blijven drinken.

Toen de avond nog normaal verliep waren ze als bijna vanzelfsprekend ter sprake geraakt over het verbouwen en opknappen van een woning. Daar was hij tenslotte volop mee bezig en het resultaat dat ze eerder die avond hadden weten te bereiken, loog er weer niet om. Het droeg eraan bij dat het onderwerp hem voor in de mond lag en hij er enthousiast over kon praten. Zonder dat er een directe aanleiding voor was kwam ook ter sprake hoe zijn vroegere schoonvader indertijd de verdieping in Delft voor zijn dochter en hem opgeknapt had. En later de woning waar ze tot hun scheiding hadden gewoond.

Uitgebreid is hij erop ingegaan hoe de beste man er op de overloop, de trap en in de kamers een laminaatvloer heeft aangelegd. Hoe alle deuren er, inclusief de kozijnen en plinten, na hun fietsvakantie netjes geschilderd waren geweest. Hij heeft verteld dat Sonja's moeder alle kasten grondig schoongemaakt had en hoe ze de planken van nieuw plakpapier voorzien bleek te hebben. Weliswaar niet helemaal in de kleuren van hun voorkeur, maar dat ze er teveel door overbluft waren geweest om erover te durven klagen.

Hij heeft zichzelf horen vertellen hoe hun verdieping zover in orde was gemaakt dat zijn ex en hij er zomaar in hadden kunnen trekken. Zonder mankeren waren alle kamers immers voor hen ingericht. Alle meubeltjes stonden er keurig neergezet en gerangschikt op de meest passende plek.

Hij deed verslag hoe zijn eigen moeder erbij betrokken waren geraakt en alles door hen gezamenlijk tiptop in orde was gemaakt. Alles tegen een geringe lening met gunstige aflossing voorwaarden voor als hij klaar zou zijn met z'n studie. Ze waren tot de conclusie gekomen dat hij niets meer zelf had hoeven doen en hoe Sonja en hij in een gespreid bedje terecht waren gekomen.

Patty merkte even later lachend op dat ze zoiets ook weleens zou willen meemaken. Maar evengoed moest hij bekennen dat het een aantal maanden duurde voordat zijn verloofde en hij zich in hun woning thuis hadden gevoeld. Dat Sonja en hij extra veel tijd nodig hadden gehad om zich alles 'geheel eigen' te maken omdat de inrichting volledig buiten hen om plaats had gevonden.

Zonder er de nadruk op te hoeven leggen trokken ze de conclusie dat het 'zelf doen' en je 'persoonlijke plan trekken' voordelen heeft. Maar het meest in het oog springende was dat hem juist dát inzicht gedurende hun relatie altijd ontbroken heeft. Het verbaasde hem vooral dat hij daar nog nooit zo tegenaan gekeken had. Eenmaal thuis en door de frisse lucht onderweg, het omkleden en tandenpoetsen weer enigszins opgeknapt van de drank inname en zijn vermoeidheid, is hij een poosje op de rand van zijn bed blijven zitten. Nu hij 't uitrekent is het ruim elf maanden sinds de scheiding. Hij mist het getrouwd zijn of wat hij met Sonja had niet, maar het daagt hem plotseling waarom hij het indertijd nodig vond om de knoop zo drastisch door te hakken. Waarom hij een nieuw leven wilde beginnen en zijn huwelijk hem plotseling zo ontzettend bleek te beklemmen.

Zojuist heeft hij gezien hoe aantrekkelijk, ronduit sexy, zijn buurvrouw is en hoe ze zonder opgelegde regels met haar man een eenheid lijkt te vormen. Hij is onmiskenbaar opgewonden geraakt door wat hij van haar te zien heeft gekregen, maar tegelijkertijd heeft het hem voortdurend voor ogen gestaan dat wat hij zag niet voor hem bestemd was. Het onvoorwaardelijke samenspel tussen Patty en haar echtgenoot liet daarover geen twijfel bestaan. Als man en vrouw vormen ze 'een stel'. De manier waarop ze met elkaar omgingen, hoe ze elkaar leken aan te voelen, het had er allemaal zo vanzelfsprekend en natuurlijk uitgezien dat hij er alleen maar jaloers op heeft kunnen worden.

Herman kan niet ontkennen dat hij met Sonja momenten van geluk heeft gekend. Ze hebben regelmatig uitgewisseld dat ze erg veel van elkaar hielden en hij weet dat hij haar met hun scheiding een groot verdriet heeft aangedaan. Maar of ze ooit net zo'n stel waren als de buren leken te zijn, kan hij zich niet voor de geest halen. Hij kan niet zeggen waar het precies in zit, maar bij de andere stellen om hem heen meent hij al vaker te hebben opgemerkt wat hem vanavond opnieuw duidelijk is geworden. Zou het zitten in het onvoorwaardelijke dat er bij die relaties vanaf lijkt te stralen?

Mag hij dat liefde noemen?

Is daar inderdaad een duidelijk merkbare niet gespeelde, en dus oprechte genegenheid bij waar te nemen?

Herman kan de gevoelens die hem bekruipen niet benoemen. Ze overweldigen hem. Hij wordt door allerlei beelden overvallen, maar kan aan de stemming die ze meebrengen geen verklaring verbinden. Net zomin als hij ooit eerder, nog tijdens zijn huwelijk of school- en studententijd zijn gevoelens heeft kunnen benoemen. Toch is er geen sprake van weemoed, noch van nostalgie, spijt, of een wil om de klok terug te draaien. Totaal niet zelfs, maar hij blijft nog even op de rand van zijn bed zitten en mijmert verder. Weer helemaal wakker twijfelt hij eraan of hij nog een klein glaasje whiskey uit de koelkast zal gaan halen.

Ondanks alles staat het voor hem vast dat hij de goede weg is ingeslagen. Dat hij de juiste beslissing heeft genomen door alleen zijn weg te vervolgen. Het idee om voortaan zonder Sonja verder te gaan, lijkt hem nog altijd 't beste.

Het komt hem voor dat hij voornamelijk en misschien wel domweg altijd, op zoek is geweest naar een relatie waarin hijzelf zijn keuzes kon bepalen. Dat alleen hijzelf of desnoods na goed overleg met zijn partner, wilde en kon uitmaken wat hij verderop tegen wilde komen. Welke uitdagingen hij op zijn levenspad aan wilde treffen. Het dringt tot hem door hoe hij al in zijn jeugd, gewend was om een eigen plan te trekken. Dat hij uitdagingen opzocht en ze telkens op een persoonlijke manier aan wilde gaan.

Hoe hij meestal op zichzelf aangewezen was en dat hij daar tijdens zijn relatie vanaf heeft geweken. Het tekent zich af hoe hij in zijn relatie met Sonja te lang gezocht heeft naar 'n evenwicht. Hij wilde een samenspel bereiken tussen toewijding aan zijn studie, zijn werk, in meerder opzichten zichzelf en de partner in wie hij een gelijke kon zien. Bij Sonja heeft hij een soortgelijke opvatting nooit aangetroffen. Helaas dus.

Hoewel ze er onmiskenbaar een hoop moeite voor hebben gedaan om hun huwelijk zo leuk mogelijk te houden, was de koek feitelijk al vroeg, misschien al toen ze nog maar pas in Delft waren gaan wonen, op. Waarschijnlijk had hij op de brug over de Moerdijk al het idee opgevat dat hij volledig aan haar vastzat. Of kwam het omdat ze hem gedurende hun huwelijk met incorrect taalgebruik en feitelijk als een flauw grapje weleens "Her Man" noemde?

O.V.

Omdat de man voor een werkafspraak naar Utrecht moest, heeft hij er de trein voor genomen. Hij wilde niet net zoals de vorige keren met de auto over de A12 om dan eenmaal aangekomen op zijn bestemming nog eens onderworpen te worden aan het eindeloze gezoek naar een parkeerplek. Vandaag wilde hij in alle rust reizen en genieten van het openbaar vervoer. Er eens eigenhandig ervaring mee opdoen. Uit eerdere bezoekjes aan de stad weet hij dat het probleem om er je auto kwijt te raken en ook nog eens bij zijn gastheer voor de deur, steeds groter wordt. Overigens jammer dat hij vanmorgen hier naartoe vergeten is om voor onderweg een leuk boek mee te nemen of dat hij in de hal een van die gratis krantjes bij zich heeft gestoken. Die zijn er tenslotte niet voor niets in grote stapels voor neergelegd.

Uit het raam naar buiten kijken is wel aardig, maar iets omhanden hebben biedt meer mogelijkheden. Het maakt het reizen leuker, maar door gebrek aan ervaring heeft hij zich daar dus niet op voorbereid. Al heeft hij intussen wel geleerd dat autorijden aanzienlijk meer afleiding biedt. Als hij nu iets te lezen bij zich zou hebben was de keuze wat uitgebreider dan alleen maar naar dat landschap achter het raam staren. Die krantjes bleken toen hij daarnet op het station aankwam trouwens allemaal op. Vanmorgen had hij opgemerkt dat de meeste mensen meteen doorbladeren naar de sudoku puzzeltjes. Of hij daadwerkelijk iets mist aan de inhoud zal hem niet duidelijk worden. In ieder geval zag hij op het perron en in de gangen wel de grote kasten staan met de naam van die krantjes erop, maar op wat zwerfvuil na waren ze allemaal leeg. Hij had alweer een hele tijd geleden voor het laatst gebruik gemaakt van het openbaar vervoer en daarom leek het hem een aantrekkelijke optie om voor een hernieuwde kennismaking te gaan. Helaas is het op de afspraak vandaag een beetje later geworden dan voorzien en nu zit hij daardoor in de avond trein terug naar zijn woonplaats. Hij weet dat er kaartjes zijn die hem, omdat hij nu buiten de zogenaamde spits reist, recht zouden geven op korting, maar het is hem niet bekend hoe hij daar alsnog voor in aanmerking komt. Waarschijnlijk had hij het van tevoren, voor zijn vertrek en meteen vanmorgen dus al, moeten bedingen.

De aanschaf van dat kaartje, bij die gele automaat in de hal van het station en niet aan een loket zoals hij nog verwacht had, was al een regelrechte openbaring voor hem. In al zijn onhandigheid bij het bedienen van de apparatuur, heeft hij de hulp van een vriendelijke dame nodig gehad. Anders had hij vast en zeker nu nog staan hannesen. Al die moeite, uitsluitend om met de juiste reisbescheiden onderweg te kunnen! Waarom in de tussentijd het openbaar vervoer ook zo ingewikkeld is gemaakt, het is hem een raadsel.

Wat was er verkeerd aan een medewerker van de spoorwegen die je vanachter een doorgeefluik met zo'n schattig plateau erin, een kaartje verkoopt? Die draaischijf konden ze met een handige hendel, die ervoor op de tafels ernaast zat gemonteerd, bedienen. Als kind heeft het ding heeft hem altijd mateloos gefascineerd. Het leek hem iets exclusiefs, dat het werk voor de spoorwegen iets speciaals verleende, of de medewerkers er een aureool door kregen.

Al heet zo'n kaartje tegenwoordig een vervoersbewijs, zoveel is er toch niet aan het principe veranderd? Als passagier wil je meerijden en het enige dat daarvoor nodig is, is een kaartje waarmee het bewijs geleverd wordt dat je voor die hoedanigheid, de uiteindelijke rit hebt betaald. Daar kan de conducteur vervolgens een gaatje in knippen als hij komt controleren.

De man wil echter niet mopperen en hij kan begrijpen dat menselijk personeel aanzienlijk duurder is dan automaten. Het gedoe dat met overuren, vakanties en ziekte samenhangt, is hem niet volledig onbekend. Uiteindelijk maakt hij het regelmatig mee bij zijn collega's. Alleen bekroop hem de vraag waarom het nog wel 'live' werkende personeel dan alleen maar als een automaat zou moeten, willen of kunnen functioneren.

Omdat de oorspronkelijke loketten in de hal allemaal dichtgetimmerd bleken te zitten en hij dus niemand kon vinden om 'persoonlijk' het plaatsbewijs bij aan te schaffen, is de man naar de informatie balie gelopen. Op dit station overigens aangeduid met uitsluitend het woordje "info" boven haar met een grote gele I op een blauw veld. Al kon hij zoiets nog best begrijpen. Letters kosten geld en iedereen kent intussen de betekenis van de eerste vier van het enigszins lange woord. Het levert vanzelfsprekend veel kleinere borden op en dat bespaart natuurlijk ook een heleboel materiaal. Zeker landelijk gezien met al die stations overal. Zoals hij onlangs op het nieuws nog heeft kunnen zien, komen er steeds meer haltes en stationnetjes bij. Internationaal voldoen de vier letters heel goed en gezien het inleveren van onze moedertaal is het bordje met alleen maar 'info' of dus uitsluitend die eenzame ' i ' er nog maar op, meer dan genoeg informatie.

De mevrouw die door haar rode hoedje, uniform en het logo op haar borst onmiskenbaar een medewerkster van de spoorwegen moest zijn, was niet bereid om de aanschaf van een kaartje aan hem te verduidelijken. Kennelijk vond ze het niet meer dan vanzelfsprekend dat iedereen, ook een onbenul zoals hij, de door haar werkgever opgestelde apparaten zou moeten kunnen bedienen. Met uitsluitend een knikje van haar hoofd wees ze hem waar hij moest zijn. Uit deze manier van doen sprak een oogverblindende minachting. Ze leek namelijk wel beledigd toen hij even later aan haar durfde te vragen hoe hij op het paneel zijn bestemming moest intypen en dus op die manier een geldig kaartje kon aanschaffen. Hij wist dat er een stempelautomaat op het perron zou staan en dat hij daarmee een aangeschaft vervoersbewijs moest valideren maar hij wilde de bijbehorende procedure even uitgelegd krijgen. Voor de mevrouw bleek het echter teveel moeite.

Later, eenmaal onderweg bedacht hij dat de medewerkster in hem waarschijnlijk een van die 'verstokte automobilisten' herkend zal hebben. Waaraan ze dat precies had kunnen zien, was hem weliswaar niet duidelijk, maar afgaande op haar manier van omgaan met klanten leek het hem zo. Overigens verwachtte hij dat ze zich er kennelijk niet van bewust was dat er met haar opstelling weinig tot geen personen bekeerd konden raken tot een intensiever gebruik van het openbaar vervoer. Zeker niet voor een relatief kleine afstand zoals hij vandaag af zou gaan leggen. Met de auto is de rit in een uurtje te doen en feitelijk heeft alleen het parkeerprobleem ter plaatse hem ertoe laten besluiten dat deze manier van reizen een redelijk alternatief zou kunnen vormen.

Zou kunnen, want hij vond dat de mevrouw er zichtbaar vanuit ging dat de vaardigheid om het apparaat te gebruiken tot de basiskennis, noem het 'algemene ontwikkeling', gerekend behoorde te worden. Hij voelde zich eigenlijk een beetje gediscrimineerd qua leeftijd. Heeft hij immers de tijd dat alles nog gewoon functioneerde niet nog meegemaakt?

Wat verwachtte ze eigenlijk van hem?

Haar nogal snibbige opmerking dat er "aanwijzingen" op het scherm stonden en dat hij zich "daaraan diende te houden", maakte hem duidelijk dat 'sociale vaardigheden' in de huidige tijden inderdaad tot een officieel schoolvak gebombardeerd zijn. Een vak dat gezien dit soort ervaringen een stuk beter onderwezen zou kunnen worden. Even kwam het bij hem op dat het misschien een idee zou zijn om, net zoals met dat inburgering examen voor buitenlanders, eens een soortgelijke eis aan iedere Nederlander te stellen.

Een burgerschapsdiploma of zoiets, laat de exacte naam maar aan de ambtenarij over. En dat men voor dat examen dan minimaal een voldoende diende te halen. Ten minste een zes plus en niet zo berekenend als op de middelbare school tegenwoordig, dat slechts een vijf punt zes ook wel voldoende geacht wordt. Misschien zou zo'n examen dan periodiek herhaald kunnen worden, zodat we weer wat meer beleefdheid in de maatschappij terugkrijgen. De man kan zich er duidelijk over opwinden als hij voor zijn gevoel onbehoorlijk behandel wordt.

Wat overigens de eventuele sanctie op het falen voor de toets zou moeten zijn is hem niet duidelijk. Maar het idee is er in principe, al staat hem evenmin voor ogen wat de meest wenselijk frequentie van die toetsing zal zijn, of het beste moment waarop ie uitgevoerd zou moeten worden. Iedereen ieder jaar, lijkt 'm wat vaak, maar hij merkt bij zichzelf op dat de ergernis over dit soort gebreken steeds vaker de kop bij hem opsteekt. Dat het tekort schieten van de sociale vaardigheid in de hem omringende maatschappij hand over hand toeneemt. Als hij het ter sprake brengt bij zijn vrouw of er eens een enkele keer met vrienden over overlegt, meent hij op te mogen merken dat hij er niet alleen in staat. Het stoort hem net zo erg als het flauwe elkaar een fijne dag toewensen, meestal zonder dat de plichtpleging gemeend overkomt.

Onderweg naar de trein bedacht hij dat de behandeling helder maakte, dat een incidentele reiziger voor de spoorwegen niet interessant zal zijn. En het spreekt inderdaad voor zich dat je op zulke mensen geen miljoenen bedrijf met internationale belangen kunt laten draaien. Dat de krant dus niet overdrijft door de service van de spoorwegen weleens "armzalig" te noemen en berichten publiceert over ontevreden reizigers. Mede door zijn ervaringen lijkt dit alles niet meer dan voor de hand te liggen.

Vanmorgen verbaasde het hem dus allemaal niks. Aangestoken door dit soort ervaringen voelt hij zich steeds vaker weggedrukt als onderdeeltje van de grijze massa. Persoonlijke omstandigheden lijken er immers steeds minder toe te doen. Tegenwoordig is het zowat een uitzondering als je in een winkel niet wordt afgeblaft als je iets durft te vragen. Of dat je minderwaardig wordt behandeld als je een vorm van deskundigheid van het verkopend personeel durft te verwachten. De man vraagt weleens aan zijn vrouw waar de beleefdheid of voorkomendheid is gebleven, maar zij weet het helaas ook niet en kan hem er dus niet verder bij helpen. De man zou wel willen dat de mensen wat hoofser met elkaar omgingen. Dat men weer eens wat onderling respect wilde tonen, of moet hij daarbij eigenlijk 'durven' zeggen?

Terwijl hij stond te stuntelen bij de grote gele kast werd ie aangesproken door een mevrouw die het kennelijk niet langer kon aanzien. Vriendelijk deed ze hem voor op welke 'knoppen', feitelijk niks meer dan velden die op het beeldscherm geprojecteerd werden, hij moest drukken. Ze vertelde hem toen alles gelukt was, hoe hij vervolgens met zijn pinpas het verschuldigde bedrag kon overmaken. Ze draaide zich er discreet voor om toen hij daartoe de cijfers van zijn pincode intoetste op het paneeltje naast het beeldscherm.

Was ie er net aan gewend om dat aanraakscherm met de virtuele toetsen te bedienen, moest het betalen juist weer met echte knoppen die daadwerkelijk en met kracht, ingedrukt dienden te worden!

Nu zit hij dus in de trein weer terug naar huis.

Op de heenreis vanmorgen, heeft hij tegen de gewekte verwachtingen in niet eens zo heel erg lang op het wegrijden hoeven wachten. Hij had zich erop voorbereid dat onder de huidige toestanden vrijwel alle treinen met vertraging

44

zouden vertrekken en uit de krant was hem duidelijk geworden dat het geen uitzondering zou zijn als de trein plotseling in *the middle of nowhere* stil zou vallen om daar een poosje om onduidelijke redenen te blijven staan. Niet voor niets wordt er in de media verslag van dit soort voorvallen gedaan. Goed op de hoogte dat hij is, zijn de berichten hem niet ontgaan.

Op het perron aangekomen bleek het boemeltje naar Utrecht al voor hem klaar te staan. Nog geen tien minuten later en dus precies op tijd volgens de dienstregeling, zette de trein zich zonder problemen in beweging. Dat hij zich gehaast had om op tijd op het station te zijn, wierp dus zijn vruchten af. Al speet het hem, toen hij eenmaal zat, dat hij niet een kopje koffie gekocht had beneden in de hal. Of dat hij iets te lezen of puzzelen bij zich had gestoken voor onderweg. Er nog even voor terug gaan leek hem teveel risico om de trein te missen.

De hele heenreis verliep overigens exact volgens het boekje. Het viel hem alleen op dat de conducteurs zich vanaf het vertrek in de cabine van de machinist, in wezen toch helemaal achteraan in het rijtuig, terugtrokken. Hij had er goed zicht op omdat hij vlak erbij een lege zitplaats had aangetroffen. Er zat trouwens verder niemand in dat deel van de trein, dus hij had zich ruim kunnen installeren. Niet alleen had hij er aan beide kanten zodoende een heel raam voor zichzelf waardoor hij naar buiten kon kijken, maar het plekje bood hem ook uitzicht op de toegang naar dat hokje voor de machinist op het platform tussen de deuren. Op de lege plek naast hem kon hij trouwens zijn tas laten staan. Die hoefde dus niet in het bagagerek boven zijn hoofd, al had hij er geen bezwaar tegen gehad om 'm erin te leggen als dat nodig was.

Onderweg naar het perron waarvandaan de trein zou vertrekken, was hem na een korte blik op de info van de gele borden opgevallen dat er tussen zijn woonplaats en de uiteindelijke bestemming een aantal stations was bijgekomen. Hij kende de tussenliggende stop plaatsen, maar er bleken er bij nader inzien wel drie bijgekomen.

In de veronderstelling dat de onvriendelijk behandeling van de mevrouw in de hal te wijten moest zijn aan haar humeur van de dag, ging hij ervan uit dat een andere medewerker van de spoorwegen hem uitkomst zou kunnen bieden betreffende welke halte voor hem de meest geschikte was om op zijn bestemming te geraken. Zodoende keek de man ernaar uit om er een van haar collega's naar te kunnen vragen. Het personeel dat voor die taak het meest voor de hand leek te liggen, waren de conducteurs. Zowel de man als de nogal dikke vrouw, hadden bij het aan boord gaan een bekertje koffie bij zich. Daar concentreerden ze zich vanzelfsprekend op, maar ze leken eigenlijk vooral oog voor elkaar te hebben. Naar wat hij ervan kon waarnemen gingen ze volledig op in het uitwisselen van onderlinge geintjes. Uitsluitend het geven van het vertreksein aan de machinist, helemaal aan het begin van het vervoermiddel, verstoorde hun aandacht. Het vormde de enige aanleiding waarvoor ze gedurende de hele reis uit de cabine tevoorschijn kwamen. Steeds de man door de deur van de cabine en de vrouw via de binnendeur en het balkon. Kennelijk diende er een soort onderscheid gehandhaafd te worden. Ze kwamen wel telkens met elkaar babbelend weer door de schuifdeuren naar binnen, om dan nogmaals te verdwijnen achter hun favoriete blauwe deurtje.

Door zijn verlegenheid durfde hij hen niet te storen. Meerdere keren heeft hij het tweetal tevoorschijn zien komen voor het verrichten van de benodigde handelingen. Dat was op ieder volgende station, maar omdat ze onmiddellijk weer bij elkaar terug het hokje in kropen vond hij niet de moed om hun gewoonte te doorbreken. Ervoor opstaan en ze opwachten tijdens het wegrijden, ging hem te ver. Het leek hem trouwens dat er in dat plekje, mede gezien het postuur van de vrouw, niet zo heel veel ruimte zou zijn. Maar hij moest ernaar raden en kennelijk voldeed de ruimte aan hun eisen qua comfort en arbeidsomstandigheden.

Het uiteindelijke stellen van de vraag waar hij het beste uit kon stappen, leek hem een goede gelegenheid als ze zijn kaartje kwamen knippen. Maar ook daar is het niet van gekomen. Waarschijnlijk hadden ze pauze of was intussen de controle van vervoerbewijzen helemaal afgeschaft. Hoewel hij iedere avond de krant zowat spelt, ontsnapt er weleens een nieuwtje aan zijn aandacht. Dit was hem dus kennelijk ontgaan.

Door alle informatie van dat bord in de hal, had de gedachte bij hem postgevat dat er wellicht een halteplaats of stationnetje dichter bij zijn bestemming kon liggen. Hij zou dan een halte, of misschien zelfs twee, eerder kunnen uitstappen omdat hij er dan al bijna was. Maar hij was niet op de hoogte van alle nieuwigheid. Snelwegen voeren toch voornamelijk langs bekende, oude paden. Daar treft hij die nieuwe namen alleen aan bij een afrit waarop hij niet van zijn route hoeft af te wijken om op z'n uiteindelijke bestemming te geraken. De nieuwe halteplaats is hem zodoende hooguit opgevallen als de naam ervan plotseling op het grote blauwe bord prijkte.

Helaas heeft de man de beambten dus niet om uitkomst kunnen vragen en is hij helemaal meegereden tot aan het eindstation middenin de stad. Al doet het er allemaal niet toe natuurlijk. Zijn werkgever betaalt de reiskosten en dat retourtje zat al lang en breed in zijn portemonnee. Maar het houdt hem bezig dat sommige zaken de laatste tijd zo onduidelijk voor hem lijken. Zou hij, zoals zijn dochter het een poosje geleden opmerkte "oud worden"? Ze bedoelde het op dat moment weliswaar als grapje, maar sindsdien staat ie er steeds vaker bij stil dat ze misschien gelijk heeft.

Aan de andere kant van het pad dat midden tussen de banken loopt, zit tegenover hem een meisje. Het is een zogenaamd 'jong ding'. De man meende eerst dat het kind begin twintig zou zijn, maar toen hij eenmaal was gaan zitten leek het hem dat ze eerder negentien dan wellicht al vier- of vijfentwintig kon zijn. In de spiegeling van het raam kan hij haar bekijken. Als de achtergrond door voorbij lopende personen er tenminste donker genoeg voor wordt.

Ze heeft haar knieën opgetrokken en zit half uitgestrekt over de bank met haar voeten op de rand van de prullenbak onder het tafeltje. Zo met haar rug naar hem toe blijft ze grotendeels verborgen en hangt min of meer weggedoken in de hoek van de zitplaats. Haar tas staat naast haar knieën en omdat ze dwars zit heeft ze de hele zitplaats, die toch feitelijk voor twee personen is bedoeld, in gebruik. Voor zover hij het kan zien staart ze naar buiten en daarmee wekt ze een verveelde indruk. Haar lamlendige manier van doen maakt d'r voorkomen extra jong. Door dit gedrag ziet ze er meer uit als een puber dan de jonge dame die ze met haar opvallend nette rok en vestje suggereert.

De rest van de coupé is leeg. Even hiervoor zijn er een paar jongens luidruchtig langsgelopen, maar die zijn door de schuifdeur achter hem door gegaan. Met alleen een keurende blik tijdens het voorbijgaan, hebben ze ingeschat dat het kennelijk beter was om verderop in de trein plaats te nemen. Die stond toen nog op het station en intussen rijden ze alweer een tijdje. Omdat het buiten al helemaal donker is, kan de man het meisje beter bekijken in de weerspiegeling van de ruit naast hem. Door het isolerende glaswerk ziet hij haar in een dubbel dubbelspiegelbeeld, al ligt die vlak naast zijn hoofd korter op elkaar als degene aan de andere kant van de wagon. Het beeld is hierdoor niet erg scherp of gedetailleerd, maar het kan ermee door. Op het station had hij haar al bekeken, maar toen heerste er buiten de coupé nog teveel licht om haar goed in zich op te nemen zonder dat het zou opvallen. De man weet dat staren niet netjes is, dus dat doet ie nooit.

De bank waarop hij is gaan zitten, was de eerste volledig lege die hij tegenkwam na het instappen. Omdat hij ervan uit ging dat de trein nog voller zou raken, heeft hij meteen van de buitenkans gebruik gemaakt en er plaats genomen. Hij heeft het kind niet willen storen door de plek recht tegenover haar in te nemen en er was immers meer dan ruimte genoeg voor hem aan deze kant van de wagon. Haar houding straalde overigens niet uit dat ze het gezellig zou vinden als hij erbij kwam zitten. Laat staan dat ze waarschijnlijk verlegen zat om een praatje aan te knopen met zomaar een oudere man.

Zo nu en dan komt er buiten de trein een straat langs. De lantaarnpalen met de eronder geparkeerde auto's geven aan dat daar niet ver vandaan geleefd moet worden. Hier en daar ziet hij dan ook mensen in de huizen. Het spoor komt er zo dicht langs dat hij er zowat in de huiskamers bij lijkt te zitten. Hij vraagt zich af waarom ze de woningen zo vlakbij het spoor hebben neergezet. Het lijkt hem dat een trein niet in volledige stilte langs zal komen rijden en een stukje verder van het talud af moet het dus aanzienlijk rustiger zijn. Periodiek

47

geraas van het spoor kan het wooncomfort niet ten goede komen komt hem voor. Maar de vorderingen in de moderne bouwtechniek, maken het kennelijk allemaal mogelijk.

Als de trein voor een volgende halte afremt en hij dus heel langzaam aan de huizen voorbij trekt, ziet hij hoe er hier en daar gekookt of zelfs al aan tafel gezeten wordt. Met wat extra moeite zou hij zelfs kunnen zien wat er op het menu staat, maar hij is er niet echt nieuwsgierig naar. Volgens goed Hollandse gewoonte hebben de meeste huizen geen gordijnen voor het raam zodat het allemaal goed te bekijken valt. In ieder geval zijn die nog nergens gesloten en het valt hem op dat er vrijwel overal een televisie aan staat. De beeldschermen staan telkens op de meest strategische plek, centraal in de woonkamer opgesteld. Iedere keer als ze een rijtje huizen passeren, valt de opvallende plaatsing hem opnieuw op. Het staat hem bij dat aansluitsnoeren tegenwoordig een vaste lengte hebben en hij begrijpt dat het kortst erbij gelegen stopcontact en de antenne aansluiting ergens midden op die muur aangebracht zullen zijn. Het gebrek aan 'n echte keuze verklaart de onpersoonlijke eenvormigheid in de gevonden oplossingen.

Het meisje heeft ergens vanuit haar tas een telefoontje opgediept en zit er fluisterend in te praten. De man kijkt even vluchtig naar haar, maar wordt weer afgeleid door een nieuwe straat achter het raam aan zijn kant van het rijtuig. Hij vraagt zich af of hij straks op weg naar huis beter een snelle hap in de snackbar kan halen of dat ie bij de chinees om de hoek neer zal strijken om er aan een tafeltje te eten. Zijn vrouw is naar haar zus en hij weet dus dat ze niet op hem zit te wachten. Gisteravond hebben ze afgesproken dat hij zelf voor zijn maaltijd zal zorgen. Het staat hem dus volledig vrij hoe hij straks in het diner gaat voorzien. Mijmerend over de verschillende gerechten die hij graag lust, probeert hij zich voor te stellen waar zijn voorkeur vandaag naar uit zal gaan. Als het een maaltijd van de chinees wordt dan neemt hij er bami bij, dat staat al wel vast. Maar een patatje met een broodje kroket of iets dergelijks lijkt hem ook wel aantrekkelijk. Een 'vette bek' kan best voor een keer. Hij kan eventueel ook even bij de hamburgertent langsgaan voor zo'n menu dat ze daar altijd in de aanbieding schijnen te hebben. Overigens hebben ze daar ook tafeltjes. Er zijn tegenwoordig toch veel opties en nu hij erover nadenkt verbaast hij zich er eigenlijk over. Hij realiseert zich tegelijkertijd dat smaak en kwaliteit ook hierbij geen hoofdpunten meer vormen. Die vereisten zijn opgeofferd aan snelheid, verloren geraakt in eenvormigheid.

De man bedenkt dat toen hij nog klein was en nog bij zijn ouders woonde, er hooguit de keuze was uit welke chinees of snackbar. Allemaal hadden ze hetzelfde menu en hooguit was er eens een 'aanbieding van de week' waarbij iets nieuws te ontdekken bleek. Chinees Indische restaurants waren nog helemaal niet gespecialiseerd in een bijzondere streekkeuken of gerechten die er op de een of ander manier uitsprongen. Gewoon een maaltijd en of die nu origineel uit China of Indonesië afkomstig was, er kwam altijd veel teveel voor hun drie uit de plastic bakken en 't dunne tasje tevoorschijn. Kwantiteit ging toen ruimschoots boven kwaliteit. Als het veel was, was het vanzelf goed.

Een indringend, knerpend piepgeluid verstoort de stilte. Hij ziet hoe alle vier de spiegelbeelden tegelijk het apparaatje beantwoorden. Wellicht is het een idee als hij binnenkort ook eens zo'n leuk toestelletje koopt. Dan kan hij naar huis bellen als het per ongeluk nogmaals laat wordt. Nu zou hij er niets aan hebben, want wat voor zin heeft het om zijn vrouw op te bellen als die er helemaal niet is? De man moet glimlachen om zijn overwegingen, wat een dilemma's toch allemaal!

Het meisje is wat meer overeind, middenop de bank gaan zitten. Kennelijk is het slome hangen haar toch gaan vervelen. Als hij even kort rechtstreeks naar haar kijkt, ziet hij hoe ze het apparaatje aan haar oor houdt en er ingespannen naar luistert. "Ja met mij waar ben je?

Hmmm.

Ik ben over een halfuur in de stad."

Mededelingen en kreten meer zijn het niet. Het lijkt eigenlijk nog het meest op de gesprekken zoals die in Amerikaanse films en tv-series worden gevoerd. Alleen 'hello' en dan losbarsten in volzinnen en oppervlakkige formuleringen, zoals die zijn voorgekauwd door het script. Het valt hem weleens op dat kennelijk niemand in lijkt te zien dat achter al die welbespraakte conversaties een heel team schrijvers schuilgaat. Men laat zich kennelijk liever door uiterlijkheden en vage suggesties imponeren. Ook al komen deze 'script' makers soms met naam en toenaam aan bod in de aftiteling.

Het valt hem steeds vaker op hoezeer de maatschappij in dat opzicht aan het veranderen is. Hoe mensen voornamelijk in cliché's lopen te leuteren en inhoudelijk niets meer te aan elkaar te melden lijken te hebben. Het persoonlijke is verloren aan het gaan en hoe men onbeschaamd allerlei privé zaken in het openbaar deelt. Dit valt hem nog het meest op in van die praatprogramma's op de kijkbuis. Hij noemt ze natuurlijk niet voor niets 'wauwel shows', maar evengoed kijkt hij er een enkele keer naar. "Om op de hoogte te blijven", want zijn vrouw vraagt hem telkens fijntjes waarom hij ze aanzet als hij zich er zo zichtbaar aan blijkt te ergeren. Men kletst erop los of het een lieve lust heeft, maar als de show is afgelopen weet je al niet meer waar het gesprek over ging of wat die personen er eigenlijk over te zeggen hadden.

Hij gaat er vanuit dat het meisje op het beeldschermpje heeft gezien, wie haar opbelt. Daarom hoefde ze zich niet eerst bekend te maken, de andere kant weet tenslotte ook aan wie hij of zij de oproep richt. Men verwacht meteen met de juiste persoon in gesprek te raken. De man verbaast zich erover hoe beknopt communicatie kan zijn. Dat zal hij zich dus moeten aanleren als hij ook zo'n toestelletje neemt. Nu meldt hij zich altijd netjes met een goede morgen, middag of avond en zijn naam. Afhankelijk van het moment van de dag hoeft hij alleen de begroeting maar aan te passen. Zo kan iedereen, als ze hem opbellen gelijk horen wie het apparaat beantwoordt. Omdat hij zich eerst beleefd bekend heeft gemaakt.

Hij realiseert zich dat dit feitelijk overbodig is geworden. Alleen hij en zijn vrouw maken gebruik van de telefoon in de huiskamer, dus wie anders dan zij of hijzelf zou de hoorn van de haak kunnen opnemen? Vroeger de kinderen, maar toen waren er nog niet van die apparaatjes die je nu overal om je heen ziet en waar iedereen er een van lijkt te hebben. Behalve hij dus nog. De man moet glimlachen om zijn overpeinzingen, hij zit zich hier een beetje op te winden over niets.

Toen hij klein was hadden de mensen nog niet allemaal een eigen aansluiting waarop ze bereikbaar waren. Als er ergens een was dan zat die pal achter de voordeur en bij de beter gesitueerden een stukje verderop in de gang. Dat waren altijd van die bakelieten gevaartes die op een speciaal PTT plankje aan de muur bevestigd waren. Zwart met een zilverkleurige draaischijf en de hoorn zat er nog met een snoer aan vast Zijn ouders hebben hem erop geleerd hoe hij netjes, precies zoals hij het nu nog steeds doet, een gesprek moest aannemen. Toen was het nog ondenkbaar dat men altijd en overal een communicatiemiddel met zich mee zou sjouwen.

Hij moet plotseling denken aan de conference van Herman Finkers. Daarin zou een van de eerste abonnees van Almelo een geheim nummer hebben. De grap is of die mensen nu nummer drie of vier als aansluiting hebben gekregen, maar het doet er vanzelfsprekend niet toe omdat er volgens het verhaal in heel die stad maar negen telefoons zouden zijn. Alle andere namen noemt hij vervolgens op dus het resultaat laat zich raden.

Het meisje is nog in gesprek. Ze beantwoordt kennelijk vragen want kan volstaan met een hmmm geluid als reactie. Hij merkt dat ze het zowel ontkennend, bevestigend als neutraal kan laten klinken. De man vindt het knap en hij zit zich er nog over te verbazen als ze plotseling de verbinding verbreekt. Met een venijnige beweging drukt ze het een of ander knopje op het telefoontoestel in en daarna blijft ze er nog even naar zitten kijken. Het lijkt erop of ze verwacht dat het dingetje uit zichzelf iets zal gaan doen. In de spiegeling ziet hij dat ze er een verbaasde blik bij heeft getrokken.

Buiten is er weer een nieuwe straat, maar daar doorheen ziet de man hoe het meisje fanatiek op de knopjes van haar toestelletje zit te drukken. Het lijkt of ze een code intoetst, maar hij realiseert zich dat ze waarschijnlijk een berichtje intypt. Hij weet dat dit met veel van die toestellen kan, maar kent het dus nog niet uit eigen ervaring, z'n dochter heeft het hem verteld. Weer klinkt er een luide toon en nu ziet hij hoe ze op het schermpje iets zit te lezen. Hij vermoedt dat ze een reactie op haar bericht ontvangen zal hebben. De snelheid waarmee dit allemaal blijkt te gaan laat hem versteld staan. De trein is in de tussentijd een stationnetje, meer een halte binnengereden en er na hooguit een halve minuut weer vertrokken. Er is niemand ingestapt, alleen een man en een vrouw zijn langs het raam komen lopen. Weer in het donker ziet hij hoe het meisje nogmaals met de knopjes van haar toestel in de weer is. Even later houdt ze 'm aan haar oor.

"Ik zit in de trein naar huis.

Nee vanavond.

Kon wel maar dat heb ik niet gedaan.

Ik wilde eerst weten of hij serieus genoeg was. Daarom heb ik even gewacht tot hij terugkwam, na het college lopen."

Het gesprek aan de andere kant van het gangpad gaat hem niet aan, maar omdat het zo stil is in de coupé en het meisje tamelijk hard praat is er geen ontkomen aan.

"Om een uur of halfvijf pas.

Ik heb zijn kamer dus een beetje opgeruimd."

Buiten is het helemaal donker. De man laat zijn hoofd tegen de raamstijl rusten en kijkt beurtelings naar buiten en het meisje. Hij hoeft er alleen zijn ogen voor aan te passen, uitsluitend zijn focus te verleggen.

"Ja dat kon natuurlijk ook - maar je kent me toch"?

"Dat vind ik gemeen van je.

Zoiets zou ik noooooit doen."

De lange uithaal illustreert dat ze in gesprek moet zijn met een kennis. De toon waarop ze spreekt is zo amicaal dat ze goed met elkaar bekend zullen zijn. Het klinkt ronduit uitbundig aan haar kant van de treinwagon.

De man begrijpt dat er een wederzijdse kennis wordt besproken. Waarschijnlijk haar vriendje.

"Ja natuurlijk heb ik dat gedaan.

Ik kon er toch gewoon naar zoeken tussen zijn papieren.

Nee vierentwintig dat stond op zijn paspoort."

"Die vond ik er ook tussen ja.

Je had die foto moeten zien!"

Weer een lange uithaal. Ze wil er blijkbaar met haar gesprekspartner mee uitwisselen wat ze ergens van vindt. Afgaande op de geluiden was er blijkbaar iets uitermate belachelijk en was daarop haar aandacht gevallen.

"Ik had hem trouwens gezegd dat ik de rommel een beetje op zou ruimen."

Onder het spreken heeft ze haar voeten op de rand van de bank tegenover haar gezet. In een klassiek Romeinse houding ligt ze nu half uitgestrekt, leunend op een elleboog over de bank gedrapeerd.

"Een ongelofelijke bende ja."

"Nog erger.
Daar is Johan echt heilig bij. Die heeft zijn spullen niet op een grote hoop over zijn werktafel zwerven. Je had het misschien moeten zien om het te kunnen geloven.
Ik overdrijf echt niet."
De man begint zich af te vragen of de rit nog erg lang zal duren. Hij heeft trek gekregen en wil graag iets te eten. Hij weet dat er op treinen tegenwoordig geen restauratie meer meerijdt. Alleen op de grote routes misschien nog een karretje met koffie, thee en gevulde koeken. Dit is slechts een lokaal lijntje.
Een soort nostalgie overvalt hem. Hoe leuk zou het niet zijn om eens een hele lange treinreis te maken. Hij probeert zich voor te stellen hoe hij met zijn vrouw langs de Rijn kan gaan rijden. Hoe ze dan tegelijkertijd van een maaltijd en van het uitzicht kunnen genieten. Dat ze dan aan een deftig gedekt tafeltje in een ouderwets rijtuig reizen. Voor zover hij zich kan herinneren loopt er ter hoogte van de Lorelei inderdaad een spoorlijn vlak langs de rivier. Het moet eruit zien als in de film over de Oriënt Express, zoiets.
Aan de andere kant van de wagon wordt het gesprek steeds geanimeerder. Het meisje is in haar enthousiasme steeds luider gaan praten. Het hindert niet, maar geneert hem. Wat moet hij met haar ontboezemingen?
"Daar zag ik inderdaad wel tegenop."
Buiten de trein is niets te zien, het is er te donker voor.
"We hadden het nou eenmaal zo afgesproken.
Hij had me wel naar huis willen brengen maar dat zou dan betekenen dat we de voorlaatste trein moesten nemen."
"Nee dat gaat niet bij ons. Hij zou echt met de laatste trein weer terug moeten naar Utrecht.
Dan hadden we dus zeer bijtijds van het feest moeten vertrekken."
In de verte ziet de man een boerderij of iets dergelijks. Dwars door de velden loopt een rij lichtjes naar een gebouw waar een schijnwerper aan de gevel hangt. De strook lampen is waarschijnlijk de weg die er naartoe leidt. Hij kan niet zien waar al dat licht voor het gebouw voor nodig is. Doordat de trein rijdt verschuift zijn beeldhoek. Zo nu en dan vallen de gebouwen weg achter iets dat dichter bij het spoor staat.
Hij schrikt op van haar uithaal.
"No way!
Ja wel leuk maar daar gaat het niet om. Je gaat niet naar een lustrumfeest om er om half elf ofzo alweer weg te moeten."
Hij kijkt naar het meisje en vraagt zich af waar haar plotselinge enthousiasme vandaan komt.
"Nee hij heeft geen rijbewijs en een auto lenen ging ook niet."
De man ziet hoe ze onder het spreken meer rechtop is gaan zitten. Hij neemt

aan dat het meisje langzamerhand wakker wordt uit haar lethargie.

"Ja dag!

Dan had ik de hele avond niks kunnen drinken.

En ook weer alleen in dat gammele ding naar huis zeker?

Midden in de nacht? Ik moet er niet aan denken dat ie weer een keer stuk gaat."

Het gesprek is onontkoombaar. Hij wordt verplicht om mee te genieten met de avonturen die het meisje de avond ervoor kennelijk heeft meegemaakt. Het begint hem steeds meer tegen te staan om mee te moeten luisteren, maar hij vindt het evenmin gepast om er iets van te zeggen. Haar gesprek is privé en daar moet hij zich niet mee inlaten of bemoeien. Het lijkt hem teveel gevraagd om op te staan om in een andere coupé te gaan zitten. Voor die laatste paar minuten die de reis nog gaat duren lijkt hem dat meer moeite kosten, dan dat het voor 't oplossen van zijn ergernis noodzakelijk is.

Ruim twintig minuten zijn ze al onderweg en de hele reis kan hooguit een goed halfuur, zeg een kleine veertig minuten duren.

"Nee een biertje kostte vier Euro dus veel hebben we er niet genomen.

Het was trouwens koud in die hal. Daarom zullen we er hoogstens vier of vijf hebben gehad."

"Nee hij en ik allebei."

"Natuurlijk niet – en het was ook nog een stuk duurder hoor.

Het leek me ook een beetje een vooroordeel om als enige aan de rosé te gaan.

Dat leek me teveel meisjesachtig. Het was toch al voornamelijk een mannen feest."

De man begrijpt dat intussen de drank consumptie aan de orde is gekomen. Het is misschien een beetje onbenullig, maar hij vindt dat er best wat meer privacy betracht mag worden. Wat heeft hij nu eigenlijk met hun biertjes of die wijn te maken? Het gaat hem toch helemaal niet aan dat ze zich stoer heeft willen voordoen en geen rosé heeft willen drinken?

Of hoeveel glazen bier dan wel?

Langzaam rijdt de trein weer een station binnen. Geen halte zoals eerder, maar deze keer staat er een echt gebouw van echte stenen. Het is er zelfs druk op het perron. Even overweegt hij om snel een kop koffie en een gevulde koek te gaan halen. Er is vast wel een loket voor in het gebouw.

Hij weet niet hoelang de trein hier zal blijven staan en betwijfelt of de conducteur zal wachten met fluiten tot hij weer is ingestapt. Even hiervoor heeft hij op de klok buiten kunnen controleren dat het oponthoud nog geen minuut duurt en hij betwijfelt of ie het in die tijd zal redden om heen en weer te sprinten. Terug zelfs met een beker hete koffie in zijn hand. Dat draait vast en zeker uit op morsen. Hij heeft op het grote station in Utrecht trouwens gezien dat de koffie per kopje, telkens vers, wordt gezet. Dat duurt uiteraard ook

even. De actie zou hem natuurlijk wel de gelegenheid verschaffen om te ver-
kassen naar een andere coupé. In wachten op een volgende trein ziet hij geen
heil en dan zou hij ook al zijn spullen mee moeten nemen. Het zou hem tenminste een halfuur gaan duren, dat gaat 'm te ver.

Terwijl hij nog zit te twijfelen wordt er buiten op een fluitje geblazen en hoort
hij het sissen van de zich sluitende deuren. Meteen als de trein weer rijdt
komt er een conducteur hun coupé binnen. Moet hij hem vragen of het meisje
haar beslommeringen ergens anders kan bespreken?

Of of het wat stiller mag?

"Nee nooit.

Het was de eerste keer dat ik er was.

We hadden in een kroegje afgesproken.

Daarna zijn we ergens verderop iets gaan eten."

"Niet echt nee.

Het was meer een grote snackbar.

Met van dat felle witte licht enzo."

Het meisje heeft met haar vrije hand een kaart tussen de paperassen uit haar
tas gehaald en houdt deze nu half voor zich uit in de lucht. Het is blijkbaar teveel moeite om de beambte er beleefd bij aan te kijken. Niet gehinderd door
deze actie vervolgt ze het gesprek over de telefoon.

De conducteur stempelt nadat hij de hare alleen maar even kort bekeken
heeft, op een nogal onverschillige manier zijn kaartje af. Hij maakt er geeneens een gaatje in, zoals vroeger nog wel gebruikelijk was. De man laat het
erbij zitten. Als al het personeel zo weinig betrokken blijkt bij het werk, dan
zal hij die interesse waarschijnlijk ook niet 1, 2, 3 wakker kunnen schudden.

Het valt de man kennelijk ook niet op hoezeer hij zich gehinderd voelt door
het gesprekje tegenover hem. Om aan een hele uitleg te beginnen heeft hij
trouwens ook geen zin. Volgens hem zullen ze binnen niet al te lange tijd in
Leiden aankomen, maar hij heeft niet opgelet welk station ze zojuist zijn uit-
gereden. Hoewel ze op het oude deel van het traject zijn aangeland weet hij
niet hoeveel ze er nog moeten en hij kan dus evenmin inschatten hoe lang het
reisje nog precies gaat duren. Was dat zoeven Woerden, Bodegraven of zijn ze
Alphen aan de Rijn gepasseerd?

"Met de fiets. Dat was heel romantisch natuurlijk."

Op hemzelf en het meisje na, is de coupé weer leeg.

"Ik zat bij hem achterop. Hij moest zich dus rot trappen om over allerlei brug-
getjes heen te komen."

De conversatie aan de overkant gaat gewoon verder.

"Ja ik ben er een keer met mijn moeder wezen winkelen. Het is er wel aardig
hoor, maar ik vind het bij ons leuker."

"Dat niet alleen. Het is er helemaal niet gezellig. Zo met die grote weg vlakbij

54

het station er dwars doorheen."

"Ja dat weer wel. Zoiets hebben wij niet inderdaad."

De man verbaast zich over het oppervlakkige gebabbel. Zonder dat hij het wil moet hij horen hoe het meisje vergelijkingen maakt met hun woonplaats. Niet zozeer het onderwerp als wel de lijzige, ietwat zeurderige toon waarop het gesprek plaatsvindt, stoot hem af. Hoe kunnen mensen toch zo weinig gearticuleerd met elkaar spreken?

Het verbaast hem dat veel mensen op die manier toch de hele dag in gesprek lijken te willen zijn. Kijk maar eens om je heen, overal op straat en soms zelfs in de rij bij de kassa in de supermarkt!

Hoewel hij er zelf ook een hekel aan heeft om te moeten wachten, kan hij zich niet voorstellen dat je dan maar even iemand op gaat staan bellen. Uitsluitend om de tijd te doden, want ook bij zulke gesprekken vliegen de onbenulligheden meestal in het rond. Het gaat hem niet aan, hij wil er niet naar luisteren, het stoort 'm alleen maar.

"Nee die waren allemaal nog op het feest natuurlijk.

Hij woont in een huis met soosleden en dat feest was het zoveelste lustrum van hun sociëteit.

We hadden het rijk dus helemaal alleen."

Het meisje zit samenzweerderig te lachen. Zo te zien is ze inderdaad vergeten dat er nog meer mensen, hijzelf bijvoorbeeld, in de coupé zitten. Nogmaals is ze behaaglijk achterover tegen de leuning gaan hangen. Net zoals hij is ze wat meer in de hoek van de bank, tegen het raam aan geschoven. Haar voeten heeft ze op de bank tegenover zich laten liggen. Ze heeft maar een kort rokje aan en daaronder is nu duidelijk een donker gekleurde onderbroek zichtbaar. Het dingetje zit strak om haar billen.

Gegeneerd wendt hij zijn blik af en kijkt weer naar buiten.

"Ik had me voorgenomen om eerst even te douchen."

"Nee niet meteen. Ik had alleen onderweg al laten doorschemeren dat ik dat niet erg zou vinden. Maar hij bleef op zijn kamer rondlummelen.

Ik geloof dat ie niet helemaal door had wat de bedoeling was."

"Denk je dat"?

"Ik kan me niet voorstellen dat ze in dat huis nooit een meisje onder de douche hebben. Jij wel?

En dan - jongens"?

Ze laat haar vraag veelbetekenend klinken.

Terwijl ze luistert naar een uitgebreide uitleg, kijkt ze om zich heen. Het spijt de man dat hij niet zo'n handig muziek apparaatje heeft. Hij zou zich dan met van die dingetjes die je in je oren propt, af kunnen zonderen. Hij doet of hij aandachtig naar buiten zit te kijken en beredeneert waar ze zich bevinden. Een snelle rekensom leert hem dat het, als ze inderdaad zijn waar hij denkt

55

dat de trein rijdt, nog maar een paar minuten kan duren voordat ze bij het kleine stationnetje in zijn woonplaats zullen aankomen.

Ze passeren inderdaad de gebouwen en silo's van de brouwerij. Hij fietst daar wel eens en weet dus dat het vandaar niet ver meer is naar de voorlaatste stop op het stationnetje aan de Lammenschansweg.

"Omdat ik hem geroepen heb natuurlijk. Ik stond daar te wachten en hij kwam maar niet.

Het water was niet eens heel erg warm."

Het meisje is nogmaals vergeten dat er iemand mee moet luisteren. Het lijkt ook totaal niet tot haar door te dringen dat de inhoud van haar gesprek niet voor buitenstaanders bedoeld kan zijn of dat hij zich ervoor kan afschermen. Nogmaals bedenkt hij dat zo'n klein muziek dingetje daar uitermate handig voor is. Het verklaart natuurlijk ook waarom je ze zoveel ziet de laatste tijd.

"Nou ja – ik weet niet of ze daar een boiler hebben.

Daar had ik eigenlijk niet aan gedacht."

"Minstens vijf minuten denk ik."

"Ik had toch wel verwacht dat het anders zou lopen. De hele avond heeft hij echt heel lief tegen me gedaan.

Charmant enzo."

De trein houdt in, de remmen piepen en een beetje schokkerig rijdt ie inderdaad het stationnetje binnen. Eerst passeren ze nog de brug over het Kanaal.

"Dat verwachtte ik wel ja. Jongens zijn toch altijd geil. Of niet dan"?

"Nou dat weet ik niet hoor.

Zoveel ervaring heb ik daar niet mee.

Dat is denk ik meer jouw afdeling."

De man hoopt op versterking. Hij vindt de inhoud van het gesprek intussen wel heel persoonlijk worden. Helaas is het hem iets te ver om hier al uit te stappen en de verdere weg naar huis te lopen. Zijn fiets heeft hij trouwens op het hoofdstation gestald en hij moet er morgenochtend weer mee naar kantoor. Het meisje heeft zich even kort wat opgericht en kijkt over haar schouder naar buiten. Ze leest de naam van het station aan haar gesprekspartner voor. Doordat ze zo overdreven articuleert lijkt het of ze alle letters van het bord apart uitspreekt.

Niemand loopt langs, buiten niet en ook niet over het middenpad tussen hen in. Ze gaat weer met haar voeten op de vloer zitten. Gelukkig komt het uitzicht op haar onderkleding erdoor te vervallen. Intussen propt ze met haar vrije hand de spullen, die ze onder het praten uit haar tas heeft gehaald er weer in. Het eindpunt komt in zicht, maar de trein blijft nog even op deze halte staan. Blijkbaar duurt het haar te lang, want onder het praten en rommelen met haar spullen, kijkt ze nog eens naar buiten.

"Viel me wel een beetje tegen eigenlijk."

"Je zou verwachten van wel ja maar dat was dus niet zo. Meer een kleintje eigenlijk. En ik weet niet of het aan de drank of het koude water lag maar helaas maatje pink."
"Nee dat zeg ik toch. Niet echt een flinke harde."
Ze merkt het allemaal luid op, zeer nadrukkelijk alsof de persoon aan de andere kant van de lijn zich heel goed moet kunnen voorstellen wat ze precies bedoelt. De man vraagt zich af hoe expliciet een mens moet zijn om begrepen te worden.
"Ben je gek ofzo. Ik ga niet aan een vent z'n pik zitten zuigen.
Ik heb m'n grenzen hoor."
Intussen durft hij haar uitroep te betwijfelen. De onbeschaamde manier van praten maakt hem bijna aan het blozen. De man weet wel dat er tegenwoordig andere normen gelden en dat ook meisjes er plezier in zullen scheppen om over sex en dergelijke te praten, dit was hem vroeger met zijn vrienden ook niet vreemd tenslotte, maar zoals dat hier tegenover hem in de trein gebeurt moet hij dat normaal vinden?
Is dat de moderne tijd en loopt hij dus eigenlijk achter?
Volgens hem traden ze in zijn tijd lang niet zo in detail. Zij bespraken hun escapades voornamelijk in bedekte termen. Iedereen begreep toch immers wat er bedoeld werd, de kleinigheden of hoe het een en ander in de praktijk verliep, dat moesten ze er zelf maar bij bedenken. Al wilden ze onder elkaar natuurlijk ook niet onderdoen als mocht blijken dat het hun aan ervaring tekort schoot. Hij kijkt weer naar buiten. Door het meisje heen ziet hij hoe er iemand langs loopt op het perron.
"Uiteindelijk na een beetje helpen wel.
Maar het ging beter toen we eenmaal op zijn kamer waren. Zeg maar toen we in zijn bed waren gaan liggen.
Nou ja meer er op dus want hij gunde me geeneens de tijd om echt onder het laken te kruipen."
Het meisje krijgt een lange vraag te verwerken. Ernaar luisterend doet ze de rits van haar jas omhoog. Dan maakt ze ook de sluiting van de tas dicht. Na een korte fluittoon bij de deuren vertrekt de trein. Heel langzaam rijdt hij naar het eindstation. Het kind is intussen rechtop gaan zitten en het ziet er daardoor uit alsof ze zich intensief concentreert op de vraag waarnaar ze luistert.
"Daar was geen sprake van nee."
"Wat"?
Haar enthousiasme is nogmaals aangewakkerd. In ieder geval begint ze weer zeer luid te praten. Of schreeuwt ze zo omdat de trein weer rijdt?
"Nee niks ervan gewoon effe vlug. Meteen er bovenop – en dat was het."
Ze pauzeert haar kreten om nogmaals naar een vraag aan de andere kant van de lijn te luisteren. De man constateert dat er daar blijkbaar veel belangstel-

ling bestaat voor de avonturen van zijn medereizigster.

"Twee keer en ik hoefde niks te spelen hoor.

Dus verder was het wel lekker."

De trein sukkelt traag verder. De man staat, als hij de gebouwen van het voormalige goederenstation herkent, op. Ze zijn bijna bij het eindpunt.

Hij blijft met zijn rug naar het meisje toe tussen de banken staan, doet zijn jas dicht. Zijn actie maakt haar er niet opmerkzaam op dat het onderwerp van haar gesprek toch tamelijk persoonlijk genoemd mag worden. Of dat hij er getuige van is en het haar zou passen er wat minder luidruchtig over te zijn.

Om wat bewegingsruimte te krijgen stapt hij een stukje het gangpad op, maar om niet om te vallen moet hij zich vastgrijpen aan de zijkant van de bank. Het spoor maakt vlak na het oversteken van de Rijn, vlak voor het eigenlijke binnenrijden van het hoofdstation een scherpe bocht. Hij was het vergeten, anders was hij voor de stabiliteit nog even blijven zitten. Nu maakt zijn optreden een wat onbeholpen indruk. Hij hoopt er niet de schijn mee gewekt te hebben dat hij haast heeft. Dat hij ergens voor op de vlucht wil slaan.

Onverstoorbaar en even luidruchtig heeft het meisje haar ontboezemingen intussen voortgezet. De laatste opmerkingen heeft ze zelfs min of meer uitgeroepen en wel twee keer herhaald. De piepende wielen en het kraken van het schuddende rijtuig maken dat blijkbaar noodzakelijk. Pas als de trein weer enigszins tot rust komt, kan de man de bank weer loslaten.

Hij gaat verder met het fatsoeneren van zijn kleding en loopt, als ze eindelijk vrijwel tot stilstand zijn gekomen, naar het platform bij de deuren. Daar komt het meisje naast hem staan. Galant, zoals het een een heer betaamt, laat hij haar voorgaan door de inmiddels open sissende uitgang. Haar telefoontje heeft ze nog steeds aan haar oor geklemd, maar het doet er niet meer toe wat ze ertegen zegt. Ze zijn niet meer aan elkaar overgeleverd, op het perron bevinden ze zich weer in de buitenwereld.

Bericht

Hoewel op zich verbazingwekkend is het helaas tegelijkertijd vanzelfsprekend dat de man gedurende de afgelopen maanden ook berichten heeft ontvangen over de maat van zijn geslachtsdeel. Bijvoorbeeld hoe die met de hulp van pillen - nu in een voordelige aanbieding - of na 'slechts' een minimale operatie, tot geweldige proporties op te werken zou zijn. Dit terwijl alleen hijzelf, zijn echtgenote en misschien de uroloog die hij jaren geleden eens heeft bezocht, van de exacte maat van het orgaan op de hoogte zijn. Of deze personen er overigens voldoende belangstelling voor op kunnen brengen om hem er zo'n email over te sturen, blijft de vraag.

Overigens heeft hij zijn vrouw nooit willen vragen of zij misschien ontevreden is. Het onderwerp is hem te exotisch om zomaar tussen neus en lippen ter sprake te brengen.

De meeste van dat soort overbodige berichten zijn trouwens in het Engels gesteld, soms zelfs van een zeer gebrekkig soort en voor zover hij weet kent hij geen mensen met deze moedertaal die van zijn eventuele details op de hoogte kunnen zijn. Zo internationaal heeft hij het liefdespad helemaal niet weten te bewandelen. Hij is dus heel goed op de hoogte van de flauwekul die langs de email weg verspreid wordt, toch keek hij toch op van dit ene, blijkbaar speciaal aan hem persoonlijk gerichte, berichtje.

Aanbiedingen voor zaken zonder welke een mens verondersteld wordt niet te kunnen leven. Of in van dat slecht vertaalde Nederlands gestelde brieven over ongevraagde vriendschappen met naar eigen zeggen 'brave' meisjes uit bijvoorbeeld Rusland, zijn eveneens zijn deel geweest. Hij heeft er zelfs weleens een fotootje bij gekregen, maar die was zo onscherp dat hij er niet op heeft kunnen ontwaren of het afgebeelde meisje inderdaad aantrekkelijk genoemd kon worden. Of dat haar haren langs natuurlijke weg zo blond waren. Dat hij die persoon ooit zou herkennen mocht hij haar levend en wel op straat tegenkomen, is ook een vraag.

De man weet dat dit soort berichten allemaal onder de zogenaamde SPAM vallen en tegenwoordig worden die berichten vrijwel vanzelf door een filter dat ervoor in zijn mail programma is aangebracht, geweerd. Zonder dat hij ze eerst nog heeft hoeven lezen, worden de verdachte zaken automatisch geselecteerd voor verwijdering. Hij kan dat vervolgens doen met een simpele muisklik door ze uit de map 'ongewenste berichten' te verplaatsen naar de speciaal ervoor ingerichte 'prullenbak'.

Deze gang van zaken behoort tot het mooie van automatisering. Hoewel oorzaak en gevolg hier natuurlijk enigszins door elkaar lopen. Uiteindelijk is de oplossing om verschoond te blijven van alle overbodige mail via hetzelfde fenomeen voorhanden gekomen. De stroom SPAM maakt een aanzienlijk deel uit van alle onnodige, nutteloze informatie die er met de de berichten wordt uitgewisseld. En de man is niet de enige die er last van ondervindt, dat blijkt omdat de soft-ware voor vrijwel iedereen noodzakelijk is geworden.

Het is hem al diverse keren voorgekomen dat de opstellers ervan, het veelvoud van de mensen die hem al de nonsens zenden komen overigens uit de USA, zich waarschijnlijk vreselijk zullen vervelen. Of dat ze ervoor betaald worden om de rommel achter hun beeldscherm in te kloppen.

Elke maandag weer komt er een flinke lijst met direct te wissen berichten in zijn inbox terecht. Meestal hebben die een afzender van de andere kant van de oceaan en steevast gaan ze over Amerikaanse producten en diensten die hier meestal niet eens te verkrijgen of zelfs verboden zijn. De bewoording van de mailtjes verschilt nauwelijks en ook de producten ontlopen elkaar niet veel.

Dan weer komen ze van de een of andere farmaceut waarvan de pillen hier uitsluitend op recept te verkrijgen zijn, of het gaat om een blijkbaar onmisbare dienst waarbij het de vraag blijft of men er inderdaad de oceaan voor over wil komen steken om 'm te leveren.

Zo krijgt hij periodiek aanbiedingen voor casino's waar hij nog nooit is geweest of zelfs naar toe zou willen, bijvoorbeeld vanwege de afgelegen plek waar ze te vinden moeten zijn. Vaak kan hij een aardig startkapitaaltje als lokker vooruitzien, maar hij heeft zich er nog nooit echt door verleid gevoeld. De meeste berichten verdwijnen tegenwoordig dus ongelezen in de prullenbak, omdat ze als zodanig herkend worden door zijn mail programma.

Het berichtje dat hem ruim een maand geleden onder ogen kwam viel om meerdere redenen op. Niet zozeer omdat het door de eerste, automatische filtering heen was gekomen, maar vooral de officiële bewoording waarmee het was opgesteld sprong hem bij nader inzien in het oog. Een advocaat probeerde namelijk kontakt met hem op te nemen. Door uitsluitend het merkteken van het SPAM-filter en niet de directe gang er naartoe die daar meestal op volgt, kwam het bericht in de lijst met te verplaatsen berichten terecht. Daarom heeft hij er alleen even vluchtig naar gekeken.

Een dag later en de volgende weer, kwam er zo op het oog nog eenzelfde bericht van dezelfde afzender. Allebei weer heel persoonlijk en duidelijk aan hem gericht. De toon leek daarnaast indringender, nadrukkelijker en 'intiemer' te worden. "Hij moest toch echt eens reageren om de hem toegevallen som geld niet mis te lopen."

Dit laatste bleek overigens pas bij die betere beschouwing, want blijkbaar had hij in het eerdere, vluchtige nalopen van de inhoud over het hoofd gezien dat er een aanzienlijke rijkdom te verwerven zou zijn. De inhoud van het bericht wekte de schijn van een buitenkans die hij onmogelijk kon laten lopen. Zijn nieuwsgierigheid werd er weliswaar door gewekt, maar hij besloot het desondanks nog even aan te zien of er geen sprake was van het soort oplichting waarvoor zoveel gewaarschuwd wordt.

Allengs kregen de berichten een vriendelijkere toon, minder afstandelijk of zakelijk zoals in de eerste serie. Er werd gevraagd of hij zijn gegevens even wilde verifiëren op hun juistheid. Zijn personalia had hij overigens nooit verstrekt en daarom klopten ze inderdaad niet. Het leek er voornamelijk op dat er wat willekeurige zaken bij zijn naam waren neergezet met de opzet om hem te verleiden tot het verstrekken van zijn echte bankrekening nummer. Dan volgde daarop natuurlijk de voor een transactie belangrijke gegevens. Hij kon het eigenlijk aan zijn water aan voelen komen en hield de informatie dus angstvallig voor zich.

Volgens het advocaten collectief dat hem de gegevens leek te willen ontfutselen, zou hij een bedrag van iets meer dan anderhalf miljoen dollar bijgeschreven krijgen als hij daartoe aan het kantoor wilde doorgeven aan wie ze het over konden maken. Hij zou alleen maar het mailtje hoeven te beantwoorden en er inzetten of aanvullen wat men van hem wilde weten. Hij mocht volstaan met het corrigeren van zijn persoonlijke data, al werd er vanzelfsprekend expliciet gevraagd naar zijn rekeningnummer en de naam van zijn bank.

Het sprak allemaal voor zich en wonder boven wonder wilden ze verder blijkbaar niets weten. Ter verduidelijking was eraan toegevoegd dat de gegevens uitsluitend dienden om daar het geld naartoe over te kunnen maken. Glimlachend stelde hij vast dat er geeneens gevraagd werd naar zijn pincode of naar andere zaken waarmee ze de bankrekening, waar doorgaans overigens hooguit een paar tientjes op staat, konden leegroven.

Het kantoor van de advocaat, die ook gerechtsdeurwaarder bleek te zijn en afgaande op de naam van de firma eveneens aan incasso's deed, bevond zich in Hong Kong. De volledige naam van het kantoor met alle vennoten stond inclusief een indrukwekkend logo en aanbevelingen van niemand minder dan de Queen of England onderaan het nieuwste mailtje. Jammer dat hij de eerste voorafgaande berichten grotendeels had weggegooid want om helemaal zeker te kunnen zijn had hij willen kijken of ze iedere keer door dezelfde, zijn eigen, zaakwaarnemer waren ondertekend.

Louter uit nieuwsgierigheid heeft de man op het internet gekeken wat de HK dollar op dat moment 'deed'. Het bleek net geen een op tien te zijn en dat viel hem toch een beetje tegen. Bij het begrip dollar was hij er toch in eerste instantie vanuit gegaan dat het om de Amerikaanse versie zou gaan. Het exoti-

61

sche benadrukte nogmaals dat dit soort berichtjes waarschijnlijk in de categorie flauwekul thuishoorden, maar toch nog ruim een ton in Euro's zou hij natuurlijk heel goed kunnen gebruiken. Wie niet?

Vervolgens bleef het een paar dagen stil uit het verre Oosten. Pas een week later kwam er weer een berichtje van het kantoor uit Hong Kong binnen. Nogmaals werd er de nadruk gelegd op het feit dat hij nog niet gereageerd had op hun verzoek om informatie. En dat ze helaas echt geen andere manier wisten om met hem in kontakt te komen. De grote som geld lag nog steeds op hem te wachten en ze zagen er naar uit om de afwikkeling van deze transactie zo spoedig mogelijk met hem af te kunnen handelen.

Als hij de zaak niet mocht vertrouwen kon hij zich eventueel laten vertegenwoordigen door een jurist ter plaatse. Heel behulpzaam was er als bijlage een lijst met kantoren gevoegd waar het bureau zeer veel vertrouwen in scheen te hebben. De enige voorwaarde die deze uitbreiding van de procedure met zich meebracht was dat hij zijn personalia onder moest brengen bij dat andere kantoor. Vervolgens moest hij hen vanzelfsprekend machtigen, omdat er anders niet namens hem in deze zaak opgetreden kon worden. Dat een viertal van deze kantoren op hetzelfde adres gevestigd waren als het kantoor dat zo naarstig naar hem op zoek bleek, deed vermoeden dat het een groot gebouw was waarin een groot aantal deurwaarders en juristen bij elkaar zaten. De man stelde zich erbij voor dat het waarschijnlijk een gerechtsgebouw of 'paleis van justitie' zou zijn. Dit daadwerkelijk uitzoeken via Google maps of een soortgelijke dienst vond hij echter te ver gaan.

Een beetje vilein merkten ze op dat de kosten van deze vertegenwoordiging aanzienlijk zouden zijn, maar de opbrengst van zijn nalatenschap waarschijnlijk niet zouden overtreffen. Als slotopmerking stond er op de onderste regel van het berichtje vermeld dat het oorspronkelijk aangekondigde bedrag door de rente en gedurende de lange periode die het geduurd had om naar hem te zoeken, met ruim 12% was gegroeid. Helaas had hij zoals gezegd de eerdere berichten al weg gegooid. Hij kon dus niet controleren hoe lang de procedure al geduurd had of waarop de som geld waarnaar hij uit kon kijken precies uitkwam. Maar in een van die oude berichten had inderdaad een overlijdensdatum of iets dergelijks gestaan. Zoiets stond hem nog bij.

Ook de naam van de persoon van wie hij die enorme som geld tegoed had, was er ooit in langs gekomen. Nu wist hij dat allemaal niet meer en kon het fijne dus niet nagaan. Het leek hem echter een beetje sullig om als reactie te gaan vragen of ze de oude berichten nogmaals aan hem konden toesturen of dat hij het een en ander nog even wilde narekenen. Voor de zekerheid maakte hij een zogenaamde map aan onder zijn email account. Daar wilde hij vanaf dat moment de berichten in bewaren. Uit de 'oude berichten' haalde hij degenen tevoorschijn die nog niet vernietigd waren en die sloeg hij er daarna ook in op. Als alles netjes bij elkaar stond, ontvangen en eventueel straks verzonden berichten op datum gesorteerd, kon hij gemakkelijk nalopen welke gegevens hij aan ze verstrekt had.

De man heeft meerdere email adressen. Vanzelfsprekend die van zijn provider waarmee hij ook inlogt en daar heeft hij geheel volgens het advies van zijn computerblad, een tweetal aliassen voor aangemaakt. Met een van die twee legitimeert hij zich wel eens op een site. Op die wordt hij dus het meeste lastig gevallen met de rommel berichten. Zijn hoofd email adres gebruikt hij uitsluitend voor berichten aan familie en kennissen. De inbox die daarbij hoort blijft dus redelijk schoon.

Het andere reserve adres gebruikt hij zo nu en dan voor het maken van een bestelling. Als naam voor het zogenaamde account dat hij bij zo'n Internet leverancier altijd moet aanmaken om de bestelling te kunnen plaatsen en uitvoeren. De bijbehorende toegangscode en ander noodzakelijk gegevens houdt hij ervoor bij in een speciaal tekstbestand dat hij onder een cryptische naam verstopt heeft staan op zijn harde schijf.

Daarnaast heeft hij een aantal mail adressen die verbonden zijn met de site van zijn zaak. Daarop ontvangt hij eveneens SPAM, maar die is meestal van zakelijke aard en betreft dan ongevraagde diensten, lidmaatschappen en vermeldingen op zakelijke zoek sites of kortingen die hem worden aangeboden als hij eerst voldoende Euro's aan een bestelling besteedt.

Zo nu en dan ontvangt hij er zelfs een sollicitatie op, meestal voorzien van een CV maar hij heeft die nog nooit willen openen. Hij is bang om inbreuk te maken op iemands privacy, vernietigt deze berichten meteen en beantwoordt de afzender per omgaande dat hij als ZZP'er nu eenmaal geen vacatures heeft. De man vindt dat hij dat aan de beleefdheid verplicht is, al heeft hij nooit om de toegezonden informatie gevraagd.

De kwestie met betrekking tot de nalatenschap uit Hong Kong is in zijn achterhoofd blijven doorspelen. Was hij nou dom geweest om het hele verhaal niet serieus te nemen en had hij alles meteen naar de prullenbak moeten verwijzen?

Automatisch via het zelflerende filter of met de hand?

Hij twijfelt of hij niet beter had moeten kijken naar de oorspronkelijke berichten. Had hij dan misschien kunnen nagaan of er inderdaad sprake was van een connectie?

Voor zover de man man weet heeft hij geen familie in die contreien. Nooit is in het ouderlijk huis een verre oom of tante uit Hong Kong ter sprake gekomen. Ook niet daar ergens in de buurt. Gezien het fortuin dat hem nu toe kan vallen verwondert het hem vooral dat zo'n blijkbaar rijke familietak, volledig buiten beeld geraakt en gebleven zou kunnen zijn. Wie is zijn mecenas en hoe kan die zomaar uit de lucht komen vallen?

Wat is de oorspronkelijke relatie die hij met hem of haar heeft?

Misschien dat hij een keer zijn zusje moet opbellen om te vragen of zij ook benaderd is. Hoe teruggetrokken leefde hun familielid daar eigenlijk?

Waarom en in hoeverre heeft hij of zij zich bij leven en welzijn voor hem en zijn verwanten in Europa verborgen gehouden?

Vooral dit laatste gegeven kan hij nog maar met moeite loslaten omdat het de enige verklaring kan vormen voor de moeilijkheden die men ter plaatse ondervonden heeft om hem te traceren. Teneinde de twijfel geen kans te geven heeft hij tot nog toe ieder bericht van het kantoor van de barrister na lezing als kul afgedaan. Ze domweg weggeklikt naar de prullenbak en later dus die speciale map. Hij heeft zichzelf ermee willen behoeden in de val te trappen die men kennelijk voor hem heeft opgesteld. De man heeft er vaak genoeg over gelezen hoe mensen ter goeder trouw een groot deel van hun hebben en houden via het internet verkwanseld hebben, door op de trucs van slimme oplichters in te gaan.

Toen hij de berichten uiteindelijk toch wat beter begon te lezen, heeft de twijfel bij hem postgevat. Vooral een van de latere berichten, waarin ze er zo nadrukkelijk op aandrongen dat hij kontakt met ze op zou nemen, had hij daarom geprint. Louter uit voorzorg. Hij heeft het een aantal keren herlezen om te ontdekken waar het addertje onder het gras verborgen zat. Hoe ze hem er nou precies mee probeerden te foppen.

Als hij tegenwoordig 's morgen zijn email binnenhaalt betrapt hij zich er op uit te kijken naar een nieuw bericht van het kantoor aan de andere kant van de wereld. Hij is toch henieuwd geworden naar de vervolgstappen die de advocaten er ondernemen om hem daadwerkelijk te vinden. Het lijkt hem intussen dat zij vanuit hun functie aangesteld zijn om zich alle moeite te getroosten het flinke bedrag bij de juiste persoon, bij hem dus blijkbaar, te bezorgen.

Overigens is 't hem eveneens bekend dat alle kosten die aan de procedure verbonden zijn, hem ten laste zullen komen. Ze worden naar alle waarschijnlijkheid verrekend en dus in mindering gebracht op het aan hem nagelaten bedrag. Daarover heeft hij onlangs zijn licht opgestoken bij een advocaat hier in de stad. Een oud klasgenoot met wie hij over deze kwestie in gesprek geraakt was toen hij 'm bij toeval tegenkwam in de kroeg.

Als die "barrister" kosten noch moeite spaart om hem te vinden dan is het inderdaad goed mogelijk dat er niet veel van die anderhalf miljoen dollars en de opgelopen rente overblijft. In ieder geval niet als hij nog langer zo kinderachtig blijft tegenstribbelen.

Om heel eerlijk te zijn is het toegezegde bedrag aanzienlijk genoeg om het risico van een eventuele Internet truc te kunnen compenseren. Het lijkt hem intussen wel interessant om er achter te komen hoe zo'n oplichter te werk gaat en wat hij ervoor moet doen om er in te trappen. Als ze alleen maar zijn bank gegevens willen hebben, ziet hij niet in hoe iemand vervolgens die rekening kan leegroven. Tenslotte is hem nog geen enkele keer gevraagd om een bijdrage en een handtekening heeft hij sowieso niet in digitale vorm.

Het staat hem overigens bij dat over die kosten een keer iets in een van de eerste berichten heeft gestaan. Maar toen vond hij dus nog dat ze, vrijwel ongelezen in de 'prullenbak' mochten verdwijnen. Hij herinnert zich er nog van dat er een tarief vermeld stond en dat hij die bedragen toen aan de hoge kant vond. Hij bedacht toen dat hij zelf ook weleens voor zulke tarieven zou willen werken. Dan kon hij met zo nu en dan een paar weekjes bezig zijn, in een jaarsalaris voor hem en zijn vrouw voorzien. Alles dus in relatie met wat hij nu bij het uitzendbureau en in zijn zaak verdient.

Aan alle twijfel is vanmorgen een einde gekomen. Op het email adres dat hij zoveel mogelijk privé wil houden kwam een bericht binnen van een advocaten kantoor uit Hong Kong. Omstandig werd er in uitgelegd dat hij de mogelijke bevoordeelde was van de een of andere koninklijke prins uit die contreien en dat hij daarom recht had op een bedrag ter grootte van minimaal anderhalf miljoen dollar. Hij had zich er dus in vergist dat er sprake was van een familielid en hij was uitverkoren om tot de mogelijke bevoordeelden te gaan horen. Dat is iets anders dan hij eerder begrepen had.

Het enige dat hij voor het ontvangen van dit geldbedrag behoefde te ondernemen was het verstekken van zijn personalia en bankgegevens zodat ze het daarop konden laten bijschrijven door de executeur testamentair in deze kwestie. De termen hadden hem kennelijk in verwarring gebracht, maar het bericht zag er weer fantastisch uit. Zo op het eerste gezicht leek het, met al die koninklijke logo's, inderdaad heel legitiem. Als service hadden ze zelfs voor hem uitgerekend wat de geldsom in Euro's waard zou zijn tegen de huidige koers. Zoals hij al bedacht had ruim anderhalve ton dus.

Alleen zijn naam was deze keer volledig verkeerd gespeld en de verdere gegevens klopten ook weer van geen kant. Het kantoor had trouwens een heel andere naam dan die uit het eerdere bericht. Al was het eveneens gevestigd in het zelfde gerechtsgebouw. Zij het dus op een geheel ander nummer.

Glimlachend omdat ze hem toch bijna tuk hadden gehad, kieperde hij alle uit Hong Kong afkomstige berichtjes alsnog in de prullenbak. Dat hij van twee verschillende personen, onmiskenbaar allebei prins nota bene, eenzelfde bedrag zou erven leek hem ondanks het aantrekkelijke vooruitzicht, te sterk om er langer geloof aan te kunnen hechten.

Bedankt

De man komt de trap af. Tot even hiervoor heeft hij boven op zijn kamer zitten werken. Dat doet hij elke avond een tijdje. Eerst na het eten even rustig het laatste stukje uit de krant doornemen en eventueel een kort dutje, dan om klokslag acht uur het journaal en vervolgens verdwijnt hij voor een poosje naar zijn kamer op de eerste verdieping. Omdat hij meestal de koffie nog niet helemaal op heeft gedronken, neemt hij zijn mok mee er naartoe. Maar eerst schenkt hij er in de keuken de laatste druppels bij uit de kan. Zo gaat het sinds hij thuis is komen werken en zijn 'kantoor' aan huis heeft. Het vormt het vaste, dagelijks terugkerende ritueel, al hoeft hij de tijd tegenwoordig niet meer te besteden aan het afmaken van een klusje, factureren of bijwerken van de boekhouding.

Soms roept zijn vrouw hem van onderaan de trap omdat er op de televisie een uitzending begint waar hij of zij, maar gewoonlijk toch samen, naar willen kijken. Over het algemeen houdt hij dat overigens zelf in de gaten en komt ie al ruim op tijd, minimaal een paar minuten voor de uitzending is begonnen, de trap af. Om ongeveer kwart over negen maar ook rond een uur of tien beginnen op de BBC de programma's waar hun voorkeur naar uitgaat. Het uurtje tijdverschil verschaft hem dagelijks de tijd om even bezig te zijn, om ergens alleen voor zichzelf, helemaal privé aan te werken. Daar is ook nadat de kinderen het huis uit zijn gegaan, geen verandering in aangebracht.

Overdag is dezelfde kamer 'het kantoor'. Dan ontvangt hij er zijn klanten of zoekt er voor hen de zaakjes uit die hij voor ze op zich heeft genomen. Steevast noemen ze dat 'de klusjes'. Maar ze komen de laatste tijd niet zo vaak meer voor. Nog slechts heel af en toe komt een klant bij hem langs om te overleggen over lopende zaken of een nieuwe opdracht met hem voor te bereiden. Hij heeft soms nog wel kontakt met een aantal van hen, maar dan gaat het meer om een vrijblijvend advies of toont men belangstelling voor hoe het met hem gaat. De man is er te trots voor om ze om nieuw werk te vragen en intussen heeft hij een aantal van zijn hobby's een vaste plaats op de werkkamer kunnen geven. Zodoende kan hij zich daarop werpen.

In een van de hoeken heeft zijn uitgebreide geluidsapparatuur 'n plekje verworven. Daar staat een keyboard, wat piep en knordozen zoals hij ze noemt en een grote ouderwetse bandrecorder met 18 centimeter spoelen. De apparaten staan er gebruiksklaar neergezet. De man hoeft ze alleen maar in te schakelen als hij erop wil spelen. Vlakbij het raam heeft hij een werktafel gemaakt waaraan elektronische schakelingen uitgewerkt kunnen worden. Hij kan er aanpassingen aan aanbrengen of een nieuw ontwerp bouwen. Ook deze plek is gebruiksklaar, compleet met een soldeerbout, meetapparatuur en de elektroscoop die hij er onlangs voor heeft aangeschaft.

Er half achter verborgen, op de grond staat een slordige stapel apparaten waar hij 'nog eens naar wil kijken'. Onder andere een ouderwets elektronisch orgel en 'n half afgebouwde synthesizer bouwdoos die hij een poosje geleden van een vriend kreeg. Daar is iets met de oscillator niet helemaal gelukt, maar hoe dat zit weet hij niet precies. Het moet ergens uitgebreid beschreven staan in de aantekeningen die erbij in de doos gestoken zitten. Maar daar heeft hij zich nog niet aan gezet. Hij heeft het zogezegd te druk met andere dingen.

Op de begane grond loopt hij de gang af naar de keuken.

Hij zet er zijn vuile vaat, hij had ook een bordje met een geschilde appel erop en een mesje mee naar zijn werkkamer genomen, op het aanrecht. Het inruimen van de afwasmachine heeft hij in de ogen van zijn vrouw gedurende de afgelopen maanden zo vaak fout gedaan dat hij zich er niet meer aan waagt. Als hij het vuile goed netjes naast elkaar aan de afdruipkant van het werkblad rangschikt, kan ze er na thuiskomst alsnog het beste plekje voor in het apparaat kiezen.

Hij gaat de kamer in en neemt plaats in de stoel tegenover die waarin zijn vrouw altijd zit. Zonder iets te zeggen kijkt hij ernaar. Het lijkt erop of hij wat zou willen bespreken maar niet helemaal weet hoe ie moet beginnen. Hij leunt tegen de rug van zijn stoel en gaat meteen weer rechtop zitten. Hij aarzelt, laten we het daarop houden want zo ziet het er welbeschouwd uit.

"Weet je dat ik het nog nooit tegen je heb gezegd?

En toch loop ik er al een tijdje aan te denken. Het kost me eigenlijk vooral moeite om de juiste woorden te vinden. De juiste woorden om erover te beginnen. Maar ook wat ik precies wil zeggen of wat ik feitelijk bedoel."

De eerste woorden kwamen een beetje mompelend uit z'n mond, nu hij eenmaal is begonnen spreekt hij hardop. Articuleert hij zorgvuldig zodat ie duidelijk te verstaan moet zijn.

"We zijn intussen bijna veertig jaar bij elkaar en dat speciale waarover ik wat tegen je wil opmerken kan ik vreemd genoeg nog steeds niet met de juiste termen benoemen. Da's dus eigenlijk raar want in feite hebben we nooit zoveel nodig om elkaar te begrijpen. Vooral omdat ik de prater ben en jij luistert altijd het beste. Het heeft er juist altijd toe geleid dat we op onze manier met problemen, als ze er ooit waren, om wisten en konden gaan. Dat gaat al jaren zo en er is volgens mij geen verandering bij nodig.

Daar gaat het me nu dan ook niet om, maar we hebben het er nooit over gehad hoe we zo ver gekomen zijn. Ik bedoel zo ver als waar we nu zijn. En ook niet hoe we verder gaan. Moeten of willen gaan dus."

Onder het spreken is hij tegen de rugleuning aan gaan zitten. Nu komt hij weer iets naar voren.

"Ik houd niet zo van plannen maken en me daarop vastleggen, dat weet je. Ik ben tenslotte geen chinees en leef niet in een planeconomie, maar evengoed hebben we nog een paar jaar samen tegoed.

Als we ons best doen en een beetje blijven opletten, misschien zelfs nog een flink aantal en daar hoop ik natuurlijk op. Dat weer wel, maar zoals je merkt vind ik 't lastig er met je over te spreken.

Ik weet niet wat ons te wachten staat en 't lijkt me trouwens helemaal niet interessant om op voorhand te weten wat er aankomt, toch zul je begrijpen dat de laatste tijd flink wat indruk op me heeft gemaakt. Ik bedoel wat me is overkomen met dat ziekenhuis en dergelijke.

Dat hebben we nooit of te nimmer aan zien komen of verwacht, Nu het min of meer achter ons ligt, moeten we constateren dat we er goed doorheen gerold zijn. Al weet ik dus nog steeds niet of jij wel blij was toen ik weer genezen verklaard werd en naar huis mocht.

Het doet er niet zo toe misschien, maar het is een vraag die me zo nu en dan bezig houdt. Vooral als ik een soort teleurstelling bij je op meen te merken.

Je zult begrijpen dat dat dan zeer doet."

Hij kijkt de kamer rond en het lijkt of hij zoekt naar een manier om zijn betoog te vervolgen. Alsof er ergens een aanknopingspunt moet staan, liggen of hangen om op verder te borduren.

"Het waren natuurlijk de dokters die me behandeld hebben en dat ik zo goed met ze op kon schieten heeft er volgens mij toe bijgedragen dat ik het het tijdens de opname in het ziekenhuis nogal naar m'n zin heb gehad.

Ik denk nog steeds dat ze me een aardige vent vonden en misschien daarom zo hun best hebben gedaan om me erdoor te helpen. Dat ze me al die persoonlijke tips en aanwijzingen gaven om mijn genezing, het proces zoals ze het professioneel noemden, te versnellen.

Zoiets zou ik voor hen in mijn vak ook doen. Maar daar hebben we het de afgelopen tijd al eens vaker over gehad. Intussen is die periode veranderd in een aardige herinnering en kijk ik er dus met plezier op terug. Laat ik het afdoen met de opmerking dat de scherpe kantjes er zijn afgesleten.

Toch mogen we vaststellen jij en ik er allebei een soort van tik aan hebben overgehouden. Jij hebt je er erg voor moeten inspannen om de boel hier in huis gaande te houden. En dat allemaal tussen de bezoekuren en later ook mijn herstel hier in huis door.

Ik heb je nooit kunnen tonen hoe ik dat op prijs heb gesteld en om eerlijk te zijn vraag ik me weleens af of ik hetzelfde voor jou had kunnen opbrengen. Elke keer kwam je op tijd. Al die weken iedere dag weer! En laten we vaststellen dat mijn aanpak beslist anders geweest zou zijn. Dan druk ik me nog tamelijk voorzichtig uit. Helaas zit ik momenteel nog met een aantal onbeantwoorde vragen."

Hij staat op en draait zijn rug naar de kamer. Als hij zo tegen de serre aan praat kan ze hem nog steeds heel goed verstaan. Dan hoeft hij niet plotseling heel hard of met aanzienlijk meer nadruk te gaan spreken.

"We verschillen nogal van elkaar, dat probeerde ik je zojuist duidelijk te maken en ik moet eraan toevoegen dat het beeld, mijn voorstelling, me nog niet duidelijk is. Hoe vaak ik er de laatste tijd ook over heb zitten peinzen, ik kan niet helder voor ogen krijgen waar onze overeenkomsten en verschillen eindigen of beginnen.

Telkens als ik denk een punt gevonden te hebben waarvan ik zeker ben dat jij daar anders over denkt, dan moet ik kort erop al toegeven dat we het er toch telkens met elkaar over eens geworden zijn. Ook als ik heel persoonlijk of nadrukkelijk iets meemaakte en dus aanzienlijke verschillen qua inzicht of ervaring meende te kunnen verwachten.

Dát vind ik erg verwarrend.

In de praktijk zal het er natuurlijk niet zoveel toe doen, maar als onderwerpen waarover we van mening kunnen of zelfs mogen verschillen, wezenlijke overeenkomsten bevatten, hoe zit dat dan?"

Hij blijft voor zich uit staan kijken, lijkt weer om woorden verlegen. Naar het schijnt kan hij zijn verwarring niet goed verwoorden.

Het verhaal wordt, voornamelijk omdat hij tussen de verschillende opmerkingen lange pauzes laat vallen en hierdoor stamelend lijkt te spreken, merkbaar onsamenhangend. De man draait zich om en gaat op zijn stoel zitten.

"Ik denk dat we tot nog toe een leuk leven hebben gehad, in ieder geval vind ik het mijne niet erg vervelend. Ik heb het altijd leuk gevonden als je bij me was, maar daar hebben we het ook nog nooit expliciet over gehad.

Natuurlijk spijt het me dat ik niets belangrijks heb bereikt. Zogenaamd belangrijk of in 't echte 'leven' iets van belang.

Soms denk ik dat niemand lijkt te willen weten wat ik kan of waartoe ik feitelijk in staat ben. Tenzij ze er een voordeel bij kunnen halen natuurlijk, maar dat wil ik geen echte belangstelling noemen.

Om kort te gaan heb ik me eigenlijk nooit kunnen bewijzen. Bijvoorbeeld door componist te worden van elektronische muziek en dat we daardoor allerlei internationale concerten af hadden moeten lopen. Zeg maar dat ik dan wereldberoemd zou zijn en jij, als mijn muze, in die faam zou kunnen delen. Als mijn érkende muze, want ik zou je er in alle openheid en natuurlijk iedere keer als ernaar wordt gevraagd, erkentelijk voor zijn.

Zij het dat jij niet van mensenmassa's houdt en laat ik eerlijk zijn, ik heb concertkaartjes altijd veel te duur gevonden. Een beetje vier tot vijfmaal de prijs

70

van een plaat, of nu dan een CD neertellen, voor een concert waar je door het kabaal van de bezoekers niet van de muziek kunt genieten of hoort wat er ge- speeld wordt.

Omdat jij zo vaak studeerde op je piano heb ik me nooit ten volle op dat com- poneren toegelegd, maar op deze manier vonden en ondersteunden we elkaar wel heel erg. Ik heb mijn muziekcollectie erdoor uit kunnen breiden. Bij deze wil ik sorry zeggen voor de keren dat ik je naar iets heb laten luisteren dat je vreselijk vond. Ik wil overigens bekennen dat ik zelf ook niet altijd heel erg blij was met de nieuwste aanschaf.

Je hebt er in ieder geval nooit over geklaagd en dat apprecieer ik. De koptele- foon die ik een paar jaar geleden met Sinterklaas als surprise van je kreeg spreekt vanzelfsprekend boekdelen, maar ik gebruik 'm trouwens met veel plezier. Nog steeds en dat weet je."

Alsof hij zijn grapje wil laten inwerken, laat hij een korte pauze vallen.

"Over andere carrière stappen zullen we het niet hebben.

Waar het om draait is dat ik me door jou altijd gesteund gevoeld heb en ik hoop erop dat je mijn waardering ten aanzien van jouw stappen ook opge- merkt zult hebben. Nogmaals, ik denk dat we nog een tijdje samen door kun- nen gaan, maar de laatste tijd weet ik niet of jij dat een leuk vooruitzicht vindt. Of het je aantrekt, zeg maar.

Mij lijkt dat dus wel, maar ik ben partijdig. Ik spreek hier voor mezelf.

Helaas ben jij in dit opzicht lastig te peilen. Hoewel mijn waardering dus nog- al groot is, is de twijfel die er tegenover staat weleens moeilijk. Doe ik het goed, behandel ik je wel precies zoals je wenst en laat ik nog voldoende blij- ken dat ik van je houd?

Zoiets zit ik dan te bedenken en ik ben me vervolgens niet zeker of ik daar een passend antwoord op heb.

Zo vraag ik me regelmatig af of jij wel gelukkig bent bijvoorbeeld."

Tijdens het spreken is hij met z'n billen naar de voorkant van de zitting van de stoel geschoven. Zo recht overeind gekomen lijkt hij wat groter en het ziet er daadkrachtig uit, maar zijn houding onderstreept de onzekere inhoud van zijn woorden niet. Hij gaat weer met zijn rug tegen de leuning zitten.

"Zo vond ik het bijvoorbeeld een heel compliment dat je indertijd jaloers was op die collega waarvan je dacht dat ik verliefd op haar was. Dat was wellicht een beetje zo, maar niet omdat ik bij jou weg wilde of je niet leuk meer vond. Ze was gewoon aardig en haar onbereikbaarheid maakte het opwindend om kontakt met haar te zoeken, meer was het niet. Ik vond het gewoon spannend om haar een brief te schrijven, die heb ik je laten lezen en dat je me de keuze liet om 'm ook daadwerkelijk te versturen vond ik erg sportief. Het toonde voor mij aan dat je van me hield en me misschien ook respecteerde."

Weer is hij naar voren geschoven op de stoel, maar nu blijft hij zo zitten.

71

"We hebben, nu mijn omzet en daardoor mijn inkomen grotendeels ingestort is, niet meer zoveel armslag als eerst.

Dat jij nu een redelijk betaalde baan hebt is meegenomen, maar de afspraak was dat jij voor de extra's zou zorgen. Nu zijn we intussen afhankelijk van wat jij verdient en is de boel dus omgedraaid.

Het is jammer dat ik geen vaste inkomsten meer heb waarop we kunnen rekenen en dat we daardoor in onzekere omstandigheden verkeren.

Ik doe mijn best, dat weet je, maar als ik nergens een leuke baan kan vinden dan blijf ik afhankelijk van wat het uitzendbureau voor me beschikbaar heeft. Jammer genoeg is dat niet zoveel en lang niet vaak genoeg, maar het ligt helaas niet anders. Al zou ik dat dus best willen."

Hij kijkt even voor zich uit de kamer in, overweegt of ie een lichtje aan moet doen, maar laat het zo. Buiten is het weliswaar donker aan het worden, maar het is nog licht genoeg voor wat ie aan het doen is.

Straks kan het ook nog.

"We hebben altijd een eenheid gevormd. Bijvoorbeeld in de strijd die we met de zorg instanties voor onze zoon moesten voeren. Altijd stonden we schouder aan schouder. We wisten wat we aan elkaar hadden en, al liet je soms de kastanjes door mij uit het vuur halen, je stond wel pal achter me.

Je nam het voor me op als de begeleiders zich tegen me keerden en zoals we allebei weten ging dat soms op het persoonlijke af.

Pal onder de gordel, durf ik zelfs te stellen. Maar alleen zo hebben we hem kunnen ondersteunen. De samenwerking stelde ons in staat om 'm te sturen in zijn zelfstandigheid. Intussen zijn we zo ver dat hij dat toch maar bereikt heeft, ondanks alle tegenwerking dus.

Daar mogen en kunnen we trots op zijn, vind ik."

De man gaat weer staan en kijkt kort op zijn horloge. Het is bijna half tien.

Over hooguit een kleine drie kwartier komt zijn vrouw thuis van de vergadering op haar werk. Die kon en mocht ze niet missen. Ze was het aan haar status binnen de firma verplicht, om erbij te zijn.

"Als ik terug kijk op ons leven, dan zie ik dat we weliswaar nooit aan de weg getimmerd hebben en in de ogen van velen zullen we weinig tot niets bereikt hebben op de wereldschaal, maar hebben we zoiets ooit gewild?

Privé hebben we altijd genoeg aan onze kop gehad.

Natuurlijk was 't leuk geweest om overal uitgenodigd te worden en te behoren bij de gevierde, heel populaire personen. Daarin zijn we echter niet geslaagd omdat we er nooit moeite voor hebben willen doen. We hebben helemaal '*nevernooit*' onszelf voorbij willen lopen om geliefd te zijn. Om bijvoorbeeld een BN'er te worden.

Dat wilden we niet en onze manier van tegen de dingen aankijken liet het niet toe. Wat moet je trouwens met dat kwartiertje faam van Andy Warhol?

Laten we eerlijk zijn, jij bent meestal terughoudend, kijkt de kat uit de boom en ik sta altijd klaar met een grap of leuk bedoelde opmerking. En ja die zijn langzamerhand steeds cynischer aan het worden of slaan de plank weleens volledig mis. Ik kan niet anders blijkbaar en het zal mijn lot wel zijn.

Zo sta ik immers in het leven en noem het intussen ervaring, zo je wilt."

De man is onder het praten naar de kamerdeur gelopen. In de streep licht die naar binnen schijnt, kijkt hij nog eens op zijn horloge. Snel loopt hij de gang op en gaat naar boven. Hij wil nog even verder werken aan een frequentie volgende schakeling die hij aan het ontwerpen is.

Hij had nog wel willen spreken over de manier waarop ze de laatste tijd zo vaak tegen hem uit lijkt te vallen. Of dat hij zich weleens genegeerd voelt als ze, ook in het openbaar, neerbuigend tegen hem doet.

Hoe onzeker hij daarvan wordt omdat ie niet zo goed kan inschatten of ze dan echt boos op hem is, of gewoon moe en een beetje humeurig. Misschien moet ie het wijten aan de overgang?

Daar heeft ze de leeftijd voor maar hij weet er niets vanaf. En ze wil er ook niet over praten. Als ze straks thuis is gekomen dan drinken ze nog even een glaasje wijn samen. Daar zal ze na zo'n avond vol gezeur wel aan toe zijn.

Terras

Vanmorgen zijn de man en zijn vrouw tamelijk vroeg van huis vertrokken. Ze moest voor het tweejaarlijkse functioneringsgesprek op het hoofdkantoor van haar werkgever in Den Haag zijn en omdat hij 'eigenlijk toch niets om handen had' zijn ze met de auto gegaan. "Dan hoef ik niet met mijn goede kleren aan in de trein. " Ze had het er als overbodig argument aan toegevoegd.

Dat ze een hekel heeft aan zelf autorijden en het dus bij voorkeur aan hem overlaat door zich te laten brengen en halen, is een gegeven waarmee ze nooit moeite hebben gehad. De zachte dwang die van haar opmerking uitging en de negatieve lading was hem dan ook niet meteen opgevallen, maar bij nader in-zien wilde hij er zich niet alsnog boos over maken. Inderdaad heeft hij de laatste tijd niet zo heel veel omhanden. Dat laat zich overigens duidelijk op-merken aan de hand van de dagindeling, die hij er op nahoudt.

Zijn 'zaak' levert hem nog hooguit een paar uurtjes arbeid op. Het aanbod aan werk is langzamerhand zo weinig dat hij het in hooguit een dagje per week gemakkelijk redt om het allemaal naar behoren uit te voeren. Feitelijk hoeft hij er alleen maar voor naar het kantoor te gaan. Dat hebben ze indertijd, toen hij zich pas als zelfstandige gevestigd had en er nog volop voor hem te doen was, naast de slaapkamer op de eerste verdieping van hun huis, ingericht.

Helemaal in het begin bleek de drukte die het werk, en alles dat erbij kwam kijken, vaak meer dan een dagtaak te vullen. Indertijd had hij meer dan zestig, misschien wel zeventig uur in de week nodig om alles stipt op tijd klaar te krijgen. Dat waren de goede oude tijden, maar die zijn nu afgelopen. Tegen-woordig kan hij zijn dagen grotendeels vrij en 'naar eigen inzicht' inrichten. Naast naast een incidenteel baantje via het uitzendbureau, heeft ie niet 'zoveel bijzonders' te doen in de rest van de week. Het kleine beetje werk laat zich eenvoudig inpassen in de dagelijkse rompslomp en kan eventueel ook nog wel een dagje of wat uitgesteld worden. Als hem dat beter uitkomt bijvoor-beeld. Exact zoals het vandaag weer eens aan het licht komt.

Het uitzendbureau waar hij ingeschreven staat, heeft inderdaad slechts af en toe een keer en dan hooguit een paar uurtjes werk voor hem in petto. Het een en ander laat zich dus tamelijk gemakkelijk met elkaar combineren. De om-standigheid verschaft hem de vrijheid om hier nu even op dit terrasje plaats te nemen voor een kopje koffie. De auto heeft hij in 'n parkeergarage gezet. Na-dat ie zijn echtgenote eerst afgezet had bij het reusachtige kantoorpand. Dat gebouw staat een paar blokken hier vandaan. Ze zullen gemakkelijk naar elkaar of de parkeergarage toe kunnen wandelen als ze er klaar is met dat gesprek. Volgens afspraak belt ze hem op als het zover is. Gisteren is ze naar de kapper geweest en vanmorgen heeft ze een tamelijk nieuwe jurk aangedaan om er zo goed mogelijk uit te zien. Op de een of ander manier wilde ze indruk maken op de beambten. Dit hoewel ze toch tamelijk zeker kan zijn over haar functie.

Het gebrek aan verplichtingen staat hem toe om 's morgens thuis uitgebreid de bijlagen van de krant te lezen. Zijn vrouw noemt het dat ie "onder het genot van een kan koffie, 'm van voren naar achter zit te spellen."

Ondanks alles spreekt 't voor zich dat hij er alle tijd voor kan nemen nu hij nog maar weinig rekening hoeft te houden met afspraken die hij bijvoorbeeld met 'n klant heeft gemaakt. Een echte agenda heeft hij overigens nooit nodig gehad en onder de tegenwoordige omstandigheden is zo'n ding natuurlijk helemaal overbodig. Desnoods kan hij verplichtingen af met een kattebelletje bij de telefoon. Voor als hij naar de tandarts moet bijvoorbeeld of als het uitzendbureau heeft gebeld dat ze hem plotseling ergens kunnen gebruiken.

Zo'n vodje dient voornamelijk als geheugensteuntje. Zijn vrouw zal hem namelijk, exact volgens de gewoonte die ze altijd al heeft gehad, aan een afspraak herinneren. Ook toen de kinderen nog thuis woonden speelde ze al vol overgave de 'secretaresse' van het gezin. Ze hield nauwgezet alle afspraken en ieders verplichtingen bij in de kleine agenda die ze er ieder jaar in januari speciaal voor aanschafte. Het dingetje droeg ze uiteindelijk niet voor niets altijd bij zich in haar tas. Zo kon ze de kinderen en hem er telkens aan herinneren waar ze zich moesten melden en hoe laat ze ergens werden verwacht.

Zijn vrouw is wat kordater, meer gestructureerd in haar handelen, dan hij voor zichzelf altijd nodig vond. Zijn bezigheden, beslommeringen zoals hij het liever noemt, laat hij bij voorkeur verlopen volgens een vaste dagindeling of per week. Dat kan hij tamelijk gemakkelijk uit zijn hoofd onthouden, al is de steun die hij van haar ontvangt vanzelfsprekend uiterst gemakkelijk. De man is blijkbaar meer in de wieg gelegd voor improvisatie en rust.

Toen ze de kamer waar zijn kantoor zou komen, helemaal naar hun zin hadden ingericht, is hij er voortvarend aan de slag gegaan. Eerst moest dat nog tussen het werken bij zijn baas door gebeuren. Hij wilde daar immers zijn zaakjes op de juiste manier afhandelen. De boel netjes tot een einde brengen en zorgvuldig afronden wat hij er in de voorgaande jaren had opgebouwd.

Na het uiteindelijke faillissement van de firma en erop volgend zijn officiële ontslag, wilde hij thuis zijn bezigheden voortzetten. Hij kon zich gelukkig prijzen dat de opdrachten zich intussen opstapelden. In het begin hoefde hij ze alleen onder eigen vlag af te maken. 's Avonds of in het weekend. Terwijl kon hij een 'portefeuille' met nieuwe orders opbouwen.

Het gegeven stelde hem overigens in staat om maar heel kort gebruik te hoeven maken van de uitkering waar hij recht op had. Al na twee maanden had hij trots kunnen melden dat z'n inkomsten voldoende waren om er van te bestaan. Aan het Arbeidsbureau doorgeven dat hij geen WW uitkering meer nodig had en ze zijn recht erop 'tot nader order' konden opschorten, het deed hem wat. Hoewel het intussen wenselijk zou zijn om de aanspraak alsnog te gelde te maken, is die na ruim twintig dertig jaar natuurlijk verlopen.

Diep in zijn hart vindt de man het een schande om geld te ontvangen zonder er een inspanning tegenover te hoeven stellen. In zijn geval zou 'zo nu en dan een keertje' een sollicitatie hebben voldaan. Hij had het daar eenvoudig bij kunnen laten als hij zich hard genoeg beriep op zijn specialisatie en het fenomeen 'passende functie' dat toen nog opgeld maakte. Maar dat idee stuitte hem dus nogal heftig tegen de borst. Vandaar dus alle betoonde ijver om zijn 'eigen praktijk' grondig en degelijk van de grond te krijgen. Hij spande zich in om een échte 'zaak' op te zetten. Met een praktijk, zijn kantoor aan huis. Z'n echtgenote heeft hem daar overigens altijd door dik en dun in ondersteund. Zij vond het evenmin passend dat ie "zijn hand op zou gaan houden."

Dat ze hem voortaan iedere dag voor haar voeten zou hebben, leek haar trouwens evenmin te deren. Veel vrouwen schijnen daar namelijk tegenop te zien. Bijvoorbeeld als hun echtgenoot met pensioen gaat en dus van het ene op het andere moment alle dagen, gedurende de hele dag thuis is. Net zoals ze het op dit moment doen, maar indertijd was hij nog maar negenentwintig, druk op kantoor en zij werkt sinds kort voornamelijk buitenshuis. Hij liep en loopt haar dus nauwelijks voor d'r voeten.

Hoewel de omzet van zijn zaak een paar jaar geleden geleidelijk aan is ingezakt, was er niet lang nadat hij helemaal voor zichzelf ging werken, kort sprake van de mogelijkheid om iemand in dienst te nemen. De vraag kwam voort uit de wens om hem tijdens drukte te ondersteunen. Het ging om misschien twee of hooguit drie dagen per week. Het risico dat ze in de wintermaanden tegenover elkaar terecht konden komen, om duimen draaiend te moeten wachten op een nieuwe opdracht, heeft hem ervan weerhouden een wervingsactie te beginnen. Als zo'n tijdelijke kracht dus al te vinden zou zijn.

Net zo min als hij dat voor zichzelf ooit wenselijk vond, kon de man zich niet voorstellen dat hij een personeelslid te verstaan zou moeten geven dat deze teveel was. Dat de collega, die hij overigens eerst grondig en persoonlijk had moeten inwerken, overbodig zou blijken. Zakelijk gezien leek zoiets misschien laakbaar, maar op het menselijk vlak leek het hem niets.

In de rustige maanden van het jaar lieten zijn werkzaamheden het toe om er, net zoals vandaag eigenlijk, eens 'n dagje op uit te trekken. Als hij het goed indeelde en het werk van de ene dag verschoof naar een andere konden zijn vrouw enhij ergens gaan winkelen. Of hij kon eens naar een museum toe om daar een mooie tentoonstelling te bekijken. Ze grepen dan met beide handen de mogelijkheid aan om de dagen waarin ze elkaar ternauwernood hadden kunnen spreken door de drukte van het seizoen, te compenseren. Meteen als de kinderen naar school waren gingen ze er dan vandoor. Ze zorgden er vervolgens voor om weer thuis te zijn als de lessen op de school van hun dochter afgelopen waren. De taxi van hun zoon volgde niet veel later.

Maar meestal al vanaf begin mei tot minstens eind september stond zijn werk ternauwernood afleiding toe. Ieder jaar vlak na Pinksteren leek de drukte van de ene op de andere week plotseling toe te nemen en duurde het maanden voordat het hem lukte om het aanbod weggewerkt te krijgen. Met een hele goede planning vooraf waren ze dan slechts in staat om er een weekje, na veel extra voorbereidingen krap twee, op uit te trekken voor een zomervakantie met het gezin. Het leek ze echter duidelijk dat zoiets tot de hebbelijkheden van het zakendoen behoorde en daarom niet weg te cijferen was.

In zulke tijden was hij tot 's avonds laat op kantoor te vinden. Hij kwam alleen met het eten en daarna even voor het journaal met een snelle kop koffie erbij, naar beneden. Regelmatig moest hij overdag de weg op om ergens een klant te bezoeken, maar dan bleef zijn vrouw thuis om de daar de lopende zaken af te handelen. Ze hield overigens ook de administratie bij, dat paste immers beter bij haar dan bij hem.

Van een echt gezinsleven was in de drukke zomermaanden op deze manier helaas ternauwernood sprake. Ook in het weekend moest hij dan namelijk het een of andere werkje verrichten. Of hij ging op kantoor zitten om nog iets na te kijken, een taak beter uit te werken dan hem eerder in de week gelukt was of de betalingen te verwerken. Dat laatste was natuurlijk een leuke bezigheid, maar helaas moest ie ook weleens een klant achter z'n vodden aanzitten. Aanmaningen behoorden vanzelfsprekend ook tot zijn taak, maar hij deed het met tegenzin. Het ging immers tegen zijn gevoel van vertrouwen in.

In dergelijke periodes stoorde alle drukte 'm vooral omdat hij er dan zoveel moeite voor moest doen om toch deel te kunnen nemen aan het gezinsleven. Het werk stond dat soms niet toe en hij zag met lede ogen hoe zijn vrouw hun beider taak alleen op zich nam. Bijvoorbeeld door er met de kinderen op uit te trekken om er eens een leuk dagje van te maken. "Dan heeft papa ruim de tijd om te werken."

Het waren de tijden waarin ze over voldoende geld beschikten om aan al hun verplichtingen te voldoen. De tijd waarin er geen tekorten waren of een negatief saldo bestond. Als alle klanten netjes en op tijd betaald hadden, voelde hij zich 'echt zelfstandig', durfde ie zich een zakenman te noemen.

Tot een aantal jaren geleden leek het werk vanzelf te verlopen. Dan hoefden ze zich weinig zorgen te maken en liet de gang van zaken zich voorspoedig noemen. Ondanks alles kon hij de uitvoering van zijn werk en de inspanningen die hij ervoor moest leveren goed met elkaar in de pas houden. Feitelijk verliep het een en ander exact zoals hij het zich kon wensen. De enige tegenslag die hun ontwikkeling remde was de zorg rond de handicap van hun zoon en de moeite die het later bleek te kosten om hem op een goede plek te krijgen. Een plek waar men met hem om kon gaan en hem de steun bood die hij nodig had. Dat bleek namelijk nogal veel voeten in de aarde te hebben.

Naast alle genoemde beslommeringen hield ook het onderhoud van hun huis ze regelmatig bezig. Het grove werk, het zogenaamde 'groot onderhoud' liet zich oppakken door er zo nu en dan eens iemand voor te laten komen. Daar bouwden ze dan eerst heel spaarzaam een budget voor op en tijdens het uitvoeren van de werkzaamheden probeerden ze zoveel mogelijk behulpzaam te zijn om de kosten enigszins te drukken. In periodes waarin het werk dit toeliet, stak de man graag z'n handen uit de mouwen. Zijn vrouw hield zich voornamelijk bezig met het schilderwerk, maar voor de uitvoering van allerlei andere dingen kon ze op hem rekenen. In het voor- of najaar bijvoorbeeld.

Het bood ze afleiding en voldoening omdat het resultaat er langzamerhand mocht zijn. Heel soms was het echter nodig om iemand, een vakman, aannemer of specialist in te huren, maar dit was uitsluitend om de erg lastige klusjes uit te voeren. Werkzaamheden waarvoor hij bijvoorbeeld het gereedschap niet in huis had of waarbij ervaring belangrijker was dan doorzettingsvermogen of nieuwsgierigheid. Als altijd leerde de man graag hoe hij zelf een aanpassing kon uitvoeren. Langs de weg van proberen en fouten herstellen lukte het vaak om via 'doe het zelven' tot een oplossingen te komen. Al doende voerden ze plannen uit om, voornamelijk voor later als ze niet meer zoveel zelf konden, het huis helemaal naar hun zin aan te passen of bouwkundig te verbeteren. Ze wilden de woning klaar te hebben voor hun "oude dag." Daarbij hielden ze elkaar in de detaillering, eventuele mogelijkheden, het gewenste comfort en de praktische uitvoering in balans.

De ene keer wilde hij iets zo oplossen dat het perfect zou gaan werken, maar dan vond zij de middelen die hij ervoor moest aanschaffen niet mooi genoeg of gewoon te duur. Een andere keer was de tegenstelling omgedraaid.

Zo lagen de voorkeuren regelmatig op andere vlakken en moesten ze zich daarop concentreren om consensus te bereiken. Het resulteerde erin dat een daadwerkelijke afwerking weleens bleef liggen tot er, in de bouwmarkt of bij een meubelgigant, uiteindelijk een oplossing voorhanden bleek. Zo hebben ze door deze hang naar perfectie anderhalf jaar op de logeerkamer geslapen. Het duurde zo lang tot de vloer van hun slaapkamer vervangen was, al het verfwerk er keurig genoeg uitzag, de wanden netjes waren gestuukt en het behang er eindelijk strak genoeg op zat. Ook op het plafond want dat was mooier.

Die tijden zijn momenteel helaas voorbij, de omzet van zijn zaak begon plotseling zienderogen terug te lopen en zonder dat hij een mogelijkheid zag om z'n inkomen te herstellen, trok deze al evenmin vanzelf weer aan. Zijn prijzen verhogen leek hem niet verstandig omdat de klanten dan zeker naar een ander op zoek zouden gaan. Zo trouw waren die niet meer. Het was hem al duidelijk geworden dat voornamelijk de prijs nog telde, niet de kwaliteit die ervoor werd geleverd. Zijn uitgangspunt wilde hij echter niet verloochenen, want als het even kon deed hij telkens zijn uiterste best. Hij deed wat hij kon en minder dan dat vond ie gewoon te weinig. Ook daarin streefde hij naar perfectie.

Drie en een half jaar geleden is zijn vrouw bij haar huidige werkgever aan de slag gegaan. Het was intussen broodnodig omdat de dreiging dat ze de eindjes niet meer aan elkaar konden knopen, steeds groter werd. Weliswaar is ze er parttime begonnen, maar toen de kinderen allebei het huis uit waren, heeft ze er toch een volledige baan van gemaakt. Ze geniet van het werk en mede door dit plezier heeft ze een positie bij die baas weten te verwerven. Daarvoor vindt momenteel het functioneringsgesprek plaats, waar ze vanmorgen naartoe moest. Qua leeftijd zal ze waarschijnlijk niet meer in aanmerking komen voor een andere functie of promotie. Misschien dat ze nog in een andere loonschaal terecht komt. Wordt ze geherwaardeerd zoals ze dat noemen.

De man wist indertijd dat een flink aantal van zijn collega's, z'n vakgenoten gestopt waren met hun zakelijke activiteiten. Hoewel begrijpelijk wilde hij daar voor zichzelf nog niet toe overgaan. Hij zag het als een overgave, 'n concessie aan de consumptiemaatschappij en zijn idealisme maakte dat hij er geen heil in zag. Op sollicitatiebrieven die hij zo nu en dan schreef, eerst uitsluitend voor het opvangen van de stille winterperiode maar later toch voor een volledige baan, had hij telkens een afwijzing gekregen.

Dat hij 'pas' negenenveertig was en zich nog niet oud wilde noemen, lag bij de 'human resource managers' aan wie hij zijn brieven stuurde, beduidend anders. Als hij navraag deed waarom een afwijzing zijn deel was geworden, hield men weliswaar vol dat er een 'andere, beter geschikte' kandidaat was gevonden, maar even kort doorvragen leverde meestal al snel de opmerking "er werken hier meer mensen van uw leeftijd hoor" op of werd er verwezen naar de "samenstelling van het team" en hoe hij daarbij "uit de toon zou vallen tussen de jongelui". De 'leeftijdsdiscriminatie' kon je uit de gebezigde toon opmaken, al werd de werkelijke toedracht wijselijk ingeslikt. Dit kwam dus bovenop de wetenschap dat er nog maar weinig personen overgebleven waren die zijn eigenlijke werk naar behoren konden uitvoeren. Het stemde hem verdrietig dat hij blijkbaar overbodig was geworden, men hem niet meer nodig had of er botweg vanuit wilde gaan dat hij 'te duur' zou zijn.

Na een tijdlang alleen maar negatieve reacties en afwijzingen, begon hij zich letterlijk afgeschreven te voelen. Deze toestand maakte dat hij voortaan op allerlei vacatures begon te reageren. Hij deed dus niet meer uitsluitend een gooi

80

naar functies die aansloten bij zijn ervaring of vergelijkbaar leken met zijn 'vorige' werk. Alles wat hem in een advertentie of op het kantoor van het UWV enigszins 'aantrekkelijk' leek inspireerde zijn fantasie. In gedachten zag hij zich dan al binnen allerlei bedrijven functioneren. Met vanzelfsprekend dezelfde inzet waarmee hij dat jarenlang voor zijn eigen zaak deed.

Tot nog toe heeft het helaas niet geleid tot een nieuwe werkkring en, nog veel belangrijker, een stabiel inkomen. Het Uitzendburo heeft inderdaad zo nu en dan een poosje werk voor hem, maar daarop kan hij geen toekomst bouwen. Voornamelijk omdat hij weer weg mag als het werk klaar is. 'Matig functioneren' zodat ie ergens langer ingehuurd moet blijven, dat werkt niet is hem reeds verteld en 't zou 'm tegen de borst stuiten, tegen zijn eergevoel ingaan.

Tegenwoordig raken de financiële reserves die ze in afgelopen jaren voorzichtig bij elkaar hebben weten te scharrelen, uitgeput. Ze moesten er steeds vaker een beroep op doen, terwijl het nu juist bedoeld was voor als ze oud zouden zijn. Als ze het rustiger aan wilden doen.

Een huisman kan of wil hij zich niet noemen, de meeste taakjes in het huishouden worden immers nog steeds door zijn echtgenote opgepikt. Dat is trouwens begonnen toen hij nog in Amsterdam werkte en laat, meestal pas vlak voor het eten op tafel stond, thuiskwam. Niet alleen het werk maakte dat hij meestal een poosje na sluitingstijd doorging, maar ook reed hij liever achter de dagelijkse file op de A4 aan, dan erin terecht te komen en z'n tijd te verdoen met stilstaan en wachten. Die handige telefoontjes, daar was indertijd nog geen sprake van, dus het moment van thuiskomst bleef daarom meestal een gok.

Maar de kinderen waren klein, dat maakte de omstandigheden flexibel. Zijn vrouw kon gewoon wachten tot hij binnengelopen kwam en dan was er voldoende tijd om op hun gemak van de avondmaaltijd te genieten. Hij probeerde natuurlijk wel om rond een vaste tijd thuis te komen, maar het forenzen liet zich niet sturen. Pas later, toen hij thuis ging werken en de kinderen naar school moesten, aten ze op een meer Hollandse tijd. Maar de situatie rond de huishoudelijke taken is gebleven hoe ie was. Ze zijn het domein van zijn echtgenote gebleven.

Uitsluitend in de drukste tijden op haar werk vraagt ze momenteel weleens of hij een handje uit wil steken. Vroeger was dat bijvoorbeeld bij het bereiden van de avondmaaltijd, assisteren bij het huiswerk van de kinderen of tijdens een klein klusje in de tuin. Z'n behulpzaamheid kwam dan als geroepen, maar door haar goede planning hoefde hij die slecht sporadisch te tonen. In de loop der tijd zijn de huiselijke werkjes op die manier vanzelf tussen hem en zijn echtgenote 'verdeeld geraakt' en, hoewel hun omstandigheden het nu anders toestaan, heeft zich geen aanleiding voorgedaan om er een drastische verandering in aan te brengen. Hij wijt het aan de 'macht der gewoonte' en ze erge-

81

ren zich er allebei niet aan eigenlijk.

Omdat ze tamelijk op zichzelf zijn, is er sowieso niemand die aanstoot aan hun omstandigheden neemt. De kinderen zijn zoals gemeld 'op zichzelf' en er zijn er maar weinig die zich bezighouden met hun dagelijkse gang van zaken. Dit alles maakt dat er geen dringende reden bestaat om de situatie in huis, zoals die in de loop der tijd is gegroeid, alsnog te wijzigen.

Nadat hun zoon, omdat er eindelijk 'n woonplek voor hem gevonden werd, het huis uit kon, wonen de man en zijn echtgenote samen in het grote huis. Soms, als het op haar werk zo chaotisch dreigt te worden, dat ze de gevraagde inspanningen rond het huishouden niet helemaal naar wens kan vervullen, beklaagt ze zich erover dat het 'een rommel is'. Hij ziet zo'n opmerking als een hint. Maar als hij de dag erop vol overgave de kamer heeft gestofzuigd, blijkt bij haar thuiskomst dat ie teveel plekken overgeslagen heeft. Ook, of beter gezegd juist, degene die hij vanwege haar vorige reprimande extra veel aandacht heeft geschonken!

Zo dient ze ze vervolgens "allemaal opnieuw te behandelen"!

Deze humeurigheid levert dus weleens wat spanning op en remt het initiatief voor nieuwe acties zijnerzijds aanzienlijk. Het verlamt hem dat ze zo gepikeerd raakt omdat "hij er alleen maar een nog grotere bende van heeft gemaakt" en dan ook nog eens met "al het extra werk van dien"!

Dat ze er zijn inspanningen mee ontkent of blijkbaar niet wil zien dat hij heeft geprobeerd het een en ander uit haar handen te nemen, legt hij met tegenzin naast zich neer. Hij 'lijdt in stilte'. Het is de vaste omschrijving die hij er als cynische grap over maakt tegen de kinderen of een kennis.

Intussen is de 'status quo' dat zij hem in bepaalde gevallen een duidelijke taak opdraagt. Hij vervult deze taak vervolgens 'zorgvuldig en geheel volgens haar nauwkeurig omschreven aanwijzingen'. Speciaal daarvoor heeft hij er al eens aantekeningen voor gemaakt. Weliswaar op een kladblaadje, maar die mocht vervolgens naast de telefoon voor nadere bestudering. Zulke taakomschrijvingen doen zich echter niet zo heel vaak meer voor. Soms moet hij er zelfs op aandringen om er een toebedeeld te krijgen.

Dat ze soms wat mopperig tegen hem doet en hij dan als 'kop van Jut' fungeert, is niet sympathiek. Het maakt hem weleens stuurs of stemt 'm verdrietig, maar verder is er in zijn ogen geen smet op hun relatie te bespeuren. In grote lijnen verlopen de zaken normaal. Zoals hij vandaag dus ook zijn rol als chauffeur naar Den Haag vice versa speelt. Zij het dat zijn vrouw daar met echt personeel natuurlijk nooit een 'leuke middag' aan vast zou knopen.

Die attractie heeft hij op dit moment toch nog mooi tegoed!

In de loop der tijd hebben de man en zijn vrouw binnen de familie en kennissenkring een reputatie opgebouwd. Ze staan bekend om hun cynisme, regelmatig bijtend zuur, maar het hindert ze niet merkbaar. Ze stemmen er gewoonweg mee in omdat ze menen de leeftijd bereikt te hebben die met zo'n houding samenhangt. Als mensen ouder worden, zeg dat ze de veertig passeren, dan strijden ervaring en verwachting om voorrang. Naarmate jaren toenemen, wint het eerste en neemt de ander langzamerhand af, op de teleurstelling die daarmee samenhangt steunt cynisme.

Door het kantoor aan huis zijn ze de laatste dertig jaar vrijwel altijd bij elkaar in de buurt geweest. Het stel onderneemt daardoor dingen die andere echtparen gewoonlijk apart van elkaar doen. Zoals nu naar Den Haag gaan voor haar werk en daarna samen een paar uurtjes winkelen. Ook deze dingen zijn in de loop van de afgelopen jaren gegroeid.

Als hij voor zijn zaak naar Duitsland of bijvoorbeeld een verre stad in het land moest, deelden ze het zo in dat ze er samen naartoe gingen. Het enige waarvoor ze dan moesten zorgen was dat ze voor het eten thuis waren. En ze dienden de speciaal ervoor opgetrommelde oppas op tijd af te lossen. De gezamenlijke maaltijd was ze altijd heilig, maar een enkele keer durfden ze een kennis voor hen te laten waarnemen. Als de reis naar het buitenland een overnachting in een hotelletje noodzakelijk maakte bijvoorbeeld en die persoon het vertrouwen waard was om de zorg voor hun zoon over te nemen.

De gewoonte om samen op te trekken is dus in de loop der tijd ontstaan en langzamerhand steeds belangrijker geworden. Ze voelen zich er allebei namelijk goed onder. In ieder geval geeft de man regelmatig aan het "nooit anders dan zo" gewild te hebben en inderdaad lijkt het er vaak op of ze niets liever doen dan samen iets te ondernemen. Hoe onbenullig in andermans ogen het soms ook lijkt, ze zijn vaak samen of ten misnte in elkaars buurt te vinden.

Wellicht lijken ze erdoor op 'n stel parkieten of paartje duiven, maar dat deert ze evenmin. Ze hechten er zichtbaar aan om elkaar te begeleiden, samen ervaringen op te doen en deze met elkaar te delen.

Ondanks dat het pas kwart over tien is, wordt het opeens druk op het terras. Zojuist zijn er een paar meisjes kwetterend bij een van de tafeltjes midden op neergestreken en er schuiven er telkens meer bij aan waardoor het lawaai toeneemt. Zonder dat een van de nieuw aangekomen dames er de moeite voor neemt om te vragen of een stoel daadwerkelijk beschikbaar is, halen ze ook de bij zijn tafeltje resterende exemplaren een voor een weg. Ze schuiven ermee aan bij de reeds gesettelde jongedames.

Ogenschijnlijk zijn ze redelijk bekend met de gelegenheid en voelen ze zich er thuis. Zo gedragen ze zich in ieder geval en de man vermoedt dat ze op de school zitten die hij een eindje verderop heeft zien staan. Het is hem van het voorbijlopen niet bijgebleven waar het instituut exact voor opleidt, maar het valt hem op dat er uitsluitend meisjes op het terras lijken neer te strijken. Er zal wel sprake zijn van een pauze, maar de overdaad aan vrouwelijk schoon

springt hem in het oog. Opvallend eigenlijk want voor zover hij het heeft begrepen staan tegenwoordig alle studies en opleidingen toch open voor iedereen, open beide seksen zeg maar?

Het beroemde 'm' schuine streep 'v' uit advertenties is al een hele tijd niet echt
noodzakelijk meer. Zelfs al is een functie qua naam wel degelijk seksegebon-
den. Dan staat er bijvoorbeeld 'secretaresse' of 'receptioniste' in een vacature,
maar is die malle toevoeging er aan toegevoegd. Er bestaat toch ook zoiets als
een 'secretaris' of 'receptionist', waarom dan niet die twee woorden desnoods
gescheiden door hetzelfde lullige streepje ervoor in de plaats neergezet?

Het meisje met een schortje voor en hierdoor duidelijk de serveerster, loopt
gedienstig op en neer naar het buffet om de koffie, de flesjes frisdrank en een
incidentele taartpunt of vroege tosti voor haar gasten te halen. De indruk dat
de dames hier vaste klant zijn wordt versterkt doordat ze zonder de kaart te
hoeven raadplegen exact weten waar ze trek in hebben. Hij bespeurt overigens geen herkenning bij de bediening, terwijl de meisjes zo op het oog toch
leeftijdgenoten, wellicht zelfs klasgenoten van elkaar kunnen zijn.

Waarom hij het denkt is 'm niet helemaal duidelijk, maar de man komt nadat
de serveerster een paar keer heen en weer is gelopen en bij nadere beschouwing van de meisjes aan de tafeltjes tegenover hem, tot de conclusie dat de
school zal voorzien in een beroepsopleiding. Hij denkt dat het meisje dat op
het terras werkt een andere volgt.

Intussen kan hij namelijk niet geloven dat de serveerster geen studente aan
'iets hogers', een hogere beroeps opleiding bijvoorbeeld, is. Het lijkt hem dat
ze hier werkt om wat bij te verdienen. Waarschijnlijk gaat het om een aanvulling op haar budget, bijvoorbeeld om er de huur van een kamer mee te betalen. Op de een of andere manier maakt het meisje op hem een veel te slimme
indruk om zich full time te hoeven lenen voor het werk dat ze hier tussen de
tafels en stoelen op de het grint uitvoert. En evengoed zou ze aan de Universiteit in zijn woonplaats kunnen studeren. Of in Rotterdam of Delft, want den
Haag biedt geen hogere opleiding dan de Haagse Hogeschool. Of je zou de
geleende onderdelen van de RUL tot Haags moeten willen rekenen.

De serveerster onderscheidt zich aanzienlijk van de meisjes die aan het tafeltje een stukje verderop plaats hebben genomen. Waarin het verschil precies zit
kan hij niet benoemen, maar ze ziet er heel anders uit dan haar klanten. Het
meisje wekt de indruk boven hen te staan maar is niet arrogant. Ze heeft over-
wicht en is leuk om naar te kijken. Ook de andere meisjes kunnen ermee door,
maar die met dat schortje heeft iets extra's. Hij weet er geen naam voor, maar
het is er en daarom kijkt hij naar haar. Blijft ie op haar letten.

Toen hij hier ging zitten was het terras nog leeg en tamelijk donker, maar zoals hij meteen bij aankomst al meende te kunnen verwachten, zit hij intussen
in het zonnetje. Die is om de hoek van de grote flats gekropen. Het groepje

84

moet overigens eveneens op de hoogte zijn van de loop van de schaduwen op het terras. Bij hem mag het gerekend worden tot beroepsdeformatie. Als fotograaf is hij immers gewend om de lichtval te letten. Zo is het een tweede natuur geworden om van tevoren op de letten waar 't zonlicht vandaan komt, hoe laat het is, waar nog schaduw heerst en het licht te verwachten is.

De schaduw kwam van achter de hoge gebouwen die er pal naast en achter hem staan. Omdat het er intussen laat genoeg voor is ligt zijn plekje nu in de volle zon en langzaamaan komt het tafeltje van de meisjes eveneens in steeds meer licht terecht. De serveerster heeft zojuist links en rechts gevraagd of ze een parasol op moest doen, maar dat vond niemand nog echt nodig. Tegen het einde van september is de zon vanzelfsprekend niet heet meer te noemen. Een moordende temperatuur hoeven ze dus niet te vrezen. Mocht het er eventueel toch op uitdraaien, dan kan ze het immers alsnog doen.

Dat het een mooie dag zou worden was in het journaal de vorige avond reeds toegezegd. Eenmaal naar zijn zin geïnstalleerd heeft de man er een boek bij gepakt. Met vooruitziende blik heeft hij er twee meegenomen om er de tijd van het wachten mee te vullen. Nu kijkt hij afwisselend over de rand van zijn leesbril naar de stoelendans recht voor hem, de tekst en de verdere activiteiten die er op het terras plaatsvinden.

Het boekje dat hij leest is een bundel met columns. Ze beslaan hooguit anderhalf tot twee pagina's voordat er een nieuwe begint en telkens mijmert hij over de woorden die hij zojuist gelezen heeft. Om ze in hun context te plaatsen moet hij even nadenken over de periode die erin beschreven werd. Hij probeert zich dan voor te stellen hoe de omstandigheden waren. Het lichte karakter van de inhoud staat toe dat hij zijn aandacht verdeelt over het lezen, peinzen over de inhoud en een steelse observatie van zijn omgeving.

De groep meisjes is uitgegroeid tot ongeveer zeventien personen en alle tafeltjes direct om hen heen zijn intussen nodig om er alle bordjes, glazen, flesjes, koppen en asbakken – de lege en die waar ze zo nu en dan een peuk in uitmaken – op neer te kunnen zetten. Hoewel ze nog niet allemaal van de zon kunnen genieten hebben de dames vanuit hun zithoek een strategisch overzicht op het terras. Ze kunnen iedereen die vanuit de zaak of rechtstreeks door het poortje opzij van zijn eigen tafeltje aangelopen komt, uitgebreid bekijken en desgewenst van commentaar voorzien. Ook passanten die over het stukje straat er vlak voorlangs lopen, laten zich zo door hen beoordelen. Al wachten ze er beleefd mee tot de persoon buiten gehoorsafstand is gekomen.

Hijzelf is blijkbaar verloren gegaan tegen de achtergrond zodat ie kan meegenieten van wat ze menen op te moeten merken. Doordat hij met zijn rug naar de straat zit heeft hij weliswaar niet evenveel zicht op de omgeving als zij wel hebben, maar als hij wil volstaat 't om zijn hoofd een stukje te draaien als nader onderzoek dat nodig maakt. Soms is hun kritiek ongezouten en kan hij zich net op tijd achter zijn boek verschuilen om zijn geamuseerdheid te verbergen. Hij wil perse geen inbreuk maken op de privacy van het groepje, maar is toch nieuwsgierig geraakt naar wat ze elkaar over deze of gene te melden hebben. Het tafereel biedt zo een aangename afleiding tijdens het wachten op zijn echtgenote.

Het stoort hem dat de dames, als ze elkaar roepen, de anderen 'meiden' noemen. Hij weet wel dat het een moderne term betreft. Ze zal dus in het dagelijkse taalgebruik normaal gevonden worden. Maar de jongedames die hij hier voor zich ziet zou hij zelf toch anders willen duiden.

Ter verklaring, als de man vroeger met zijn vrienden op het strand was, bedoelden ze een heel ander soort meisjes met de term dan hij hier voor zich ziet. In die zin wil hij ze dus perse geen 'meiden' noemen. Hij zou liever spreken van jonge dames, zo niet gewoon 'dames'. Hun manier van doen mag, hoewel behorend tot het zogenaamde groepsgedrag, ronduit beschaafd genoemd worden namelijk. De meisjes zijn weliswaar luidruchtig aanwezig maar ze domineren het terras niet te veel. Het is gewoon een groep jongedames die met elkaar samen van een kopje koffie geniet.

Vijf van de meisjes hebben een hoofddoek om en twee daarvan hebben daarnaast ook nog een bijpassend lang gewaad aan. Alleen hun handen en gezichtjes zijn strikt gezien dus 'bloot' en zichtbaar voor zijn blikken. Al hebben ze nu hij erop let, ook blote voeten in elegante schoentjes. De man verslijt ze voor Marokkaans, maar een van hen zou ook heel goed een Turkse kunnen zijn. Het onderscheid kan hij niet maken, maar hij ziet een verschil. Wat hij Marokkaans denkt te mogen noemen ziet er wat ronder, meer gevuld, beter doorvoed uit. Die ene Turkse is ronduit mager. Voor zover het zich onder het overvloedige textiel van de gewaden laat onderscheiden.

Van de anderen kan hij de herkomst niet een, twee, drie plaatsen. Er zijn negen blonde meisjes bij, maar ook die hebben door hun jeugdigheid allemaal iets exotisch over zich. Het valt hem op hoe beweeglijk ze allemaal zijn en hij durft ze een voor een 'knap' of 'leuk om te zien' te noemen.

In zijn ogen is het hele gezelschap een 'lust voor het oog', de meisjes kunnen daarom zijn goedkeuring wegdragen. Vanzelfsprekend is het seksistisch om op die manier naar vrouwen te kijken, maar uit de keurende blikken die hijzelf al mocht oogsten en de manier waarop ze commentaar zitten te leveren op de voorbijgangers, heeft hij opgemaakt dat ook zij het niet flauw vinden om een oordeel over anderen te vellen.

De man valt, alleen al door het leeftijdsverschil, volledig buiten iedere voor hen interessante categorie. Maar juist omdat ze ongezouten hun oordeel voor de andere gasten gereed hebben, durft hij die van hemzelf op ze los te laten. Het is tenslotte niet bindend en hij houdt 'm keurig voor zichzelf.

Hij moet glimlachen om zijn rechtvaardiging. Het lijkt erop of zijn echtgenote zijn gedachten kan lezen en hem, zij het op afstand, terecht wijst. Als hij overigens een verslag aan haar zou moeten uitbrengen, van de handelingen die er aan die andere tafels plaatsvinden, kan daar niet aan ontbreken dat minimaal een van de meisjes telkens met een telefoontje in de weer is. Voor zover hij het kan zien gebeurt er van alles op de schermpjes en hebben ze de apparaten niet uitsluitend in gebruik om ermee op te bellen. Al gebeurt dat zo nu en dan ook wel eens!

Dan gaat met 'n heftig knerpend geluid of speels muziekje een van de toestellen af en schakelt het gezelschap als bij toverslag om naar een lager volume. Het valt hem op dat degene die het gesprek binnen krijgt zich op een onopvallende manier van het groepje afwendt. Hij zou het 'steels' willen noemen en de anderen kijken dan even niet meer naar de spreekster om. De betreffende juffrouw zondert zich met een kleine draai van haar schouders af en wordt door de andere dames, vooral die het dichtst bij haar in de buurt zitten, met een zelfde minimale beweging tijdelijk buitengesloten. Zo maken ze dus geen oog contact meer en kan de persoon ongestoord telefoneren.

Opvallend vindt hij de manier waarop de meisjes zo weten te bereiken dat ze hun collega zo min mogelijk storen. Zoveel consideratie hebben ze namelijk niet met de rest van de mensen op het terras. Als niemand van hen telefonisch in gesprek is, neemt het lawaai dat ze weten te produceren, weer het kennelijk normale volume aan. Overigens merkt hij op dat een meisje bij haar gesprek niet wordt afgeluisterd of geïnterrumpeerd, maar het groepje is er deelgenoot van zonder er een actieve rol bij te spelen. Het lijkt alsof de anderen een gereserveerde houding aannemen, of ze tijdelijk op 'stand-by' staan.

De jongedame aan de telefoon geeft namelijk met zo nu en dan een knikje of een kreetje aan waarover het gesprek dat ze aan haar oor heeft, gaat. Of de spreekster draait zich van het gezelschap af om aan te geven dat het dit keer een privé onderwerpje betreft. De man begrijpt dat ze op die manier tegelijkertijd afstand kunnen nemen en ook betrokkenheid weten te tonen. Hij vindt het knap hoe dit verloopt en omdat het een aantal keren zo gaat raakt hij erdoor geïmponeerd. Voor hem is het een nog onbekend onderdeel van de moderne communicatie techniek!

Dat er plaatjes op de schermpjes van die toestelletjes te toveren zijn, is hem bekend. Hij heeft 't gezien op degene die zijn dochter onlangs heeft aangeschaft. Een paar weken geleden heeft ze, net terug van de wintersport, daarop de eerste foto's aan hem en zijn vrouw laten zien. Het appartement waar ze gezeten heeft en vanzelfsprekend een aantal plaatjes die zij en haar vriend onderweg van elkaar geschoten hebben op de hellingen. Ook van een terrasje hoog op de berg in de zon stonden er een aantal op hun toestel. De foto's die ze er met hun echte camera genomen hebben mocht hij even snel op zijn laptop zien, maar ze moesten die nog samenvoegen. Ze zouden er een album van

87

gaan bestellen. Online via een foto servicedienst op het Internet, dat spreekt voor zich.

Aan de tafeltjes een stukje bij hem vandaan levert het uitwisselen van afbeeldingen een eindeloos heen en weer geschuifel op. De dames scharrelen ervoor tussen de diverse stoelen en om de schooltassen. Ze hebben telkens blijkbaar een andere voorstelling op hun telefoontje getoverd en ze geven de dingen vervolgens door om de betreffende afbeelding door de hele kring te laten beoordelen. Een enkele keer lopen ze ermee naar degene die het plaatje 'moet bekijken'. Kennelijk om duidelijker aan te wijzen waar de aandacht zich exact op dient te concentreren. Waar ze het over hebben weet de man natuurlijk niet maar hij kan zich er een goede voorstelling van maken als hij afgaat op de kreten en uitroepen die de dames er onderling bij uitwisselen.

Nu de zon intussen ook op de rest van het terras schijnt en dus alle tafels in haar warmte hult, lijkt het wel of de activiteiten erdoor toenemen. Het is in het hoekje van de dames in ieder geval een drukte van belang. Vooral omdat ze geen van allen meer dan een paar minuten achter elkaar op dezelfde plek lijken te kunnen blijven zitten. Ze domineren er nu toch de sfeer op het terras mee, maar het gaat er opgewekt aan toe dus hindert allerminst.

Overigens zijn er nog pas twee andere tafels waaraan iemand heeft plaats genomen. Aan de ene, helemaal achterop het terras tegen de muur van de zaak aan, zit een ouder echtpaar en vlak naast hem achter de boom, heeft een man plaats genomen. Die kwam zojuist aangelopen met een telefoontje aan zijn oor, Deze heeft hij er nog niet vandaan gehaald. Hij heeft het er dus ook maar druk mee. Op z'n tafeltje heeft ie zoveel spulletjes neergelegd dat hij onmogelijk nog lang alleen zal blijven. Waarschijnlijk zal hij zich net zo min aan het gedrag van de meisjes storen als hijzelf. Het oudere echtpaar is trouwens volledig verwikkeld in het bestuderen van de kaart die de serveerster hen in het langslopen heeft aangereikt.

De man wordt uit zijn mijmeringen opgeschrikt als in zijn borstzak zijn eigen toestelletje begint te tsjilpen. Niet gewend om het apparaat meteen tevoorschijn te toveren, duurt het even voordat hij ook nog de juiste knop gevonden heeft om 'm in te schakelen. Dan pas kan hij er een antwoord in spreken. Het is zijn vrouw, het overleg is afgelopen en ze wil weten waar hij zit.

Hij vertelt het en vraagt of hij naar haar toe moet komen of dat ze hier samen eerst een kopje koffie nemen. Onder het spreken ziet hij hoe vanaf de andere tafel de meisjes naar hem zitten te kijken. Hoewel hij van huis uit toch tamelijk zacht spreekt, lijken ze hem plotseling opgemerkt te hebben.

Schroeiplekken

Het eerste dat me opviel toen mijn vriend aan kwam lopen was zijn ietwat wijdbeense gang. Om het plat te zeggen leek het erop of hij in zijn broek had gescheten en of hij, door zo met zijn knieën een stuk uit elkaar te lopen, wilde voorkomen dat de plak stront tegen zijn billen aan kwam. Zo zag het er uit, maar toen hij bij de stoeltjes die we tussen onze tenten hadden neergezet, aankwam ging hij er tot mijn verbazing gewoon op zitten. Wel steunde hij er opvallend zwaar bij op de dunne leuninkjes toen hij zich er heel voorzichtig in liet zakken, zodat ik bang was dat ze wellicht zouden breken.

Ik had zijn actie met gemengde gevoelens zitten bekijken. Toen hij zoeven opstond en naar het toilet gebouw liep, was me nog niets opgevallen, maar nu vond ik dus dat hij 'opvallend voorzichtig' terug was gekomen. Hij liet zich tegen het rug leuninkje aan zakken en slaakte een zucht. Alsof hij opgelucht was om weer te kunnen zitten. Ik zei niets, wachtte af, nam alleen een slokje bier uit het glas dat ik in mijn hand hield.

We keken samen langs het pad hoe de kinderen een eindje verderop op het veld met elkaar aan het ravotten waren. Mijn dochter had even hiervoor het camping schepje en een van de pannetjes uit onze kookset opgehaald. Ze was bij de kranen aan het knoeien met modder en grind. De attributen had ze er kennelijk bij nodig.

Naast me kwam mijn vriend naar voren om ook zijn glas van het tafeltje te pakken. Ik keek even naar hem, maar zag aan zijn blik dat ik 'm op het moment niet lastig moest vallen met vragen of opmerkingen. Noem het humeurig, hoe hij voor zich uit keek. We waren op vakantie, dus ik liet het zo. Zelf had ik trouwens ook nergens zin in, het trok me niet om op te staan of iets te gaan doen. We zaten goed zo en konden uitgebreid genieten van onze rust.

Bijna tegelijk dronken we onze glazen leeg. Ik zette het mijne tussen de lege flesjes op de tafel en Peter die van hem in het gras naast zijn stoeltje. Nogmaals slaakte hij een diepe zucht. Alsof hij zorgen had en zijn hart wilde luchten. Ik keek hem aan en zag dat het goed was om te vragen wat er speelde.

Hij wuifde mijn vraag weg met een vage veeg met zijn pols in de lucht.

"Ach niks, eigenlijk."

Aarzelend zei ie het laatste er achteraan. Ik bleef naar hem kijken en wachtte of hij er uit zichzelf nog iets meer aan wilde toevoegen. Het bleef bij wat hij gezegd had en samen keken we weer naar de kinderen. Er kwam opeens een heleboel lawaai van het veld namelijk, maar ogenschijnlijk was er niets aan de hand. In ieder geval niet iets waarbij onze directe hulp of enige vorm van ingrijpen noodzakelijk leek.

Nadat de rust weer was teruggekeerd keek ik hem opnieuw aan.

"Waarom loop je eigenlijk zo moeilijk?

Ben je gevallen?"

Ik had geen schaaf plekken op zijn knieën of kuiten gezien, maar ik wist uit ervaring dat de trappen onderweg naar het hoofdgebouw hier op de camping verraderlijk glad konden zijn. Vooral als de mede kampeerders hun auto aan het wassen waren of met gieters heen en weer liepen om hun tuintjes te besproeien. Als ze eenmaal nat waren kon je gemakkelijk over de treden uitglijden, zeker als iemand er zeepsop gemorst had.

De baas van de camping heeft met grappige verbodsborden weliswaar uitdrukkelijk aangegeven hoe hij aankijkt tegen water verspilling, maar intussen onderkent ie de noodzaak van dit soort acties. Hij stelt er namelijk geen sanctie tegenover. Vooral de vaste bezoekers van de camping sjouwen dus regelmatig rond met water en daarom leek het me voor de hand liggen dat mijn vriend op de trappen uitgegleden zou kunnen zijn.

"Je kent die truc met een lucifer toch"?

Ik kende verscheidene kunstjes die je met een lucifer kon uithalen, dus ik begreep niet meteen op welke mijn vriend doelde. Het klonk in feite ook een beetje verveeld, de manier waarop hij het zei. Meer alsof het 't er niet toe deed. Ik vroeg me daarom af of ik hem naar de hoed en de rand moest vragen of dat hij vanzelf wel verder zou gaan.

"Ik heb 'm van Jacques geleerd, die ken jij toch ook"?

Jacques is een wederzijdse vriend van ons. Op de middelbare school zat hij een klas hoger dan Peter en ik, maar toen we gingen studeren hebben we een tijdlang bij elkaar in hetzelfde huis gewoond. Peter en hij zijn zelfs een keer tegelijk naar een ander huis verhuisd. We noemden hem indertijd overigens meestal Sjaak omdat dat beter aansloot bij de volkse eenvoud de we nastreefden. Daar werd hij gelukkig nooit door gehinderd.

Ik realiseerde me dat we hem tegenwoordig niet meer zo vaak zien, maar een aantal jaren geleden toen we allemaal nog volop met onze studie bezig waren, was dat dus beduidend anders. Op zowat alle verjaardagen en partijen was hij aanwezig. Ook later kwamen we elkaar op de feesten die hij regelmatig bij hem thuis gaf, tegen. Niet dat een van ons een echt fuifnummer genoemd kan worden dat gaat wat ver, doch we trokken regelmatig met elkaar op.

Het zorgde ervoor dat we met z'n allen aan allerlei festiviteiten deelnamen en elkaar dus ook tipten als er weer eens ergens iets te beleven viel. De laatste jaren is het kontakt onzerzijds echter wat verminderd. Voornamelijk omdat we met de kinderen niet altijd genoeg tijd konden vinden om bij hem langs te gaan of een reden zagen om hem voor een partijtje uit te nodigen. Ik vertel er maar even bij dat Jacques niet is getrouwd of kinderen heeft.

Dat Peter en ik allebei weleens bij hem thuis geweest waren en dus min of meer op de hoogte konden zijn van zijn gewoontes, leek me voor de hand liggen. Toch was het mij niet duidelijk welke specifieke truc er nu door Sjaak ooit met lucifers was uitgehaald. Ik begreep dus niet waar mijn vriend hier op doelde en stond op nadat ik gevraagd had of hij ook nog een biertje wilde. Het leek me dat het mijn beurt was om even naar de koelbox op en neer te lopen. Het zou Peter trouwens de moeite van het opstaan en naar de tent strompelen besparen.

Vriend Jacques woont net buiten de stad op een oude boerderij. Omdat de kinderen, z'n drie broers en twee zussen, hun ouders zoals dat heet 'uit gingen kopen', heeft hij als jongste voor een zacht prijsje het reusachtige gebouw, het erf en de schuren kunnen overnemen. In het voorhuis heeft hij na zijn afstuderen de praktijk gevestigd en in de rest is hij zelf gaan wonen. Maar het huis moest indertijd nog flink worden opgeknapt.

Met alle vrienden hebben we hem onder andere geholpen bij de werkzaamheden aan de grote schuur. Hij wilde daar een werkplaats voor zijn antieke Austin Healy Sprite maken. Maar dat was dus nog maar aan het begin van zijn activiteiten daar. Toen hij zich nog voornamelijk bezighield met het plannen maken voor hoe het allemaal zou moeten worden na zijn studie. Als hij het hele huis in gebruik zou gaan nemen en er zich ging 'vestigen'.

Die wagen is overigens nooit helemaal af gekomen, want Jacques heeft 'm verkocht voordat hij de motor ging reviseren. Later heeft hij er wel op de basis van 'n oude lelijke eend, een soort sport wagentje in elkaar gezet. Het was een zogenaamde kitcar zoals hij 'm noemde. Als ik weleens bij hem op bezoek kwam liet hij telkens trots zien hoever hij ermee was. Om eerlijk te zijn begreep ik niet zo goed waarom hij niet gewoon een kant en klare sportwagen kocht. Intussen was hij dierenarts en had hij al tamelijk snel een goedlopende praktijk weten te verwezenlijken. Mijns inziens kon hij het zich best veroorloven om, al was het dus voor de lol, een leuke auto aan te schaffen. Een echte sleutelaar vond ik hem eigenlijk evenmin.

Om kort te gaan, tijdens onze studie was Jacques altijd wel ergens op de boerderij aan het opknappen en klussen. Er was telkens wel het nodige aan het pand te doen en dat deed hij, als hij er wat tijd voor vrij had weten te maken of als er voldoende hulp voorhanden was, met overgave. Dat wil dus zeggen, als wij tussen de colleges door of in een periode waarin we minder hard aan onze studie hoefden te werken, de tijd vonden om in het huis van Sjaak het een of andere 'werkje' ter hand te nemen. Hem te assisteren.

Daarbij werden zowel de oude alsook nieuwe huisgenoten gemobiliseerd.

91

Omdat Jacques zo'n aardige vent is, kostte hem dat maar weinig moeite. Indien nodig was hij dus in staat om een flinke ploeg assistenten en hulpkrachten over de vloer te ontvangen. Zoals opgemerkt hebben Peter en ik ons daar ook diverse keren voor laten strikken, maar wat mij betreft ging dat altijd zonder tegenzin. Als ik luister naar mijn collega hier naast me, durf ik ervan uit te gaan dat dit voor hem ook opgaat.

De ouders van Jacques waren uit het huis getrokken omdat ze, mede gezien hun leeftijd, het aanzienlijke onderhoud niet meer aan konden. Hun vertrek was mogelijk geworden omdat ze het boerenbedrijf aan een van de buren hadden kunnen overdoen. Mèt het er omheen liggende land ofwel 'de grond' zoals ze het indertijd liever noemden.

Hoewel er nog geen sprake was van melkquota en meer van dergelijke regelingen, die de waarde van een boerenbedrijf bij de bank financieel beïnvloeden, verschafte de verkoop hen de mogelijkheid om 'ermee op te houden'. Zowel zijn vader als moeder hadden plannen die ze wilden verwezenlijken en waren diep in hun hart niet erg verknocht aan het boeren bestaan. Als oudste zoon had hij de boerderij van zijn ouders overgenomen, net zoals die dat eerder van de zijne en zo voort hadden gedaan. De niet onaanzienlijke opbrengst werd grotendeels verdeeld onder de kinderen en zoals gezegd kreeg Sjaak de opstallen onder zijn beheer. Zijn vader en moeder wilden verhuizen naar zijn oudste broer die in Canada een boerderij was begonnen. Het geld hadden ze voor hun emigratie niet allemaal nodig en zo konden ze de kinderen stuk voor stuk 'bedenken'.

Ten tijde van het vertrek van zijn ouders was Jacques derdejaars en had ie er nog minimaal vier à vijf te gaan. Hij woonde toen op een kamer ergens bij ons in de stad. Net als wij allemaal verhuisde hij trouwens met regelmaat naar een volgend huis. Bijvoorbeeld met het oog op een ruimere kamer, dichter bij de colleges of het lab en andere redenen die het studentenleven aantrekkelijk en mobiel houden. Daarom leek het zijn familie een goed idee om hem voortaan het ouderlijk huis te laten bewonen.

Als bijkomend voordeel bleef het pand hierdoor voor hen 'behouden', maar dat was dus niet de belangrijkste reden waarom Sjaak zich er vestigde. Zijn familie kon op deze manier echter, als ze op bezoek gingen bij hun broertje, ruimschoots hun nostalgie bevredigen. Allemaal waren ze er geboren en getogen, zoals dat heet. In de boerderij lagen zodoende hun wortels. Nadat Sjaak eerst met onze hulp, een bevriende aannemer, beschikbare tijd tussen de colleges en zodoende bijna twee jaar aan de constructie van het huis gewerkt had, is hij zelf een voor een de kamers op gaan knappen.

Iedere keer als er weer een deel van het immense huis klaar was gaf hij een feest om de vrienden, familieleden en kennissen die hem bij de werkzaamheden geholpen hadden, te eren en bedanken. We hadden langzamerhand allemaal onze specialiteiten en konden hem telkens, afzonderlijk of in een groepje, behulpzaam zijn. Totdat we dus 'vaste verkering' kregen, verloofd raakten, trouwden en onze kinderen gingen opvoeden. Het maakte dat 'n periode bij hem over de vloer, zich steeds lastiger lieten inplannen in ons gezinsleven.

In de tussentijd bouwden we zelf trouwens aan een carrière. Daar ging vanzelfsprekend veel tijd in zitten en intussen was Jacques ook aan het afstuderen. Maar het was altijd erg leuk om bij hem aan het werk te zijn. Mijn echtgenote vond het bijvoorbeeld geen bezwaar om 'n hele zaterdag en zondag in de weer te zijn met grote lappen gordijnstof. Ook niet toen ze, kort erop al, zwanger werd van onze oudste.

Het grootste voordeel van het werken bij Sjaak bestond eruit dat we in tegenstelling tot de werkzaamheden aan ons eigen huis, de rommel niet achter ons hoefden op te ruimen. Geen extra werkzaamheden voordat we eindelijk konden gaan slapen of omdat de volgende dag weer 'een gewone werkdag' zou worden. Als er bij Jacques een klus geklaard was, dan konden we gewoon naar huis of, meer gebruikelijk, aan de borrel.

Hij had in huis voldoende ruimte om, indien nodig of omdat we nog niet helemaal klaar waren, de boel de boel te laten. Hij woonde ergens in het achterhuis of tijdelijk op zolder en vond ogenschijnlijk alle rotzooi die we maakten of achter ons lieten slingeren, geen bezwaar. De week erop ging hij gewoon weer verder waar we gebleven waren. Niet altijd met dezelfde ploeg personeel om zich heen, maar altijd vol enthousiasme en overgave.

Een toegevoegde waarde was Jacques' gewoonte om op zondagmiddag een maaltijd voor alle aanwezigen klaar te maken. Koken kon hij namelijk net zo goed als klussen en het sprak wel degelijk mee dat we hem mede daarom graag behulpzaam waren. Ook als je tussen vrijdagavond of zondagmiddag, slechts een paar uurtjes productief geweest was, was je welkom om voor het diner op zondag aan de lange tafel in de opkamer aan te schuiven. We hebben daarvan allemaal regelmatig gebruik, of in sommige gevallen misschien misbruik, gemaakt.

Dan ging bijvoorbeeld op zaterdagochtend de telefoon en vroeg een van de maten, soms Jacques zelf, of ik iemand wist die "even een paar pijpjes aan elkaar kon komen solderen."

Een enkele keer was de nood zo hoog dat ie er ronduit voor uitkwam "niet verder te kunnen zonder hulp." Vanzelfsprekend was zo'n verzoek niet tegen dovemansoren gericht en de wens liet zich meestal nog redelijk eenvoudig inpassen in de rest van het programma voor zo'n weekend. Zoals ik al vertelde ook mijn echtgenote, toen nog verloofde, vond het geen bezwaar om desgevraagd onze behulpzaamheid te tonen of aan te bieden.

Een enkele keer kwam ze me dan in de loop van de zondag ophalen of was ons behulpzaam om het klusje dat we onderhanden hadden, volledig af te krijgen. In ieder geval was het vanzelfsprekend dat we dan met z'n allen een glaasje dronken en de maaltijd die Jacques gewoontegetrouw bereid had, liet zich altijd goed smaken. We konden erop rekenen en soms namen we uit voorzorg een bijdrage mee in de vorm van een fles lekkere wijn of een mooie whiskey. Bij veel puin en te verwachten rommel namen we zelfs iets te eten mee, dat hadden we dan thuis klaargemaakt en hoefde alleen maar in de oven van Sjaak te worden opgewarmd. Hij voegde daar dan overigens altijd iets aan toe, waardoor het nóg smakelijker werd dan we eerder bedacht hadden.

Op een middag, terwijl ik hem in de keuken hielp bij het snijden van de uien en groenten, heeft hij me eens toevertrouwd dat hij voor speciale gerechten wel eens een aantal keren doordeweeks geoefend had, om de juiste bereiding volledig onder de knie te krijgen. Vaak had hij inspiratie ervoor opgedaan tijdens een etentje in het een of andere restaurant. Daar kwam hij dan tijdens zijn stage of als hij waarnam op de praktijk van een collega. We mogen Jacques in meerdere opzichten een perfectionist noemen en dat kon hij met zijn kook kunsten uitstekend bewijzen.

Het dringt tot me door dat Peter en ik elkaar toen inderdaad weleens ontmoet zullen hebben. Als student waren we nog gewoon kennissen, collega's werden we namelijk pas later, nadat we afgestudeerd waren. Indertijd zullen we ons voornamelijk bezig gehouden hebben met onze verkeringen en later met trouwen. Mijn vrouw en ik kregen daarna al snel kinderen en, nu ik er even over nadenk, Peter is niet zo lang na ons ook in het huwelijksbootje gestapt.

Door de kleintjes wisten onze echtgenotes hun band te versterken. Omdat ze elkaar van de middelbare school kenden en bevriend gebleven waren, kostte ze dat totaal geen moeite. We woonden niet heel ver bij elkaar vandaan, dus dat maakte het gezamenlijk boodschappen doen of winkelen voor de hand liggend. Of Peter zijn vrouw inderdaad op onze bruiloft voor het eerst ontmoet heeft, is me trouwens nooit duidelijk geworden, maar op het werk houden we die anekdote er al jaren in.

Intussen zijn we al bijna twaalf jaar collega's. Daardoor zien en spreken we elkaar tegenwoordig bijna elke dag, alleen al tijdens het werk of erna. Onze gezamenlijke vakantie hier op de camping is erdoor tot stand gekomen.

Hoewel we door alle omstandigheden dus niet meer zo regelmatig bij hem thuis kwamen, bleek iedere keer als we er waren dat de woning onder Sjaak z'n handen uitgroeide tot 'een paleisje'. Iedere kamer die gereed kwam, richtte hij vol toewijding en met smaak in met de spullen die hij er blijkbaar in overvloed voor beschikbaar had.

In de loop der tijd bleek het zijn hobby geworden om tijdens ritten door het land, veilingen te bezoeken. Hij bezocht ze overigens niet uitsluitend om er meubels of schilderijen voor de woning aan te schaffen, vaak bracht hij er een blind bod uit op zaken die hem "ook wel leuk" leken. Weken later werden die door een bode bezorgd omdat er geen tegenbod op was uitgebracht en hij ze zodoende tegen de afslagprijs aangeschaft had.

Tijd om de veiling zelf te bezoeken had Sjaak over het algemeen niet en zijn interesse ging niet diep genoeg om ervoor om te rijden of terug te komen teneinde er live aan biedingen mee te doen. Het was de gewoonte die hem dreef naar de bijbehorende kijkdagen en of 'n lot aan hem toeviel deed 'm vervolgens niet zoveel. Hij vertrouwde er klakkeloos op dat een volgende keer de gelegenheid voor een buitenkansje even groot zou zijn.

Op deze manier vulde het huis zich met steeds meer mooie, vaak prachtige spullen. Maar ook met snuisterijen en curiosa. Die zette hij dan op de randen die we boven de lambrisering in de huiskamer hadden getimmerd, een verloren hoekje en 'n richeltje elders in huis. Of de spullen stonden opgeslagen ergens op de zolder of in de schuur totdat ze van pas kwamen. Vaak moesten ze eerst grondig schoongemaakt of nog een beetje opgeknapt worden, maar ook daarvoor vond Jacques altijd wel een vrijwilliger.

Doordat hij zoveel op veilingen rondhing kon onze vriend ruimschoots rondsnuffelen in oude boeken en tijdschriften. Mede daardoor deed hij vaak vondsten die uit lang vervlogen tijden stamden. Omdat niemand zulke ouderwetse dingen gebruikte of nodig had, kon hij die zogenaamde troep vaak voor een gering bedrag, zelf noemde hij dat dan "een prikkie", aanschaffen. Maar ik verbaasde me er er weleens over hoeveel geld hij kennelijk aan de oude rommel kon besteden. Bij navraag bleek overigens dat het de vervoerskosten van de bode niet veel hoger opdreef. Die reed toch al en hij betaalde voor de rit.

Omstandig kon Jacques een door hem aangeschaft "handig dingetje" demonstreren en vaak verbaasde hij ons met de vindingrijkheid waarmee in het verleden oplossingen gevonden waren voor alledaagse zaken. Daar had men dan helemaal geen computers of elektronica voor nodig gehad. Soms maakte hij er een soort quiz van.

Dan vroeg hij bijvoorbeeld of wij wisten waartoe een bepaald voorwerp diende. Glimlachend keek hij toe hoe we een voor een het betreffende apparaat ter hand namen en er over speculeerden waar het voor gemaakt of bedoeld was. Pas later op de avond, als het feest al goed en wel aan de gang was, showde hij hoe het onderwerp van zijn eigen en intussen onze vragen, gebruikt kon worden. Meestal leverde zo'n ontknoping hilarische momenten op omdat wij uit onszelf nooit op zulke toepassingen gekomen zouden zijn en er in de loop van de avond vele fantastische mogelijkheden waren gepasseerd.

Kortom Jacques had door zijn hele huis spullen staan en van vele ervan was ons het doel pas duidelijk na een terdege uitleg. Als onderdeel van deze nostalgie maakte hij trouwens ook graag gebruik van middeltjes en tips uit groot-moeders tijd. Vaak had hij die tijdens het snuffelen en rondneuzen tussen de uitgestalde waren van zo'n verkoping opgedaan. Hij noteerde de vondsten en paste ze toe waar dat mogelijk was. Ook als hij er lang naar moest zoeken voordat hij alle benodigdheden die erbij nodig waren verzameld had. Deze voorkeur hing misschien ook wel een beetje samen met zijn werk, want uiteindelijk kwam hij vaak op hele oude boerderijen waar tradities nog in ere werden gehouden. Vaak juist als er moderne alternatieven of 'nieuwerwetse apparaten' en vindingen voorhanden waren.

"Weet je nog dat Jacques altijd een doosje lucifers op het toilet had liggen? Hij deed immers niet aan lucht verfrissers of sprays."
Inderdaad was dat een van de talrijke huis middeltjes waar onze vriend gebruik van maakte. Naar zijn voorbeeld ligt er bij ons thuis overigens ook altijd een doosje op het randje in het toilet. Al zit er op het plafond dus een ventilator gemonteerd, die gaat draaien als het licht wordt ingeschakeld. Dat is overdag natuurlijk niet zo vaak het geval maar daarom gebruiken we soms de truc om een lucifer aan te steken als de lucht in het gemak te 'geparfumeerd' is geraakt tijdens onze aanwezigheid. Weliswaar is het eenvoudiger om even een paar tellen het licht aan te doen, die ventilator loopt na het weer uitschakelen van de lamp immers een paar minuten door, maar uit milieuvriendelijke overwegingen gebruiken we dus ook weleens zo'n lucifertje om de vreselijkste geuren te verdoezelen. We hebben het handigheidje van Jacques overgenomen, mijn ouders bijvoorbeeld kenden de truc helemaal niet. Ter goeder trouw zetten we er een traditie mee voort.
Ik beantwoord Peters' vraag bevestigend door een hum geluid te maken. Naar ik begrijp heeft hij ook even aan onze vriend zitten denken. Waarschijnlijk heeft hij dezelfde herinneringen als ik en zal hij eveneens tot de conclusie gekomen zijn dat we hem de laatste tijd te weinig hebben gezien. De vakantie is uiteindelijk een tijd van bezinning en het opbouwen van frisse moed. Zo heb ik me al voorgenomen om binnenkort een feestje te geven en al onze vrienden ervoor uit te nodigen. Mijn veertigste verjaardag vormt daarvoor vanzelfsprekend een goede aanleiding. Daar zal mijn vrouw zich niet tegen kunnen of willen verzetten. We zullen Jacques er ook voor uitnodigen, dat staat bij dezen vast.
Peter is tijdens mijn overpeinzingen een beetje omhoog gewipt met zijn zitvlak en haalt een doosje lucifers uit zijn zak. Ik herken ze, het zijn van die exemplaren die ook als ze nat geworden zijn aan te steken zijn. Het maakt ze ideaal voor op de camping, al regent het momenteel dus gelukkig niet.
"Deze heb jij toch ook altijd"?
Nogmaals hum ik mijn bevestiging. Ik blijf in zijn richting kijken en vraag me af waar hij op aanstuurt. De lucifers van ons liggen naast het gasstel dat in

de voortent op een kist staat. Ik heb ze daar zoeven nog gezien toen ik de verse biertjes uit de koelbox haalde. Of Peter en zijn vrouw ze ook mee hebben genomen weet ik niet, maar gezien het feit dat onze echtgenotes vaak samen boodschappen doen is het niet uit te sluiten.

"Die van ons liggen in de tent.

Heb je deze ergens gevonden?"

Voor de zekerheid kijk ik toch even over mijn schouder. Er ligt inderdaad zo'n zelfde doosje naast ons kook toestelletje. Voor zover ik me kan herinneren zitten ze per drie verpakt in een cellofaantje en liggen de andere twee doosjes tussen de boodschappen in de bak met voorraad.

Bij het inrichten van ons vakantieverblijf heb ik ze zelf opgeborgen waar ze nu liggen en we hebben ze nog niet nodig gehad. Daar is het weer tot nog toe te mooi voor geweest. Peter pakt de opener van tafel en maakt allebei onze flesjes ermee open. Hij schenkt zichzelf een nieuw glas bier in. De andere fles schuift hij in mijn richting.

"Net op het toilet vond ik dit doosje. Terwijl ik zat te poepen leek het me een goed idee om wat aan de stank te doen.

Van die worsten hier ga je nogal ruiken namelijk."

Of de vreselijk geur inderdaad van het worst eten komt vraag ik me af. Ik verdenk er de bier consumptie van dat de gasproductie zo hoog is komen te liggen. Gist zal er een invloed op hebben vermoed ik.

"Helaas was ik vergeten dat ik voordat ik ging zitten eerst de bril had afgeveegd."

Deze gewoonte is me goed bekend, ik heb aan de kinderen geleerd om 'm toe te passen als ze op een vreemd toilet zijn en maak er zelf ook altijd gebruik van. Dat heb ik van mijn moeder ooit zo geleerd.

"Dat er dus een berg papier in de plee lag was me eventjes ontgaan.

Precies zoals het hoort heb ik de vlam eventjes groot laten worden en dus gewacht tot bijna het hele steeltje mee aan was gegaan. Toen ik even later, vlak voordat ik mijn vingers zou branden het lucifertje tussen mijn benen door in de pot gooide moet de boel in de hens gevlogen zijn."

Peter laat even een pauze vallen. Kennelijk wil hij me in staat stellen om een beeld te vormen van de omstandigheden waaronder hij verkeerde toen hij op het toilet was.

"Eerst merkte ik nog niets, maar het werd opeens heel erg heet onder me en nu heb ik me flink verbrand."

Ik durf mijn vriend niet aan te kijken. Ik ben veel te bang om in de lach te schieten en 'm recht voor zijn raap uit te gaan zitten lachen. Dat wil ik hem besparen, maar evengoed hij zit me hier doodgemoedereerd te vertellen hoe hij zijn achterwerk en scrotum heeft verschroeid, door in de pot er onder een kampvuurtje te stoken!

97

We zeggen allebei geen woord, maar voor mijn oog doemt het beeld op hoe hij in het nauwe hokje verschrikt opgesprongen moet zijn boven de vlammenzee die opgelaaid zal zijn. Het kost nauwelijks moeite om me voor te stellen hoe hij verschrikt de brandende haren uit heeft staan slaan.

De hokjes hier op de camping zijn niet ruim en het laat zich eenvoudig voorstellen hoe Peter, ook schoon aan de haak toch een forse gestalte, zich in allerlei bochten heeft moeten wringen om genoeg ruimte voor zijn acties te krijgen. Voldoende armruimte om overal bij te kunnen. Waarschijnlijk is hij er flink bij gehinderd, door de broek die naar z'n enkels gezakt zal zijn.

Ik moet intussen mijn knieën strak tegen elkaar houden om niet in die van mij te piesen. Het beeld hoe mijn vriend, natuurlijk zo ver mogelijk bij die fik vandaan en dus waarschijnlijk in een hoekje gedrukt, zichzelf billenkoek staat te geven, maakt dat de tranen over mijn wangen beginnen te lopen.

Vanaf het andere stoeltje zit Peter me meewarig aan te kijken. Als ik even opzij durf te kijken zie ik in zijn blik hoe de verbazing over mijn ingehouden proesten en het verlangen naar medelijden met zijn pijnlijke achterwerk om de voorrang strijden. Hierdoor moet ik nog erger lachen.

Als ik mezelf niet langer kan inhouden en hikkend in een aanval van de slappe lach uitbarst, dringt het potsierlijke van de situatie gelukkig ook tot hem door. Hij is snel in staat om ook de humor in te zien, al weet ik niet of hij moet lachen om mijn reactie of dat hij intussen het lachwekkende van zijn zelfverbranding inziet. Uiteindelijk proesten we het allebei zo uit dat we niet meer bij dreigen te komen. Slechts een korte blik op de ander maakt dat we weer helemaal opnieuw beginnen.

Verbaasd komen de kinderen een voor een kijken waar hun papa's zoveel lol om hebben. Ik moet intussen met mijn vlakke hand op mijn dij kletsen om enigszins tot bedaren te komen en Peter onderwerpt zich eveneens aan een soortgelijke actie. Hierdoor zijn we niet in staat om het hen naar behoren uit te leggen.

Telefoon

18 hr. 02 "Ja hallo, met mij.
- Luister eens, ik ben met de collega's even wat drinken dus wacht maar niet op me met het eten.
- Nee joh, ik had je toch al eens zoiets verteld. Gewoon, met een ploegje van onze verdieping.
- Nee........, ze doen dat elke maand een keer.
- Ja, die is er ook en John, die naast mij zijn kantoortje heeft weetjewel, die is er ook bij. Ook met zijn secretaresse.
- Nee verder alleen dus een paar lui bij ons van het kantoor en nog iemand uit het magazijn. Die wou graag mee, geloof ik.
- Maar ik ga nu naar ze toe, ik wilde alleen maar even bellen om te zeggen dat ik wat later kom.
- Nee dat heeft geen zin. Bewaar maar wat, dat warm ik dan wel op als ik vanavond thuiskom.
- Oh, dat vind ik lekker ja. Hoezo?
- Doe dat dan maar. Maar ik weet echt niet hoe laat ze het gaan maken, dus ga vooral niet op mij zitten wachten. Ga maar gewoon eten, ik red me wel.
- Lekker ja. Neem jij dan alvast een glaasje bij het eten.
- Ik maak het echt niet laat. Als ik weer thuis ben, dan drinken we de rest wel op.
- Nou ja, als jij alles opdrinkt dan neem ik straks wel wat anders. Ik heb toch nog wat whisky staan en we hebben ook nog een paar biertjes in de koelkast toch? We zien wel waar ik hier mee begin.
- Ja bedankt en tot straks ik ga het echt niet laat maken hoor. Het zijn maar collega's moet je maar bedenken.
- Goed dan, dag."

18 hr.45 "Hi met mij weer. Het schijnt de gewoonte te zijn dat we met zijn allen uit eten gaan. Niks fancy ofzo, maar wel in het een of andere restaurant hier in de buurt. Heb jij intussen al wat gegeten?
- Nee joh, ik had toch gezegd dat je dat niet moest doen. Dit vind ik nou echt flauw van je.
- Ik had je er toch speciaal voor opgebeld.
- Nou ja, je hebt zelf gezegd dat ik me niet zo afzijdig moet houden en ik had

99

je toch verteld dat ze vorige maand met zijn allen een uitje hadden gehad?

- Zie je wel, je hebt toen trouwens zelf gezegd dat ik een volgende keer mee moest gaan. Je vond het zelf ook maar raar dat ze me de vorige keer niet ge-vraagd hadden.

- Ja dat wel.

- Ik zal wel eens vragen of ze dat inderdaad van tevoren al weten.

- Ja, in feite wel ja.

- Nee joh, alleen maar de collega's. We zijn gelijk uit werk weggegaan en hebben in dat cafeetje vlak bij de oprit naar de snelweg afgesproken.

- Ja die, die op dat pleintje. Jeweetwel.

- Nee, ik ben alleen gegaan. Ik kon er trouwens vlakbij, eigenlijk zo'n beetje pal voor de deur, mijn auto kwijt.

- Ja dat viel heel erg mee ja. Er is zo'n kleine parkeerstrook voor en die was bijna helemaal leeg.

- Nee dat dacht ik niet. Nu je het zegt, ik heb er eigenlijk niet op gelet. Nou ja, ik kijk dan wel even als we hier weer weggaan.

- Of weetje, ik loop straks gelijk even naar buiten om te kijken. Dan gooi ik er wel wat in als er toch een meter staat.

- Ja, dat kost een hoop geld ja, maar ik leefde in de veronderstelling dat je hier nog gewoon gratis kon staan.

- Ik heb er gewoon niet op gelet. Je hebt gelijk, het is een beetje dom.

- Nou hopelijk heb ik mazzel en is er intussen niet gecontroleerd, als het toch verplicht is, hier.

- Wanneer was dat?

- Oh toen, maar dat was in de winkelstraat in die buurt hierachter. Da's nog een flink stuk verder naar het centrum hoor.

- Daar stonden toen trouwens van die grote blauwe borden. Weet je nog?

- Ja precies, nou iedereen heeft intussen z'n jas aan, dus ik ga. Ik zal wel even kijken, buiten.

- Ja, dank je, zal ik doen, dag tot straks. Eet wat!"

19 hr. 08 "Nou iedereen zit te bellen, dus ik doe maar even mee.

- We zijn in het restaurantje aangekomen en het ziet er inderdaad uit als een leuk ding.

- Nee, daar hadden ze geen zin in. Vonden ze niet leuk ofzo. Misschien lusten ze geen pizza, die mensen heb je ook hoor. Ze schijnen hier elke keer naartoe te gaan.

- Weet je trouwens of mijn salaris al is bijgeschreven? Ik heb hooguit drie tientjes in mijn zak, dus dat zal wel niet genoeg zijn. Ik wil dus graag kunnen pinnen, maar wil natuurlijk niet voor gek staan als dat ding blokkeert.

- Ik lees wel even wat voor, ik heb de kaart hier voor me tenslotte. Wacht

100

even.

- Ze hebben slakken als voorafje, dus die neem ik.

- Achtvijftig. Alle prijzen zijn hier zo'n beetje als bij Berend en Armand, zie ik. Ik denk dat ik aan een voorgerechtje en een hoofdschotel wel genoeg zal hebben.

- Ik heb net twee biertjes op en ze hebben, toen we binnen kwamen, een karaf wit en rood besteld.

- Ja dat weet ik, maar ik eet er toch bij. En ik drink er heus niet meer dan twee. Je kent me, dus daar blijft het bij. Echt.

- Nee, dat doe ik toch nooit. Wanneer heb ik trouwens voor het laatst een toetje genomen. Dat was vlak voor de kerst, toen waren we samen en lopend gekomen.

- Jij wou toen trouwens ook een likeurtje, dus nou moet je niet gaan zeuren.

- Ik weet heus wel dat ik nog moet rijden. Ze moeten volgens mij trouwens allemaal nog rijden.

- Nee, die is met zijn eigen auto gegaan.

- Zij ook, ja. Iedereen is met zijn eigen auto gekomen. Oh trouwens, ik mocht daar inderdaad gratis staan. Ik zei het toch al.

- Ja een dikke zestig Euro hoorde ik net. Dat heb ik dus alweer mooi bespaard. Zou ik na het eten toch een cognacje kunnen nemen.

- Grapje. Jeetje, waar is je gevoel voor humor gebleven.

- Ja dat is goed. Ze komen er trouwens aan om onze bestellingen op te nemen, dus ik ga hangen.

- Een entrecote ofzo, ik moet nog even kijken.

- Ja o.k. Tot vanavond."

20 hr. 17 "Nou het is weer zover. Iedereen zit in zijn mobieltje te kleppen, dus ik dacht dat ik jou nog wel even kon bellen.

- Wat ben je aan het doen?

- Oh.

- Nee, het is hier wel leuk hoor, maar ze zijn niet erg snel. We zitten nu te wachten op het hoofdgerecht.

- En steak met paddestoeltjes in een armagnac roomsaus. Volgens John is dat een van de specialiteiten van het huis.

- Dat is dan toch allang verdampt joh.

- Ik heb net mijn tweede gekregen.

- Rood.

- Nee die heeft een entrecote besteld, geloof ik. De bediening is misschien traag, maar ze laten ons hier zodoende wel met rust. We redden ons dus wel.

- Met, wacht even ik zal even tellen........ elf man. Wij van onze afdeling en dan John met zijn secretaresse. Een paar mensen van de boekhouding uit het

101

kantoor naast ons en een vent uit het magazijn beneden.

- Nee joh, het is woensdag dan is zo'n tent toch hartstikke blij met iedere klant die binnen komt wandelen. Ze hebben alleen maar even vlug een paar tafeltjes tegen elkaar hoeven schuiven.

- Ja, maar heel kort maar. Aan de bar en in het halletje dat ernaast was. Het was zo gebeurd. Die *muts* van John had net haar jas uit toen we al konden gaan zitten.

- Ja, ja dat kun je je niet voorstellen. Niet gewoon dom, maar dat kind heeft het zeker weten uitgevonden. Misschien moet John haar maar eens flink aan-pakken. Het is zo nu en dan namelijk best gênant wat er allemaal uitkomt.

- Nee die zitten aan het einde van de tafel. Dit kunnen ze niet horen.

- Hé, ik ben niet lijp hoor.

- Nee inderdaad. Ze moeten me trouwens niet afluisteren. Dat is onbeleefd toch? Hé, ze komen eraan dus ik ga hangen.

- Ja da's goed, tot straks.

- Dankje, dag."

21 hr. 26 "Hi, zeg het is nog niet afgelopen hoor.

- Nee, daar zijn we net weg, we gaan nu nog even naar een leuke koffietent met zijn allen.

- Nee, nee ik heb me keurig aan mijn taks gehouden. Het was trouwens ze-venentwintig vijftig.

- Dat gaan we nu doen geloof ik. Ze hadden het in ieder geval over designer koffie en espresso. Dat zou erg lekker moeten zijn.

- Nee, inderdaad. Nooit te oud om te leren, nee.

- Zo bedoel ik het niet. Dat weet je best. Ik mag toch trouwens ook wel eens een leuke avond hebben?

- Goed ja. Nou o.k. ik ga hangen, ik bel wel weer als het afgelopen is.

- Ja, voordat ik naar huis kom ja. Dag."

21 hr. 59 "Hé met mij. Ik loop nu naar de auto.

- Ja dat viel wel mee overigens, ik begrijp niet wat daar zo speciaal aan zou moeten zijn. Nou ja, de prijs misschien.

- Nou ik vind acht euro voor een kopje espresso nogal aan de prijs.

- Ja acht.

- Nee, maar ik heb even een tientje kunnen lenen van John.

- Ik heb daar niet gepind. Dat hoefde toch niet, ik had inderdaad nog ruim dertig euro in mijn portemonnee.

- Nu nog? Een stuk of vier, ik heb natuurlijk een fooi gegeven.

- Nee, ik heb er dertig van gemaakt. Ik had er toch nog wat kleingeld en een paar euro's bij inzitten.

102

- Ik dacht dat die koffie een euro of vier zou gaan kosten, wist ik veel!
- Nou, John heeft ons uitgenodigd bij hem thuis. Hij schijnt hier ergens in de buurt te wonen.
- Voor een kopje huiselijke koffie, zoals hij het noemde. Ik lust trouwens best wel een echte bak, voordat ik straks die rit naar huis moet maken.
- Tja, het is nu natuurlijk rustig op de weg dus ik denk dat ik er dan binnen hooguit twintig minuten zal kunnen zijn.
- Ja, maar dat wordt niet laat hoor. Ik ga na een bakje koffie weg, dan heb ik meer dan genoeg.
- Ik kon dit echt niet afslaan, vind het juist veel te leuk dat ze me nu eindelijk lijken te accepteren.
- Om heel eerlijk te zijn voelt het wel zo ja. Ik ben zelfs toegesproken in het restaurant. Had je niet verwacht hè?
- Nou John natuurlijk. Die is eigenlijk een soort gangmaker van het collega clubje. Hij zei dat ik er intussen helemaal bij hoorde.
- Allemaal ja. Ik kreeg ook nog een een kort applausje.
- Hé ik ben bij de auto. Ik ga hangen, dag."

22 hr. 17 "Ja hi, met mij weer. We zijn bij zijn huis aangekomen. Het was toch verder dan ie gezegd had.
- Nee, hij staat naast zijn auto op ons te wachten.
- Oh, Gerda een collegaatje. Ze is met me meegereden. Wil je haar even spreken?
- Ook goed ja, ik zie trouwens dat er nu bij John uit z'n auto, nog twee mensen klauteren. Ik dacht dat die met hun eigen auto zouden komen.
- Nou ja, dan is er meer parkeerruimte voor mijn auto, moet je maar denken.
- Ik zie hier trouwens een plekje en ga hangen. Dag."

22 hr. 42 "Hé, met mij.
- Ik zag natuurlijk dat jij het was.
- Nee, nog niet. We zitten nog steeds bij John.
- Ja, heel erg leuk eigenlijk. Bel je me speciaal, om dat te vragen?
- Nou dat kan nog wel een half uurtje duren. John heeft koffie voor ons gezet en die hebben we hier in de kamer met z'n allen op zitten drinken.
- Nee, die heeft hij niet, geloof ik.
- Het is hier trouwens net zoals jij het altijd noemt een echt mannen huishouden. Jij zou het hier ook wel leuk vinden, denk ik.
- Nou gezien de rommel enzo. Wel alles op keurige stapels hoor, maar toch een soort chaos. Nou ja, je weetwel. Jij zegt toch altijd dat het er op mijn werkkamer niet uitziet van de troep. Zo is het hier ook een beetje.
- Nee, geen foto's nee.

- Nee joh, hij had wel van alles wat in huis, maar ik moet straks nog een heel stuk autorijden.
- Nou cognac natuurlijk, en allerlei verschillende likeurtjes.
- Ja, die ook.
- Hij heeft trouwens wel zeventien verschillende soorten whisky in huis.
- Die is nu even die Gerda en nog een andere collega aan het uitlaten.
- Nog met z'n zessen, om precies te zijn. We hebben nog wel een tijdje op die vent uit het magazijn staan wachten, maar kennelijk was die intussen toch maar naar huis gegaan. Eigenlijk best wel onbeleefd om zonder wat te zeggen weg te blijven.
- Hier, buiten, voor John z'n appartement natuurlijk.
- Hij zou zo nog wat te drinken meebrengen als hij de meisjes uit had gelaten, dus ik blijf nog even een Spaatje drinken.
- Tja, een half uurtje ofzo. Anders ga je toch alvast naar bed. Ik kom heus wel thuis.
- Ja dat kan ook. Moet ik je dan nog bellen als in eraan kom, of zal ik je maar met rust laten?
- O.k. ook goed. Ja, dat is dan afgesproken.
- Zal ik doen.
- Oh, ze komen binnen, dus je hoort nog van me.
- Tot straks. Dag."

23 hr. 47 "Hé ik blijf denk ik maar hier slapen.
- Bij John, ja. Kijk hij had de Spa vergeten te pakken of die was op en toen heb ik daarvoor in de plaats nog een klein glaasje wijn gedronken. Voor de gezelligheid.
- Nee twee, maar toen was alles op.
- Ik had je toch al verteld dat ie wel zeventien verschillende soorten whisky in huis had. Nou, daar zijn we toen van gaan proeven.
- Nee, die zijn intussen een voor een weg gegaan.
- Ja, die proeft ook mee natuurlijk.
- Hij is nu even wat ijs uit de vriezer aan het halen. Hij was al eerder begonnen. Bij de koffie had ie er al een voor zichzelf ingeschonken. Die was van zijn favoriete soort en inderdaad heel erg smakelijk. Maar we gaan nu ook nog wat andere proberen.
- Alleen wij twee nog, ja. Hoezo?
- Nee op de logeerkamer natuurlijk. Hé, Gerard je bent toch niet opeens jaloers aan het worden?"

Voorstel

De man is met zijn lege koffiekopje de huiskamer in komen lopen. Alsof zo-iets volkomen vanzelfsprekend is heeft hij 'm bij zijn vrouw neergezet, op het bijzet tafeltje naast haar stoel. Ze concludeert dat er kennelijk niks meer te be-kijken is op de televisie. Haar veronderstelling wordt gesteund door de stilte achter 'm. Hij zal het apparaat dus uitgeschakeld hebben. Normaliter blijft hij hele avonden in de serre, naar het toestel zitten kijken. Volgens hem is er al-tijd wel iets leuks of een bezienswaardig programma op te bekijken. 'Uitein-delijk kunnen ze niet alle achtentwintig zenders even saai maken en het is na-tuurlijk wèl de bedoeling om die programma's aan de kijker te verkopen'.
"Weet je wat mij een goed idee lijkt"?
Hij maakt de opmerking terwijl hij zich in zijn stoel tegenover haar laat zak-ken. Het stoort haar dat hij zonder er rekening mee te houden dat ze zit te le-zen, zomaar om alle aandacht vraagt. Haar tijdschrift heeft ze echter al laten zakken. Met een zucht en 'n hum geluidje hoopt ze hem duidelijk te maken dat ze maar matig geïnteresseerd is. Toch richt ze haar blik naar zijn stoel en kijkt toe hoe hij erin gaat zitten.
Pas als hij ervan overtuigd is dat hij haar volle aandacht gevangen heeft, ver-volgt hij met wat hij kennelijk wil bespreken. "Ik stel voor dat jij en de kinde-ren naar die camping in Brabant gaan.
Je weet wel die ene waar we samen ook een aantal keren zijn geweest."
Hij laat even een stilte vallen om zijn woorden op haar in te laten werken.
"Dan gingen we in de omgeving fietsen.
En een dagje winkelen in Den Bosch. Dan reden we er langs het water, een kanaal met dat smalle bruggetje bij die sluis erin, naartoe."
De man kijkt of hij aan haar blik kan zien dat ze begrijpt over welke camping hij spreekt. Hij wacht even op een knikje of nogmaals een hum geluidje ter bevestiging. Als de stilte blijkbaar lang genoeg heeft geduurd, gaat hij verder.
"Weet je nog dat we daar een keer onze Nordic Walking poles mee naar toe hadden genomen?
Toen waren we er samen.
Het was die keer dat we er allebei geen dekking hadden op onze telefoontjes.
We zaten te wachten op een berichtje van de begeleiding en moesten telkens helemaal naar het volleybal veld lopen om te kijken of er misschien iets was ingesproken. Weetje nog?"

Er is geen ontkomen aan, ze zal nu aan hem duidelijk moeten maken dat haar hoofd niet staat naar zijn beslommeringen of zich overgeven. Het wordt zo te merken een lang verhaal. Ze zat een artikel te lezen dat haar interessant leek en wil daar nu eigenlijk mee doorgaan. Ze kent haar man lang genoeg om te weten dat hij zich eigenlijk verveelt.

Het stoort haar en ze vraagt zich af waarom hij niet, net zoals zij, ook een tijdschrift pakt. Of een boek. Er liggen er genoeg die hij nog moet lezen. Dat zegt hij immers zelf ook te pas en te onpas tegen hun gasten. Trots wijst hij hun bezoek er dan op dat er nog 'minstens een stapel van een meter' op hem ligt te wachten. Ze zou hem weleens aan willen sporen 'doe het dan, begin er eens aan', maar ze laat het erbij en kijkt naar hem. Tegen de zijkant van hun boekenkast, nog geen meter bij haar vandaan, staat die hele stapel met nieuw gekochte boeken te wachten om te worden ingekeken. Ze weet dat er een aantal tussen zitten waarin hij ooit is begonnen er steken dan boeken leggers of een stukje papier uit om aan te geven tot hoever hij is gekomen.

Hun blikken kruisen elkaar. Ze knikt om te bewijzen dat ze luistert en begrepen heeft dat hij met haar wil praten. Omstandig laat ze het tijdschrift helemaal op haar schoot zakken, ze wil ermee benadrukken dat hij haar aandacht nu volledig heeft gevangen.

"We zijn toen een wandeling gaan maken aan de overkant van de weg.

Eerst liepen we door het bos bij de camping.

We kwamen toen over dat modderige zandpad tot aan de straat en aan de overkant hebben we daarna een poosje nog een ander pad gevolgd. Dat stond het eerste stuk nog helemaal vol met hoog gras in het midden, maar later werd het beter omdat het daar kennelijk meer gebruikt werd.

We kwamen ook langs een boerderij. Dat weet ik vrijwel zeker en een eindje verderop langs datzelfde pad liggen de Loonse en Drunense duinen."

Hij pauzeert weer even om zijn vrouw de gelegenheid te geven zich een beeld te vormen. Hij weet vrijwel zeker dat ze zich die wandeling nog zal weten te herinneren. Daar ergens, in de middle of nowhere, had hij een flinke hypo gekregen. De koekjes die ze anders altijd bij zich heeft, lagen echter nog bij de tent. Ze hadden er allebei niet aan gedacht om ze mee te nemen. Het was net na het eten toen ze even een korte wandeling gingen maken. En zulke aanvallen kwamen alleen als hij nog aan tafel moest. Als hij honger had bijvoorbeeld of zich erg aan het inspannen was.

Ergens helemaal onder uit zijn rugzakje had ze zo'n klein Mars reepje opgediept. Het dingetje was half geplet en de chocolade wit uitgeslagen omdat ie er al zo lang in had gezeten, maar ze had het hem desondanks in zijn mond gepropt. Eigenlijk is zoiets meer een bonbon dan de suiker bom die hij in zulke gevallen nodig heeft om hem weer op de been te helpen, maar ze hadden het ermee moeten doen.

Zelf herinnert hij zich vooral de paniek gevoelens die zich onder het lopen van hem meester hadden gemaakt. Zoals altijd was hij door het plotselinge tekort aan suikers verward en onrustig geworden. Het leek er toen vooral op dat hij bang was dat ze verdwaald waren en nooit meer terug zouden raken op een vertrouwde plek. Alsof het vertraagd aan hem voorbij ging, had hij op de acties van zijn vrouw gereageerd. Om hen heen de zandverstuivingen en slechts hier en daar begroeide duinen.

Toen het weer een beetje beter met hem ging, was ze hem voorgegaan terug naar de camping. Zonder om te kijken is ze voor hem uit blijven lopen tot ze weer bij de autoweg aankwamen. Daar hoefden ze alleen nog maar over te steken en een kort stukje over het voetpad te lopen naar de hoofdingang. Terug de camping op en dwars over het veldje naar hun tent. In een roes en hevig zwetend is hij achter haar aan gekomen. Zich exact volgens de instructies, links en rechts afzettend met de stokken bij elke stap.

"Dat vond ik een mooi stukje landschap. Er was een hartstikke leuk uitzicht met doorkijkjes tussen de duinen door.

We waren niet eens zo heel ver weg van het dorp en de rest van de bewoonde wereld. Maar het zag er daar toch ruw en vrijwel ongerept uit."

Hij laat zich tegen de rugleuning zakken. Onder het praten is hij wat naar voren gekomen, maar nu zoekt hij weer het gemak van de stoel op. Z'n vrouw heeft haar tijdschrift neergelegd.

Allebei hebben ze naast hun zitplaats een stapeltje liggen. Zij vooral woon tijdschriften en de verschillende dames- en modebladen die ze een keer per maand van hun dochter krijgt. Naast de stoel van de man zijn de bladen te vinden waarop hij een abonnement heeft. Twee over computers, een Engelse en een Nederlandse en nog een maandblad dat uitsluitend over fotografie gaat. Omdat hij er meestal nog iets in op wil zoeken of na moet kijken, liggen er zowel recente die hij nog niet helemaal uit heeft en een enkele van soms wel maanden terug op hem te wachten. Zo nu en dan krijgt hij van zijn echtgenote op z'n donder.

Ze maant hem dan dat hij ze "eens uit moet zoeken."

Het betekent voornamelijk dat ze de stapel te hoog vindt worden en graag zou zien dat hij er een paar, zo niet allemaal, weg doet. Meestal mogen er inderdaad een of twee in de bak voor het oud-papier worden gegooid. De informatie en een eventuele aanbieding die er in staat, blijkt intussen vaak verouderd of is verlopen.

"Als je tegen de kinderen zegt dat ze naar die camping moeten komen, dan kun je met ze naar datzelfde paadje gaan. Ik vond het er vooral mooi in de avondzon.

Eigenlijk precies zoals die keer dat wij er waren. Dat was toen een mooie zomeravond en niet te warm. Het was er erg aangenaam."

107

Hij spreekt het woord langzaam uit, alsof hij iedere lettergreep een voor een wil benadrukken. Even laat hij een pauze vallen.

"Misschien is dat het juiste woord.

Ik vond het er aangenaam." Nogmaals legt hij de nadruk op zijn bevinding.

De man geniet duidelijk van zijn woord vondst. Ze heeft geen idee waarop hij aanstuurt. Zijn vrouw is zijn beschouwingen gewend en begrijpt soms al na een half woord waarover hij het heeft, maar nu ontgaat de clou haar volledig. Waarom wil hij nu opeens terugkomen op een weekend waarin ze samen waren gaan kamperen?

Het was niet de eerste keer geweest dat ze erop uit getrokken waren, of dat het die keer uitzonderlijk was of heel erg speciaal. Ze zijn inderdaad diverse keren naar Brabant gegaan om er te fietsen. De omgeving bevalt ze erg goed en de camping is comfortabel genoeg om aan hun eisen te voldoen. Het was er altijd tamelijk stil.

Ook de keren dat het er erg druk en er met moeite een plaatsje op het veld of tussen de caravans te vinden was, hadden ze genoten van de natuur en de rust die er heerste. Ze denkt inderdaad met plezier terug aan de vakanties en weekenden die ze er samen hebben doorgebracht.

Om zichzelf meer bedenktijd te gunnen staat ze op en haalt 'n fles uit de kast. Terwijl ze er een glas bij pakt vraagt ze of hij ook iets wil. De man wil een glaasje rosé dus staat hij op om uit de koelkast op hun slaapkamer, boven op de eerste verdieping, een fles te halen. Als hij terug de kamer in komt, is zijn vrouw alweer in haar stoel gaan zitten.

Het tijdschrift ligt met de rug omhoog, opengeslagen naast haar. Ze zit net haar glas vol te schenken met de rode wijn. Naast zijn stoel heeft ze voor hem de flessen koeler neergezet. Op de hoek van het tafeltje staat ook een glas klaar. Hij maakt zijn eigen fles open en schenkt zich in.

"Je kunt de koker dan mee nemen en de rest daar ergens verstrooien.

Op een rustig, windstil plekje tussen de duinen. Niet alles, want ik wil ook wat hier in de tuin hebben.

Maar het moet wel met de kinderen erbij.

Dat wil ik zo."

Voorzichtig neemt de man een slokje. Hij laat de koude drank door zijn mond heen en weer stromen voordat hij het duidelijk genietend doorslikt. Een poosje geleden heeft hij de film met onder anderen Jeff Bridges over het leven van 'the great Lebowsky' weer eens gezien. Hij moet glimlachen bij de herinnering aan de scène waarin de hoofdrolspelers de as van hun vriend verstrooien.

Hij zet het glas terug op het viltje op de tafel en gaat weer achterover geleund zitten. Hoe die andere acteur heet weet hij niet meer, maar onlangs heeft ie hem zien spelen in een serie die op zondag werd uitgezonden. Daar heeft hij ook van genoten.

"Zeg maar dat het mijn laatste wil is. Maar let wel op waar de wind vandaan komt, als het toch een beetje waait."

De vrouw kijkt naar haar man. Voor zover ze zich kan herinneren hebben ze nog nooit over begraven of cremeren gepraat. Er is nog geen aanleiding voor geweest, beiden zijn ze gezond. De diabetes van haar echtgenoot is toch helemaal geen levensbedreigende aandoening?

Vanmiddag heeft ze, zoals iedere dag haar gewoonte is, in het programmaboekje gekeken wat de televisie te bieden zou hebben. Er is niets waarvan ze zich nu voor de geest kan halen dat haar man op deze vreemde gedachte gebracht kan hebben. Vaag herinnert ze zich een programma op de BBC, zijn favoriete zender, dat over iets uit de geschiedenis zou gaan.

In Engeland hebben ze elke avond wel iets over de natuur, hun landschap, kust of hun historie te melden. Ze kijkt met hem mee als de uitzending over koken of huizen gaat. Ze vindt dat het ding sowieso te vaak aan staat en bladert liever in haar tijdschriften. Op de achtergrond hoort ze dan waar hij naar zit te kijken. Als het echt interessant lijkt, dan roept hij haar erbij of neemt ze uit zichzelf even naast hem plaats om een programma af te kijken.

Het blijft een tijdje stil en ze kijkt weer even naar haar man. Kennelijk in gedachten verzonken zit hij voor zich uit te staren. De vrouw pakt haar tijdschrift weer op en gaat verder op de bladzij waar ze even hiervoor gebleven was.

At the Zoo

Hoewel hij al een flink aantal jaren geleden voor het laatst in een dierentuin is geweest, viel het hem zojuist op dat er in dat liedje van Paul Simon niet eens zo heel erg overdreven wordt. Het is natuurlijk maar een 'song' en uiteindelijk dateert het uit de begintijd van zijn carrière. Toen vormde hij nog samen met Art Garfunkel een duo uit New York en trokken ze als 'a poet and a one man band' * over de wereld. Maar in de tekst heeft hij de zaken allerminst veel te groot gemaakt of dus overdreven!

Zo viel het hem in het voorbijgaan meteen op dat olifanten inderdaad reusachtig en onmiskenbaar goedmoedig lijken. Toch komen ze zoals bezongen door het duo, nogal dom op je over als je er toch wat beter op let! Daar leggen ze dus terecht de nadruk op. Zelf is hij er even speciaal voor stil blijven staan om het goed op zich in te laten werken, vooral omdat het 'm zomaar opeens opviel. Intussen heeft hij plaats genomen op een bankje in de afdeling waar de apen bij elkaar verzameld zitten.

Onder het lopen viel 't hem overigens ook op hoe 'de natuur' hier ogenschijnlijk heeft weten te 'overleven'. Hij zag het omdat de verschillende dieren in grote lijnen hun natuurlijkheid lijken te hebben bewaard. Hoe ze zich, ondanks de omstandigheden hier in het park, op hun eigen manier en op het oog dus nog grotendeels geleid door hun specifieke instinct, lijken te gedragen. Voor zover hij, met zijn nogal beperkte kennis hierover, het gedrag in de kooien tegenover hem natuurlijk mag noemen natuurlijk. Hij heeft er niet speciaal op gelet maar het kwam onder het voorbijgaan plotseling bij hem op. En daarna heeft hij er wat aandacht aan geschonken.

Of, zoals gesuggereerd in de songtekst, Orang Oetangs nogal sceptisch staan tegenover veranderingen in of rond hun kooien, heeft hij overigens niet kunnen onderzoeken. Afgaande op de bordjes zitten de beesten een stuk verderop en daar is hij nog niet geweest. Daardoor heeft hij het niet nader kunnen bestuderen. Maar, voor zover zijn oppervlakkige kennis reikt, hij durft het gedrag in de kooien waar ie langs is gekomen over het pad hiernaartoe, al met al toch min of meer natuurlijk te noemen.

Niet omdat hij vreselijk vaak naar zulke programma's kijkt op de tv, maar het lijkt hem dat de dieren hier onder verantwoording van de verzorgers, in hun

* Uit: Homeward bound (1967)

111

meest natuurlijke staat worden getoond. Hij vertrouwt erop dat niemand ge-
fopt wordt of dat de commercie de macht in het park volledig heeft overgenomen. Dieren lijken hier voornamelijk de toon te bepalen en niet de gladde wereld van bijvoorbeeld Walt Disney of zo'n andere Hollywood-achtige onderneming. Alleen hier en daar de vermelding van een bedrijfsnaam die kennelijk aan moet geven dat deze onderneming het dier ernaast geadopteerd heeft,
ze het beest steunen, is de knieval die het management ervoor gemaakt heeft.

Het is er trouwens rustig genoeg voor om de dieren ongestoord hun gang te
laten gaan. Hij is zowat de enige bezoeker die zich op de paden van de dierentuin laat zien. Al heet het hier in verband met de internationalisering dus al
wel een ZOO. 'Blijdorp Zoo' zag hij staan op het bord bij de ingang. Het staat
overigens netzo op het foldertje dat hij kreeg en ook op het toegangsbewijs.

De geluiden van de stad, toch heel dichtbij en rondom hem, manifesteren zich
uitsluitend in een zacht ruisen. Het verkeer dat hierachter op de weg – ergens
in de verte – langs komt, domineert niet en is slechts op de achtergrond hoorbaar. De uiteindelijke ruis die erdoor waar te nemen is, stoort allerminst want
wordt overstemd door de geluiden die de dieren hier onderling maken. Alleen
als je 't echt horen wil, exact wil weten waar de geluiden vandaan komen, is
het brommen hoorbaar. De man wil daar echter niet naar luisteren, hij wil uitsluitend de stilte horen, met rust gelaten worden. Hij wil alleen zijn.

De schoolreisjes zijn nog niet gearriveerd en daardoor ontbreken de kreten die
daar onmiskenbaar bij zullen horen. Ook dat maakt dat het ronduit stil is in
het park. Het staat hem toe om de rust, de stilte die hem omringt, over zich
heen te laten komen. Hij ervaart 't als een weldaad. Het maakt dat hij kan proberen om zijn gedachten op een rijtje te krijgen. Nu hij er al even zit merkt ie
trouwens pas dat de ochtend ronduit fris genoemd mag worden. De dagjes-
mensen zullen zich dus ook nog niet in de buitenlucht durven te wagen.

Alles maakt z'n verblijf hier momenteel speciaal. De stilte, de ongestoorde
sfeer in het park, 't heeft hem feitelijk overvallen. Hij mocht op voorhand niet
verwachten dat de wandeling die hij moest maken om hier te komen, hem tegelijkertijd over zo'n grote afstand zou verplaatsen. Eerst was er de hectiek
rond de op gang komende activiteiten in het reusachtige gebouw, toen onderweg hier naartoe, het lawaai op straat. Alles verliep zoals 't in een drukke och-
tendspits normaal gaat. Die omstandigheden waren te verwachten en ze ver-
dienden daarom geen extra aandacht. Het maakte dat de tocht hiernaartoe, ternauwernood indruk op hem heeft gemaakt. Hij hoefde zich slechts op zichzelf
te concentreren, kon zich verliezen in het lopen. Intussen probeert hij de rust
over zich te laten komen, zichzelf te hervinden.

De vraag dringt zich overigens op of, net zoals in dat liedje van zijn held, alles hier daadwerkelijk ècht gebeurt. Moet hij geloven dat wat er om hem heen
aan de hand lijkt, de enig echte waarheid is?

112

Die Paul Simon heeft gemakkelijk praten, voor hem blijft het namelijk een vraag. Wat moet en kan ie er allemaal van denken?

Indertijd thuis luisterden zijn vrouw en hij graag naar het duo. Onwillekeurig moest hij tijdens het lopen naar deze bestemming, glimlachen om de woorden uit juist dit lied. Hoe het langzaam zijn herinnering binnen begon te sijpelen. Nog voordat hij om tweederde van de rotonde gelopen was begon ie als vanzelf eerst voorzichtig de melodie te neuriën. Maar toen die allengs helderder werd, kwamen ook delen van de tekst weer bij hem naar voren. Eerst voornamelijk kreten, flarden en soms in een volgende regel alleen een enkel woord, maar het ritme van zijn lopen stelde hem in staat om steeds meer van de context uit het liedje te herstellen.

Intussen weet hij weer hoe de song in elkaar steekt en kan hij het zich weer grotendeels herinneren. Jammer dat hij geen zangstem heeft, want het lied zeurt nu aldoor in zijn hoofd verder. Alsof het eruit moet, komt het telkens terug en met alleen hummen krijgt ie het niet afdoende uit zijn systeem verwijderd. Het lijkt of de geluiden om hem heen ervoor zorgen dat er iedere keer delen van het liedje terugkomen in zijn hoofd, dat hij het uit zou moeten schreeuwen om er helemaal vanaf te komen. Associaties en herinneringen zijn ermee in de pas gaan lopen.

Onderweg naar dit zitplekje is hij voorbij gelopen aan kooien waar grote en kleine apen door elkaar in de verschillende verblijven opgesloten zitten. Het spreekt voor zich dat er naast volwassen exemplaren ook hun kinderen, kleinkinderen en de andere jonkies, die in menselijke begrippen dus kleuters of baby's genoemd worden, in de groepjes aanwezig zijn. Hij heeft gezien hoe de beesten elkaar vredig zitten te vlooien. Ze zijn ook maar net wakker natuurlijk en zo de dieren over deze eigenschap beschikken, zullen ze zich hogelijk over hem verbazen mocht hij inderdaad plotseling in luidkeels gezang uitbarsten. Als er überhaupt een reden voor zulke uitbundigheid zou zijn, want die ontbreekt hem op dit moment. Evenals het zangtalent om 't ook in dat opzicht enigszins aangenaam te houden.

In het oerwoud of de bergen, beter gezegd in hun natuurlijke habitat, zullen de beesten onmiskenbaar beschikken over aanzienlijk meer ruimte om te bewegen. In ieder geval meer dan de paar vierkante meter in de kooien aan weerskanten van het pad. Hij bedenkt dat de dieren van huis uit gewoon zullen zijn om middenop een open vlakte, tussen heel dicht struikgewas of juist hoog op een stel rotsen te leven. De bordjes bij de verblijven, op een paaltje of aan de spijlen ervan bevestigd, kunnen hem daarover uitsluitsel verschaffen, maar 't komt bij hem op dat de dieren blijkbaar vrede met hun bestaan hebben. Ze berusten er zichtbaar in, hoewel ze op deze manier toch een beduidend ander leven hebben gekregen.

Het is hem in het voorbijgaan opgevallen, toch deed 't ook pijn toen hij zag hoe alert de apen nog zijn. Dat ze nauwlettend op hem en de omgeving in het park letten, maar tegelijkertijd stralen ze 'n soort gezapigheid uit. Dat contrast verontrust hem. Hij verwacht dat de beesten op tijd hun natje en droogje zullen krijgen en hoe dit er al generaties achter elkaar aan bijgedragen moet hebben dat het instinct om daar zelf voor te zorgen verloren is geraakt. Het verzorgde bestaan zal er in zijn ogen toe geleid hebben dat er geen besef meer bij de beesten bestaat over wat hen eigenlijk toe zou moeten komen. Hoe ze de strijd om hun bestaan zouden moeten leveren en hij bedenkt dat de 'struggle to survive' door die behandeling weg gesleten zal zijn.

Even vond hij het opmerkelijk dat de apen zo zichtbaar vrede met de omstandigheden leken te hebben. Maar na enig nadenken drong het tot hem door dat hijzelf, immers ook een primaat, zich net zo gemakkelijk zou voegen in zo'n aanbod. Bijvoorbeeld als iemand hem goed zou komen verzorgen.

In plaats van een kooi met een stevig gaas eromheen, zitten de apen tegenover zijn zitplaats op een eilandje en worden ze alleen door het water van de bezoekers gescheiden. Door het hier en daar geplante struikgewas is er zowel voor de dieren als voor hem, 'de willekeurige bezoeker', een soort privacy gecreëerd. Het beeld dat hij aan de overkant van het grachtje aantrof vertederde hem zodanig dat hij er even voor stil is blijven staan. Vervolgens heeft hij op een van de bankjes plaats genomen om er een poosje naar te blijven kijken.

Het bankje staat half verscholen tussen wat hogere struiken zodat hij, noch voor de voorbijgangers vanaf het voetpad of de apen op het eiland opvalt. Zijn donkere jas zal hem trouwens ook grotendeels laten wegvallen tegen het groen dat hem links, rechts en achter omringt. Hij zal er weinig tegen afsteken, geen opvallend contrast vormen met de omgeving. Hoewel het niet zo heel erg waait, zit hij er tamelijk beschut.

Toen zijn vrouw, indertijd nog zijn vriendinnetje, en hij pas bij elkaar op een kamer woonden mocht hij vaak met z'n hoofd bij haar op schoot op de bank liggen. Die hadden ze zo gezet dat ze er zo lang mogelijk van de door het raam naar binnen vallende namiddagzon konden genieten. Het was er daardoor altijd lekker warm en, omdat ie met de rugleuning naar de kamer stond, ook ronduit knus. Wandelde een van de huisgenoten eens spontaan binnen, dan viel tegen het volle licht in lastig voor ze op te maken wie zich waar in de kamer bevond. Zo zaten ze er heel privé bij elkaar en een enkele keer streelde ze hem dan over zijn voorhoofd of ging met haar vingers door zijn haren. Ze lazen dan allebei bijvoorbeeld iets of keken naar een programma op hun kleine televisie. Die stond in verband met de ontvangst naast de wastafel in de hoek, vlakbij het raam.

Als hij zo bij haar lag genoot hij van haar rustige ademhaling maar was vooral onder de indruk van het nieuwe van de omstandigheden. Er ging een tot dan toe ongekende rust uit van het gestage op en neer gaan van haar buik, zo

114

dicht was hij nog nooit bij iemand geweest. Met de verbondenheid die ze zo samen hadden, had hij nog totaal geen ervaring opgedaan. Als ze dichtbij en bij elkaar waren raakte hij eenvoudig onder de indruk van de tederheid die uitging van haar aanrakingen. Hoewel hun verbondenheid voor haar natuurlijk even nieuw was en het tonen van die genegenheid waarschijnlijk spontaan bij haar opkwam. Heel veel leeftijdsverschil was er niet tussen hen.

Hij probeerde iedere keer om zo lang mogelijk bij haar te blijven liggen, maar meestal wilde hij alsnog een kopje koffie, een vers biertje, een ander tijdschrift of boek pakken. Soms was de elpee waar ze naar luisterden afgelopen en dan moest hij daarvoor dus even opstaan om de andere kant op te zetten. Als hij terugkwam was de comfortabele houding lastig weer terug te vinden en kwam er al snel weer iets anders aan de orde. Vrijwel altijd net voordat hij zich nogmaals helemaal in de juiste positie had weten te manoeuvreren. Ze had dan bijvoorbeeld gevraagd of hij iets uit de keuken of van het tafeltje achter hen wilde pakken. "Als je zo bij me ligt kan ik het niet zelf doen."

De hele procedure van nogmaals een lekkere houding, het kontakt en de meest genoeglijke positie vinden, herhaalde zich dan telkens van voren af aan. Maar hij moest het na twee of drie pogingen opgeven, omdat ie niet meteen lekker en net zo vertrouwd als ervoor, bij haar kon kruipen. Een enkele keer was ze intussen iets anders gaan zitten en was het alleen daardoor al onmogelijk om het oorspronkelijke comfort te hervinden. Ze berustten er dan in dat gewoon naast elkaar zitten, braaf schouder aan schouder, ook een zekere huiselijkheid inhield. Nu hij erover nadenkt bleek zijn vrouw het intieme van hun gezellige samenzijn ook uitermate prettig te vinden.

Het merendeel van de apen aan de overkant van het water zit aan elkaar te frunniken. Hoewel er ook hier een aantal tussen loopt dat duidelijk op de omgeving let, alert is. Ze treden op als een soort wakers met hun blik continu gericht op alles buiten het eiland. De rust die van de groep afstraalt blijkt plotseling op te lossen als de beesten met elkaar overgaan in bekvechten. De aanleiding laat zich niet gelijk opmerken. Het kan zomaar zijn dat er een te dicht bij de ander gekomen is of misschien op iemands tenen is gaan staan. Misschien hebben ze gewoon een hekel aan elkaar? De schijngevechten duren telkens maar heel even en de lieve vrede wordt meestal met een paar rondjes om elkaar heen draaien, snel hersteld. Het lijkt hierdoor meer op een spel dan dat er daadwerkelijk iets verschrikkelijks aan de hand kan zijn.

De man heeft weleens gehoord dat er sprake zou zijn van een alpha mannetje en dat er een bepaalde rangorde heerst binnen zo'n groep. Nu hij de sociologie daadwerkelijk eens zelf kan bestuderen, ontgaat hem wat er toen allemaal over is opgemerkt. Hij heeft het niet onthouden omdat ie niet wist dat het ooit van pas zou komen of er een noodzaak zou komen om ervan op de hoogte te zijn. Voor hemzelf was het namelijk niet belangrijk, hij heeft nooit ruzie gehad. Nu hij erover nadenkt met niemand eigenlijk, nooit echt in ieder geval! Tussen hem en zijn echtgenote is er gedurende alle jaren van hun huwelijk geen enkele onenigheid voorgevallen. Nooit was er een kwestie die hun relatie zou hebben kunnen verstoren. Ze zijn er altijd samen uitgekomen als er iets speelde of dreigde de kop op te steken. De manier waarop de apen met elkaar omgaan maakt dat hij moet denken aan welke problemen zijzelf op hun weg zijn tegengekomen. Feitelijk waren dat alleen de strubbelingen rond de handicap van hun zoon.

Die speelden al van tijdens z'n opgroeien. Toen leken ze de situatie weleens niet helemaal aan te kunnen. Met name de periode waarin het accepteren van de handicap zich begon af te tekenen dringt zich op. De man realiseert zich hoe zijn vrouw en hij juist in die tijd altijd op zoek zijn gebleven naar oplossingen en een eventuele uitweg. Hoe het er weleens op leek dat ze met de rug tegen de muur stonden. Toch is er nooit sprake geweest van opgeven.

Nu hij erover nadenkt moet hij toegeven dat ze nimmer een kwestie hebben kunnen of willen afschepen aan zogenaamd officiële instanties. Als de zaken zich bijvoorbeeld weer eens hadden opgestapeld, want een vraagstuk bleek helaas nooit alleen te komen. Toch hebben ze hun rug altijd recht weten te houden, pal gestaan als het nodig was. Ze hebben altijd alles gedaan om hun kinderen zoveel mogelijk te ondersteunen, vanzelfsprekend ook hun dochter.

Onlangs hebben zijn vrouw en hij ingezien dat ze ten opzichte van haar weleens tekort zijn geschoten. Alle nadruk kwam immers voornamelijk terecht op haar broertje, maar ze konden toch niet anders? Ze moesten handelen naar wat hen als beste voorkwam. Het joch stond niet sterk genoeg in zijn schoenen en de problemen die hij tegen kwam waren soms enorm. Het dringt tot hem door dat ze er tot nog toe stilzwijgend op gerekend hebben dat ze dit, mede door het verschil in leeftijd dat tussen hen bestaat, begrepen zal hebben.

Al peinzend komt het hem voor dat ze dezelfde houding ook bij allerlei beslommeringen die zich rond zijn zaak voordeden hebben verkozen. Vrijwel altijd hebben ze zich alle moeite getroost om onafhankelijk van derden hun boontjes te doppen. Ze gingen daarbij uit van zichzelf, hun eigen voorwaarden en ze wilden de verantwoording telkens zelfstandig dragen. Als ze ooit ergens assistentie bij hadden kunnen krijgen, dan is ze dat waarschijnlijk gewoon ontgaan. Ze hebben een eventuele steun, bijvoorbeeld omdat het teveel in zou gaan tegen hun 'eigenheid', liever aan zich voorbij laten gaan of ronduit afgewezen. Onder elkaar noemden ze het gekscherend 'ontwijkend gedrag'. En zo hebben ze het ook weg gelachen toen een goede vriend hen ooit 't verwijt maakte dat ze zijn 'uitgestoken hand' niet hadden willen aanvaarden. Ze zouden zijn hulp afgewimpeld hebben. Daarover deed hij die avond nogal teleurgesteld zijn beklag. Later hebben ze het gezamenlijk afgedronken met een fles mooie wijn.

De man moet glimlachen om de herinneringen die hem overvallen, Voor hem staat het vast dat zijn vrouw altijd heel goed naar hem kon luisteren. Bijvoorbeeld als hij weer eens teleurgesteld of zelfs gefrustreerd terugkwam van een vergadering of overleg. Hij neemt het maandelijkse verslag dat de zorgverleners aan hem aflegden in gedachten. Bedenkt hoe hij dan telkens thuiskwam na het gesprek met de begeleiding die hun zoon terzijde had moeten staan. Hoe alle ondersteuning weliswaar gebeurde vanuit expertise en dat het honderd procent verantwoord was, maar desondanks schoot het vaak flink tekort. Daarover waren ze het meestal snel eens.

Het dringt tot hem door hoe zijn ze, toen de jongen nog klein was de verantwoording grotendeels aan hem over leek te laten. Als verklaring is hij er altijd vanuit gegaan dat de verwerking van zijn handicap en alles dat daarmee samenhing, haar te ver ging en dat hij de sterkste moest zijn. Hij ging dan alleen naar ouderavonden en later de bijeenkomsten waarop hij kennis maakte met verzorgers en de vele vertegenwoordigers van allerlei instanties uit de zorg.

Ze wekte er naar die buitenwereld toe misschien de indruk mee zich afzijdig op te stellen. Dat ze zich niet helemaal kon vinden in zijn opvatting of manier van doen. Maar ze steunde hem in die zelfgekozen rol vanuit de achtergrond. Zo is ze dat altijd door dik en dun blijven doen!

Hij moet toegeven dat ze vooral zijn koers leken te varen, maar dat zij die corrigeerde als de situatie mis dreigde te lopen. Als iets op de een of andere manier onduidelijk werd, bood zij uitleg, gaf hem steun. Zo vormden ze alsnog een eenheid, waren ze een team dat verenigd bleek. Dat was zo in alles waarvoor ze stonden en het vaarwater waarin ze terecht kwamen.

Een heel enkele keer heeft ie moeten toegeven dat hij te kort door de bocht wilde scheren. Als zij hem dan niet tot de orde geroepen had was het een en ander wellicht misgegaan. Door bijvoorbeeld de tijdsdruk had hij zich kwaad laten maken of hij was opgewonden geraakt over een onrecht dat hen werd aangedaan. Hij realiseert zich dat het haar in die gevallen waarschijnlijk veel moeite gekost zal hebben om hem op andere gedachten te brengen, ziet voor zich hoe ie met zachte dwang in kalmere wateren werd geloodst.

Van huis uit wil de man dat zaken zo helder mogelijk, efficiënt en per omgaande geregeld worden. Feitelijk zoals hij dat evenzo en ten allen tijden voor zijn klanten geprobeerd heeft te bewerkstelligen. Al kreeg hij daar ook niet iedere keer de waardering die hij ermee verdiende.

Hij vindt dat professionaliteit valt of staat met inzet en volharding. Al leidden zijn inspanningen ertoe dat men hooguit inzag of erkende dat hij zijn best had gedaan. Tegenwoordig noemt hij dat 'het consumentisme', omdat men lijkt te ontkennen dat ergens nog mensenwerk aan te pas komt. Hij voelt zich er een slachtoffer van de wegwerpmaatschappij door en hoewel hij telkens heeft geprobeerd om aan de hoogste verwachtingen te voldoen, wekte hij die verwachtingen zelf op door zich nogal dienstbaar op te stellen. Regelmatig had hij zoiets daarom wat 'zakelijker' aan moeten pakken. Maar dan druiste dat tegen zijn gevoel van menselijkheid, z'n eigenwaarde in. Het liefst wilde hij ermee tonen dat zijn ijver niet louter werd ingegeven doordat hij er geld voor kon vragen. Dat hij dezelfde uitgangspunten van z'n omgeving verwacht, wordt helaas niet altijd begrepen of komt daar niet helemaal uit.

Als ie eerlijk is moet hij vaststellen dat zijn vrouw hem iedere keer, zakelijk zowel als maatschappelijk, door dik en dun heeft gesteund. Eigenlijk precies zoals het een echtgenote binnen een goed huwelijk betaamt. Vanuit hun opvoeding en achtergrond hebben ze op elkaar leren bouwen. Doordat hun ouders het nooit anders aan ze hebben voorgedaan kunnen ze niet anders.

Zijn schoonmoeder aanhoorde ook geduldig de verslagen van haar echtgenoot. Net zoals zijn eigen moeder altijd deed bij papa. Zij gaven hun mening pas als ze er de kans voor hadden gekregen om die voldoende op te bouwen. Als zijn vrouw zich op soortgelijke manier op de hoogte had gesteld, nuanceerde ze inderdaad ook de gerezen boosheid of teleurstelling. Als het nodig was bracht ze hem met haar eigen argumenten tot andere inzichten. Dan stelde ze bijvoorbeeld voor hoe ze samen nog eens nader, tegen een probleem aan konden kijken. Om op die manier de kou uit de lucht te halen.

Maar daarmee wachtte ze niet meer heel ouderwets tot haar beeld compleet geworden was. Naarmate de tijd vorderde droeg ze meer en meer aan acties bij door overleg te plegen, vanaf het begin en ook naar buiten toe haar betrokkenheid te tonen. Ze nam initiatief, stelde zich op de hoogte door bijvoorbeeld op de bibliotheek 'n boek over zo'n gerezen vraagstuk te halen. Met haar overtuigingskracht heeft ze hem vaak in de gelegenheid gesteld om enige rust te vinden. Om, indien nodig, voldoende afstand te nemen van 'de verstoringen' die er plaats vonden. Die deden zich namelijk telkens voor als er weer eens afgeweken werd van hun verwachtingen of er nogmaals tegen gemaakte afspraken werd ingegaan, ze niet serieus genomen werden.

Als ie naar de apen op het eilandje kijkt herkent hij hoe ze elkaar er eveneens steun verlenen. Dat ze, net zoals thuis in het gezin, gezamenlijk hun reacties bepalen. Daar aan de andere kant van het slootje, functioneren de dieren vanzelfsprekend als troep, maar op de een of andere manier ziet hij dat er ook sterk individuele factoren aan de orde komen. Hij merkt hoe de beesten uitgaan van een inbreng, maar wil die niet meteen als persoonlijk benoemen. Het blijven beesten tenslotte. Toch maken ze, zonder hun eigenheid te verliezen, onmiskenbaar stuk voor stuk deel uit van de groep.

Bij hen sprak dat minder vanzelf. Na verloop van tijd leken zij er weleens hopeloos alleen voor te staan. Dan was er kennelijk niemand meer op wie ze terug konden vallen. Niet voor advies, noch voor steun of warmte. Na al een half woord konden de familie en vrienden blijkbaar raden waar het gesprek

over zou gaan en er waren er maar weinig die voldoende interesse konden opbrengen om telkens hun frustraties te aanhoren. Die kwamen voort uit de er-
gernissen die ze over hielden aan de zorgverlening en de taakopvatting die de
medewerkers daar hanteerden. Die bleken er in hun ogen soms maar weinig
van te begrijpen namelijk. Zo zijn ze langzamerhand afgezonderd geraakt, de
man, zijn vrouw en ook hun dochter tegenover de rest van de wereld.

Dieren worden in hun handelen niet gehinderd door beleefdheidsformules of
terughoudendheid. Dat zijn menselijke trekjes en zij kunnen hun instinct als
uitgangspunt nemen. Bij mensen valt alles samen met beschaving en daar
hebben ze zich met het gezin misschien teveel naar gedragen. Ze wilden niet
onbeleefd zijn en hielden hun mond. Maar ze merkten ook hoe ze sterker werden onder de ervaringen en de tegenslagen op hun weg. Allengs is het onbegrip voor die zogenaamde werkelijkheid gegroeid. Daarmee nam ook hun
boosheid toe. Maar ondanks alles getroostten ze zich de uiterste moeite om
een evenwicht te bewaren tussen de dagelijkse realiteit en de confrontaties.
Na verloop van tijd leken ze uitsluitend bij elkaar de kracht te vinden om
daaraan het hoofd te blijven bieden.

Nu hij erover nadenkt wordt het hem duidelijk hoeveel moeite het gekost
heeft om telkens tegen die stroom van onbegrip of de regelrechte tegenwerking die ze voelden, op te moeten roeien. Het dringt tot hem door dat hij haar
daar nooit echt voor heeft bedankt.

De man let op de beesten op het eilandje. Hij kijkt hoe ze elkaar bejegenen,
hoe de dieren dan weer een heftige strijd lijken te leveren om vervolgens in
pais en vree met elkaar verder te gaan. Het maakt dat ie voor zich ziet hoe
hun familie en de vriendenkring zich soms totaal geen voorstelling kon maken van de onwil die zij op hun weg tegen leken te komen. Hoe het daardoor
vaak beter was om er maar helemaal over te zwijgen en dat ze in zulke gevallen uitsluitend bij elkaar het benodigde begrip konden vinden.

Ook ziet hij nu hoe slechts in een heel uitzonderlijke geval, de frustraties tussen hen in zijn komen te staan. Dat confrontaties dan te overweldigend waren
geworden en ze als gevolg daarvan niet genoeg hadden aan hun gedeelde verzet. Soms bleek 't dan onmogelijk om onder zulke omstandigheden naast elkaar te opereren. Dan leken ze in tegengestelde kampen gedreven.

In alle eerlijkheid moet hij erkennen dat ze ondanks alles tegenover de 'boze
buitenwereld' samen hun kop op hebben weten te houden. Ondanks alles en
ogenschijnlijk 'fier en ongeschonden' hebben ze zich staande weten te houden
in de woelige wereld. Het doet hem dus pijn dat hij daarvoor nooit zijn waardering heeft laten blijken, hoe hij haar opstelling, haar steun en inbreng gewoonweg voor lief heeft genomen.

Een van de apen heeft het in de ogen van zijn soortgenoten te bont gemaakt
en wordt nu door een van de grotere exemplaren, achterna gezeten. Handig

119

dat ze met de klauwen aan hun voeten aan vanalles een houvast kunnen vinden. In razende vaart springen en rennen de apen achter elkaar aan tussen de struiken en bomen door. Een keer lijkt de jager te vallen en ziet het ernaar uit dat hij de jacht op zal moeten geven, maar dan vindt ie toch een manier om de vluchtende snoodaard nogmaals de bocht af te snijden en te slim af te zijn. De prooi benut intussen de meest ingewikkelde routes van het repertoire en kan zodoende de dans een poosje ontspringen. Zo voeren ze letterlijk een choreografie uit tussen het gewas.

Intussen lijkt het of de andere apen aanwijzingen schreeuwen naar het rennende stel. De groep raakt steeds meer betrokken bij de opwinding en reageert uiterst onrustig op wat er gaande is. Ook in de kooien achter hem klinkt gekrijs en het lijkt of plotseling de hele apenbevolking van de dierentuin in rep en roer is geraakt. Dan geeft het tweetal de strijd op en lijkt het niet meer dan een spel geweest te zijn. De opgejaagde aap biedt zich nederig, zich kennelijk bewust van haar onderdanigheid, aan aan de jager. Even heel kort neuken ze met elkaar om met 'het vluggertje' de vrede te herstellen.

Ook voor de rest van de groep lijkt daarmee de kous af te zijn en iedereen gaat over tot de orde van de dag. De man moet er om glimlachen. Waren alle problemen maar zo eenvoudig op te lossen. Mensen zijn weliswaar geen Bonobo's of Chimpansees, maar een heleboel zaken zouden een stuk minder gecompliceerd blijken als er op deze manier in de mensenwereld eveneens een oplossing in het verschiet lag. Hij stelt zich een paar wereldomvattende problemen voor en bedenkt er een soortgelijke resolutie bij.

Bijvoorbeeld een kwestie in de Verenigde Naties of het voortdurende conflict in het Midden Oosten. Als trouwe journaal kijker kost 't hem weinig moeite om zich voor te stellen hoe er krijgertje te spelen is tussen de tafels in de grote vergaderzalen of hoe de paring na afloop van een conferentie tot stand zal komen. Zij het in dit geval uitsluitend om de boel onderling te verzoenen, als diplomatiek spel, en niet ingegeven door lust of politieke ambities zoals nu weleens het geval schijnt te zijn.

Op het eilandje zijn de apen gedurende de achtervolging verspreid geraakt, maar er vormen zich alweer duo's en groepjes. De rust keert eigenlijk verbazingwekkend snel weer terug en daaruit blijkt nogmaals duidelijk dat het leven van deze dieren er beduidend anders uitziet dan het gecompliceerde bestaan van mensen.

De man kijkt op zijn horloge. Hij heeft trek in koffie gekregen en zo te zien is het er inderdaad tijd voor. Bij half elf geeft het klokje aan en daarom staat hij op om op zoek te gaan naar een gelegenheid waar hij in zijn vraag kan voorzien. Bij voorkeur zou hij nu een kopje espresso willen drinken. Goed wakker willen worden, zich oppeppen.

Het rusteloze van de afgelopen nacht en de wandeling van vanmorgen, eisen

120

tijdens het opstaan hun tol op. Voordat hij helemaal overeind is gekomen begint het in zijn hoofd te bruisen. Het lijkt of het opeens minder licht wordt en het park om hem heen draait. Hij moet zich aan de leuning van de bank vastpakken om niet om te vallen. Het duurt even voor het over is en alles weer stil blijkt te staan. Mochten ze bij die koffie iets te eten hebben, dan moet hij dat dus ook maar doen.

Hij heeft behoefte aan in iets zoets en verwacht dat ze er wel een brownie of cupcake bij zullen verkopen. Die zijn erg in de mode weet hij uit de tijdschriften die hij de afgelopen dagen heeft doorgebladerd. Hij recht zijn rug en kijkt of ie een richtingbord ziet waarop hij kan opzoeken of er ergens een restaurant of koffiebar te vinden is. Hoe hij er naartoe kan wandelen.

Alsof hij afscheid van ze wil nemen, kijkt hij even over zijn schouder naar de dieren achter zich. Ze hebben zijn bewegingen echter niet opgemerkt of storen zich er niet aan. Het ziet eruit of de apen hem totaal negeren. De hand die hij uit een automatisme al iets omhoog had gedaan, alsof hij daadwerkelijk naar de beesten had willen zwaaien, stopt hij snel in zijn jaszak.

Vroeger, toen hun dochter nog een kleutertje was, zijn ze op een zondagmiddag met een stel vrienden naar Artis geweest. Hij heeft haar toen verbaasd door er een pinguïn over zijn kopje te aaien. Dat je een beest dat ze alleen kende uit de plaatjesboeken van school of uit de kast thuis, zomaar in levende lijve kon aanraken, vond ze zo vreemd dat ze alle dieren wel even een blik van haar aandacht had willen schenken.

Daar hebben ze haar vanaf weten te houden, al was het natuurlijk spannend om zo nu en dan een dier daadwerkelijk aan te kunnen raken als ze ervoor bij een kooi waren gaan staan. Alleen kleine dieren, geen grote of de lama's bijvoorbeeld, die vond ze toch te eng. Heel erg leuk vond hun gezelschap het toen hij bij verrassing door een giraffe over zijn wang werd gelikt. Om eens met eigen ogen te kunnen zien hoe hoog die dieren op hun schoften stonden, vergat hij dat er ook nog een lange nek aan zat. Daarmee kon het beest over het hek heen met zijn tong uitvinden wat die man daar stond te doen.

Later zijn ze met hun vieren een paar keer naar Amersfoort geweest en daar hebben ze verschillende apen een handje kunnen geven. Hun zoon was de eerste keer nog zo klein dat hij de hele wandeling door het park in zijn wagentje moest blijven zitten. Alleen voor de rit met het treintje, tussen de dierenverblijven door, mocht hij eruit en tijdelijk bij zijn zus op schoot. Nu hij erover nadenkt realiseert de man zich dat ze ook een keer naar het dierenpark in Wassenaar waren. Hun dochter moet toen nog een peuter zijn geweest, want die dierentuin is intussen al vele jaren gesloten.

De laatste keer dat ze er samen waren, was hier in Blijdorp. Hun zoon was op dat moment een jaar of acht, hooguit negen. Omdat hij ongeveer een uur na

121

hun aankomst plotseling onwel werd, hebben ze een tijdlang met hem op een bankje gezeten. Later hebben ze op de EHBO post zitten wachten tot de epileptische aanval over ging of mogelijkerwijs toch 'door zou zetten'. Het was in de buurt waar indertijd de runderen, okapi's en een hele grote os opgesloten zaten, maar vandaag is hij daar niet langs gekomen. Bij de herinrichting van de dierentuin, een paar jaar geleden, hebben ze het een en ander grondig veranderd, ook dat zal dus wel ten prooi zijn gevallen aan vernieuwingen.

Dat laatste bezoek vond meer dan vijftien jaar terug plaats. Hij probeerde al eerder om het exact uit te rekenen, maar weet niet meer precies wanneer het een en ander plaatsvond. Ongetwijfeld zou z'n vrouw het hem hebben kunnen voorrekenen, die hiel dat soort zaken beter bij dan hij. Hoe ze het flikte heeft hij nooit geweten, maar ze wist altijd precies te melden wanneer iets had plaatsgevonden, of stond te gebeuren.

Vanmorgen om tien voor halfzeven is een van de zusters naar hem toe gekomen. Ze informeerde of hij misschien iets wilde eten, maar daarvoor vond hij het te vroeg. Zich verontschuldigend is hij snel opgestaan, heeft de tas opgepakt en zijn jas aangetrokken. Om de een of andere reden durfde hij niet nog een keer naar het bed te kijken en is de gang op gesneld. De zuster was nergens meer te bekennen, vervolgens is hij met de trap naar beneden gegaan.

In de grote hal hield zich vrijwel niemand op, alle balies waren nog onbemand en alle rolluiken zaten dicht. Er liepen alleen drie mensen van de schoonmaakdienst. Snel is hij naar buiten de frisse lucht in gelopen. Hij was er voornamelijk aan toe om even op zichzelf te zijn.

Hij wilde niet meer omringd worden door de bedrukkende sfeer in het hospitaal. Weliswaar stinken ziekenhuizen niet meer naar ether zoals hij dat vroeger bij zijn oma altijd zo indringend vond, maar hij was het tussen de vier muren meer dan spuugzat. Hij wilde alleen zijn, zijn gedachten ordenen en is gaan lopen. Gewoon, zonder dat hij een duidelijke richting of bestemming voor ogen had, is hij op weg gegaan. Alleen de tas en de spullen die hij van het bed heeft meegenomen deed hij in de auto.

Daarna wilde hij zijn geest leeg laten waaien, moest weg uit de omklemming van het gebouw. De atmosfeer binnen benauwde hem te zeer. Toen hij even later bij een soort gracht aankwam en daar de keuze tussen links- of rechtsaf moest maken is hij naar links gegaan. Maar bij het eerstvolgende bruggetje is hij het water overgestoken en aan de andere kant toch rechts, richting de stad uit, opgelopen. Overigens nog steeds zonder precies te weten waar hij naartoe wilde. Het bewegen, lopen in plaats van slenteren, niet meer stil te hoeven zitten, zijn eigen tempo aanhouden en niet geleid worden door zaken waarmee hij rekening diende te houden, het deed hem allemaal goed. Pas toen hij merkte dat hij naar de noordelijke rand van de stad onderweg was, begon het plan om naar de dierentuin te gaan, post te vatten.

Na even kort rekenen kwam hij erop dat hij daar een kleine twintig jaar geleden voor het laatst geweest zou kunnen zijn. In gedachten verzonken heeft hij zijn weg vervolgd. Hij vroeg zich af hoe oud hun zoon nu en toen precies was en kon zich voor de geest halen dat hun dochter indertijd al aan het puberen was. Maar de exacte details is hij helaas vergeten. Precies op het moment dat hij zijn berekeningen toch maar opgaf, herkende hij de rotonde en de weg die hem naar de ingang van het dierenpark zou voeren. Het maakte dat zijn vage voornemen van even ervoor, veranderde in een resoluut besluit.

Tijdens dat laatste bezoek had hun zoon die nare epileptische aanval gehad en daarna wilde zijn vrouw er nooit meer heen. Overigens ook niet naar een andere dierentuin of ZOO dus. Ze verklaarde niet meer bij "al die opgesloten beesten" op bezoek te willen. Het zou er "stinken", was er altijd "veel te druk met die toeristen massa" en ze vond het "zo zielig", al stond het voor hem vast dat dit niet de exacte redenen waren voor haar afwijzing.

Tot de diergaarde open ging heeft hij op een bankje tegenover de ingang zitten wachten tot hij achter de ramen van de kassa bewegingen opmerkte. Om niet meteen de eerste gast te zijn heeft hij 'rustig aan gedaan' tijdens het ernaartoe lopen, het oversteken van de trambaan en de weg. Desondanks hoefde hij niemand voor te laten gaan en eenmaal binnen is hij zo snel mogelijk langs de vogels gelopen. Die zaten in hun kooien vlak achter het automatische toegangshek. Het stonk er vreselijk en de beesten zeiden hem niets. Daarom is hij vlug doorgelopen.

Verderop naar achteren in het park, het nieuwste deel aan de andere kant van de spoorlijn, vond hij te ver om naartoe te gaan. Na een korte wandeling is hij neergestreken bij de apen op het eilandje in hun vijver, alles nog in het oude deel. De indeling blijkt sinds zijn laatste bezoek trouwens zo veranderd dat hij zich nauwelijks kan voorstellen welke route zij er die keer hebben gewandeld. Hij is hier natuurlijk niet vaak genoeg geweest om er een te hebben. Het maakt 't huidige bezoek wat willekeurig, maar dat doet hem niet zoveel.

Het besef om 'ergens aan te moeten voldoen', is plotseling helemaal komen te vervallen. Het maakt 't gevoel dat hij opeens vrijgesteld is van allerlei verplichtingen, alleen voor zichzelf verantwoording draagt heel sterk. Het verschaft hem de mogelijkheid om te gaan en staan waar hij wil. Mede daarom doet het huidige uitje hem goed. Van het ene op het andere moment zijn er geen bezoektijden meer die zijn dagelijkse doen en laten beheersen. Hij kan zich overgeven aan dit oponthoud in de dierentuin, in deze verre stad, aan het mooie weer en als het lukt een poosje genieten van de rust.

Het is het soort bezoek waar ze door alle beslommeringen en drukte, al een hele tijd niet meer aan toe gekomen zijn. Dat maakt het juist zo opvallend hoe 't nu letterlijk 'terloops' op zijn pad kwam. Al lopend overviel hem immers deze mogelijkheid, dus inderdaad terloops nadat hij domweg in een onbestemde richting was vertrokken. Er dieper over nadenken, zoeken naar de een of andere verwijzing of een teken, lijkt hem overbodig. Daarom heeft hij zomaar een poosje naar die apen zitten kijken. Oppervlakkig maar wel geboeid en enigszins verbaasd.

Als hij het inderdaad zo graag had gewild was het natuurlijk eerder mogelijk geweest om een keer naar de dierentuin te gaan. Eventueel helemaal alleen, zonder vrouw en kinderen. Het behoorde allemaal tot de mogelijkheden en zo hij niet alleen wilde had hij eventueel iemand mee kunnen vragen. Ook al omdat zij er zo'n tegenzin bij ondervond. Toch is die mogelijkheid ondenkbaar gebleven. Zijn familie en voor alles zijn gezin, de kinderen, hebben altijd op de allereerste plaats gestaan. Het vraagstuk is daarnaast nooit groot genoeg geweest om het tot een conflict te laten komen. Hoe graag hij er ook naartoe had gewild, hij heeft zich telkens zonder morren bij de voorkeur van zijn vrouw neergelegd. Er nooit zin in gehad om er strijd over te voeren, uiteindelijk bleven er meer dan genoeg andere dingen om te doen.

Een aantal weken geleden is ze geopereerd in het grote ziekenhuis hier een halfuurtje lopen vandaan. Omdat het om een nogal omslachtige ingreep ging, op een blijkbaar moeilijk toegankelijke plaats en waarbij zich allerlei complicaties zouden kunnen voordoen, moest de ingreep helemaal in Rotterdam plaatsvinden. Alleen hier was er een afdeling met de expertise om het tot een goed einde te brengen. De specialist die haar in het ziekenhuis in Leiden behandelde, zou erbij aanwezig blijven. Zij het uitsluitend als arts-assistent en voornamelijk om er zelf zoveel mogelijk van te leren.

Achteraf bleek dat de operatie naar wens was verlopen. Volgens 'het team' was dit voornamelijk te wijten aan haar kracht, positieve instelling en doorzettingsvermogen. Trots stonden ze elkaar te feliciteren met het behaalde resultaat. Daarbij vergaten ze overigens niet om zijn echtgenote hun welgemeende complimenten te maken. Toch lag ze er als een klein verslagen vogeltje bij en dat wekte bij hem en zijn dochter vooralsnog weinig vertrouwen. Vooral omdat zijn vrouw in de dagen meteen na de operatie alleen maar achteruit leek te gaan.

Bij ieder bezoekuur dat hij aan haar bed uitzat, tweemaal daags, zag ze er weer bleker uit. Hij ging eenmaal in de voormiddag en later nog een keer na het avondeten, maar zag niet veel vooruitgang in haar situatie. Ze leek telkens kleiner, petieteriger geworden en straalde persé niet meer de daadkracht uit die hij altijd van haar gewend was.

Als hij na de lunch haar kamer opkwam leek 't of ze in een nog groter bed was neergelegd. Dat de ruimte er omheen langer en breder geworden was. Het zag eruit alsof het plafond een stukje hoger boven haar bed uit was gekomen en zelfs het uitzicht uit de ramen leek steeds weidser te worden. Ondanks dat ze volgens de gegevens op de status aan de voet van haar bed, 'flink' aan leek te sterken. Tot er vanwege 'wat complicaties' een tweede operatie noodzakelijk bleek, heeft de verpleging volgehouden dat het goed ging en dat ze redelijk aan het opknappen was.

Die hernieuwde ingreep hebben ze gisteravond, meer vannacht eigenlijk, in allerijl uitgevoerd. Als privilege mocht hij in een kamer op de gang wachten tot ze ermee klaar waren. De operatie zou 'een uurtje of anderhalf tot hooguit twee' gaan duren en hoefde alleen met spoed uitgevoerd te worden. De man kon er dan na afloop bij zijn als ze wakker werd gemaakt en uitsliep. Ondanks alle haast was de verkoeverkamer ervan op de hoogte gesteld dat hij er naast haar bed te gast zou zijn.

Helaas is ze niet meer wakker geworden. Verslagen, nog niet helemaal terug in de werkelijkheid, vervolgt hij zijn weg naar het restaurant waar hij 't kopje koffie dat hij zichzelf beloofd heeft, kan gaan gebruiken. Misschien hervindt hij er zijn tegenwoordigheid van geest en kan ie eindelijk hun dochter op de hoogte brengen. Natuurlijk is ze op haar werk en waarschijnlijk zal ze intussen de uitslag van de operatie vernomen hebben, maar hij moet haar even zelf opbellen.

Vanmiddag zal hij naar het huis gaan waar hun zoon woont, dan kan ie het slechte nieuws omtrent zijn moeder ook met hem delen. Hij hoopt dat zijn dochter in de gelegenheid is om hem erbij te vergezellen, zodat hij er niet helemaal alleen voor staat.

Joepie

De man, indertijd meer een jongetje natuurlijk, zal om en nabij de tien jaar oud geweest zijn. In ieder geval en geheel volgens de indertijd geldende telling, zat hij in de vierde klas van de lagere school. Intussen heet dat door alle vernieuwingen in het onderwijs groep zes. Bij hem in de klas zat een meisje dat in het grote huis naast de hoge standerd molen woonde. Haar naam was Maria of Marja dat weet hij niet zo goed meer. In ieder geval betrof het een verwijzing naar de moeder van Jezus waarmee veel gezinnen hun jongste dochter opzadelden. Later, toen hij op de middelbare school bij de paters zat, heeft hij weleens bedacht dat dit voor de gelovigen kennelijk een manier was om aan God duidelijk te maken dat deze jongste de laatste zou worden. Alle opa's en oma's werden natuurlijk bij de oudste kinderen vernoemd.

Op de fiets onderweg naar school of huis kwam hij elke dag langs haar woning. Vanzelfsprekend was hij op dat moment nog te jong om belangstelling voor meisjes te hebben of stond zijn Roomse opvoeding het toe om fantasieën omtrent dat andere geslacht te koesteren. Het maakte de omgang tussen de klasgenoten echter zo dat alle kinderen als gelijke met elkaar omgingen. Als hij haar of een van de ander kinderen uit de klas, achterop kwam dan liepen ze samen verder naar school. Of ze mochten bij hem achterop. Laten we de manier van met elkaar omgaan onbevangen noemen, al werd er door de ouders wel degelijk een onderscheid gemaakt tussen zogenaamd 'betere families' en de kinderen van een andere, ogenschijnlijk mindere, komaf.

Vaders met een eigen zaak of praktijk, maar zeker degenen met een zogenaamd academische achtergrond, waren ver verheven boven wat toen nog arbeiders of handwerkslieden werden genoemd. Hetzelfde ging op voor de heel speciale mensen die een baan als ambtenaar op konden voeren. Het maakte dan niet eens uit of ze plaatselijk, in Leiden of een omliggend dorp, of zelfs helemaal in 'den Haag' dat werk deden, voorwaarde was slechts dat het een functie betrof waarbij er aan een bureau gewerkt werd. Dus niet achter de vuilniswagen aan lopen of bijvoorbeeld kantonnier.

Bij hem in de familie waren het trouwens vooral zijn moeder en tantes die dit onderscheid hanteerden. Sowieso leek het idee voorbehouden aan vrouwen, want het bleek voornamelijk 't werk van de echtgenoten die het onderscheid, de indeling bepaalde. Zelf heeft de man nooit gezien waar de verschillen lagen of vandaan kwamen. Ze schenen echter te bestaan en omdat zijn vader bij

een heel groot bedrijf werkzaam was en daar een kennelijk 'belangrijke functie' bekleedde, werd ook zijn familie tot de bovenlaag gerekend. Zonder dat
hij het zich bewust was, werd de man dus bij die 'elite' ingedeeld. Dat heeft
hem nooit een voordeel opgeleverd overigens en hij kon of wilde zich er
evenmin ooit op beroepen.

Van de keer dat hij bij het meisje thuis geweest is, staat hem niet veel meer bij
dan de boterham die hij er in de keuken heeft gegeten. Of het brood door haar
moeder, een bediende of misschien een oudere zus werd klaargemaakt weet
hij zich niet meer te herinneren. Alleen dat er twee vrouwen in de keuken aanwezig waren en die hadden allebei een schort aan. Zoveel staat nog vast, maar
hun exacte rol kan hij zich niet meer voor de geest halen.

Gezien zijn leeftijd waren alle volwassenen voor hem hetzelfde. Daarom behoorde in zijn beleving van alles en nog wat tot de mogelijkheden en omdat
Maria thuis dus de jongste was, bleek ze eveneens heel RK, een flink aantal
oudere zussen en broers te hebben. Eventueel kon die andere vrouw dus net
zo goed een zus geweest zijn, of zoals bij hem in huis een dienstmeisje. Al
had die heel andere taken dan boterhammen smeren en deze beleggen voor
toevallig aanwezige klasgenoten. Joke was er maar tweemaal per week en
haar werk kwam vooral neer op het schoonhouden van hun huis.

Zijn klasgenootje had waarschijnlijk een verjaardag, in ieder geval was er
sprake van 'n gebeurtenis die met een feestje gevierd diende te worden. In zijn
herinnering was er namelijk een hele groep kinderen, klasgenoten voor zover
hij nog weet, bij haar thuis aanwezig. Ze zaten met zijn allen rond de grote tafel die middenin de met witte tegels beklede ruimte stond. Zwarte en witte tegels op de vloer en naar hij weet was er een lang aanrecht met boven de bak
in de hoek een koperen kraan. De man had, omdat ze dat thuis niet zo vaak op
tafel hadden, een boterham met chocoladehagelslag gevraagd. Het strooisel
stond midden op de tafel, vlak voor zijn neus aantrekkelijk te zijn. Spontaan
had hij het aangewezen toen 'm gevraagd werd wat ie "erop wou".

Bij hem hadden ze meestal vleeswaren of kaas om als beleg op het brood te
doen. En op vrijdag was er altijd vis. Hartig beleg wilde zijn moeder het
liefst, omdat het volgens haar zo gezond was. Dus vrijwel nooit jam of andere
zoetigheden, dat noemde ze 'het voedsel van de armoe'. Wat dat ook mocht
betekenen want het smaakte wel lekker als hij het eens kreeg. Iets prettigs
hoorde toch niet direct bij armoede leek hem.

De tamelijk dik uitgevallen boterham, witbrood wat op zich natuurlijk al een
traktatie betekende, was rijkelijk met boter besmeerd. Dat wel, maar de hagel-
slag was er slechts dun, ronduit mondjesmaat overheen gestrooid. Het resultaat zou niet misstaan hebben in de nouvelle cuisine maar daar was indertijd
nog lang geen sprake van. In zijn ogen was er vooral krenterigheid in het spel.
Het voelde of hij ergens voor terecht gewezen moest worden, alsof de moeder

van het meisje iets tegen hem had. Wat hij echter misdaan kon hebben, dat wist hij niet. Lang erover nadenken ging niet, het feest moest verder.

Gelukkig kon hij nog wel een hint van chocolade proeven, maar deze was beduidend minder dan dat er daadwerkelijk sprake was van de 'volle smaak gewaarwording'. Zoals waar later in de tv-reclames voor dit merk gewag van werd gemaakt. De man weet nog dat hij uit teleurstelling over deze tegenvaller, niet om een tweede boterham heeft willen of durven vragen. De andere kinderen waren intussen trouwens al van tafel verdwenen en alleen hijzelf met twee andere treuzelaars zaten nog aan het brood. Al kwam dat in zijn geval voornamelijk omdat hij als een van de laatsten zijn boterham had gekregen. Anderen zaten toen al lang en breed aan hun tweede. Het feestvarken was intussen met de rest van de klas naar ergens anders in het reusachtige huis vertrokken.

Maria had een oudere broer Joep, die zat twee jaren boven hen in de zesde klas bij de hoofdmeester. Hoewel hij een flink stuk ouder was dan zij, zat hij toch pas daar. Zijn zusje sprak meestal neerbuigend, nogal onvriendelijk over hem. Ze noemde hem dan "die achterlijk" of sprak kortaf over "de lomperik." Omdat hij inderdaad een tamelijk grove, nogal onbeholpen indruk maakte wisten ze altijd precies over wie zij sprak. Overigens werd ze voor haar woordkeus meteen door de onderwijzer gecorrigeerd want "zo behoorde je niet over familieleden te praten." Zoals al opgemerkt spreken we over het Roomse leven en daar horen tamelijk 'eigen' omgangsvormen bij.

Die dingen had ze vanzelfsprekend moeten weten en het werd haar zichtbaar aangerekend dat ze in zulke termen en op die toon over haar jongste broer durfde te spreken. De meester bleek daar heel beslist in en zijn boosheid maakte telkens 'n diepe indruk. De rest van de klasgenoten zag er echter geen bezwaar in. Ze hadden meestal geen oudere broer die net zo afweek als die van haar en de man wist als 'enig kind' sowieso niet hoe je precies over een oudere of jongere, zus en broer moest spreken.

Joepie liep altijd wat voorover gebogen en liet daarbij zijn armen los naast zijn lichaam hangen. Hierdoor ging zijn bovenlichaam altijd een beetje zwaaiend heen en weer. Als hij zich omdraaide leek het zelfs wel of zijn schouders enigszins vertraagd achter hem aan bewogen. Zijn gang versterkte hierdoor de nogal slome indruk die hij al maakte. Meestal stond hij helemaal alleen op het speelplein omdat hij nauwelijks omging met zijn klasgenoten. Joep werd domweg nooit door hen in hun spel betrokken. Uitsluitend als de hoofdmeester de jongens erop wees dat hij mee moest doen, dan was ie welkom in een team. Zij het dat dit vrijwel altijd gepaard ging met duidelijk merkbare tegenzin bij de jongens met wie hij werd ingedeeld.

Door het leeftijdsverschil was Joep minstens een kop groter dan de andere leerlingen en hij maakte ook hierdoor een grove indruk, zeker in vergelijking

129

met de snellere kinderen om hem heen. Daar had zijn zusje dus gelijk in als ze hem zo noemde. Door zijn bouw was hij niet lenig en kon alleen al door zijn postuur dus geen sportieve indruk maken. Ook als hij mee moest doen leken zijn bewegingen min of meer vertraagd tot stand te komen. Dit maakte het overigens wel interessant om naar hem te kijken. Het was fascinerend om te zien of hij een bal nu wel of 'net niet' te pakken zou krijgen. En kon of hij 'm dan vervolgens in de juiste richting weer wegschoppen?

Waarschijnlijk was Joep daarom bijna altijd de keeper als hij meedeed. In die rol leverde hij vanzelfsprekend het minste gevaar op verlies op en kon hij de andere jongen niet voor de voeten lopen tijdens het dribbelen en overschieten. Dat de ruimte om te kunnen scoren door zijn aanwezigheid al aanzienlijk minder werd, namen ze voor lief. Het compenseerde zijn onhandigheid en trage manier van reageren namelijk ternauwernood, bleek vaak.

De speelplaats van de school was door een rij rode tegels in twee bijna gelijke delen verdeeld. Aan de ene kant van de lijn, de zijde waar de kleuterschool haar poort had, was het de bedoeling dat de kleintjes speelden. Dat wil zeggen de kinderen uit de eerste, tweede en derde klas. Voor alle duidelijkheid, de kleuterschool had andere tijden voor hun pauze, het begin en slot van de schooltijden. De omstandigheid maakte dat er nooit kinderen met de kleuters door elkaar konden lopen.

De 'grote kinderen', die in de klassen vier, vijf en zes zaten, moesten aan de de andere kant van de rode streep blijven. Op dat deel stond de fietsenstalling met daar weer naast het tuintje waarin de jongens met hun zakmes 'landje veroveren' deden. Tegen de rand van de opstaande stenen en bij het trapje voor de ingang van de gymzaal konden de leerlingen knikkeren.

Aan deze kant van de afscheiding was het eveneens toegestaan om met een bal te spelen en er mocht ook geholld worden. Dat was aan de kant voor de kleintjes namelijk strikt verboden, dus bijvoorbeeld tikkertje spelen was voorbehouden aan de hogere klassen. De grotere leerlingen konden als er niets anders te doen was, rondjes lopen om de fietsenstalling. Bij de muur die rondom het plein stond konden ze eveneens knikkeren of er de tijd doden door er alleen maar een beetje te staan kletsen. Dat laatste is waar de meisjes uit de zesde zich voornamelijk mee bezig hielden zodat er langs de muur altijd groepjes vriendinnen rondhingen. Bij regen was het mogelijk om onder het afdak, dicht opeengepakt staand tussen de fietsen te schuilen.

De jongens bleven voornamelijk op het vrije deel van het plein. Daar deden ze 'ruwe spelletjes' of voetbalden er in groepjes. Daar hield de man toen al niet van zodat hij in de pauzes vaak alleen maar rondjes liep rondom de fietsenstalling. Braaf met een hoedje op want zijn moeder stond er op dat hij er altijd netjes uitzag. Zoals gezegd maakte het voor hemzelf niets uit, maar als kleine jongen schikte de man zich vanzelfsprekend nog gemakkelijk.

Hij vond het zelfs wel grappig als de hoofdmeester een denkbeeldige hoed voor hem afnam als hij 's morgens langs hem heen het schoolgebouw binnenliep, onderweg naar zijn klas. Een aantal van de andere jongens droeg weleens een pet of bij schaatsweer een ijsmuts.

Een paar dagen na het feestje bij Maria thuis, stond hij vlakbij de rode tegels van de demarcatielijn op het schoolplein, toen de jongen uit de zesde op hem af kwam lopen. Het oudere joch keek 'gemelijk' naar hem. Dat woord hadden ze de middag ervoor van hun meester geleerd tijdens het voorlezen. De manier waarop Joep naar hem keek verbaasde de man een beetje.

Zijn ogen loensten en hoewel hij altijd al wat voorovergebogen liep, leek het erop of dit nu nog erger het geval was. Vergelijk het met de Hulk, al werd die televisieserie indertijd nog niet uitgezonden en was de held als stripfiguur hier totaal onbekend. Geïllustreerde boekjes waren sowieso in de ban vanwege hun verderfelijke inhoud, maar de man stond zich er voornamelijk over te verbazen hoe een pas geleerd woord, plotseling zo ontzettend goed uitgebeeld werd. Joepie bleef vlak voor hem staan. Hij leek met die 'gemelijke blik' volledig op te willen gaan in zijn rol van 'grote broer'.

Waarschijnlijk had de man zich nederig, wat onderdaniger moeten gedragen, in ieder geval probeerde de jongen op hem neer te kijken. Hij snoof erbij en keek de man met een afwachtende, tevens dreigende blik aan. Gemelijk was echt de enige omschrijving die erbij paste, want Joepie handelde exact zoals de meester het de vorige middag aan de klas had uitgelegd. Plotseling haalde hij uit om de man een enorme stomp uit te delen.

Omdat ie de actie niet had zien aankomen of maar verwachtte, kon Joep hem vol in zijn maagstreek raken. De aarde draaide daarna een paar keer heel snel rond en alles om hem heen werd opeens donker. Happend naar lucht zeeg hij machteloos ineen op zijn knieën. Zijn rug kromde zich van de plotselinge pijn in z'n buik. Alle lucht was met de overweldigende klap uit zijn longen geslagen. Hij hoorde hoe het bloed dreunend, met een kennelijk enorme kracht door z'n aderen werd gejaagd. Zo bleef hij op handen en knieën, zo klein mogelijk in elkaar gedoken, op de stenen zitten. Bang voor nog zo'n dreun, duizelig en volledig in de war omdat hij zich afvroeg waar hij deze behandeling aan te danken kon hebben. Dat dit er ook bij hoorde hadden ze 'm er niet bij verteld, dus nu werd hij erdoor overvallen.

Even later, achter hem en voor zijn gevoel ver weg, hoorde hij hoe de bel ging. Weer enigszins bij zijn positieven komend zag hij hoe Joep in de richting van de ingang bij hem vandaan slofte. Zelf kon hij zich, nog herstellend van de klap, niet verroeren. Met grote teugen hapte hij zoveel mogelijk lucht naar binnen. Hij moest er iedere keer een beetje voor omhoog komen uit zijn ineen gedoken houding. Het leek of hij er steeds duizeliger bij werd, maar het ging niet anders. Hyperventileren was overigens nog niet als term voor zijn actie ingevoerd. Zo naar lucht happend kreeg de pijn in zijn buik een plaats en concentreerde zich ter hoogte van zijn maag. Het voelde of hij moest braken, maar er kwam niets toen hij kokhalsde. Er was voornamelijk die kramp, het drukkende gevoel in zijn buik. De man hoorde zijn naam roepen, gevolgd door aansporingen dat hij naar binnen moest komen, zich moest haasten. Verongelijkt vroeg hij zich af of de meester soms dacht dat hij daar voor z'n lol zo zat. Dacht hij misschien dat het een onderdeel van een spelletje was?

Was er wel een spel waarbij hij deze verkrampte houding aan moest nemen en hoorden zijn benauwdheid, de ademnood en pijn daar dan gewoon bij?

Met moeite kon hij zich na een paar tellen toch oprichten. Het schoolplein was intussen opgehouden met draaien. Hij had alleen nog 'n zurige smaak in zijn mond en het ruiste vreselijk in zijn oren. Alles maakte hem misselijk. Hij moest nogmaals kokhalzen, weer bijna spugen. Zo wankelde hij naar het opstapje bij de deur.

Aan het muurtje ernaast zocht hij even steun, haalde nog eens heel diep adem, ging ervoor rechtop staan en strompelde vervolgens naar binnen. Hij was de laatste die de klas in kwam en moest de deur achter zich sluiten.

De man ziet een schim. Vaag kan hij een soort gezicht onderscheiden en hoort hoe in de verte iemand zijn naam roept. Beter gezegd, zijn naam wordt ergens genoemd en hij kan niet bepalen waar. De stem klinkt op een rustige toon, maar het lijkt of er een vertraging in zit. Het geluid komt van een andere plek dan waar hij de contouren van die ogen, neus en wat door kan gaan als mond, meent te zien. Zijn ogen nemen alleen een beweging waar, het komt omdat hij zich niet kan concentreren. Het gezicht kijkt naar hem, alsof het op iets wacht. Hij kan niet terugkijken, op het roepen reageren, kontakt maken.

Achter het hoofd ziet hij witte of lichtblauwe lappen hangen, waarschijnlijk zijn het gordijnen. De persoon naast hem is ook in lichte kleuren gehuld. Hij merkt hoe het gezicht zijn naam weer zegt en begrijpt dat er gevraagd wordt of hij wakker aan het worden is. Zijn oren horen het niet specifiek, maar hij neemt waar dat het hem zoiets wordt gevraagd. Vaag, maar de bedoeling is 'm duidelijk genoeg voor nu. Al kan hij er dus niets mee aan.

Hij kan niet zien hoe ver de schim bij hem vandaan staat, waar hij is of hoe hij er zelf bij ligt. Voor zover hij het kan inschatten kan het evengoed een meter als enige kilometers zijn. Zijn gevoel voor afstand is verdwenen. De persoon naast hem torent boven hem uit. Het gezicht kijkt op hem neer omdat hij er een stukje lager, voor zijn gevoel achterover gekanteld, bij ligt.

Hij is beneden het hoofd, ligt naast de gestalte die vlakbij hem staat. Hij moet ervoor omhoog kijken en ziet dat het gezicht details krijgt. Er was al dat witte gewaad, nu ziet hij daarboven het hoofd duidelijker worden. Op het haar, zit een mutsje, het steekt lichtblauw bijna alsof er licht vanuit gaat, af tegen de achtergrond. Hij kan niet onderscheiden of er een man of vrouw onder zit. De mond, het halve gezicht, zit verborgen achter een lapje.

Vermoedelijk ligt hij op een bed en kijkt in de richting waar zijn voeten zullen liggen. Hij kan helaas niet even vlug een andere kant op kijken. Zijn mond doet het niet en hij is vergeten hoe hij naar de schim kan knikken. Z'n hoofd functioneert helemaal niet, doet niet mee met wat hij zou willen. De schim verandert langzamerhand in een persoon, zo te horen een vrouw. Waarschijnlijk is ze verpleegster, of dokter. Zijn omstandigheden beginnen tot hem door te dringen.

Hij probeert of hij haar kan bereiken door te wuiven, maar ziet hoe ze zich omdraait en naar een plek bij de gordijnen loopt. Daar staat een toren van apparaten, ze kijkt ernaar. Daarna doet ze er iets mee, draait ergens aan zonder dat hij kan zien waaraan of wat ze precies verandert. Dan loopt ze weg, het is niet mogelijk om te zien waar de gestalte blijft.

Hij ziet alleen slangen en snoeren, hoort hoe er om hem heen apparatuur aan het sissen of piepen is. Aan haar postuur, de elegantie van de bewegingen die ze maakte en het duidelijk zichtbare paardenstaartje op haar achterhoofd heeft hij gezien dat de schim inderdaad vrouwelijk zal zijn. Maar het is onbelangrijk omdat ze er nu niet meer is. Ze had een mondkapje voor, dat maakte haar gezicht zo lastig te herkennen. Duidelijk zichtbaar zat er blauw achtige make-up rond haar ogen, maar dat doet er evenmin meer toe.

Hij zou wel willen weten waar hij is, maar het wordt er te donker voor om iets te kunnen zien. Kennelijk heeft iemand de verlichting lager gedraaid of is het zomaar vanzelf donkerder aan het worden.

Hij hoort nogmaals zijn naam noemen, opnieuw roept iemand of hij wakker wordt. Het eerste dat hij herkent van zonet zijn de gordijnen. Het lijkt wel of ze op de een of ander manier langzaam naar voor en achteren wapperen. Nu de man ze ziet, blijken ze toch stil te hangen. Erachter schijnt licht. Het is slechts een klein beetje, maar voldoende om te kunnen zien dat het er is. Hij probeert zijn blik naar beneden te richten, daar moeten zijn voeten zich bevinden en was eerder die schim. Dat herinnert hij zich.

Het lukt niet om zijn hoofd al goed te laten bewegen. Intussen stapt iemand zijn gezichtsveld binnen, komt naderbij en buigt zich over hem heen. Hij probeert te glimlachen of te knikken, hij weet zelf niet goed wat hij precies wil of kan. Hij wil laten zien dat hij wakker is, dat hij leeft. Hij zou wel iets tegen de persoon willen zeggen, maar zijn mond laat hem in de steek. Ook zijn handen kan hij niet bewegen. "Blijft U maar rustig liggen meneer. Uw handen zitten vastgebonden omdat U nogal onrustig was vannacht.

Ze mogen zo weer los. Als U een beetje tot rust gekomen bent."

Terwijl ze het zegt dringt het tot hem door dat zijn handen inderdaad slechts

133

een klein stukje met hem willen meewerken. Hij merkt dat hij ze niet verder omhoog kan krijgen dan een beperkt stuk. In plaats daarvan probeert ie zijn hoofd iets op te tillen. Dan kan hij ernaar kijken en zien waaraan ze zijn vastgemaakt, maar hij krijgt er geen beweging in. Zijn hoofd is te zwaar. Hij heeft blijkbaar niet genoeg kracht in zijn nek. Hoe hebben ze dat voor elkaar gekregen?

Het lukt hoe danook niet om omhoog te komen. Eigenlijk zou hij zich een beetje willen oprichten. Bij zijn knieën voelt hij een deken of laken. Het houdt zijn voeten vast op het bed. Iedere verdere beweging is echter onmogelijk. De man kan alleen nog maar recht omhoog kijken, al het andere is hem teveel. Hij voelt in zijn nek hoe hij moet zweten van de inspanning. Hij besluit rustig te blijven liggen, zich volledig over te geven en af te wachten wat ze voor hem in petto hebben.

Hij voelt hoe ie om zich heen ligt te schoppen, ziet en voelt hoe hij met zijn armen zwaait en krampachtig probeert om zich op te richten uit die liggende positie. Tegelijkertijd realiseert ie zich dat dit dus eerder gebeurd moet zijn, toen het hier nog veel donkerder was. Nu ligt hij stil op dit bed, maar het getrappel is waarschijnlijk de aanleiding geweest voor dat vastbinden. Nu kan hij uitsluitend met zijn ogen knipperen, zijn handen een paar centimeter omhoog brengen. De controle over zijn benen is hij ook volledig kwijt. Alleen al het idee om op te staan, overeind te komen, uit bed te gaan, het maakt dat 't zweet 'm uitbreekt.

Hij probeert te onderscheiden wat er zich binnen die traag bewegende gordijnen bevindt. Hij kan zijn ogen naar links of recht bewegen, het hoofd gaat er langzaam achteraan. Naast hem kan hij alleen maar slangen en apparaten waarnemen. Die staan stil, hij kan zich er niet mee verbonden voelen. Erachter zijn openingen tussen de lappen. Daar tussendoor kan hij, als ze inderdaad heen en weer bewegen, die apparatuur van het geluid en zo nu en dan ook langslopende mensen zien. Ze verplaatsen zich te snel om te kunnen opmaken wat ze er aan het doen zijn. Het textiel maakt dat hij telkens maar heel even ziet dat ze er zijn. Het kost 'm teveel moeite om er lang genoeg naar te blijven kijken wat er allemaal gebeurt.

Waar al die mensen heen gaan of vandaan komen blijft onzichtbaar. Hij hoort uitsluitend een hoop lawaai. Het komt van de spullen die om hem heen staan te ruisen en knorren. Er borrelen pompen en van overal uit de ruimte klinken piepjes. Hij hoort klikken, tik geluiden, bellen en alarm tonen. Die komen vast van al de verschillende apparaten die hij ook om hem heen ziet staan. Ergens ter hoogte van zijn voeten staat een stofzuiger te loeien en dan hoort hij daar bovenuit ook nog een continu ritmisch weerkerend geluid.

Hij voelt dat hij het zelf maakt, waarschijnlijk zal het samenhangen met zijn hartslag of ademhaling. De man weet dat hij in een ziekenhuis ligt, maar om

134

hem heen is het grotendeels grijsachtig soms zwart, eigenlijk vooral donker. De inspanning om alles uit elkaar te houden en tegelijkertijd te begrijpen wat er met hem gebeurt wordt hem teveel. Die zuster van daarnet is trouwens ook alweer weggelopen. Hij hoeft helemaal geen antwoord te geven op haar vragen, zich te bewegen of te laten zien dat hij er is.

De man komt bij zijn positieven. De geluiden lijken minder te zijn geworden, ze laten zich wat beter afzonderlijk waarnemen. Hij kan intussen het ritmische piepen naast zijn hoofd plaatsen, dit is een zogenaamde monitor. Hij meent aan het ritme van 't gepiep te herkennen dat het een hartslagmeter zal zijn, hij kent ze uit films en deze zal hem wel in de gaten staan te houden. Hij besluit er even naar te blijven luisteren.

Het piepen echoot ergens in zijn achterhoofd en hij wil graag de connectie met zichzelf leggen. Als het apparaat een piepje geeft lijkt het inderdaad of er in zijn hoofd een bevestiging klinkt, het gevoel stelt hem op z'n gemak. Net als hij er aan gewend is om mee te drijven met het ritme van het geluid en denkt ze terug te voelen in zijn vingertoppen, voeten en schouders, wordt zijn rust verstoord door een stem die tegen hem spreekt. Ditmaal is het een mannenstem. Heel langzaam realiseert hij zich dat die steeds duidelijker wordt. Het lijkt wel of hij intussen ook in staat is om een reactie te geven.

De man opent zijn ogen om te reageren op de broeder die naast zijn bed is komen staan. Hij hoort een hol, rochelend geluid als hij probeert te spreken. Het lukt hem intussen dus om te reageren op wat er met hem aan de hand is, maar het is nog niet duidelijk wat hij doet of hoe hij er controle over krijgt.

"Ik ga de verdoving wat minder intensief maken meneer.

U zult zo dus wat wakkerder worden.

Probeert U rustig te blijven."

De stem klinkt vriendelijk en maakt dat ie zich aangenaam voelt. Hem inderdaad enigszins verdoofd maar nu door de rust die hem omgeeft. De sterker wordende pijn in zijn buik maakt dat hij plotseling moet denken aan de enorme stoot in zijn maag die hij als kleine jongen van Joepie heeft gekregen.

Een paar tellen geleden heeft een broeder hem geholpen bij het op de tafel klauteren voor zijn operatie. Met een ruk heeft hij het tijdelijke vestje van de man z'n schouders getrokken. Geheel naakt is hij op de tafel gaan liggen. Aan zijn rechterzij zaten de zusters die hem van de wachtruimte naar deze zaal hebben gereden. Ze hebben allemaal een groen schort aangetrokken. Het bed hadden ze eerst zorgvuldig naast de tafel gemanoeuvreerd en daarna zijn ze er omheen gelopen. Behulpzaam zorgden ze ervoor dat hij er niet aan de andere kant vanaf gekukeld is tijdens het overstappen. Daarna is er een warme deken over hem heen gelegd. Ze hebben deze bij zijn benen ingestopt.

135

De broeder heeft intussen een slangetje op het infuus in zijn linkerarm aangesloten. Zojuist vroeg hij om zijn geboortedatum, maar de man is niet verder gekomen dan de dag en de maand. Toen is hij in de ruimte getuimeld, naar nergens weg gezweefd. Nu komt hij langzamerhand weer terug onder de mensen, al verloopt het proces in stappen die hij niet begrijpt of kan sturen. Is de operatie gestopt of zijn ze al klaar?

Moeten ze misschien nog beginnen?

Of ligt hij hier omdat ze ermee zijn opgehouden?

Omdat hij niet te redden was?

De man weet niet precies wat ze oorspronkelijk afgesproken hebben. Gejaagd probeert hij zich te herinneren hoe en wat er allemaal besproken is. Weer merkt hij hoe het zweet in zijn hals loopt, hoe hij sneller begint te ademen maar er geen controle over heeft. Hij ligt hier wel, maar kan niet sturen wat hij moet doen, of hoe dat gaat. Hij weet niet hoe laat het is en kan daardoor zijn huidige situatie niet inschatten. Afgaande op het licht dat door de ramen achter de gordijnen naar binnen komt, kan het hooguit heel vroeg in de ochtend of misschien nog steeds laat in de namiddag zijn. Al lijkt het hem dat het even hiervoor nog donkerder was. Hij weet niet welk seizoen het is. Is het nog steeds lente?

Hij haalt zich voor de geest hoe het eerder was en hoe laat het was bij ditzelfde licht. Dan kan het het niet anders dan een uur of zes, zeven zijn. Of zijn ze al verder in het jaar en is het dus beduidend vroeger, nog nacht?

Hoe lang is hij zo helemaal weg, onder narcose, geweest en ze zouden hem toch een poosje in slaap houden, is dat nu voorbij?

De geluiden in de zaal wekken de indruk dat het inderdaad nog nacht zou kunnen zijn. Het maakt 't hem onmogelijk om te beslissen wat de exacte tijd is. Het gepiep naast hem gaat trouwens ook een stuk sneller. Het lijkt opeens veel intensiever te klinken. De tonen worden luidruchtiger en beginnen de hele omgeving te overheersen. Het duurt niet lang voordat het nog het enige is dat hij kan horen.

Een andere pieptoon mengt zich door alle geluiden en overstemt nu plotseling alles. Horen en zien vergaat hem door het kabaal.

De man krijgt zijn ogen niet meer open. Hij voelt hoe ie ze stijf toegeknepen houdt, maar niet kan ingrijpen of ze alsnog open krijgt. Het indringende lawaai jaagt hem op. Hij heeft totaal geen idee van wat er gaande is, hoort boven alle geluiden uit hoe de broeder naar hem is toegesneld.

"Probeert U zo rustig mogelijk te blijven. We zijn U wakker aan het maken, maar maakt U zich geen zorgen. U komt nu bij uit de narcose.

Blijf rustig, maakt U zich vooral geen zorgen."

De broeder heeft een hand op de man z'n schouder gelegd en drukt hem ermee terug op het bed. Nadrukkelijk heeft hij gezegd dat hij zich geen zorgen moet maken. De man probeert te knikken om aan te geven dat hij begrijpt wat er van hem verlangd wordt. Dat de operatie afgelopen is neemt hij onmiddellijk aan, maar is het gelukt en wat is er dan gebeurd?

Ze hadden hem beloofd dat de operatie een paar uur zou duren en dat ze hem daarna een tijdje zouden laten rusten. Hij neemt aan dat hij hier op de zogenaamde 'intensive care' afdeling is. Voor zover hij kan zien is het heel vroeg in de morgen. De man doet een poging om, al is het bij benadering uit te rekenen hoelang hij buiten westen kan zijn geweest. Dat is door het gebrek aan informatie onmogelijk, maar hij probeert het toch. Hoe intensief hij zich ook concentreert, hij komt er niet uit. Al doet 't er niet toe, wat voor dag is het?

Het maakt niet uit of het vroeg of al later in de ochtend is.

De broeder is naast hem blijven staan. Nog steeds heeft hij zijn hand op z'n schouder. De man doet zijn ogen een stukje open en kijkt naar hem.

"Zo daar bent U weer."

De broeder kijkt hem vriendelijk aan en geeft 'm een klein duwtje.

"Uw vrouw en uw dochter zijn al op bezoek geweest."

De broeder spreekt rustig maar zijn woorden dringen niet gelijk tot hem door. Wat hij precies zegt duurt even. Hoewel hij hoort dat de broeder een tijd noemt en uit de toon van spreken begrijpt dat het uren geleden moet zijn geweest, kan hij zich alleen voorstellen dat het gisteren was. Afgaande op hoe hij 't vertelt, zal het allemaal nog ruimschoots voor de dienst van deze broeder hebben plaats gevonden. Waarschijnlijk kan ie hem dus helemaal niet naar de exacte omstandigheden vragen. Hoe laat is wat hij allemaal zegt voorgevallen en waar zijn ze nu?

"Uw dochter is niet goed geworden.

Ze zijn een tijdje gebleven maar omdat U zo ver weg was, zijn ze weer vertrokken."

Het klinkt geruststellend, dat is alles. Het komt waarschijnlijk door de toon waarop de broeder tegen hem spreekt. Hij hoort eraan af dat hij zich rustig moet houden. Het ontneemt hem de lust om zijn vragen te stellen. Nu moet hij klaarblijkelijk eerst wakker worden.

Waar is ze trouwens ziek van geworden?

Heeft ze iets verkeerds gegeten?

Kwam het door hem?

"Nu bent U al goed wakker aan het worden. Blijft U maar rustig liggen dan gaan we U straks een beetje schoonmaken."

Hij zou willen vertellen dat hij niets kan. Dat hij er dus heus niet vandoor zal gaan. En waar is hij trouwens 'vies' van geworden?

Hoe gaat dat schoonmaken er straks aan toe?

Moet hij dat zelf doen en kan hij dat dan wel?

Hij kan alleen een sputterend geluid voortbrengen. Er zit iets in zijn mond

137

waardoor hij niet kan spreken. Hij wil even voelen wat het is maar kan zijn hand niet ver genoeg omhoog krijgen. Die zit nog vastgebonden.

De broeder kijkt ernaar. "Ik zal straks Uw handen voor U losmaken. Eerst moet U nog wat wakkerder worden. Windt U zich alstublieft niet weer zo op, raak niet in paniek. Het komt allemaal heus wel in orde.

We letten goed op U hoor."

De broeder geeft hem nogmaals een kneepje in zijn schouder. De man zou naar hem willen glimlachen, de jongen ervan willen overtuigen dat hij hem inderdaad volledig vertrouwt. Hij kan alleen maar met zijn ogen knipperen. De rest van zijn lichaam wil nog steeds niet meedoen.

De broeder kijkt hem nogmaals aan en loopt naar de apparaten die vlakbij het voeteneinde staan. Daar tikt hij een paar keer op een aantal verschillende plekken van een paneel en loopt weg tussen de gordijnen door. Aan het licht dat kort naar binnenvalt te zien, kan het inderdaad niet anders dan heel vroeg in de ochtend zijn. De man maakt het op aan de heldere kleur van het schijnsel. Hij meent er de opgaande zon in te kunnen onderscheiden. Zag hij niet hoe een deel van het gebouw, buiten achter de ramen achter die gordijnen, erdoor verlicht werd?

Ergens achter de gordijnen zullen dus ramen zitten, dat heeft hij net gezien.

Het piepen verloopt in een rustiger tempo. De man weet dat het te maken heeft met zijn omstandigheden en probeert of hij het ritme kan sturen. Of hij het tempo van het gepiep kan beïnvloeden.

Hij concentreert zich op het geluid. Hij zal zich niet opnieuw opjutten.

Door rustig zijn adem wat langer binnen te houden rekent hij erop de interval tussen de tonen te kunnen beïnvloeden.

Het werkt niet, binnen de kortste keren begint de vervelende janktoon er weer doorheen te loeien. Hij stopt met nadenken over het ademen en probeert uitsluitend te luisteren naar de tonen die er naast zijn hoofd klinken. Het gejank stopt vrijwel meteen weer. De rust die erop terugkeert voorkomt dat de broeder nogmaals naar zijn bed komt.

Elders in de zaal klinken weer de verschillende piep, tik, ruis en alarm geluiden die hij eerder al kon horen. Daar heeft hij geen belangstelling voor, voelt niet dat hij er iets mee te maken heeft. Dat hij er wat aan kan doen.

De man moet in slaap gevallen zijn want hij schrikt wakker. Het licht is nu overal om hem heen. Er loopt een zuster naast zijn bed. Ze beweegt zich op en neer tussen de apparaten bij zijn voeteneind en die naast zijn hoofd. Intussen spreekt ze tegen hem maar hij verstaat niet wat er gezegd wordt. Ze moet gemerkt hebben dat hij ergens van wakker geschrokken is, maar kijkt slechts even heel kort naar hem. Hij krijgt de indruk dat ze voornamelijk geïnteresseerd is in de apparaten.

138

Hij wil iets tegen haar zeggen, laten zien dat hij er is. Opmerken dat hij zich al veel wakkerder voelt dan daarnet. Er volgt alleen een sputterend geluid. Ze staat stil en draait zich naar zijn bed.

"Er zit een tjoep in uw mond dus U kunt niet spreken.

Houd U zich maar rustig. Als alles weer goed met U gaat, dan halen we 'm eruit."

De broeder komt ook tussen de gordijnen door gelopen. Vriendelijk kijkt hij naar de man en schenkt hem weer zijn breedste glimlach. "Zo U bent er weer zie ik.

U heeft nog even geslapen."

Met zijn handen maakt de man een vragend gebaar.

Hij wil weten wat de operatie heeft opgeleverd. Hebben ze uitgevoerd wat er afgesproken was, of moesten ze stoppen?

De broeder loopt naar de andere kant van zijn bed en buigt zich over hem heen. Met zijn hand schrijft de man een 'w' een 'a' en een 't' op het laken. De broeder leest het en vraagt of hij iets wil vragen. De man z'n hoofd doet het gelukkig weer, want hij kan een korte bevestiging knikken.

Nogmaals schrijft hij "wat" op het laken en voegt er "is er gebeurd" aan toe.

De broeder volgt zijn vinger en zegt hardop wat hij meent te lezen.

"Wilt U weten wat er gebeurd is"?

De man knikt, hij wil het inderdaad weten. Laten ze hem nu maar vertellen of het gelukt is. De zuster is intussen klaar met haar werk. Ze groet haar collega en verdwijnt tussen de gordijnen.

"De dokter komt zo en dan zal die U precies vertellen wat ze hebben gedaan. Voor zover ik weet is de operatie geslaagd. U bent gisteravond laat hier naar de afdeling gebracht."

Dat hij de operatie overleefd heeft is hem duidelijk, maar hebben ze de kanker weg kunnen halen?

Waren er complicaties?

Hebben ze, waar ze bang voor waren, ook wat aan zijn hart moeten doen?

Dat maakte de operatie immers risicovol en zou ervoor gezorgd kunnen hebben dat ze hem "onverrichter zake" dicht moesten maken. "Of erger." Zo hadden ze het genoemd. "Dat U misschien niet meer wakker wordt."

Op aandringen van het team chirurgen hadden zijn vrouw en hij, de kinderen daarop moeten voorbereiden.

Waar is dat rare ding in zijn mond trouwens voor nodig?

Het irriteert hem want drukt ergens diep in zijn keel op een plek die pijn doet. Zo nu en dan klinkt er ook een reutelend geluidje uit en daar heeft hij geen controle over. Hij schaamt zich ervoor dat hij de boertjes niet in kan houden.

"U moet nu even goed wakker worden en dan gaan we U straks wassen."

De broeder tikt gewoontegetrouw tegen zijn schouder.

139

Hij loopt om het bed heen naar de apparatuur bij het voeteneind. Daar toetst hij een aantal keren op het paneel. Kennelijk zitten er knopjes of schakelaars op en kan hij er iets mee instellen of veranderen. De man concentreert zich om er beter naar te kunnen kijken. Bij nader inzien hangt er waarschijnlijk een beeldscherm en zit daar weer onder een soort toetsenbord. Het lijkt nog het meest op een computer zoals hij die thuis ook heeft staan. Als hij wegloopt knikt de broeder nog even naar hem.

De man realiseert zich dat hij naakt is en onbedekt op het bed ligt. Alleen op zijn onderbenen ligt iets, een laken of een dekentje. Verder moet hij er helemaal bloot bij liggen. Hij voelt het aan de tocht die over zijn benen, schaamstreek en schouders strijkt. Waarschijnlijk is zijn dochter van die aanblik onwel geworden. Ze heeft haar vader natuurlijk nog nooit helemaal bloot gezien. De man moet glimlachen bij de gedachte aan zichzelf in een zwembroek, hij heeft er een gruwelijke hekel aan om voor gek te lopen. Dat maakt het een regelrechte zeldzaamheid dat ze hem ooit eerder bloot heeft kunnen bekijken. Hij rekent uit dat het op de camping, jaren geleden voor het laatst geweest zal zijn dat ze hem in een korte broek en misschien wel een ontbloot bovenlichaam heeft gezien. Het was erg heet die zomer en waarschijnlijk de laatste keer dat ze met zijn allen als gezin op vakantie waren. Kort erna heeft ze verkering gekregen, was ze opeens voor een heleboel dingen te groot, volwassen geworden.

De zuster komt tussen de gordijnen door zijn tent binnen gelopen.

"Zo U bent al wakker hè. We laten U nog even liggen en dan kom ik U zo schoonmaken. U zit nog helemaal onder de jodium." Ze raakt zijn zij aan.

Hij kan het niet controleren, maar gelooft haar op haar woord. De man voelt zich plotseling dood en doodmoe, het liefst wil hij alleen nog maar slapen. Wat hem betreft mogen ze hem nog heel lang, desnoods een paar uur maar minimaal een tijdje, met rust laten.

Flexibel

Sinds het afgelopen voorjaar is er bij het bedrijf waar de man in loondienst is een regeling waardoor hij en zijn collega's niet meer exact om half negen aan hun werk hoeven te beginnen. Ze mogen overigens ook zelf bedenken wanneer ze weer eens op huis aan willen. Zij het dat er tussen de oude aanvangstijd van half negen tot de vorige sluitingstijd rond vijf uur, tenminste een personeelslid met voldoende ervaring aanwezig moet zijn om de lopende zaken af te kunnen handelen. Bij het ingaan van de flexibele werktijden is namelijk vastgesteld dat de continuïteit gehandhaafd diende te blijven. Tenslotte moet een eventuele klant tijdens de voormalige kantooruren zo nodig te woord gestaan kunnen worden. Niet iedereen is tegenwoordig zo modern dat ie de oude tijden 'zomaar' overboord zal kunnen gooien.

Weliswaar is er een callcenter dat de honneurs nu waarneemt, maar daar wilden ze de mogelijkheid om ruggespraak te kunnen houden met het bedrijf, niet verliezen. Zeker tijdens de zogenaamde 'leercurve' leek het ze een voorwaarde. Daarom is er dus voorlopig de regel, dat een vertegenwoordiger van de firma aanwezig moet zijn, in het leven geroepen.

Dat maakt 't niet helemaal uitgesloten dat de nieuwe werktijden ooit voor eenieder gaan gelden. Maar het geven van passende antwoorden en bieden van oplossingen voor prangende vragen, zou verloren gaan als er plotseling sprake zou zijn van teveel variabele factoren. Vandaar dus het qua dienstbaarheid nog niet helemaal loslaten van de oorspronkelijke tijden, de kantooruren zoals ze altijd zo braaf genoemd werden. Daarover heeft Dollie Parton, zij het een half uurtje korter dan hier, ooit een liedje gezongen. *)

Afgelopen zaterdagmiddag is de man terug gekomen van vakantie. Om die gepast af te sluiten is hij, precies zoals het in de afgelopen jaren de traditie is geworden, gisteravond naar de pizzeria geweest met de kinderen. Eerder, nog 's middags heeft hij zijn vrouw geholpen met het opruimen van de kampeerspullen. Alleen de tent hangt nu nog op zolder om helemaal goed te drogen en te 'luchten'.

Ervaring heeft ze geleerd dat ie dan keurig netjes opgeruimd kan worden voor

---

*) **Nine to five**, uit de gelijknamige film waarin zij tevens debuteerde als actrice.

de volgende vakantie en gereed is om dan nogmaals achter in de auto te worden gepakt. Weer volledig gereed voor vertrek.

Het bespaart ze het getob dat je weleens ziet in een park als mensen vergeten zijn hoe de tent opgezet moest worden of er van alles kwijt is geraakt en ze daar dan aan het oefenen slaan. Dat men vlak voor de vakantie alle spulletjes nog even moet controleren omdat ze vergeten zij hoe het ook alweer zat.

De man en zijn vrouw zorgen er altijd voor dat aan het einde van de reis alles in orde is voor de volgende keer. Wat er verloren is gegaan of aan vervanging toe, wordt voordat de boel opgeruimd kan worden, aangevuld of vernieuwd. Ze houden ervan om op die manier het vakantiegevoel nog enigszins te prolongeren en 't zorgt ervoor dat ze geheel voorbereid aan de volgende kunnen beginnen. Ze kunnen immers zo weer weg.

Het gasstel, de pannen, borden, bekers, tafel, stoeltjes en andere kampeer benodigdheden zijn na eerst grondig afgewassen en zo nodig schoon gepoetst te zijn, naar de vliering verhuisd tot volgend jaar. Misschien dat ze het komende voorjaar weer een weekendje naar een camping in Brabant of de Achterhoek gaan om er in de buurt een paar fietstochten te gaan maken, maar het is natuurlijk zinloos om tot die tijd alles zomaar te laten staan of het dan pas helemaal in orde te maken.

Sinds gistermiddag staat het kampeergerei dus netjes opgeruimd naast de kerst spullen en het sleetje. Die bewaren ze er al van toen de kinderen nog klein waren, omdat er indertijd nog weleens sneeuw viel.

Met betrekking tot zijn werk, waar hij vandaag dus met frisse moed de draad weer op heeft gepakt, moeten we constateren dat de man een voorliefde heeft voor 'grappen'. Hij houdt er ontzettend van om practical-jokes uit te halen. De collega's weten intussen vrijwel meteen wie er het kopje aan die schotel vastgeplakt heeft. En een succesnummer is het met een plakbandje de voeler van de telefoon vastzetten onder de hoorn. Die blijft dan in de ingedrukte stand verankerd zitten, zodat het apparaat, als er wordt opgenomen, blijft rinkelen. De paniek die de opgebelde vervolgens overvalt is hilarisch.

Ronduit mysterieus is het of hij degene zou kunnen zijn die hen met verdraaide stem, desnoods aangevuld met een raar aangezet accent, opbelt met een nonsens verhaal. Hij kan heel goed stemmetjes nadoen namelijk en zich zodoende gemakkelijk voordoen als een potentiële klant met vragen. Vreemd of voor de hand liggend, hij draait er de zijne niet voor om. Tijdens z'n vakantie heeft hij vanzelfsprekend weer de nodige talen en accenten leren kennen. De ervaring heeft geleerd dat men zich de komende weken dus schrap kan zetten. Vooral bij nieuwe collega's draagt zijn grappenmakerij bij aan het inwijdings- ritueel. Eenieder verwacht momenteel niet anders meer eigenlijk en de vaste medewerkers spelen een spel desgevraagd graag met hem mee.

Menig collega heeft hem daartoe, en meestal min of meer vertrouwelijk, op de hoogte gebracht van een opgemerkte zwakheid in het gedrag of de werkwijze van zo'n nieuweling. Aan medeplichtigen heeft hij dus geen gebrek en andere collega's gaan intussen evenmin vrijuit. Als er zich dus een mogelijkheid voordoet om iemand eens flink in de maling te nemen, dan staat de man voorop om er zijn medewerking aan te verlenen. Hij neemt desnoods het initiatief en zijn bijna dertig dienstjaren staan het ook toe. Ze bieden hem onderhand een ruim repertoire waaruit naar hartenlust geput kan worden.

De geschetste manier van doen maakt het weleens lastig om in 'n gesprek met een mogelijke klant, het moment te bepalen waarop men door meent te hebben dat degene die aan de lijn zit, oprecht handelt en het dus niet een grappen makende collega betreft. Diverse keren is het intussen voorgekomen dat een klant verbaasd uit moest leggen, dat ie niet een medewerker was die zo'n grap uithaalde. Dat, zeg maar zijn 'domme onwetendheid' niet gespeeld was, maar oprecht genoemd moest worden. In alle verwarring werd dan omstandig uitgelegd dat hij of zij daadwerkelijk met deze klacht, opmerking of vraag opgebeld had en dat er door hem of haar, helemaal niemand van de firma in het ootje werd genomen.

Al deze toestanden verhoogden de effectiviteit van de grap vanzelfsprekend in aanzienlijke mate en menig collega heeft zich nog lange tijd afgevraagd of de man niet gewoon het spel tot het einde heeft volgehouden. Dat hij zijn rol zodanig speelde dat ze er met open ogen ingevlogen zijn of dat collega's er in mee zijn gegaan 'tot het gaatje'. Zelfs als hij tijdens zo'n gesprek gewoon langs hun werkkamer was komen lopen, bleven die twijfels knagen.

Later draaide het er dan wel eens op uit dat er bij de klant, die zich tekort gedaan voelde, diep door het stof gegaan moest worden. Dat dan de 'oprechte excuses' niet van de lucht waren. Ook zoiets leverde natuurlijk de nodige hilariteit op. Overigens is het, en ondanks alles, de ervaring, dat klanten erg dom over kunnen komen. Alleen al omdat ze niet volledig op de hoogte zijn van de manier van werken bij het bedrijf natuurlijk, maar het is de algemene indruk dat tegenwoordig niemand meer een gebruiksaanwijzing leest. Dat men zich met een half woordje opgedaan via het internet, 'een deskundige' meent te mogen noemen.

Menig collega is tegenwoordig dus blij dat dat callcenter ertussen zit. Geen gevraag meer naar de bekende weg, verzoeken om informatie die gewoon in de papieren staat of opmerkingen die feitelijk nergens op slaan. Bijvoorbeeld omdat de door de klant verwachte functie helemaal niet op het geleverde apparaat aanwezig is. Of dat er ergens een verwijzing naar een blauwe knop bestaat, terwijl die dus duidelijk zichtbaar in het grijs is uitgevoerd.

Alleen de zware gevallen worden nog aan ze voorgelegd, maar meestal komt het er dan op neer dat ze zelf contact met de betreffende klant moeten opnemen. Dat omzeilt de mogelijkheid van een practical joke in sterke mate, al is die ook hierdoor nooit helemaal uit te sluiten.

Binnen de firma is het de man z'n taak om voor de apparaten die ze leveren de gebruiksaanwijzing te schrijven. Hij krijgt dus als eerste de nieuwste apparatuur op zijn bureau en moet vaak aan de hand van trial and error uitzoek welke functies en mogelijkheden erin verborgen zitten. Het in het steenkolen Engels opgestelde 'manual' dat Chinese, Koreaanse of Japanse fabrikanten bij een monster voegen, brengt hem namelijk niet veel verder. Hij kan overigens geen Kanji-tekens ontcijferen, dus een eventuele gebruiksaanwijzing in de taal van de fabrikant biedt sowieso ternauwernood aanknopingspunten.

Geheel radeloos is hij echter niet en eventueel kan hij met een ingenieur van de fabriek van gedachten wisselen, mocht een functie voor hem onduidelijk blijven. Men ziet weliswaar op tegen de kosten en de door het tijdverschil vreemde momenten waarop zulke gesprekken moeten plaatsvinden, maar het maakt dat hij als een van de besten op de hoogte is van alle 'ins en outs' van de door het bedrijf gevoerde producten. Dit maakt hem voor de collega's tot een vraagbaak en deze taak vervult hij eveneens graag. Zij het dus soms op zijn 'geheel eigen wijze'.

Niet uitsluitend hierdoor maar mede omdat hij er dus al een flink aantal jaren werkt, is hij intussen een van de 'best ingevoerde' werknemers. Zo heeft hij binnen de kring van medewerkers een aanzienlijk langere staat van dienst dan de directeur of de chef van het magazijn. Deze is bijna toe aan zijn pensioen maar pas na hem binnen het bedrijf aangenomen. Terwijl beiden dus een flink stuk ouder dan de man zijn, gelden ze samen met nog drie andere collega's als het 'senioren sextet'. Zij het dat ze door de jongelui uitsluitend achter hun rug zo genoemd worden. Uit "eerbied voor hun grijze haren" heeft hij er al eens over opgemerkt. Al kent buiten het zestal vrijwel niemand het liedje van Gert en Hermien en wordt dat op de radio ook nauwelijks meer gespeeld.

Begin November twee jaar geleden ontving het bedrijf een verzoek van de beheerder van het industriegebied of die een lijst met kenteken nummers en de erbij horende namen van het personeel mocht hebben. Vanwege zijn anciënniteit zadelde de directeur hem op met de taak, maar ze kwamen overeen dat de man eerst uit zou zoeken waar die informatie allemaal voor nodig mocht zijn. Beide mannen leefden in de veronderstelling dat de parkeerplaatsen aan de straat voor hun bedrijfspand, deel uitmaakten van de openbare weg en vonden het daarom vreemd dat een particuliere beheerder zomaar om de privé gegevens van personen kon vragen. Maar het bleek voornamelijk om de bezetting ervan doordeweeks, zowel overdag als in de avonduren en in de weekenden te draaien. Het een en ander vond plaats op last van de brandweer en politie.

Het maakte de eventuele medewerking al wat minder verdacht, maar het leek ze toch beter om bij deze instanties nader te informeren waar de noodzaak van de gevraagde lijst precies lag. En wat er met de gegevens werd gedaan. Er werd hem op het hart gedrukt dat de brandweer er in geval van nood over moest kunnen beschikken. Ze zouden alleen dan hun werk optimaal kunnen uitvoeren en kennelijk was de lijst dus inderdaad noodzakelijk.

Een soortgelijk antwoord gaf de afdeling voorlichting van de politie, het zou inbraken en andere criminaliteit voorkomen. En niet onbelangrijk, het spaarde de installatie van camera's voor deze bewaking en dus een beambte voor het bekijken van de video's uit. De lijst leek hierdoor niet in strijd met welke regel dan ook dus besloten ze om 'm voor de afgesproken datum van 1 januari in orde te maken.

Overigens zit de man met zijn werkkamer aan de voorkant van het kantoorpand. Het biedt hem vanuit het raam dus een prachtig uitzicht op wie er dagelijks aankomt en 's middags weer vertrekt. Nog belangrijker, hij kon zo tamelijk eenvoudig op een lijst in de vensterbank noteren welke auto er bij welke persoon hoort. Daarbij was het dus gemakkelijk dat hij alle collega's minimaal van gezicht kent.

Hij kwam met de directeur overeen dat hij gedurende een drietal weken zijn waarnemingen bij zou houden en aan de hand daarvan de noodzakelijke gegevens op een definitieve lijst vast zou leggen. Zo kon hij het gevraagde papier eenvoudig maken. Het is niet belangrijk om te vermelden, maar omdat de vaste kantooruren nog van kracht waren, zou er nauwelijks werktijd mee verloren gaan. Iedereen kwam immers vrijwel gelijktijdig aan, zodat hij er zo nu en dan een kwartiertje eerder voor aanwezig hoefde te zijn op kantoor. Dat mocht ie eventueel compenseren door een keer wat vroeger weg te gaan. Zoiets was echter z'n eer te na, waardoor hij ervoor bedankte.

Fijntjes voegde hij eraan toe dat de directeur vanzelfsprekend de eerste keus zou krijgen voor een mooi plekje op de parkeerstrook, al waren alle plekken even groot. Hij stelde een plek voor die niet te ver van de voordeur lag, maar zijn baas zag af van zo'n voorkeursbehandeling. Heel modern stelde hij voor dat degene die het vaakst aanwezig was, het dichtste bij de voordeur terecht zou kunnen komen. Voornamelijk omdat die dus het meest gebruik moest maken van de faciliteit. Het zou iets te maken hebben met tijdverlies en dergelijke. De man kreeg gewoonweg de vrije hand om de zaken te regelen zoals het hem goed dunkte. Dit was niet tegen dovemansoren gezegd!

Omdat hij niet meer dan zeven minuten fietsen van het bedrijf verwijderd woont is het begrijpelijk dat de man nooit met de auto naar zijn werk gaat. Zelfs bij enorm slecht weer is het korter lopen onder een paraplu dan eerst instappen, omrijden via de rondweg naar het industriegebied en dan daar zoeken naar een plek om te parkeren. Het rijden gaat niet sneller, duurt zelfs langer omdat eerst de auto schoon moet gemaakt en betekent evengoed dat er door de regen of sneeuw gebaggerd moet worden. Zij het alleen het laatste stukje. Het maakt dat ie ervoor kiest om de hele weg te voet af te leggen.

Voor eventuele bezoekers reserveerde hij aan het einde van de straat een aantal plekken. Indien noodzakelijk konden daar ook personeelsleden, mensen zoals hij die uitsluitend zo nu en dan, mocht het eens niet anders kunnen bijvoorbeeld, met de auto naar de zaak komen, hun voertuig neer zetten.

De lijst moest namelijk het voorstel bevatten op welke plek welke auto voortaan geparkeerd zou gaan worden. Deze indeling zou ter zijner tijd door de beheerder met paaltjes worden vastgelegd. Netjes voor iedere aparte parkeerplaats een eigen houten paal met erop aangegeven het nummerbord van de betreffende auto. Die moest daar dus staan als de brandweer kwam of onverhoopt geroepen mocht worden. Het scheelde niet veel of er kwam ook een naam onder te staan, maar het bedrijf mocht er tegen een kleine vergoeding het eigen logo op laten aan brengen.

Half januari vorig jaar was het een en ander gereed. Een kleine week later pas viel het de eerste collega op dat de auto's op volgorde van kleur over de parkeerstrook verdeeld stonden. Netjes van zwart via diep blauw naar steeds lichtere varianten en groen. Dan na wit en geel verder naar donker oranje en rood. Toen iemand er iets van had gezegd, merkte ook de andere werknemers op wat de volgorde was geworden en dat het parkeerterrein op die manier een mooi spectrum aan kleuren bood. De man ging hierbij overigens vrijuit, want alleen hijzelf en de directeur waren maar op de hoogte van de hand die hij er in gehad zou kunnen hebben.

Zo hielden ze zich van de domme en lieten het erop lijken dat er een hogere macht, een niet nader te noemen medewerker van het bedrijf van de beheerder of gewoon toeval, aan te pas was gekomen bij de ontstane indeling.

Na de zomer van vorig jaar werd de kleurenpracht voor de eerste verstoord toen collega Johann in plaats van een gele plotseling een groenige auto aangeschaft bleek te hebben. Hij werd er vervolgens links en rechts op aangesproken dat hij de orde verstoord had met zijn toch enigszins ondoordachte aankoop. Hiermee bleek hij immers niet meer aan de zijde van de blauwe tinten te staan, maar was aan de andere kant van het tweetal witte terecht gekomen. Hij werd niet in de laatste plaats aangesproken door de man zelf, want die nam zijn kans op een grappige opmerking sowieso met verve waar.

Zomaar het bordje dat bij zijn gereserveerde plek hoorde verplaatsen bleek overigens niet zo eenvoudig. Bij de officiële instantie, die de brandweer toch is, liet het zich niet zomaar aanpassen. Dat diende met formulieren en stempels gepaard te gaan en voor slechts een auto leek dat teveel moeite. Maar het was vanzelfsprekend geen gezicht.

Pas in het najaar was het nodig om de lijst alsnog officieel bij te werken. Een nieuwe collega en nog twee aangeschafte wagens die de orde op het parkeerterrein verstoorden, maakten het wijzigen verantwoord. De verdeling van de kleuren werd erdoor hersteld, maar de verrassing was er natuurlijk wel vanaf. Toch bleek men aan de aanblik van de voorzijde van het gebouw gehecht te zijn geraakt. De harmonie die ervan uit ging had intussen vertrouwen ingeboezemd. Toen deze eenmaal weer hersteld was, leek er een zucht van verlichting op te gaan tussen de werknemers van de verschillenden afdelingen.

Een aantal jaren hiervoor, het was begin maart maar in welk jaar het allemaal speelde is niet meer zo duidelijk, kwam er een zending binnen met een monster uit Japan. Het hele jaar door was zoiets het geval en gewoontegetrouw was het de man die de verantwoording kreeg over het uitpakken en installeren van zo'n nieuw ding. Hooguit vroeg hij de hulp van een collega bij het sjouwen met de doos of liet een van hen zich als vrijwilliger hiervoor zien, als hij ermee bezig was. Overigens kwam er zowat iedere maand een monster binnen en de verrassing was er meestal snel af.

De doos werd steevast in het lege kamertje naast die van de man gezet en dan wees het zich vanzelf wat er verder mee gebeurde. Soms mocht het nieuwtje stof gaan vangen in het magazijn, bijvoorbeeld als het niet 'in het programma' bleek te passen. Niet alle monsters waren namelijk bruikbaar op de Nederlandse markt. Of ze waren reeds leverbaar bij de concurrentie. Duurder of goedkoper deed er dan meestal niet meer toe, 't hing voornamelijk af van wat er 'nog meer' aan producten verkocht werd binnen het bedrijf.

Noch op het kantoor van de directeur, de kamer van zijn secretaresse of in de grote vergaderzaal was er plaats om het gevaarte, nadat het eenmaal in elkaar was gezet een 'ruimte opslokkend ding', op te stellen. Het apparaat een passende plek geven bleek dus een lastige kwestie. De kamer van de man was daarom de enig logisch overgebleven ruimte om 'm met goed fatsoen met zijn computer te verbinden.

Die computer stond er trouwens voornamelijk omdat hij er met de tekstverwerker op kon werken. Hoe onvoorstelbaar nu ook, het was er een van de totaal vier die in de firma werden gebruikt. Indertijd wellicht een indrukwekkend aantal maar tegenwoordig, nu iedereen er minimaal een op z'n bureau heeft staan, een lachertje. Ze hadden er twee voor de administratie, een bij de secretaresse en die andere dus bij hem op de kamer.

Zoals beschreven kwamen nieuwe producten normaliter in de kamer naast die van de man terecht. Alle medewerkers, de meest nieuwsgierigen eerst, kwamen zich er dan aan vergapen. Het behoorde tot zijn taken om er z'n licht over te laten schijnen en er een gebruiksklare machine van te maken. Het nieuwe apparaat verhuisde dan enige tijd later vanzelf naar de showroom. Daar werd met een korte demonstratie, het ding vervolgens geïntroduceerd.

De nieuwste aanwinst zou misschien het begin van een 'nieuwe lijn' gaan vormen. Een reeks gaan vormen met andere producten binnen de rest van het programma van de firma. Enige omzichtigheid diende dus in acht genomen te worden met het eventuele tonen ervan aan bezoekers en klanten. Of aan een concurrent die 'toevallig' zijn licht mocht komen opsteken. Voornamelijk omdat er een computer voor de werking nodig was, kwam het nieuwe ding zoals beschreven bij hem op de kamer te staan.

Het was binnen het bedrijf niet de gewoonte om zeg maar, 'voor de fanfare uit te lopen'. Alleen de man en een aantal collega's van de afdeling inkoop waren dus op de hoogte van het doel van dit speciale apparaat. Zo ging dat meestal en het maakte de omgang met hem aantrekkelijk, als je op de hoogte wilde blijven van alle nieuwigheden die eraan zaten te komen. Omdat niemand door deze werkwijze exact wist waar het ding voor diende, stierf de belangstelling ervoor een snelle dood. Zeker toen er nog nieuwere handigheden waren binnengekomen die wèl aan het assortiment toegevoegd zouden worden.

Van veel monsters stond al wel het een en ander bekend en men kon dus vanuit ervaring, met eerdere apparatuur bedenken wat ermee mogelijk was. In de meeste gevallen betrof het namelijk een nieuwere of meer uitgebreide versie van de reeds binnen het zogenaamde programma gevoerde apparaten. Het maakte de verrassing aanzienlijk minder, maar vooral de verkopers zagen er al snel allerlei mogelijkheden in om hun omzet ermee te verhogen.

Dat was met dit nieuwe monster niet duidelijk en geen van de collega's taalde meer naar het immense ding toen eenmaal de nog nieuwere apparaten in de showroom terecht waren gekomen. Die machines, noem het desnoods speeltjes, moesten met voorrang behandeld worden. Er dienden trainingen en cursussen voorbereid te worden. Alleen al om ze te kunnen verkopen. Deze procedure maakte deel uit van wat ze binnen 't bedrijf 'het programma' noemden. De apparatuur moest immers zo snel mogelijk bij klanten gedemonstreerd kunnen worden. En, niet onbelangrijk op de juiste manier geïnstalleerd.

De voorbereiding hiervoor viel onder de verantwoording van de afdeling met de prachtige naam 'onderzoek en ontwikkeling' en die ressorteerde geheel onder de man z'n verantwoordelijkheid. Zij het dat hij het werk vrijwel geheel solo deed. In de gevallen dat hij er niet helemaal uit leek te komen, was er telkens een collega van de afdeling verkoop, een van de vertegenwoordigers bijvoorbeeld, die hem met raad en daad terzijde kwam staan.

Door de manier van werken lag de prioriteit telkens ergens anders. Men concentreerde zich met name op de nieuwigheden en vergat dus dat ene ding dat hij bij zichzelf op kantoor neergezet had. Het bedrijf bestaat van de verkoop en zoals overal heeft men voornamelijk belangstelling voor zaken als omzet en te behalen verkoop bonussen. Mede daardoor was er besloten om het apparaat niet op te nemen in dat al eerder genoemde programma.

Nu het er toch stond kon hij zo nu en dan de tijd nemen om de mysteries ervan beter te leren kennen. Men wist dat 't de mogelijkheid bood om documenten te kopiëren naar de computer, maar dat was alles. We noemen zulke apparaten natuurlijk scanners en vinden ze nu heel gewoon, maar indertijd waren ze nog tamelijk bijzonder. Een fotokopieerapparaat was dat immers al!

Hij merkte al snel dat gescande afbeeldingen zich ermee lieten vergroten, verkleinen, omdraaien of spiegelen. Toen hij de bijbehorende soft-ware op zijn computer beter leerde doorgronden, werden hem allengs meer functies duidelijk die met de wonderlijke machine en zijn computer mogelijk bleken. Het ligt dus voor de hand dat hij ook 'applicaties' tegenkwam die hem uitzicht boden op het uitvoeren van zijn werk of zelfs het voorbereiden van een grap.

De opmaak en vormgeving voor de uitnodiging van het jaarlijkse bedrijfsuitje bijvoorbeeld, liet zich er prachtig mee uitwerken. Eenmaal door de drukker op papier gezet zag het er uitermate professioneel, indrukwekkend zelfs, uit. Voor de man was het intussen een karweitje van niks, maar in al z'n bescheidenheid wilde hij geen goede sier maken met z'n verworven vaardigheid.

Ieder jaar zag de uitnodigingsbrief er vooral zakelijk uit en deze keer was ie 'gewoon iets beter' uitgevallen. Met actuele plaatjes, verschillende letter groottes en het bedrijfslogo er prominent voorop. Er is voor alles een eerste keer en wat betreft de uitnodiging zag die er ditmaal 'nogal gelikt' uit. Feitelijk maakte het niet uit wie en hoe die 'm had gemaakt. Het ging er voornamelijk om dat de personeelsleden wisten wat het programma voor het jaarlijkse uitje inhield. Voor de meeste collega's was wat er op het menu stond voor het afsluitende diner slechts belangrijk.

Zo zou de bus, een uit een boekje gekopieerd plaatje, om half negen vertrekken vanaf het parkeerterrein bij het kantoor, een plattegrond van het industrieterrein met ingekleurd het kantoor. Als grapje had hij een kleurenspectrum als achtergrond genomen voor het parkeerterrein. Na de koffie onderweg gingen ze, in groepjes een speurtocht maken over de Loonse en Drunense duinen. Deze waren verluchtigd met de kopie van een stafkaart. Daarna een uitgebreid 'Brabants thee buffet' en de dag werd gewoontegetrouw afgesloten met het etentje in Voorbrug. Daarna weer terug naar het bedrijf waar ze tussen half twaalf en twaalf uur aan zouden komen.

De man had er veel werk van gemaakt en een tweetal foto's van het jaar ervoor stonden op de achterkant. Die hadden tot voor kort op het mededelingenbord bij de kantine gehangen en een oplettende kijker had er sporen van de gaatjes die de punaises erin hadden achtergelaten, op kunnen waarnemen. Al had hij die plekjes dus zoveel mogelijk weg geprobeerd te werken met de soft-ware op z'n computer.

Binnen het bedrijf bestond weinig belangstelling om de markt met allerlei nieuwe apparatuur te betreden. Hun handel richtte zich vooral op minder spe-

149

cialistische producten dan computers. Indertijd zeker, werden die toch nog voornamelijk bruikbaar geacht voor de administratie en aan administratieve taken verwante zaken. Mede daardoor raakte langzamerhand een ruimere aandacht voor de machine bij de man op z'n kamer op de achtergrond.

Soms kwam een collega bij hem en informeerde er dan met al dan niet geveinsde belangstelling naar, maar het werd een algemeen aanvaard punt dat de markt voor dergelijke apparaten verdeeld raakte over de zogenaamd grote merken. Dat ze het dus maar beter daaraan over konden laten, ze namen het voetstoots aan. Hele jonge collega's zagen wel iets in de groeiende computermarkt, maar ze waren in de minderheid en maakten geen deel uit van de directie. Die deed het af als "nieuwigheid die wel zou overgaan".

Zoals reeds opgemerkt vanouds wordt er binnen het bedrijf niet hard aan de weg getimmerd in de richting van moderne techniek. Men draait een goede omzet en er wordt flink winst gemaakt met wat ze hebben en hadden. De behoefte aan veranderingen was er dus niet zo groot.

De man kon als antwoord op de getoonde interesse en geheel in overeenstemming met de mening van de directie, verklaren dat ze er 'niet veel' meer mee gingen doen. De functies van 't ding pasten naar die mening niet in de 'bedrijfsfilosofie'. Het apparaat zou voornamelijk 'in de weg staan' en waarschijnlijk binnenkort opgeruimd of weg gegooid worden. Vaak gaf hij met een puffend geluid aan er feitelijk schoon genoeg van te hebben om het reusachtige apparaat nog langer op zijn kamer te laten staan verstoffen.

Hierdoor afgeschrikt wilde zo'n collega de zware taak zeker niet meer van hem overnemen. Omdat de man de ruimte op zijn kamer geheel voor zichzelf alleen had, wist niemand dus exact wanneer of hoe vaak de machine daadwerkelijk ingeschakeld stond. Door deze omstandigheid bleven de eventuele mogelijkheden volledig in nevelen gehuld.

Allengs en al 'hobbyend' ontdekte de man dat er nog tot een flink formaat bestaande plaatjes mee te bewerken waren. Feitelijk werden de mogelijkheden uitsluitend beperkt tot het formaat van de glasplaat van de scanner-unit en die bedroeg bijna een meter bij een meter. Ook de bijbehorende soft-ware bleek tamelijk geavanceerd en hij toverde door gewoonweg te proberen, allerlei geavanceerde mogelijkheden tevoorschijn. Zo kwam de optie om met de machine op meerder formaten te kunnen printen bijvoorbeeld pas enige weken na de installatie aan het licht. Dat het apparaat daartoe in staat was, werd hem duidelijk toen er uit de verpakking een paar 'patronen' ofwel cartridges tevoorschijn kwamen. Daar bleek inkt in te zitten en ze zaten er natuurlijk niet voor niets bij!

Met enig passen en meten en door eenvoudig de Japanse plaatjes in overeenstemming te brengen met wat hij in zijn handen had, kreeg de man ook deze ongekende mogelijkheid onder de knie. Het droeg er aan bij dat hij nu proef versies, zoals bijvoorbeeld die uitnodigingen voor dat uitje, er compleet op kon voorbereiden en uitwerken. Dat hij het ontwerp uitgewerkt en dus klaar voor de drukker kon aanleveren, zonder dat daar anderen bij nodig waren.

Dat de fabrikant van zulke apparaten er van huis uit zorg voor draagt dat de uiteindelijke bediening niet te ingewikkeld uitpakt, was hem vanuit zijn functie vanzelfsprekend bekend. En dat zelfs een kind na wat aanwijzingen eenvoudig de was moet kunnen doen ook. Maar de oorspronkelijke angst voor dit soort geavanceerde apparaten had hem eenvoudigweg parten gespeeld bij het doorgronden ervan. Daar was de desinteresse binnen het bedrijf dus nog bovenop gekomen. Het had hem daardoor grotendeels in de hoek van de 'goed bedoelende hobbyist' gedrukt.

Door knip- en plakwerk, overigens niet helemaal zoals tegenwoordig in Windows en dergelijke de gewoonte is geworden via de soft-ware, maar nog letterlijk met een schaar en echte lijm, wist de man een reeks certificaten te vervaardigen. Omdat die vervolgens qua uitgeprinte grootte niet beperkt bleven tot een heel of half A4'tje zagen deze er reuze officieel uit. Trots reikte hij er soms een een uit aan een medewerker.

Kortom de mogelijkheden bleken gedurende zijn experimenten vrijwel onbeperkt. Zo maakte hij speciaal voor een collega uit het magazijn, een rijbewijs die hem toekwam voor het interne vervoer op de vorkheftruck. Door de jongen z'n handicap zat een echt 'roze papiertje' of ander certificaat er niet in, maar nu kon hij desgevraagd een officieel uitziend bewijs leveren van zijn vaardigheden op het voertuig. Trots deed hij dat vervolgens te pas en onpas, maar niemand stoorde zich eraan omdat hij er zo van groeide.

Voor de vertegenwoordigers lagen er op het einde van de zomer, bij de aanvang van het verkoop offensief dat er in het najaar zou volgen, een 'diploma' klaar waarop hun scores aan verkopen als prestatie aangetekend waren. Met een cijferlijst als op een ouderwets schoolrapport! Alleen het persoonlijk bedoelde berichtje van de juffrouw ontbrak eraan, maar in overleg met de intussen in vertrouwen genomen directeur waren er wèl doelen vastgesteld. Omdat dat er vanzelfsprekend erg Amerikaans uitzag groeide de vrees dat de firma ook in de toekomst op die leest zou worden geschoeid.

Toen een van de inktpatronen leeg raakte, kon de man nog wel overstappen op het intensievere gebruik van de resterende kleuren, maar langzamerhand raakten ook die een voor een op. Het apparaat bleef daardoor vaker werkeloos op zijn kamer staan. Heel jammer natuurlijk, maar omdat ie niet in het assortiment werd opgenomen was het onmogelijk om de cartridges, te vervangen.

Commercieel waren nergens passende exemplaren te verkrijgen, vullen ging evenmin en dat bracht de grap tot een snel einde. Wel heeft de man voor zichzelf en een naaste medewerker een paar diploma's vervaardigd.

Voor originelen kon hij uit de voorraad CV's putten die ze van sollicitanten bij de afdeling personeelszaken buitmaakten. Overigens heeft hij er nooit een als officieel durven aan te wenden en hangen ze dus te vergelen aan de muur van zijn werkkamer of liggen te verstoffen tussen de papieren thuis. Het bedrijf heeft de machine kort daarna ter vernietiging aangeboden bij het grofvuil.

Nu ze er binnen het bedrijf gewend aan zijn geraakt dat de collega's te pas en te onpas wel of niet aanwezig zijn binnen het kantoor, is de behoefte om onderling grappen te maken of gezamenlijk een practical-joke uit te voeren wat aan het verminderen. Maar dat herstelt zich misschien over een tijdje als iedereen weer terug is van vakantie. Nu zijn er nog een flink aantal mensen die nog weg moeten, net vertrokken zijn of dankzij al hun harde werken alweer toe zijn aan een kort uitje.

Tuin

De man stuurt de kruiwagen over het paadje langs het grasveld. Het pad leidt naar de twee boompjes die achteraan in de tuin, vlakbij de vijver staan. Behoedzaam probeert hij het wiel midden op de tegels te houden. Het is nog tamelijk lastig om er niet vanaf te glijden en alsnog met de grove rubberband op het gras terecht te komen. De grond is van alle regen die er de afgelopen dagen is gevallen nogal drassig geworden en daarom is hij bang dat ie de tuin er teveel mee zal beschadigen. Hij heeft trouwens opgemerkt dat het gras intussen te lang is geworden en dat hij het daarom nodig weer eens moet maaien. Als hij de halmen nu plat rijdt duurt het minstens een paar dagen voordat ze zich weer enigszins zullen hebben opgericht. Er speelt dus een soort eigenbelang dat hij zo omzichtig te werk gaat. Het zal het fatsoeneren morgen minder moeilijk maken. Als het droog blijft.

Hij heeft er een hekel aan als de tuin er zo slordig, onverzorgd bij ligt. Helaas is er de laatste weken niets van terecht gekomen om een begin te maken met de boel eens flink op te knappen. Er heeft zich geen tijd en gelegenheid voorgedaan om bijvoorbeeld minstens een uurtje of halve middag aan het onderhoud te besteden. Vandaag heeft hij zich echter voorgenomen om ten minste de Taxus en Hulst boom te gaan snoeien. Eindelijk, moet hij toegeven, want het is alweer een tijdlang nodig dat hij er wat extra aandacht aan besteedt.

Op het internet heeft hij een paar maanden geleden al opgezocht wat de beste periode was om ze in fatsoen te brengen of hoe hij zoiets het beste aanpakt, maar intussen is het optimale moment alweer geruime tijd verstreken. De beslommeringen en het slechte weer van de afgelopen dagen hebben hem natuurlijk eveneens verhinderd om er daadwerkelijk aan te beginnen.

Bij het herinrichten van de tuin, intussen een flink aantal jaren geleden, wilde zijn vrouw de toen nog twee kleine boompjes laten staan. Alle struiken met doornen maar vooral de rozen, waaraan ze immers altijd al een uitgesproken hekel had gehad, mochten met wortel en tak verwijderd worden. De boompjes echter, die mochten blijven staan. Het leek haar een goed idee om ze tijdens hun groei in een bolvorm te leiden. Ze wilde er een "bal op een stam" van maken en hij moet toegeven dat ze er langzamerhand aardig in is geslaagd om ze zover te krijgen.

De boompjes zijn allebei tot een goede twee en een halve meter hoogte gekomen en zien er vanaf alle kanten inderdaad rond uit. Eerst had hij er wat vreemd tegenaan gekeken dat je bomen en struiken, feitelijk planten in het algemeen, moest en kon verzorgen. Al is er in 't geval van de boompjes voornamelijk sprake van 'naar je hand zetten'.

Zoals zijn vrouw ze heeft gesnoeid, geleid in hun huidige vorm, valt er niet meer te spreken van een natuurlijke verschijning. Maar het resultaat, inderdaad een bol op een stam zoals ze zich gewenst had, misstaat niet. Het tegennatuurlijke valt alleen op als er rondom en bovenop de bol kleine takjes aan het uitlopen zijn. Als de harmonie van de perfecte vorm verstoord wordt. De rest van de tijd valt het uitsluitend op dat ze er mooi rond en blijvend groen uitzien. Dat hoort er bij dit soort planten bij.

Tweemaal per jaar klom ze ervoor op het trapje om de bovenste uitlopers in te korten. Ze deed dat met de snoeizaag die ze gekocht hadden om er dikkere takken mee weg te halen van een stam. Door het bijknippen van ook de kortere takjes onderaan herstelde ze vervolgens de door haar gewenste vorm van de bomen. Daar leken ze trouwens sneller te groeien dan bovenop, maar hij heeft daarover niets bijzonders kunnen vinden.

Van huis uit heeft hij nooit zoveel aan tuinieren gedaan of erom gegeven, maar hier in het grote huis hebben ze de tuin van meet af aan grondig aangepakt. Al gelijk samen, terwijl zijn vrouw zelf ook nauwelijks een achtergrond bleek te hebben in de omgang met zogenaamd groen, dus met planten en struiken. Hij verzorgde het grove werk en heeft naast het terras ook de vijver aangelegd. Evenals het heuveltje waarop ze verschillende kruiden liet groeien. De grond ervoor kwam uit de kuil van die vijver.

Het kwam er eigenlijk op neer dat hij haar plannen uitvoerde en zijn vrouw zich beperkte tot het periodieke snoeien. En vanzelfsprekend het bij elkaar zoeken van de juiste planten die ze er wilde hebben. Zorgvuldig hield ze in allerlei boeken de verschillende groei snelheden of periodes van bloei bij.

Op vakantie verzamelde ze zaadjes van planten die ze vervolgens in hun tuin probeerde op te kweken. Daarvoor liet ze ze eerst kiemen en kweekte ze de kleine scheuten op in bakken. In de serre of het kasje dat ze ervoor naast het terras hadden ingericht. Ze legde er telkens erg veel ijver bij aan de dag zodat het resultaat dat ze ermee wist te behalen, hem regelmatig verbaasd heeft laten staan. Hoe een plantje binnen een paar weken van niets meer dan een paar korrels, uit kon groeien tot een bundel stengels, bladeren en bloemen.

Haar ouders hadden maar een bescheiden tuintje achter hun stadswoning, dus van huis uit beschikte ze niet over een geërfde aanleg voor echte groene vingers. En die van hem woonden tweehoog op een flat en waren dus nooit verder gekomen dan wat planten in de vensterbank of jaarlijks een bak rode en witte geraniums aan de reling rond het balkon. Een volkstuin naast een buitenwijk van de stad had tot de mogelijkheden behoord. Bijvoorbeeld omdat het feitelijk om de hoek was, maar het lag niet in de aard van zijn vader om

154

aan zulke dingen mee te doen. Al had hij er dus het volste recht op als hij zich tenminste durfde te laten leiden door de statuten van de woningbouw vereniging waarbij ze hun flat huurden.

De man en zijn vrouw hebben zich met de aanschaf van hun nieuwe huis een flinke lap grond naast, voor en erachter verworven. Het zag er indertijd sterk verwaarloosd uit dat wel, maar volgens de makelaar konden ze er voor lange tijd al hun 'zorgen' aan kwijt. "Als ze er wat van wilden maken en het hun passie zou worden of misschien al was."

Wijs hebben ze zich er niet over uitgelaten. De tijd zou hen wel leren of hij gelijk kreeg. De hele boel laten betegelen ging ze echter te ver, dus die optie hebben ze naast zich neergelegd. Naar een flink terras ging hun wens nog wel uit. Ze hebben er bijna twee jaar over gedaan om allerlei verschillende mogelijkheden tegen elkaar af te wegen. Hoe die zich vervolgens moesten laten uitwerken, zocht ze op in boeken en boekjes uit de bibliotheek. Vooral 's winters kon ze zich daar vol toewijding op werpen. Het kostte haar dan weinig moeite om allerlei plannen tot in detail uit te zoeken. Ze maakte aan de hand van haar bevindingen ontwerptekeningen en haalde alles tevoorschijn dat noodzakelijk was om tot een grondige voorbereiding te komen.

Vlak nadat ze hun intrek in de woning namen, hebben ze bij wijze van eerste ontginning een groot deel van het grasveld omgespit. Het was noodzakelijk om de ergste wildernis van overwoekerde struiken, veel te ver uitgelopen begroeiing die zeker weg mocht en een half verzakt hek, op te ruimen. De vrijgekomen grond liet zich in het erop volgende voorjaar eenvoudig inrichten en benutten als moestuin. Ze hebben zelfs geprobeerd om er aardappelen in te verbouwen, maar al hun ingespannen zwoegwerk ten spijt was er dat jaar niet meer dan een kleine vier kilo hele kleine aardappeltjes vanaf gekomen. Eenmaal gewassen en geschild was het zelfs minder dan dat.

Er was hen op het tuincentrum een aanzienlijk grotere opbrengst voorgespiegeld, maar het zielige bakje aardappeltjes bleek net voldoende voor een tweetal maaltijden. Geen stamppot of kruimig gekookt met wat jus erover, maar gebakken toch heel smakelijk. Helaas met een hoop schilwerk omdat de knolletjes zo klein gebleven waren.

Misschien was de bodem van de tuin toch minder kleiig dan waar ze eerst vanuit waren gegaan? Of hadden ze meer en vaker moeten mesten?

Waarschijnlijk had een heel ander soort piepers het er beter gedaan?

Toch was de kweek van sla, tomaten en kruiden wel heel aardig gelukt. Deze aanplant hebben ze dan ook een aantal jaren achter elkaar volgehouden. Netjes elke keer een rij nieuwe sla plantjes, om niet maar een week een heleboel en dan verder niks meer als oogst over te houden. Winterpenen erbij voor de natuurlijke afweer tegen vliegjes en andere, nog kwalijkere insecten. Ze had het allemaal opgezocht in haar boeken.

Op de oorspronkelijke plek van de aardappels bleken bonen het overigens wèl heel goed te doen. Ook de aardbeien, geplant in een klein zonnig hoekje van de tuin en daarom als Beatle fan zijn eigen 'Strawberry Fields', met wilde en verschillende gecultiveerde soorten door elkaar, leverde iedere zomer voldoende oogst op om er zo nu en dan een plakje cake mee te beleggen. Vanzelfsprekend met een flinke dot slagroom er bovenop als finishing touch.

Nog steeds staan er achter het vijvertje wat tijm, salie, oregano en rozemarijn plantjes. Ze leveren door het jaar heen telkens nog een handvol bruikbare kruiderij op. Vers geplukt als het seizoen er is en in het najaar de rest van de opbrengst te drogen gehangen in de schuur. Vooraan, vlak achter het huis op de rand van wat ze hun terras zijn gaan noemen, zetten ze ieder jaar een paar potten met peterselie, basilicum en selderij erin neer. Ze moeten er telkens een strijd met de slakken om voeren, willen ze er zelf iets van kunnen oogsten, maar ook qua decoratie staat het erg aardig. De vier à vijf bakken met jonge fris groene plantjes verzachten visueel de overgang tussen het betegelde en de rest, het natuurlijke deel, van de tuin.

Afgelopen zondagmiddag heeft hij de accu's van de elektrische snoeischaar opgeladen. Nu vervoert hij het ding samen met een emmer, het trapje, de schep en een hark naar de achterkant van de tuin. Alles heeft hij uit de schuur gepakt om de bomen weer terug in hun vorm te brengen. De uitlopers van de taxus en ook de verse blaadjes van de hulst zijn niet meer mooi lichtgroen, maar nog wel goed herkenbaar als teveel. Ze moeten eraf, zodat de bolle vorm weer herkenbaar terugkeert.

Links en rechts van hem kijkt hij naar wat er is overgebleven van het grasveld. De aanblik maakt dat hij moet glimlachen om het plan dat ze ooit een kleine tractor hadden willen kopen. Het had hen allebei namelijk wel een leuk idee geleken, om zittend op zo'n ding, het gras te maaien. Of om er bijvoorbeeld de grond mee te verticuleren. Niet dat ze wisten wat het inhield, maar het leek ze een leuke bezigheid en ze wilden toen de tuin nog grondig aanpakken en dus gaan onderhouden.

Het gaf ze een alibi om er zulke speciale apparatuur voor aan te schaffen, maar het zou natuurlijk gekkenwerk zijn om voor zo'n kleine postzegel van een gazon een machinepark neer te zetten! Met hun gewone hand maaier bleek het veldje al te klein om er eens flink voor uit te kunnen halen. En tot nog toe hebben ze met drie tot vier maal per jaar op die manier maaien, kunnen volstaan. In hooguit een uurtje heen en weer karren met het ding en later grof afwerken met de heggenschaar, is het werk gepiept. Ze hebben er niet eens een elektrische voor hoeven te kopen.

Eenmaal per jaar 't afsteken van de randen langs de borders. Hij doet hij er niet eens drie uur over om met handwerk het hele grasveld weer tiptop in orde te maken. In het voorjaar als het weer er goed genoeg voor is. De ervaring

156

heeft geleerd dat je er dan ook nog gemakkelijk tussendoor een kopje koffie bij kunt drinken. Terwijl je ermee bezig bent dus en rustig aan doet. Dan in de nazomer nog eens als het gras te lang is geworden of, zoals nu aan het begin van de herfst, omdat het echt nodig is.

Maar in de boeken over tuinen wordt vaak gerept over behandelingen die bij een flinke tuin het beste met een machine kunnen worden uitgevoerd. Vandaar hun terugkerende wens om dat tractortje ooit eens aan te schaffen. Ten minste een paar keer per jaar hebben ze het erover gehad, maar verder dan het bezoek aan een showroom zijn ze er niet mee gekomen. Op vakantie in Duitsland was er eens een bouwmarkt waar ze ze opgesteld hadden staan. Als proef hebben ze er even een voor een op plaats genomen, maar ook toen vonden ze het een veel te grote grote aanschaf. Zelfs het allerkleinste model en hoe aantrekkelijk misschien ook geprijsd in die aanbieding. De kinderen waren erbij en ook die vonden het een leuk dingetje. Toch moesten ze verstandig zijn en hoe kregen ze het ding zonder aanhanger helemaal in Nederland?

Kort bedachten ze dat ze er met de buren ooit een uit konden zoeken. Om 'm dan, alsof ze een coöperatie waren, met hen te gaan gebruiken. Het is er echter niet van gekomen, bleek nooit nodig en kon dus iedere keer worden afgedaan als een bevlieging. Te duur in aanschaf of gebruik, geen ruimte voor opslag in de garage, veel onderhoud en last but not least volledig onnodig.

De laatste paar stappen naar de boompjes toe moet hij toch van het pad af en over het gras lopen. Inderdaad zakt de kruiwagen enigszins in de zachte grond weg en raakt het gras vertrapt, maar er zit niets anders op. Voorzichtig zet hij het trapje naast de eerste boom neer en duwt met zijn voet op de onderste trede om te voelen of het ding stevig genoeg blijft staan. Misschien kan hij voor de veiligheid beter nog een paar planken gaan halen. Dat kost meer schade aan het gras, maar dan blijft het trapje natuurlijk wel beter staan. Hij besluit het erop te wagen. Als hij niet te ver opzij leunt zal het ding vast niet omvallen en mocht hij er niet meer bij kunnen, dan kan het desnoods altijd nog.

Nog voordat hij de derde sport bereikt heeft voelt hij hoe de achtste pootjes dieper wegzakken, maar dan wordt de ondergrond plotseling stevig genoeg en stopt het. Hij stapt op het platte stukje en brengt de snoeimachine in de aanslag. Voorzichtig maait hij links en rechts de takjes en takken weg zodat de bolvorm weer herkenbaar zal worden. Het lukt hem zelfs om zonder zijn evenwicht te verliezen, verder naar opzij te leunen. Naar voren reiken gaat ook goed omdat hij daarbij met zijn buik tegen de boom steun vindt.

Als hij niet meer verder durft, klimt hij van het trapje af en verplaatst 'm iets verder naar de zijkant. Daar vandaan kan hij ook de hulst boom onder handen nemen, hij hoeft er zich alleen maar een kwartslag voor de draaien. Als hij het trapje optilt duwt hij met zijn voet de gaten die er in het gras ontstaan zijn, dicht. Ze lopen al langzaam vol met water.

157

Na ongeveer anderhalf uur is hij klaar met de taxus en heeft hij ook de hulst voor meer dan twee derde in vorm geknipt. Hij is even op het pad terug gestapt en bekijkt het resultaat. Er is geen reden om ontevreden te zijn, de ronde vorm is helemaal terug en als het zo verder gaat moet de rest van het werk niet meer dan nog een uurtje duren. Hij besluit om alvast het afgeknipte loof onder de taxus boom op te rapen en doet de werk handschoenen aan. De hark legt hij tijdelijk in het gras, daar kan hij straks de laatste takjes mee bij elkaar vegen. Misschien laat het gras zich er zelfs weer wat mee rechtop zetten. Terwijl hij aan het werk is bedenkt ie dat het misschien handiger geweest was als hij een zeil of doek onder de boompjes had gelegd. Dan was het snoeisel waarschijnlijk makkelijker op te rapen. Zij deed dat eigenlijk ook altijd.

Als de kruiwagen vol is rijdt hij ermee naar de compostbak achter de schuur. Die heeft hij drie jaar geleden voor haar gekocht. Ze wilde toen die hoop 'ongeregelde rotzooi' niet meer tegen de muur aan hebben. Het moest er intussen maar eens "netjes" uit gaan zien en dat kon beter met zo'n speciale bak. Een paar dagen ervoor hadden ze op de televisie gezien dat zulke bakken bestonden. Het ding bleek weliswaar van plastic te zijn en zag er in de winkel niet echt mooi uit, maar op de verpakking stond vermeld dat het materiaal waaruit ie is vervaardigd voor 100% was gerecycled. En dat de bak zich eenvoudig zou laten inpassen in iedere omgeving. Dat blijkt in de praktijk inderdaad het geval. Het valt de man nogmaals op onder het naderbij lopen.

Indertijd waren het deze argumenten waarmee ze hun aanschaf hadden verantwoord. Indien gewenst kon hij er ter zijner tijd een houten omheining omheen timmeren om de bak aan het zicht te onttrekken. Dat was in de praktijk dus niet nodig. Op z'n huidige plek achter de schuur staat de bak al grotendeels buiten het zicht en eigenlijk valt het ding er inderdaad niet op. Na een paar maanden had zijn vrouw er trouwens al de eerste compost uit kunnen scheppen, dus daarmee werd het nut al voldoende bewezen.

Omdat hij toch bezig was, heeft de man ook meteen het buxus haagje aan de achterkant van de tuin weer in fatsoen geknipt. Vanuit de woonkamer is die net zichtbaar onder de bolvormige bomen door en nu die er weer als vanouds uitzien wilde hij de rest afmaken. Het schemerde al een beetje toen hij eindelijk klaar was met het opruimen.

Zorgvuldig heeft hij het gereedschap schoongemaakt en weer op zijn plaats in de schuur teruggezet. Het is kwart voor zeven en qua etenstijd is dat tamelijk laat voor zijn doen, maar de inspanning heeft hem tot rust gebracht. Ondanks het vele werk dat hij zojuist heeft verricht is hij niet moe, hij voelt zich eerder voldaan. Straks kan hij waarschijnlijk heel goed een pizza opwarmen, dan is er nu even tijd om rustig een biertje te drinken. Hij zal er de krant bij pakken en 't zal exact zo zijn als het er vroeger aan toeging. De man in de serre met zijn drankje, leesbril en de krant.

158

Intussen was zijn vrouw dan meestal bezig in de keuken. Geduldig wachtte ze erop tot hij haar gezelschap kwam houden. "Om te helpen bij het roeren" zoals hij het noemde. Het was hun grapje en stamde uit de tijd dat de kinderen klein waren.

Hij was dan even ervoor thuisgekomen uit zijn werk en was zogezegd toe aan een 'momentje rust'. Liefdevol gunde zijn vrouw hem het half uurtje voor zichzelf. Ze hield zich op de achtergrond met haar huiselijke beslommeringen bezig, maakte bijvoorbeeld alvast een 'mise en place' in de keuken of ging op de slaapkamer verder met het opvouwen van de was. Ze "plande haar dag er omheen", vertelde ze weleens. Samen het eten klaarmaken was hun geliefde bezigheid en elke dag zagen ze uit naar het moment om ermee te beginnen.

De man is in de serre op de bank gaan zitten, maar staat meteen weer op. Hij loopt naar de kelder en pakt er een biertje uit de krat. Zijn keuze komt uit op een dubbel gebrouwen kloosterbier. Vorige week heeft hij samen met zijn dochter een aantal verschillende soorten ingeslagen bij de groothandel, er is dus genoeg keuze. Onderweg terug naar zijn zitplaats haalt hij een glas uit de kast. De opener moet ergens naast de bank op het richeltje liggen, die hoeft hij er dus niet bij te zoeken. Hij zet het flesje op de tafel naast het glas.

Op de mat bij de voordeur moet de krant liggen, die gaat hij er nog even bij pakken. Met alles compleet neemt hij eindelijk plaats en maakt het zich gemakkelijk. Als hij zich tegen de rugleuning aan laat zakken en naar buiten kijkt voelt hij pas zijn spieren. Zoveel beweging als vanmiddag, heeft hij de laatste maanden niet meer gehad. Zijn rug lijkt opeens stijf te worden en hij kan een voor een de spieren achterop zijn benen, in z'n dij en kuiten, aanwijzen. Vlak boven zijn hiel gloeien de pezen na van de inspanning die het evenwicht houden bovenop het trapje hem heeft gekost.

De krant laat hij nog even liggen, hij pakt de opener die keurig op z'n plaats ligt, maakt het flesje ermee open en schenkt zich het biertje in. Hij kijkt hoe de schuimlaag zich vormt, dan neemt ie een grote slok en laat zijn rug opnieuw tegen de leuning van de bank rusten.

Iets meer dan een jaar geleden, het was net als vandaag een 'mooie najaarsdag na een periode met aanhoudend regen' geweest, zat hij ook op deze bank. Volgens de gewoonte nam hij het er even van en genoot van zijn dagelijkse momentje 'rust en bezinning'. Terwijl hij er zat hield zijn vrouw zich in de keuken bezig met uien snijden of andere voorbereidingen voor het koken.

Iedere dag deed ze dat immers en zo zorgde zij ervoor dat de ingrediënten klaar stonden om te worden toebereid. De afgelopen jaren begonnen ze daar altijd om kwart voor zes exact mee en zij trof daarvoor de voorbereidingen. De man voegde zich dan bij haar en samen maakten ze het eten klaar. Soms bakte hij alleen maar de aardappels of lette op de stukken kip die ze op de grillpan had gelegd. Een andere keer keek zij toe hoe hij een maaltijd klaar-maakte. Niet omdat ze zich geweldige koks wilden noemen, maar ze vonden het prettig om zich samen ergens mee bezig te houden. Het resultaat mocht er trouwens wezen, oefening baart tenslotte kunst.

Soms maakten ze gezamenlijk een speciaal recept, maar ook daaraan voegden ze iets toe om het 'nog lekkerder' te maken. Als het resultaat ze niet beviel of teveel afweek van wat het kookboek beloofd had, dan maakten ze het een paar dagen later nog eens. Het duurde desnoods drie tot vier keer experimen-teren tot het gerecht helemaal naar hun zin lukte en smaakte zoals ze het zich gewenst hadden. Als ze hun vrienden uitnodigden, stelden ze een menu samen van de specialiteiten waarvan ze wisten dat die intussen goed genoeg door hen konden worden toebereid. Dat het 'volgens het boekje' zou smaken.

Omdat ze hem niet zoals op andere dagen had geroepen, schrok hij ervan dat het al vijf over zes was toen hij op z'n horloge keek. Een beetje ongerust, maar ook boos liep hij naar de keuken. Hij wilde haar vragen waarom ze hem in het zonnetje had laten zitten. Zijn kwaadheid kwam waarschijnlijk uit een soort voorgevoel. Het sloeg eigenlijk nergens op, maar hij was geschrokken van de afwijking van de dagelijkse gewoonte. Maar ook bang dat ie even was weggedoezeld en haar daardoor niet had gehoord.

Zijn vrouw zat op een keukenstoel en keek 'afwezig' naar hem op toen ie in de deuropening verscheen. Het is de omschrijving die hem het eerste opviel. Hij heeft het later net zo aan de ambulance broeder verteld. Ze was "kompleet van de wereld" en leek niet te weten "wie hij was, of waar hij plotseling van-daan kwam." Ze keek niet boos of verstrooid maar was duidelijk niet zich-zelf. Hooguit lag er ook een sprankje verbazing in haar blik, maar het meest opvallend was die 'afwezigheid'. Ze leek er wel te zijn, maar tegelijkertijd ook weer niet.

Meteen nadat hij weer de keuken was uitgelopen, pakte hij de telefoon van de houder en toetste een, een, twee in. Het ging in een reflex. Hij had in een oog-opslag gezien dat er iets niet klopte en wist eenvoudig dat hij dit niet op kon lossen zonder professionele hulp. Natuurlijk was op dit uur de huisarts onbe-reikbaar, hij moest dus grovere middelen inzetten.

Binnen vijf minuten was de ziekenwagen voor komen rijden. Intussen had hij geprobeerd haar weer enigszins bij te brengen, haar toegesproken alsof ze uit een diepe slaap wakker gemaakt moest worden. Kinderlijk, half roepend, aan-geslagen, geschrokken en niet wetend hoe te handelen of wat hij exact kon doen, was hij voor haar op zijn hurken gaan zitten. Hij had haar handen ge-pakt en herinnert zich dat hij ze heen en weer heeft geschud. Zijn vrouw keek hem alleen maar aan en draaide langzaam haar hoofd in zijn richting. Het ging vertraagd, alsof ze aan een film meedeed die op de verkeerde snelheid werd afgespeeld.

160

Kort daarna ging de voordeur bel en kwamen de ziekenbroeders met hun grote koffers binnen. Ze hebben haar op de grond gelegd en gemeten of haar bloedsuikers in orde waren. Maar ze was geen diabeet en had evenmin ooit last gehad van haar bloeddruk. Voor de zekerheid werd ook die namelijk gemeten en maakten ze daarna snel een 'hartfilmpje'.

Het leverde alleen het inzicht op dat ze haar wilden meenemen naar het ziekenhuis. Daar zouden ze haar in de gaten kunnen houden. Een diagnose konden de broeders natuurlijk niet stellen, maar uit de haast die ze plotseling aan de dag legden meende hij een zekere ernst af te kunnen lezen. Toch was er geen reden om met gillende sirenes de weg op te gaan. De man mocht eventueel met de ambulance meerijden, maar hij kon "misschien beter in zijn eigen auto" achter ze aan komen. Het leek hem inderdaad beter om dat laatste te doen. Dan kon hij haar er weer mee terug naar huis nemen, als alles in orde was gekomen. Hij kan zich herinneren dat ie nog even snel gecontroleerd heeft of alle gaspitten uit waren voordat hij op weg ging.

De opname duurde bijna zeven weken en het kwam niet helemaal goed. Een kleine hersenbloeding was de oorzaak van haar vreemde manier van doen die avond. Volgens zeggen niet ernstig, doch de dokters wilden haar pas ontslaan als ze weer enigszins 'onder de mensen' was. Ze moesten iedere week opnieuw, ook als zijzelf had bedacht 'eigenlijk al best' naar huis te kunnen, een aantal tests doen. Het duurde hierdoor lang voordat ze zeker waren van hun zaak. Intussen moest zijn vrouw de controle over zichzelf 'herwinnen', dat wil zeggen 'voldoende opknappen om naar huis te kunnen'.

Iedere dag ging hij bij haar op bezoek en heel langzaam bleek ze weer de oude te zullen worden. Aanvankelijk ging praten nog erg moeilijk, omdat haar kin een beetje scheef was blijven hangen. Gelukkig bleek dat al snel bij te trekken. Ze kon toen weer verstaanbare klanken vormen. Ze bleef echter nog een tijdlang traag reageren. Het leek of haar begrip niet meewerkte en het haar dus moeite kostte om zich een beeld te vormen van wat er gezegd werd of er om haar heen gebeurde. Daarnaast reageerde ze ook vaak tamelijk vreemd, want ze bleek vaak een heel ander antwoord te geven dan je mocht verwachten. Haar woordkeus 'week af', om het zachtjes te zeggen.

Ze maakte er een afwezige indruk door en krabbelde maar langzaam uit de put waarin ze hierdoor terecht kwam. Altijd was ze een zelfbewuste, stevig in haar schoenen staande vrouw geweest. Zijn echtgenote mankeerde buiten een verkoudheidje nooit iets, nam deel aan het leven en toonde voor van alles en nog wat belangstelling. Nu opeens leek ze kwetsbaar en dat stoorde, het paste niet bij het beeld dat ze zo zorgvuldig van zichzelf had opgebouwd. Van dat trage en haar vreemde reacties leek ze zich namelijk wel bewust te zijn.

Na thuiskomst moest ze iedere dag medicijnen slikken. Omdat ze bang was ze te vergeten vroeg ze hem telkens of ze het al had gedaan. Traplopen ging niet meer zelfstandig, hij moest haar aan een arm ondersteunen en liep half achter haar zodat hij haar kon opvangen als ze het evenwicht dreigde te verliezen.

Haar bed beneden zetten was echter uitgesloten. Ze wilde het persé niet en liet zich er ook 'voor tijdelijk' niet toe overhalen. Als ze iets niet alleen kon, dan zou hij haar er toch bij helpen. "En anders wachtte ze wel tot de zuster kwam." Vanaf de dag dat ze weer thuis kwam veranderde hij hierdoor in een ziekenbroeder. Maar hij deed het vanzelfsprekend met liefde. Net zoals zij het waarschijnlijk ook voor hem zou doen, verwachtte hij.

Onder deze omstandigheden durfde hij zijn vrouw niet meer alleen thuis te laten. Dat deed hij dus hooguit voor de tijd die het kostte om snel een paar boodschappen te doen. Gelukkig vond hun dochter het geen probleem om een keer per week de bulk voor ze te halen. Ze "vulde dan de voorraden aan", zoals ze het noemde. Zo was er altijd iets te eten in huis. Al hadden ze allebei niet meer zoveel trek als vroeger, omdat het toch voornamelijk neerkwam op 'opgewarmd diepvries eten'. Iets waarvoor ze vroeger hun neus ophaalden.

Langer dan hooguit een halfuur durfde hij de deur dus niet meer niet uit. Als hij door de supermarkt liep of ergens op zijn beurt stond te wachten, zag hij in gedachten weer de wezenloze blik waarmee ze hem de eerste dagen in het ziekenhuis had verwelkomd. Het maakte dat hij gehaast afrekende, snel terug naar huis wilde en zich geen tijd gunde voor een praatje onderweg. Even stoppen voor het rode licht op de rondweg duurde hem dan al veel te lang, al kwam hij daar vanzelfsprekend niet onderuit.

Drie en een halve week geleden wilde de huisarts haar opeens nogmaals op laten nemen. Hoewel ze de afgelopen maanden al flink was opgeknapt, vertrouwde ze haar metingen en het onderzoekje van het lab niet helemaal. Misschien maakte ze "een dipje" door. Waarschijnlijk was er alleen maar sprake van "een kleine terugslag". Ze mochten zich beslist geen zorgen maken, de opname zou uitsluitend voor de zekerheid zijn!

In augustus hadden ze erover gesproken om binnenkort eens naar hun zoon te gaan. Hij was in het afgelopen jaar wel twee keer naar Nederland gekomen om zijn ouders, en vooral moeder, op te zoeken, maar sinds zijn verhuizing waren ze pas een enkele keer bij hem op bezoek geweest. Dat was nog op zijn studenten kamertje in de binnenstad van Freiburg. Later zijn ze er weliswaar nog een keer geweest, maar dat was voor zijn huwelijk. Intussen ook alweer ruim twee jaar geleden!

Het was 't laatste bezoek dat ze aan hem hadden afgelegd. Onlangs hadden hij en zijn echtgenote er echter een huis gekocht en ze schenen beiden in de buurt een goede baan gevonden te hebben. Die Duitse woning hadden de man en z'n vrouw nog uitsluitend op foto's en in een filmpje op zijn telefoon kunnen bewonderen. Toen was hij bij hen op bezoek en onlangs, nadat zijn zus er met

162

haar gezin op vakantie gevierd had, bleken die ook een aantal foto's te hebben genomen.

De hoop dat hij hen 'n kleinkind, een stamhouder zou gaan schenken, speelde zo nu en dan bij ze door 't hoofd. Al vormde het geen voorwaarde, diep in hun hart verlangden ze ernaar. Soms en voornamelijk 'en passant' bracht een van hen het weleens ter sprake. Dan bleek het bij allebei te leven, hoewel ze dat vanzelfsprekend ook zonder dat het uitgesproken werd van elkaar wisten. Het behoefde geen uitleg of nader betoog, het verlangen leefde in stilte in hun gedachten. Al hebben ze het nooit met hem zelf besproken.

Zijn vrouw stelde op een avond voor dat ze er best een keer naartoe konden. Binnenkort zou ze daar genoeg voor opgeknapt zijn, vond ze zelf. Eventueel moesten ze onderweg dan maar een nacht in een hotel slapen. Ook daar voelde ze zich eigenlijk goed genoeg voor. Als ze er ruim de tijd voor namen om de reis naar het zuiden van Duitsland te maken, was er vast en zeker geen vuiltje aan de lucht. Bijtijds vertrekken, genoeg pauzes inlassen onder het rijden en genieten van het landschap. Had hij niet met Sinterklaas zo'n handig navigatie apparaatje van hun dochter en haar man gekregen?

Dan hoefde zij onderweg helemaal niet meer de kaart voor hem te lezen. Met behulp van dat dingetje zouden ze ook geen ruzie meer krijgen als hij fout reed of ergens de weg per ongeluk kwijtraakte. Met een vriendelijke stem werd immers verteld wat de beste route was. En als ze het van tevoren door hun schoonzoon lieten instellen, werd ie ook geïnformeerd als er ergens onderweg een Umleitung of Stau zou zijn. Daar werden ze dan automatisch omheen gestuurd. "Zo'n ding zoek de beste weg voor je uit."

Hij had de gebruiksaanwijzing toen al twee keer helemaal doorgelezen en wist dat ze gelijk had. Er kon heel veel met het apparaat en inderdaad zou het dingetje hen om het grootste oponthoud heen leiden. Het kon met de stem van een vrouw of man en volgens hun schoonzoon waren er ook grappige andere stemmetjes van het Internet te halen. Het had hem gerustgesteld dat het navigatiesysteem automatisch een aangepaste route uit zou rekenen, mochten ze ongelukkigerwijze ergens de fout ingaan.

De zogenaamde lab uitslagen en het meet apparaat van hun huisarts wezen helaas anders uit. Op de tweede dag van de opname, die ervoor had moeten zorgen dat het een en ander beter hij haar ingesteld werd, verloor zijn vrouw het bewustzijn en raakte ze in een coma. Toen hij er na het telefoontje van de verpleegkundige zo snel mogelijk naar toe was gefietst, leek het of ze alleen maar in een diepe slaap was gevallen.

Samen met zijn dochter heeft hij de avond en nacht aan de rand van haar bed doorgebracht. Maar de situatie verbeterde niets. Ze reageerde niet meer op hun stemmen en hoe de artsen haar ook met lichtflitsen en een heel assortiment martelapparatuur provoceerden, een voor een toonden de meters aan dat

163

ze dieper wegzakte. Ze werd niet meer wakker.

In allerijl is hun zoon naar Schiphol gekomen. Zijn zwager is hem en z'n vrouw daar gaan ophalen. Zo zat de man met zijn kinderen en hun partners aan haar bed toen een arts in de aangrenzende kamer de apparatuur uitschakelde. Het lijkt nu al veel langer geleden, maar 't is allemaal toch pas begin vorige week gebeurd.

Zijn zoon en schoondochter hebben tot gisterochtend bij hem gelogeerd op de logeerkamer boven. Geen plezierige manier om beter met haar kennis te maken, al had ze al wel een mondje Nederlands leren spreken. Alledaagse opmerkingen gingen haar goed af, zodat ze met elkaar konden spreken.

Ze hebben geholpen om de boel enigszins op orde te krijgen en uitgezocht wat hij het beste 'maar meteen' weg kon doen. Er is opgeruimd wat hij wilde bewaren en voor een paar dagen is er eten in huis gehaald. In Duitsland krijgt men ruim de tijd voor persoonlijke zaken, maar toch moesten ze gisteren alweer terug naar huis.

Ze zijn met de snelle trein gegaan. Het vliegen op de heenreis was ze met al het geharrewar dat ermee gemoeid gaat, niet zo goed bevallen. Vanmorgen heeft de man van zijn dochter, hen ervoor naar het station in Utrecht gereden.

Patat

Ze zijn er allebei niet helemaal zeker van of hij hem, net als even hiervoor, weer een handje moet geven of dat hij dat juist niet moet doen. Daarnet in de parkeergarage is het min of meer vanzelf gegaan. Toen moesten ze ervoor zorgen elkaar in het immense gebouw niet kwijt te raken. Dat maakte het fysieke contact noodzakelijk. Het ging vanzelf, automatisch, omdat het daar eigenlijk toch wel een beetje duister en spookachtig leek. De man kon het zich tenminste voorstellen dat ie dat zou vinden. Hij had hem immers ook al moeten helpen bij het lastige naar buiten klauteren uit z'n auto. Die was voor kleine jongetjes natuurlijk aan de hoge kant. Optillen moest ie 'm om het kind veilig op de grond, op z'n voetjes te laten belanden.

Toen ze samen tussen de auto's door onderweg waren naar de uitgang, had hij opeens gevoeld hoe z'n hand beet werd gepakt. Kennelijk deed het jochie het uit gewoonte, maar de man was het niet gewend en daardoor schrok ie er een beetje van. Maar met al die nare richels en stoeprandjes was het lopen, kriskras tussen alle wagens en obstakels door inderdaad een beetje lastig. Zelf kon hij door de ramen van de auto's zien waar ie liep, dus omdat het ventje nog zo klein is kon die dit extra beetje houvast wel gebruiken. Maar intussen lopen ze gewoon op straat, veilig op de stoep.

Al van vlak voorbij de uitgang van de garage was het pad te smal om nog naast elkaar te blijven lopen. Eenmaal buiten was het daarvoor te gevaarlijk vanwege het kleine stoepje en de uitrit die er vlak langs liep. Daarom is de man de jongen door de deur voorgegaan naar buiten en hebben ze elkaar dus los moeten laten. Daarna is hij hem tamelijk dichtbij, schuin achter 'm maar telkens nadrukkelijk aan de kant waar de gebouwen staan, blijven volgen. Kennelijk is het zo aan hem geleerd. Door zijn moeder of misschien wel op school. Voor de zekerheid heeft de man een paar keer over zijn schouder gekeken om te zien of hij nog achter hem aan loopt, maar trouw als een hondje is hij bij 'm gebleven.

Het kereltje is een jaar of zeven. Een goed kwartier geleden heeft de man hem bij zijn school in een van de buitenwijken opgehaald. Volgens afspraak zal hij deze middag op het jongetje passen. Nu gaan ze eerst samen lunchen.

Meteen nadat ze in de auto waren gestapt en hij even snel controleerde of de jongen zijn veiligheidsgordel goed heeft omgedaan, heeft hij voorgesteld om naar een van de vestigingen van MacDonalds te gaan. Hij wist er drie en heeft ze allemaal opgenoemd. Het kereltje liet de keuze echter aan hem over en haalde zijn schoudertjes op. Niet stuurs of onverschillig, maar precies zoals kleine kinderen dat doen als ze het maken van een keuze willen overlaten aan een volwassene. De opties hen overweldigen. Ook voor hem was dit 'n eerste kennismaking, al wist de man niet of zijn moeder vaker een collega vroeg om een middag op haar zoon te passen.

Tijdens het ritje naar het centrum van de stad, heeft hij zich af zitten vragen of hij hem inderdaad naar de hamburgertent moet meenemen. Hij zal daar heel gemakkelijk de grote kindervriend uit kunnen hangen natuurlijk, dat maakt de reclame op de televisie duidelijk genoeg. Er wordt in die filmpjes niet voor niets voorgesteld dat kinderen een eldorado in de keten zien. Maar dat ging dus kennelijk niet op voor zijn huidige gezelschap. Misschien is het er ook wel te druk eigenlijk.

De man gaat er als vanzelfsprekendheid vanuit dat het het beste zal zijn om erbij te zitten onder het eten. Al ziet hij op tegen de formica tafeltjes en de meestal plakkerige banken en gammele stoelen die in zulke fast food zaken noodzakelijk lijken te zijn. Het lawaai van rondhollende kinderen wil hij nog wel voor lief nemen en eventueel mag het joch zelfs in de ballenbak spelen, als hij dat wil. Maar het vooruitzicht op een gebrek aan comfort en gezond, smakelijk voedsel staat hem tegen.

Toen hij in zijn spiegel keek hoe het kind zich op de achterbank hield, bleek dat ie stil door de raampjes naar het verkeer links en rechts van ze zat te kijken. Het ziet eruit of het jongetje zich helemaal op zijn gemak voelt. Het had evengoed gekund dat ie bang zou zijn, maar dat blijkt dus mee te vallen. Voor hen allebei is dit een rare middag.

Nog onderweg naar de school, rijdend dwars door de binnenstad heeft de man bedacht dat het geen pas geeft om naar een echt restaurant te gaan. Helaas is 't momenteel geen weer voor een terrasje, dat is een wat meer neutrale omgeving natuurlijk. Hij kende het kind niet en wist dus evenmin of hij zich daar zou kunnen gedragen. Op dat moment had hij er nog totaal geen beeld van wat hij aan zou gaan treffen. Hij betwijfelde of het kind in een wat betere tent op z'n plaats zou zijn. Wellicht voelde hij zich enorm opgelaten in een chique zaak. Vooral met alleen maar volwassenen om hem heen. De overwegingen hadden hem op het idee van die hamburgerketen gebracht. Nader beschouwd blijken die reclames dus wel te werken.

Al is het maar voor een eenvoudige lunch, je moet er toch al gauw minstens een halfuur tot drie kwartier voor uittrekken. Dat is tamelijk lang voor 'n kind, zoveel weet hij er nog wel vanaf. Dat hij daarom uit moet zien naar wat afleiding staat voor hem intussen vast. Zo'n ballenbak is dus zo gek nog niet, maar hij ziet op tegen het vooruitzicht dat hij daar met allerlei moeders omheen moet zitten. Die zullen de aanblik van hem erbij vast vreemd interpreteren.

166

Eenmaal aangekomen bij de school stond zijn besluit grotendeels vast. Het enige waaraan nog moest worden voldaan was het kind ervan overtuigen met hem mee te gaan. Ook dat viel in de praktijk enorm mee. Zijn moeder had hem blijkbaar goed op het verloop van de middag voorbereid en ze had de juf er ook al van op de hoogte gesteld dat hij 'm mee zou nemen. De man heeft zich aan haar voorgesteld en met z'n paspoort gelegitimeerd, dat leek haar wat formeel. Ze heeft desondanks en lachend zijn pasfoto vergeleken met wie in levende lijven voor haar stond.

Eventueel zou zo'n lunch minder formeel en op een koopje kunnen. Dan konden ze lopend op straat iets nuttigen. Als het joch vervolgens nog meer trek mocht hebben zou er vast verderop, nog 'n kroketje of een frikadel te koop zijn. Uiteindelijk is er in elke stad altijd wel een snackbar of loket met gefrituurd voedsel in de nabijheid. Toch staat het hem tegen. Het is niet omdat hij niet op straat wil eten, maar hij wil erbij zitten. Het lijkt hem leuk om kennis te maken met het kind.

Uit de krant is het hem bekend dat scholieren niet bewust en gezond eten. Of hij het jongetje echter lastig moet gaan vallen met allerlei verantwoordelijkheden, lijkt hem wat te ver gaan. Volgens hem ging het trouwens voornamelijk om middelbare scholieren in dat onderzoek. Daar kan hij het jochie hier bij hem niet toe rekenen. Eigenlijk gunt hij 't hem om een keertje te zondigen. Zijn moeder kennend kan hij bevroeden dat ze hem niet vaak een vette hap voor zal zetten. Daarvoor is ze te zorgzaam.

Hij heeft nog even in overweging genomen om de verschillende keuzes aan zijn metgezel voor te leggen, maar die heeft zich intussen omgedraaid op de achterbank. Hij kan het zien in de spiegel. De jongen zit er geknield en met zijn ellebogen op de hoedenplank, naar buiten te kijken. Hij ondersteunt z'n hoofdje erbij. De man vindt het niet nodig om hem met zijn overwegingen en twijfels lastig te vallen. Bij de volgende bocht zal hij wat voorzichtiger remmen, dan rolt het ventje niet om. Hij zal nu immers de veiligheidsgordel niet strak genoeg om zich heen hebben zitten.

Het restaurant bovenin in het warenhuis biedt waarschijnlijk het beste alternatief. Daar zal hij waarschijnlijk een verhouding kunnen vinden tussen de uitersten die hem onder het rijden te binnen zijn geschoten en het kind er een gezonde maaltijd laten eten. De jongen kan er zelf iets kiezen. Wellicht is dat uit alle mogelijkheden de meest verstandige. Het is trouwens maar een korte wandeling vanaf de garage naar het warenhuis. Ze kunnen vooraf eventueel een kopje soep nemen. Er zijn toch ook van die kleine koppen?

De jongen kan er voor zichzelf bepalen waar hij trek in heeft en hoeveel hij precies wil eten. Dan hoeft hij hem niet te betuttelen of iets op te dringen. Hij wil zeker geen vaderrol gaan zitten spelen of de opa uithangen. Dat laatste zou men kunnen zeggen en het lijkt hem een gruwel om zo gezien te worden.

167

Al is de rol nog zo plaatsvervangend omdat de jongen er zelf een heeft natuurlijk. Maar evengoed heeft de man daar totaal geen zin in. Heeft hij er geen uitgesproken hekel aan als hij mannen van zijn leeftijd in de weer ziet met kleine kinderen?

Kleinkinderen of zelfgemaakt, als zulke mannetjes aan de tweede leg zijn bijvoorbeeld. Hij moet glimlachen om zijn eigen gemopper en kan zich intussen een aantal frappante voorbeelden voor de geest halen. Zijn eigen directeur bijvoorbeeld en de man die verderop bij hun in de straat is komen wonen. Die is ook zo blij met 't hele jonge meisje dat hij op de nieuwjaarsreceptie heel bezitterig voorstelde als 'zijn echtgenote'. Hij sprak dat toen ook nog zo lullig uit met de nadruk op "ècht genoten." Het wicht had wel om de weinig subtiele toespeling gelachen, maar het ging toch meer alsof het zo afgesproken was dan uit echte pret. Blijkbaar was ze het van hem gewend. De man had de voorstelling vooral meelijwekkend gevonden. Hij had met haar te doen omdat hij niet eens een stoel voor haar was gaan pakken. Naar zijn idee ga je zo niet om met een hoogzwangere vrouw.

Vanuit het restaurant, helemaal op de bovenste verdieping van het gebouw waarin het warenhuis is gevestigd, is er een prachtig uitzicht over de binnenstad. Het patroon van de oudste grachten is er nog duidelijk te onderscheiden, in de directe omgeving staan een paar hoge gebouwen onder anderen van de Universiteit en er is uitzicht op wel drie kerken. Hij kan het jongetje aanwijzen wat de loop van Rijn is en vertellen hoe deze in het ontstaan van de stad zijn rol heeft gespeeld. Een van de overgebleven oude stadspoorten is er te zien en vlak voor het warenhuis was de oorspronkelijk doorwaadbare plaats. Alsof hij een wijze oom is kan hij het kind onder het eten een mooi verhaal over de geschiedenis van z'n woonplaats vertellen. Bijvoorbeeld over het beleg van de Spanjaarden gedurende de zestiende eeuw. De tachtigjarige oorlog. Aan de overkant kijk je recht tegen de eeuwenoude ommuurde Burcht op haar heuvel aan, die zie je niet vanaf de straat. De verschillende kerken en nog andere gebouwen zullen in het verhaal te betrekken zijn. Zo'n kasteelmuur moet imposant zijn voor kleine jongetjes. Ze stamt misschien nog uit de tijd van de Romeinen en in ieder geval ziet het er heel erg middeleeuws uit. Door er allerlei details in te verweven kan hij hem, onder het spreken de aanknopingspunten van zijn verhaal lijfelijk aanwijzen. Onmiskenbaar moet zoiets het een en ander interessant genoeg maken.

Hij kan het verweven met de folklore van de stad en de jaarlijkse 3 oktober viering. Dat feest moet de jongen minimaal kennen het wordt immers zeer uitbundig gevierd. Voor zover de man weet wonen zijn moeder en hij alweer een aantal jaren in de stad, ze zullen dus zeker een keer op de kermis geweest zijn. Dat laat niemand aan kleine kinderen voorbij gaan. Misschien hebben ze zelfs de optocht of de taptoe wel eens bekeken. Omdat de jongen hier in de stad op school zit krijgt hij er sowieso vrij voor van school. De man neemt zich voor om het straks eens aan hem te vragen.

Als hij niet al te bangelijk is aangelegd kan hij 'm trouwens ook vertellen van de arm van burgemeester van der Werf. Volgens de overlevering heeft hij die tijdens het beleg van de Spanjaarden aan de bevolking aangeboden toen ze zich, door de honger gedreven, aan de Spaanse beleggers over wilden geven. Omdat ze zelf dan aan het eten zullen zijn hoeft de anekdote niet al te gruwelijk, maar hij denkt dat kleine jongetjes er wel van zullen smullen. Het is allemaal interessant genoeg om er een spannend verhaal van te maken.

Hij kan aan die hongerige burgers, stoere schouten en deftige schepenen toevoegen. Als hij goed op het gezicht van het kind let, kan hij waarschijnlijk wel zien of zijn relaas op de juiste manier overkomt. Dat hij hem er niet mee traumatiseert, maar juist wijzer maakt. Hij zal aan zijn gezichtje beoordelen of het nog iets spannender moet of beter van niet. Overigens betwijfelt ie of het joch op school al vaderlandse geschiedenis zal krijgen. Dan loopt hij met zijn verhaal dus mooi op de feiten vooruit. Ze kunnen er ruim de tijd voor nemen, want de hele middag staat tot hun beschikking. Om heel eerlijk te zijn heeft de man er geen flauw benul van hoe hij de middag op een aangename manier voor het ventje moet invullen.

Zelf vond hij, toen hij nog op de lagere school zat en de meester verhalen vertelde over de middeleeuwen, juist die altijd heel interessant. Boeiender in ieder geval dat het in zijn ogen eindeloze geleuter over de bezetting van de Duitsers waar de leraren en zijn ouders elke keer over begonnen.

Kunnen ze 'n bezoekje brengen aan een van de musea, of misschien een matinee voorstelling in de bioscoop?

Hij heeft vergeten om in de agenda van de krant na te kijken wat er op een doordeweekse woensdagmiddag voor middelbare mannen met kleine jongetjes te beleven is in de stad. Als het verhaal over die burgemeester aanslaat kunnen ze ook even naar het park lopen dat zijn naam draagt. Daar staat een standbeeld van de held. Het heeft die uitgestrekte arm, alleen is de sabel ooit uit zijn hand verwijderd. Hij weet niet waarom dat is gedaan, maar het zal wel te maken hebben gehad met veiligheid of regels uit Brussel. Hij weet dat je er vlakbij hele lekkere ijsjes kunt halen. Italiaanse dus dat zal het kind ook wel een attractie vinden. Er staan bankjes genoeg om er samen op te gaan zitten en er dan in alle rust eentje op te likken.

Iets meer dan een maand geleden heeft de man via het uitzendbureau, een baan gevonden. Zijn dochter wees hem op het speciale kantoor dat zich voornamelijk zou richten op wat oudere werknemers. Mensen van zijn leeftijd en ze had er nadrukkelijk op aangedrongen dat hij er zich eens zou gaan oriënteren. Ze bracht het onderwerp om eens aan een baantje te denken ter sprake toen hij zich durfde te beklagen over de allengs teruglopende omzet van zijn zaak. Het viel hem namelijk steeds vaker op dat het minder druk werd in zijn praktijk. Mede daarom had hij zijn tarieven al wat verhoogd en was ie van plan om voor zijn inzet 'onderzoek kosten' te gaan rekenen, doch 't ging hem nog te ver om die op voorhand van zijn klanten te verlangen.

Het was hem overigens onduidelijk of dit gegeven in enige mate bij de zakelijke teruggang meesprak. Vast stond het alleen dat er aanpassingen noodzakelijk waren, om nog van de opbrengsten rond te kunnen komen. Hij deed al een hele tijd zo zuinig mogelijk en feitelijk kon het natuurlijk niet meer dat hij nog steeds gemiddeld ongeveer een tientje per uur rekende. Dat hij zich ermee voor de gek hield wist hij intussen ook wel, maar het werk leverde hem nog teveel bevrediging op. Daardoor heeft hij het al lange tijd genoeg gevonden om 'z'n zaak' niet helemaal op te geven.

Hij had trouwens het idee opgevat dat z'n ervaring en de uitgebreid opgebouwde expertise, hem een zekere status verschaften. Dat hij dankzij al z'n geleverde inspanningen iets voorstelde en men hem daardoor nodig had bij het uitvoeren van z'n hobby. In eerste instantie compenseerde dit gevoel de terugloop in omzet enigszins, maar dat dezelfde klanten hem feitelijk in de steek lieten was desondanks bij hem beginnen door te schemeren.

Deze omstandigheid maakte het vasthouden van de balans tussen de vervulling van zijn droombeeld en de werkelijkheid weleens lastig. Vanzelfsprekend hoeft een lager wordende omzet, idealisme niet in de weg te staan, maar hij moest zich allengs steeds meer moeite getroosten om van de opbrengst van z'n zaak rond te komen. Om van de werkzaamheden te kunnen leven. Volwaardig leven, niet slechts overleven en geleidelijk had hij zich aan dat nieuwe beeld moeten aanpassen. Eerlijkheid gebood hem om toe te geven dat wat hij deed niet genoeg meer opleverde. Hoewel hij er gedurende een flink aantal jaren z'n gezin goed van had kunnen onderhouden, leek zijn werk langzaamaan te veranderen in een hobby. Terwijl dat dus lange tijd juist het tegenovergestelde was geweest.

Anderhalf jaar geleden bleek plotseling dat er voor zijn grootste klant het faillissement was aangevraagd. Kennelijk waren er onbetaalde rekeningen aan de orde of speelden er andere betalingsmoeilijkheden. Een leverancier van 'm had daarom de regeling aangevraagd. Zelf had de man in de periode eraan voorafgaand uitsluitend gemerkt dat er steeds minder opdrachten bij hem binnenkwamen. Ondanks dat hij zichzelf altijd free-lancer noemde, weersprak deze terugloop zijn verwachtingen. De ervaring had 'm immers geleerd dat er hooguit een seizoen component meesprak. In het voorjaar trok de omzet altijd bij tenslotte en in de zomer had hij het vaak uitermate druk.

De betalingen van deze klant hadden inderdaad iets langer op zich laten wachten, maar hij kreeg tot op de laatste factuur alles keurig verrekend. De bui rond de rechterlijke uitspraak had hij daarom niet zien hangen. Hij werd voornamelijk door het faillissement overvallen, omdat hij meer dan vijftien jaar, wekelijks en noem dat eens niet regelmatig, zijn diensten, service en inzet aan deze klant had mogen leveren.

Dat er in de laatste paar maanden steeds minder werk aan hem werd toegestuurd, leek hem een onderdeel van de trend die er kennelijk heerste. Oorspronkelijk leek 't hem van tijdelijke aard. Van al zijn klanten viel immers het aanbod weleens tegen. Volgens stemmen heerste er 'pessimisme' in de markt en daar deden ze op het journaal zowat elke dag, en vast niet voor niets, uitgebreid verslag van. De zogenaamde consument was zijn vertrouwen aan het verliezen of zoiets, daar scheen het allemaal door te komen. Er waren wijze mannen genoeg die de werking van de conjunctuur wel even wilden komen uitleggen. Zij konden er aldus een verklaring voor geven. Dat ze elkaar overigens tegen leken te spreken, viel kennelijk alleen hem op. Net zoals hij het zich afvroeg of 'die deskundigen' niets beters te doen hadden.

Feit bleef dat niet alleen de aantallen opdrachten meer en meer tegen bleken te vallen, het leek er ook weleens op dat ze voor hem werden uitgezocht. Het kwam bij hem op dat hij nog uitsluitend lastige, de meer ingewikkelde klusjes aangeboden kreeg. Het leek hem daardoor dat het eenvoudigere werk waarschijnlijk aan anderen werd gegund of men het zelf probeerde. Als een klant dacht dat zijn diensten te duur werden, dan boden ze hem het werk kennelijk niet meer aan. Helaas zonder dat hij er nader over geconsulteerd werd of er een duidelijke, bevredigende uitleg voor mocht ontvangen.

Normaal had hij redelijk veel kontakt met zijn klanten en ze wisten feitelijk heel goed dat er met hem te overleggen was. Maar de omzet werd dus aanzienlijk minder en geleidelijk aan was de conclusie gerechtvaardigd dat er niet meer zoveel vraag naar zijn bezigheden was. Dat zijn specialisme niet meer gerespecteerd werd en men spullen liever weggooide. Of dat ze zomaar bleven staan om te wachten tot het vanzelf beter ging.

Zakelijk gezien spreekt het voor zich dat nieuwe apparatuur verkopen veel interessanter is dan service bieden. Het kost immers veel inspanning en levert te weinig op, om open te staan voor reparaties of onderhoudswerk. Omdat dat nou juist zijn branche is, deed deze constatering hem pijn. Alles, de verminderde vraag, het gebrek aan belangstelling en de terugloop in zijn inkomsten maakte dat hij beneden een redelijk bestaansminimum terecht kwam. Helaas zag hij geen alternatief.

Eerst had hij het nog druk genoeg met het afstemmen van zijn zaken. Daar was gewoon meer tijd voor beschikbaar en bijvoorbeeld zijn administratie werd opeens elke dag tot in de puntjes bijgewerkt. Eerder deed hij dat slechts een keer per week in het weekend. Of zelfs minder vaak omdat hij het er ge-

171

woonweg te druk voor bleek te hebben. Dan betaalde hij alleen de rekeningen en deed zijn boekingen pas op het einde van een kwartaal als de omzetbelasting weer moest worden aangegeven.

Zijn vrouw en hij hadden, ondanks alles en door flink wat zuiniger te doen, nog een tijdlang kunnen rondkomen van wat er aan daadwerkelijke inkomsten binnenkwam. Nu de kinderen het huis uit waren, konden ze de behoefte aan luxe en extraatjes verminderen. Zo planden ze bijvoorbeeld ritjes met de auto zo dat ze met elkaar gecombineerd werden en er dus ternauwernood overbodig te noemen kilometers gereden werden. Sowieso deden ze zoveel mogelijk op de fiets natuurlijk, maar zijn ritten naar de klanten bleken zich heel goed met elkaar te laten combineren. Soms ging z'n vrouw met hem mee, om er samen een gezellig dagje van te maken. Ook daarvoor was aanzienlijk meer tijd beschikbaar.

Als onderdeel van de maatregelen om zich staande te houden, is zijn echtgenote het afgelopen voorjaar niet meer naar dat seizoensbaantje bij het attractiepark in het naburige dorp gegaan. Ze heeft ervoor in de plaats een aanstelling gevonden bij het tuincentrum in de buitenwijk. Dat werk leek haar eveneens aardig om te doen en hoewel ze haar vroegere collega's meende te gaan missen, bleken die ook vrijwel allemaal ander werk gevonden te hebben. Daar kwam ze toevallig achter toen ze een van hen op de markt in de stad tegen het lijf liep. Maria, Toos en Gerda, ze waren evenals Irene naar een andere baan op zoek gegaan. Werken in het park bood niet de vastigheid waar ze, gezien de omstandigheden naar op zoek waren. Ook hún mannen bemerkten allerlei invloed op hun inkomsten.

Het was haar trouwens in dat laatste seizoen, al een aantal keren opgevallen hoe zwaar het viel om iedere dag, en voor al de negen weken waarin het park open was, op de fiets heen en weer te rijden. De speciale bus die tussen de stad en de attractie op en neer reed, vertrok pas als het park al geopend was. Dat was voor het werk te laat en met de lijnbus vond ze teveel tijd kosten omdat die niet vaak genoeg ging en dichtbij een halte had. Ze zou er dan of veel te vroeg of net te laat aankomen. De halteplek houdt namelijk in dat ze daarvandaan minstens een kwartier moest lopen naar de ingang. Het resultaat was dat ze er net zolang over deed als op de fiets. Zo'n bus neemt ook nog 'ns niet de kortste weg namelijk.

Natuurlijk had de man zijn diensten kunnen uitbreiden, maar welke activiteiten hij naast zijn huidige kon aanbieden of wat er misschien aan extra's door hem kon worden uitgevoerd, zag hij niet. Vanzelfsprekend had het werk in de loop der tijd een specialisatie in de hand gewerkt. Hierdoor wist hij exact waar ie in uitblonk. Dit maakte waarom hij juist zo goed met zijn klanten kon overleggen waarop ze, qua kosten en te besteden tijd, uit gingen komen. Een

172

goede verkoper was hij daarentegen niet, dus loze praatjes en overdrijvingen waren hem vreemd. Dit werkte een eerlijkheid in de hand, die door zijn klanten hoog werd ingeschat. Het schonk ze, naast de door hem uitgedragen expertise, vertrouwen. Deze werkwijze beviel iedereen uitermate goed en daarom heeft hij zijn werk gedurende meer dan dertig jaar met plezier gedaan en volgehouden. Uitbreiden naar andere fronten had hem soms wel wat geleken, maar de eventuele cursus die daarvoor noodzakelijk was, die kon hij zich niet veroorloven. Zo er al een was die aansloot bij zijn vooropleiding en hem de mogelijkheid bood om zijn opgedane ervaring te benutten.

Wat voor opleiding danook, die zou zeker in 'n richting moeten gaan waarvoor hij belangstelling op kon brengen en diende een uitbreiding op te leveren op z'n diensten. Zijn zaak behoefde niet persé vervangen of totaal vernieuwd te worden, maar deze kon zich op die manier verbreden. Een uitbreiding zou hem wellicht wat meer zekerheid hebben verschaft, maar de investering heeft ie niet gedaan. Door zijn interesse voor techniek verdiepte de man zich graag in het nieuwste van het nieuwste. Zo maakte deze nieuwsgierigheid dat hij al vanaf de introductie open stond voor computers.

Eerst verschillende home-computers en later ook de onvermijdelijke PC. Hoe hij echter op dit nieuwe, voor hem volledig andere terrein te werk zou moeten gaan, is hem nooit voor ogen gekomen. Gevoelsmatig achtte hij zich voornamelijk 'een belangstellende', meer een gebruiker dan iemand die alle ins en outs kon begrijpen. Zo liet hij zich gemakkelijk overdonderen door de vele mogelijkheden en hoewel allengs steeds handiger met de apparaten, durfde hij zichzelf nooit een expert te noemen. Programmeren deed ie wel en soms waren die applicaties uitermate effectief, maar desondanks zag hij er voor zichzelf qua specialisatie geen glanzende toekomst in weggelegd.

In de praktijk bleken cursussen, zeker op het gebied van automatisering, vaak veel meer te kosten dan ze hem ooit op zouden kunnen leveren. Garanties werden er nimmer geboden en in een bijdrage in de studiekosten was van rijkswege, of wat voor instantie danook, niet voorzien. Als zelfstandige bleek hij er alleen voor te staan. Hoe logisch danook, een ZZP'er moest klaarblijkelijk alleen z'n boontjes doppen, al kostte hem dat dan moeite.

Dit kwam dus allemaal naast het gevoel dat hij niet precies wist wat hij nog zou willen of moeten leren. Het ontbrak hem aan de ambitie om een totaal andere richting op te gaan. Z'n werk was hem altijd gemakkelijk afgegaan omdat de uitvoering hem geen moeite kostte. Het leek 'm overigens potsierlijk om na 't volbrengen van een cursus, zichzelf opeens opslag te moeten geven. Tarieven verhogen omdat hij bijvoorbeeld een 'management aantekening' had verworven of vervolgens zijn administratie foutloos en geautomatiseerd kon invoeren. Aan het eigenlijke werk veranderde feitelijk niets en aan de uitvoering hooguit een heel klein beetje. Hij nam wat minder inkomen voor lief.

Het uitzendbureau waarnaar zijn dochter verwezen had, bleek 'Ervaringstijd' te heten. Het bemiddelde, zoals het een en ander al deed vermoeden, in mensen met een 'ruim arbeidsverleden'. Mensen met ervaring. Vandaar natuurlijk de omgekeerde samentrekking in de naam. Volgens de vrouw die hem er ontving ging het voornamelijk om personen die "zich nog niet helemaal afgeschreven" voelden voor de arbeidsmarkt. "Vutters en mensen die na hun pensioen nog een poosje wilden doorwerken", noemde ze die.

De man moest begrijpen dat ze blij was met zijn inschrijving omdat hij geen dagelijkse verplichtingen bleek te hebben. Ze leek vooral in haar nopjes dat hij geen oppas of voorlees opa was. Het maakte hem "heel gemakkelijk" inzetbaar, omdat hij tijdens kantooruren en niet pas "als de kindertjes allemaal in bed liggen" of "weg gebracht zijn naar de crèche" beschikbaar was. Ze vertelde met nadruk dat veel anderen wel aan zulke eisen moesten voldoen en dat het haar aantrekkelijk leek dat hij met zijn vijfenvijftig jaar "nog goed genoeg ter been" zou zijn.

Dat laatste heeft hem een beetje aan het lachen gemaakt. Hij kent in zijn omgeving jongere kerels dan hijzelf die juist ternauwernood meer iets blijken te kunnen. Zo loopt een van zijn vrienden al zeven jaar voor 100% in de WAO en zit zijn buurman van een paar deuren verderop om diezelfde reden al vele jaren aan de waterkant van de Singel te vissen. Die laatste kan misschien hooguit twee of drie jaar ouder zijn dan hijzelf.

Voor hem zou het sterk z'n eer te na zijn om van een uitkering te moeten leven. Of er zelfs maar van afhankelijk te zijn. Toen hij een poos geleden uit ging zoeken of er voor hem misschien een tijdelijke subsidie te halen was, bijvoorbeeld om de moeilijke tijden op te vangen, bleek hij nergens voor in aanmerking te komen. Volgens de uitleg die de geconsulteerde ambtenaar hem verschafte, kwam het door "gebrek aan anciënniteit." Wat dat precies betekende en in hoeverre je een voorgeschiedenis ontbeert als je toch al ruim boven de vijftig bent en zowat dertig jaar deelneemt aan het arbeidsproces, is hem ontgaan. De term "afgeschreven" kwam dus nogal vreemd op hem over toen de mevrouw van dan uitzendbureau 'm gebruikte. Kun je jezelf zomaar afschrijven, of kan "de maatschappij" dat iemand aandoen?

De meeste baantjes die ze er beschikbaar hadden, betroffen "licht administratief" en "niet te zwaar lichamelijk" werk. De kandidaten moesten bijvoorbeeld "mutaties" bijhouden en invoeren. Het ging daarbij voornamelijk om het maken van boekingen op een computer. Als hij er belangstelling voor had dan mocht ie eventueel ook call-center werk gaan doen.

Het werk zou in ieder geval, niet "te inspannend", nauwelijks "fysiek belastend" en ook ideaal voor een man "met zijn achtergrond" zijn. Ze zei het toen ze enige voorbeelden uit het aanbod opnoemde. Dat hij eraan gewend was om in een eigen tempo te werken, vond ze ook al een enorme pré. Aan het eind

174

van hun gesprekje benadrukte ze nogmaals dat hij een van de jongste werkzoekenden was die ze had mogen inschrijven. Het feit dat hij zich helemaal niet 'zo oud' voelde was haar kennelijk al pratend ontgaan.

Officieel is de man bij het bedrijf aangesteld als 'account manager'. Wat de functie inhoudt hebben ze hem moeten uitleggen, maar het gaat inderdaad om niet te zwaar administratief werk. Hij doet het part-time, per week twee ochtenden en drie middagen zodat hij bij elkaar voor ongeveer twintig uur onder de pannen is. Alleen op de dagen dat het er heel erg druk is zal hij soms wat langer moeten blijven of eerder komen. Dat wordt overigens uitbetaald als overwerk en omdat normale uren al beter betalen dan hij normaliter voor zichzelf durft te rekenen, is hij er aanzienlijk op vooruit gegaan.

De groothandel 'doet' in papierwaren en kantoor benodigdheden. Hij weet er overigens alleen van dat de firma zich sinds een paar jaar geleden net buiten de stad op een industrie terrein heeft gevestigd. De grote reclame borden zijn daartoe onontkoombaar tenslotte. Voor zijn eigen business ontvangt hij ieder kwartaal een stapel foldertjes met aanbiedingen. Bij het persoonlijke kennismaken werd 'm met trots verteld dat het bedrijf deel uitmaakt van een "wereldwijd opererend conglomeraat."

Hij nam de opmerking voorlopig voor wat ie waard was. Op dat moment vond hij zijn werkplek en vooral de nieuwe collega's belangrijker. Als eenmanszaak had hij, buiten het overleg met zijn vrouw of een praatje met z'n kinderen als ze uit school kwamen, nooit veel aanspraak gehad onder het werk. Het maakte hem dus weleens jaloers als andere mensen zomaar een hele tijd over bijvoorbeeld hun vakantie bleken te kunnen ouwehoeren. Bij de koffie automaat, zomaar op de gang of tijdens het wachten op de kopieer machine. Hij prees zich overigens gelukkig, niet van voetbal te houden. Soms merkte hij namelijk op dat er binnen een bedrijf van 'n klant veel tijd verloren ging met het bespreken van de wedstrijden. Alsof er op maandagochtend nog iets aan de afloop te doen zou zijn. Als gast werd hij vanzelfsprekend niet in het overleg betrokken.

Het kantoor waar hij moest gaan werken zit in een groot bedrijfsverzamelgebouw. Er zijn daar meerdere kleine bedrijven en deze reus met het gigantische magazijn, bij elkaar gebracht. Het pand is nog geen tien minuten fietsen van zijn huis en dat maakte 't baantje al ronduit aantrekkelijk. In de afgelopen weken is de moeder van het jongetje ermee bezig geweest om hem voor zijn functie in te werken.

Het jochie en hij zijn aan een van de ramen gaan zitten. Ze hebben er zowat het mooiste uitzicht dat ze zich konden bedenken. Daar waren ze het snel over eens toen het kind er het laatste lege tafeltje voor in beslag kon nemen. Zonder zich om andere bezoekers te bekommeren was hij er meteen uit de lift naartoe gehold en had er zijn jasje over de leuning van een van de stoelen gehangen. Omdat de man eerst even wilde kijken wat er zoal te eten zou zijn, kwam hij wat later bij het tafeltje aan. Hij had het kind niet willen corrigeren, zag er meer enthousiasme in, dan een vorm van ongemanierdheid. Er waren trouwens geen andere bezoekers die zich er wel aan leken te ergeren. De zaak werd druk bezocht en vrijwel alle tafels zaten vol, maar er liepen geen zoekende mensen die misschien ook aan het raam hadden willen zitten. Het kind bleek er intussen geboeid naar buiten te staan kijken en nam zeer beleefd pas plaats nadat de man zich op een van de andere lege stoelen neerzette. Plechtig kondigde hij aan de wensen rond het menu te willen bespreken.

Het werk dat hij bij de groothandel doet komt er in feite op neer dat hij de belangen van zijn 'accounts' in de gaten moet houden. Feitelijk gaat het natuurlijk om niets meer of minder dan een andere, meer Amerikaanse naam voor bestaande klanten. Nieuwe heten namelijk 'prospects'. De belangen van een aantal vaste klanten zijn bij hem persoonlijk neergelegd en hij vertegenwoordigt hen zodoende bij de aansturing door de afdeling accountbeheer van het bedrijf. Het is zijn taak om kontakt op te nemen met de personen, die verantwoording dragen voor het op peil houden van de voorraden.

Hij moet aan de hand van eerder geplaatste orders en via statistieken, die overigens opgesteld worden door deskundigen elders in de top van het bedrijf, beoordelen of een aanvulling nodig mocht zijn. Vervolgens mag hij de contactpersonen opbellen met een passende aanbieding. In de praktijk komt het erop neer dat de verschillende secretaresses en hoofden van afdelingen hun bestellingen bij hem plaatsen of dat hij ze er aan herinnert dat de voorraden op beginnen te raken. Het is eveneens z'n taak om ervoor te zorgen dat de eenmaal bij elkaar gezette spullen, op een afgesproken tijdstip bij de cliënt worden afgeleverd. Het afstemmen van de verschillende handelingen voor 'n account binnen het bedrijf maakt dus onderdeel uit van 't 'managen'.

In z'n functie zal hij, vanzelfsprekend afhankelijk van de eventuele afname, kwistig met cadeautjes en kortingen mogen strooien. Het draait er voornamelijk om het account ertoe te verleiden meer te kopen dan er feitelijk nodig is. Soms zal hij er dus voor moeten zorgen een grotere slag te slaan. Zoiets gaat bijvoorbeeld door zijn klant te verleiden om nog andere producten bij de groothandel af te nemen of hem iets te laten bestellen bij een met 'n aan hen verbonden collega. Een ander onderdeel van het conglomeraat.

Wat hem betreft vallen de presentjes trouwens onder de prullaria. Het gaat immers voornamelijk om pennen met een grappig bedoelde opdruk en andere door de diverse fabrikanten ter beschikking gestelde kleinigheden. Merchandise, waarvan het directe nut soms niet helemaal duidelijk is, maar waar wel altijd het merk van een bepaalde fabrikant op staat. Kennelijk zijn ze echter geliefd bij de mensen die hij moet benaderen voor zo'n bestelling, want sommigen durven er rechtstreeks om te vragen.

176

Zelf zou de man zijn nieuwe beroep omschreven hebben als 'klant gebonden telefonisch verkoper' of iets dergelijks, maar hij heeft in de afgelopen jaren het zicht op de arbeidsmarkt een beetje uit het oog verloren. Hoe allerlei nieuwe functies dus heten of wat men precies met de moderne terminologie bedoelt, is hem soms niet helemaal duidelijk. Bijna dertig jaar heeft hij als zelfstandige zonder personeel z'n bedrijf gerund. Maar dat was vanuit zijn eigen kantoor, op de eerste verdieping thuis. Klanten noemde hij gewoon bij hun naam en iedereen die van zijn diensten gebruik wilde maken behandelde hij op een eigen, persoonlijk manier. Zonder gebruik te maken van formules en vage aanduidingen. Werk was iets dat gedaan moest worden en dat ging meestal het beste door er gewoon aan te beginnen. Zelf ging hij ermee door tot het helemaal af was, tot ie het afgesproken resultaat bereikt had met zijn inspanningen. Aanbiedingen zoals hij nu naar zakenlieden uitbrengt, wist hij meestal eenvoudig af te wimpelen als ze op zijn weg kwamen.

In zijn zaak heeft hij alle verantwoording telkens zelf gedragen. Hij deed het voorkomende werk immers ook allemaal zelf. Het stelde hem in staat om heel gemakkelijk over zijn budget, voorraden en aankopen, eigen beslissingen te nemen. Alleen de administratie werd een keer per kwartaal door zijn echtgenote bijgewerkt. Ze deed het in verband met de aangifte van de omzetbelasting en het resultaat bood hem de gelegenheid om te bekijken of de zaken nog gingen zoals ze moesten gaan. Dat was de laatste tijd dus een beetje tegengevallen, vandaar dit baantje en dat uitzendbureau.

Als het papier voor de printer op dreigde te raken haalde hij nieuw. Hij liet de drukker facturen of bonnen printen als de stapel te klein werd en ook voor inktpatronen, eens een speciaal stempel of potloden en balpennen, zorgde hij gewoon zelf. De benodigdheden haalden zijn vrouw of hij altijd tijdens het boodschappen doen, bij een winkeltje in de binnenstad. Als ze het eens vergaten of er was daar geen voorraad dan kwamen ze er later nog eens terug om de rest op te halen of 't alsnog in orde te maken.

Bij de winkel had hij geen accountmanager die hem bestookte met aanbiedingen, maar werd er te woord gestaan door een verkoper die hun eventuele vragen beantwoorde. Soms lagen bij de kassa hebbedingetjes in een bakje, ook daar, maar de verleiding die daarvan uitging liet zich meestal eenvoudig weerstaan omdat ze geen direct nut of noodzaak vertegenwoordigden.

Hij kende zijn huidige werkgever overigens wel en was er ook weleens met een vriend geweest om er een computer aan te schaffen, maar hij had er geen klantenkaart of zo'n account. De gehanteerde manier van handelen was hem grotendeels vreemd en hij moest het vak daarom nog in alle facetten leren.

Begin vorige week heeft de man de moeder van het jongetje wat beter leren kennen, dat gebeurde tijdens een dienstreis. Het tripje viel buiten de beslommeringen van het werken op kantoor omdat ze er naar de andere kant van het land voor moesten. De vrouw vond de reis een noodzakelijk onderdeel van het inwerken en daarom hebben ze 'm gemaakt. In het begin van het inwerken had ze aan hem duidelijk gemaakt, dat ze al een halfjaar geleden haar baan had opgezegd. Hij wist ook dat de vestigingsmanager en zij hadden afgesproken dat ze alle contacten en relaties persoonlijk aan haar opvolger zou overdragen. Deze opvolger is hij voorlopig en als alles goed gaat wordt hem misschien een contract aangeboden. Zo gaat dat.

De manager van dit filiaal is feitelijk haar oude, voormalige baas. Lange tijd hebben ze samen zijn winkel in het centrum draaiende weten te houden. Deze werd later door het Amerikaanse bedrijf overgenomen en zodoende hebben ze er hun huidige functie van algehele vestigingsmanager en zij als account manager, verkregen. Oorspronkelijk ging het erom de vestiging op poten te zetten. Maar 't draaide erop uit dat hun invloed op de dagelijkse gang van zaken en dus in feite van allebei hun functie, geleidelijk afgebouwd werd. Exact zoals dat tegenwoordig in het bedrijfsleven gaat werd 'dat leuke winkeltje uit de binnenstad' door de reusachtige handelsfirma opgeslokt en dat ze in dat proces hun oude klanten meenamen, vormde hooguit een aardige bijkomstigheid. Haar baas werd echter allengs op een zijspoor gerangeerd en omdat zij daar geen zin in had, heeft de vrouw haar baan opgezegd. En omdat hun positie dat toestond kwamen de twee overeen dat zij voor de overdracht van het werk, alle benodigde aandacht en tijd mocht, zo niet kon en moest inruimen. De man heeft zelfs horen zeggen dat haar baas er nadrukkelijk op had aangedrongen dat ze dit "met de grootst mogelijke zorgvuldigheid" zou doen.

In de afgelopen weken heeft hij een aantal keren aan den lijve ervaren, hoe populair de vrouw is bij haar accounts. Hij heeft opgemerkt hoe ze in relatief korte tijd de nodige 'goodwill' heeft weten te bereiken. Waarschijnlijk liet zich dat verklaren door haar ervaring en de historie dat ze er al van voor de overname door die Amerikaanse groothandel werkt. Ze kent uit ervaring alle factoren van de firma, ze heeft ze van heel dichtbij meegemaakt. Het verschil tussen haar en de man is trouwens dat zij geleerd heeft om in allerlei moderne termen te werken en handelen. Omdat ze de oude nog kent en hij leergierig genoeg is om zich op de hoogte te stellen, kan ze hem gemakkelijk inwerken.

Dit zo zorgvuldig mogelijk overdragen van haar functie houdt de mogelijkheid in zich om haar geleidelijk afscheid te laten nemen en geeft haar baas de gelegenheid om een tijdlang nog optimaal van haar inzet gebruik te maken. Al heeft hij waarschijnlijk ook op kunnen merken dat de overdracht haar pijn lijkt te doen. Ze heeft namelijk geen haast om weg te gaan bij de firma.

Eerst heeft de vrouw hem verteld dat ze de behoefte voelde groeien om na ruim zeventien jaar "eens verder te kijken." Ze noemde het toen dat ze zich wilde "oriënteren." Gelijk na de middelbare school, nog geen maand na haar

178

eindexamen en een korte vakantie, is ze bij het toen nog zelfstandige zaakje gaan werken. Haar baas runde de winkel en zij zou achter de schermen een aantal administratieve taken toebedeeld krijgen en bijspringen als het ervoor te druk werd. Die taak nam ze indertijd over van zijn echtgenote. Die had lange tijd geprobeerd om haar man vanuit hun huis te helpen, maar het viel haar te zwaar om tussendoor ook nog de kinderen op te voeden.

De vrouw had zodoende het factureren, beheren van de voorraad, telefoon beantwoorden en dergelijke op zich genomen, maar al snel was de organisatie van de kleine onderneming door de overname op Amerikaanse leest geschoeid geraakt. Oorspronkelijk was haar baas, gebaseerd op de eerdere ervaringen met zijn winkeltje, vanuit de garage met het bedrijf begonnen. Maar het bleek hem dus al snel dat er meer aan vast zat dan hij en zijn vrouw samen konden 'behappen'. Feitelijk groeide de vraag hen boven het hoofd. De keuze om òf de winkel op te geven òf zich helemaal toe te leggen op zijn handelsfirma kon hij niet maken. Zijn vader en moeder waren met de winkel begonnen tenslotte. Die droeg zijn naam, maar de handel leverde meer op zodat het pandje in de binnenstad beter verhuurd kon worden en hij zich kon concentreren op het bedrijf thuis. Nadat hij deze van zijn garage naar een locatie met meer ruimte verhuisd had, bleek kort daarna het aanbod van de Amerikanen wel zo aantrekkelijk.

Opeens hoefden ze niet meer op een voormalige slaapkamer van zijn kinderen, het geïmproviseerde kantoor, hun werk te doen. Er zou altijd voldoende magazijnruimte zijn en de aanvoer van hun voorraad werd efficiënter geregeld. Niets stond een verdere groei van zijn firma meer in de weg en door de aansluiting bij het wereldwijde concern groeide de kansen aanzienlijk!

Zoals al opgemerkt moest de man erg wennen aan alle nieuwe termen en benamingen die plotseling opgingen voor vaak heel alledaagse functies. Soms leverde het verwarring op omdat vooral hun baas krampachtig aan de oude vast wilde houden, maar meestal konden ze er om lachen. De vrouw en hij schepten er namelijk genoegen in om het belachelijke ervan te benadrukken of nieuwe erbij te bedenken. Deze fantasie termen vonden vervolgens snel hun weg onder de rest van het personeel dat hen, de mensen van kantoor, als voorbeeld zag.

In de dagelijkse praktijk was ooit gebleken dat "meneer", hun baas dus, zeer bedreven was in het delegeren van voorkomende taken. Hij noemde het samenwerking en was er gelukkig niet vies van om zijn handen ervoor uit de mouwen te steken. De medewerkers stelden het in ieder geval op prijs dat hij zich er niet te goed voor voelde om zo nu en dan eens vuile handen te maken. Toen het bedrijf haar enorme groei doormaakte moest hij echter steeds meer verantwoordelijkheden aan zijn assistente overgelaten.

De vrouw nam het graag van hem over, zag er meestal een kans in en greep

179

die iedere keer met beide handen aan. Het werk ging haar namelijk gemakkelijk af omdat ze snel leerde. Door de geleidelijke groei kon ze voor elke volgende stap zichzelf de tijd geven om zich aan te passen. Ze vond het dragen van alle verantwoordelijkheid leuk en op haar beurt was ze die nu, zo goed en zo kwaad als dat mogelijk was, aan het overdragen op hem.

De omstandigheid dat ze op de vestiging voornamelijk met stagiaires en uitzendkrachten werkten, droeg eraan bij dat de vrouw tot de spil van de firma was uitgegroeid. Het personeelsverloop bood immers geen vastigheid en zij was lange tijd de enig goed ingevoerde medewerker. Deze manier van handelen is tenslotte zeer Amerikaans en juist omdat vast personeel 'vreselijk duur' zou zijn, werden er vrijwel geen mensen aangenomen. Ook hij zou pas een contract aangeboden krijgen als ie volledig was ingewerkt, voldeed aan de eisen en vanzelfsprekend zou die aanstelling slechts voor een afgepaste periode gaan gelden. Hooguit was er zodoende eens een caissière en, toen de chaos er niet meer te overzien was, de chef van het magazijn in dienst genomen.

Voor de dienstreis die ze gingen maken, stond een kennismakingsgesprek met een van de grotere klanten op het programma. Van hem werd het de eerste die hij voor de groothandel of zelfs maar überhaupt in zijn carrière ging maken, maar de vrouw maakte er volgens zeggen meerdere per jaar. De klant op hun bestemming had een tijd geleden zijn kantoor vanuit Leiden naar de Achterhoek verplaatst. Omdat de vrouw er na die verhuizing nog nooit was geweest had ze het plan opgevat om persoonlijk een bezoekje aan de andere kant van het land af te gaan afleggen.

Op de dag waarop alle agenda's het reisje toe stonden, stond zijn auto helaas voor een reparatie bij de garage. Ze moesten daarom de trein nemen, er was namelijk op de zaak geen alternatief vervoer voorhanden. Daar was door het hoofdkantoor in Seattle nooit in voorzien.

Officieel zou ze hem en de directeur van het bedrijf met elkaar in contact brengen. Zo hoopte ze hun zakelijke verbintenis te behouden. En hoewel er daar in de buurt ook een vestiging van de groothandel is, mocht ie zijn bestellingen bij hen blijven onderbrengen. Uiteindelijk spreken we van een wereldomvattend bedrijf en kunnen leveringen overal vandaan uitgevoerd worden.

Dat 'account managen' is eigenlijk helemaal geen ingewikkelde job, maar omdat vertrouwen er belangrijk bij is, dient de overdracht van de aangelegde contacten inderdaad goed te gebeuren. Het is hem duidelijk geworden dat het persoonlijke karakter van de omgang met de cliënten voorop staat. Hoe sterker je als manager een band met je klanten kunt opbouwen en hij heeft al opgemerkt dat dit weleens op het heel persoonlijke af kan gaan, hoe minder een klant weg zal lopen naar de concurrent. Al is er van een echte competitie ternauwernood meer sprake, nu de kleine winkels en speciaalzaken een voor een overgenomen worden door die 'conglomeraten'.

180

Het is hem intussen duidelijk dat haar zorgvuldigheid de vrouw een manier biedt om 'geleidelijk aan' afstand te nemen van haar werkzaamheden. Deze bijkomstigheid zal haar waarschijnlijk vooral welkom zijn omdat ze zo het definitieve afscheid van haar carrière ermee kan uitstellen. Op het oog blijkt ze namelijk nogal gehecht aan de omgang met haar contacten. Of hun directeur met zijn ruimhartige opstelling de Amerikaanse terreur op de hak neemt. is overigens niet helder. Hij heeft die man slechts eenmaal ontmoet en het leek 'm toen dat hij niet alleen met die moderne functienamen moeite had.

De werkzaamheden die hij binnen het kantoor dient uit te voeren blijken hem mee te vallen. De man heeft er alleen aan moeten wennen dat hij actief de klanten moet benaderen. In zijn praktijk thuis zoeken klanten hem altijd op. Hij hoeft alleen maar af te wachten en op vaste tijden thuis te zijn. In zijn eigen werk komt het daar op neer, maar bij deze baan is het de bedoeling dat er binnen de bedrijven waarvan hij het 'account beheert' een persoonlijker contact wordt opgebouwd. Èn dat deze onderhouden blijft. Daarom dient ie de verschillende contactpersonen regelmatig te benaderen met een verkooppraatje. En hij mag ze daarbij bestoken met aanbiedingen. Dat laatste is blijkbaar het belangrijkste, want iemand zo nu en dan met 'een smoesje' opbellen levert blijkbaar de meeste verkopen op. Daarmee had hij nog geen ervaring. Desgevraagd bleek zijn intercedente bij het 'buro Ervaringstijd' er trouwens vanuit te gaan dat hij "door zijn leeftijd" vele "anekdotes en ervaringen" met de klanten zou kunnen delen. Ze vond zelfs dat hem dat uitermate geschikt zou maken voor het werk.

Op het behalen van resultaten staan overigens diverse premies. Volgens goed Amerikaanse gebruik wordt er hard aan gewerkt om de onderlinge competitie binnen het bedrijf tot de grootste hoogten op te drijven. Wekelijks worden er dus 'targets' gesteld en men werkt er met diverse 'assets'. Nadrukkelijk prijkt het 'company statement', ingelijst met een gouden rand, boven de fotokopieer machine. Of de foto van het hoofdkantoor er eveneens verplicht hangt is 'm niet duidelijk, maar 'het sfeertje' verbaast hem nog steeds.

De vrouw heeft hem in een paar dagen de hoognodige kneepjes van het aanleggen van een dossier van contactpersonen bij gebracht. Die van haar mag hij straks zonder meer overnemen, zodat hij wat dat betreft in een gespreid bedje terecht komt. Voor een aantal cliënten lijkt het haar echter noodzakelijk om daar gezamenlijk en dus persoonlijk kennis te gaan maken. Het is de reden waarom ze samen met de trein op reis zijn geweest.

De betreffende relatie is naast een oude bekende uit de tijd van de winkel en zaak aan huis, ook een persoon met wie ze al een hele lange tijd, een "hechte band" onderhield. Zakelijk gezien en door de premies die ze erdoor verdient, zeer interessant want als klant is hij, ook na de verhuizing, al zijn kantoorbehoeften via haar blijven bestellen. Voor de kennismaking hebben ze een af-

181

spraak op zijn bedrijf gemaakt. Niet te vroeg in de ochtend omdat ze er zo'n grote afstand voor moeten afleggen. Al waren ze door de treinreis helaas alsnog verplicht er toch al vroeg voor op pad te gaan. Oorspronkelijk was het de bedoeling dat ze met zijn auto zouden gaan, maar precies een paar dagen voor de reis ging die stuk. De enige dag dat er in de garage tijd was voor de reparatie, was er precies sprake van hun afspraak. Ze moesten ervoor in de plaats dus de trein nemen. Altijd opgeruimd konden ze volgens haar onderweg "nog fijn een paar uurtjes werken."

Inderdaad is ze het grootste deel van de reis met haar laptop in de weer geweest. Hijzelf heeft voornamelijk naar buiten zitten kijken en ook een flink stuk gelezen in het boek dat hij voor onderweg had meegenomen. Van praten of overleggen kwam niet zoveel terecht, daarvoor was het te onrustig met telkens die langslopende mensen in het gangpad en de medereizigers om hen heen. Er is weliswaar geen sprake van geheimen, maar die lui hoeven niet allemaal mee te luisteren. Daar bleken ze allebei een hekel aan te hebben.

De vestiging van het bedrijf moest zich op een 'bedrijvenpark' naast het stationnetje bevinden. Daardoor konden ze het korte eindje er naartoe wandelend afleggen. Zo hebben ze toch nog kunnen bespreken hoe ze hem voor zou gaan stellen en wat er met dit account overlegd moest worden qua nieuwe producten. Keurig op tijd kwamen ze bij hun afspraak aan, de eerste indruk die hij bij dit 'prospect' maakte was daarmee dik in orde.

De lunchbespreking met het bedrijf, die ze voor de gezelligheid in een restaurant er niet ver vandaan voerden, verliep geheel naar wens. Het werd zelfs zo gezellig dat ze ter afsluiting een 'hele leuke' order meekregen. De vrouw gaf hem later in de trein terug een compliment over zijn manier van handelen. Ze had zich er over verbaasd hoe snel hij dit blijkbaar geleerd had. Het zorgde ervoor dat hij zich door haar gewaardeerd, erkend voelde. Hij kon blijkbaar tevreden zijn met de afloop en volgens haar mocht ie in vertrouwen de toekomstige samenwerking met de Achterhoek tegemoet zien.

Of ze dit van tevoren zo bekokstoofd had, werd hem trouwens niet helemaal duidelijk. Ze liet zich er niet over uit, maar het leek hem dat dit reisje met alle kosten vandien natuurlijk wel terug verdiend moest worden. Bij nader onderzoek in de boeken, later op kantoor, merkte hij op dat deze klant alweer een hele poos geen echte bestelling had gedaan. Hoewel dus in eerste instantie tevreden met de order die ze op het reisje hadden verworven, bleek deze de optelsom van de normale bestellingen van de afgelopen twee maanden.

Het klopte tot op zowat de laatste cent, dus van een echte bonus mochten ze feitelijk niet spreken. Dat zijn gesprekspartner, het account om in termen van zijn werkgever te blijven, een leeftijdgenoot was en dat ze elkaar goed bleken te begrijpen, had blijkbaar dus niet zoveel aan het succes van de bespreking bijgedragen. Maar ze hadden inderdaad tijdens de nazit wat grapjes uitgewisseld en daar hadden ze allemaal smakelijk om zitten lachen.

Het was voor het eerst sinds zijn aantreden bij de groothandel dat de man het idee kreeg dat zijn carrièrestap wellicht terecht was. Na de dienstreis durfde hij de oorspronkelijke scepsis, die hem de afgelopen weken nog regelmatig overvallen had, van zich af te werpen. In gedachten was hij zijn dochter dus dankbaar dat ze hem ertoe had aangezet de overgang te maken.

Tijdens de wandeling naar het station, meer een halte eigenlijk, om er op te kunnen stappen voor de treinreis terug naar de randstad, heeft hij lopen mijmeren over zijn vroegere werk. Gedrieën waren ze na de geslaagde lunch, te voet onderweg gegaan. Het plaatsje van de nieuwe bedrijfsvestiging is tenslotte niet zo heel erg groot en dat maakte een taxirit wat overdreven. Het feit dat ze er een stationnetjes, hoe eenvoudig danook, hebben is al een heel pluspunt in vergelijking met andere plaatsen en dorpjes. Om de vrouw ruimschoots de tijd te gunnen om op haar eigen wijze afscheid te nemen van dat account, is hij langzaam voor ze uit gelopen naar het perron.

Hij is altijd heel gelukkig geweest als zogenaamde ZZP'er, maar nu hij blijkbaar een plekje heeft gevonden in het 'grotemensen' bedrijfsleven ziet de toekomst er beter uit dan in de voorafgaande periode. Hij realiseerde zich dat hij de laatste tijd niet altijd even vrolijk en daarom waarschijnlijk minder prettig gezelschap moet zijn geweest. Hij zag in dat hij de laatste tijd weleens cynisch was. Onder het wachten op de trein nam ie zich daarom voor om eens een feestje te geven. Hij kan er zijn kennissen laten zien hoe hij is opgeknapt. Dat je, net zoals vroeger, weer met hem kan lachen en dat zijn verbittering grotendeels weg is. Dat hij weer positief in het leven staat, zich prettig voelt.

De vrouw voegde zich pas weer bij hem toen hij daadwerkelijk het perron op ging. Ze hadden echter niets met elkaar te bespreken, zaten vol met hun eigen beslommeringen en bleven in stilte op de trein staan wachten. Het bleek dat ze de verbinding naar Arnhem op twee minuten na gemist hadden. Inderdaad had hij een wit met rode trein zien vertrekken toen ze vlakbij de halte waren aangekomen, maar hij heeft er dus even op haar staan wachten. Het resulteerde erin dat ze een heel uur min die twee minuten, moesten wachten op de volgende verbinding. Het leidde tot de conclusie dat hoewel de Achterhoek een deel van Nederland is, het toch tamelijk ver van hun woonplaats verwijderd blijkt te liggen. Het gebied tamelijk lastig bereikbaar is.

De wijn die ze bij de lunch genoten hadden begon al na korte tijd zijn werk te doen. Om niet buiten in de kou te hoeven blijven staan, waren ze in een hoek van de wachtruimte op een van de houten banken gaan zitten. Het was er warm en zoals het hoort zaten ze er beschut. Zonder iets te zeggen of vragen trok de vrouw na een paar minuten haar benen op en ging met haar rug tegen hem aan zitten. Al na een paar tellen leek het erop of ze in een diepe slaap was gevallen.

183

De man had intussen zijn boek tevoorschijn gehaald en zat erin te lezen. Hij was al over de helft aangekomen en het verhaal begon hem steeds meer te intrigeren. Vanmorgen op de heenreis had hij er ook al van zitten genieten. Als het leuk genoeg is geschreven kan ie intens opgaan in een verhaal. Vooral als het, zoals in dit geval, boeiend is geschreven en over een onderwerp gaat dat hem aanspreekt. Hem raakt.

Eenmaal is hij anders gaan zitten. Zijn been was gaan slapen en het harde hout van de bank begon in zijn billen te steken. De tinteling begon pijn te doen. Onder het wiebelen ging de vrouw even iets meer rechtop zitten, maar had zich meteen toen hij eindelijk goed zat, weer behaaglijk tegen hem aan laten zakken. Zonder iets te zeggen ging ze verder met haar dutje. Uit de rustige manier waarop ze ademhaalde maakt hij op dat ze inderdaad in 'n diepe rust verzeild was geraakt.

Vijf minuten voordat hun trein aan zou komen heeft hij haar voorzichtig iets van zich af geduwd en op die manier wakker gemaakt. Ze was inderdaad onder zeil geweest, maar eenmaal weer wakker begon ze gelijk haar verfomfaaide haren in fatsoen te brengen. Nog terwijl ze ermee bezig was, kwam de trein het station binnengereden. Om 'm niet weer te missen zijn ze er op een holletje naartoe gerend. Nadat ze eenmaal een zitplaats gevonden hadden, duurde het overigens nog meer dan vier minuten voordat het daadwerkelijke vertrek uit de Achterhoek plaatsvond. Alle haast bleek dus overbodig, maar de man voelde zich duidelijk opgelucht bij de gedachte dat ze weer onderweg naar huis waren. Al moesten ze er nog op hopen dat ze straks, eenmaal aangekomen in Arnhem de eerstvolgende aansluiting naar Utrecht zouden gaan halen. Daar vandaan naar hun woonplaats rijdt er ieder halfuur een boemeltje.

In de trein ging hij gelijk verder met lezen. De vrouw bleef nog enige tijd met haar haren in de weer en hoewel er buiten nog teveel licht voor was, probeerde ze in de weerschijn van het raam een glimp op te vangen van haar vorderingen. Met even een klein knikje heeft hij over zijn boek heen naar haar geglimlacht toen hij vond dat ze er weer toonbaar genoeg uitzag. Hij deed het voornamelijk om te laten blijken dat ze op kon houden met frunniken en 't gelukt was om haar kapsel te herstellen.

Nog voor Arnhem schakelde ze haar computertje even in, maar al na een paar minuten moest het apparaat uit. De accu stond niet toe dat ze er langer mee verder werkte. Omstandig begon ze het ding weer op te bergen en is ze naar buiten gaan kijken. Sinds hij de zakenrelatie een hand heeft gegeven en d'r voor is gegaan naar het station, hebben ze geen woord gewisseld. De hele verdere rit is ze niet meer verder gegaan met haar middagslaapje.

Ook de volgende trein liet trouwens even op zich wachten, maar dat zou niet lang genoeg gaan duren om ervoor plaats te moeten nemen in het station. Ze konden gemakkelijk even op het perron blijven staan of er een paar keer over heen en weer wandelen. Helaas bleek er in het hok op het perron geen koffie te koop, allebei bleken ze wel een bakje te lusten namelijk. Het was de eerste opmerking die ze tegen hem maakte. Het was er in de buitenlucht warm genoeg voor om heen en weer te wandelen en door de ligging van de sporen in een soort dal, hadden ze geen last van een eventuele wind die zou waaien.

Dat was die ochtend allemaal heel anders, maar op dat moment was het natuurlijk ook een stuk vroeger geweest. De zon had haar werk toen nog niet kunnen uitvoeren. Dat maakte de huidige omstandigheden een stuk aangenamer. Hun trein vertrok overigens van hetzelfde perron als waar ze op aan waren gekomen, dus ze hoefden nergens de trappen op te klauteren of zich een weg zoeken in een doolhof binnen het stationsgebouw.

In Utrecht moesten ze meer dan twintig minuten wachten op de trein die hen uiteindelijk naar Leiden zou brengen. Intussen was het kwart voor zes en ze kwamen op het idee dat ze allebei wel trek hadden in iets te eten. Er zou tijd genoeg zijn om boven in de grote stationshal even een snelle snack uit een van de automaten te trekken, maar omdat het die dag zo gezellig geweest was stelde de man voor om er een restaurant voor op te zoeken. Het zou immers niet meer uitmaken of ze nu de eerstvolgende trein zouden nemen of een latere. Spontaan, in een opwelling, gooide hij zijn voorstel eruit.

Het leek hem gezellig om de dag op die manier een soort bekroning te verlenen. Het samen wachten op een aansluiting en het vervelende doden van de tijd die dit telkens met zich mee had gebracht, hadden in zijn ogen de band die tussen hen was ontstaan sterker gemaakt. Hij voelde zich trouwens prettig in haar gezelschap en meende te merken dat zij het ook niet vervelend vond om met hem, toch uit 'n beduidend andere generatie, op te moeten trekken.

Het leek haar meteen een goed idee en ze stelde voor om het een en ander bij hun werkgever te declareren. Uiteindelijk was haar voor het inwerken van hem, de vrije hand gegeven en dit was de eerste keer dat zich de gelegenheid voordeed dat ze op het genereuze aanbod in kon gaan. Ze hoefden niet meteen te overdrijven, maar een "dagmenuutje in een leuke bistro" of desnoods als hij niet teveel trek had een "eenvoudige pizza", kon ze waarschijnlijk wel verantwoorden. Ze stelde dat de order van die middag een viering wel toestond. Zulke grote bestellingen haalde ze immers niet elke dag binnen en de man was op dat moment niet op de hoogte van de omstandigheden waaronder het een en ander tot stand was gekomen.

Overigens was hij, nog voordat hij 'm helemaal had uitgesproken, geschrokken van zijn voorstel en erg blij dat zij er zakelijk op in ging. In ieder geval zag ze die kant van het verhaal als belangrijkste reden en dat stelde hem gerust. Hij wilde geen verkeerde indruk op haar maken. 'Macho gedrag' is hem vreemd, dus dat ze hem een haantje zou vinden stond hem tegen.

Dat ze eenvoudigweg in de eerstvolgende trein zouden stappen, naar hun woonplaats zouden afreizen en daar allebei hun eigen weg vervolgden, speelde bij zijn overwegingen een belangrijke rol. Zij het ergens op de achtergrond, voelde hij dat de dag was veel te gezellig verlopen was om elkaar zomaar los te laten. Hij had zich onderweg vanaf Arnhem naar dit voorlaatste station, een paar maal geprobeerd voor te stellen wat hij tegen haar zou gaan zeggen als het afscheid zover was. Weliswaar waren ze het grootste deel van de tijd in hen eigen gedachten verwikkeld geweest, maar de reis vroeg om een passende afsluiting. Hoe, wat en op welke manier dat zou moeten gaan kreeg hij niet voor ogen. Dus daarom volgde zijn spontane voorstel om samen de stad in te gaan. Het verschafte hem de mogelijkheid het afscheid nog even uit te stellen, zich er beter op voor te bereiden.

Hun keuze viel op een bistrootje in een van de souterrains aan de lager gelegen walkant van de Oude Gracht in het centrum. Geen dure speciaalzaak, maar het zag er van buitenaf gezellig uit toen ze door een van de ramen naar binnen stonden te kijken. Hoewel er wel stoelen en tafeltjes op de straatstenen tussen de deur en de waterkant klaar stonden, het terras, vonden ze het er nog te koud voor om daarop plaats te nemen. Er zat sowieso niemand buiten.

Het was al bij halfzeven toen ze er aankwamen en daardoor vielen ze middenin de Hollandse etenstijd. Als het binnen erg druk zou zijn waren er vast wel bezoekers buiten gaan zitten. De menukaart in het verlichte bakje naast de ingang beloofde overigens dat ze binnen van heel erg lekkere dingen konden gaan genieten.

Tijdens vergaderingen en trainingen, ofwel de 'meetings', die ze gedurende de afgelopen tijd gezamenlijk hadden bijgewoond, was het de man een aantal keren opgevallen dat de vrouw iets speciaals bij de aanwezigen los leek te maken. Overigens niet alleen op mannen had ze die uitwerking. Op het merendeel van de aanwezigen bleek ze een zekere impact uit te kunnen oefenen. Hij had eerst bedacht dat het aan haar mooie ogen, haar kleding of goede figuur kon liggen, maar deed dat al snel af als te seksistisch. Ze was voornamelijk vriendelijk, attent en voorkomend. Ze sprak op een besliste toon over zaken waar ze ogenschijnlijk verstand van had en zonder autoritair te worden kwam ze kordaat, overtuigend op haar gehoor over. Charmant zonder dat het hinderlijk werd of dat je je er bij nader inzien door 'ingepakt' zou voelen. Die uitwerking had ze dus zowel op mannen als vrouwen, viel hem op.

Het leek er trouwens op dat ze de eigenschap spontaan aan en uit kon zetten, want niet altijd in elk gezelschap liet haar invloed zich gelden. Nadat hij er op was gaan letten leek het er weleens op of ze vanuit het niets zomaar op die innemende houding kon overschakelen. In de dagelijkse omgang op het werk was ze namelijk veel afstandelijker. Daar leek ze zich meer op de vlakte te houden en liet ze veel minder van zichzelf doorschemeren. Aanzienlijk minder dan ze bijvoorbeeld vandaag tijdens de vergadering en lunch had laten zien. Het was op hem overgekomen alsof ze dan iets van zichzelf toonde, haar gesprekspartners een soort vertrouwen schonk.

Vanmiddag stelde hij zich voor dat ze zich kennelijk af liet schrikken als zij één op een in het directe gezelschap van vreemden was. Dat ze zich zichtbaar beter op haar gemak voelde in grotere gezelschappen leek hem evident. Voor hem was het een hele tijd geleden dat hem zoiets opviel. Eeuwen geleden dat hij überhaupt op zoiets gelet had. Hij keek vrijwel nooit naar vrouwen. Hij is gelukkig getrouwd en heeft naast zijn eigen eigen vrouw ternauwernood met anderen kontakt onderhouden. Door de situatie waarin ze verkeerden was dat ook niet nodig of mogelijk. Hij was hele dagen thuis, daar werkte hij. Zijn vrouw had alleen een part-time baantje zodat ook zij meestal ergens in huis te vinden was. Het echtpaar zegt natuurlijk niet voor niets dat zij een 'tropen huwelijk' onderhouden. Al jaren!

Het heeft vanzelfsprekend wel mogelijk gemaakt dat zowel zijn vrouw als hij, zich intensief met de opvoeding van hun kinderen bezig hebben kunnen houden. Niemand heeft hier ooit een bezwaar in gezien, hooguit heeft de school er weleens misbruik van gemaakt dat er tijdens de lesuren een vader beschikbaar was om in te kunnen zetten als begeleider. Hij. Naast hun dochter hebben ze ook nog een zoon, maar die heeft in het speciale onderwijs gezeten vanwege z'n handicap.

De moeder van het jongetje is nooit getrouwd geweest. Zoals ze al bij hun eerste kennismaking zei is ze "een bewust ongehuwde moeder." "Zelfverklaard" voegde ze er toen lachend aan toe. Ze komt daar kennelijk graag, maar zonder dat het militant wordt, voor uit. De man kon er zich niet gelijk een voorstelling bij maken toen ze zichzelf zo benoemde, maar intussen heeft ze een paar keer geprobeerd hem uit te leggen wat ze ermee bedoelt. Ze hebben samen over het onderwerp gediscussieerd, maar dit kwam vooral omdat de man zich zo'n principiële houding moeilijk kon voorstellen.

Over begrippen als links of rechts, heeft hij tot voor kort nooit nagedacht. Het is volledig aan 'm voorbij gegaan dat zo'n indeling ooit nodig of wenselijk kon zijn in een maatschappij. Voor hem zijn alle mensen gelijk. Dat heeft hij ook geprobeerd aan zijn kinderen mee te geven in hun opvoeding. Het idee vervolgens aan haar uitleggen bleek nog tamelijk lastig overigens.

Voor zichzelf bestelde de man een trappistenbier, die kon hij onder het doornemen van de kaart opdrinken. De vrouw wilde liever een glas witte wijn. Na enig overleg besloten ze om een van de voorgerechten samen te delen. Volgens de beschrijving op de kaart leek deze namelijk nogal groot.

Al bij vrijwel de eerste blik op het menu was voor allebei de keuze op vis bij het hoofdgerecht gevallen, dat maakte verder overleg tamelijk gemakkelijk en op een prettige manier eenvoudig. De man wilde een gepocheerde moot zalm en de voorkeur van de vrouw ging uit naar een forel. Ze zou 'm gerookt krijgen. Die vissen had hij al genoeg gegeten op zijn vakanties in het Sauerland en daarom liet hij deze traktatie aan zich voorbij gaan.

Zijn vrouw en hij logeerden de laatste jaren regelmatig bij een pension in die streek en omdat de echtgenoot van de eigenaresse ernaast een kwekerij drijft, staan die vissen vrijwel altijd op de kaart. Hetzij gerookt of gebakken, maar ook gepocheerd en zelfs rauw is hem gebleken dat ze eetbaar, klaar te maken zijn. Het is dus niet dat de vissen hem intussen de strot uit komen, maar hij had er op dat moment geen trek in. Dat stuk zalm zou immers ook heel lekker kunnen zijn en die vis eet hij beduidend minder vaak.

Nadat ze allebei hun glas leeg hadden, heeft hij voor bij het eten een fles rosé besteld. Niet na eerst een paar minuten 'interessanterig geneuzel' met de wijnkaart, maar gewoon degene van het huis. Wel verbond hij er de uitdrukkelijke voorwaarde aan dat de wijn koud zou zijn. Van hem mochten ze er "desnoods" een klontje ijs bij doen. De man had er helemaal geen zin in om zich tegenover de vrouw beter voor te doen dan hij is. Hij weet niks meer van wijn dan dat ie lekker smaakt en in de meeste gevallen goed valt. Al komt dat laatste helaas pas de volgende ochtend aan de orde als ie er al of niet koppijn aan overgehouden blijkt te hebben. Bij het 'kopje koffie toe' vonden ze het nog wel kunnen dat er ook een glaasje likeur bij neergezet werd.

Het eten was erg lekker geweest, maar het verdiende een bekroning. Ze hadden genoeg op hun bord gehad en wilden niet ook nog eens een toetje. Hoewel het meisje van de bediening het zeer verleidelijk maakte toen ze opsomde wat de kok nog wel voor ze klaar wilde maken. Maar ze zijn verstandig gebleven en hebben het bij die koffie gelaten. Met alleen dat ene kleine glaasje erbij.

Onderweg weer terug naar Hoog Catharijne heeft ze, nadat ze eerst de trap naar de oude gracht weer waren opgeklauterd, zijn arm gepakt. Alle tijdens het eten en erna genoten drank maakte haar gang wat onzeker, al moest hij toegeven dat de schoenen die ze aanhad daar onmiskenbaar eveneens hun invloed op uitoefenden. Het kwartiertje lopen zou haar zeker goed doen veronderstelden ze. Anders kon ze in de trein wel weer tegen hem aan komen zitten. Wat hem betreft mocht ze onder het rijden wel weer even een dutje doen. De rit naar Leiden duurt iets meer dan een halfuur dus misschien zou ze dan bij aankomst weer voldoende zijn opgeknapt om haar taak als huismoeder op te vatten.

Onder het eten heeft ze hem terloops een aantal van haar beslommeringen beschreven en naar het hem leek was dat 'ongehuwde moederschap' niet echt ideaal te noemen. Zo had ze er bijvoorbeeld alle moeite voor moeten doen om tijdens haar afwezigheid gedurende hun dienstreis, voldoende oppas te regelen voor haar zoontje. Het jongetje, dat net een paar maanden op de lagere school zat en dus aan die uren gebonden was, gaat weliswaar naar de buitenschoolse opvang en wordt dagelijks door haar daarvandaan opgehaald maar dat lukte die dag niet omdat ze zo laat terug zouden komen. Rond etenstijd was weliswaar het oorspronkelijke plan, maar daar hadden de uitgebreide lunch plus het missen van de trein in de Achterhoek een spaak bij in het wiel gestoken. En natuurlijk het etentje in Utrecht dat ze eraan hadden verbonden.

Na het overleg dat zij vanuit een telefooncel op het perron in Arnhem met haar moeder gevoerd had zou deze, en uitsluitend voor deze keer, het jongetje in haar plaats ophalen. Na het eten zou de opvang worden voortgezet door een buurvrouw uit de straat, want daar ging het kind wel vaker een paar uurtjes naar de tv kijken. Dat de vrouw het daardoor niet zo heel erg laat kon of wilde maken begreep de man ook zonder de toelichting. Toen zijn kinderen nog klein waren had de ouderlijke plicht ook een aanzienlijke invloed uitgeoefend over zijn dagelijkse bezigheden. Al had hij dus wel een partner waarmee hij, althans een deel van de taken, kon delen.

Omdat ze voor haar afspraken van vandaag, geen 'passende oppas' kon vinden heeft de man haar aangeboden om vanmiddag op haar zoontje te letten. Overmoedig heeft hij erbij aangeboden om er ook nog een leuke middag van te maken. Nu zit de jongen een bord patat te nuttigen. Vanwege de hoeveelheid heeft de man er een extra grote portie mayonaise bij laten scheppen, dat vond zijn eigen zoon vroeger ook heel erg lekker. Zijn zoon is trouwens alweer drie jaar geleden op zichzelf gaan wonen bij de stichting die hem een 'goede opvang' aangeboden heeft. Daarover later meer.

Glimlachend stelt de man vast dat het bij die jongen gelukt is om een zekere belangstelling op te wekken. Al is het helaas beperkt gebleven tot kermis attracties op het Internet en het lawaai van zogenaamde 'house' muziek. Helaas 't niveau dat hoort bij zijn beperkingen.

Aan een soortgelijke taak is hij bij dit kind nog niet toegekomen. Dat verhaal over de Spanjaarden en het beleg van hun stad zal hij het jochie straks vertellen. De middag is nog jong en omdat het niet regent zullen ze door een paar van de binnen straatjes in het oudste deel van de stad kunnen gaan wandelen. Als het voor het kind te lang gaat duren kan hij ook een verhaal ophangen over Rembrandt van Rijn en hoe die ooit geboren is in deze stad. Nu bekijkt hij hoe ie voorzichtig een voor een de staafjes gefrituurde aardappel naar binnen zit te werken. Het joch geniet er overduidelijk van.

Zelf heeft de man een kom soep genomen, broccoli met rivierkreeft en het smaakt hem goed. Het personeel heeft er klaarblijkelijk zijn best op gedaan om er een pittige smaak aan te geven. Daarin zijn ze wonderwel geslaagd zonder dat het er vreselijk 'pedis' door is geworden. Al heet de soep dus Thais te zijn.

Publicaties van D.F.Verplancke:

W - 1x kort 2x lang(er) (2007)

Een drietal verhalen (1 korte en 2 lange pips vormen, in het morse alfabet de code voor de letter W) waarmee de schrijver onder de knie heeft willen krijgen wat er komt kijken bij het voorbereiden, opmaken en geschikt maken van zijn teksten voor publicatie via deze zogenaamde Printing On Demand (zelf!) uitgeverij.

2 - een Dubbelroman (2010)

Twee romans die qua inhoud en thema dicht bij de wereld van de schrijver staan. In verband met de ziekte van zijn zus, aan wie hij vooral een van de twee wilde opdragen, is de publicatie van deze roman versneld tot stand gekomen. Ingeven door het overhaaste karakter hiervan, wordt een herziening, met een enigszins andere opmaak, overwogen.

Blauw Druk - 14 schetsen over mannen (2012)

Dit boek, dat U waarschijnlijk zojuist heeft uitgelezen met, naar de schrijver hoopt, evenveel plezier als waarmee het door hem is geschreven.

Deze uitgaven zijn gepubliceerd bij POD internet uitgeverij Lulu. De boeken kunnen direct via http://stores.lulu.com/dfverplancke *besteld worden.*

in voorbereiding: (voorlopig zonder titel)

* Een roman waarin verslag wordt gedaan van het leven en welzijn van de architect Mol van Egteren (voorlopige naam/functie). De schrijver beoogt het intrigerende levensverhaal van deze fictieve man te beschrijven en wil er in weergeven hoe deze ogenschijnlijk in het leven geslaagde persoon, ertoe komt er een einde aan te maken. Is het ziekte, tegenslag, scheiding of spreken er andere motieven mee?

* Bundel(s) verhalen die de schrijver samenstelt uit de diverse dingen die hij 'tussendoor' over zijn belevenissen en waarnemingen opschrijft.

www.ingramcontent.com/pod-product-compliance
Lightning Source LLC
Chambersburg PA
CBHW032147020726
47496CB00003B/762